He lunged his head [...]
rattlesnake, and tried t[...]
yanked one wrist free, [...]
waist and pulled her back towards him.

'I said are you going to be *accommodatin'*!' he shrieked.

She heard somebody screaming. She didn't realize at first that it was her. Uncle Casper gripped the hair at the back of her neck and clamped his mouth against hers, trying to force his rigid tongue in between her lips.

She pushed against him wildly, and staggered back, two steps, and then fell against the bolts of linen and percale that were stacked on the floor between the shelves. Uncle Casper scrabbled himself on top of her, forcing her down on to her back, grunting, grunting, and grabbing for her wrists.

She couldn't find the breath to scream again. She kicked and struggled, but Uncle Casper knelt astride her waist, gripping her tight between his thighs.

He looked down at her, panting. He sniffed, and twisted his head so that he could wipe his nose against the shoulder of his shirt. Then he said, 'What was all that for? Hunh? What was all that? What kind of a way was that for a niece to treat her uncle?'

EMPRESS

Graham Masterton

SPHERE BOOKS LIMITED

A SPHERE BOOK

First published in Great Britain by Hamish Hamilton Ltd 1990
This edition published by Sphere Books Ltd 1991

Printed and bound in Great Britain by
BPCC Hazell Books
Aylesbury, Bucks, England
Member of BPCC Ltd.

ISBN 0 7474 0064 4

Sphere Books Ltd
A Division of
Macdonald & Co (Publishers) Ltd
Orbit House
1 New Fetter Lane
London EC4A 1AR
A member of Maxwell Macmillan Pergamon Publishing Corporation

For Wiescka

When Henry came home that thundery afternoon and stood in the hallway shaking his umbrella and called out, 'India, my darling! They've given me India!' her immediate thought was not of palaces or elephants or princes with diamonds in their foreheads. As if they had flown open in her mind with a sudden and general clatter, she thought of those black tinplate boxes on the back shelves of the Darling general store; and how she had breathed in their mysterious dust-dry pungencies; and wondered what kind of extraordinary country it could be where people ate foods that tasted of shoe-leather and gunpowder and dried flowers and fire.

She had seen real live elephants, of course, whenever the circus had come to town, and she had seen pictures in magazines of snake-charmers and bazaars and the Taj Mahal. But prising open those lids and smelling those spices had given her the immediate understanding that for all of its farness, and for all of its strangeness, India was not a story but *real*.

And now Henry had returned home with rain spots on his shoulders and cheerfully announced that to all intents and purposes this far, strange country was actually *his*, and consequently *hers*, too.

'Fenugreek and cumin,' she recited, holding out her arms for him. 'Chili and turmeric and garam masala.'

'What?' he laughed.

She kissed him. His sidewhiskers were wet. 'India!' she told him. 'India!'

Yet – when she lay in their brass-pillared bed that night and Henry slept – she realized that Fate had brought her India

I

much earlier in her life. Fate had brought her India almost five years before and four thousand miles away, in Kansas, in early June; that day her Uncle Casper had reappeared.

She hardly ever allowed herself to think of what had happened that summer. It still made her feel dry-mouthed and upset. She stared up at the ceiling in the overwhelming darkness and wondered if God had given her India in belated consolation for what had happened; or if what had happened had been the price that she had been obliged to pay for a dream that she had never really asked for.

I

She was balancing like a tightrope-walker on Mrs Sweeney's back fence when she heard the train whistle; but of course she didn't know that Uncle Casper was aboard it, and so she paid it no attention.

Quite apart from which, it required all of her concentration to balance on top of the fence, arms held wide, parasol held high, one foot in front of the other, swaying a little, hesitating, and then high-stepping forwards. She looked as if she couldn't be real, a pretty mechanical marionette. The sunlight shone through her long blue-and-white striped skirt, and her white cotton bonnet.

'Steady, now! Back straight!' called Mrs Sweeney. She was watching Lucy intently; as if she could will her to keep her balance. 'And whatever you do, don't look down at your feet!'

The train whistled again, high and doleful. Lucy took two more steps, paused, then another three, paused, and then teetered quickly to the guttering, and held on.

'Well, that wasn't too bad,' said Mrs Sweeney. 'Not sure what Forepaugh and Sells would've thought about it; but it'll do for me.'

She helped Lucy to jump down. Lucy tugged her skirts out of her bloomers, brushed them down, and then perched herself on a backless kitchen chair to put on her button-up boots.

'Do you think we could dance some more?' she asked Mrs Sweeney, one eye squinched up against the sun.

'Oh, no, no, I'm all danced out, thank you very much,' Mrs Sweeney told her. ''Sides, I have to go along to Leonard Judd's in just a while, and deal with his correspondence.'

Mrs Sweeney always finished up Lucy's dancing-lessons by making her balance along the fence. 'It makes your feet strong; it gives you balance.' Before she married, she had walked the slack-wire for Forepaugh and Sells, travelling all over the country. The stories she could tell, the hearts she had broken.

'Just one more waltz?' Lucy begged her. 'You know me, I could dance all day!'

Mrs Sweeney took her to the gate, and opened it. 'You're just like my Samuel. I could die dancing, he used to say! And bless him, he did! The Lord called him at the Stock-breeders' Ball, right in the middle of a polka.'

Lucy tightened the ribbons of her bonnet. 'He's still dancing, I'll bet you, somewhere in Heaven.'

'Well, that's as may be,' sniffed Mrs Sweeney. 'But not the polka. I can't see the Lord God and his Heavenly Throng dancing the polka. Not with him, anyhow.'

Lucy was never quite sure if Mrs Sweeney was serious. Her pinched, triangular face appeared to be permanently vexed, and she always wore mourning-black. But she had an irreverent Irish wit; and because of that, and because of the dancing-lessons she gave, most folk in Oak City called her the Skipping Widder. She probably wasn't much more than forty-two years old; she could have passed for sixty.

But Lucy adored Mrs Sweeney because she chattered endlessly while they danced together round and round her creaky upstairs room, *one*-two-three, *one*-two-three. Like

3

two little people on the top of a musical-box. Mrs Sweeney told her all about the dances she had been to in New York, when she was a young girl, before she had fallen with a capital F and joined the circus. Oh, those dances, my dear! White gloves, ostrich feathers, gaseliers and sparkling jewellery! High-varnished carriages, and men with collars so tall they had to spend the entire evening staring at the ceiling!

By contrast, there was very little dancing in Oak City, Kansas; and not much reason to dance, either. Oak City wasn't much more than a wind-sucked collection of wooden buildings on the Kansas Pacific railroad track between Hays City and Fort Wallace. From time to time, some of the local sodbusters got up a barndance; and every year the Army arranged a Christmas ball at Fort Hays, where a local girl might have the chance of dancing with one of the officers (but what an ignorant, spotty, bay- rum-smelling collection of stumbling young giddy-goats *they* were!).

But apart from that, only the grass danced, only the dust danced; and the only music you could hear was the roller-organ in the corner saloon, or singing in the church on Sunday mornings. '*Rock of Ages, cleave to me . . .*' Oak City had more than its fair share of sky; and more than its fair share of wind; and when there wasn't any wind, like today, it had more than its fair share of silence.

'See you next Thursday, Mrs Sweeney!'

Lucy closed the yard gate behind her, and held up her skirts as she negotiated the alley that led to the main street. Today, the street was hot and silent; not even the rattling of a buckboard disturbed the quiet. That distinctive smell of prairie filled the air: hay, dust, and cattle, intermingled with a fragrance like dried spices.

She began to walk back towards her father's store. The heels of her button-up boots echoed on the plank sidewalk. She was seventeen years old, very small-breasted, very slim-hipped, and very tall; but then her mother had been tall, too. Her hair was so fair and fine that her mother used to

4

tease her that Rumpelstiltskin had spun it. Her nose was quite long but very straight, with just a sprinkling of freckles on the bridge, and her eyes were such an intense blue that people used to look twice, because they couldn't believe that anybody could have eyes as blue as that, as if she had tinted them with two meadowsful of squeezed-out cornflowers.

The only part of her face that Lucy didn't like was her mouth. It could look pouty and sulky, even when she wasn't feeling pouty and sulky in the least.

She hummed the *German Hearts* waltz, and skipped around in a circle. *One-two-three! One-two-three!* Over at the depot, she heard the deep-chested chuffing of the train, and blossoms of black smoke rose up into the sky.

Most of the doors of the stores along Main Street were open, because of the heat and the lack of wind. Inside, the shops and offices were shadowy, and each harboured its own particular smell. The musty ripeness of the Meat Market, where the butchers chopped up steer carcasses in their derby hats and their brown-bloodied aprons; L. Judd Real Estate & Loan Agent, where Mrs Sweeney worked in the afternoons, letter-writing, all lavender-water and papers; the Helmsley Drug Store, cough-candy and cloves; J. A. Overbay's Dry Goods & Clothing, sour new denim and boot-polish.

Two of the younger butchers were leaning outside the Meat Market with their arms folded, one high-coloured and the other white as milk. They were smoking cheroots and narrowing their eyes against the brightness of the morning. Lucy knew them both: Bob Wonderly and William Zang. They had attended the Oak City school together.

'Lucy! You been dancing, you pretty thing?' the ruddy one shouted out. 'How about a dance for your old pal Bob?'

Lucy smiled at him quickly under the shadow of her hat-brim, but shook her head.

'Hey, Lucy!' the butcher-boy persisted. 'Hey, come on over here! Don't you go acting all high'n'mighty-like! Listen here, how'd you care for some ox-liver?'

His colleague exploded with mirth. 'Smack me, Bob! Ox-liver! Romance aint dead yet! Hey, look! She's walking on! Maybe you'd better ask her if she'd fancy some washed tripes thrown in!'

'You can fun,' Bob Wonderly complained. 'I'm sure glad some folks can afford to turn up their nose at it. First-grade ox-liver, damn it. Don't grow on trees.'

Lucy crossed the street, and passed the wide dusty tract of land in front of the railroad depot. As she did so, a tall broad-shouldered young man appeared from the shadows of the entrance, his chestnut-coloured hair shining bright in the sun with brilliantine. In his right hand he was carrying a heavy brown-paper parcel tied with twine: his left arm was raised to balance the weight.

She stopped and waited for him and smiled, shading her eyes against the sun.

'Jamie!' she called.

He came up to her, and set the parcel down on the ground. He wiped his forehead on his shirtsleeve. 'Ned wouldn't wait for me,' he told her. 'Said his haircut was urgent, case he met Dorothy Oosterman.'

Lucy kissed the tip of her fingers and touched Jamie on the nose. 'Didn't expect to see you in town today.'

'Oh. Well, no. I wasn't coming till tomorrow. But since Ned was coming in anyway.'

He hefted up the parcel again, and together they began to walk slowly along Main Street. She and Jamie weren't exactly courting; not formally; but when the Cullens had settled close to Oak City just over two years ago, Lucy and Jamie had immediately made friends, and everybody naturally assumed that they would marry one day. People talked about them in the same breath, 'Jamie'n'Lucy.'

'What's that?' Lucy asked Jamie, nodding towards his package. 'Not more Bibles?'

'Bibles?' said Jamie. 'Not on your life. These are law-books.'

'That won't please your father,' Lucy told him.

'Don't care if it doesn't,' Jamie replied. 'Respecting your father is one thing. Pleasing him, well, that's another.' He paused, and then he added, 'Specially since he's so darned difficult to please.'

Jamie's father Jerrold Cullen was religious to the point of spontaneous incandescence, and had given a Bible to every man and woman who worked for him, and a few to people who didn't. He held every word in the Bible to be true indisputable fact, and you could guarantee that even if you started talking to him about cattle-diseases, or the price of feed, he would soon be lauding the suffering of Job, or discussing how Jonah got out of the whale, or considering the lilies as they grew.

Jerrold Cullen was sorely displeased by what he regarded as Jamie's unnatural determination to be a lawyer rather than a granger, and he frequently said so. To toil on the land was divine, as far as he was concerned. Jamie should be out in God's good air, ploughing and fence-mending and branding calves, not sitting in stuffy schoolrooms squinting at lawbooks. Book-learning in Jerrold Cullen's estimation came somewhere a little lower than taking the Lord's name in vain and only a little higher than coveting thy neighbour's maidservant.

To be truthful, Lucy didn't really understand Jamie's passion for the law, either. She had tried to read some of his books on Precedent, and they were boring beyond all human reason. But she liked Jamie. She liked him because of his slow, serious manner; and she liked him because he was so tall. She stood five-feet-seven in her stockings, overlooking most of the short squat Oak City boys by almost an inch. But Jamie was six feet two inches clear, and when he wore his riding-boots he stood out in a crowd like a man taking a leisurely swim in a lake of bobbing hats. He always made her feel small and delicate and feminine.

He was handsome, too; at least Lucy thought he was.

With age and experience his face was developing some edges. An angular chin, and a nose with the hint of a bump in it, and deep-set eyes which were grey like thunderstorms and very bright. He looked as if he couldn't make up his mind whether to hit you or laugh.

She liked him so much that she almost loved him; but she still had her secret dream of marrying a prince, or a lord, or a millionaire.

'Hudson's Law of Torts, in seven volumes,' Jamie explained. 'Had to order them special from Monkey Ward.' He used the derisive nickname for Montgomery Ward in deference to the bitterness that Lucy's father felt for the big Chicago mail-order houses. Montgomery Ward and Sears Roebuck had brought scores of small main street stores close to the brink of bankruptcy, Lucy's father included.

A farm wagon for $50, sent by railroad express? Seventy-two dozen shirt buttons for 35c? Which small-town store-keeper could compete with that? Especially when — once read, and re-read, and dreamed over, and ordered from — the mail-order catalogues supplied the entire Western frontier with an inexhaustible supply of free toilet-paper?

'Torts? What are torts?' Lucy asked him. 'They sound like some kind of cookie.'

Jamie said, 'Pfff!' in derision and shook his head. 'You must know less than just about any girl I ever met!'

'I'm going to be a socialite,' Lucy retorted, sticking her nose in the air. 'A socialite doesn't have to know what torts are. *Do* have another tort, Mrs Vanderbilt.'

'Are you trying to make a clown out of me?' Jamie demanded.

'I'm sorry! Oh, Jamie, I'm sorry! Don't sulk! Tell me what torts are! Do!'

Jamie could see that she was teasing him; but he cleared his throat and said gravely, 'A tort, see, is when you cause injury or damage, either by something you did, or by something you should've done and didn't.'

'Well that's as clear as mud,' said Lucy, skipping as she walked.

'Listen –' said Jamie. 'Suppose your father left the lid off the blasting-powder and then one of his Saturday boys went looking for a pound of nails with a lighted candle?'

'And then what?' asked Lucy.

'And then the boy got himself smithereened, of course, because your father should have put the lid back on the blasting powder!'

'And that's a tort? When a boy gets smithereened?'

Jamie gave her a serious nod. 'Well, yes. That kind of thing. Smithereened boys, trampled crops, ladders not fixed, you name it. Mr Collamer says there's a good steady future in torts.'

Lucy held on to his sleeve. 'It all sounds gigantically dull to me. I thought you were going to be a crime lawyer. You know, defending murderers and bank-robbers.'

'You know something about you?' Jamie asked her.

'No, what?'

'You'd tease the fleas off of a mule, you would. No mistake about it.'

They had almost reached Jack Darling's General Store. It was a two-storey frame building, painted stray-dog yellow; store below, living accommodation upstairs, the very last building in the street; where Oak City finished and the rest of Kansas began. To Lucy, the house where she lived had always marked the definitive end of the world. Street one side: High Plains the other. She sometimes felt that it was like living on the very edge of the Earth.

There are no mountains in Kansas. The plains-dwellers called it the land 'where you can look farther but see less'. But on days when the distant sky was gun-barrel black and the whitish-yellow prairie grass waved like a soft and silent sea, Lucy could still feel an alarming sense of vertigo.

In Kansas, it was easy to remember that you were glued on to the world only by the soles of your feet.

9

Jack Darling was waiting on the store verandah, a grey-haired man with a frame as bony as a bicycle, in a long shopkeeper's apron. Above his head, a weather-blistered sign announced that he was Jack Darling Leading Merchant of Western Kansas, and that he had a stock of Farm Supplies, Fine Groceries & Family Provisions; Clothing in Suits Nobby & Modest; and Stetson's Hats in all the Latest Styles.

The sign said nothing about him being a widower; and times being so hard.

'Poppa!' Lucy called out, and waved; and her father inclined his head to acknowledge that he had already seen her.

'Care for a sarsaparilla?' Lucy asked Jamie.

'Sure. But I can't stay too long. Ned said to meet him at twelve. I have to help out with the herd this afternoon. Dehorning, something real grisly like that.'

They climbed the steps on to the verandah, and Jamie set down his parcel and lifted his hat. Jack Darling smiled and said, 'How're you keeping, Jamie? Your pa working you hard?' And then, to Lucy, 'I've got a surprise for you, sweetheart, of sorts. Guess what just arrived on the eleven o'clock train?'

'Not those eyeglasses you sent away for?'

Jack Darling shook his head. 'It's not a what, it's a who.'

'Oh, pity. I'm dying to see you in eyeglasses.' She put her arm around him and kissed him. 'I expect you're dying to see me, too!'

Jack Darling gave his daughter a playful smack. 'You're going to be the death of me, one day, with all your teasing.'

'Takes after her mother,' he told Jamie, as they went inside. 'Never could be serious, not about nothing.'

'Yes, sir,' said Jamie, but that was all. Lucy had warned him that Jack Darling had almost died from grief when he lost his wife. Hadn't eaten, hadn't slept, and still groaned into his pillow at night.

Jack Darling was sallow-faced, with a drooping grey

moustache, and a slight stoop to his shoulders; but he was still good-looking. Most people reckoned that was where Lucy's eyes had come from; and that clear, determined profile of hers. It was her mouth that was different. You would have to look in the parlour, at a photograph of her mother, to find that alluring, pouting, wilful mouth.

'Sarsaparilla or lemonade?' asked Lucy.

'Either. Or a Prickly Ash tonic, if you have one.'

'Ugh! I don't know how you can drink that stuff!'

'Supposed to be good for the married side of life,' Jack Darling remarked. He was a moral man, a good churchgoer, but he wasn't prudish.

'Jamie's not married,' Lucy retorted.

'Not right now,' Jamie told her, defiantly. 'But when I get my law degree, and hang up my shingle – well, then, there's one or two girls in this town that better watch out.'

'There's one or two girls in this town that better watch out, already,' Lucy warned him, as her father topped up a glass of Prickly Ash bitters with soda-water.

'How about you, sweetheart?' her father asked her. 'Sarsaparilla?'

Lucy shook her head. 'Where's the surprise?' she wanted to know. The store didn't look any different from usual; shadowy and cool with the green blinds drawn down over the windows; its rafters hung with hams; its shelves crowded with everything from apple-butter to bushel-baskets to women's winter long-johns.

Around the stove (cold, of course, because it was summer, but still Oak City's social focus) the usual loungers were sitting, playing poker and sipping the whisky that Jack Darling provided for free. Henry McGuffey, a bearded old-timer who had somehow become beached on the High Plains on his way to the goldfields of California: 'run out of funds and enthusiasm'. Samuel Blankenship, former engineer for the Leavenworth, Lawrence and Galveston railroad (known in Kansas as the 'Lazy, Lousy and Greasy') who had crushed his best friend while he was shunting and lost his nerve for driving locomotives. Osage Pete, half-Indian, half-Norwegian, able to speak five different languages and all of them badly.

Jack Darling smiled, and called out, 'Cass!'

There was a moment's pause, and then the stockroom door opened up and a stocky black-bearded man appeared, dressed in a tight tan-coloured suit. He had a large leonine head, a deep barrel of a chest, but disproportionately short legs. His face had been barbecued crimson by the sun, so that to begin with Lucy didn't recognize him. He came forward with a sly smile on his face; and then stopped and held out his arms.

'Uncle Casper?' breathed Lucy. She turned to her father. 'It's Uncle Casper!'

'It surely is!' her Uncle Casper told her; and then smacked his hands together, and picked her up in his arms and twirled her around. 'Heyyyy-hooooooo!!'

Lucy hugged him and kissed him. His hair was still wet from washing his face, and his hands smelled strongly of Peet's Almond Cream soap.

'Did you *know* Uncle Casper was coming?' Lucy asked her father, bright-eyed and excited, and when her father nodded, she said 'Why didn't you tell me?'

'Your daddy thinks I'm not to be relied on, that's why,' Uncle Casper told her. 'Thought I wouldn't show up, see, and didn't want you to get your hopes up unnecessary-like.'

'But you've never let us down before!' Lucy replied. 'You never forget my birthday, do you? And you never forget to send me the flower-money on momma's anniversary!'

'Couldn't forget my dear sister and my dear sister's little girl, now could I?' Uncle Casper asked her. 'What do you think of the beard?'

Jack Darling was smiling cautiously. They had seen Casper only twice in the last five years. The first time, on that stark February day when Lucy's mother had been buried in the snow. And the second time, two years gone, when he had arrived late one night to beg for money; and Jack Darling had given him a hundred dollars for the sake of his dear dead wife.

Casper had eventually paid most of the money back. All the same, Jack's expression showed that he was still wary and reserved about his brother-in-law. Jamie noticed it, even if Lucy didn't. Enough bad news had come through the door of the Jack Darling General Store in the past few years for Jack not to know its face when it put in yet another appearance.

'How long are you staying?' Lucy asked Uncle Casper. 'Oh, Jamie, meet my favourite uncle!'

'Fav'rite and only,' Uncle Casper remarked, laying his hand proprietorially around Lucy's shoulders. He ignored Jamie's outstretched hand, and said to Jack Darling, 'How about shot of that genr'l-store liquor, Jack, just to ease the old pie-eating equipment? And –' nodding to Jamie '– some for my friend here.'

Jamie said, 'Thanks, but I have to go. My father's expecting me back before lunch.'

'Come on, you've still got time for a shot,' grinned Uncle Casper, his eyes glittery and black. 'The first time I ever tasted whisky, my father was expecting me back before lunch, too. That was thirty-five years ago, and I haven't been back for lunch yet.'

Jamie shook his head. 'Thanks all the same. I have my law-studies, too.'

'Law-studies, huh?' asked Uncle Casper. 'Let me tell you something, young fellow – no man ever got rich by studying *nothing* – nothing except for life.' Jack Darling handed him a shot-glass of whisky, and he tossed it back as if he were throwing a bucketful of water on to a blazing barn. 'Women, and fighting, and how to make money, that's all you have to study.'

'And that's what you studied?' Jamie asked him. Lucy

13

didn't much care for Jamie's tone of voice. It was throaty and expressionless, the voice he put on when he was upset, or jealous, or angry.

Uncle Casper nodded and grinned. 'Women, and fighting, and how to make money.'

'And that's the way to get rich?'

Uncle Casper carried on nodding.

'By that token,' said Jamie, 'I guess you must be richer than most?'

Uncle Casper's eyes narrowed, and he sniffed in one nostril. 'No need to get smart, Sonny Jim.'

'Millionaire, are you?' asked Jamie. 'Multi-millionaire? Billionaire?'

There was a lengthy pause. Then Uncle Casper said, 'There's rich and there's rich. I may not be rich now. Not rich in the sense of having much money –'

'Is there another kind of rich?' asked Jamie, in exaggerated surprise. 'I always thought that rich, by definition, meant having a lot of money.'

'I'm right on the *edge* of being rich.' Uncle Casper snapped back at him. 'I'm rich in ideas, rich in plans, rich in assets. If'n my plans turn out the way they're s'poster, I'll be rich in money, too.'

He held out his empty glass without even looking at Jack Darling; but Jack Darling refilled it for him. He was a storekeeper after all; and it was a long-standing tradition that storekeepers kept one or two bottles for the sake of sociability.

'Oil,' said Uncle Casper. 'That's what I'm after. I'm taking the railroad clear to California, and I'm going to drill myself a fortune, right out of the ground.'

'Fixed your lease?' Jamie asked him. 'Sorted out your drilling rights?'

'Things are arranged,' Uncle Casper told him, offhandedly.

'Good,' said Jamie. 'In that case, all I can say is good luck,' and turned to go.

Uncle Casper snatched his hand out and caught hold of Jamie's sleeve. 'Don't you turn your back on me, Sonny Jim. When I come back here from California, you're going to be turning your back on a man of means.'

Jamie gently but firmly prised Casper's fingers away. 'I did wish you good luck, sir.'

Casper let out a loud, braying laugh, and tossed back his second shot of whisky. He said, 'Sure. Sure you did.' He was too much weakened by alcohol and poor eating habits to take on a burly young man like Jamie. He held out his glass with a noticeably trembling hand for another shot. Jack Darling hesitated, but then poured it out for him.

'Will you have a drink with me, then, to show that you mean what you say?' Uncle Casper challenged Jamie.

'Sir, I *always* mean what I say,' Jamie told him. 'I don't need to take a drink to prove it, to you or anybody else. Besides, I don't want to get home smelling of liquor. My father's a temperance man, can't tolerate the breath of Satan.'

Uncle Casper squeezed Lucy's shoulder and smiled. 'The breath of Satan, hey? Upright lad you've got here, young Lucy. Upright!'

Lucy didn't catch the sarcasm in Casper's voice, but Jamie did. Apart from that, Jamie didn't at all care for the way that Casper was hugging Lucy and kissing her hair, as if he owned her. Lucy didn't mind. Lucy didn't think anything of it. To her, Uncle Casper was Uncle Casper, and that was all.

Tightly, Jamie said, 'Believe me, sir, I can drink with the rest of them, when the time's right.' He hesitated, and then he added, 'Unlike some, I can hold my liquor.'

'How's that?' Uncle Casper demanded. 'You trying to tell me that I can't take my drink?'

Jamie stayed calm. 'No, sir. I'm not telling you anything at all. I'm just leaving. Goodbye, Lucy. Goodbye, Mr Darling.'

But Casper said, 'Ho no!' and reached across and tugged the bottle of whisky out of Jack Darling's grasp. He held it up high above his head, noisily sloshing its contents from side to side.

'Come on, now, you're a God-fearing young man, I'll bet you five dollars that you can't drink five shots of whisky without breathing in between; and then say the Lord's Prayer backwards.'

'Casper, that's foolishness,' said Jack Darling. 'Give me the bottle.'

Jamie looked away. 'I'm not taking any bets on anything, sir, least of all liquor, and certainly not prayer. My brother Ned's meeting me outside the barber-shop at twelve noon precisely, and he's going to be plenty sore if he has to wait.'

Casper glanced up at the clock. 'Come on, friend, plenty of time! No wonder you're studying law! You're just like a lawyer, you're all puff! Lucy – you should watch yourself with a fellow like this! All puff and no stuff!'

Jamie looked quickly at Lucy, then lowered his head.

'Puff! Puff! Puff!' mocked Uncle Casper, and sloshed the whisky with every word.

Jamie lifted his eyes. 'Mr Darling,' he said, in a quiet voice, 'would you give me a shot-glass?'

'Oh, *no*, Jamie,' Lucy begged him. 'Uncle Casper was only ribbing. Weren't you, Uncle?'

'Sure,' grinned Uncle Casper. 'I was ribbing, that's all. You High Plains folk don't know a leg-pull even when you trip right over it.'

But without a word, Jamie walked around the stove, and took down a glass from the shelf. He came back, twisted the whisky bottle out of Uncle Casper's hand and uncorked it.

'Jamie!' Lucy protested. 'If you drink so much as one drop of that whisky, I shall never speak to you again, ever!'

But Jamie stared at Uncle Casper and said, 'A bet's a bet. Do you think I'm going to walk out of here with your uncle or *anybody*'s uncle thinking I'm a coward?'

'Be serious, Jamie,' Jack Darling told him. 'Casper's a joker, that's all.'

But Jamie took a deep breath, then another, and filled up the shot-glass to the brim. He paused for a moment, and then knocked it back. Without hesitating, without breathing, he filled the glass again, and knocked that back, too.

'Jamie!' Lucy protested. 'Jamie – it was only a joke!'

Red in the face, Jamie filled his glass again, and swallowed it. Two more to go, and already tears were running down his cheeks. Uncle Casper put his arm around Lucy's shoulders and squeezed her tight and said, 'He's plucky! I'll give him that much! Most men would've breathed by now!'

Jamie splashed more whisky into the glass, and drank it with shaking hands. The liquor dribbled down his chin and trickled on to his shirt. One more to go. Jack Darling turned away, shaking his head. Old Henry McGuffey whooped hoarsely and called out, 'That's showin' 'em, son! That's showin' 'em!'

Almost purple, his forehead bursting with sweat, Jamie poured out a final shot. He hesitated for a moment, struggling not to breathe, struggling not to choke. Then he tilted his head back, and swallowed it.

He wiped his mouth with the back of his hand, set down the empty glass, and then breathed out.

'Don't nobody light no matches,' Samuel Blankenship cackled. 'That boy's going to have dangerously inflammable breath for just a while.'

Lucy clapped her hands. 'The Lord's Prayer backwards!' she laughed. 'Oh, come on, Jamie, you can do it!'

Jamie swallowed two or three times. Then he said, 'Amen, ever and ever for, glory the power the –' and recited the entire prayer from end to beginning with scarcely a single hesitation.

When he had finished, Lucy broke free from Uncle Casper and waltzed up and down the store with him. 'Whoopee! You did it. Jamie! You did it!' Uncle Casper watched them wryly, picking in between his front teeth with his thumbnail.

At last Jamie came up to Uncle Casper and held out his hand. 'That's five dollars you owe me.'

Casper gave him a sloping grin. 'I told you, didn't I? Didn't I make myself clear? That was a leg-pull, that's all. No bet. Just a leg-pull.'

Jamie took a deep, patient breath. 'Sir, that was no leg-pull, and you know it. That was a legal bet, square and legal; and what's more I won it square and legal.'

Casper looked around the store, smiling at everybody; Henry and Samuel and Osage Pete. 'What did I tell you? No sense of humour west of Leavenworth.'

Lucy said, '*Uncle* – you're cheating! Jamie drank the whisky and he said the prayer.'

Casper looked back at her, and shrugged. 'No concern of mine if the boy's too fond of the bottle, and an atheist to boot.' But when Lucy folded her arms and frowned at him crossly, he shrugged, and sniffed, and dug into the inside pocket of his suit, and one by one brought out a handful of crumpled-up bills. Painstakingly, he smoothed out a five-dollar bill, and held it out. 'Here – seeing that you won't take a joke for what it's worth; and seeing that it's Lucy here who's appealing on your behalf, here's your money. I wish you joy of it.'

Jamie let his hands drop to his sides. 'Forget it,' he said. 'I'm not a betting man, in any case.'

'Come on,' Uncle Casper encouraged him, flapping the money up and down. 'Take it, you've earned it.'

Jamie said, 'Forget it, do you mind?' and took hold of Lucy's arm. 'Will I see you Sunday?' he asked her. 'I thought we could go horseback-riding, down along the river. We could take those two new bays from the Williams place; they're really special.'

Lucy nodded. 'All right, then. Two o'clock. Three?'

'Two o'clock's fine by me.'

'Take the money,' Casper insisted. 'Come on, now. You've won it. Take the money.'

'Unh-unh,' Jamie told him, without taking his eyes away from Lucy. 'If it hurts you so much to give it away, then I'd rather you didn't. But you can pay Mr Darling for his whisky.' He swayed a little, and sidestepped. He was obviously beginning to feel drunk.

'Hmh. Suit yourself.' Uncle Casper folded up the five-dollar bill and tucked it back into his pocket. 'If that's the way you feel.'

Lucy took Jamie's arm and stepped out on to the verandah with him. 'I'm sorry,' she said. 'Uncle Casper can be kind of sharp sometimes. He doesn't mean any harm.'

'Sure he doesn't,' said Jamie. 'But, you know, be careful, all the same. A man who drinks that much.'

'Oh! You can talk! Five straight whiskies and no breathing!' Lucy stood on tiptoe and kissed his cheek. Jamie caught hold of her hand and pressed it tight between his.

'I think I like you, Mr Jamie Cullen,' Lucy told him.

'Well, yes, Miss Lucy Darling; and I think I like you, too.'

He picked up his parcel of books; and then lifted his hat to her, and began to make his way down the street towards the barber-shop. Lucy could see Jamie's brother Ned waiting in his buggy, dressed in black, his black hat lowered over his eyes, as motionless as a photograph. Jamie turned around to wave Lucy goodbye. As he did so, he lost his balance and fell flat on his back in the dust, with his legs in the air.

'Jamie!' screamed Lucy, and ran to help him up.

Jamie sat up with dusty-white shoulders and a glassy smile. 'It's those damned books!' he protested. 'Shifted my weight from left to right; and these damned books – swung around and tippled me over!'

Lucy was almost breathless with laughter. 'You're drunk! You're totally drunk! Ned's going to kill you! And what's your father going to say!'

'I'm all right, I'm all right,' Jamie told her, and started to laugh, too. 'But you tell that uncle of yours –'

He paused, and then he looked serious. 'You keep an eye on that uncle of yours. I've seen men like that before.'

'Men like what?'

'Cardsharps, riff-raff. Devilish so-and-sos.'

'Jamie, he's not riff-raff. He's my *uncle*!'

Jamie climbed on to his feet, and collected his books. 'All the more reason.'

Lucy watched him teeter across the street towards his brother's buggy; and over the warm soft noises of the morning, she heard them arguing. '*Where the blue blazes have you been? Have you been drinking? Smell like a darned saloon!*'

At last, Ned whipped up the buggy, and it turned a circle in the street and headed back towards the Saline River. Lucy called, 'Jamie!' and waved, and Jamie waved wildly back. 'See you Sunday! Two o'clock! And you take care!'

Over a supper of pan-fried corned-beef hash, with a bottle of whisky on the table, Uncle Casper told them stories of what he had been doing since he had last visited. They sat in the cramped little dining room upstairs, with its greyish wooden furniture and its red chequered curtains. By contrast to the meanness of the room, the view out of the window was startling: an endless undulating ocean of grasses; an evening sky so clear and so wide that it could make your head spin.

Uncle Casper kept the whisky bottle beside his plate and drank almost three-quarters of it during the meal. Lucy loved him. The more he drank, the funnier he became; until the two of them were screaming with laughter. Lucy's father joined in, too; but less wholeheartedly, and sometimes Lucy caught him grimacing instead of laughing, or simply staring out of the window.

'I've made a fortune and I've lost a fortune,' Uncle Casper declared when they had finished eating, rolling a Durham cigarette one-handed. 'But this time, I'm out to make a fortune so big that it can't be lost. This time, I'm going to have silk shirts and velvet collars, and beautiful naked women to warm up my long-johns before I put 'em on.'

'Come on, Casper', said Lucy's father, with a smile. 'Let's keep the smoking talk till later.'

'Lucy doesn't mind, do you, Lucy?' grinned Uncle Casper, resting his hand heavily and affectionately on Lucy's arm, and breathing whisky fumes at her. 'Lucy and me, we're friends; and always will be; and always *have* to be. Because Anna was exactly like Lucy. My poor, poor Anna; rest in peace. But Lucy has the same looks, what do you think, Jack? And the same way about her. You can't deny it. Anna all over again.'

Lucy's father said nothing, but cleared away the plates, and went through to the kitchen to find them some plain cheese and an apple pie.

Uncle Casper leaned forward. 'Let me tell you something, darling. A schoolteacher told me this one, on the train from Leavenworth. He said the definition of good education is the ability to be able to describe a woman without using your hands.'

'Oh, Uncle,' Lucy protested, although she didn't understand the joke at all.

Uncle Casper laughed and tilted back in his chair and swallowed another mouthful of whisky. His eyes were pink around the edges and his words were beginning to sound blurry. 'You've grown up beautiful, do you know that? Beautiful! I can't even understand why you stay here, out in this –' he turned towards the window, where the grass waved for mile after mile. '– this isn't even a *place*.'

'It's home,' said Lucy, defensively.

'And you're going to stay here all your life?'

'Of course not. I'm going to be a socialite.'

Uncle Casper sucked at his cigarette, and blew smoke out of his nostrils. 'A socialite, hmh? All diamonds and pearls, I suppose, and ostrich plumes? I've seen women like that; in Washington, and Baltimore, and Charleston.'

Lucy lowered her eyes. She didn't mind being teased; but not about that one particular dream. That dream was precious. Without that dream, she didn't know how she could have tolerated the long glaring summers and the bitterly-cold winters and the weather-scraped faces of men and women who were trying to scratch a living out of nothing much.

'Need money, if'n you want to be a socialite,' Uncle Casper told her. 'Need money and plenty of it. And what have you got?'

Jack Darling came back into the room, carrying a plate of strong yellow cheese. Uncle Casper looked up and said, 'How's business, Jack? Thriving, is it? Can't hear yourself think for the register ringing?'

Jack sat down. He glanced at Lucy first, because she looked a little upset, but then he said, 'Look around you, you can see for yourself. Times have been nothing but thin since the cattle-drives finished. Everybody's living off credit, including me.'

Eleven years ago, when Jack Darling had first opened his general store, Oak City had still been a thriving railhead for Texas longhorns, and every cattle-drive between May and November had brought thirsty, hungry, and well-paid drovers – a seasonal trade for sure, but enough to keep Jack Darling's General Stores and most of the other Oak City businesses bustling.

But the prosperous days of the cattle-drives had been short-lived. Immigrant grangers like Jerrold Cullen had started to complain about the ticks which the Texas cattle brought with them – ticks to which the Texas cattle themselves were immune, but which had decimated the domestic herds with splenic fever.

In the end, the Kansas legislature had been forced by the grangers to declare a quarantine line, north to south, halfway down the territory. No Texas cattle were to be driven into Kansas anywhere to the east of that line; and as the grangers moved further westward, so the quarantine line had to be moved further westward, too.

One by one, the riotous railhead towns had lost their seasonal trade. 'The wild and reckless sons of the Plains' no longer congregated in towns like Abilene, Ellsworth, Wichita, and Ellis; and community after community dwindled and died. At the very last, even Dodge City, the wildest and wealthiest of all the railheads, had collapsed into poverty, too.

Lucy could remember the days when her father's store had been crammed with luxuries and fancy goods. Canned oysters, silks, perfumes from Paris, and nickel-plated .45s with carved ivory handles. At one time he had even sold diamond rings and stickpins. She could remember him giving her pretty new dresses almost every week; and soft kid boots, and ribbons, and bonnets. These days, he was hard put to keep them both in bacon and flour.

Uncle Casper nipped out his cigarette between finger and thumb and cut himself a stout chunk of cheese. 'Lucy wants to be a socialite,' he remarked. 'But that takes a whole consideration of money, being a socialite. How're you going to manage to dress her in furs, Jack? How're you going to decorate her with pearls, and such?'

Now Jack Darling understood why Lucy had been looking upset. He reached across the table and grasped her hand. 'Everybody has the right to have a dream, Cass. It's written in the Constitution. I have mine, you have yours.'

'Ah, yes!' Casper replied, with his mouth full. 'But the difference beween your dream and my dream is that my dream is going to come true! When I bring in that oil-well, I'm going to be rich, Jack, I'm going to shine with diamonds from top to toe. Lucy can dream about being a socialite, by all means; she can dream and dream. But only money can make a dream like that happen for real. Otherwise believe me it's Oak City, Kansas, for ever, and marriage to a hayseed lawyer with as much sense of humour as a half-a-pint of buggy paint, and five squalling babies, and lose your looks before you're turned thirty.'

Jack said, 'Cass, you listen to me, I'm a patient man, and you're Anna's brother, God rest her poor spirit, but don't try my goodwill.'

Casper leaned forward with an unabashed grin. 'Oh, you know me, Jack! I speak my mind, that's all; and sometimes it aint so difficult for people to take offence. But I don't mean nobody no harm, especially you, and especially young Lucy. If'n I've done you any discourtesy, well then, accept my apologies.'

He took hold of Lucy's hand again, and squeezed it tightly; and gave her an exaggerated wink. 'Trouble is, you know that I'm telling you the truth. It's money, or else it's Oak City. And Oak City's no place for a girl who looks the way you do.'

Casper smoked, and smiled, and poured himself another whisky. Lucy had never seen a man drink so much whisky and still remain coherent. At last Jack Darling looked up at the clock and said, 'I'd better get back downstairs. Sam's being taking care of the store. God knows, he's probably given everything away for free.'

'Good for him!' Casper remarked. 'I like a man with a generous heart.'

That evening, when the store was all closed up, Jack Darling and Uncle Casper sat in the parlour for a drink and a smoke. Lucy joined them for a while, sitting at the table with her crochet, but all Casper wanted to talk about was money and how to make it, and so at nine o'clock she made her excuses and left them to it.

She had just finished turning down the beds and lighting the lamps in the bedrooms; her father came out of the parlour and took hold of her arm. She was already in her nightdress; a plain cotton gown with a high-buttoned neck and a yellow-ribboned yoke.

'Goodnight, sweetheart,' he told her.

She kissed his prickly cheek. 'Goodnight, poppa.'

Jack Darling hesitated. He looked strangely old tonight; and tired. 'You know, sweetheart, if I *could* take you away from here. . .'

Lucy kissed him again. 'Was momma content, being here?'

Jack Darling pulled a face. 'Sure, in her way, she was content. But your momma, well – she was my wife, she had a duty to be content. She always stood by me, no matter what.'

'Then you don't have to worry. I'll stand by you, too, if you want me to.'

Jack Darling tried without much success to smile. 'I know that, sweetheart. But I've been thinking about what your Uncle Casper said at supper.'

'Poppa . . . if momma was content, then *I'm* content. You always do your best.'

'But you should have dresses, parties, dancing. That's what you really want.'

Lucy gave him another kiss. 'Everybody's entitled to have a dream. You said so yourself.'

'Even if it never comes true?'

She looked away. She didn't say anything. Her dream was too important for her to risk it by tempting fate. *You should have seen them*, Mrs Sweeney had told her. *The ladies in their white silk gowns, with all their ostrich feathers; and the men like gods.*

Jack Darling said, 'Lucy, what can I give you? Nothing but hard work, and more hard work, and when the good Lord calls me, what do you get? A patch of dry land, and a general store in a town where nobody can't scarcely afford to buy nothing.'

'Poppa, I'm content!'

Jack Darling looked away, disconsolate. 'The things I promised your mother! The jewellery, the high life! All that turned up was ruin and more ruin, and then the enteric fever.'

Lucy squeezed his hand. 'Poppa . . . don't blame yourself for everything. It wasn't your fault that they stopped the cattle-drives. And momma getting sick, that wasn't your fault, either.'

Her father looked back at her, and his cheeks were glistening with tears. 'Just so long as you never curse me, Lucy, for all of my failures.'

'Poppa, you never failed me once. Not once.'

He held her tight. 'Goodnight, sweetheart. Sleep well. Me and Cass'll be turning in, too, in just a while.'

'Don't drink too much. And don't let Uncle Casper drink too much.'

Jack Darling wiped his eyes with his fingers, and grunted in amusement. 'That man must be hollow from the neck down.'

He went back to the parlour. As he closed the door, Lucy glimpsed Uncle Casper opening up another bottle of whisky. She stood where she was for a while, thinking. Then she went into her room.

Lucy had always felt secure in her room. It was small, wallpapered with roses, just big enough for her mahogany-veneer bed with its patchwork quilt, and a light-oak cupboard which a German family had brought all the way from Münster, in Westfalia. Jack Darling had accepted the cupboard in settlement of five months of unpaid credit. It wasn't worth anything, but it was handsomely carved, and to Lucy it represented the first time that she had been grown-up enough to understand an act of human charity.

She could remember the faces of the Hartmann family as they delivered the cupboard on their handcart. Grim, undernourished, with that defiance that characterizes people who face poverty and hardship without any foreseeable end to it, but who have come too far to go back.

When they had gone, Lucy had asked her father what the cupboard was worth.

He had walked around, slapped it, and shrugged, 'Four or five dollars, maybe nothing at all. Folks around here may be short of cash and food and shoe-leather, but they aren't exactly short of furniture.'

'But how much did the Hartmanns owe you?'

'One hundred and eight dollars and four cents.'

'But you told them that if they gave you this cupboard, that would leave them square!'

Her father had nodded, opening and closing the cupboard door. 'Well-made piece. We could put it in your room.'

'I don't understand,' Lucy had protested. 'If you didn't mind losing a hundred dollars, why did you take their cupboard at all? That was plain mean!'

Jack Darling had looked at his daughter for a while, and then he had said, 'If I hadn't taken their cupboard, Lucy, I would have taken their pride. They have to believe that they can pay their way, otherwise they don't have no reason for carrying on. In one moment of thoughtlessness, I would've done to them what five thousand miles of travelling and ten years of suffering couldn't do, and what ten more years of suffering won't do, either.'

He had laid his hand on Lucy's shoulder – and, tonight, all these years later, Lucy unconsciously laid her own hand on her shoulder in fond imitation.

'A man can live without a place to hang up his clothes, Lucy. But he can't live without hope.'

She sat on her bed brushing out her curls and thinking about what her father had said. Sunday-school talk, really; cracker-barrel kindness. But if a man showed genuine charity, it was always easy to accuse him of being sentimental and simple-minded.

Lying back on her pillow, she thought about Uncle Casper, too. Now that she was older, she felt that she could perceive in him some complications of character that she had never noticed before. It was not so much that he was a mischief-maker (although the more she thought about the way in which he had taunted Jamie into drinking all that whisky, the more deliberate devilishness she saw in it). It was his self-destructiveness that unsettled her – the way he drank whisky as if he wanted to drown, and the relish with which he had told them about his catastophic schemes for making money, as if he revelled in ruination and disaster.

He had lost thousands of dollars of his own and other people's money trying to set up a steamboat service on the Platte River in Colorado (too shallow). He had fitted out an expedition to go to Peru, to dig for silver (it had never left Charleston harbour.) He had built the grand façade of a fifty-room hotel in Huron, South Dakota, believing (mistakenly, as it turned out) that Huron would be chosen as state capital.

Whether he was planning majestic follies on the Western plains, or keeping himself in whisky money by playing faro and find-the-lady in small-town saloons, it seemed to Lucy that her Uncle Casper was constitutionally incapable of doing anything successful – that he *needed* to lose; that he *needed* to be hurt.

But for all that, he had a louche magnetism that Lucy found hard to resist. He spoke his mind, even when it was impolite or offensive or even downright dangerous; and seemed from experience to know the price of everything, especially the price of dreams. This evening, he had disillusioned Lucy deeply, by telling her just how much her dream would cost. But by putting a price on it, he had somehow made it seem more possible. Yes, she would need a fortune to enter high society, but wasn't America a land in which there were still fortunes lying around to be made?

She opened the top drawer of her bedside table, and lifted out the inlaid jewellery-box which had once belonged to her mother. She unlocked it, and opened it up, and took out the pieces of jewellery one by one, and arranged them on the bed.

One cameo brooch; two necklaces, one pearl and one

sapphire; three pairs of earrings, one pearl, one jet, one silver; two rings.

In the prosperous days, her mother had owned much more; but by the time she died, this was all she had left. Lucy picked up the silver earrings and stood in front of her mirror, holding them up to her ears.

One day, she would dance, with these earrings on. One day she would have diamonds and rubies and emeralds.

She heard Uncle Casper laughing in the parlour; then her father's voice, lower and less distinct. Then Uncle Casper again. '– can't fail. They've already spudded three wells and every one of them's –' A long pause. The clinking of glasses. Then her father's voice. '– just don't have that kind of cash available – everything's tied up in stock – not to mention two-and-a-half thousand dollars' worth of credit – and who knows when that's going to be –'

Lucy put away the jewellery box; and then tiptoed across to her bedroom door, and opened it. She could just see a triangle of lamplight shining across the rumpled Indian blanket on the landing floor. However, she could now hear her father and Uncle Casper very much more distinctly.

Uncle Casper was saying, '– Jack, I can't deny that I've had my share of thin luck. Sure I've had some failures! The old Peruvian silver expedition didn't work out too good. Bold idea, bad organization. Probably just as well. Turned out the ship's captain thought Peru was someplace in Africa. But anybody can make mistakes, and I've sure learned by mine.'

Jack was silent for a while. Then he said, 'Cass, I simply don't *have* five hundred dollars; not to hand; and even if I did I'm not too sure that I'd give it to you.'

Casper coughed. 'Well . . . I guess I could scrape by with less. Say three hundred and fifty? Especially if I stay with acquaintances, and eat plain, and manage to pick up some second-hand drilling equipment. Come on, Jack, I'd cut you in for ten per cent.'

'I don't know,' said Jack. 'It took you two years to pay me back the last loan I gave you, and I was a whole lot flusher then.'

'I paid you back, though, didn't I? With interest, too!'

Jack said, 'Yes, you did. But this drilling for oil . . . you don't even know if there's anything down there!'

'My friend in California, John Ferris, he's sure of it. That's why he wrote me, asking me to come in with him. You might say they owe me a favour.'

'It still sounds like a long shot t'me,' Jack replied.

'Oh come on, Jack,' Casper urged him. 'Stop acting so damn glum! Just take a look at me! What do you see in my eyes? What's that brightness you see? Aint that the shine of good luck? Don't you see luck? Hey? Look in my eyes!'

There was another protracted pause. Then Jack said, 'Cass, when I look into your eyes, I'm not too sure *what* I see. I'm worried I might be seeing myself, reflected back.'

Casper laughed. 'You just won't trust me, will you, Jack? You plumb refuse to trust me!'

'The question of trust doesn't even arise,' Jack Darling told him, rather stiffly. 'I don't have the money, and that's all there is to it.'

'What about y'r property? Couldn't you raise five hundred with an extra mortgage?'

'Casper, it's taken me twenty years to build up this business. These days, I'm scarcely breaking even. If I went bankrupt now, I wouldn't have nothing. Not even the clothes I stand up in. And I have to think about Lucy, too.'

'Oh, well,' Casper sighed. 'Anna was always saying about you that you was the cautious sort.'

'The hell you say!' Jack barked at him. 'You leave Anna out of this!'

Casper sniffed. 'All right, all right! Don't get yourself aerated! Sometimes the liquor says somethin' what the heart don't mean. But think about it, Jack. Don't dismiss it out of hand.'

'Cass – let me put it to you this way,' Jack Darling told

him. 'I could raise the money, I guess, if I had the mind to. But I was never a man who believed in something for nothing. If you want that money bad enough, well, I'm not preaching at you, but I think you should earn it.'

Lucy heard the clinking of bottle against glass, and guessed that Casper was pouring himself another drink.

Then she heard him say, 'Every man has to take a chance, Jack, just once in his life. Otherwise – well – he might as well climb into his grave here and now, and whistle f'r his dog to fill it in for him.'

Later that night, after the moon had set, Lucy was woken up by Uncle Casper stumbling heavily against the corridor wall. There was a pause, and then her bedroom door swung open. She slitted her eyes open, and she could see him leaning against her closet, peering at her in the darkness. He was breathing harshly and heavily.

'Weave 'em up and weave 'em down,' he sang, under his breath. 'Weave 'em pretty girls round and round . . .'

He suppressed a cough. Then, 'Lucy?' he whispered, after a while.

She didn't answer.

'Lucy, you awake?'

Again she didn't answer.

Uncle Casper took three shuffling steps into the room. He hit his foot against the end of her bed, and almost fell over. 'Sssh!' he told himself, and giggled.

He came right up close, and knelt down beside her. She could smell the sourness of whisky on his breath, and the sweetness of Durham tobacco.

'Lucy? You sleeping? I just came to say goodnight. Goodnight kiss.'

She closed her eyes and kept them closed. *I'm asleep, can't you see that I'm asleep?* although her heart was beating in long slow bumps, and her fists were clenched so tightly that her fingernails dug into the palms of her hands.

'You've grown up a treat, Lucy, did you know that?' Uncle Casper slurred. 'You've grown up beautiful, Lucy like a – like a princess.'

He leaned right over her, and brushed his beard against her cheek. 'Just like a princess,' he repeated.

He waited for a long time, so near that she could feel his breath on her neck. Then he climbed back on to his feet again, staggered, and muttered to himself. 'Goddamn call o' nature.' He swayed back out of her room, colliding with the cupboard door as he did so. Lucy heard him wrestling open the kitchen door so that he could go down to the yard and use the privy.

Immediately, she jumped out of bed, hurried breathlessly across to her bedroom door, and turned the key.

She lay awake for almost an hour, waiting for Uncle Casper to return, but she heard nothing. At last she fell asleep, and dozed until sun-up, dreaming of frocks and silk stockings and people laughing. A little after five, the kitchen door slammed again, and Uncle Casper's footsteps came trudging through the parlour. She heard him cursing to himself as he passed her door. 'Goddamned stiff neck, stiff as a goddamned board.'

He must have fallen asleep in the privy and stayed there for most of the night. Lucy buried her face in her blanket to stop herself from laughing out loud. She heard him drag his way along to the spare room, and collapse on to his bed with a crunching of springs.

Sunday was windy and bright. Lucy and Jamie rode down to Overbay's Bend by the Saline River, and tied their horses to the scrubby bushes that grew right down to the water's edge. Overbay's Bend wasn't much more than a shallow oxbow, but the river had eroded the soil deeply enough to give some protection from the wind.

'So how long is this beloved uncle of yours going to be staying?' asked Jamie, shaking out a blanket and laying it on the grass.

Lucy shook her head. 'I don't know. Three months maybe. It depends how long it takes him to make enough money to go on to California. He's working in the store, and he's been doing some vet work, too. Poppa says that he's a wonder with animals.'

'He must have been pretty mad at your father for not grubstaking him.'

Lucy shrugged. 'If he was, he didn't show it. But it's hard to tell what he's thinking, most of the time. He talks a lot but he never really tells you anything about himself. And he has this peculiar smile, too, like something's funny, but he's not going to tell you what it is.'

'Here, sit down,' Jamie told her.

Lucy perched herself as elegantly as she could on the edge of the blanket. This afternoon she was wearing her maroon embroidered blouse and a long camel-hair riding-skirt. Her hair was brushed up under a plain-straw pillbox hat, which she had renovated by sewing a maroon velvet band around it. Primly, she covered her buttoned riding-boot with the hem of her skirt.

Jamie sat down beside her and scooped up a handful of pebbles. 'You should have seen me! I was drunk as a duck all afternoon, after drinking that whisky. At least Ned didn't snitch on me, that was one thing. But drunk! I nearly dehorned the dog, instead of the cow.'

'Well, serves you right. Uncle Casper was only ribbing.'

'Oh, no,' said Jamie, tossing pebbles across the wind-ruffled river. 'That man wasn't ribbing. Not one bit of it.'

'He'll be gone before too long, anyway,' Lucy replied.

Jamie glanced at her. 'What's wrong? He hasn't upset you or anything?'

'I don't know. I used to love him so much, when I was younger. But – I don't know – he seems different now. Kind of *mean*, in a way. Kind of strange. But definitely different.'

'Most likely it's *you* that's different,' Jamie suggested. One

33

of his pebbles skipped and skated across the river, and then *plopped* out of sight. 'Maybe you've grown up, that's all, and now you can see him for what he is.'

Lucy took off her hat and lay back on the grass and watched the clouds sailing by. Huge cumulus clouds, dreamily floating fortresses, with battlements and towers and walkways and bridges. She could almost imagine people living in them, kings and queens and princes.

'I'm not sure what he is,' she replied. 'He talks real strange. He frightens me sometimes. But you can't stop yourself from listening. He can make you feel that you can do anything, anything at all — that anything you ever wanted can come true. Just so long as you're strong enough, and so long as you don't care what people think about you, and so long as you're ready to give up absolutely everything.'

Jamie frowned at her. 'Would you do that?'

'Would I do what?'

'Give up absolutely everything?'

Lucy looked at him. 'I don't know. I think I'd be scared to.'

'How about me?' Would you give me up?'

She didn't answer. Jamie rolled over and lay on his stomach and looked into her eyes, really close. He said, in a different kind of a voice, 'You know that I want to marry you, the day that I get my law degree.'

He hesitated for a second, and then he kissed her; a brush of a kiss at first, and then more deeply, his tongue-tip touching her teeth.

She closed her eyes and slowly wound her arms around him. They kissed again and again, and she could feel the wind blowing her hair across her forehead.

'Oh Jamie,' she whispered; but suddenly she had to open her eyes and stare at him, to make quite sure that he wasn't Uncle Casper.

★

On Monday morning, summoned by the president of the Kansas Farmers' & Stockbreeders' Bank, Lucy's father took the ten-oh-five train to Hays City. Lucy saw him off at the Oak City depot, which was little more than a lock-up warehouse and a gingerbread ticket-office that had once belonged to a now-defunct town called Willis. You could still see the name Willis in faded paint on the side.

It was a grey, overcast day, not too cold, but overnight the wind had grown friskier. Jack Darling leaned out of the passenger-car window and waved his hat as the train pulled away across the plains. Its smoke was visible for miles before it finally dwindled below the horizon. It was like watching a steamship sail off across a windy sea.

On her way back to the store, Lucy almost collided on the corner of Main Street with the Skipping Widder, who was hurrying to the depot to collect Mr Judd's mail. 'Been to the store,' Mrs Sweeney told her. She sounded very Irish. 'Who's the fellow serving today? Can't say that I've seen him before. Can't say that I'm sorry!'

'Oh, that's my Uncle Casper. My poor momma's brother.'

Mrs Sweeney narrowed her eyes and looked back towards the store. 'He staying permanent?'

Lucy shook her head. 'He's saving up enough money to go to California.'

'Hm! Best place for him, I'd say! Or China, maybe! That's further!'

Lucy was startled by Mrs Sweeney's vehemence. 'He wasn't rude to you, was he? He does have a way of speaking his mind, sometimes.'

'Rude? No. But I've met men like him, met 'em before. Not the kind of man you ought to dance with.'

Lucy couldn't think what to say. She smiled, and shrugged, and said, 'I must be getting back.'

Mrs Sweeney clasped her wrist. 'Well, you watch your step, young Lucy. That uncle of yours has got the devil perched on his shoulder, in my opinion. The very devil.'

Without saying anything else, she hurried off towards the depot, her black skirts billowing in the wind. Lucy shielded her eyes against the whirling dust, and watched her go. Then, puzzled, she headed back along Oak City's deserted main street, to the yellow-painted building where Oak City ended and the rest of Kansas began.

Uncle Casper was up on a stepladder at the back of the store, sorting out boxes of shoes. Samuel Blankenship was there, too, sitting by the cold stove with his sippin' whisky and a three-day-old copy of the Kansas City *Daily Journal*. Lucy closed the store door behind her to keep out the wind, and untied the ribbon of her bonnet.

'Your poppa make the train okay?' asked Uncle Casper. He wrote a large cardboard notice Shoes At Cost and propped it up on the shelf.

Although there were only two trains a day to Hays City, and you could see them coming for miles, Uncle Casper's question wasn't so strange. Western trains had a disconcerting habit of sliding out of stations and depots unannounced; with no whistle, no flag, and no cry of 'All aboard!' They arrived with a fanfare, left silent.

Uncle Casper said, 'You could sort them notions out, Lucy, if you've got a mind. They're all of a-tangle.'

'Oh, sure,' said Lucy, absent-mindedly.

Uncle Casper climbed down from the stepladder and came towards her, wiping his hands on his long white storekeeper's apron. 'Something wrong?' he asked her. 'You look kind of distracted.'

'I was just talking to Mrs Sweeney.'

'Oh, yes? You mean the little old Irishwoman? She wanted pickled fish and ground coffee. She wanted a bottle of Dr Kilmer's, too, but we're out.'

'Was she – was she *unhappy* about something?' Lucy asked him.

'Unhappy?' he sniffed.

Samuel Blankenship looked up from his newspaper. His expression was oddly expectant.

'I mean, was she upset about something?' Lucy asked.

Uncle Casper slowly shook his head. 'Not that I could see. Maybe dithering, you know, the way that old women do. But not upset. Why – what did she say to you?'

Lucy began to sort through a cardboard box full of tangled-up elastic. 'Nothing. It was just that –'

Uncle Casper was standing very close to her. He must have been drinking already that morning because she could smell the whisky, mixed with eau-de-cologne. An alarmingly masculine smell: the smell of vanity and self-destruction, mixed.

'Do you know something, Lucy,' he told her, and his voice was soft enough for Samuel Blankenship not to be able to make out what he was saying, 'you're going to waste here; here in this store; here in Oak City. Truly going to waste.'

Lucy blushed. She felt hot and cold at the same time. Uncle Casper smiled at her and she wanted desperately for him to go; but also for him to stay. She had never come across anybody who confused her so much. She glanced at him quickly and his eyes were dark and glittering like widow's beads, and he was still smiling.

Just then the store door gusted open and Mrs Barnaby came in, fussing and brushing the dust from her skirts. Uncle Casper gave Lucy a long slow wink, and then turned away. 'Good morning, ma'am; how are you today, ma'am? Mr Darling aint here today, but my name's Casper Conroy and I'm his brother-in-law, and whatever I can do to please you, I surely will.'

He dragged over a bentwood chair so that Mrs Barnaby could sit down, and fuss with her fraying ginger hair. 'Well, you wouldn't have three cans of wrinkled peas, would you, and a cake of that white floating soap?'

Lucy carried on tidying the drawers and boxes of notions;

but for the rest of the morning she was aware that Uncle Casper was staring at her.

He caught her in the stockroom during the lunch-hour, when Samuel Blankenship had at last eased himself out of his chair, and gone off to the Demorest Home Restaurant for pie and boiled potatoes. She was looking for more mother-of-pearl blouse buttons, right at the back of the stockroom, between the narrow rows of shelves, amongst the musty-sweet bolts of fresh fabric. She heard the door close but she didn't pay it any mind; the wind was up, and the draught was always banging doors around the house.

It was only when Uncle Casper appeared around the side of the shelving, smiling, and without his apron, that she began to realize that something was different; something was wrong.

He approached her, quite close, and watched her without saying anything as she sorted through cards of pearly buttons.

'You haven't left the store empty?' she asked him. 'The kids'll be coming back from school soon. They're always pilfering the cough-candy.'

'Store's locked,' said Uncle Casper, unblinking.

'Locked? Who locked it?'

Uncle Casper didn't answer, but looked around the stockroom as if he were trying to make up his mind about something.

'We don't close for lunch,' Lucy told him, aware that she sounded faint.

'Oh, we do today,' Uncle Casper replied. 'Staff meeting.'

'Uncle Casper, if poppa finds out that you shut for lunch –'

'Oh, yes? And who's going to tell poppa that we shut for lunch?'

'Well, me, of course!'

Without warning, Uncle Casper snatched her left wrist,

and held it tight. He kept on staring at her, and smiling, although his smile was frighteningly tight-stretched. He was breathing deeply, whisky and tobacco, as if he had been running hard to catch up with her.

'Now, why would you choose to do a thing like that?' he asked her.

'Uncle, will you please let *go* of me,' Lucy asked him. She was beginning to feel the first quick surges of panic, but something inside of her warned her, *stay calm, don't over-excite him, don't make trouble.* She had the fearful idea that he might have gone mad, tipped over the edge of sanity by whisky and bankruptcy and her father's refusal to lend him any more money.

'Let you go?' he grinned at her. 'I aint likely to let *you* go! I aint *never* going to let you go! A prize like you! A prize like you, in Oak City, Kansas! Ha!'

He suddenly lunged forward and snatched at her other wrist. She dropped the cardboard box of buttons, and they sprayed over the floor. 'You're hurting!' she gasped at him, but he took no notice. He jerked her closer, so that they were almost face-to-face.

'What did I tell you?' he whispered. He was so near that she could see the open pores in his cheeks; the grey curly hairs in his black tangly beard. She could hardly breathe for the foulness of his breath. 'You grew up just beautiful. Better'n any man could've wished for.'

'Uncle Casper,' she pleaded, both wrists raised. 'Uncle Casper, please let me go. If you let me go now, I won't say a word to poppa. I won't tell anybody. I promise.'

Uncle Casper looked intently into her eyes. Then his gaze dropped to her white linen blouse, and the slight swell of her breasts. 'You grew up a looker, you know that? Even better'n Anna.' His breath went in and out, in and out.

Lucy swallowed. She was trying not to cry, but she could feel the tears springing into her eyes. 'Uncle Casper, please.'

For a moment, she really thought that he was going to let

her go. He lowered her wrists, although he didn't release them, and he dropped his head so that she could see the irregular parting in his scalp.

'Are you going to be accommodatin' to me?' he asked her, without looking up.

'Of course I am.'

He looked up. No smile now. 'I mean, are you going to be *real* accommodatin'?'

'Uncle, I –'

He lunged his head forward like an attacking rattlesnake, and tried to kiss her. She twisted away, yanked one wrist free, but he caught her round the waist and pulled her back towards him.

'I said are you going to be *accommodatin*'!' he shrieked.

She heard somebody screaming. She didn't realize at first that it was her. Uncle Casper gripped the hair at the back of her neck and clamped his mouth against hers, trying to force his rigid tongue in between her lips.

She pushed against him wildly, and staggered back, two steps, and then fell against the bolts of linen and percale that were stacked on the floor between the shelves. Uncle Casper scrabbled himself on top of her, forcing her down on to her back, grunting, grunting, and grabbing for her wrists.

She couldn't find the breath to scream again. She kicked and struggled, but Uncle Casper knelt astride her waist, gripping her tight between his thighs.

He looked down at her, panting. He sniffed, and twisted his head so that he could wipe his nose against the shoulder of his shirt. Then he said, 'What was all that for? Hunh? What was all that? What kind of a way was that for a niece to treat her uncle?'

Lucy was gasping and her eyes brimmed with tears. She shook her head. 'Uncle, let me go, please.'

'I told you, I wouldn't let you go. A princess like you? A man would have to be crazy in the head to let you go.'

Keeping her wrists held fast, Uncle Casper looked around

at the scattered boxes of notions. Buttons, reels of thread, crochet hooks. At last he saw what he wanted, a roll of red silk ribbon. He shifted his grip so that he was holding both of Lucy's wrists with one hand, and then he leaned over, grunting, and picked the ribbon up. He held the end of it between his teeth, and let it unroll from his mouth like a long lascivious tongue.

Dear Jesus, she thought, *he's going to strangle me!*

'Uncle, please!' she begged him. All she could manage was a throaty whisper. 'Uncle, please, don't strangle me. Please don't strangle me! Please!'

Uncle Casper let the ribbon drop out of his mouth. He stared at her in bewilderment. Then suddenly he realized what she meant, and picked up the ribbon, and brayed with laughter. 'You think I'd –? You must be crazy in the head! Strangle you? I aint going to strangle you! Have to be crazy in the head, to strangle you.'

Still laughing, still shaking his head, he wound the silk ribbon around Lucy's wrists and lashed them tightly together, two or three dallies and a half-hitch, above her head. He did it with all the deftness and expertise of a man who has tied up struggling heifers and panicking horses.

'Good strong stuff, silk, for something that comes out of a worm's rear end.'

He was calmer, now that he had tied her up; less jittery. He lifted himself off her – although when she tried to struggle herself up into a sitting position, he shoved her roughly back down. 'You just stay there, princess. Don't you move.'

'What are you going to do?' she whispered. Her lower lip was trembling uncontrollably. She felt as if she were just about to faint.

'Do? What am I going to *do*?' He heaved her further up on the stack of fabrics, so that she was lying flat on her back with her bound hands almost touching the wall. There were four or five iron hooks in the wall, and he unwound two more feet of red ribbon and tied it around the largest hook, using the figure-eight knot that trailhands favoured when they had to lash down a really wild steer. He checked that the knots were tight by tugging at them, and sniffed.

'Uncle, it hurts! Please, it hurts! Please let me go! Please! Think of momma!'

Uncle Casper bent over her and kissed her directly on the lips. 'Well, I *am* thinking of momma,' he smiled. 'Believe me, I am.'

With that, he took out his clasp-knife, and opened it with a bitten thumbnail. Lucy thought for a moment that he was going to slit her throat, but he hardly looked at her. He cut the remaining ribbon free, and then he climbed down from the bolts of fabric, lifted Lucy's right ankle, and wound the ribbon around it, knotting it tight.

'Weave 'em up and weave 'em down,' he hummed to himself. 'Weave 'em pretty girls round and round.'

He bound the other end of the ribbon around one of the slatted shelves where the notions were stacked. Lucy screamed, '*Let me go! Let me go! Let me go!*' and kicked at him furiously with her free left leg. But Uncle Casper simply dodged, and said, 'Hey . . .' and batted her kicks away with his hand. Then he caught hold of her flailing ankle, and tied that, too, to the shelves on the opposite side.

The rows of shelves were nearly five feet away from each other, and so Lucy's legs were stretched painfully wide apart.

'There, tied up good and tight,' Uncle Casper told her. 'Chinese woman showed me how to do that. Chinese.'

Uncle Casper loosened his black spotted necktie. Lucy stared up at him wide-eyed, shivering. She knew there was no use in screaming, nobody could hear. She wrenched and twisted at the silk ribbons, but they were far too tight for her to break free. Uncle Casper said, 'You can struggle all you want, princess. You won't get away.'

'How can you call me a princess when you're doing *this*

to me!' Lucy screeched at him. 'Poppa's going to *kill* you! He'll *kill* you!'

Uncle Casper's eyes looked peculiarly distant, as if he were thinking about somewhere else, and somebody else. 'Well, princess, you know what they say. Love comes in all kinds of different disguises. Love wears all kinds of different masks. This just happens to be mine.'

Oh, Jesus save me, she thought. *He is mad! He's completely mad!*

He climbed back up on to the bolts of cloth next to her, and stroked her cheek. His fingers were gentle and surprisingly soft. She tried to turn her face away, but he wound his fingers into her hair, and breathed, 'Still! Keep still!'

He kissed her forehead, then her eyes, then her nose and her lips. His beard and his breath almost suffocated her, and she couldn't stop herself from retching.

But Uncle Casper didn't seem to be offended by her disgust. In fact, it seemed to arouse him all the more. He kissed her and kissed her, and stroked her face, and after a while his hand strayed down the side of her neck, until he was touching the cameo brooch that pinned together the collar of Lucy's blouse.

'Oh, don't break it,' she gasped, in desperation. 'Please, don't break it. It used to be momma's.'

Uncle Casper carefully unfastened it, and held it up for a moment, turning it this way and that. 'I wouldn't break it,' he told her. 'Where d'you think your momma got it from?'

He laid the brooch aside, and started to unbutton her blouse. She wanted to scream, she wanted to plead with him to stop, but somehow she couldn't make her jaws work. Perhaps it was fear that was keeping her silent. Perhaps it was pride. She knew that he wasn't going to let her go, no matter what; and that he would only relish it more if she begged.

Perhaps more than anything else she was silenced by shame. Nobody had seen her undressed before, not Jamie,

43

not anybody. And worse than that, there was the shame of feeling excited. In spite of her helplessness, in spite of her panic, in spite of her revulsion, she felt a dark breathless anticipation, as if something inside her *wanted* it to happen.

'Oh please dear Jesus,' she murmured, and closed her eyes for a moment, and tried to picture Christ. 'Oh please forgive me.'

Almost matter-of-factly, Uncle Casper opened her blouse to the waist, and tugged it out of her skirt. She opened her eyes again, and stared at him. He stared back, and then smiled. 'You've grown up pretty, princess,' he told her. 'Pretty as a picture, that's what they say.' He reached out with both hands, hesitated for a moment, and then grasped her breasts through the thin muslin of her corset cover.

'Stop,' she mouthed, although she wasn't sure that she was speaking out loud. Could he hear her? Perhaps he couldn't even hear her.

'You know what my rule-o'-thumb is, for the perfect woman's breast?' he asked her. 'My rule-o'-thumb is that the perfect woman's breast should fill a man's hand, no bigger, no smaller. That's my rule-o'-thumb. The perfect woman, that's her proportion. Filling a man's hand.'

Between finger and thumb, he rolled her nipples through the muslin. She swallowed, she shivered; but at least he had stopped kissing her. Those foul kisses, bristly and suffocating and thick with sour-tasting saliva.

'I saw a girl once, in San Francisco,' Uncle Casper remarked. 'She danced naked, in a parlour-house on Commercial Street. And do you know something? Not a man in the place so much as took off his hat. Stark, stark naked, she was; and all those men there dressed to the nines. And do you know something, she was the most beautiful girl I ever saw, ever. After Anna, that is; and now you.'

Slowly, Uncle Casper lifted Lucy's corset cover. He smoothed the palm of his hand over her flat white stomach, around and around. 'Of course, she's probably dead now,

44

poor creature,' he added. 'Once their looks go, those parlour-house girls ... well, they usually prefer the razor. Once across the throat! Then it's goodbye despair, hallo heaven!' He carried on smoothing for a while, thinking and smoothing. Then, with sudden impatience, he seized the muslin corset cover in both hands and tore it the rest of the way up. Lucy cried out, and thrashed from side to side, but Uncle Casper immediately leaned his weight on her and clamped his hand against her mouth and ordered, 'Sssh! Now, sssh, now!'

She said, '*Mmmf!*' and tried to bite his fingers, but he pressed his hand so tightly over her mouth that she could hardly breathe.

After a moment, he took it away.

'You goin' to be quiet?' he asked her.

'I hate you,' she raged at him. 'I *hate* you!'

'Good,' he smiled. 'But stay quiet.'

He lowered his head and kissed her lightly between her breasts. 'Beautiful,' he said, 'you smell of violets. What's that, violet soap you use, eau-de-violets, something like that?' He cupped her right breast in his hand, and closed his mouth around her nipple. She could feel his beard brushing her bare skin. She could feel his tongue-tip, drumming her nipple against the roof of his mouth.

'Please let me go,' she whispered. 'Please let me go.'

But she was sure now that Uncle Casper wasn't listening to her. It could be that he wasn't listening to anything at all, except some private carnival that was going on inside his head. Roll up, roll up, and see them dance. Roll up, and claim your prize. Prize princesses, yours for the taking! Lucy strained her head up a little to look at him. He was kissing and licking and squeezing her breasts, and occasionally murmuring, '*Perfect* ... perfect ... and tastes of violets, too.'

She watched his tongue-tip circle around her nipples until they tightened. Tight, and hard, and tiny, like unripe buds. For a split-second he gripped each nipple between his teeth, nipped it, as if he were going to bite it off. Then he looked up and smiled at her, triumphant.

With two twists of his hand, he unfastened the waistband of her brown cotton skirt. It was impossible for him to pull her skirt right off, because her ankles were both tied. But he took out his knife and cut through the hem, so that he could rip it from top to bottom. It dropped on to the floor, leaving Lucy in nothing but her calf-length drawers and her white lisle stockings.

Uncle Casper stood watching her for a while, no longer smiling, distant, mad, and she wondered if he were going to go away now and leave her. Please, God, let him leave! But what would her father say, if he came home and found her like this! She was just about to ask Uncle Casper to untie her when he started to unbutton his shirt, and then to unbuckle his belt.

He undressed calmly, humming as he did so, although in time-honoured Western tradition he dropped all his clothes on the floor ('so's they don't fall off the hook and get lost'). He wore no underwear. He must have known since he woke up this morning what he was going to do to her. His chest was bosomy and suntanned and marked with a diamond of black hair, but he didn't look fit. His belly was slack from years of whisky, he wore a girdle of fat around his hips, and beneath their black shagginess, his short shapely legs were as white as Lucy's stockings. He must have caught the sun on his chest when he was labouring at some time with his shirt off, gardening or ploughing or laying railroad track.

'I was in Bodie once,' he said, as if he were continuing a conversation that had been briefly interrupted. 'I saw a girl dive off the roof of a hotel. Naked, she was, too. Death was what *she* wanted. What did she care about modesty? She was pretty. Redhead, I recall. But she lay in the street naked, with everybody looking at her, and of course she didn't care. Women take on a special kind of beauty, when they're dead.'

He approached Lucy slowly and stood next to her, naked. In his fist he held the totem of his perversity. He was gripping it so tight that its clefted head was almost maroon.

'You see this?' he asked her.

She turned her head away. Her heart was racing.

He grabbed her hair again, and forced her to face him. He held his swollen glans within an inch of her nose. 'You see this?' he repeated. His voice was beginning to crack.

She closed her eyes, nodded.

'Open your eyes,' he demanded.

She kept them shut.

'Open your eyes!' he shouted at her, and wrenched her hair until she felt her scalp crack.

She opened her eyes. They were sparkling with tears.

'This is yours now, princess,' Uncle Casper told her. 'This is your pleasure, morning, noon'n night.'

She stared at it. It looked more like a blind, angry creature than part of Uncle Casper. She didn't know what he wanted her to say. That she was so terrified that she was numb? That she was close to being sick? That she wished that God would strike him dead? In an unexpected release of fright, she wet herself; the way that a child does when there seems to be no escape, anywhere, in any direction. She sobbed with humiliation; but Uncle Casper hadn't appeared to have noticed, or if he had, to care.

Uncle Casper climbed up on to the fabric between her thighs, picked up his knife, and cut open her sopping muslin drawers. 'Beautiful . . .' he breathed. Then he looked at her, sharply. 'Have you been touched?' he snapped. 'Has any man touched you before? That hayseed lawyer? Any of them bug-ridden butcher boys?'

Lucy, trembling, shook her head. This response seemed to please Uncle Casper, because he smiled, and reached out, and stroked her gently with his hand.

The feeling of his fingers made Lucy shiver with cold. She

47

strained desperately at the ribbons that bound her hands until they cut into her flesh. She tried to heave her body from side to side, to break her ankles free. But she was tied up too securely, there was nothing she could do. The tears poured down the sides of her face, but she was too overwhelmed to sob; too frightened to cry out.

His fingers opened her and explored inside. She closed her eyes tight and bit her tongue and tried to believe that this wasn't happening, that she was back in bed, dreaming; and that she would soon wake up.

Her eyes were still closed when Uncle Casper shuffled himself forward, and began to press his glans against her.

'Defloration, that's the proper word for this,' he murmured. 'Dee-flaw-rayshun.'

He pushed, and he pushed again, and as he forced his way into her, Lucy screamed out loud. 'It's too big!' she screamed. 'It's too big! Take it out! It's too big!' But Uncle Casper forced himself all the way into her, and then crouched over her, panting with achievement.

'You know what you are now?' he breathed into her face. 'You're a woman. You've got yourself a man inside you. You should be proud of yourself. A woman.'

He drew himself out, and for a split-second Lucy thought that it was all over. But then he rammed himself back in again, harder this time; and then again; and then again. He went on and on, gasping and panting and spitting, until he roared out 'Aaaaahh!' and shuddered, and shuddered again, and then abruptly collapsed.

He sat on the bolts of fabric for a long time, still naked, smoking and drinking whisky out of the bottle. He didn't take his eyes away from her once.

At last, he said, 'Time to open up the store. People're goin' to start wonderin'.'

Lucy said nothing, but lay on her back staring at nothing, her eyelashes spiky with dried tears.

'Question is,' said Uncle Casper, 'what are you going to say to your poppa?'

Still Lucy said nothing. She could hear him talking but her mind was empty. All she could think of was the plains, the plains that stretched for ever and ever, and the silvery-grey grass that waved like the ocean in the wind.

Uncle Casper stood up, and found his pinstripe pants. He struggled his way into them, and buttoned them up. 'Tell you what you're going to say to your poppa. Nothing, that's what you're going to say. Nothing at all.'

He leaned over her, buttoning up his shirt. His eyes were crimson from drinking. 'You're not going to tell your poppa nothing.'

'Please untie me,' Lucy whispered.

Uncle Casper fastened his cuffs. 'You just listen to me first, princess. You're not going to tell your father nothing; and there's a very good reason why you're not going to tell him nothing.'

Lucy turned away. Her wrists hurt and her ankles hurt and her whole body felt swollen and bruised.

Uncle Casper said, 'You're not going to tell your father nothing because if you do, I'll have something to say to him, too, about your mother and me. Oh, yes. Don't you turn your face away from me. Your mother and me, we was only half-related, you know that, different mothers. And when we was young, your mother and me, we was close like two spring chickens in the same pot. We was lovers for a while, your mother and me. Might have been a sin in the eyes of God; but we was lonesome and friendless and each other was all we had.'

'You're lying,' whispered Lucy. 'I hate you.'

'Certainly you hate me, but I aint lying. It's the Bible truth, so help me.'

'My momma would never have done anything like that. Never.'

'Maybe she did and maybe she didn't,' said Uncle Casper. 'But you'll never know, will you? And if you want to keep

49

your poppa sane and happy, you'd better make sure that *he* never knows, neither.'

Lucy couldn't think of anything to say in reply. She was beginning to tremble with shock; and with the dread that Uncle Casper would never let her go. She let her head fall back on the bolts of fabric, and the tears streamed out of her eyes and into her ears.

Uncle Casper leaned over her again. 'How about it, then?' he asked her. 'What you going to say to your poppa?'

Lucy shook her head. She was too distressed to be able to speak.

'You goin' to tell him what happened? You goin' to tell him what we did? That aint goin' to please him much, now is it? His own little girl, playin' parlour-house girls with his brother-in-law? Because then I'm goin' to have to tell him all about me and your momma; and then I'm goin' to have to tell them that you was leading me on, to show that you was just as good as your momma used to be.'

'No!' Lucy choked.

Uncle Casper seized hold of her hair. 'No, what? No, you're not goin' to tell him? Or what?'

'No,' whispered Lucy. 'I'm not going to tell him.'

Uncle Casper stared at her for a moment, and then slowly smiled and nodded his head. 'You're a good girl, Lucy. I could tell that, moment I saw you again. No witchery, no bitchery. Just the kind of girl I go for.'

He cut her ankles free, and then her wrists. He stood and watched her as she miserably buttoned up her blouse, and dragged her skirt up from the floor. 'There has to be a first time sooner or later,' he told her. 'No point in waiting till you're too darned old. I mean the best age is sixteen, for a girl. That's the best age. You've wasted a year already; don't want to waste no more.'

Lucy climbed off the stack of fabric, and stood up, holding her skirt around herself with her hand. She didn't look at Uncle Casper; couldn't; but he didn't take his eyes away from her once, even when he lifted up his bottle of whisky to take another swig.

'You'd better open up the store,' she told him, so quietly that he could scarcely hear her.

Uncle Casper swallowed whisky, and wiped his mouth, and sniffed. 'Okay.' Then, 'Are you all right? Didn't hurt you or nothing?'

Lucy shuffled past him, opened the stockroom door, and went back into the store. Samuel Blankenship and Henry McGuffey were both outside, their faces pressed against the window. When they saw Lucy, Samuel Blankenship rattled the doorhandle, and waved.

'All right, you old coot, keep your goddamned wool on!' Uncle Casper shouted at him. He reached out and laid his hand on Lucy's shoulder.

'Listen . . . if I hurt you or anything –'

Lucy twisted herself away. 'Don't you dare to touch me,' she shivered. 'Don't you dare to touch me, ever again.'

Uncle Casper was about to say something, but decided against it. He blew out his cheeks in silent acceptance of what she had said, and picked up the keys from the counter. 'You'll want to change y'r clothes, right?' he suggested.

Without a word, Lucy unlocked the side door, and stepped out, and closed it behind her. The wind was gusting even more strongly now, and she had to keep her skirt together with both hands. Unsteadily, she climbed the stairs at the side of the store, and let herself in. She went straight to her bedroom, locked the door behind her, and sat on her bed.

Her face in the mirror looked like the face of another girl altogether; a girl she didn't know.

'Who are you?' she whispered. The girl didn't reply.

Jack Darling came back just after dark. Lucy had closed the store at six, and now she was serving out pork and beans in the kitchen. Uncle Casper was already eating, hunched over his plate, a half-empty bottle of whisky close to his elbow.

'Well,' said Jack Darling, briskly chafing his hands together, 'you'll be happy to know that the Farmers' & Stockbreeders' Bank is more than happy to extend my credit.'

'Is that good?' asked Casper, with his mouth full. 'Gettin' yourself even deeper in debt?'

'Oh, times'll turn,' said Jack, as he sat down at the table. 'I'll have some of that buttermilk, Lucy, if there's any left.'

'Interest you in a whisky?' Casper asked him.

Jack shook his head. 'One drunk a month is enough for me.'

He began hungrily to fork up beans. It was only after the third mouthful that he realized that nobody was talking. He looked from Lucy to Casper and back again.

'Something wrong?' he asked them.

'Not as far as I know,' Casper remarked. He had only eaten half his supper but now he pushed his plate away. 'Everything's fine, as far as I know.'

'How was the store today?' Jack inquired.

'Fine,' said Casper.

'What was the take?'

'Sixteen dollars and nine cents cash money; thirty-seven dollars and fourteen cents credit.'

Jack turned back to Lucy and said, 'Mrs Barnaby come in?'

'Sure,' Casper told him. 'Mrs Barnaby came in. Bought herself some peas, and some soap, and one of them self-righting cuspidors.'

'The twenty-cent or the forty-one cent?'

'The twenty.'

Jack put down his fork. 'You should've sold her the forty-one cent, the way John Barnaby spits.'

Lucy brought over a glass of buttermilk. She tried, but she couldn't bring herself to look her father in the eye. As she turned back towards the sink, her father said, 'Lucy? What's the matter, sweetheart?'

52

'Nothing,' she said, without turning round. *Oh God*, she thought. *If I try to talk to him, I'll burst into tears.*

'Come on,' Jack coaxed her. 'I know when there's something wrong.'

He looked at Casper but Casper simply shrugged, and swallowed more whisky.

'Lucy –' Jack began; but Lucy untied her apron and hung it up on the back of the door and covered her face with her hands. Jack got up from the table and stood beside her.

'Lucy, what the heck's wrong?'

She smeared tears away from her eyes. 'I've got a headache, that's all. It's the weather.'

'Hey, now! Did you take anything for it?'

She shook her head. Her throat was too tight for her to speak.

Jack put his arm around her. She stiffened, but she managed to tolerate it. Jack said, 'Listen, sweetheart, you're looking awful flushed. Take yourself off to bed. Cass'n'me, we'll do the cleaning-up. I'll bring you some hot milk and some Bromo Vichy later on. You've probably tired yourself out, that's all, what with two thoughtless men to take care of.' He winked at Uncle Casper.

Lucy nodded. She allowed her father to kiss her on the cheek; then she walked woodenly off to her room. She locked the door behind her and stood with her back to it, her eyes tightly shut, trying to make herself believe that today had never happened; that it had all been a nightmare.

But her face was flushed because she had been scrubbing around her mouth with a nailbrush and witch-hazel soap, to take away the taste and the memory of Uncle Casper's saliva. She had rubbed her breasts, too, with a rough flannel facecloth, and douched herself over and over with a Wearever syringe she had taken from the store. She had hidden it behind her closet, and prayed that her father wouldn't discover that it was missing.

'Oh, Lord Jesus, please forgive me my terrible sin,' she

prayed. Then she sat down on her bed, her hands in her lap, her eyes closed, too exhausted to cry any more.

After a while, however, she turned to look at her bedside table. She frowned at it for a moment, thoughtfully. Then she reached over and opened her bedside drawer, and took out her mother's jewellery box.

She was still sitting there half an hour later when her father knocked at the door.

The pawnbroker spread the jewellery out on top of the counter. He was a tiny man, with wild white hair and pince-nez eyeglasses. Lucy noticed that his shirt-cuffs were frayed, and from that she assumed that he was probably a widower. He took out a handerchief and blew his nose, and then he said, 'What did you think this was worth?'

Lucy looked down at it. The necklaces, the rings; everything except the cameo brooch, which she was wearing. 'I don't know. It used to belong to my mother.'

'It's good quality,' the pawnbroker told her. 'Modest, but good quality. The trouble is, I have to think about market values. Know what I mean by market values?'

'I think so. My father owns a general store.'

'Ah well, in that case. But take a look at my poor emporium! Most of this stuff I can't give away for nothing, and it's supposed to be security.'

The tragedy of what had happened to western Kansas since the quarantine laws was illustrated nowhere better than here, at Lilienthal's Pawnbroker, in Hays City. Scores of Sunday-best suits hung from the ceiling; as well as hats and umbrellas and walking-sticks and violins. The window was crammed with dusty silverware; one corner of the floor was crowded with shoes. The saddest cabinet was filled with wedding-bands, dozens of them, many of them inscribed. *For Ever and Ever, Your Joshua.* But nothing was forever when your children were hungry and the bank was threatening to foreclose.

54

'Folks around here can't afford to buy bread, let alone violins.'

Lucy waited while the pawnbroker inspected the necklaces through a magnifying-glass. He nodded a couple of times, and then he said, 'Two hundred eighty. That's the very best I can do. It's worth more. To be honest with you, it's worth four hundred, maybe five. But two hundred eighty is the very best I can do.'

'Can't you make it more?'

He picked up one of the earrings, and turned it over. 'Maybe three hundred, but that's stretching it.'

'But I need three hundred-fifty.'

The pawnbroker shook his head. 'I'm sorry. I'm truly sorry. It's just not possible.'

'Please,' Lucy begged him. 'It's real important. I just have to have three hundred-fifty dollars.'

'Miss − what can I do? Put yourself in my shoes. You want me to cut my own throat? You want me to open my veins in front of you, so that you can watch me bleed to death?'

Lucy said, 'I can pay you back the extra fifty in six weeks' time. Or maybe even a month.'

The pawnbroker took off his pince-nez. 'You *say* you can pay me back the extra fifty in six weeks' time. But what happens if you don't? I wouldn't have a leg to stand on.'

Lucy felt as if she were suffocating. She watched with rising panic as the pawnbroker began to wrap up the jewellery in the chamois-skin she had brought it in. If *he* didn't give her the money, she didn't have any place else to go. She couldn't take the train all the way east to Salina. It had been difficult enough persuading her father to let her come to Hays, on the pretext of seeing her childhood friend Marjorie Smith, whose parents used to run the Smith Hotel in Oak City (empty these days, and derelict). If she went on to Salina, she wouldn't have any hope of getting back home before tomorrow morning.

She placed her hand protectively over her cameo brooch. *Momma, I'm sorry, I know how much you loved this brooch.* Then — as the pawnbroker held out her chamois-skin — she unfastened it, and held it up.

'If I give you this, too?' she asked him. 'It's French, genuine French. From France.'

'French, from France? No kidding.' the pawnbroker took it and inspected it through his eyeglass. 'This your mother's too?'

Lucy nodded, and swallowed. 'It was her favourite.'

'Well, I'm not surprised. It's very fine. It's Dutch, as a matter of fact, not French.' He turned it over and scrutinized the back, and then he said, 'Sure.'

'Pardon?' asked Lucy.

'I said, sure, yes, I'll give you the money. Golden eagles suit you?'

Lucy was shivering as she watched the pawnbroker count out three hundred-fifty dollars in $10 gold coins, and shake them into a small canvas bag. He escorted her to the door, and then handed them to her. 'You take care, young lady. That's a whole lot of money you're carrying there. People have been killed for a whole lot less.'

'Thank you,' she whispered, and stepped out of the shop on to the wide windy sidewalks of Main Street, Hays. It was five after twelve. There was a train back to Oak City at twenty after, if she hurried.

It was only when she was back in her room that evening, and emptied the gold coins on to her quilt to count them, that she discovered at the bottom of the bag a small package wrapped in brown tissue paper. Puzzled, she unfolded it; and there was her mother's cameo.

She held the cameo tightly in her hand, and her eyes filled with tears. How could the same world contain people who were so generous, and people who were so irredeemably foul? She waited until well past eleven o'clock. Her father had gone to bed at nine-thirty after a hard day's stocktaking, and she could hear by his breathing that he was deeply asleep. When she heard the parlour clock chime a quarter after eleven, she quietly left her room, and crept along the corridor to the small spare room where Uncle Casper was staying. She hesitated for a moment, with her heart pounding, and then she knocked.

'Who is it?' Uncle Casper demanded, in a thick voice.

'It's me, Lucy.'

There was a pause, and then the bedsprings scrunched. Uncle Casper opened the door and stood there tousle-haired in his long-johns, a hand-rolled cigarette dangling out of one side of his mouth. His room was dense with tobacco-smoke and the stink of whisky.

'Well, well, well,' said Uncle Casper, his cigarette waggling. 'If it aint my fav'rite princess. Acquired the taste for it, have we? Come back for some more of your old Uncle Casper's special treatment?'

Her skin felt freezing-cold, and her mouth was dry. She was wearing her nightgown and a dressing-robe, both tightly fastened, and she had taken the precaution of wearing a pair of winter drawers as well. 'I want to talk,' she told him.

'Well, certainly!' slurred Uncle Casper, in a genial tone. 'Come on in. How about a drink? This is the last of the real good whisky.'

Hesitantly, Lucy entered the room. The smoke was so thick that she could hardly breathe. Uncle Casper sat on the iron-framed bed and patted the mattress beside him, to indicate that Lucy should sit down.

'I think I'll stand, if you don't mind,' said Lucy.

'Whatever position takes your fancy,' Uncle Casper grinned at her.

Lucy licked her lips. 'I want you to leave,' she said, her voice breaking with nervousness.

Uncle Casper looked her up and down, but said nothing.

'You came here to borrow money from my father, so that you could go to California and look for oil.'

Still Uncle Casper remained silent.

'Well, I have some money ... enough for you to start drilling, anyway. You can have it, all of it, as long as you promise to go.'

'How much?' asked Uncle Casper.

'Three hundred–fifty dollars.'

Uncle Casper raised one eyebrow. 'Is that in gold, or paper?'

'It's in gold. You can see it if you don't believe me. But you have to promise to leave tomorrow. There's a train for Denver at ten after twelve.'

Uncle Casper swallowed whisky, and sniffed. 'You're in some kind of a rush to see the back of me, Lucy.'

'Yes,' she quivered, keeping her back pressed against the wall, and the doorhandle well within reach. She had never been so much afraid of anybody in her life: not even the Oak City schoolmistress, who used to scream at her, and thrash hysterically at her hands with a leather strap.

'Is that it?' asked Uncle Casper. 'You give me the money, and I go?'

'No,' she told him. 'It's my money. I pawned momma's jewellery to get it. Everything except the cameo.'

'Ah,' grinned Uncle Casper. 'So *that's* why you went rushing off to Hays this morning. Nothing to do with visiting no friends. You aint so apple-pie innocent as you look, are you, my lady? Still – glad you kept the cameo. That was always sentimental, that cameo. Worth something, too.'

Lucy said, 'You must promise to pay me back. You know – as soon as you've found your oil.'

'Well, princess. There's no cast-iron guarantee that we *will*, or even if we do, when. Could take years. You may lose your shirt along with the rest of us, if you'll excuse the expression.'

'I know that,' said Lucy. 'But poppa doesn't know what I've done. I must redeem momma's jewellery if I can. He'll be so angry.'

'Well, princess, sure. If God decides to smile on us and we *do* strike oil –'

'And a percentage,' said Lucy, swallowing hard.

Uncle Casper stared at her, one eye wide, one eye half-closed. He had been drinking so much that he found it difficult to keep her in focus.

'A *percentage*?'

'You offered poppa a percentage.' Her voice was shaking; and even though she tried to sound brave and confident, she didn't feel it.

'Well, now,' said Uncle Casper, 'what I said to your poppa, that was a different kettle of fish altogether. Your poppa wasn't trying to ride me out of town on a rail.'

'But you want to go anyway, don't you? And if I give you my three hundred and fifty dollars, that's an investment, isn't it? That's what you told poppa. Ten percent, that's what you said.'

Uncle Casper sniffed, and swallowed phlegm. 'You got yourself a cold ear, from listenin' at keyholes?' he asked her. ''Sides,' he added, 'now I'm here, and cosy, and now you and me are rubbin' along so well, there aint such a burnin' attraction for me to move on, is there?'

'I still think you ought to pay me a percentage.'

Uncle Casper laughed, a cracking, humourless laugh. 'You're a tough nut, and no mistake. All right. You can have a percentage. Say, two-and-a-half percent of whatever profits I make, net of expenses, and net of your original stake.'

Lucy didn't really understand what he meant, but she countered, 'Five percent. You offered poppa ten.'

'I keep telling you, princess, that was different. But, all right, for the sake of peace'n'tranquill-ity, let's say five.' He held out his hand. 'How about shaking on it?'

Lucy opened the bedroom door. 'I never want you to touch me again, ever, as long as you live.'

'Come on, princess,' Uncle Casper cajoled her. 'Don't take it so hard. I'm still your good old Uncle Casper. You'll look back on this, one day, and you'll think different about it.'

He stood up. 'Come on, let's shake on it. Make it legal.'

Lucy backed away. 'I'll get it all down in writing. Then you can sign it. I don't want you to touch me again, never.'

'You're a tough nut, Lucy, no mistake about that.'

'I loathe you and I despise you,' Lucy whispered at him. 'I'll see you in the morning with the money, and the paper to sign. Make sure you pack your bags. And if you say one single word to poppa about the jewellery, I'll kill you. I swear on the Holy Bible, one night when you're asleep, I'll kill you.'

Uncle Casper raised his whisky glass. 'Sleep tight, princess. Don't let the bugs bite. I always liked a girl with fire.'

Lucy closed the door, and stood in the darkened corridor with the blood rushing through her head with a sound like longhorns stampeding through dry prairie grass. She stayed where she was, taking one deep breath after another; but then she heard his bedsprings squeaking, and so she hurried back to her room, and locked the door behind her.

She heard Uncle Casper lurch his way noisily outside to the privy. She took off her dressing-robe and her winter drawers, and climbed into bed, and prayed; every prayer she could think of. The moon was setting, but her room was still burnished with silver light. '*In my trouble I cried to the Lord*,' she prayed. '*Deliver my soul, O Lord, from lying lips, from a deceitful tongue.*'

On his way back to bed, Uncle Casper rapped softly at her door.

'Lucy?' he called her. 'Lucy?'

She didn't reply. She lay rigid; willing him to go away.

'Lucy . . . I want to tell you this. I'm sincere now, Lucy,

so you listen. I love you, Lucy. I love you more than you can ever know.'

'But, Lucy, I can't, I'm not qualified,' Jamie insisted. 'Supposing I make some kind of terrible mistake. It could ruin my legal career for ever.'

'Jamie, I *can't* ask anybody else. Mr Judd would go directly to poppa, and tell him all about it.'

Jamie propped his rake against the side of the stall, and brushed down his shirt with his hands. He had been mucking out his father's horses when Lucy had arrived. His sleeves were rolled up tight and there was straw in his hair. Lucy thought he looked very scruffy and very handsome.

'All I need is a simple piece of paper,' she pleaded. 'And all it has to say is that I'm lending Uncle Casper three hundred and fifty dollars to help him drill for oil; and that if he actually makes any money, he has to pay my three hundred and fifty dollars back, as well as a five per cent royalty.'

'Well,' said Jamie, reluctantly, 'I guess it doesn't have to be all that complicated. A simple deed should be sufficient. Even exchanging letters would stand up in a court of law.'

'And it doesn't matter my being under age?'

Jamie shook his head. 'Not at all. Minors enter into legal contracts every day of the week. When a kid buys a poke of cough-candy, that's a legal contract. Actually, the advantage is yours, because if your Uncle Casper fails to pay your money back, you can sue him; but if *you* break your contract in any way, there's nothing much that he can do about it, because you're too young.'

He closed the stable door, and pinned it. 'Mind you, I still think you're wasting your time. A deed's only as good as the intentions of those that put their names to it; and I wouldn't trust your Uncle Casper's intentions further'n the next corner. But come on across to the house. I'll look up something in Sansom's Contract Law.'

Lucy followed him out of the stables and along the track that ran beside the corral. On the far side, shaded by three gigantic red oaks, stood the Cullen farmhouse, an L-shaped weatherboarded building with a split-shingle roof and vivid green shutters.

Jamie's brother Ned was in the corral, yanking at the reins of a wilful chestnut pony. As Jamie and Lucy walked past, he called out, 'Where you sloping off to this time, Jamie? Thought pa told you to muck out them stables!'

'Ladies first, muck later!' Jamie retaliated, and took hold of Lucy's arm.

They went into the house. Through the open door at the end of the hallway, they could see Jamie's blonde-haired mother busy in the kitchen. She was baking biscuits, and the whole house was tuneful with the aromatic music of pecans and syrup and gingersnaps. The house was decorated austerely, in a godfearing fashion, with whitewashed walls and simple furniture. The only decoration was provided by religious samplers, embroidered by Jamie's two sisters.

'Come on upstairs,' said Jamie; and led Lucy up to his room. It was a small room in the eaves, with a view to the north-east, toward the Saline River, and Oak City beyond. Down below, tethered to the fence, Lucy could see the grey pony she had borrowed from Mr Overbay to ride down here. Next to the window stood a home-made bookshelf crammed with leather-bound lawbooks. Jamie sat on the bed, and tugged out Contract Law.

'Hey, don't close the door,' he told Lucy. 'My father doesn't approve of unmarried people being in the same room together. Not with the door closed.'

Lucy said nothing. *If only you knew what had brought me here*, she thought to herself.

Jamie thumbed through the book for a while. Then he tore a sheet of paper out of his study-book, and began to draft an agreement. After a lot of scratchings-out, Jamie produced a deed between Casper Conroy, of Wappoo Creek,

Charleston, South Carolina, and Lucy Darling, of the Jack Darling General Store, Main Street, Oak City, Kansas.

'You're sure you want to do this?' Jamie frowned. 'I wouldn't trust your uncle with a bent nickel.'

Lucy stood with her arms folded. 'I'm sure.'

'Three hundred and fifty, that's a lot of money. Supposing he comes up with nothing but dust?'

'Then I'll have spent all my savings on nothing at all.'

Jamie waved the agreement dry. 'You don't seem unduly perturbed about it.'

'A person has to take risks, sometime,' said Lucy. 'Otherwise a person might just as well crawl into her grave and let her dog fill it in for her.'

'That sounds like your Uncle Casper talking.'

Lucy didn't answer. She read the deed quickly, and then handed it back.

'I suppose you want me to come into town with you, to sign it?' Jamie asked.

'Would you mind?' I'm sorry I'm such a nuisance.'

'No,' he told her, giving her a quick kiss on the cheek. 'You're a princess.'

She swallowed a dry swallow and stared at him. 'Please don't call me that,' she told him.

'What's wrong?' he asked her. 'Something's upset you, hasn't it?'

She tried to smile. 'It's nothing. It's just that I don't like deceiving poppa that's all. If I told him that I was giving Uncle Casper all of my savings – well, he'd go crazy. He thinks that Uncle Casper ought to work for his grubstake.'

'Well, personally, I agree.'

'Don't argue about it, Jamie, please. It's something I want to do, that's all.'

'I don't know,' said Jamie. 'It's pretty hard to believe that you're so darned fond of your dear old uncle that you're prepared to give him all of that money, no questions asked, regardless of what your father thinks about it. Holy smoke,

Lucy, you don't even know if he has the legal rights to drill anywhere!'

Lucy looked away. She made it plain that she wasn't going to discuss it.

Jamie watched her for a moment, and then said, 'All right, if that's what you want. But let me tell you this, Lucy, I don't approve of what you're doing, not for one second.'

'You don't have to,' she replied.

Uncle Casper was waiting with theatrical patience at the railroad depot, pacing this way and that, and fanning himself with his hat. His two carpetbags were packed, and he was wearing his tan suit and his best brown boots. There was no sign of the train yet; but at this time of the year it was very rarely late.

He greeted Jamie with a broad grin, and pumped his hand. 'Here's the fellow who can drink,' he said, loudly, turning around to smile at two elderly ladies who were also waiting for the train.

Lucy could hardly bear to look at him. 'We have an agreement,' she said, with her eyes lowered. 'Five per cent, that's what you said, wasn't it?'

'That's c'rect, five per cent. And darned generous, too, if you don't mind my saying so.' He snatched the agreement and scanned it quickly and sniffed. 'Looks all right t'me. Show me where it says five per cent.'

Jamie stood beside him and pointed to paragraph three. 'Ah, yes,' said Uncle Casper. 'That's good. That's fine, then.'

Jamie unscrewed his pen and offered Uncle Casper his back. Uncle Casper signed his name, and then Jamie signed his. They were just shaking hands when they heard the train whistling, piercing and mournful, as it approached Oak City across the prairie.

'Time for the money, then,' said Uncle Casper.

Lucy opened her leather squaw bag and took out the canvas sack.

'Do you think I should count it?' asked Uncle Casper, loosening the drawstring and peering inside.

'You can if you want to. It's all there,' Lucy told him.

'All right then, I'll trust you,' grinned Uncle Casper. 'If an uncle can't trust his niece.'

The train drew in to the depot with its bell clanging and its brakes squealing as if it were running over a litter of piglets. Uncle Casper climbed aboard, and then walked along the car so that he was right next to Lucy and Jamie. He slid open the window and stuck out his head.

'You wait,' he told Lucy. 'I'll be back here before you know it, richer'n My-das.'

The train waited at the depot for almost fifteen minutes, chuffing and clanking with monotonous regularity. Jamie wanted to get back home, but Lucy didn't want to leave the depot until she had seen Uncle Casper disappearing into the distance with her own eyes. Only then would she feel safe about leaving her bedroom door unlocked at night.

At last the conductor climbed up on to the step; and the locomotive blew out a deafening salvo of steam. Uncle Casper said. 'That's it, looks like we're off.'

Lucy stepped nearer. 'Uncle Casper!' she called him. Her voice was white.

He looked down at her. 'You wait,' he promised her. 'I'll be back.'

She was almost choking, having to talk to him. But she had to know. 'Uncle Casper – what you said about you and momma –'

'What about it?'

'You made it up, didn't you, just to keep me quiet?'

Uncle Casper grinned. 'What do *you* think, princess? What's your opinion?'

'I think you made it up.'

'If that's what you think, it's not my place to try to change your mind.'

'Uncle Casper! Tell me the truth!'

He shook his head. 'Bye-and-bye, princess – as you grow older – there's one thing you're goin' to find out for yourself. And that is – the only truth is, that there aint no truth.'

The train pulled away from the depot, and Jamie came up and took hold of Lucy's arm. She stood quite still until the train was out of sight.

'Do you want to tell me what that was all about?' asked Jamie, quietly.

Lucy whispered. 'No. Not yet, anyway.'

They left the depot building and walked across to Jamie's buggy. Jamie handed her the deed and said, 'You'd better keep this paper someplace safe. You never know.'

'Jamie,' said Lucy, 'thank you for everything. Thank you for not asking too many questions.'

Jamie climbed up on to the buggy and released the brake. 'I can wait. Will I see you on Thursday, when I come into town?'

She nodded and smiled.

Jamie cracked his buggy-whip and drove off back towards the Cullen Farm. Lucy watched him for a while, and waved, and then walked home, feeling empty and tired.

'Casper gone?' her father asked her, as she walked into the store.

'Yes,' said Lucy.

'Well, he's probably gone for good this time,' her father remarked. He was weighing out tea by the half-pound; and the brass scales made a clonking noise as he reached full measure.

'I hope so,' said Lucy.

'You didn't get on with him too good this time, did you?' her father asked her.

'No,' said Lucy. 'Not too good.'

'He drinks like a whale, I'll allow you that. Never seen a man drink like that before.'

Jack Darling wrapped up another packet of tea, and then he said, 'I'd love to know where he managed to get hold of three hundred and fifty dollars, though, just like that.'

'Didn't he tell you?' asked Lucy.

Jack Darling shook his head. 'He's a conundrum, that man. Never did understand him, nor trusted him much, neither. If he weren't your momma's brother –'

Lucy went upstairs to change into the plain blue cotton dress she usually wore in the store. She brushed up her hair, and then she opened her jewellery box to find her barrettes. When she looked inside, she went cold. She sat down on the bed with a feeling of grief deeper than anything she had felt since her mother died.

Apart from her tortoiseshell barrettes, the jewellery box was empty. The cameo had gone.

2

It was mid-January when Jamie rode up to the store in the middle of a snow-blizzard, and tied his blanketed horse to the hitching-rail outside. He came in through the door in a whirl of snowflakes and a high shriek of wind.

The stove was hot and all the usual loungers were sitting around it, drinking whisky and discussing President Cleveland's love life. The President was fat and ugly and nearly fifty. Was he truly going to marry twenty-two-year-old Frances Folsom, or was he more interested in her mother?

Henry McGuffey said it didn't matter how old a man was, he still enjoyed the company of pretty young women.

Lucy was serving Mrs Ottinger with Rubens shirts for her one-year-old son Thomas, who was sitting in the corner of the store solemnly sucking a stick of bright crimson candy. Jamie gave Lucy a smile and a wave, and waited by the stove until she had finished, warming his hands.

'How's Saint Jerrold today?' asked Samuel Blankenship, referring to Jamie's father. 'Saved any more sinners, has he?'

Jamie grinned. 'A little religion never did anyone any harm, Mr Blankenship.'

'Couldn't agree more,' said Samuel. He chewed off another cheekful of Union Leader Cut Plug. 'Trouble is, I never could understand having a taste for it, breakfast, lunch, and dinner.'

'You want nourishment, Mr Blankenship?' Jamie told him. 'My father says the scriptures are just as good for you as pork'n'beans.'

Samuel laughed, and spat tobacco-juice into the pan of ashes in front of the stove. 'Never argue with the son of a saint.'

At last Lucy was finished with Mrs Ottinger. She never hurried the farm women when they came into the store to browse and to buy, even when they asked to see muslins and calicoes and ready-to-wear dresses that they obviously couldn't afford. They would stand transfixed in front of the old cheval-glass in the corner, holding in front of their plain wool dresses some of the finest and prettiest fabrics, and for a moment their faces would light up, and their eyes would be far away. It didn't matter that the fashions were already a year behind the times in the East, and two years behind in Paris. They were new in Oak City, Kansas.

Jamie leaned across the counter and kissed Lucy on the cheek. She smiled, but these days it was always the same – she never let him kiss her on the lips. She never let him put his arm around her, either, and when he asked her why, all she ever said was, 'I'm sorry, but I think we ought to wait.'

He tugged a folded letter out of his glove. 'I just picked this up at the depot.'

'Did you see if there was anything for us?' Lucy asked him. Today's train had been the first in four days, because of the snow.

'Couple of cases of Heinz fruit,' Jamie told her. 'Didn't see anything else.'

He handed Lucy the letter and she read it slowly. It was headed Kansas State University, Manhattan, Kansas.

'You're going to study law at the State University?' she asked him, in surprise.

He nodded. 'That's right, the whole three-year course.'

'When do you start?'

'Next semester, isn't it great? Well, I have to ask father about it first. I mean he's going to have to pay for it. But he's been a little more easy-going about my law studies lately. You couldn't say enthusiastic, but more easy-going.'

'What about Mr Collamer?' asked Lucy. 'I thought Mr Collamer was teaching you just fine.'

Jamie shrugged. 'Well, sure, but Mr Collamer doesn't have anything else to teach me. He admits it himself. He hasn't practised for fifteen years, and what I need now is proper up-to-date lectures, you know, and real practical experience. There aren't even any proper law firms in Oak City, only Lloyd Judd's.'

'Does that mean you're going to be living in Manhattan?' Lucy felt breathless and upset, as if the world had suddenly come unstuck at the seams. She hadn't realized until now how much she had depended on Jamie since Uncle Casper had assaulted her. Not as a lover; she still couldn't help tightening up whenever he touched her; but as a constant friend. Somebody who protected her, and reassured her that some men could be gentle and protective.

'I'll *have* to live there,' said Jamie. 'But I'll be back for vacations, and maybe some weekends.'

Lucy hardly knew what to say. She folded up the letter and handed it back to him.

'You don't look too pleased,' Jamie told her.

'Of course I'm pleased. I'm really proud of you.'

'I'm pretty proud of myself, to tell you the truth.'

Lucy called to Henry McGuffey, 'Hear that, Mr McGuffey? Jamie's been accepted for the State University, to study law.'

Henry McGuffey raised his whisky-glass. 'Congratulations, young Cullen! How about a drink?'

'How about five drinks, without taking a breath, and the Lord's Prayer back'ards?' Samuel Blankenship suggested, and slapped his thigh in amusement. The social circle around the general store stove hadn't let Jamie forget last summer's wager. It had now become part of Oak City folklore.

Jamie shook his head. 'I have to get back. The cattle need feeding something desperate, with all this snow on the ground.'

Lucy walked to the door with him. She was looking white, and the reflected light from the snow outside made her appear whiter still. It was partly the winter, and the lack of sunshine. It was partly the memory of Uncle Casper, and what he had done to her. She had imagined that it would fade, and that one morning she would be able to wake up and go through the day without thinking about it once. But it remained raw and recent and startlingly vivid, as if it had happened only yesterday. Sometimes when she thought about it she found herself rubbing her wrists, as if Uncle Casper had only just cut her free.

Jamie touched her fine blonde hair. 'You look like you could use a tonic. Mother always swears by Dr Bradfield's.'

Lucy smiled faintly. 'I'm not surprised. It's two-fifths alcohol.'

'I'll call in to see you on Sunday, okay? If the snow's not too bad,' he told her.

'All right,' she said. Then, 'Do you really *have* to go to Manhattan?'

He looked at her questioningly. 'Of course, if I want to be a lawyer.'

'But what about us?'

Jamie took a deep breath. 'Us?'

'Well, if you're gone for three years —'

Jamie waited for her to finish, but she didn't. Instead, she reached out and touched the horn button of his coat, twisting it between her fingers.

'Lucy,' said Jamie, in a low, gentle voice, 'the way I see it, right now, there isn't any "us". Leastways, there hasn't been for six or seven months. You never kiss me, you never let me hold you, you never say you love me. You didn't want to come to the barndance; you didn't want to come to the carnival; you didn't want to come to Hays City, for the cavalry dance. Whenever we're together, you scarcely say two words to me. Now, let's be fair about it, we're still friends, but you can hardly call that "us".'

'Jamie –' she said, suddenly tugging at his button.

'I'm sorry, sweetheart,' he replied. 'There's so much I want to see; so much I want to do. The world is *huge*, Lucy, and I want to be part of it. I don't want to spend the rest of my days mucking out horses in Oak City, Kansas.'

Even more softly, he said, 'Remember, you used to have a dream too. All that stuff about being a socialite, going to dances. Rubbing shoulders with the rich. What happened to that?'

'Maybe I grew up,' said Lucy; although she didn't mean it. She didn't feel any more mature. She just felt dirty, and spoilt, like a brand-new doll that somebody stepped on, and then carelessly dropped into a muddy ditch.

Even now she couldn't convince herself that her lost purity didn't somehow show on her face.

Uncle Casper had robbed her of her dream that day in the stockroom. She didn't even bother to take dancing lessons any more. What was the use? She lived hour by hour, working in the store, cleaning the house, sweeping the floors and cooking the meals and ironing her father's worn-out shirts. Life at least seemed safe that way.

Jamie said, 'I promise I'll write.'

'I thought you wanted to marry me,' she persisted.

'Well . . .' he said, 'sure . . . but things can change.'

'Does that mean you don't love me any more?'

'Of course I love you. But, come on Lucy, it isn't easy to go on loving somebody who doesn't show any signs of loving you back.'

She lowered her head and looked down at the floor. Jamie stood watching her for a while, and then said, 'I have to go. I'm sorry.'

'You don't have anything to be sorry for,' she said.

'Well, maybe not. But I'm sorry things didn't turn out different.'

She looked up, and then she kissed him, on the lips. 'Me too,' she said, and turned away.

Jamie tugged on his gloves, and opened the door. Snow came tumbling into the warm interior of the store, and Samuel Blankenship looked up gravely.

'You inning, young fellow, or outing? Whichever it is, make up your mind before this stove freezes over.'

Lucy lay in bed that night and silently wept to herself. Then she stopped weeping and lay staring at the ceiling. The wind had died a little and the town lay eerily silent. She could hear icicles dripping along the eaves; and the roof cracking under the weight of the snow.

She thought of her dream. She thought of dancing, and laughter, and varnished carriages. She thought of silk ball-gowns and rows of pearls.

Uncle Casper had been right. It had been one of those fantasies that would never come true. She didn't even have her mother's jewellery to wear to the Oak City barndance; let alone diamonds to wear to a New York ball.

Ever since she had been able to read the labels in her father's store, she had fancied that she would travel all over the world. Bourjois' Violette de Parme, from Paris, France. Myron Parker's Bay Rum, from Puerto Rico. Lea & Perrins' Worcestershire Sauce, from England. And all those extraordinary spices from the Bombay Trading Company, Bombay, India.

But now the names had shrunk back to being nothing more than names; far-sounding cities, in tiny print, on dull-coloured labels. Lucy felt as if the whole globe had dwindled to the size of the Jack Darling General Store, and that she would never escape.

She was almost asleep when she heard a train-whistle blow. The blizzard must have died down for a train to be able to get through. She wondered which direction it had come from, east from Kansas City or west from Denver. Trains from the east usually brought them goods they had ordered, and they were running very low on sugar and washing-powders and navy beans. Well, she would find out in the morning, when she took the buckboard along to the depot.

Not a quarter of an hour had passed, however, before she heard footsteps on the wooden sidewalk below her window, and then somebody climbing slowly up the stairs at the side of the building. There was a knock at the kitchen door, then another, then another. The knocking went on and on, loud and insistent. Whoever it was, they weren't planning on going away.

Lucy sat up. She doubted if her father had heard it. His bedroom was at the back, overlooking the yard, and he was usually so tired by the time he got to bed that he slept like a dead man.

She climbed out of bed, took down her dressing-robe from the hook on the back of the door, and went through the parlour to the kitchen, tying up her robe as she went. A dark shape was visible through the spiderweb glass in the kitchen door, one arm lifted as it beat against the frame.

Lucy went up to the door and called, 'Who is it? What do you want?'

There was a long pause. She could hear the wind whining through the cracks around the sides of the door. Then a hoarse voice said, 'Lucy? That you?'

She felt as if she had been dropped into a tub of freezing-cold water. There was no mistaking that voice, however hoarse it was. Uncle Casper had returned.

'Uncle Casper?' she whispered.

'Open the door,' he demanded. 'I'm dyin' of frostbite out here.'

Lucy took hold of the door-key, but she found it impossible to turn it. Something inside her simply wouldn't let her do it. Her heart danced a slow waltz, *one-two-three, one-two-three*.

Uncle Casper drummed at the door yet again. 'Lucy, I'm dyin'! For Christ's sakes, let me in!'

But she couldn't turn the key. He rattled and banged and shouted out 'Lucy! Will you open the damned door!' but she couldn't turn the key.

At that moment, however, her father came into the kitchen. She couldn't see his face because it was so dark. But she could see the silhouette of his sleep-scruffed hair and his worn-out robe. 'Lucy?' he said. 'What in hell's going on? Who's making all that noise?'

'It's Uncle – Casper,' she told him, turning away from the door.

'Uncle Casper? Well, let him in, for pity's sake! You can't leave a man standing outside on a night like this!'

But Lucy stayed where she was, with her back to the door, unable to touch it. She was shaking with fear, as if she expected Uncle Casper to come roaring through the door like Satan himself, and to rape her where she stood.

Jack reached out and held her arm. 'You're cold, sweetheart,' he said. 'You're freezing.'

Lucy said, 'Poppa, I –' but then without hesitation, Jack turned the key in the lock and opened up the door. Uncle Casper came stamping in, whacking his gloves together, as big and as black and as shaggy as a bear.

'Jesus, Jack! A man could have perished!'

Jack shut the door and locked it again. Then he went over to the hutch and lit the lamp. Uncle Casper was wearing a huge fur coat and a huge fur hat, and black boots. He was carrying a large leather portmanteau. His beard and his eyebrows were encrusted with ice, and there were thick icicles underneath his nostrils. When he saw Lucy standing with her back to him, he didn't say anything, not even 'hello', but he didn't take his eyes away from her as he eased himself out of his coat. Underneath he was wearing a well-tailored Norfolk jacket and knee breeches. He sat down on one of the kitchen chairs and Jack handed him the bootjack.

'Taken me over a week to make it here from California,' he remarked, easing off his boots. 'We were stuck solid for a day and a night in the High Sierras. It's taken me two clear days to get here from Denver.'

'How are things in California?' Jack asked him. He went across to the range and picked up the blue-enamel coffee-pot. 'What about some coffee? The hob's still hot.'

'Not for me,' said Uncle Casper. 'Keeps me from sleeping.' He reached into the inside pocket of his suit for a silver flask. He unscrewed it, lifted it up, and said, 'Good health. Here's to the dollar, and to whisky, and to immoral ladies wherever they may be!'

He took three long swallows of whisky; then burped into his fist. 'Don't know if I would've survived that journey, without this flask here. Jesus, it was cold in them railroad cars. Cold? We considered setting light to the seats, just to keep ourselves warm.'

'You're looking real good, if you don't mind my saying so,' Jack remarked. 'Did you find any oil?'

Uncle Casper was about to take another pull from his flask, but he lowered it and stared. 'Did I find any oil? Didn't you get my wire?'

Jack shook his head. 'Telegraph service is pretty irregular around here.'

Uncle Casper threw back his head and let out a great shout of laughter. 'Did I find any oil! Here —' he said, and opened his coat, and lifted his pocket-watch out of his vest pocket. 'Look at this, and then ask me if I found any oil!'

Jack took hold of the watch and held it in the palm of his hand. The watch was solid gold, its face engraved with scrolls.

'Turn it over,' said Uncle Casper; and when he did so, Jack saw a rose design, on a background of pavé-set diamonds, with petals of real rubies and leaves of real emeralds.

'Well, I'm damned,' he said. 'You actually struck oil.'

Uncle Casper nodded. 'Ferris and Conroy Oil Company, of Seal Beach, California.'

'Well, I'm damned, ' said Jack.

Uncle Casper took his watch back and grinned widely. 'Now, Jack! You regret you didn't back me now, don't you? Hunh? Just think about it! If you'd have been a little more foresighted – if you'd have been a little more trusting, a little more free-and-easy with your money . . . well, you could have been a wealthy man, as of today. They told us we was mad, me and Ferris, drilling where we did . . . but we kept on drilling and we kept on drilling, and November first we struck oil. And now I'm rich, Jack, and I'm making a thousand dollars a day without lifting a finger.'

Jack slowly rubbed his unshaven chin. 'A thousand dollars a day?'

'A thousand dollars a day. Maybe more, by now! Maybe fifteen hundred.'

'Fifteen hundred?' Lucy's father turned away with such a look of defeat and injustice on his face that Lucy could hardly bear it. He filled the coffee-pot with water and put it on the hob to boil.

'You're sure you don't want a whisky?' Uncle Casper asked him. 'You sure look like you could use it.'

Jack said, 'No thanks, Casper. I have to get up early tomorrow. I have a store to run.'

'Ha!' laughed Casper. 'Sure you do! Sure you do! Weighin' out butter, shovellin' out beans! It's a hard life, Jack! It's a real hard life!'

'You can use the spare room again, if you like,' Jack told him. 'Lucy – would you make sure that the bed's made up?'

Lucy nodded. She kissed her father, and then crossed the kitchen towards the door. As she did so, however, Uncle

Casper stuck his leg out in front of her to block her way, and gave her a wary, suggestive grin. 'Aint yo goin' to kiss your old Uncle Casper? He's a man o' means, now. Somebody to look up to. Why – you aint said one p'lite word to me since I walked through that door.'

Lucy stood stiffly with her hands by her sides. 'I have to make your bed,' she told him, in a cold voice.

'Not one little kiss?' Uncle Casper asked her, tapping his lips with his finger.

'I'm sorry,' said Lucy. 'I'm tired.'

Uncle Casper smiled at Jack and shifted his leg out of the way, but as Lucy tried to walk past him, his arm came out as quick as a bullwhip and snatched at her sleeve, pulling her on to his lap. Before she could struggle free, he kissed her, wetly and ferociously, right on the mouth.

Lucy wrenched herself away from him, and struck at him with both fists. As he tried to protect his face, he lost his balance and toppled sideways off his chair. He landed noisily on the floor, surprised and winded. Lucy wiped her mouth with her sleeve, almost hysterical, again and again, and spat out Uncle Casper's saliva. She felt as if he had infected her with every kind of foul disease there ever was.

'Lucy! What the heck!' Jack exclaimed, shocked. 'Casper, are you all right?'

Uncle Casper heaved himself up again, laughing. 'Bruised my butt, I think, Jack! But nothin' more serious than that! What a spitfire, hey? What a spitfire!'

Lucy stared at him wide-eyed; still shaking; still rubbing at her mouth with the sleeve of her robe.

'Come on, Lucy,' her father told her. 'I think you'd better say you're sorry to your Uncle Casper for that. He was only funning.'

'Funning?' said Lucy. 'Look at him, he's drunk! I can't stand to be kissed by drunks!'

Uncle Casper laughed, and sniffed, and took out his flask.

'How many drunks have you been kissed by, Lucy Darling my darling?'

'One too many,' Lucy retorted. She stared at her father to make it quite clear that she didn't have the slightest intention of apologizing, and then she stalked out of the room and slammed the door behind her.

She heard her father say, '. . . little upset . . . her boyfriend's going off to law school . . .'

'Oh, you mean the drinker,' Casper replied, and laughed some more. 'Five whiskies, without a breath; never saw anybody do that before. Never did it myself! Didn't even think it was possible!'

Lucy didn't make up Uncle Casper's bed. Goddamn him, he could sleep on the floor for all she cared. She hated him so much she could hardly breathe. She locked her bedroom door, then she filled her washbasin and scrubbed at her mouth with her facecloth.

She blew out her lamp and went to bed; but she couldn't sleep. She lay on her back listening to the murmuring of voices from the parlour. Then she heard the kitchen door open and close; and she could guess what was happening. Her father was going down to the store to fetch up another bottle of whisky. She could almost have hated her father for being so weak; but of course he didn't know what Uncle Casper had done to her, and she knew that he was entertaining him only because her mother would have wanted him to.

It was just after two o'clock in the morning when she heard her father retire to bed. She heard him tread carefully along the darkened corridor to the spare room; and then pause and murmur, 'Goddamn it,' when he discovered that she hadn't made up Uncle Casper's bed. She waited, holding her breath, expecting him to knock at her door, but he didn't. She heard him open the blanket chest, and make up the bed himself.

'Oh, poppa,' she whispered to herself. 'I'm sorry.' She

loved him so much for his patience and his kindness and his daily suffering. If only she could have told him what had happened.

She closed her eyes and tried to imagine her mother. She tried to remember her all dressed up in her blue silk dress, laughing. She tried to remember her at Christmas-time, singing carols and stirring the puddings. She tried to re-member her dancing. But all she could picture was a hunted desperate face, white as ivory, and wrists as thin as wooden spoons, and eyes that were losing all of their life.

Her mother had died the week after her thirty-sixth birthday. Lucy wondered what it would be like when *she* was thirty-six – and when she was thirty-seven, and older than her own mother.

She was almost asleep when her doorhandle was clumsily turned around; and then there was a scratching at the door. She went cold. She lay with her eyes open, not moving, not even breathing.

'Lucy . . .' whispered Uncle Casper. 'Lucy, c'n you hear me?'

She didn't reply. She waited and waited, and for a moment she thought he might have given up and gone away, but then he scratched at the door a second time.

'Lucy . . . I came to give you y'r money back . . . y'r three hundred–fifty dollars. I've got it all here . . . golden eagles just the same like you gave me. C'n you hear me, Lucy? Are you awake? I've got your money. So's we're quits, you understan' . . . you can buy back y'r momma's jewellery.'

Still Lucy refused to reply. Uncle Casper sniffed and shuffled his feet, and then he said, 'I've come a long way, Lucy, just to square things up. All I want is for us to say that we're quits. I don't want nothing; nothing at all. C'n you hear me, princess? Just that bitty paper, that's all I want, so's we're quits.'

So that was why Uncle Casper had toiled all the way back to Kansas, in the middle of winter! He wanted to revoke their agreement, so that he wouldn't have to pay her five per cent of his oil profits.

No, she thought. *Five per cent is your punishment for what you did to me. I'm not letting you out of this one, uncle. I'm going to take my share and I'm going to go on taking my share until you die or your oil-well runs dry, and I know which of those two things I want to happen first.*

Uncle Casper scratched at the door-panel yet again. 'Lucy, are you hearin' me? I've got y'r money, Lucy, plus interest if you want it. Two per cent, now that's fair. You're lucky to get y'r stake back so quick, princess, plenty of people lose their money for good. And let me tell you this – I'm givin' you back this money before I've earned it. We aint broke even yet, me and Ferris, and I aint going to see any kind of profit out of that well for years and years. Maybe never will.'

My God, thought Lucy. *You're so grotesque!* She had seen the word 'grotesque' in a magazine, under a steel-engraving of gargoyles at Rouen Cathedral, in France. There had been something about the bulging eyes and stretched-open mouths of those gargoyles that had reminded her of Uncle Casper, that day that he had assaulted her.

'Lucy?' called Uncle Casper; but this was followed by an even longer silence.

Lucy strained her ears. Had he tiptoed off to his room? Had he fallen asleep in the corridor? She was just about to climb out of bed and go to look when he cleared his throat, and said, 'Lucy? If you're awake, you sweet thing, you listen to me. I'm tryin' to do right, you understand me? I'm tryin' to make up for treatin' you wrong. You can have y'r money, and another hundred besides. How's that? And, there's somethin' else, too. Your momma's cameo brooch? I guess you realized it was me that took it; but believe me, Lucy, I had to have all the money I could lay my hands on, and I pawned that brooch and got me thirty-nine dollars and that bought me all the drilling-bits I needed.

'But I redeemed it, when the well came in; and I've brought it with me. And if you give me that bitty paper, princess, you can have it back, and welcome, even though it's sentimental to me, too.'

Lucy sat up rigidly in bed. She was tempted for one moment to open the door and demand her mother's brooch back right away. But she took a deep breath and gripped the blankets and stayed silent. Uncle Casper was wily and violent, and there was no telling what he might do.

No, she thought. *He's going to bed now. He must be exhausted after travelling all the way from Denver in this weather; and apart from that he must have drunk the best part of a bottle-and-a-half of whisky. He'll sleep like a log.*

She felt a thrill of fear at what she was thinking. But she was determined that Uncle Casper had got the better of her for the very last time. She would have her five per cent; and her mother's cameo brooch; and Uncle Casper would never touch her or kiss her again.

I'll wait till he's asleep, and then I'll go through his pockets and steal the brooch back again.

There was a bumping noise. It sounded as if Uncle Casper was pressing his forehead against the door. 'Let me tell you somethin', Lucy . . . you may not think it, sometimes, but I'm real fond of you. When I was out in California, I used to think about you . . . you're a fine-lookin' girl, Lucy, I tell you that true. I used to think of you tied up in them ribbons . . . and I used to *shake*, Lucy, I used to *shake*! And it weren't them California earthquakes, neither.'

He paused, and sighed, his forehead still pressed against the door. 'Tied up in them ribbons, Lucy . . . you was a man's exotic-est dream come true.'

At last, after sniffing and coughing and shuffling a little longer, Uncle Casper dragged himself along the corridor to the spare room. Lucy heard the clunking of the whisky bottle that he was carrying against the door-jamb. Then the door shut, and she heard him collapsing into bed.

She was deeply tired, and it was hard for her to stay awake. She waited until three o'clock struck, then half-past three. At last, when she was sure that Uncle Casper must be sleeping, she climbed out of bed and wrapped herself in her robe.

Outside her bedroom window, Oak City lay white and silent under two feet of snow, a collection of wooden dollhouses out of a child's wintry dream. She unlocked her door and stood in the corridor for a long time, listening. All she could hear was her father's deep, regular breathing; and a crackling snoring from Uncle Casper's room.

She had never thought of herself as brave; and she never imagined that she would ever feel vengeful. But she was so determined to punish Uncle Casper for what he had done – no, for even less than that – for being alive, for being what he was – that she made her way along the corridor with a set face and clenched fists and nothing but the abrupt appearance of the Devil himself could have persuaded her to go back.

She reached Uncle Casper's door. He had closed it; but his lamp was still lit, and she could smell tobacco-smoke. She waited for a moment, keeping her eyes on the dull little picture of Charlotte, North Carolina, which her mother had always kept in the corridor to remind her of home. A farmhouse, in Mecklenburg County, with ducks in the yard. Then she turned the doorhandle, and eased open the door.

Uncle Casper was lying on top of his quilt, still dressed, still wearing his boots. His eyes were closed and his mouth was open and if he hadn't been snoring Lucy would have taken him for dead. The smell of whisky and sweat was so overpowering that she had to clamp her hand over her mouth to prevent herself from gagging.

As Lucy crept around the foot of the bed, she saw that

Uncle Casper had taken a bottle of whisky to bed with him. He must have fallen asleep while he was drinking it, because the bottle had fallen over sideways and emptied all over his vest and his trousers. One hand curled lightly around the bottle, twitching every now and then as Uncle Casper dreamed.

Dear God, she thought, *what kind of dreams can a man like this be dreaming*.

She went to the bureau, where he had scattered his loose change and his tobacco-pouch and cigarette-papers. There was no sign of the cameo brooch there. She slid open the top two drawers, one after the other. One was empty; in the other lay a hammerless .32 pocket revolver, and some grey-looking handkerchiefs.

All the other drawers were empty. Uncle Casper hadn't bothered to unpack yet. He must have the cameo in his bag; or in one of his pockets.

Watching him carefully, Lucy knelt down beside the bed and unfastened the clasps of his bag. He snorted, and stirred, and said something that sounded like, 'Ferris, you sumbitch . . . no damn good at all.' Lucy froze, her knees trembling with the strain, her eyes wide; but Uncle Casper went on snoring.

It was difficult to see inside the case when it was opened. The lamp was on the opposite side of the bed, and so Lucy was crouching in shadow. She lifted out one or two silk shirts, and a handful of crumpled silk drawers, and a pair of corduroy trousers with some stiff yellowish stain on them. But she couldn't make out what was in the bottom of the case. She could feel some papers, and some pens, and some metal bits and pieces that must have been something to do with drilling for oil.

She stood up, and made her way around the bed, and cautiously picked up the oil-lamp. It was a heavy glass Bordeaux parlour-lamp, embossed with bunches of grapes coloured true-to-life. It had been a Christmas present from some friends of her mother's, and even though it must have cost more than three dollars, her mother had always hated it.

Lucy took the lamp around to the case, and held it up while she explored inside. The bottom of the case was awash with rubbish – railroad schedules, police suspenders, buttons, hairbrushes, Kissingen Salts (for obesity), Methylene Compound (for gonorrhea), valves, spring-loaded catches, a box of four barbers' razors, and a dog's-eared copy of *Illustrated Day's Doings and Sporting World* with a cover-line which promised pictures of 'frisky women' inside.

She didn't dare to tip up the entire contents of the case on to the carpet, but she was fairly sure that the cameo brooch wasn't there. She pushed back the shirts and the underwear, and stood up again, holding the oil-lamp like the Statue of Liberty. Uncle Casper must have the brooch in one of his pockets.

Biting her lip, she approached the bed. Uncle Casper had stopped snoring now, but his breathing was harsh and slow and regular. Carefully, Lucy tugged the purple silk handkerchief out of the breast pocket of his coat, and then slid two fingers inside, to see if the brooch were there.

Next, she lifted the other side of his coat, and explored his inside pockets. Nothing, except for a folded-over pamphlet.

She tried the ticket pockets at the front of his vest, then his side pockets. All of them were empty. She was shivering with cold and concentration, and with the effort of holding up the heavy lamp. She was just about to try his trouser pockets, however, when a strong hand closed around the wrist in which she was holding the lamp.

'*Ah!*' she cried, and looked up in fright. Uncle Casper, bleary-eyed, was smiling at her.

'Well, well . . .' he said, in a voice still clogged with sleep. 'I was right, then, was I? You want some more pleasurin'? You came back to your old Uncle Casper for more of them fun and games.'

'Let go of me!' Lucy hissed at him. 'Let go!'

Uncle Casper tightened his grip. 'What you whisperin' for? Frightened your poppa's goin' to find out? Well, we can keep quiet about this, if that's what you want . . . I don't mind. Romantic chatter aint totally necessary, in spite of what the women's papers say.'

'Let go of me! I want my mother's brooch!'

'Oh . . . so that's it? You didn't want no lovin' at all! You just came in here to steal my property! Well, let me tell you somethin', I don't take kindly to that. I don't take kindly to that at-all!'

He squeezed her wrist so tight that the lamp shuddered in her hand. 'I'll tell you what, though, princess, we can make a deal, you and me. An agreement, let's say! You can give me some of your lovin' now, and maybe I'll think about giving your momma's brooch back!'

Lucy thought of the revolver in the top bureau drawer, and wondered wildly if it were loaded. And, if it were – if she would have the courage to pick it up and use it.

But Uncle Casper was holding her in such a vicious grip that she couldn't get free. He was grinning at her, showing his teeth, as if he were quite prepared to bite a chunk out of her living flesh. *That uncle of yours has got the devil perched on his shoulder*, that's what Mrs Sweeney had told her, and Mrs Sweeney had known her men.

'Please, uncle,' she pleaded. 'I'm going to drop this lamp in a moment.'

Uncle Casper blew her a kiss, then smiled again, with strings of saliva stretching between his lips like spiderwebs. 'You and me, I do believe we was born for each other. Even if we wasn't, I must say that I've taken a fancy to you.'

He sniffed, and then he said, 'Seems to me like you've got yourself a choice, princess. Either you treat me nice; or else I shout out to your poppa that you came to my room, lookin' to misbehave yourself. And what's he goin' to say to that? Because the supportin' evidence is, that here you are.'

'Uncle Casper, I'm asking you, let go!' Lucy demanded;

and she knew that she wasn't going to ask him again. If he didn't release her, she would scratch his face.

Uncle Casper reached out with his free hand to take the lamp away from her. But as he did so, Lucy twisted her arm, and the lamp dropped on to his chest. The globe rolled off on to the floor, and the wicks flared up, and before Uncle Casper could say, 'Son-of-a-bitch!' his whisky-soaked clothes roared up into a sheet of flames.

Uncle Casper yelled. Lucy screamed, although it was more of a moan than a scream; and stumbled back, suddenly free of him.

'I'm on fire!' Uncle Casper raged at her. 'I'm on fire, Goddamn it!'

His coat and his vest were furiously ablaze. He tried to knock the lamp off his stomach, but the glass shattered, and he was suddenly awash with a lapful of fiery oil. He screeched a terrible high, harsh screech, and jumped off the blazing bed, enveloped in flames from the knees upward.

'God help me! I'm burning!'

He spun and danced and flapped his arms and screamed, trying to beat the flames out with hands that were themselves alight. His beard was alight, his hair was alight, fire rippled out of his cheeks. Backing away from him, horrified, Lucy could see his agonized face, eyes wide open, as it wrinkled and shrivelled and melted right in front of her.

'Poppa!' she shrieked 'Poppa!' She knew that you were supposed to roll people on the ground, if they were burning, or cover them up with a blanket. But the bed was burning, too, and the room was filled with whirling fragments of cotton quilt and smouldering hanks of horsehair; and through this maelstrom of fire, Uncle Casper was blazing like a tar-barrel, so hot that she couldn't get close.

The bedroom door hurtled open, and Jack Darling tumbled into the room, in his nightshirt. The draft of the door opening fed the flames with a huge rush of fresh oxygen, and Uncle Casper virtually exploded in front of them, in an incandescent pillar of human flesh. Lucy glimpsed his arms, held up in front of him in the stiff fetal posture that everybody adopts when they are burning to death; and his diminutive blackened head, like a lump of tarry coal.

Then her father snatched her out of the room, and pushed her whimpering and hysterical into the corridor. He slammed the bedroom door shut, and shouted at her, 'Fire-extinguishers! Go down to the store and bring me up as many as you can carry!'

Lucy hesitated, shaking. She felt as the night were closing in on her from all sides. But Jack Darling hustled her along the corridor and into the kitchen. He opened the kitchen door for her, and pressed the keys to the store into her hand. 'You understand me! Fire-extinguishers! I'm getting to work with the bucket!'

In bare feet, slipping and stumbling, her robe snapping in the penetrating wind, Lucy went down the icy steps to the back of the store. Behind her, she heard her father furiously trying to prime the kitchen pump. If it had frozen during the early hours of the morning, there would be no hope of putting out the flames, and the store could easily burn down to the ground.

Fumbling with cold and shock, Lucy opened up the stockroom and hurried to the far end, where they kept the blue glass hand-grenades for putting out fires. She cleared six or seven parasols off the top of the crate of hand-grenades with a sweep of her arm, and hefted it up. Panting, almost losing her balance, she climbed back up the stairs to the smoke-filled kitchen.

She needn't have hurried. When she reached Uncle Casper's room, coughing and gasping, the hand-grenades rattling in their crate, she found that the flames were already out. Her father had drenched the bed with two bucketfuls of water, and now it was simply smouldering. Behind the bed – although she hadn't wanted to look at it – she saw the twisted branch–like creature that had been her Uncle Casper lying face-down on the floor, its blackened teeth exposed.

Jack had opened the window, and already the smoke was shuddering off into the night. He took the crate of fire-extinguishers out of Lucy's hands, and said quietly, 'It's all right, sweetheart. It's over.'

Lucy covered her face with her hands. Her eyes were watering from the smoke, but she wasn't crying. She didn't feel anything at all. She felt completely detached from herself, as if she were somebody else altogether, the girl she had seen in the mirror after Uncle Casper had raped her.

Dearest Jesus, she had wanted revenge; but nothing like this.

As the night began to fade, and the sky lightened to the colour of ice-water, they sat in the parlour, wrapped up in their overcoats, and shared a potful of black coffee and brandy. The smell of smoke was piercing and sour.

'He must've reached out to turn off the lamp, and toppled it over,' said Jack, trying to be calm, trying to be logical about it, trying not to give way to shock, although he couldn't stop himself from flapping his hands as he spoke, like two snared doves. 'God above ... I told him that whisky was going to be the death of him ... but I didn't expect it to kill him *this* way.'

Lucy asked hoarsely, 'What are we going to do now?'

Jack said, 'I don't know. I guess we'll have to call Ernie Truelove, down at the funeral parlour. Then we'll have to get word to the county coroner, one way or another, to see if he feels like travelling two hundred miles in the snow to look at a man who was burned up to nothing but ashes. Don't suppose the sheriff'll want to know. Accidental death, after all.' He paused, and then he said, 'You heard him screaming, was that it, and you ran into his room and there he was, burning?'

Lucy nodded, tight-mouthed. She didn't want to think

about it. She knew already that she was going to have nightmares about it.

Jack was quiet for a while, blowing the steam from his cup of coffee. 'Natural justice, I guess. The hand of God. It was bound to catch up with him sooner or later. The drink, you know, or the drunkenness.'

Lucy said, 'Do we have to talk about him any more?'

Jack reached out and laid his hand on hers. 'No, of course not. I'm sorry. Why don't you ride out to Jamie's place, and spend the day there, while me and Ernie Truelove clear the place up?'

Lucy thought it about for a while, and then said, 'All right, poppa, that's a good idea. I don't think I can stand to – well, I think I will, that's all. Jamie's always been kind; even when I didn't deserve it.'

'Maybe you can persuade him to make an honest woman of you,' said Jack; in an off-key attempt to say something light-hearted.

Lucy stood up, and went across to her father's chair, and kissed him on the forehead. He took hold of her hand, and said, 'Whatever you do, you make sure you rest. You look tired out.'

'Yes, poppa. I love you, poppa.'

'I love you too, sweetheart.'

She filled up a kettle of water to heat on the kitchen stove. While Jack went down to see Ernie Truelove at the Truelove Funeral Parlour on Cross Street, she washed her hair in the basin in her bedroom, and combed it out. At least it didn't reek of smoke any more. While she was rouging her cheeks, so that she wouldn't look so tired and ghastly, she thought she heard a creaking noise from Uncle Casper's room, and the skin on her scalp crawled in instantaneous terror. She could imagine him lifting himself up off the floor, charred and black, and walking stiffly along the corridor to take his revenge.

She listened and listened, but then the creaking came

again, and she realized that it was only the bedroom door, creaking in the wind from the open window.

She dressed in her blue-velvet riding-habit. It was warm, even if Jamie had seen it dozens of times before. Then she put on her dark blue broadcloth overcoat, and her white-fox scarf, and her riding-boots. By the time her father came trudging back up the stairs, she was ready to leave for the Cullen farm.

'I'm off now, poppa,' she told him, as he coughed and sniffed and stamped the slush from his boots.

'Okay, sweetheart, you take care. It looks like more snow before lunchtime.'

'That's all right. If it snows too much, I'll just stay over.'

She kissed him, and squeezed his hand.

'You'll be all right, won't you?' she asked him, glancing back towards Uncle Casper's room.

'Sure. I'm afraid of one or two things in this life. I'm afraid of God, and being alone, and I'm afraid of the Devil. But I'm not afraid of the dead.'

Lucy left the store and made her way along the snowy street to Overbay's to borrow their grey pony. Although the drifts were so deep, a few people had stuggled in from outlying farms for provisions or medicines or human company, and their blanketed horses stood patiently tied to the hitching-rails.

Oak City was silent; a tiny silent town on a vast silent plain. But somehow Lucy felt *shut in*, as if she could hardly catch her breath — as if the world ended where the buildings ended, and the snowy landscape and the snowy sky were pressing in on all sides like fat suffocating pillows. She took two deep lungfuls of ice-cold air, and then she lifted her skirts and stepped over the snowdrifts to the Overbay's store.

She found Jamie up in the hayloft, bundled up in a sheepskin coat, his ears covered by the flaps of a havelock cap, forking bales of hay down to his younger brother Martin. It was gloomy and cold and aromatic in there, and Martin kept sneezing.

'Lucy!' called Jamie, brushing the hay from his overalls. 'What brings you down here?'

'Can we talk?' asked Lucy.

Jamie said, 'Sure,' and forked down one last bale. It thumped on to the floor of the barn only inches in front of Martin's feet.

'Hey, watch it!' Martin complained. 'You darn near beaned me with that one!'

Jamie climbed down the rickety loft-ladder, pulling off his gloves. 'Martin – how about loading up the wagon? I'll give you a hand in just a minute.'

Martin lifted up a bale in each hand, and sneezed yet again.

'Bless you,' said Lucy.

'Oh, don't fret yourself, it's always me that has to do the hard work,' Martin grumbled. 'Soon as anything that looks like effort rears its ugly head, Jamie finds a nickel-plated excuse for quitting.'

Lucy smiled. 'I'm glad to know that I'm nickel-plated, anyway.'

Jamie took hold of her arm. 'Surprised to see you down here,' he told her.

'Why are you surprised? We're still friends, aren't we?'

'Well, sure. But things haven't exactly been lovey-dovey between us, have they?' His eyes were bright: he was provoking her on purpose.

'Oh, Jamie,' she said. 'Have I really been that much of a shrew?'

Jamie pushed open the barn door. 'Come on over to the house,' he said. 'Mother's been baking hermits.'

'Can I talk to you alone?' Lucy asked him.

Jamie shrugged. 'Of course you can.'

'I mean now, out here.'

'Well, okay, sure. I don't mind the goddamned perishing cold if you don't.'

She covered her eyes with her hand. She hardly knew where to begin; or what to say. Out here in the snow, on the Cullen ranch, the events of last night seemed absurdly theatrical, like some kind of monstrous marionette-show, as if they hadn't happened at all. Lucy looked away, towards the empty corral, and the house, and the snow-burdened oaks. She wanted to cry but somehow she couldn't. She felt shocked; but she felt no grief for Uncle Casper. She hoped that he would continue to burn in hell, the same way that he had burned in front of her eyes.

'Something's happened,' said Jamie.

Lucy nodded. 'Last night . . . Uncle Casper came back from California.'

'Oh shoot, not that chiseller.'

'Jamie, please listen,' Lucy begged him. 'He came back because he struck oil.'

'He struck oil? You're kidding me! He actually struck oil?'

'Yes,' said Lucy. Her eyes were watering in the wind. 'I'm not exactly sure where, or how. Some place called Seal Beach, that's what he said.'

'Well,' Jamie replied, 'I guess that's good news. You get your five per cent. Congratulations, you're rich! Or you could be, anyway!'

'Jamie . . . he came back because he wanted to cancel our agreement.'

Jamie vigorously shook his head. 'Unh-hunh, that's not possible, he can't do that. That agreement is legal and binding. You're entitled to your five per cent no matter what.'

'I suppose I would have been,' said Lucy. 'But he's dead.'

Without warning, she found that she was crying. Not quietly weeping, but scrunching up her face like a small child, and sobbing in deep, frosty gulps. Jamie held her

tight, and patted her back, and said rather lamely, 'Hey now
. . . *Dead*? How come he's dead?'

'He – burned,' Lucy sobbed. 'He – stole my mother's –
brooch and I – was looking for it – when he was asleep.
And I was holding – the lamp and he – grabbed hold of my
arm – and he was all soaked in whisky and he –'

'Jesus,' Jamie exclaimed. 'You mean he really caught fire?'

'He was all burned up. I mean, like firewood. It was
awful.' She pushed herself away from Jamie, though gently,
and pulled her handkerchief out of her glove. The tears on
her eyelashes sparkled in the pearly, unfocused daylight.
'Poppa's called the funeral parlour . . . he told me to come
down here, to ask if I could spend the day.'

'My God, Lucy, of course you can spend the day! You
can stay here as long as you like! Look, come on in. It's cold
enough to freeze the cluck out of a chicken.'

They walked across the snowy yard. Jamie put his arm
around her, and squeezed her tight, and for the first time in
a long time she didn't find a way to duck him or dodge him
or twist herself free. Inside the house they hung up their
coats, and Jamie took Lucy through to the parlour.

Unlike most parlours in High Plains farmhouses, which
were ostentatiously stuffed with clocks and china and plants
and pictures, and thickly draped with lace and bobble-fringed
velvet, the Cullens' parlour was modest and severe. A large
leather chair stood by the fireplace (father's); and next to it,
slightly further away from the fire, a smaller sewing chair
(mother's) with an unfinished sampler resting on the seat.
Apart from two lamp-tables, the only other furniture was an
upright piano and a glass-fronted china cabinet, displaying
the plainest of German china; and the only decoration was a
framed Currier & Ives' lithograph showing a faintly-smiling
husband and an idealistically devoted wife reading the scriptures together.

The fire had burned low; and so Jamie stacked more logs
on to it. 'Here – come warm youself up. No, you can sit in

93

father's chair, he won't mind. He's a little short on temper, but not on Christian charity. You look just awful.'

Lucy took hold of his hand. 'Dear Jamie. You're the first person who's ever said that to me without my minding.'

'Mother'll bring you some hot milk and cinnamon.'

As the fire crackled up, Lucy began to feel better, although she still couldn't stop her hands from trembling.

'You should have seen Doctor Satchell,' Jamie told her. 'Shock can make you pretty ill. We had a cousin back east who saw his baby get caught in a feed-grinder. He couldn't speak for months. Just literally couldn't speak.'

'I'll be all right,' Lucy assured him. She gave him a rueful smile, and touched his hand. 'The worst of it is, I do believe I'm *glad* he's dead.'

Jamie said nothing. Asked no questions, expressed no surprise. Lucy glanced up at him with a quick, forced smile, and said, 'I suppose you think I'm dreadful, saying that.'

'I don't know,' said Jamie. 'What do you want me to think?'

'I'm not sure. I'm confused. It seems so much like justice, what happened to Uncle Casper, but it can't be right. It can't be right for *anyone* to die like that?'

Jamie shrugged. 'Father says that you shouldn't try to gainsay God.'

Just then, Jamie's mother came in with a blue china mug of hot milk on a tray. She was a handsome fair-haired woman, half Swedish; and Jamie and all his brothers looked strikingly like her. 'You'll stay for supper, yes?' she asked. 'We have fried salt pork and apple dumplings.'

'I'd love to,' said Lucy. The thought of sitting at a crowded supper table with a friendly and devoted family like the Cullens seemed very appealing. When she thought about home, all that she could picture was the burned-out bedroom where Uncle Casper had died, and that grinning stick-like body.

That body was going to haunt her. She knew that with

dreadful certainty. Still grinning, it would run after her in dreams.

When his mother had gone, Jamie drew up the sewing-chair and sat close to her. 'Listen, there's one thing that you *don't* have to worry about, and that's your share of your Uncle Casper's oil money.'

'I don't understand you. He's dead now, isn't he? How can I share his money when he's dead?'

'Lucy,' said Jamie, 'did you read that agreement?'

Lucy hesitated, shook her head. 'It just said five per cent, didn't it?'

'What kind of a lawyer do you think I am? That was a model partnership agreement copied out of Newman's *Contracts, Agreements, Deeds, Indentures & Bonds*. You could have smacked me with a bellyband when your uncle signed it without even reading it. Mind you, I got the distinct feeling that he couldn't read too good.'

'But what does it *say*?'

Jamie leaned forward and said. 'The agreement provided for you to receive five per cent of your uncle's oil profits when he was alive. Yes? But if he were to die – and the way I saw him drinking, that wasn't exactly a remote possibility – you inherit his entire interest.'

Lucy stared at him. She could scarcely understand what he was saying; but somehow she knew that it was moment-ous.

'Lucy,' Jamie repeated, 'now that your Uncle Casper is dead, you own not just five per cent of his oil, but all of it.'

'All of it? How can that be? He said he was making a thousand dollars a day. Maybe more. Maybe fifteen hundred.'

'Are you complaining? You're rich!'

Lucy didn't know whether to squeal out loud, or cry, or dance, or what to do. 'You're not fooling me? You wouldn't be mean enough to fool me? The agreement really said that?'

Jamie took hold of her hands between his, and held them tight. 'Lucy – I don't know what in the world possessed you to give your uncle all of your savings, and if you don't want to tell me, then I don't want to know. It's your business. But whatever the reason, Lucy, sweetheart, you surely did yourself a good turn.'

Lucy's eyes brimmed with tears. She had never felt so guilty or so wretched in her life; but at the same time she was ridiculously happy. How could you feel so bad and so good, both at the same time? She had treated Jamie so off-hand, all of these months; she had pushed him away and rejected him, and all the time he had already made sure that the dream for which she had been craving all her life had actually come true.

It was a fairytale; like looking under your bed and discovering a brimming chestful of gold and diamonds from a pirate story, or the Arabian Nights.

'There's one thing, Jamie . . .' she whispered. 'The money I gave to Uncle Casper. It wasn't my savings. I pledged my mother's jewellery.'

'You pledged it?' Jamie demanded. 'You took it to a pawnbroker? Shoot! What the heck did you do that for?' He sat back, angrily; and almost crushed his mother's embroidery. But then she could see the realization breaking in his mind that – the way things had turned out – it was just as well that she *had* pledged her mother's jewels. 'It was heck of a risk, wasn't it? A heck of a risk! And why?'

'I wanted – to be rid of him,' said Lucy. She didn't think that she could admit to any more; not yet, anyway. Jamie, of course, thought that she was still a virgin. She didn't know what he would say if she were to confess that she had already been taken by Uncle Casper. She knew that Jamie would be furiously jealous and deeply hurt; and all the more jealous and hurt because Uncle Casper was already dead, and there was nobody on whom Jamie could take his revenge. Nobody, that is, except Lucy herself.

She could still feel with unnerving clarity the bright red ribbons cutting into her wrists and ankles; and Uncle Casper grunting and spitting and bludgeoning himself into her. It made her feel as if the floor were tilting beneath her feet. She had tried desperately to drown the feeling in the bottom of her mind, but it proved as futile as trying to force a sodden mattress to stay under water. It surfaced, drearily, time and time again, as ugly and as unforgettable as ever.

Jamie said, 'Lucy – your uncle didn't ever upset you, did he?'

'What do you mean? Of course not.'

'It's just that I don't understand why it was so all-fired important for you to be rid of him. You told me you loved that jewellery; it was all you had to remember your momma by.'

Lucy picked up her milk, and stirred the cinnamon powder into it. 'I didn't like him, that's all. He drank too much. I don't know. He was crude. He cussed a lot. He upset poppa.'

'And that's all? He didn't try to get too friendly?'

Lucy blushed and lowered her eyes, but didn't answer.

'All right,' said Jamie. 'I'm sorry. I shouldn't have asked.'

They sat by the fire in silence while the flames took hold of the logs. After a few mintues, however, they heard the back door slam, and voices in the kitchen. Jamie's father appeared, brambly-bearded, meaty-shouldered, with piercingly clear green eyes and a big fleshy nose that had always reminded Lucy of some variety of ripe vegetable squash.

'Lucy!' he smiled, his voice thick with phlegm. He cleared it, and blew his nose, and said, 'I'm sorry. It's that cold wind. Makes your nose run faster than your feet.'

'Old joke, father,' Jamie complained. 'Listen – you don't mind if Lucy warms herself up a bit. She had a shock last night. Her uncle came back from California and ended up setting fire to himself in his bedroom.'

'Dear God!' said Jerrold Cullen, sitting down on the sofa. 'Was he badly hurt?'

'Dead, I'm afraid,' Lucy told him.

'Dead! That's terrible! Lucy, I'm so sorry!'

Lucy caught her breath. 'To tell you the honest truth, Mr Cullen, my uncle and I weren't exactly the best of friends.'

'I see,' said Jerrold, soberly. 'But all the same, he was a human soul; and his Maker has now drawn him back to the place from whence he came.'

'Amen,' said Jamie. His father turned and glared at him, not quite sure if he were serious or not. A pious man had a great deal to put up with in a household of irreverent sons.

'Can you tell me how it happened?' he asked Lucy.

But Jamie interrupted, '– Father, I don't think that Lucy really wants to talk about it.'

'Are you her advocate?' Jerrold inquired. 'Can't she speak for herself?'

He turned back to Lucy and said, 'This boy and his passion for the law, I never knew a boy so stubborn.'

'You must be proud of him, though, winning a place at the State University.'

Jerrold said, 'Hmph! The only place with which any man needs to concern himself is his place in the Kingdom of Heaven.'

'You're letting him go, though?'

'All the tribes of Israel couldn't have stood in his way,' Jerrold replied; and although he knit his eyebrows and tried to sound stern, Lucy had the feeling that he was secretly proud of Jamie's determination. Jerrold knew himself to be a formidable father, and if Jamie could stand up to *him*, Jerrold reckoned that he could stand up to anyone.

'Guess Jamie and me don't see eye to eye on what constitutes the law,' said Jerrold. 'As far as I'm concerned, the law was given by God, at Sinai. God is the moral governor of the world, and the redeemer of his people, and because of that, only God has the authority to legislate for the wellbeing of all of his creatures, and for righteousness on earth.'

'Amen,' said Jamie.

'Oh, you can mock me,' snapped Jerrold, turning around on the sofa. 'But you're breaking a fine family tradition, too. The Cullens have always been grangers, ever since they came here from Scotland, granger fathers and granger sons, and heartily proud of it, and the Lord be praised.'

He reached into his pocket for his pipe. 'But what can I do?' he asked. 'I can't do anything more than speak my mind; and then help him on his way. At the end of the day, that's all fathers are good for.'

Just then, Mrs Cullen called for Jamie to pump up some water for her. Jamie stood up, kissed Lucy on the forehead, and then went through to the kitchen.

Lucy said, 'You're going to miss him.'

'Hmph!' Jerrold replied. 'I'm going to miss his appetite, and I'm going to miss his argufying; but that's about the sum of it. He's the slowest stable-mucker I ever saw, and he rides about as elegant as a sack of beets. The law's welcome to him, that's my opinion. He sucks bullseyes in church and he never remembers the words of his hymns and he's always provoking his kith.'

'*I'm* going to miss him,' Lucy told Jerrold.

Jerrold looked at the fire, and tiny orange flames pirouetted in his eyes. 'Jamie's not the man for you, Lucy. You should be looking for somebody well-heeled, and reliable, a man of good stock.'

'I didn't say that I was going to *marry* him, Mr Cullen. I simply said that I was going to miss him.'

'Well, don't miss him too much. He's a wayward character, at best.'

Lucy was about to tell Jerrold that she had never met anyone more loyal and reliable than Jamie, but something in his expression cautioned her not to; and so she stayed silent, while the fire sizzled and crackled, and the minutes passed, and Jerrold Cullen stared unfocused into the flames as if he were remembering things that might have been, but which had never come to pass.

★

Jack Darling listened thoughtfully while Jamie explained about the deed; and to Lucy explaining that she had pawned her mother's jewellery; and then he untied his long brown apron.

'I never heard anything like it,' he said. He sounded angry, but controlled, and in some way, defensive. 'But – well – if you say that it's true, then I'll have to believe it, won't I?'

'I'm sure sorry about your brother-in-law, sir,' Jamie told him. 'My father sends his condolences, too. But it's an ill wind that blows nobody some good fortune.'

'What do we have to do now?' Jack asked him. 'Do we have to register our interest, something like that?'

Jamie said, 'I was going to suggest that you went to California, or sent somebody on your behalf, to look into things. After all, we don't even know the well's exact location, do we? Neither do we know whose land it's on, or who granted the lease, or who was supposed to be taking care of it while your brother-in-law came back here to Kansas, and if *they* have an interest in it, too.'

Jack sat down. It was still early morning, the thin sunlight was arranged across the floor like cut-up pieces of dress-pattern. The regular loungers hadn't shown up yet: in this weather, Henry McGuffey didn't usually ease himself out of the sack until he grew too hungry to stay there any longer.

'Who can I send?' asked Jack. 'I can't go myself. I can't leave the store.'

'Poppa, we're *rich*,' said Lucy. 'You can leave the store for ever if you want to. You can close up right this minute, and walk out of the door, and never come back.'

Jack looked at her with serious, unfocused eyes. 'Your mother and me built this store up together, Lucy. It's not just a store to me, it's part of my life. When I stand in here, and I'm alone, I can still hear your mother singing. I can still see her smiling at me, the way she used to, when she was weighing out the sugar for me.'

He lowered his head. 'Besides, this supposed oil-well may not turn out to be anything at all. Nothing else that Cass ever did was any darned good. I could close up the store and find myself bankrupt.'

Lucy suggested, '*I* could go, couldn't I?'

Jack looked up again. 'You? A seventeen-year-old girl all on your own? That's the dumbest thing I ever heard. 'Sides, it's more than likely a wild-goose chase.'

Jamie put his arm around Lucy's shoulders. 'Sir – I really believe it's worth going. And if you allowed Lucy to go, I could go along, too, sir. I've always had a strong yen to see California; and I have two clear months before I have to start college. That's if you'd trust me.'

'Trust you?' Jack seemed distracted, gruff. 'Any reason why I shouldn't?'

Jamie grinned. 'Then you wouldn't mind?'

'Well . . . I don't know. Let me think on it. I guess it would make some kind of sense for you to go, seeing that you're a lawyer. Or nearly a lawyer, anyhow.'

He tilted back his chair and reached for the bottle of sipping whisky. 'I'd better open up,' he said. 'You want a warmer before you go? That's a long cold ride back to your place.'

'No, thank you, sir,' said Jamie. 'I shouldn't be here at all. I just thought I'd better come along with Lucy to explain the way things stood.'

'You realize you're turning your back on a man of means?' teased Lucy.

Jamie smiled broadly. 'Yes, I do. And congratulations.'

Jack poured himself a drink. 'Thanks, Jamie. 'Preciate what you've done.'

When Jamie had left, however, Jack put down his drink untasted and turned to Lucy with a serious face.

'I think you owe me some kind of an explanation,' he said, clearing his throat.

Lucy was spooning coffee into the chipped red enamel pot. 'What do you mean?' she asked him. 'I've told you everything.'

'You and your Uncle Casper, that's what I mean, and you know it. There's more to this business than meets the eye.'

'I told you. Uncle Casper said that he needed the money really quickly, otherwise he might have lost his chance of drilling the oil-well altogether. I guess I felt sorry for him, that's all.'

'Don't lie to me, Lucy,' her father told her. He reached into his shirt pocket and took out her mother's cameo brooch and held it up in front of her. 'I found this in your Uncle Casper's valise. I thought it was dear to your heart. And all the rest of your mother's jewellery. I thought it meant something to you. Something precious.'

'It does,' whispered Lucy. 'It did.'

'Then how could you think of pawning it? Was your Uncle Casper more precious to you than your mother's memory? You've hurt me, Lucy, you've hurt me bad! Just — just giving away those things that meant so much! And then flying straight in the face of what I told you was right! You knew darned well that I wanted Cass to work for his grubstake! Even if I'd had the money, cash in hand, I *still* would've made him work for it! But what did you do? You not only gave him the money for nothing, you pawned your dead mother's jewellery to raise it! And by cracky I believe I'm entitled to know why!'

Lucy was shaking. 'Poppa —' she said. But her father was too angry to let her speak.

'Don't you 'poppa' me! I wasn't going to shout at you in front of your Jamie. He did his best, and he just about saved your skin, with that agreement of his. But I'm going to shout at you now! What you did was wrong, Lucy. It was disrespectful, it was disobedient, and it flew straight in the face of what was right!'

Lucy felt the tears coursing down her cheeks. She opened

her mouth but the words refused to come out. All she could do was shake her head, and then cover her face with her hands.

Jack stood up and watched her for a while, fidgety and uncomfortable.

'Do you want a drink or something?' he asked her.

Lucy whispered, 'No. No, thank you.'

'Well . . . I guess I'm sorry I yelled,' Jack told her. 'But the trouble is, Lucy, we only have you and we only have me. We don't have anybody else. If we can't trust each other, then who the heck can we trust?'

Lucy wiped her eyes. 'I'm sorry, too,' she told him.

'Do you want to try and tell me what was going on?' he asked her.

She was silent for a very long time, like a woman who has suddenly forgotten who she is. She and her father became a tableau, two figures standing motionless in a store filled with shadows, their faces pale as lamp-globes in the snowy light from the street outside.

After a while, however, Lucy sat down, her grey skirts arranged around her, and told her father what her Uncle Casper had done to her.

The weather eased a little the following week, although it was still far too early for a thaw. The skies were brilliantly clear and the snow was dazzling and the north-west wind was as hard as a hammer.

Lucy and Jamie took the Kansas Pacific Railroad west to Denver, where they spent two nights at a cheap but well-scrubbed boarding-house on 16th Street, waiting for a delayed connection to Cheyenne.

Lucy was delighted by Denver. She had visited Kansas City, on a hot summer weekend two years ago, but Denver by comparison was glorious: proud and high and rich with silver. Almost all of the buildings, by city ordinance, were built of brick; and some of them were astonishingly grandiose, like the Windsor Hotel, which boasted 176 rooms, and flags snapping on its Gothic rooftops, and a taproom (which Lucy peeked into) with three thousand real silver dollars embedded in the floor.

They went to Riverfront Park and listened to band music in the snow. They visited Elitch's Zoological Gardens, and saw a tiger and a lion and a camel, morose and sleepy in the mile-high winter, but fascinating all the same.

Horse-drawn streetcars rolled along the wide city thoroughfares. Lucy was particularly taken by the streetcars which travelled up neighbouring hills, and then rolled back down again, with their horses riding on the rear platform as passengers. And the stores! You could buy absolutely everything, from a solid gold watch-fob to a silk Paris gown to a 'festive Bowie knife'.

And everybody strolled the well-swept sidewalks looking so fashionable and wealthy and nonchalant.

But, more than anything else, Lucy was enchanted by the mountains. If she stood on her chair in the Miller Boarding-house and leaned out of the back window, with the brisk sub-zero wind blowing directly into her face, she could see the high clear summits of the Rockies, and the distant crest of Pike's Peak. She could scarcely believe what she was seeing. The mountains seemed completely unreal; as if they had been cut out of cardboard. After a lifetime spent on the Kansas plains, she couldn't believe that the people of Denver could walk the streets and not even give the mountains a second glance.

On their second night in Denver, as Lucy was brushing out her hair in readiness for bed, Jamie knocked at her door, and called, 'Lucy? Lucy, it's me. Can I talk to you?'

Lucy fastened the ribbon of her robe, and opened the door for him. He was dressed in shirtsleeves, with fancy embroidered suspenders. Lucy thought that he looked tired, and a little flushed.

'All right if I come in?' he asked her.

'I guess it is,' she smiled. 'Just so long as Mrs Miller doesn't see you.'

They sat on the iron-framed bed. The room was very small, but a hot fire fumed in the grate, and heavy brown drapes kept too much of the draught from blowing in from the window. On the yellow-papered walls hung uninspiring engravings cut from religious magazines, such as *The Faithful Seneschal* and *Titus and His Family*.

Jamie said, 'I didn't feel like sleeping. Too excited, I guess.'

'What time are we supposed to leave tomorrow?' asked Lucy.

'Six o'clock, if the train's running. We should reach Cheyenne by lunchtime; and then we join the Union Pacific at three-thirty. Again – that's always provided that it's running.'

Lucy gave her hair a last quick brush. 'I love it here. When we come back from California, I'm going to come here again. In fact, I might even live here. Can you imagine that?'

'You'll be rich by then,' Jamie reminded her. 'You'll be able to go anywhere you like. New York. Paris, even.'

'No,' said Lucy. 'I want to live somewhere with mountains.'

Jamie shrugged. 'Guess you can grow tired of mountains, same way that you can grow tired of anything else.'

Lucy laid down her hairbrush and stared at him. 'You don't think that I'm tired of you, do you, Jamie?'

'Heck, no, you're only seventeen. I don't have any right to think anything like that. Now you're rich, well, you can go out and find yourself anybody you care to. Maybe one of those princes you were always talking about.'

'Oh, Jamie . . . we'll probably get to California and find out that I'm not rich at all.'

Jamie smiled ruefully. 'Forget it, Lucy. You're rich right enough. I looked at your Uncle Casper's clothes. A family with ten children could live off his shoes for a month.'

'So you think that I'm going to go off and leave you behind, and never think about you again?' Her blue eyes were dark in the lamplight, dark as ink.

'There's no "think" about it. If you had seven thousand dollars a year, you wouldn't stay in Oak City for a minute. And if what your Uncle Casper said was correct, you're going to have seven thousand dollars a *week*.'

'Jamie –' Lucy began, but Jamie shook his head.

'You know it's true. You're going to go off and be a socialite; and I'm going to go off to learn to be a lawyer. It's our calling, that's all. You can't fool around with your calling.'

'But if I'm *very* rich, you wouldn't have to be a lawyer, would you? We could both live off Uncle Casper's oil! We could stay together all the time!'

Jamie said, 'Lucy, you don't understand. I *want* to be a lawyer. It's my vocation. I haven't been fighting my father all these years, just to sit around on my duff all day, eating Turkish delight.'

Lucy giggled. 'Is that what rich people do? Sit around on their duffs all day and eat Turkish delight?'

'You're impossible, you know that?' Jamie told her.

'But I want you with me! If you study law, I won't see you for three years! And, who knows, I might meet somebody else.'

Jamie looked at her gravely. 'That's a risk I'm going to have to take. I always knew that.'

'But what if I get married? And have children?'

'I don't know. I'll have to think about that when it happens. *If* it happens, which I hope it doesn't.'

Lucy held his hand between hers. 'Jamie – I know things have been difficult between us – but it wasn't your fault, it was mine. I'm still fond of you. I still love you.'

She believed at that moment that she was telling the truth, that she really did love him. Sitting next to her in this boarding-house bed on a freezing-cold night in Denver, he looked tonight like the man who had everything she wanted. Handsome and gentle, but strong, too; and unselfish.

At the same time, she was conscious that she might not love him forever: that if he didn't agree to stay with her now, she might not give him a second chance. Life was too exciting for second chances.

Jamie said, 'I can't give up the law, Lucy. It's something I have to do, whether I lose you or not.'

He gave her a quick, buttoned-up smile. 'I suppose you're angry with me.'

'Why should I be angry with you?'

'For loving the law more than I love you. Isn't that what you're thinking?'

She squeezed his hand tight. 'I'm not angry with you. I never could be. I love you. It's only me I feel angry with.'

'Oh, yes? And what do *you* have to be angry about? You're young, you're rich, and you're pretty. What more could a girl want?'

For one unbalanced second, Lucy was about to tell Jamie about Uncle Casper. But then something inside her warned her not to; that he would take it too hard. She turned her head away, and stared unfocused at the hot sparks rushing up the chimney, although she could still feel Jamie watching her profile.

'Can I ask you something?' said Jamie.

She nodded.

'Do you really want to stay with me for the rest of your life?'

She turned back to him. 'Right this minute, that's what I want, more than anything else in the world.'

'Why? Because I won't give in to you?'

'No,' said Lucy. 'Because I really need you.'

He kissed her, two pecks on the lips, and then another; and then he stopped and looked straight into her eyes. She could see the little green flecks in his irises; the fine blonde hairs on his cheekbones.

They kissed each other again, very slowly this time and Lucy thought it was just like the sun sinking below the prairie on a clear winter evening, when you look and it hasn't quite gone, and you look again and it still hasn't quite gone, and at the very end there's a glimmering molten bar along the western horizon, the day clinging to the edge of the world by its fiery fingernails. Lucy closed her eyes. She couldn't think that she was cold; that this was winter-time. All she could feel was the heat from the fire and the heat from her cheeks and the heat from her own blood.

'Lucy. . .' said Jamie, touching her hair, touching her cheek.

'I'm sorry, Jamie,' she whispered. 'I was so *stupid*, and so selfish; and everything went so wrong.'

Jamie kissed her again. 'It doesn't matter. Everybody's selfish sometimes. You and I were born for each other. You know that, as well as I do.'

'How can people be born for each other?'

'You'll see,' said Jamie. He tugged the plain silver ring off his little finger, and slipped it over Lucy's wedding-finger. 'What's mine is yours, no matter what happens. You'll see.'

They held each other tight. Jamie kissed her again and again; her lips, and then her neck. His shirt rustled; her robe rustled; his breath rustled in her ears. The bedsprings creaked, the fire popped, the mountain wind sang through the window-frame. She did love him! She *did* love him! Even when she became a socialite, and she was surrounded by admiring young men – men like gods, men wearing starched collars so high that they had to stare at the ceiling all evening, Jamie would always be there to take care of her, in a way that her father had never been able to take care of her. She loved him! She loved him more than life itself! She could feel an extraordinary sensation rising up inside her, as if her womb were being flooded with warm water. She murmured, '*Jamie, Jamie. . .*' and it sounded like somebody else altogether.

Jamie's hand traced the long curve of her back, and the flare of her hips. He was breathing hard, and his eyes were closed. He reached upward, and his hand brushed her breast through her robe. He took hold of the ribbon that fastened it, and pulled it.

It was then that Lucy opened her eyes and saw Uncle Casper staring at her, his face on fire. Flames poured out from between his teeth, and his eyes were wrinkling like frying eggs.

She didn't cry out. She couldn't. But she pushed Jamie hard in the breastbone with the heel of her hand, and snatched her robe tightly together, and sat panting and shivering and staring at him in horror.

'Lucy?' he frowned at her. 'Lucy, what the hell's the matter? Jesus Christ, Lucy! Are you all right?'

She opened her mouth and closed it again. 'Jamie, I –'

Jamie gently put his arms around her, and shushed her. 'Lucy . . . we were always meant to be together, you and me. No two ways about it. Lucy, I *love* you!'

'I can't,' she whispered. 'Just – can't –'

He kissed her cheek. She could feel for herself how cold and sweaty her skin was. 'Lucy you darling bobbasheely,' he coaxed her, 'there's nothing for you to be afraid of. Nothing! It's the naturalest thing in the world. And I love you, there's no question about that. Hey!' he joked. 'Maybe we could get married in Cheyenne, make it legal!'

She swallowed tightly, and shook her head.

'Well, just a suggestion,' he told her. He took his arm away, and clasped his hands together, and looked at her warily.

'It's not me, is it? I don't smell or something? You know, cheesy feet, something like that?' He was trying to be funny but she could tell that he was badly upset.

She shook her head, and said, 'It's not you.'

'Well, I'm sorry,' he told her. He kissed her quickly on the forehead and stood up. 'I guess I'd better get some sleep. Don't know how easy it's going to be, but I'd better try.'

109

Lucy, with tears in her eyes, reached up and took hold of his hand. 'Jamie, it's not you. I promise.'

'It's all right,' he told her, with the petulance of chronic frustration. He tried a smile.

'You do understand, don't you?'

'Sure. Sure thing. I understand.'

He left her room and closed the door quietly behind him. Lucy stayed where she was, sitting on the bed, with her robe wrapped tightly around her. She had wanted Jamie so desperately that she was trembling, the way you tremble when you have to hold the same position for too long. But she was terrified that he would immediately discover that she was no longer a virgin, and refuse to have anything more to do with her. In spite of his defiance of his father over the matter of law studies, she knew how religious he was, and she knew what it said in the Bible about harlots.

She was even more terrified of those incendiary visions of Uncle Casper; and the way that he was still clinging on to her, even in death.

She could picture her father's face, when she had told him at last what Uncle Casper had done to her. He had sat like a man chiselled with infinite patience out of ironstone.

She had tried to tell her father everything. She had spoken quietly and slowly, her eyes brimming with tears, occasionally pausing to compose herself, so that she wouldn't distress him too much.

At the last moment, however, with the words already taking shape on her lips, she had choked on Uncle Casper's lascivious claim to have slept with her mother. She had wanted desperately to talk about it, to find out the truth. The poisonous doubt that Uncle Casper had planted in her mind troubled her just as sorely as the memory of his raping her. But she hadn't been able to bring herself to hurt her father as much as that; and now that Uncle Casper was dead, it no longer seemed to matter whether he knew or not.

To Lucy, however, it remained just as much of a nightmare as ever. *We was close, like two spring chickens in a pot.*

At last her father had laid his hand on her shoulder, the way he always did, and had said hoarsely, 'I don't understand why you didn't tell me at once. I would have killed him.'

'I was ashamed,' she had told him.

'Good grief, Lucy. I'm the one who ought to be ashamed, for doubting you,' her father had replied. He had hesitated for a moment, his mouth working with emotion, and then he had said, 'I'm the one who ought to be ashamed, because I never protected you; same way I never protected your mother, neither.'

With tears sliding down his face, he had smacked his fist into the palm of his hand, and said, 'I wish to God I had burned him myself! I wish to God I had burned with him!'

After that, they hadn't spoken about it any more. There was nothing more for them to say. But Lucy's father had remained edgy and withdrawn for the rest of the day; and even Henry McGuffey's hilarious reminiscences about his boyhood in Mobile, Alabama, had failed to tickle him. Twice during the afternoon, Lucy had found her father standing and frowning at nothing at all, his hands by his sides. And when they were sitting together in the parlour in the evening, she had caught him staring at her over his newspaper as if he couldn't think who she really was.

When the morning had arrived for her to leave with Jamie for California, their railroad fares paid for by selling Uncle Casper's jewel-studded pocket-watch, she and her father had kissed each other goodbye with a brief display of forced tenderness that had almost amounted to relief.

Hatred can cool; envy can be assuaged; but guilt never forgets, and guilt never forgives, and guilt eats the spirit like fire consumes flesh.

According to Jamie's guide-book, Cheyenne was the largest city on the Union Pacific railroad between Omaha and

III

Sacramento; and after the luxuries of Denver, Lucy could scarcely wait to see it. As the train came clanking in to the depot, however, she was disappointed to see that Cheyenne was nothing more than a ragamuffin assembly of wood and canvas buildings.

Gathered around the station was a solemn audience of stray dogs, Indians wrapped in filthy blankets, and dangerous-looking men with big boots, broad-brimmed hats, and revolvers. It was just beginning to snow.

The train slithered to a halt on the icy rails, and immediately the more experienced travellers jumped down from the steps and made a rush for the railroad dining room. This was a flat-fronted barn of a building beside the tracks, set out with rows of refectory tables and wheelback chairs, its walls hung with stuffed buffalo heads. By the time Lucy and Jamie managed to push their way in, the noise inside had grown tremendous: an ocean-like roar of shouting and laughing and clattering cutlery. They had to wait for over twenty minutes before they could catch the eye of the harassed Chinese waiter, and then they were served (without being consulted as to choice) with two large steaks, sizzled black on the outside and bleeding-raw on the inside, fried eggs, boiled Indian corn, and a heap of hoe-cakes and syrup.

The price was one dollar – but only seventy-five cents if you paid in silver.

As she sawed at her meat with a knife as blunt as a bricklayer's trowel, Lucy shouted to Jamie, 'What kind of steak is this? It's like trying to eat a horse-blind!'

A red-bearded man sitting opposite shouted back, 'It's beef, miss, if you'll forgive me; but when it's tough they usually call it antelope. Kind of makes it sound more enticing; you know, for your tyro traveller.'

He sniffed, and swilled hot tea around his mouth, and then added, 'I don't know which way you're headed, but you should keep clear of the dining station at Sidney, Nebraska. They do you an excellent-tasting stew they call chicken-stew, but I know for a sure fact that it's made from prairie-dog.'

They crossed Wyoming in an endless blizzard, although the hot-air stove in their Pullman car kept them as warm and comfortable as if they had been sitting in their own parlours. The only excitement was that now and again the train had to be halted, and the passenger-cars had to be disconnected for half an hour, so that the locomotive could be run ahead of them at full speed into a snowbanked cut, to clear the track. This procedure, the conductor laconically informed them, was called 'bucking the snow.'

The snowstorms whirled themselves away when they entered Utah, and Lucy couldn't keep herself away from the window as the train ran through roaring tunnels into Echo and Weber Canyons, where rocks towered above them in fantastic and dreadful shapes. The landscape was so strange that nobody on board the train seemed to be able to agree if they were travelling through God's sublime wilderness or the playground of Satan.

She and Jamie remained courteous to each other, but much more guarded than before. Neither of them was in the mood for a serious conversation about Lucy's abrupt disinclination to carry on with their love-making, although Lucy couldn't help turning it over in her mind again and again. *I want him; I'm sure that I love him; and perhaps he can help me to forget about Uncle Casper. But what if I see that blazing face for ever and ever? What good would I be as a wife?*

She smiled at him from time to time, and he smiled back, but their smiles were both strained with uncertainty.

At the moment, however, they were both too tired to think of much more than reaching California. They were both much farther away from home than they had ever been before. They had passed the Thousand-Mile Tree, one thousand miles west of Omaha, and the journey was both awe-inspiring and exhausting. They ate, slept, talked to their fellow-passengers; read books and newspapers supplied by the train attendant; and stared sightlessly out the window.

At last, however, the train began to climb the Sierras, the last great natural barrier to California. For almost forty miles they toiled upwards through gloomy wooden snowsheds, which kept the track clear in mid-winter. The snowsheds covered not only the main tracks but also depots, turntables, switch tracks, and even houses where railroad workers lived in permanent eerie twilight with their wives and children.

Still inside a snowshed, the train reached Summit station, seven thousand feet above sea level, in time for breakfast. The passengers ate a huge meal of rainbow trout and fresh-baked bread and good hot coffee. Lucy wrapped herself in her coat and took a walk outside. The air sparkled. The Sierras rose all around her, snowy and shining and forested with pine. She felt that she was standing on the threshold of Heaven. 'Mother,' she whispered, as if her mother would be able to hear her more easily.

Jamie came to stand beside her. He pulled off his glove and took hold of her hand. For a long time he said nothing, but at last, with his breath smoking, he said quietly, 'There's no need for you and me to be so chilly.'

She turned to him. Her eyes were watering with the cold. 'It's my fault,' she said. 'If only I didn't feel so darned muddled.'

'You're muddled? Muddled about what? Muddled about us?'

'No,' she told him. 'Muddled about myself. And about being rich, and you going off to university. I thought it was all going to be wonderful, but I don't understand it. I feel like I'm being swept away.'

Jamie held her tight. The train whistled, to gather its passengers. 'You're growing up,' Jamie told her, his breath smoking against her fur collar. 'That's all that's happening.' He smiled. 'It happens to everybody, sooner or later.'

★

The western slopes of the Sierras drop from seven thousand feet to thirty feet in less than a hundred and fifty miles, and the train flew down without using steam — coasting so fast and so silently that Lucy felt as if she were dreaming.

The train rushed round curves with nothing but its brakes to hold it. The axle-boxes smoked with the friction, and the Pullman cars were acrid with the smell of burning wood. The wheels were red-hot, and when they ran through the darkened snowsheds, they glowed like discs of fire.

They sped round embankments with a harsh metallic whisper, they glided softly through cuts and snowsheds; and then suddenly burst out into the sunlight and swung around the stomach-turning curve of Cape Horn, at which point Jamie's guide-book advised nervous passengers not to look out of the windows.

There, two thousand feet below them, was the American River, a silvery artery in the morning sunlight.

Lucy stared in fascination as the train twisted and turned its way around the head of the canyon, sometimes doubling back on itself so tightly that she felt she could throw a breadroll from her table and hit the tracks on which they had just been travelling.

Throughout the morning, they descended into the Sacramento Valley; and Lucy nodded in her seat and slept. She dreamed about her father, sitting mortified and silent in the parlour ('*Why didn't you tell me sooner? I would have killed him.*') and for some reason he was counting dry beans from hand to hand. She dreamed about her mother's picture on the shelf. Her mother spoke to her, in a tiny voice, almost inaudible. *Lucy! Lucy!*

When she opened her eyes again, the train was running swiftly through orchards and fields of flowers. The sky was clear blue and the air was so warm that the passenger-car windows had been opened. She sat up, and rubbed her eyes.

Jamie appeared, freshly-shaved, wiping his towel around

his neck. He smiled at her, and leaned forward and kissed her. 'Welcome to California,' he told her.

Lucy had conjured up in her mind all kinds of wonderful visions of the Puebla de Los Angeles, the town of the angels. But when they arrived on the steamer from San Francisco, she discovered that it was far from being the city in the clouds which she had imagined. Although some of the stores looked prosperous and well-stocked, and there were one or two impressive business buildings and a scattering of elegant private dwellings, the rest of the town was a higgledy-piggledy collection of adobes, saloons, warehouses, and flaking hotels.

The weather, however, was hazy and warm; and there was no real need for grandiose architecture to keep out the weather. Orange groves and vineyards clustered around the town on all sides. When Lucy unpacked her trunk at the Pico House and leaned on her elbows on the clay-tiled windowsill, she could look directly out over a small dark-green orange grove, while the mission-church bells clanged dolorously over Sonora, the Spanish quarter.

And there were flowers everywhere, on the last day of January! Tuberose and jasmine and fragant stock in the hotel garden; and heliotrope trained up the side of the open brick-paved court which you had to cross to reach the dining rooms.

They spent their first morning in Los Angeles resting. Lucy slept, fully-dressed, stretched on her bed. When she woke up, the sun was shining brightly, and she lay still for a while, thinking about her father, in snowbound Kansas; and about Jamie, in the next room.

For the first time, she allowed herself the heretical thought that she might not need either of them, now that she was rich. Perhaps she had been feeling muddled because she didn't love them as much as she felt she ought to.

But she still couldn't manage completely on her own. She

116

admitted that much. The thought of striking out completely alone, without anybody to take care of her – well, she wouldn't know where to start. Even if you were rich, how did you go about finding someplace to stay? How did you buy a house? How did you get yourself introduced into society?

She felt, however, that she was at a momentous turning-point in her life. She felt as if every step she had ever taken, every word she had ever spoken, had brought her at last to this: to an unexpected paradise where oranges ripened in mid-winter, and farmers went by with carts heaped with pumpkins, and strawberries, and green pod-peas, and lemons, and even lambs!

And what would be next? Society, fortune, and a thousand dollars a day!

She reached out to the table beside her bed and took down the photograph of her mother. Anna Darling, soft of eye, in a sepia picture that was already fading away. She kissed it; and she felt closer to her mother than ever; as if she hadn't died at all, but was always there, watching, waiting, and protecting her.

'He's dead, you tell me?' asked the russet-whiskered attorney, sucking at his empty pipe, his brown boots perched up on his desk like two glossy red squirrels.

'Yes, sir, dead,' said Jamie. He reached into his coat pocket, and produced Doctor Satchell's death certificate. The two squirrels jumped off the desk as the attorney swung himself around to read it.

'Burned dead, it says here,' he remarked. '"Cause of death, burned".'

Lucy was about to interrupt, but Jamie lifted his hand to hush her. 'That's correct,' he said. 'Burned dead. Accidental house-fire.'

The attorney cracked his knuckles, one by one. The plaque on his desk said that his name was Thurloe Daby, and Lucy had thought that if anybody in the world could have fitted such a peculiar name, it was him. He looked very Thurloe; and very Daby, too.

'What happens now?' Thurloe Daby asked handing the death certificate back.

Jamie unfolded a copy of the deed which Uncle Casper had signed at Oak City depot. 'This deed provides that, in the event of his death, all of Mr Casper Conroy's oil-leases and the proceeds thereof should pass to Miss Lucy Darling.'

Thurloe Daby grimaced at Jamie's tiny handwriting. He found his eyeglasses, and wound them around his whiskery ears, and scrutinized the agreement narrowly.

'Looks reasonable to me,' he drawled. He was a very slow speaker. 'I'll have to authenticate the signature, of course. But otherwise ... well, it's all written in plain English, aint it? And I can't see any court in the Union denying the rights of a young lady so charming as this.'

The squirrel-shoes obediently bounded back up on to his desk, and Thurloe Daby settled himself back in his chair. 'You can't say that it hasn't been a story of dire tragedy, Ferris and Conroy Oil Company, now can you? One tragedy after another. But I guess that all's well that ends well.'

'I'm sorry?' said Lucy.

'Well, my dear, the whole shooting-match is yours now, the whole kit and caboodle.'

'What about Mr Ferris?' asked Jamie.

Thurloe Daby pulled a face. 'What you mean is, what about the *late* Mr Ferris.'

'You mean he's dead, too?'

'That's right. Last Thursday before Christmas. Shot dead. Clean as a whistle.'

'Well, I'll be darned,' said Jamie. 'How did that happen?'

Thurloe Daby shrugged. 'Nobody correctly knows. But the circumstantial evidence points to Mexicans, trying to rob his house. Surprised them, you see; and they were too fly with a forty-five. No head left, excusing your sensitivities.'

Jamie was obviously finding it difficult to suppress his excitement. 'So what you're trying to tell us is that the whole oil-well now belongs to Miss Darling?'

Thurloe Daby nodded. 'That's what I said. The whole shooting-match. The whole kit and caboodle. I'll have my clerk rustle up the lease for you. It's Congress land, which is one blessing, rather than railroad land. Less in the way of paperwork; and a whole lot less interference. Encouragement rather than avarice, if you know what I mean.'

He leaned over his desk and lifted the lid from a pottery cookie-jar in the shape of Charles Frémont's head. Lucy had already recognized Frémont's sad, worried eyes, and his neatly-trimmed beard.

'Cookie?' Thurloe Daby asked, taking out a handful. 'They're good. My maid bakes them for me. Never got married, don't know why. A radiant face and a well-shaped ankle – well, I always had an eye for a radiant face and a well-shaped ankle. But marriage? I don't know. Maybe I care too much for my peace and privacy.'

He walked around his desk, snapping cookies in half as he did so. He went to the open window of his ochre-washed office, and sprinkled cookie-crumbs on to the sill. Outside, the winter sunshine to which Lucy still hadn't become accustomed sparkled and danced on the leaves of palo verde and fan palm.

'Leave these out for the quail,' Thurloe Daby explained.

Jamie said, 'What's happening about the well now? Who's in charge?'

'Oh, it's pumping; and it's pumping good. No need to worry yourself about that. Mr Ferris was a stickler for organization. There's a foreman out there; fellow called Griswold; and sixteen or seventeen men; all properly pay-rolled. No need to worry yourself about that. The Ferris and Conroy Oil Company just about runs itself. With a little assistance from yours truly, of course.'

'Do you want to quote me some output figures?' asked

Jamie, taking out his pen and his notebook. 'How many barrels a day, and what price they're fetching?'

'Offhand, no,' said Thurloe Daby. 'But there won't be much risk of Miss Darling here having her bank account swelled by less than twenty-five thousand dollars a week.' He sniffed, and brushed cookie-crumbs off his button-strained vest. 'John Ferris hit the spot first time; pay-dirt; and after that he never looked back.'

'But surely they did it together,' Lucy put in. 'Uncle Casper told me they were partners; and that they drilled and drilled all over the place before they first struck oil.'

Thurloe Daby shook his head, his jowls wobbling. 'John Ferris had this oil-well spudded some time in May.'

'Then why did my uncle need money to buy drilling equipment? He even pawned my mother's cameo brooch to buy drill-bits!'

'Well, he may have *told* you that,' said Thurloe Daby, returning to his desk. 'But the truth was that John Ferris bought that lease, all on his own; and John Ferris drilled that well, all on his own; and your Uncle Casper didn't appear in the picture for quite some pretty time. Then, when he did, he and John Ferris were always shouting and arguing. They weren't friends. I saw them fight two or three times. I witnessed them fight in this very office. Throwing punches, tossing paper all around. You see that canary?'

They all turned to inspect a small yellow-and-white bird perched in a cage in the corner of the office. 'They threw that canary across the office, cage and all. Poor darned creature hasn't uttered a cheep since. His name's Chorus, on account of the way he used to sing. Now he's so silent I'm thinking of changing his name to Grave.'

'What percentage of the well did Mr Ferris give to Mr Conroy?' asked Jamie.

Thurloe Daby sat down again. 'Near on half. Forty-nine per cent or thereabouts. They signed a paper about it.'

'Mr Ferris gave Mr Conroy forty-nine per cent of an oil-well that was already producing oil?'

'That's correct.'

'But *why*?' asked Jamie. 'Did he ever tell you why? People don't usually go around giving other people any per cent of a fortune, let alone forty-nine per cent, and for no reason whatsoever.'

'Do you want to know the truth?' asked Thurloe Daby. 'The truth is, I don't know, but I have my suspicions. You don't like to speak ill of the dead, do you? They're dead, they can't answer back. But on the other hand, if they can't answer back, what does it matter *what* they think?'

'What are your suspicions, Mr Daby?' asked Lucy, loudly; although she found him quite intimidating.

'You want to know what my suspicions are? Well, I'll tell you. My suspicions are that Mr Ferris and Mr Conroy knew each other from way back. They always talked as though they did; although they never fessed up to it in so many words. My guess was that they'd probably been involved in some kind of business arrangement together, back east. Who knows? The one thing I *do* know for sure is that Mr Ferris wasn't Mr Ferris's real name. And my suspicions are that Mr Conroy had been looking for him for quite a time; and that when he got wind of the fact that Mr Ferris was out here in California, pumping up the old black gold, he came hotfooting it out here to claim his share of the proceeds.'

Lucy turned to Jamie, and frowned. 'I still don't understand why Uncle Casper needed three hundred and fifty dollars so badly?'

Thurloe Daby opened one desk drawer after the other, searching for his tobacco-pouch. 'Who knows? Probably we'll never know. My suspicions may be completely groundless. But let me put it this way: I've been working out here in California ever since the war, and I know two fallen-out thieves when I come across them; and Mr Ferris and Mr Conroy were two fallen-out thieves.'

He licked his finger and made the sign of the cross in the air. 'May they enjoy eternal tranquillity, of course.'

He leaned forward, and told them in a harsh whisper, 'My suspicions are that Mr Conroy had a little bit of business on Mr Ferris; a little bit of business that Mr Ferris was reluctantly willing to give him forty-nine per cent of his oilwell for, just to keep it under his hat.'

'Oh, yes?' said Jamie.

'Oh, yes, Mr Cullen; because the commonest cause of a changed name is a shady past.'

'That still doesn't explain why he wanted three hundred and fifty dollars from Miss Darling here.'

Thurloe Daby found his tobacco-pouch, and flapped it open, and stared at the contents in disappointment. 'You're right,' he said, as if he were speaking to the tobacco-pouch. 'It doesn't explain it. Not unequivocally. But my suspicion would be that Mr Conroy wanted three hundred and fifty dollars to buy the testimony of Certain Parties who might have been willing to establish that Mr Ferris wasn't Mr Ferris at all; but that Mr Ferris was in actuality Somebody Else – a Somebody Else who was wanted by Certain Other Parties for – what? Who knows? Enbezzlement, cheating, making off with funds that weren't quite his? I mean, let's consider for one sober moment where Mr Ferris might have found the money to purchase his oil-lease and start drilling operations. There's a thought, yes?'

'But the oil-well still belongs to Miss Darling?' asked Jamie.

'Oh, yes. Legal and watertight. Mr Ferris and Mr Conroy signed a partnership agreement; and since Mr Ferris had no wife and no issue; and nobody else laid a claim to it; his share passed to Mr Conroy when he died.'

He held up Lucy's deed, and waved it from side to side. 'And here it is – provided the old John Hancock pans out. Mr Conroy's share and Mr Ferris's share; both. Congratulations, Miss Starling, you're an exceedingly wealthy woman!'

'Darling,' Jamie corrected him.

Thurloe Daby stared at him; and then fidgeted in his seat, and said 'Aha!' and adjusted his polka-dot necktie.

That afternoon, they walked on the beach; watching the grey-gold Pacific foaming and thundering on the sand. Lucy took off her shoes, so that her small bare feet made waif-like tracks. The breeze ruffled and flapped at her primrose-yellow dress, and made her ribbons fly.

'So that's it, you're really rich,' said Jamie, his eyes squinched up against the wind.

'I still can't believe it,' Lucy told him.

'You saw the oil-pump. You saw the oil!'

'I don't know, it all looked so scruffy. All those men in red-flannel shirts, and all those filthy black barrels.'

'You're rich, Lucy,' Jamie insisted.

She took hold of his hand, and together they walked barefoot into the foam. Although the weather was so warm, the water was bone-cold, and Lucy was soon shivering.

'I won't believe that I'm rich until I go out and buy my first diamond necklace.'

'Is that the first thing you're going to do?'

'No. The first thing I'm going to do is redeem all of my mother's jewellery; and then I'm going to buy my father a new Sunday-best suit; and then I'm going to buy myself one of those three-dollar walrus handbags I saw in the Sears catalogue. *Then* I'm going to buy myself a diamond necklace.'

'You'll be able to buy yourself a hundred diamond necklaces,' Jamie grinned. Then – watching her narrowly out of the corner of his eye – he asked, 'You think you'll leave Kansas?'

She stopped, and looked around her; at the sand-dunes; and the sunshine; and the gulls turning in the wind.

'Oh yes,' she said. 'I think I'll leave Kansas.'

They walked up the dunes towards the dilapidated surrey

that they had rented. Their old grey horse was tearing at the salty beach-grass with its teeth.

As she climbed up into her seat, Lucy turned to Jamie and said, 'I wish you'd come with me.'

Jamie shook his head. 'Sorry, sweetheart, it just isn't possible.'

'No duff, no Turkish delight?'

'Hit it in one,' he told her.

He climbed up beside her and took hold of the reins. Then, before he geed up the horse, he leaned across and kissed her, a long lingering kiss.

'Don't forget me,' he told her. 'I won't forget you.'

3

It was his voice that first attracted her attention: high, clear, and crisp as an English apple. She could hear him all the way from the tennis-court, in spite of the string quintet, and the children chasing the peacocks across the lawn, and the laughter of four hundred fashionable guests.

She turned, frowned, and said to Evelyn Scott, 'Who *is* that man? He sounds very pleased with himself, whoever he is.'

'Oh, you mean *him*!' said Evelyn, lifting her lorgnettes and peering at him across the garden. 'I should think that he has every right to be pleased with himself. That my dearest dearest, is Henry Carson.'

'Should I know him? I don't think I've heard of him.'

'My dearest dearest!' hissed Evelyn, between clenched teeth. 'He's just about the best-connected Englishman ever! He's a Member of Parliament, very well thought of! The Coming Man! You really must make more effort to become *oh coorong*. Especially when it comes to men.'

Lucy gave her a rueful pout. 'There seem to be *so* many

people one has to know. And I can never work out if I'm allowed to like them or not.'

'For goodness' sake don't say that you "like" people,' Evelyn chided her. 'You may as well eat mashed-potatoes with your knife.'

'I don't *like* mashed-potatoes, so I don't eat them with anything.'

'Oh, Lucy! Heavens! You'll be the death of me!'

Lucy twirled her parasol and gave a little skip and laughed. She knew just how much she irritated Evelyn when she 'behaved Kansas'. Evelyn was so shiveringly sensitive to etiquette that if a man took his gloves off when he was visiting for only ten minutes she positively *shrank*; and the sight of finger-bowls on a breakfast-table could make her quite nauseous.

Of course Lucy used to tease Evelyn on purpose – calling to see her well before two o'clock, and leaving well after five – asking the servants how they cared for the weather – or picking up her skirts and kicking off her shoes so that she could run in her silk-stockinged feet along the corridors of the Scotts' enormous cottage. Being rich was still too much fun for her to fret about etiquette.

But Evelyn was very dear to her. The whole Scott family was very dear to her. They had advised and protected her ever since she had arrived in the East, and Evelyn had been the sweetest of all.

Evelyn's father was Dawson Scott the Pennsylvania coal baron (walrus moustache, hair parted dead-centre, eye for the ladies, current market value $32 million.) When Lucy and her father had left Oak City in a fanfare of local publicity, they had been commended into Dawson Scott's care by Colonel George McNamara, the owner of the *Kansas Daily Journal*, who had grown up with Dawson Scott on a slummy street in North Side, Pittsburgh. Both George McNamara and Dawson Scott remembered whey-faced fathers with flour-sack pants and mothers with two dresses to last the year; and how frightening it could be to find that you were suddenly wealthy.

Evelyn was the Scott's middle daughter. All three Scott daughters were tiny and 'well-covered'; but Evelyn was particularly diminutive and plump-breasted and sweet-faced, with bushy coppery hair. She spoke in a high educated chirrup, like a caged canary; and had a special fondness for yellow. Yellow dresses, yellow gloves, and yellow hats.

She and Lucy went almost everywhere together, and Mrs Cornelius Vanderbilt (with unaccustomed wit) had christened them Primrose and West, after the famous burnt-cork theatrical entertainers. Primrose, of course, being Evelyn; and West, of course, being Lucy.

Lucy's Kansas accent had been described by Mrs Stuyvesant Fish as 'rather like a Jew's-harp, continually twanging, entertaining, not unpleasant in any way that one could name, but altogether *strange*.' The Fishes were old money but not too much of it, and so they couldn't afford to be rude to the Johnny-come-latelys like the Lehrs or the Darlings. There was a point at which wealth became so prodigious that it overwhelmed class.

Of course Lucy and her father were parvenus; but they had been accepted by the leading ladies of established society with far more gentleness than most of the newly-rich. For one thing, Lucy was very pretty to look at, and always laughing; while Jack Darling remained bemused and melancholy and gentle. He might not yet have learned that one raised one's hat only on the *first* occasion that one happened to pass an acquaintance on an afternoon drive; and that one certainly didn't wink and wave and shout out, 'How's tricks?' even to the Belmonts or the Goulds.

But he rarely offended anybody, and the husbands liked him because he wasn't boastful, and he could tell one or two robust stories after dinner, especially the one about the woman who could smoke three cigars at once. He turned out to be useful on a yacht, too, because he could tie knots, and sing songs, and even rustle up steak-and-eggs. Yachts were important to the monarchs of America's burgeoning wealth. They were an ideal way of showing off one's money in the guise of being 'sporty' and 'athletic'.

Lucy occasionally caught her father looking sad and a little lost; as if he were daydreaming about being back in Oak City, shooting the breeze with Henry McGuffey and Samuel Blankenship round the old general-store stove; but he never complained that he was homesick, and most of the time he seemed to enjoy their wealth as much as she did.

At the moment, he was sitting on the stone balustrade at the far side of the house, eating strawberry sorbet with a little spoon and telling an entranced audience of large-hatted ladies about the hard life that was daily endured by women living on the High Plains of Kansas. They listened with gasps of delicious dismay, as if he were describing the life of a primitive African tribe.

'And then of course it's time for them to leave, and they have to make their choice between the rustling Lucinta petticoat and two weeks' worth of kitchen-soap. But who's going to hear that petticoat, out on the farm, except their husband, and he's too tired to see, let alone hear.'

Lucy heard Henry Carson let out a sharp, brisk laugh. It sounded like the echo of somebody chopping down a tree.

'Oh, do introduce me,' Lucy begged Evelyn. 'He sounds such fun.'

'My dearest, I'd be amazed if Mrs Harris lets you approach within fifty feet of him,' said Evelyn. 'She's absolutely *frothing* to pair him off with Henrietta. He's thirty-one, he's one of Lord Salisbury's favourites, he's so intelligent he makes me feel ill, and his family own a house in Derbyshire, England, that makes The Breakers look like a toolshed.'

Lucy stared across at Henry Carson, one hand prettily raised to her cheek, as if she were posing for a Valentine fan. After studying him for a very long while, she said, 'Well, y'know, he must be a *lunatic* if he's thinking of marrying

Henrietta. She's so darned *plain*! And I don't think she can even read. There you are! Listen! He sure *laughs* like a lunatic.'

'You're incorrigible,' said Evelyn. 'All Englishmen laugh like that. Well, all rich ones, anyway. It's something to do with the schools they go to. Or inbreeding, or something.'

She hesitated, and then she sniffed, 'Papa says the only sure way you can tell if an Englishman is sane is to ask him what he thinks about the Irish. If he says that he finds them quite decent, on the whole, then that's it.'

'What's what?'

'He's mad. One hundred per cent guaranteed.'

Lucy was silent for a while, watching Henry Carson with unselfconscious absorption, occasionally moving her head from side to side when passing picnickers obstructed her view.

'Don't *stare* so,' whispered Evelyn, uncomfortably. 'He'll think you're interested in him.'

'I *am* interested in him.'

'Well, I know you are, but it's not done to show it,' said Evelyn. As far as Evelyn was concerned, almost nothing was 'done' when it came to men. It even offended Evelyn's sense of propriety if her boyfriends tried to pay for her theatre tickets, in case she was morally compromised.

'He's short, too, isn't he?' Lucy observed, after a while.

'Well, most Englishmen are,' Evelyn told her. 'It's the diet. They eat too much variety meat, that's what mamma told me. Liver and brains and things.'

'Short and mad,' said Lucy, opening her parasol and thoughtfully spinning it around on her shoulder. 'He's handsome, though, isn't he? And he must have the highest collar I ever clapped eyes on.'

'*Saw*,' Evelyn corrected her.

'Beg pardon?' asked Lucy.

'The highest collar I ever saw. Apart from the fact that it's coarse to make remarks about gentlemen's collars.'

The string quintet played a lilting polonaise. Some of the children danced on the verandah, the little girls garlanded in flowers. Behind them, the house that the Harrises called their summer cottage rose grandiose and marble-flanked amongst mature elms; a forty-room mansion in the style of a German *Schloss*, with towers and spires and a hundred-foot ballroom, and stabling for eight carriages.

The Harrises' summer cottage was just like one of the cloud-castles that had sailed over Lucy's head as she lay by the Saline River in Kansas, a cloud-castle translated by sheer wealth into stone and stained-glass and imported marble.

Mrs Harris adored picnics and today was perfect for a picnic. A warm south-westerly breeze blew across the gardens, and the peacocks wailed like lonely children, and rich and stunningly beautiful women strolled the greensward in linen and lace and hats that burst from their heads like flowering gardens in their own right. Occasionally the music and the laughter were punctuated by the civilized knock of a croquet mallet.   A man passing close by said to his lady companion, ' – but then again, it takes a high level of surrounding culture for – say – the invention of bicycles.'

Lucy said, 'I think I'll go say hello.'

But Evelyn snatched at once at her sleeve. 'Lucy, you can't do that!'

'Why ever not? He's only a man!'

'Exactly! He's a man! And you haven't been introduced!'

'I know, Evelyn. That's why I'm going to go introduce myself!'

Still Evelyn clung on to her. 'You can't introduce yourself until somebody else has introduced you first!'

'Well, *you* introduce me, then.'

'I don't know him! Besides, it's just not done. Mrs Harris will explode.'

'Oh, good! I love explosions! Do you know, in Kansas once the Army fired cannons into the clouds, to see if they could make it rain. It made such a noise! It was wonderful!'

'And did it?' asked Evelyn, almost hysterical with apprehension at what Lucy might do.

'Did it what?' said Lucy, and began to walk across the lawn towards Henry Carson and his companions. Evelyn hurried in pursuit.

'Did it rain?' Evelyn panted.

Lucy frowned at her. 'When?' she wanted to know.

Henry Carson had already glanced at her once or twice. No man really could have resisted glancing once or twice at a tall blonde girl in a silk day-dress the colour of poured cream, with a wide cream hat heaped with yellow silk roses, and a four-strand pearl choker that must have cost the better part of thirty thousand dollars.

He had smiled, too. Or half-smiled. Or looked amused, anyway. Lucy was in no doubt that she would like him the moment she spoke to him; and that he would immediately warm to her.

But (after the famous Mrs Pembroke Jones) Mrs Harris was the most experienced society hostess in Newport, and she was sensitive to the slightest tremor in the social fabric. Before Lucy could approach within thirty feet of Henry Carson, Mrs Harris fluidly excused herself from the conversation in which she was engaged and sped across the lawn at a sharp diagonal, intercepting Lucy beside the steps.

'Miss Darling!' she exclaimed, in a purposeful coo. 'I've been meaning to tell you all morning how *interesting* you look!'

'Well, thank you,' Lucy replied; not realizing that *interesting* was a small but calculated insult. 'I'm enjoying myself.'

Mrs Harris took hold of Lucy's elbow, and piloted her away from the steps and back across the lawn. Mrs Harris' complexion was uncannily flawless for a woman of sixty, as if she were wearing a pale mask of porcelain bisque, and she always dressed herself in the frilliest and fussiest of frocks. This morning's frock was white, with burgundy ribbons.

'You must meet young Charlton Bright,' she said. 'He

comes from Omaha, so you and he must have been neighbours, almost!'

'I was sort of hoping you might introduce me to Mr Carson,' said Lucy.

Mrs Harris tightened her mouth, as if she had just discovered an ulcer on the end of her tongue. 'Well, my dear! Mr Carson is far too busy for girlish chit-chat, I'm afraid! He's here on official business, for the British government.'

'He's *laughing*,' Lucy observed, turning her head.

'My dear girl, even politicians are allowed to laugh. And he is so fond of Henrietta! Look! Here's Charlton!'

'Mrs Harris —'

'Charlton! You dear boy! Come and meet Lucy Darling! Isn't she just a picture!'

Charlton Bright turned out to be as tedious as he was tall. He was beakynosed, with a straggly brown moustache, and a concave chest. He stood six inches away from Lucy and addressed three one-minute sentences about horsebreeding to somebody who (judging by where he fixed his eyes) must have been sitting on Lucy's hat. Three sentences was all that Lucy could endure. She excused herself when he made it clear that he was going to attempt a fourth sentence, and made her way back to Evelyn.

'Told you so!' said Evelyn, triumphantly.

'If I hear one more word about the private life of horses, ever, in the whole of my life, I shall *drown* myself!' Lucy told her. 'Charlton's *sweet*, once you get to know him,' said Evelyn. 'He'll do anything, if you ask him! Anything at all!'

'I don't care for men who do anything at all,' Lucy replied; trying to sound airy. 'I only care for men who say no; or that they *might* if you say pretty-please.'

Evelyn gave her an odd look that was partly regret and partly envy. 'I knew another girl like you, once.'

'Oh, yes?'

'Well, she married an actor, and she was famous for a

while. But he beat her; and in the end he beat her so hard that she died. Or else she went mad, nobody quite knew.'

'That's not going to happen to me,' Lucy protested. 'I think you've got yourself an all-fired cheek to say that it might!'

'Lucy, it isn't *done* to say "all-fired".'

Luncheon was served at long tables under the trees; on starched white tablecloths and flower-decorated Limoges porcelain. Lucy ate a little cold lobster salad and a small slice of game pie; and drank only one glass of champagne. She was too interested in keeping her eye on Henry Carson to concentrate on eating.

She was fascinated by his obvious authority; and by the way in which everybody around him nodded and laughed at what he said. And now that she was closer, she could see that he was very handsome indeed. He had a high forehead, and a short nose with a slight bump on the bridge, and a firm cleft jaw. If she hadn't known him to be a politician, she would have taken him for a sportsman.

Lucy's father had been talking to Mrs Curwen Phelps, a fussy woman with huge white ostrich plumes on her hat; but now he turned to Lucy and smiled at her. 'I forgot to tell you. I heard from Mr Hardenbergh this morning. The house should be ready in about six weeks.'

'As soon as that?' said Lucy. 'That's marvellous!'

'I offered them a bonus if they finished quick. Well, I guess you'd call it a bribe.'

Since they had arrived in the East, Lucy and her father had been staying in a suite of rooms at the Holland House, on Fifth Avenue at Thirtieth Street, while a house was being built for them in the up-and-coming neighbourhood of Central Park West. Their bankers had advised them that they would soon be able to afford to build a cottage at Newport, too; although not on the scale of the Harris mansion.

The oil kept on pumping, and they had become what Evelyn liked to call 'medium-rich'.

Jack Darling sipped his champagne, and then turned around in his chair to see what Lucy was staring at so intently.

'Got your eye on some feller?' he asked.

Lucy smiled. 'Henry Carson. I wanted Mrs Harris to introduce me, but she wouldn't. And Evelyn said it wasn't "done" for me to introduce myself.'

Jack laughed. 'All this etiquette. Must say it gets good and tedious at times. I'd give fifty bucks to pick my teeth.'

'I'm going to meet him, though,' said Lucy.

'Oh, yes? And how're you going to manage that?'

'I'll manage.'

Jack looked down at his champagne glass. A curved reflection quivered on the tablecloth. 'Sometimes I wonder if you and me was meant for this kind of life.'

She took her eyes away from Henry Carson. 'Aren't you happy?' she asked her father.

'Oh, I guess so, sweetheart. Mustn't complain. I've got everything a man could wish for. But sometimes I feel like loosening my collar and putting my feet up and pouring myself a glass of sipping-whisky and just being myself.'

He paused, and then he said, 'I wish your mother was here, too. All those years of hard work, and she never lived to see the reward. I miss her real bad, Lucy, to tell you the truth. I miss her badder now than I ever did before. I don't even have her ghost to look at.'

Lucy held his hand. 'Oh, poppa, you'll get over it.'

But Jack shook his head. 'I don't want to get over it, Lucy. I want to mourn that mother of yours till the day I go to join her.'

The luncheon continued. The cloud-shadows sailed silently across the lawns. When the meal was finished, the forty-strong chorus from the New York musical *Father's Day* sang a selection of light operatic songs, and were rewarded with garlands of flowers and glasses of champagne.

After the entertainments, the women went to play croquet, while the men changed to swim in the indoor swimming-pool, or to play tennis. Lucy and Evelyn sat under an elm by the tennis-court, sipping champagne.

'You're quiet,' Evelyn remarked.

'Am I?' said Lucy.

'Yes,' Evelyn replied. 'I do declare that you're almost behaving yourself.'

At that moment, however, Lucy sat up stiffly, because Henry Carson and his friends had appeared from the direction of the house, dressed in tennis whites. They were laughing loudly, and Henry Carson was swishing his racket from side to side, as if he were clearing his way through some invisible underbrush.

'— you simply won't get the Bengalis to lift a single finger if you talk to them like that,' he was saying, as he passed Lucy by. 'You have to make the beggars feel that it was *their* idea, and that they're doing you some kind of tremendous favour.'

Lucy stared at him as he walked past; and for a split-second he looked over his companion's shoulder and stared back at her. He didn't smile. He didn't even blink. But there was something in his eyes that told her that he was interested in her. And what eyes! Dark brown and disturbing; the sort of eyes that could melt chocolate.

'Criminies, he's handsome,' she said breathlessly.

'I'd loosen my corsets if I were you,' Evelyn told her, tartly.

'And that *accent*! Snip-snip-snip! Doesn't it just make you quiver all over!'

'Lucy, for goodness' sake, I thought you were going to behave.'

The men began to play doubles; not particularly energetically, although Henry Carson hit two or three hard and accurate backhand shots. There were polite smatters of applause whenever anybody scored, and occasional cries of 'bravo!' All the time, Mrs Harris' footmen weaved their way discreetly through the guests, refreshing their glasses with champagne.

Henry Carson and his friend won the first game. While they were changing sides, and chatting to each other, and patting their faces with towels, Lucy abruptly stood up. She was still breathless, not because of her corsets, which were tight enough; but because she had made up her mind what she was going to do to attract Henry Carson's attention, and she knew that Mrs Harris wasn't going to approve one bit, let alone Evelyn, and she didn't suppose that her father would be particularly pleased, either.

'Where are you going?' Evelyn demanded.

'For a walk, that's all,' Lucy told her, and began to make her way towards the tennis court, dragging her chair behind her.

'Lucy!' Evelyn called her. But Lucy was determined to be deaf. She walked right up to the tennis-net post, and set her chair down beside it. Then she took hold of the net, to test how tight it was; and turned the crank-handle three times more, so that it was stretched to the maximum.

'Now, then, what are you up to, Miss Darling?' called Barry Wentworth in a jocular voice, walking towards her. 'We leave that kind of thing to the ground staff.'

Lucy said nothing; didn't even turn to look at him. Instead, she climbed up on her chair, and then placed one foot on top of the net post.

'Hey now, you better come down!' said Barry Wentworth.

But Lucy took a quick breath, and balanced herself on one foot; then carefully put out the other foot, and placed it on the net itself.

There was a sudden hush around the tennis-court as people turned to look. Lucy swayed a little from side to side. *Concentrate*, she told herself. *And remember what Mrs Sweeney told you. Don't look down at your feet. Back straight, eyes front. And be utterly, utterly confident.*

She stepped out on to the net. She kept her arms outstretched, judging the way the net was swaying, feeling for that perfect centre of gravity. Unlike Mrs Sweeney's fence, the tennis-net had a disconcerting way of double-wobbling beneath her feet, and as she took a second step, and then a third, she began to fear that she wouldn't be able to do it, that she would have to jump down, even though everything depended on her crossing from one net post to the other, without a slip.

To tightrope-walk across Mrs Harris' tennis-court would be dramatic. To try to tightrope-walk across Mrs Harris' tennis-court and to fall off halfway through would be ridiculous.

There was a hush on all sides as she reached the centre of the net. Even the quintet stopped playing. She hesitated for a moment as the net gave a sudden sharp swing to the right; and for one moment she was sure that she was going to lose her balance. She put another foot forward, then another. She heard somebody gasp; and somebody else say, 'No! No! She's doing it! She's doing it!'

Now she was making her way 'uphill', towards the post on the other side of the court. There were only six or seven more steps to go; and the garden-party guests began to gather around her in fascination and amusement.

The soles of her feet felt as if they had been cut in half; and her calves were trembling uncontrollably. She closed her eyes for a second, admonishing herself, *confidence! back straight! you can do it!* and when she opened them again she saw that her exhibition had already brought her what she wanted. Henry Carson had elbowed his way discreetly forward through the crowd of guests, and was standing by the net post, his hands on his hips, smiling, and waiting for her.

Three more steps; two; she couldn't even smile back at him, she was concentrating so hard. But then he held up his arms for her; and she swayed once; and wobbled; and jumped lightly down on to the grass.

Henry Carson held up her hand, and called out, 'Three cheers!'

There were whistles and applause and laughter, and somebody shouted out, 'We ought to start a circus! Barry, old man! You can ride a bicycle, can't you?'

Lucy, flushed with effort and embarrassment, turned around and curtseyed, and there was more applause; although she glimpsed Mrs Harris at the back of the crowd with a face like a prairie cyclone. She couldn't see Evelyn anywhere.

Henry Carson was taller than he had appeared from the other side of the lawn. He smiled at her and said, 'Well! That was jolly impressive, I must say! Did you have to train for it?'

'My dancing-teacher showed me. She used to walk the slack-wire for Forepaugh and Sells.'

Henry Carson laughed that sharp woodcutting laugh. 'Forepaugh and Sells! There's a name for you! Nothing to do with dogs and prisons, I shouldn't suppose?'

'No, Mr Carson. Travelling showmen. They used to be famous, in the West.'

'Now, look here,' said Henry Carson, 'you really mustn't call me "mister". Plain Henry will do. George, would you bring us two glasses of champagne? You do care for champagne, I suppose, Miss Ah –?'

Mrs Harris had now managed to bustle her way across the tennis-court.

'Mrs Harris, you've been very remiss,' Henry Carson complained, before she could open her mouth. 'You haven't yet introduced me to this delightful tightrope-walking protégée of yours.'

Despite the porcelain smoothness of her face, Mrs Harris' eyes were pink with annoyance. 'Well, Mr Carson,' she said, between tight-stretched lips, 'the fact of the matter is that we didn't know that she could perform in public. She's been hiding her light under a bushel as it were.'

'Is that true?' Henry asked Lucy. 'I wish you'd show me how you do it. The Prime Minister keeps telling me that I ought to keep my lights hidden under bushels. Ha! Ha! Can't manage it!'

'Mr Carson, allow me to present Miss Lucy Darling,' said Mrs Harris. The words stuck to her tongue like fine-grained sand. 'Miss Darling, I have the honour of introducing the Honourable Henry Carson, member of Parliament for Southport.'

Henry Carson took Lucy's hand and kissed it, and Lucy bobbed a little curtsey.

'I'm charmed,' he told her.

'Well, I guess I am, too,' Lucy replied.

Mrs Harris raised her eyes to heaven.

They strolled across the lawns together, and down to the artificial lake which the Harrises had created by damming a tributary of the Wansicut River. A flotilla of bafflehead ducks came swimming up to them, hoping for bread-crumbs.

'You know, this reminds me awfully of home,' said Henry Carson, standing with his hand in his pocket, sipping champagne. 'Well, the family park, actually, at Brackenbridge. Not so Capability Brown, of course. But, still, awfully similar. I've been trying to build a cascade – you know, a kind of staircase of water.'

Lucy watched him for a while without saying anything.

'You come from Kansas, they tell me,' he remarked. 'I can't say that I've ever had the pleasure of visiting Kansas.'

'It's not much of a pleasure. Most of it's flat.'

'You're not sorry you left it, then?'

Lucy looked away. 'I don't know. I miss it sometimes. I miss the people more than anything. In Oak City, there was no pretending you liked folk if you didn't; and you never had to worry which fork you picked up.'

Henry Carson laughed. 'I never pretend that I like people

if I don't! And I certainly don't worry which fork I pick up! In fact I eat with my fingers whenever I can. It's only these dratted society matrons who worry about etiquette. They're so terrified that they're going to betray their' — and here he whispered confidentially, — *'lack of breeding.'*

'Well, I don't *have* any breeding to speak of,' said Lucy, quite defiantly. She didn't like to think that all of those lessons that Evelyn had given her in which fish-server to use for buttered haddock and what to do with your napkin after you had finished eating (*never* refold it!) were all in vain.

Henry Carson looked at her closely but she couldn't read the expression on his face. It was too complicated, too masked. She had never spoken to a man with this much poise, this much maturity. She suddenly felt as if she were very seriously out of her depth.

'You shouldn't worry yourself about it,' Henry Carson told her. 'Some people work all their lives at acquiring breeding, and never do; while some are simply born with it. I know at least three peers who are absolute pigs. Besides, why give a fig about breeding, when you have so much oil?'

Lucy turned to him suspiciously. 'You seem to know a whole lot about me.'

'Of course I do. I asked.'

'When?' she retorted.

'The moment I first saw you. I said to George, who's that entrancing creature? And George said, Lucy Darling, daughter of Jack Darling the oil millionaire. Jack Darling inherited his oil from his late brother-in-law; and now he's well on the way to being a very wealthy chap indeed. And everybody thinks that Lucy is the prettiest debutante of the season.'

Lucy blushed. She wished she had brought some cake to throw to the ducks. Anything to divert Henry Carson's attention. He wouldn't take his eyes off her, and it was so *embarrassing!*

Henry Carson said, 'I couldn't possibly have left Newport

without meeting the prettiest debutante of the season, could I? Blanche would never have forgiven me.'

'Blanche?'

'My sister. She's dying to see me married. She says it'll be good for me. Well, a great many people want to see me married. Especially Mrs Harris.'

'Mrs Harris tells everybody that you and Henrietta are practically engaged.'

Henry Carson nodded. 'I know. Frightful, isn't it? How can you tell a doting American mother that her beloved daughter is tiresome and fussy and plain as a pikestaff?'

He paused, and then he said, 'I shouldn't have said that. She's quite a sweet girl really. But the ladies of Brackenbridge have always been rather special. And when I get married, I want my wife to be the most special lady of all.'

Lucy didn't know quite what it was, but there was an inflection in Henry Carson's voice that seemed to suggest that he was talking about *her*, as if he had already made up his mind that it was *she* that he wanted.

They walked a little farther around the lake. They reached some low stone steps where a rowing-boat was moored, and where the whole Harris house was reflected in the water.

'The drowned palace,' said Lucy.

Henry Carson glanced at her. 'You should see the Taj Mahal.'

'In India? I'd love to go to India.'

'You'd adore it,' he told her. 'India is – well, India is beyond words.'

'You've really been there?'

Henry Carson nodded. 'Twice now. And each time I loved her more. Sometimes I feel that my whole destiny lies in India.' He smiled. 'That's if the Prime Minister allows it, of course. I may end up in Ireland, God forbid.'

'Don't you care for the Irish?'

'Of course not. They're beyond all comprehension, and they smoke their pipes upside-down.'

'You're sane, then,' said Lucy.

'*What?*' Henry Carson laughed.

He took hold of her elbow and escorted her slowly back up the hill. The grass was poisonously green and shiny, as if it couldn't be real. Lucy would have loved to have lain on her back on it, and watched the clouds go sailing past. It was one of those afternoons when she felt that everything was changing, that the world was pivoting beneath her feet, and carrying her away with it.

'I think I've monopolized you too long,' said Henry Carson, as they reached the parapet around the back of the house. The orchestra was playing a minuet; sprightly, prissy, and light. 'I really must go and talk about trade tariffs.'

Lucy said, 'I hope you don't think it was too forward of me. The tightrope-walking.'

Henry Carson laughed, and kissed her hand. 'I thought it was magical. I'm not sure that Mrs Harris approved, but don't worry about that. If we let ourselves worry about the Mrs Harrises of this world, nobody would ever walk on tennis-nets, would they? or swallow swords, or misbehave themselves, or fall in love at first sight.'

He grasped her hand. 'I would like very much to see you again, Lucy, before I return to England. May I call on you?'

Lucy suddenly felt hot and confused. She knew from Evelyn that the etiquette of accepting gentlemen callers was extraordinarily sensitive; and that she must avoid compromising herself at all costs. She opened her mouth and then she closed it again. The simple truth was that she didn't know whether it was proper to say yes; or if no would really be understood to be no; or whether there was something else she could say that would make it clear to Henry Carson that she would adore him to call, but that she couldn't say so in so many words.

'You're staying in Newport all summer?' Henry Carson asked her.

Lucy nodded, still flushed with confusion. 'Until the second week in August.'

'Well, I have ten more days here. Then I have to take the train to Boston, and the ship back home.'

'I – I'm not used to callers,' Lucy managed to choke out. 'In Kansas, when a gentleman called –'

'Yes?' Henry Carson encouraged her.

'Well, he just came up, and said, "how about a soda?"'

Henry Carson laughed out loud, and smacked his thigh in amusement. His eyes were bright, and Lucy thought that she had never seen a man so handsome and so darned debonair in all of her life.

'You really shouldn't worry,' he told her. 'I shall call on you with the greatest of propriety. You are a very rare specimen indeed, and I shall treat you with all the respect to which any rare specimen is entitled.'

Mrs Harris reappeared, off-balance and flustered. 'You *will* dance with Henrietta, Mr Carson?'

'If you insist, Mrs Harris, just a quick scurry.'

Mrs Harris linked arms with Henry Carson, and tugged him away; but not before she had swivelled her head around and glared at Lucy with an expression that could have crushed glass. Lucy airily looked away. After all, what had Henry Carson said to her? If we all took notice of the Mrs Harrises of this world, nobody would tightrope-walk on tennis-nets, or swallow swords, and nobody would fall in love at first sight.

She was about to walk back across the lawn to rejoin Evelyn when she hesitated; and turned; and frowned intently at Henry Carson as he accompanied Mrs Harris to the garden steps. Love at first sight? Had he really meant it? Love at first sight with *her*?

She returned to Evelyn looking preoccupied.

'Lucy! you look as if you've seen a ghost, my dearest dearest!' Evelyn exclaimed. 'You'd better have some more champagne.'

'No, no thank you,' said Lucy. 'I think I'd just like to sit down, as a matter of fact.'

'You never told me you could walk on a *tightrope!*' gushed Evelyn. 'You ought to hear what people are saying! They can't make up their minds if you're the debutante of the year, or a circus-performer! It's such fun! And, of course, when Henry Carson was there to help you down! What did he *say*? He's so dazzling! And Henrietta went absolutely *green!*'

'Yes,' said Lucy. 'I expect she did.'

She sat down under one of the elms. She felt giddy and strange, as if she had drunk too much. She was still sitting there when Mrs Stuyvesant Fish came past. Mrs Stuyvesant Fish hesitated, almost passed her by; but then stopped, and came back, and laid her hand on Lucy's arm. She was veiled and perfumed; her diamond rings flashed in the afternoon sunlight.

'My dear Lucy,' she whispered, 'I thought you were *en-croy-able!* I haven't seen Wilhemina Harris so cross in *years!*'

'Thank you,' said Lucy; and it was then that she saw her father walking towards her, his white yachting pants flapping in the breeze. To think of Jack Darling wearing yachting pants! He took off his hat and she could see that he was smiling; and it was then that she knew everything was going to be dandy.

She dreamed about Henry Carson every night for the next three nights. The dreams were magnetic and dark and exciting, but also peculiarly frustrating. In each one she heard that clipped English voice calling, 'Lucy! Lucy!' But when she approached him, he immediately turned away from her, so that she couldn't catch sight of his face.

In one dream he was on the lawn at Mrs Harris' house; in both of the others he was in Oak City, just outside her father's general store. In the last dream she almost managed to reach him, but at the last moment he turned away again, so that all she could see was the dark straight hair on the back of his collar.

There was music in the dreams, too, but she didn't know what kind of music it was. It was thin, sad, pipe-like music, carried on the wind.

On the third morning the dream woke her just after seven o'clock. She lay with her eyes open looking up at the buttermilk-coloured curtains that hung over her bed. She had the prettiest of bedrooms; with tiny scarlet flowers on the wallpaper, and gilded walnut furniture that had been imported from France.

They had rented the house from the McPhersons, who had made their money in real estate. It was bijou by Harris or Vanderbilt standards; only eight bedrooms, and seven reception rooms, and stabling for two broughams and a tea-cart; but it was idyllically located on a small wooded hill overlooking the sea, and on a bright day you could see as far as Sakonnet.

She turned to look at the little enamelled clock on her bedside table. Then she drew back the quilt, and climbed out of bed. She was wearing her hair tied up in pale blue ribbons, and a pink French nightdress with a lacy bodice. She crossed to the window and looked out at the gardens. The waters of Rhode Island Sound glittered through the cedar trees, and gulls were sloping in the morning wind.

She slipped her feet into her white silk mules, and picked up her dressing-gown. Then she opened her bedroom door, and stepped out on to the galleried landing. In the hallway below her, illuminated by the muted amber sunshine that fell from the skylight, one of the maids was mopping the marbled-tiled floor, while another was polishing the doorhandle. From the direction of the breakfast room Lucy could hear the cutlery being set out for breakfast. She padded downstairs to the hall, and said, 'Good morning, Jane! Good morning, Dorothy!'

'You're powerful early, Miss Lucy,' smiled the maid with the mop. She was plump and white-faced and Irish, and had once thought of taking holy orders. 'First time I seen you up and about before nine o'clock.'

'Couldn't sleep any longer,' Lucy told her. 'It's such a beautiful day!'

'That's one thing that comes free,' the maid replied. 'God's good sunshine.'

Lucy tiptoed over the wet marble tiles, and Dorothy stepped back and opened up the front door for her. Dorothy was mulatto, graceful and calm, almost beautiful except for one wandering eye.

'You going *out*?' Jane asked her, in disbelief.

'Of course I'm going out,' Lucy replied.

'Well, then, you take good care of yourself,' the maid told her, as she skipped down the steps. 'If your poppa finds out that I let you go dancing around the garden in your nightclothes, why, he's going to skin me like a squirrel.'

Lucy turned around and waved at her, and called back, 'Tell him I was sleepwalking, and you didn't dare to wake me!'

She crossed the formal gardens in front of the house, past semi-circular rosebeds and stone statues of lions and gryphons, until she reached the woods.

She passed through the fragrant shadows beneath the trees; and at last emerged on the hillside overlooking the sea. The waves were as bright as smashed-up sugar; and already the first yachts of the day were leaning into the wind.

She stood with her arms stretched wide, so that the wind caught her dressing-gown, too, and made it ripple and flap. She closed her eyes, and thought to herself, this is what it's like to be a bird; this is what it's like to be a yacht.

This is what it's like to be in love.

'How happy I am!' she sang. 'How happy I am! How happy! how happy! how happy!' She opened her mouth, so that the wind made a hollow blowing sound across her lips. She felt that she could almost eat the wind, like bread, it blew so strongly, and it tasted of salt and freshness and sunshine.

Her eyes were still closed and her mouth was still open

when she heard somebody cough. A polite, formal cough, obviously intended to warn her that she wasn't alone. Immediately, she opened her eyes and crossed her hands over her breasts.

Half-concealed in the shadow by the edge of the woods, smiling at her mischievously, his hat and his riding-crop held in his hand, stood Henry Carson. On the far side of the woods she could see his Arab horse silhouetted amongst the trunks of the cedar trees.

'Good morning, Miss Darling!' he called out. 'You'll have to forgive my fearful lack of manners; but when I saw you there I simply couldn't resist coming to investigate!'

Lucy swallowed, and blushed, and all she could do was to chirp at him 'Oh! It's you!'

She was thrilled to see him. At least she would have been, if she hadn't been standing on this windy hill in her dressing-gown, with no powder or rouge or jewellery, and her hair all tied up in ribbons. She didn't know whether to run off down the hill, or hide behind a tree; or pretend that she wasn't there at all.

'Please, Miss Darling, don't be distressed,' Henry told her, moving out into the sunlight. 'You make a perfect picture. Perfect! But I'll go away if you want me to.'

'No, well, you don't have to go,' Lucy flustered. Her cheeks felt as if they were shining like plums. 'I was only – looking at the sea.'

Henry lifted his head up and sniffed the morning breeze, and nodded. 'It's a very fine day. Reminds me of the Isle of Wight, rather.'

'It was such a beautiful day I came out early,' said Lucy. 'I don't usually get out of bed until it's almost lunchtime.' She bit her lip. She wasn't sure if it was 'done' for a young lady to mention 'bed' to a man she scarcely knew.

However, Henry didn't seem to be at all scandalized. 'I wish to goodness that *I* could lie in bed all morning!' he replied. 'Got out of the habit, though; and once you're out of the habit, you can't go back to it. Myself, I always go for an early ride. Tones up the brain for the day's business. Sharpens the wits. This morning I thought I'd kill two birds with one stone; and leave you my calling-card while I was out.'

'You don't have to leave a card now,' said Lucy.

'Oh, Miss Darling, I must! Otherwise it wouldn't be proper. Besides, I was going to ask you and your father whether you would care to come to dinner with me tomorrow evening. Rather sadly, I have to leave on Friday; it's going to be my last opportunity to entertain you.'

'You're leaving so soon?'

'Affairs of state have to take priority over affairs of the heart, I'm sorry to say.'

Lucy looked up at him, with an unspoken question on her face.

In return, Henry lowered his eyes and tapped at his hat with his riding-crop, as if he expected to be able to conjure a rabbit out of it.

'I know I'm laying waste to all of the usual social conventions; especially here in Newport where they count for so much. I shouldn't be talking to you at all, let alone talking to you alone, in your night-attire, unchaperoned, in a field. But the plain fact of the matter is, Miss Darling, that when I saw you at Mrs Harris' the other day, you did something that no woman has ever done to me before.'

Lucy had already anticipated what he was going to say; and her heart began to rise inside her ribcage like a hot-air balloon.

Henry looked up. 'The plain fact of the matter, Miss Darling, is that you have quite captivated me. Ever since the day of that picnic, I have thought about nothing else but you; and seeing you again.'

'Well,' said Lucy.

Henry's expression was oddly little-boyish, almost plaintive.

147

'Well,' Lucy repeated; and then laughed. 'Here I am! You're seeing me!'

Henry nodded, and smiled. 'I am, yes; as clear as day; and it is the greatest imaginable pleasure.' He held out his arm to her, and said, 'If it isn't too bold a favour to ask, Miss Darling, perhaps you would allow me to escort you back to the house, so that I can leave you my invitation in the conventional manner.'

Lucy dipped him a mocking little curtsey. 'Am I still allowed to call you plain Henry?'

'But of course! You must!'

'In that case, hadn't you better call me plain Lucy; instead of "Miss Darling"?'

'Lucy isn't plain at all! But very well, Lucy it shall be! If I may offer you my arm?'

'Delighted,' smiled Lucy; and together they walked arm-in-arm through the woods. A squirrel scampered up a tree right beside them, and Lucy said, '*Psshh!*' and laughed to scare it even more.

'I sense a teaser in you,' said Henry.

'Isn't it done, in England, to tease an Honorable?'

'You mustn't call me that,' said Henry. 'I'm only a man, after all. No better and no worse than any other.'

'I haven't met any man better,' Lucy replied. 'But I've sure come across worse.' She thought this was quite a witty retort.

Henry looked at her narrowly. 'I can't believe that you know any men at all.'

Lucy turned away; suddenly alarmed that her lack of purity might somehow show in her eyes. 'Well, no, of course not,' she said.

'You're not – walking out with anybody?' Henry asked her. 'You're not engaged, perhaps, or spoken for?'

Lucy shook her head. 'I did know a boy in Kansas. His name was Jamie. Everybody thought that we were going to be married one day; but of course that was before we had any money. He went off to study the law in Manhattan, Kansas, and I came here.'

Henry said, 'Did you love him?'

Lucy couldn't think what to say to that, but he added quickly, 'Please — forgive me if I'm being too inquisitive. It really is none of my affair.'

'Oh, I don't mind,' said Lucy. 'I suppose I did love him, in a way. I surely depended on him. But depending on somebody, that's not the same as being in love with them, is it?'

'It can certainly be *part* of loving them,' Henry observed. 'But, no, it's not really the same thing at all. When you're in love, well —' he looked down at her, and his eyes were dark-brown, and alive with amusement. 'When you're in love, you're on fire.'

For one horrific and unexpected instant, Lucy had a furious vision of Uncle Casper, with his face blazing. Then she found that she was standing in her slippers on the sunlit lawn, staring at Henry instead.

'Lucy?' he asked her. 'Lucy, is something the matter?'

Lucy shook her head. 'I'm all right. I felt a little queer, that's all.'

'Let me take you inside. It's not terribly warm, is it? Perhaps you got up too early!'

'Yes,' she said. Her mouth felt dry. 'Perhaps I did.'

He helped her up the wide stone steps into the hallway. Jane and Dorothy stopped their floor-washing and their polishing and curtseyed.

'Jane, would you go tell Herrick to come to the door?' Lucy told her. 'Mr Carson wishes to leave his card.'

'Whatever you say, Miss Darling,' Jane replied, disapprovingly, and bustled off to find the butler.

Henry grasped Lucy's hands between his. 'I'm sorry. It seems that I've upset you somehow.'

'No,' said Lucy. 'It wasn't you. I guess I need my breakfast, that's all. Too many late evenings, too much backgammon, too much champagne.'

'A young lady should take care of herself,' Henry told her, and pressed her hands warmly and strongly, as if they were two flowers he wanted to preserve. In that particular downward-straining light in the hallway, she noticed for the first time the curving scar over his right eye. It gave him a quizzical expression, like a man surprised at his own good fortune. She didn't dare to remark on it, or to ask him how he had come by it.

Henry was staying in Newport as the guest of the Widgerys; who were friends of the President; and rich as all hell; but comparatively cultured. That is to say, they were cultured enough to have heard of Mozart, and not to think that the plays of Shakespeare were what he had done at weekends, when he had finished his works.

The Widgerys were dining that evening with the Pembroke Joneses, a big Yacht Club do; but they had made a point of waiting for Lucy and her father to arrive at The Seasons, so that they could welcome them. The Seasons was a titanic Second-Empire mansion set in a seventy-acre park. It had cost Milford Widgery more than four million dollars to build, an exact reproduction of the Château de Larroque, in Gascony, France, except that the quality of the stonework was very much finer.

As they jostled and squeaked in their brougham up the two-mile drive, Lucy saw The Seasons appear in the summer twilight huge and dark, with rows of lighted windows; more like a cliff than a house; a cliff in which scores of cave-dwellers lived, and kept their fires.

Jack Darling coughed, and said, 'I heard that Milford Widgery didn't exactly live in no outhouse. And, by Jiminy, look at this bulger.'

'Poppa,' Lucy admonished him, squeezing his hand. 'Stop talking so *Kansas*.'

Jack Darling grunted. 'Don't give me that society nonsense. You should hear some of the conversations that go on over the port'n'cigars. If you ask me, the richer the fellow, the fouler his mouth.'

They arrived at the door. One green-liveried footman opened their carriage-door, and put down the steps, while another was on hand to help them out. Henry was waiting for them at the top of the steps, immaculately dressed in tie and tails, with a high white collar.

'Mr Darling, Miss Darling. I'm delighted to see you! Come inside and meet Mr and Mrs Widgery. They're off in a moment; but they wanted to say hello.'

They entered a hallway as vast and echoing as a cathedral. Sparkling chandeliers hung high above their heads, and a curving marble staircase swept down from the landing to the highly-polished floor. Milford Widgery obviously had a taste for the acceptably erotic, since every niche around the hallway was occupied by a hefty mock-classical Venus, and the staircase was hung with oil-paintings of romping pink nudes and grinning satyrs.

Mr and Mrs Widgery were ready to leave; but they were still talking to each other with fierce animation in one corner of the hallway.

'Henry!' called Milford. 'Come right on over, let's see if your friends can settle an argument for us.'

Milford was small and neat and smooth, like a seal that had just emerged from the water; while Ethel his wife was large and blurry, as if she hadn't had the patience to keep still while she was posing for a daguerrotype. She had frayed silk fringes and fraying white hair and a disconcerting habit of suddenly swinging her arms to emphasize what she was saying, so that her circle of listeners were constantly ducking and diving and stepping back out of range. She welcomed Lucy with an exclamation of delight, drawing her towards her bejewelled bosom as irresistibly as a flood tide drawing a dinghy on to the rocks.

For one awkward moment, their brooches became entangled.

'My dear,' cried Mrs Widgery. 'I heard *all* about your exploits at Mrs Harris'! What a marvel! I would have given the Perry Diamond to have seen it! You know that Milly gave me the Perry Diamond, don't you? I always said that the Harris' picnics needed pepping up, didn't I, Milly? And to walk the tightrope on her tennis-net! Henry was quite breathless about it!'

'I was admiring, certainly,' smiled Henry.

Milford said, 'She's a charming young lady, Henry. No mistake about that.'

'You said you wanted us to settle something,' put in Lucy. She loved compliments, but she still wasn't sure how she should deal with them. Saying 'thank you' seemed so vain, as if you knew darned well how charming you were; so she had taken to smiling and blushing instead.

Mrs Widgery replied, 'It's our daughter's fifteenth wedding anniversary next month. Milford says it's her ivory wedding but I say it's crystal.'

Henry shook his head. 'Not my line of country, I'm afraid. Haven't the foggiest.'

But Jack Darling said, 'That's an easy one. Crystal.'

'Well, that's jolly knowledgeable of you, Mr Darling,' Henry remarked. 'How did you happen to know that?'

Jack said, 'Lucy's mother died the day before *our* crystal wedding.'

'Oh, I'm fearfully sorry,' said Henry. 'I didn't mean to upset you.'

'Pay it no mind,' Jack told him. 'She was sick for quite a while. I bought her a chandelier, though. Real crystal. She always hankered after a chandelier. She'd have loved this'un. She never saw the one I bought her. Died without opening her eyes.'

'Well!' Milford exclaimed, in an attempt to break the moment of morbidness. 'We really must be going! Mrs Pembroke Jones is a stickler for punctuality. The sport of princes!'

'The *courtesy* of princes, you mean,' Mrs Widgery corrected him.

'The politeness of kings, actually,' said Henry. 'Attributed to Louis the Eighteenth.'

'I didn't even know there *was* a Louis the Eighteenth,' Milford replied, in surprise. 'He sounds like a golf-caddy.'

'Oh, you don't know *anything*,' Mrs Widgery chided him.

'I was joking, for God's sake,' Milford protested.

The Widgerys' butler brought them their coats, and they left for their dinner, Mrs Widgery waving as if she were going on a day-trip by train to the seaside. They were still arguing – whether it was 'cabbages and kings' or 'cauliflowers and kings.' Henry said to Lucy and her father, 'Please, come on through to the drawing room, I'm sure you'd like some champagne.'

He took Lucy's arm, and together they walked through to the principal drawing room. Lucy's sky-blue silk dress whispered on the Persian rugs. The drawing room was the size of the main concourse of a railroad terminus; with chandeliers and a painted ceiling and vast gilt-framed mirrors. An entire family of Kansas sodbusters would have been quite content to set up house inside the fireplace alone.

'Always bickering, the Widgerys,' said Henry, as he led Lucy to one of the eight velvet-cushioned ottomans. 'They're delightful people, though. Rich enough to make one's eyes water, but completely unaffected by it. And every year they personally give more money to charity than the entire state budget of Delaware. They never stop telling me; but then it's something worth telling, don't you think?'

Lucy saw herself in one of the mirrors. She had curled up her hair, and pinned it with diamond-and-sapphire combs, which flashed as she turned her head. Her gown was watered silk, very low-cut, and on her bosom wore a diamond-and-sapphire necklace.

'You look marvellous,' Henry complimented her. 'Mr Darling, you have a captivating daughter.'

'Well, takes after her mother,' said Jack, sitting himself

down and tugging at the knees of his pants to make himself comfortable.

The butler came into the room on soft kid-soled shoes, carrying a silver tray of champagne glasses. After he had taken his, Jack glanced at Lucy, and sniffed, and cleared his throat, and then said, 'Mr Carson, would you be offended if I asked for a shot of sipping-whisky?'

'Not at all,' said Henry. 'Leonard, would you mind?'

The butler brought back a glass of whisky. Jack accepted it, and winked; and then promptly tipped it into his champagne.

'Well, that's fairly novel,' Henry remarked. 'That's an eight-year-old Prieur-Pageot.'

'Too weak, that's the trouble,' Jack replied, taking a large mouthful and swilling it noisily between his teeth. 'Measure of whisky gives it a decent kick.'

Lucy blushed at her father's Kansas manners; but Henry said, 'That sounds like a capital idea to me. Leonard – bring us some more whisky.'

The butler brought the bottle, and Henry tipped a measure into his own glass of champagne.

'A toast!' he proclaimed, rising to his feet. 'To Lucy, who is easily the most alluring girl that I have ever met in the whole of America, if not the world; and to you, Mr Darling, for giving us not only Lucy, but the most practical cocktail that I have ever encountered!'

They drank. Henry coughed, and his eyes widened. 'That's wonderful!' he gasped, pummelling his chest with his fist to get his breath back. 'Absolutely magnificent! My friends in London will adore it!'

'Well, it's better than a poke in the eye with a bradawl,' said Jack, although he was obviously pleased.

'It has to have a name!' Henry exclaimed.

'What about the Oak City Special?' suggested Jack.

'No, no! Let's call it the Tightrope!' Henry told him. 'Then I shall always remember how I first made its acquaintance.'

'Sounds all right t'me,' Jack replied, pouring a little more whisky into his glass before the butler could hurry round to do it for him, and topping it up with champagne.

Dinner went on for four enchanted hours. The three of them sat together at one end of the Widgerys' hundred-foot mahogany dining-table, their eyes sparkling in the light from a twenty-branch candelabrum, eating and laughing and drinking Tightropes.

The Widgerys' servants discreetly came and went with asparagus soup, lobster timbales, broiled wild duck, and fruit. Milford Widgery was almost as serious about food as he was about money, and he had bribed one of the best chefs at Delmonico's to take over his kitchens.

Henry talked ceaselessly and enthusiastically throughout the meal. As Lucy's father said afterwards, 'He sure wasn't short of chin music.' He told Lucy and her father all about Brackenbridge, his family home, and how much he revered and adored it. 'In January, in Derbyshire, it can of course turn fearfully cold and depressing. But to approach Brackenbridge from the north, and to see the winter sun shining on the statues over the portico; to walk through the park and see the geese flying through the mist; there is no enchantment like it.'

He told them about his schooldays at Eton, and how he had confounded his tutors by pretending to be lackadaisical and ill-disciplined. 'I used to sneak up to Ascot races; not because I cared for racing particularly, but because it was forbidden.' In the First Hundred Examination, however, he had come well ahead of absolutely everybody. 'First of the whole school! My tutors were furious! But of course they hadn't understood that I will *always* be first, in whatever I undertake.'

After his fifth Tightrope, Jack began to ramble about Lucy's mother again, his voice squashy with drink. But with considerable care, Henry steered him off the subject, and consoled him in a strange way, too, by describing the death of his own mother. A corroded pipe had exuded sewer gas into her bedroom, and eventually she had caught a fever. (It was nothing unsual, he remarked. The sewers at No 10 Downing Street were so foul that the Prime Minister himself was frequently feverish, and one of his private secretaries, a good friend of Henry's, had almost died.)

'Once her spirit had left her, you know, my mother lay in bed smiling, the way I always remembered her; although her face was grey, like marble. My Aunt Elisabeth had strewn the entire bed with white camellias. I still have one of them, pressed in the first copy of my first book.'

'You've written a book?' asked Lucy, deeply impressed.

'It didn't sell very well, I'm afraid,' said Henry. 'It's rather portly, and it costs two guineas.'

'But all the same! Is it an adventure?'

Henry laughed. 'I'm afraid not! But it was certainly an adventure to write it. It's called *Persia and the Persians*. It covers absolutely everything that you would wish to know about Persia, and quite a few things that you *wouldn't* wish to know, too.'

'Persia! It sound so romantic!' said Lucy.

'Don't you believe it! They're elegant, the Persians. More scrupulous than any Parisian. But they're filthy beyond any description, and corrupt, and they make a science of lying, and they have an indifference to suffering which I can only describe as bestial.'

He forked up a slice of duck, and then he added, 'Do you know, the last time the Shah of Persia visited London, he had sheep killed in sight of his suite every morning, blew his nose on the curtains, and offered to buy Lady Margaret Beaumont for his harem for half-a-million pounds.

'I have travelled through Persia more than any other European observer, and if there is any romance anywhere, I have yet to come across it.'

'In that case, I guess I'll stay right here in Newport,' Jack remarked, peering into his drink.

'I can't say that I blame you,' smiled Henry. 'But some of us have a duty to save the Oriental races from their own ignorance and cruelty. Quite apart from protecting our Indian Empire from the ambitions of the Russians.'

'You're an educated man, Henry,' Jack told him. 'You've got yourself a destiny, too. You're way above *my* head, I'm sorry to say.'

'Yes,' said Henry, without even a hint of false modesty. 'But all of us have our part to play, Mr Darling; and no man who can bring a daughter such as Lucy into the world can be thought of as anything but blessèd.'

He paused for a moment, and then he said, 'I have a proposition to put to you, to both of you. I have to return to England next week as you know; and after that I have to spend some considerable time on Parliamentary business. In the autumn, however, I should like you both to visit England as my guests. I can make all the arrangements from London, and write to you.'

'Oh, Henry! England? Truly?' Lucy cried out.

'England, how about that!' said her father, trying to focus his eyes. 'I never thought for one solitary moment that I'd ever see England!'

The only sign of agitation that Henry betrayed was his re-arrangement of his knives and forks. 'The truth of the matter is, Mr Darling, that I cannot bear to think that it might be months or even years before I see Lucy again.'

Jack raised his eyes, and looked at Henry carefully. He knew what Henry was saying: that his feelings for Lucy were serious. 'What do you say to that, sweetheart? It's your decision.'

Lucy gave Henry a coy little smile. She didn't mean to be coy. She didn't *feel* coy. But Henry was so direct about his interest in her, and she had never come across such candour before, especially when it came to courting. Bob Wonderly had at least tried to offer her a pound of liver, by way of foreplay.

'I'd like to come, very much,' she said, trying to sound demure.

Henry's face broke into a broad, satisfied smile. 'I knew you would! Thank you! We shall have such a splendid time! I can show you London, and Brackenbridge, and introduce you to all of my friends! And I know that my father will adore you as much as I do!'

'Henry —' said Lucy, cautiously. He seemed almost to have taken her acceptance of a trip to England as an acknowledgement that she would marry him.

'No ifs and buts!' said Henry. 'Let's have another Tightrope, to celebrate! To England! And to happy chances! And to you, Lucy, for lightening up my life!'

It was past midnight before they left. The footmen were yawning behind their white gloves. Jack Darling weaved his way off to the lavatory, because his back teeth were afloat, while Henry and Lucy waited for him in the hallway.

Henry gently took hold of Lucy's hand. 'I hope you don't feel that I've been too obvious,' he told her. 'There's been so little time; and you struck me so devastatingly. I really had no choice at all.'

'I'm flattered,' said Lucy. 'And at least you've been truthful.'

'Well, I told you before, didn't I? I'm no good at all at keeping my feelings to myself. Not very English, I suppose, but there's so little time. I want so much out of life; and I'm not particularly rich. I have to write, and work, and there's never much time for being social. I don't want to end up like Robert Browning, who dinnered himself away.'

He hesitated for a moment, still holding Lucy's hand, and then he said, 'You must forgive me for being so immediate, Lucy. The very last thing I want to do is to frighten you off.'

'I don't think you've managed to do that,' Lucy replied; conscious of her long-drawn-out drawl. 'But everything's still so new to me. New York, Newport, picnics, yachts. I'm trying to take it calm and easy; but sometimes I can't believe it's me.'

She squeezed his hand quickly; then released it. 'Just be understanding, Henry, that's all I ask. Up until· last spring, I'd never seen a house, ever, that didn't have its privy standing out back.'

Henry laughed out loud. 'I love you! You're perfect! You'll scandalize everybody; and rightly so! I can't wait to take you to London!'

'Henry,' said Lucy, 'I don't want you to make any kind of show of me.'

'My dearest Lucy,' Henry told her, and reached into his coat pocket to produce a neatly-folded sheet of paper. 'I wrote you a poem last night. Take it home and read it; and when you read it, please understand that I mean it with all my heart.'

Lucy accepted the sheet of paper with bewilderment. 'A poem?' she asked him. 'You've written a poem?'

'Of course! It's for you!'

'You've written a book, and you've written a poem?'

'My dearest girl, I've written thousands of poems, and I shall write more books! At Oxford, we wrote a poem about almost everything! Our tutors, our chums, the government, anybody we didn't care for, and anybody we *did*.'

At that moment, Lucy's father reappeared, smiling and blinking. Lucy quickly tucked the poem into her reticule.

'Goodnight,' said Henry. 'I shall never forget this evening as long as I live.'

Jack slapped him on the back. 'You're lucky, my friend! I haven't just forgotten this evening, I've forgotten who I am!'

Lucy deliberately tantalized herself by waiting until she had washed and changed into her nightgown before opening Henry's poem.

She drew the bedside lamp closer, and unfolded it. It was written in dark blue ink, in a firm, sloping hand. It read:

Yes, though I saw the rising day,
In Hindostan and far Cathay,
I never saw it shine so fair,
As on Miss Darling's golden hair.

I never saw in any time
A beauty that was so sublime.
I never saw in any place
A vision that could match her face.

Now, though I toil to Samarkand,
Through rain and snow and stinging sand
I'll see Miss Darling's darling smile
Which shrinks by half each weary mile.

She read the poem again and again, her eyes dewy. She had read poetry at school, of course. She remembered *The Ancient Mariner*, and the wedding-guest beating his breast. But somehow it had never occurred to her that somebody had actually sat down and written those poems; that they had been invented out of somebody's head. And she had never realized that real people could be included in poems; not just kings and princes and heroes; but real ordinary people like her.

She felt light-headed; almost uplifted; as if by becoming a character in a poem she had somehow become more beautiful, more radiant, more famous.

I am so happy! I am so ha-a-ppy! I am so happy I could die!

There was a soft knock at her door. It was her father, in his quilted smoking robe, pink-eyed from too many Tightropes. 'Can I come in?' he asked her.

'Of course you can,' said Lucy. 'I thought you'd have dropped straight off to sleep.'

He sat down on the bed beside her and gave her a kiss. 'I don't know; my head's whirling tonight.'

160

'I'm not surprised, with all that whisky-and-champagne.'

He nodded at the poem which still lay on the embroidered pillow. 'What's that you're reading? Billay-doo?'

'Henry wrote me a poem.'

Jack Darling picked up the piece of paper and read the poem, softly moving his lips as he did so.

'That's pretty,' he nodded. 'That's a real pretty sentiment.'

Lucy said, 'You do *like* him, poppa?'

'Sure. Sure I like him. I thought he was kind of a blow the first time I met him, but he grows on you, don't he? I mean you'd think he'd stand on ceremony being English and a member of Parliament and all, but he's straight and fair, even if he does talk the leg off the table.'

Lucy watched her father for a while and she could tell that something was troubling him. She held his hand, and gently squeezed it, and said, 'You're worried.'

'Well, I don't know,' he replied. 'Maybe I'm fearful for no good reason at all. But you were always so happy, back in Oak City.'

'I'm happy now.'

'Sure you are. But you understand that if you take up with this Henry, you'll be starting a whole new 'nother kind of life. Dukes and duchesses, that kind of company. I mean you've got to decide if that's what you truly want.'

Lucy smiled, and kissed him. He smelled of Hilbert's Wood Violet Toilet Water. She had tried to wean him on to French colognes, but Hilbert's had always been his favourite, because it was made in Milwaukee and it was good and strong.

'Poppa, you mustn't worry. I can hold my own, even with dukes and duchesses.'

'There's something you should know,' he told her. His voice was low and hoarse. 'I never told you before, because it didn't matter, and it was best all round that we just let sleeping ducks lie. But now you're growed, pretty well, and

161

you've started courtin', and it looks like sooner or later some fellow is going to want to marry you – well, I guess it had better come out.'

'Poppa, tell me,' Lucy insisted.

Jack gave her a wry smile. 'The truth is, Lucy, that – damn it, I don't even know how to begin to say this.'

'Poppa, you can tell me anything, you know that. Since when did you and me ever have any secrets?'

'Sweetheart, I've kept a secret from you all your life.'

She reached out and touched his cheek, he was so obviously distressed.

'Poppa – what secret?'

'That's it,' he said miserably. 'That's the secret. I'm not your poppa. Not *truly* your poppa.'

'What?' she asked him, in astonishment. 'What do you mean?'

'I raised you,' he explained. 'I always took you for my own. But the fact of the matter is that it says on your birthing papers that your true poppa wasn't known.'

'I can't believe it,' whispered Lucy. She couldn't stop herself trembling. 'Why didn't you tell me before?'

'Your momma didn't want you to know. She was ashamed of it, I guess. And besides, what good would it have done you, even if you *had* known? You loved your momma and you loved me, and that was all that was important.'

'But why does it say that my true poppa wasn't known?' Lucy asked him. 'Momma must have known who he was.'

Jack nodded sadly. 'Yes, she knew. But she never told me. She wouldn't. I asked her once, that was all. Just once, one Sunday morning. She said that if I asked her again, she'd pack her bag and she'd leave me for ever, and I knew that she meant it.'

Lucy suddenly realized that she was holding hands with a man who wasn't even her father. She couldn't believe that her mother could have deceived her all those years. Even when she was dying, she hadn't told Lucy the truth. Lucy felt her throat tightening and tears prickling in her eyes, and she didn't know which of them she felt sorrier for – her poppa or herself.

Jack Darling said, 'It was soon after we moved out to Kansas. We had a bad winter and everything seemed to go wrong. I started drinking because I was so worried; and when I drank I used to hit her. She said she couldn't take it any more; and rightly so; and so she went back to Charlotte where she was raised.'

He sniffed, and wiped his nose on the back of his hand. 'She stayed away till spring. By that time, I was beginning to get things straight, and make some money. It isn't too difficult to work your butt off when you're all on your own, without nothing to distract you but your own unhappiness.

'One day in early May she just appeared in the doorway, with her bag, and said she loved me, and would I take her back, I said yes, of course. But before she would take even one step inside, she told me that she was pregnant, and that she wanted to keep the child; and that she expected me to raise it like my own, no matter what.'

'And you said yes to that, too?'

'Sweetheart, I loved your momma with every single bone in my body. She could've told me she was expecting sextuplets, I still would have said yes.'

Lucy took out her handkerchief and dabbed at her eyes. 'And she never gave you any idea who my father might have been?'

Jack looked at her, his face disassembled by tiredness and drinking and grief. 'It could have been some beau she'd known from childhood. That's what I like to think. Some fellow she loved from way back before I met her. I sure don't like to think that it was anybody casual, a man on a train, or a hotel porter, or whatever.'

He cleared his throat, and then he added, 'I'm sorry I had

to tell you. But it's time you knew. I didn't want it coming out on your wedding-day, and ruining everything.'

'Poppa . . .' she said.

He leaned over and held her tight. 'Sweetheart, I'm still your poppa, and I always will be. I'll love you just the same as always.'

'Do you know something?' said Lucy touching his dear face. 'I always thought that we looked so much alike, you and me.'

Jack kissed her. 'Guess that was God, being kind to us.'

They sat together for a while, and then Jack eased himself up off the bed. 'It's time I hit the hay.'

When he reached the door, Lucy said, 'Poppa!' and he turned and looked back at her, although he wasn't smiling.

'Poppa,' she repeated. 'I love you, poppa.'

'I love you too, sweetheart,' he replied, and quietly closed the door.

She lay for a long time in the darkness after everybody else had gone to bed, listening to the house creaking. The night was still and humid, with only the slightest wind stirring the curtains. It was what the Eastern farmers called 'corn weather,' ideal for ripening the corn crops, and the darkness was intermittently illuminated with distant flashes of 'corn lightning'.

When Lucy heard the clocks chiming two, she climbed out of bed and went to the window, and opened it wider. The lightning was close now; and she could hear the banging of thunder, over to the south-west. A heavy rainstorm was making its way up the coast from Westerly, and it wouldn't be long before it was overhead. The trees began to rustle and whisper among themselves, and a wave of wind ran across the lawns.

Lucy brought over her dressing-table stool, and positioned it under the open window. She stepped up on it, and carefully climbed out of the window on to the parapet outside.

She peered down to the garden. The gravel path was forty feet below her, but she wasn't afraid of heights. She balanced her way along the guttering until she reached the corner of the roof, where she could see Rhode Island Sound, beyond the trees, and the white foam breaking over the shoreline. She sat down cross-legged, in her white nightdress, and felt the warm breeze blowing against her face.

I wonder who I am, she thought to herself. *I wonder where I came from. Lucy Darling, whose little girl are you?*

She raised both hands in front of her face and turned them this way and that. Whose fingers had she inherited? Whose talents? She had always believed that her personality was an equal mixture of her mother's vivacity and her father's gentle reserve. Now she felt completely fragmented, like a broken jug that wouldn't fit back together again. How could she begin to understand the world around her if she couldn't even understand herself?

She watched the lightning flicker on the ocean; catching the waves in an instant photographic flash, so that they looked as hard as hammered glass. She said, 'One grass-hopper, two grasshopper –' but the thunder rumbled almost immediately. The first few drops of rain pattered on the roof, and on to her shoulders.

Whose little girl are you, Lucy Darling? You're not even a Darling at all.

Her mother had gone back to Charlotte. But who had she met there? Some childhood beau, as her poppa liked to believe? Or some stranger? Some carpetbagger with an eye for a pretty young wife?

The trouble was, there was one thought that wouldn't stop repeating itself, over and over, in the darkest part of her mind.

'*We was lovers for a while, your mother and me,*' that's what Uncle Casper had said, with that sly mischievous grin on his face. 'Might have been a sin in the eyes of God; but we was lonesome and friendless and each other was all we had.'

The lightning crackled so close now that Lucy could smell the air scorching. The thunder collapsed right over her head. The rain started abruptly, trailing in fuming sheets across the lawns and pattering on the slates.

At once, Lucy was soaked. The rain dribbled from her nose and her chin, and her hair was stuck darkly on to her scalp. Her nightgown hung heavily and chilled, like the shroud of a girl found drowned.

'*We was lovers for a while, your mother and me.*' My God, supposing her mother had gone back to Uncle Casper. Supposing he had told her the truth. Supposing Uncle Casper had been her real father?

The rain clung to her eyelashes like tears, and turned the whole world to blurry stars. Gasping with effort, Lucy pulled herself up into a kneeling position, and began to tug off her wet nightgown. It stuck to her body and her face like cold slime, but at last she managed to drag it over her head, and unbutton the wet lace cuffs, and pull it right off.

Now she knelt naked in the guttering, her face lifted to the rain. The lightning flickered again, so that her skin gleamed blueish-white. Then the sky split open, and the whole house shook, and the rain pelted down even harder than before.

Still gasping, still trembling, Lucy washed her face with her hands; then her shoulders and her breasts. She gripped her breasts tight, twisting her nipples until they hurt. She had to be clean. She had to be utterly pure. She had to wash off every single trace of Uncle Casper, and what he had done to her.

Her discarded nightgown had blocked the drain outlet behind the parapet, and so the guttering gradually filled with two or three inches of water. She knelt forward and frantically washed her hair, rubbing and massaging her scalp until it was sore. Then she lay back in the water, and parted her legs wide. She splashed herself again and again with scooped-up handfuls of chilly rainwater, her eyes squeezed tightly shut, her teeth clenched, praying that this would purify her.

Dear God, I want to be clean again. Dear God, I want to be clean!

After a few minutes, she turned over and lay on her stomach in the gutter, panting and shuddering with cold. The worst of the storm was already passing; like a circus striking its tents and moving to another town; and the grumbling of thunder was muffled behind the ridge of the roof. The gutters gurgled; the chimneys dripped. The lightning lit up the gardens again, but fitfully.

Lucy closed her eyes, but she wasn't crying any longer. She was too cold to cry. The rain fell steadily on to her naked back, her hair trailed in the gutter like weed.

At last, however, she climbed to her feet, and wiped the rain away from her face, and sniffed. She felt calmer now, after her moment of hysteria. She felt at least as if she had purged her own sins; if not her mother's, or Uncle Casper's. Dragging her sodden nightgown after her, she climbed back in through her bedroom window, and tiptoed across to her bathroom.

She wrapped herself up in a deep white Turkish towel, and sat for a moment on the edge of the bath, shivering, trying to quieten herself, and to get her breath back.

At last she stopped shaking, and her skin began to tingle with warmth. She stood up, and slowly combed her hair in the bathroom looking-glass, pausing between every stroke.

Facing her, expressionless, was a pale-faced girl with unnaturally blue eyes and a faint sprinkling of freckles on her nose. She snarled at herself. Then she stared at herself with her eyes popping. Do you *look* like Uncle Casper? she asked herself. Do you have Uncle Casper's eyes; or Uncle Casper's nose? When you smile, do your lips curl up like Uncle Casper's?

She couldn't tell. She would never be able to find out. Her mother had left her with nothing but a legacy of doubt and bewilderment. She went back to her bedroom, and sat down, still combing her hair, over and over.

When she had left the window open, the rain had spattered in, and blotched the poem that Henry had written for her. It looked as if the poem were stained with tears. Lucy picked it up, and read again,

> *I never saw in any time*
> *A beauty that was so sublime.*

But the line which she liked the most, the line which made her smile again, and the one which she repeated over and over, was *'I'll see Miss Darling's darling smile.'* When she whispered that line, she knew that Henry was telling the truth, and that he had really fallen for her.

Her bedside lamp was still burning when she fell asleep. By dawn it had flickered out. But Lucy slept and slept, undisturbed, while the sun came up, and dried away the puddles from the night's rainstorm; while yachts angled their way across Rhode Island Sound; while gardeners trimmed the roses and clipped the lawns; a girl in a dream.

It was early September before they could move into their house on Central Park West. It stood two blocks north of the Dakota building; between 74th and 75th Streets; and directly fronted the park.

The whole district was in riotous turmoil. Only a few years ago, it had been nothing but rocky fields and shanties and market-gardens. The Dakota building had been given its name because it had been so far away from the genteel homes of Fifth Avenue that it might as well have been built in the Dakotas. But all around it, streets were being graded and buildings were being thrown up, and the Darlings' accountants reckoned that building a house on Central Park West was the best investment they could have made.

Lucy wasn't at all sure that she liked the house when it

was finished. It was a four-storey limestone building in the style of a Loire château, with a circular turret at each corner. Sixteen bedrooms, five bathrooms, a huge mirrored drawing-room, and a mosaic-floored hall with *two* staircases, one undulating down on either side like twin waterfalls.

She was pleased with the view from her turreted bedroom: an uninterrupted vista of Central Park, which had recently been cleared of most of its garbage dumps and pigsties, and was now one of the handsomest city parks in the world. She felt like a princess up here, aloof from everything: the noise of traffic and the hammering of construction, and the metallic clashing of the Ninth Avenue elevated.

She felt, however, that there was something about the house which was rather cold. Everything was just a little too elegant, and a little too stylish. Marble-clad walls, perfectly-proportioned pillars, banister rails that were heavily silver-plated. Perhaps it was her fault, too. Perhaps she wasn't yet ready to lend it her own enthusiasm, and her own radiance.

Jack's delight in his new home, however, was huge – at least to begin with. For the first week after they moved in, he kept stepping out on to the front porch, and standing with his thumbs in his waistcoat, so that passers-by would realize that the house was his. Occasionally, if one of them lifted his hat, or nodded in his direction, he would take his cigar out of his mouth and announce, 'Lit by electric light! Whole place, totally lit by electric light! And an elevator, too!'

He sent wires to Samuel Blankenship and Henry McGuffey and several more Oak City cronies, inviting them to visit New York at his expense (although Lucy drew the line at Osage Pete.) None of them answered, but Jack told Lucy that they were probably daunted by the length of the journey, and by the prospect of having to put on 'fancy manners'.

But one rainy morning in the middle of September she found him in the morning-room, standing by the window, watching the raindrops dribbling down the glass; and when she came up to him, and touched his arm, she saw that his eyes were filled with tears.

'Poppa?' she said, gently. 'What's wrong?'

He sniffed, and wiped his eyes with the heel of his hand. 'Oh, nothing. Just regrets, I guess. And why should you call me poppa, when I ain't?'

'I'll always call you poppa. You're not crying for that, are you?'

'I don't know. Maybe I'm feeling lonesome, that's all. Maybe I'm feeling out of my depth. Maybe it's raining and I just feel low.'

Lucy tiptoed up and kissed his cheek. Her affection for her father had not been diminished by his revelation that he wasn't her real father. She still loved him as much as ever; and she still trusted him to take care of her. But a distinct note of reserve now strained their relationship, mostly on Lucy's part and mostly unconsciously. She no longer sat on his lap in the evenings, when they were talking beside the fire. She no longer kissed his lips. She no longer talked about her boyfriends, and the way she felt about them, not in the same way. The unavoidable truth was that in spite of their closeness, in spite of the fact that he had brought her up, she could no longer treat him as if he were flesh of her flesh.

'Why don't you go out, try to make some new friends?' Lucy suggested. 'Harold Stuyvesant had you elected to the Sportsman's Club, didn't he? You could always go down there.'

'What, and listen to a whole lot of stiffnecks talking about stocks and futures and who's married into whose fortune; and why the price of copper keeps falling? Some sport! I spent two hours at the Sportsman's Club last Thursday afternoon, and nobody so much as said "how d'ye do", or knew the latest baseball score, and none of them would have known a joke if it had stood up on its hinder legs and bitten them in the backside.'

'But poppa, we're in society now! You can't expect men to spit and chew tobacco and tell bawdy stories around the stove.'

Jack loudly blew his nose. 'Maybe they ought to try. Maybe it would do them some good.'

'Poppa – maybe you ought to give it another go.'

Jack looked at her. The sun suddenly came out, and reflected dazzling gold light from the stable rooftop outside, and for a moment Jack appeared quite different. All the colour was bleached out of his hair and his eyes and he could have been a hundred years old.

'All right, maybe you're right. Maybe I'll give it another go.'

Jack went upstairs to dress; and not long afterwards Evelyn called to take Lucy out shopping, and then for lunch. Lucy was measured at Francine's for four new gowns; one of them sewn all over with patterns of tiny seed-pearls, one black taffeta, one scarlet silk, and one in sumptuous pale-velvet, with a wide collar made of Brussels lace. They lunched at the New Netherland hotel, lobster mousse and rocket salad, and then they shopped for evening purses and shoes.

Lucy stayed at the Scotts' house until well after five o'clock, and by the time the Scott four-wheeler had taken her home, it was nearly six.

'Is my father back?' she asked Amy the housemaid, who let her in.

'Yes, miss,' Amy replied, and then pressed her lips tightly together.

'Just here will do, thank you,' she said to the Scotts' footman, who was carrying in her shopping. But as he carefully set down her parcels on the marble bench beside her, she heard bellowing laughter from the drawing room. It wasn't Jack's laughter, either; and it was followed almost immediately by the high-pitched screaming of a strange woman.

'Amy?' she frowned.

'Friends of Mr Darling, miss,' said Amy, and bobbed her a hurried curtsey.

Lucy took off her gloves and her osprey-plumed hat, and Amy helped her out of her coat. Then she walked with a brisk step to the drawing-room doors, and opened them wide.

At first she could scarcely believe what she was seeing. Jack was sitting crosslegged on the floor, with a bottle of champagne beside him, smoking and dealing out playing-cards on to the polished parquet. Beside him, laughing, knelt a blowzy-looking girl with raven black hair and huge white bosoms that were almost spilling out of her gown. Opposite him, lying back luxuriously on a heap of cushions, reposed a plump young man with black pomaded hair and one of those shiny emerald-green satin vests that Jack's store card would once have described as 'nobby'. He was alternately puffing at a large green cigar and swigging champagne out of the neck of a bottle, and busting himself with laughter in between.

It wasn't the blowzy black-haired woman or the plump young man in the vest who startled Lucy so much, however. At the end of the room, half-silhouetted against the window, a very slender young girl was dancing, although there was no music for her to dance to. She was naked except for an embroidered silk bustier and rolled-down silk stockings. Her scraggly fair curls had been heaped up on top of her head and pinned with tortoiseshell combs. Her eyes were closed, and she was singing to herself. Although her bottom was bare, she sported a huge and luxuriant blue tail of ostrich plumes, which bobbed and dipped as she danced; and it was only as she raised one leg in a mock-balletic step that Lucy realized where the plumes had been inserted.

Lucy turned to Jack in shock. The drawing room was dense with cigar-smoke, and the smell of strong perfume. Jack was laughing so much that at first he didn't notice her.

The plump young man on the cushions had seen her at once, however, although he didn't seem unduly concerned. He set down his bottle of champagne and lay back comfortably admiring her through slitted eyes, his podgy fingers laced over the front of his vest, his green cigar tilted between his teeth.

'Now that,' he declared, 'is class with a capital K.'

Jack stopped laughing and looked up. When he saw Lucy, he stiffened, and nervously wiped at his nose, and stopped dealing, and sat watching her, wary as a hunted stag. The girl by the window opened her eyes, and stopped dancing, and tippytoed quickly to the piano, where she had left her petticoats. Her ostrich-plume tail bounced behind her. Both girls made a great bustling fuss of covering themselves up.

'Poppa,' said Lucy, walking around the back of the sofa.

Jack nodded towards the plump young man. 'Lucy, want you to meet Tom Brach.'

The plump young man made no attempt to rise from his heap of cushions. 'How dedo,' he grinned, saluting Lucy with his cigar.

Lucy said coldly, 'Don't get up.'

Jack cleared his throat. 'This is . . . Alice,' indicating the girl with the basque and the raven-black hair. 'This here is . . . what's your name, honey?'

'Mavis,' lisped the young dancer. She couldn't have been older than thirteen or fourteen.

'That's it, Mavis, my little songbird,' said Jack, and blew her a kiss. The girl smiled uneasily at Lucy.

Lucy said, 'They can leave now.'

Jack stared at her, then shook his head emphatically. 'Ho, no. You said find yourself some friends, I found myself some friends.'

'Not at the Sportsman's Club,' Lucy retorted. She felt so furious at Jack that she could hardly speak. It was everything she could do to stop herself from bursting into tears.

'Well, yes, as a matter of fact, at the Sportsman's Club. I

sat in the lounge of the Sportsman's Club for twenty minutes, and believe me those twenty minutes were the most tedious twenty minutes of my whole life, bar none. I've had more fun watching paint dry. So I asked Cyril the doorman if he knew where there was anything lively going on, and I tipped him twenty bucks, and lo and behold he directed me to Miss Collings' on West 25th Street, and there I met Tom here, and Alice and Mavis, and we've had nothing but fun all day.'

'Poppa,' Lucy declared, 'I want these people out of my house.'

'Well, that ain't at all what I call sociable,' Tom Brach remarked.

'Uppity, I call it, 'specially when we've been invited,' added Alice.

But Lucy held her ground, staring at her father with such fury that after a moment or two he flung down his cards, and climbed up on to his feet, hobbling for the first two or three steps with pins-and-needles, and said to his friends, 'Come on, now, ladies and gentlemen, time to call it a day.'

'You don't mind if we dress,' said Alice, pointedly.

'Poppa, you and Mr Brach can wait outside,' said Lucy.

She stayed with Alice and Mavis while Mavis removed her tail and they helped each other into their clothes. Even when they were fully dressed they were a pretty bedraggled pair. Half of the plumage was trailing off the side of Alice's hat, and Mavis in her tight green velour bodice and her frayed straw skimmer looked like nothing much more than a scruffy schoolchild.

They shuffled out of the front door on worn-down shoes, watched by Amy with a mixture of awe and disgust.

When the door had closed behind them, Lucy went to find Jack. He was sprawling with feigned disinterest in the library, with a huge glass of whisky balanced on his knee. The tail of his shirt was hanging down in front. He took a large defiant swallow, and then he stared at Lucy with reddened, resentful eyes.

'When I'm lonesome I get on your nerves. When I find myself some friends you get angry. What the hell else am I supposed to do?'

'Your friend gone?' asked Lucy.

'You bet. Said he had all the frosty women he needed at home.'

'Poppa, I'm not being frosty. But this is our home. You can't bring gamblers and women back to our home. What would momma have thought?'

Jack banged his glass down on the wine-table beside him. 'Do you think what your momma did was any more moral than me bringing a couple of women back home?'

'I don't know what my momma did, except look for love, and raise me the best she could, and die.'

'Your momma was my wife. But you aint my daughter. God only knows whose daughter you are, your momma never said. That's what she did to me. That's what your momma did. And you have the sheer barefaced gall to say that I can't bring a couple of women back home, just for the fun of it?'

Lucy stepped forward, and swung her arm to slap Jack's face, but Jack snatched her wrist and stopped her. She twisted her hand away, and glared at him in white-hot temper. 'You call those women? One was not much more than a child! And that drunk of a cardsharp! What kind of friends are those?'

'Friends who ain't sour or snobby, that's what kind of friends they are. Friends I can laugh with.'

Lucy said, 'You didn't . . .? Not with those girls?'

Jack blew out his cheeks dismissively, and shook his head. 'They danced for us, that's all. Dance of the seven veils.' He waved his arms from side to side in a cursory imitation of an Egyptian houri. 'Christ, Lucy, I aint had so much fun since we left Oak City.'

Lucy was tempted to snap back at him, but she stopped herself. She walked across to the window and stood looking out at the street. She heard Jack swallow more whisky, cough.

After a moment or two, she said carefully, 'I think it's about time you remembered whose money this is; whose house this is.'

'I haven't forgotten. But no matter whose house this is; no matter whose money this is; that doesn't mean that I have to live like St Jack the Pure. None of those other rich guys live like that. You should of seen some of things they got up to on those yachts, back at Newport. That was an education and no mistake.'

Lucy turned around, her silk dress swishing on the rug. 'Poppa, you brought me up. What's mine is yours. But believe you me, this money cost me more than you could ever understand, and you're not bringing home gamblers or whores and that's final. If you want that kind of fun, go find it someplace else. I don't want to see even a whiff of it. Because if you ever bring people like that home again, you and me are finished for good and all.'

Jack considered this with sudden sobriety. He sniffed, and said, 'You know that I love you, don't you, Lucy?'

'Yes,' said Lucy, 'I believe that you do.'

'Well, then, for the sake of that, I'll keep my fun to myself. But don't think I'm going to live like St Jack the Pure, because I won't.'

That day changed everything between them; not just for a week or two, but for ever. Jack seemed increasingly to regard their wealth as an enraging kind of fairytale curse; money which had to be spent and enjoyed at an ever more furious pace. The simple shopkeeperly morals by which he had lived his life up until now collapsed under the sheer weight of wealth, like the rotten floorboards of a robber-baron's counting-house. Lucy, finding him drunk or depressed or boastful or over-elated, began to take pains to avoid him, and to lead a life that was more and more fanciful.

She stayed in bed longer in the mornings, daydreaming about being married, and having a husband of her own. By the time she came down to breakfast, Jack had usually left the house, either to gamble or to go drinking, or to go to the new Polo Grounds to watch the Giants. In common with thousands of others all over America, he had developed a passion for baseball.

During the last two weeks of September, they hardly saw each other at all. Every morning she lay in her French four-poster bed, in her grey-and-gold bedroom, with her Burmese cat Rangoon sitting on her feet, doodling Henry all over her writing-paper. Henry, Henry, Henry, with curling 'ys' and 'Hs' as elaborate as the Brooklyn Bridge.

After straightening her pillows for her, her red-headed maid Nora picked up one of the sheets of doodles, and remarked, 'Sure, you're fond of this Henry! Which one is he? It wouldn't be Henry Massenheim would it? He doesn't look like the type to interest you! Well, what with his nose!'

'Henry Carson, MP,' Lucy replied. She was growing her hair, and every night she curled it in ribbons. 'An English gentleman of the first water.' She had learned that phrase from Evelyn.

'Do I know him?' asked Nora. She was green-eyed, direct, with a sharpish tongue and a very busy way about her, but Lucy had preferred her to the prim and prissy 'yes-miss-no-miss' maids that she had interviewed first of all.

'No, you don't know him,' Lucy sighed. 'He's in England and I'm supposed to be going to England to visit him. But I haven't heard yet. So I'm moping, you see, and writing Henry all over everything, and dreaming.'

'But a prosperous young lady like yourself shouldn't be moping. You could have any man you want. Just a snap of the fingers. Any man in New York.'

'My dear Nora, Henry is the man I want.'

With an oil fortune worth close to $11 million, there was no question that Lucy was highly eligible, and there was no shortage of wealthy young bachelors who wanted to make her acquaintance. The tightrope story had spread like wildfire, and so wherever Lucy went heads would turn and fans would be spread so that women could whisper, 'That's the girl who –'

Evelyn introduced her to scores of amusing boys, and steered her expertly away from adventurers and dandies, and those with a vaguely unsavoury reputation. The two of them were escorted almost every day to the theatre, or to supper-parties, or out dancing. Life became one glittering carousel of shining carriages and chandeliers, and men whose collars were so high they had to stare at the ceiling all evening.

They went to see William Gillette's *Too Much Johnson* and *The Prisoner of Zenda*, which Lucy found thrilling. They went to supper with the Jeromes and the Stewarts and the W. K. Vanderbilts. Lucy ate truffles for the first time, and decided she was going to live off nothing else. Truffles and champagne! They went to Mrs Douglas' September Charity Ball on the third floor of Delmonico's, overlooking the brightly-lit greenery of Madison Square, and Lucy danced and danced under the sparkling lights, exhilarated and laughing and prettier than ever.

With Evelyn guiding her, Lucy charmed New York society, and was named by the *New York Post* as 'Miss Lightbulb', because the men clustered around her like moths at every social function.

But although she met five or six boys whom she really liked – especially John B. Harriot IV, whose father owned most of Nevada – she was still waiting for her invitation from England. Her daydreams of being married were daydreams of him; and of that smile of his; and Derbyshire in winter. She could close her eyes and see the sunlight on the statues of Brackenbridge House, and the geese flying through the silver mist.

Henry's poem lay pressed in the front of her Bible,

together with a pink rose from the dinner-table at the Widgery's house. She read the poem every day. She watched herself in the mirror. She began to wonder if he had been deceiving her; if he were ever going to write.

On the first day of October, their newly-appointed butler came in to the drawing room while Jack was warming his back by the fire and Lucy was embroidering a handkerchief. With a great deal of ceremony, he handed Lucy a card on a silver tray. Jeremy had once buttled for Mrs James P. Kernochan, and he was the acme of haughty discretion. Jack had wanted to hire him for his imposing profile – 'like a bald-headed eagle wondering whether to lay an egg or not' – but Lucy had been entranced by his English accent. He came, in fact, from Massachusetts, but he had worked hard to develop an impressively butlerish voice.

'There is a gentleman without,' he remarked, inclining his head.

'Without what?' Jack cracked, although he cracked the same joke every time anybody came to visit.

Lucy read the card. 'It's Jamie! Poppa, it's Jamie! Oh, Jeremy, do show him in!'

Jeremy said, 'Certainly, Miss Darling,' and turned around on a rubber heel; but Jamie had already entered the open doors, and was standing with his hat on his hand, staring around the drawing room in open-mouthed admiration.

'Your hat, sir?' asked Jeremy, icily, quite unused to people who thought they were welcome to wander around his employer's house without being invited.

'Oh, sure, thanks,' said Jamie, quite oblivious, and handed it over. Jeremy flicked from it the tiniest speck of invisible dust, and carried it away.

Lucy stood up, and rushed towards him. Her hair was curled; she was wearing an exquisite dress of rust-coloured velvet, sewn with pearls. She took hold of his hands and said, breathlessly, 'Why didn't you wire? You could have wired! This is such a surprise!'

Jamie kissed her, and grinned. 'I didn't know I was coming till just about an hour before the train was due.'

'How're you doing, Jamie!' called Jack, from over by the massive marble fireplace. 'Good to see you, glad you could come! You're our first guest from Kansas, very first one!'

Jamie went over and shook his hand. He still couldn't stop himself from gazing around the room; at the arched and gilded ceiling, at the long drapes of pale-yellow velvet, at the three gilded chandeliers, at the mirrors and paintings and curvaceous French furniture.

'Some house,' he breathed. 'Never saw anything like it.'

'Electric light all through,' Jack told him. 'Got our own elevator, too.'

'How long are you here for?' Lucy asked. 'You are going to stay with us, aren't you?'

'I can only stay for a week,' said Jamie. 'I'm on my way to Washington. I'm attached to a law firm in Manhattan, Van Cortland & Paley – you know, doing some practical training. We're handling a land claim case against the Indians, and I have to check up on a whole lot of stuff at the Office of Indian Affairs. You know, land treaties and all that kind of thing.'

'So, they've finally got you doing some real work,' Jack remarked.

'Well, not really, sir,' said Jamie. 'I'm running errands, that's all.'

Jack nodded. 'You like the house? It's what they call a shat-oh. A Loo-wah shat-oh. Cost more'n three million dollars, and that's *excluding* the gold dinner-service. You ever eat with gold knives and forks? I mean, real gold knives and forks? You stay for supper tonight!'

Lucy said, 'I'm so pleased to see you. You look so well! And is that a moustache?'

Jamie sheepishly rubbed his upper lip. 'It could be. I guess it's still trying to make up its mind.'

Lucy hugged him and kissed him. 'You didn't *write!*' she protested.

'Write?' laughed Jamie. 'I haven't had time to eat, let alone write. But then neither did you write. Well – not that it mattered. I've been reading all about you in the newspapers. The *Kansas City Journal* always keeps us up to date on the doings on the Sunflower State's favourite daughter.'

'The banister-rails are plated in real silver,' Jack put in. 'Made in France, hand-made. Fifty-two thousand dollars, banister-rails alone.'

'I read about you tightrope-walking on somebody's tennis-net,' said Jamie. 'Was that really true?'

Lucy nodded, and smiled. 'It caused a terrible commotion! But I think they got over it. I was only showing-off.'

Jack said, 'How about some champagne? Jamie?'

'Well, sure, that'd be swell,' Jamie replied. 'But I don't want to make any kind of nuisance of myself.'

'You could never be a nuisance,' said Lucy. She couldn't believe how pleased she was to see him. 'Come and sit down. Where are your bags? You must come and stay here! We've got plenty of company rooms!'

'I'm booked in at the Metropolitan,' Jamie told her. 'Mr Van Cortland recommended it.'

Lucy wrinkled up her nose. 'When was the last time *he* stayed in New York? You can't stay at the Metropolitan! It's so – *urrgghh!* It's so down-at-heel!'

'It looked all right to me,' Jamie replied, a little defensively. 'Mind you – when you're used to a place like this –'

'Oh, I'm sorry,' said Lucy, reaching out and holding his hand. 'I didn't mean to be cruel. It's just that everybody in New York society is so worried about which places are fashionable and which places aren't! It's all they talk about! Things change so fast here! I mean that's why we've built our house way up here on the upper west side! People have built six-million dollar mansions on Fifth Avenue, and by the time they're finished the neighbourhood's gone to the dogs!'

'Kind of different from Oak City, then,' Jamie remarked.

Lucy looked at him closely and warmly. He was older, maybe a little tireder, but still very handsome – although handsome in a way that now seemed very Western and countrified. His suit was too tight across the shoulders and he wore boots instead of pumps and how *anybody* could walk around with a stringy necktie like that! She couldn't help noticing, too, how drawling his accent was. Every word seemed to drag on for ever. And Evelyn accused *her* of talking like Calamity Jane! Evelyn hadn't been having much luck in trying to train her to say 'fine' instead of 'faahn' and 'particular' instead of 'puhtickulluh', but Lucy had already managed to clip most of her vowels and sharpen most of her consonants, so that at least the Mrs Vanderbilts of this world didn't keep frowning at their friends and saying, 'Is that girl speaking Chinese?'

'You will stay, won't you?' asked Lucy. 'I'm dying to hear all of your news.'

'You're sure it's no trouble?' asked Jamie.

'Fourteen bedrooms, all going begging. Take your pick. I'll send a boy down to the Metropolitan to collect your bags.'

Jamie paused, and lowered his head; and then glanced across at Jack. But Jack was busy relighting himself a cigar now, and was out of earshot.

'I guess I should tell you that I purposely didn't write to you,' said Jamie.

Lucy hesitated, and then she said. 'You *purposely* didn't write? Why?'

'Well . . . look at us, Lucy. We could never be any kind of match for each other, now could we? The society princess and the hayseed lawyer? What could I ever hope to give to you now? A frame house in Manhattan, Kansas? A law business turning over three thousand dollars a year? You and I said goodbye to each other that day on the beach, in Los Angeles. You know that.'

He paused, and then smiled. 'I loved you once, Miss Darling, and I still love you just as much now. I've been thinking about you day and night, day and night, ever since you went away. I don't want you to feel obliged to have me stay here if you really don't want me to. But I don't want to have to sit this close to you and kiss you and hold your hand and pretend that it doesn't make my heart go bump and my stomach turn over, because it does; and I guess it always will, for ever and ever.'

'Oh, Jamie,' said Lucy. 'I love you, too. You know that.'

'Well,' he replied, 'there's love and there's love. I guess that you and I might have been married, if your Uncle Casper hadn't showed up. Everybody expected us to. But he did show up, didn't he, and maybe he saved the both of us from making a fool mistake.'

Lucy said, 'Oh, Jamie, it wouldn't have been a mistake. How can you say that?'

Jamie looked around the drawing room. 'It may not have been a mistake then, but *now* – well, just look at this place! I thought it was going to be grand, but I didn't have any idea. You've got to marry into society now, Lucy. You've got to marry into wealth. Some man who can walk into a place like this and not stand around like a Rocky Mountain trout with his mouth wide open.'

' Jamie –'

'Ssh,' he said, and raised his finger to his lips. 'I just wanted to be honest with you, that's all. I just wanted you to know where you stood.'

'I want you to stay,' she whispered.

'You can say it louder if you like.'

She grinned broadly, and threw her arms around his shoulders, and kissed him on the nose. 'I want you to stay! So there!'

Jack, puffing cigar-smoke, turned and grunted in amusement.

'There's something else,' said Jamie. 'I brought somebody with me.'

'Somebody from home? Who?'

Jack nodded. 'She's waiting outside. She wouldn't come in, not straight away. Not till I'd talked to you first.'

He gestured towards the doors. 'May I?'

Lucy watched him in pleased bewilderment as he crossed the drawing room, opened the doors, and disappeared out into the hallway. She heard him open the front doors; then heard him talking, although she couldn't make out who he was talking to. Then he returned; caught for a moment in the pearly October daylight; and he was ushering ahead of him the diminutive figure of Mrs Sweeney, the Skipping Widder, in a store-bought hat heaped up with artificial roses and swooping thrushes, and a worn but well-brushed fur-coat, and a duck's-head umbrella.

'Oh, Mrs Sweeney, you darling!' said Lucy, and hurried across the room to greet her. 'I can't believe that you're here!'

Beneath her fur-coat, Mrs Sweeney's ribs felt as fragile as a cat's; but she smiled so broadly that her eyes filled up with tears, and she held Lucy tight. 'I read all about you in the papers! How you walked along the tennis-net! And I said to myself, Molly you taught that girl to do that, and wasn't I proud! And when I heard that you were Belle of New York; well, I just had to come to see it for myself; I had to see you dance; and I had to see New York again, too, just once before I died. The varnish, the gaseliers, the young men like gods!'

'How did you get here?' asked Lucy. 'Poppa – look, it's Mrs Sweeney!'

Jack Darling had never liked Mrs Sweeney overmuch. Too fussy a customer, always complaining that he diluted his boot-polish with white spirits, and that he short-weighed his sugar. But she was Irish; and he had always had a soft spot for the Irish; and he knew how much she had delighted Lucy with her dancing-lessons.

'Well, well, Mrs Sweeney,' he said, waving his cigar at her. 'Fancy seeing you here.'

'Fancy seeing *you* here,' retorted Mrs Sweeney, looking querulously about her at the opulent drawing room. 'Jack Darling, the storekeeper. In a house like this! In New York!'

Jack clenched his cigar between his teeth and thrust his hands into his trouser pockets, and rocked back on his heels like a man with plenty to say if he had a mind to be sharp; but who had decided that there are times when it is better to say nothing, and this was one of them.

'Mind you,' said Mrs Sweeney, 'I wouldn't have known New York, the way it is now! All the railroads, and the cable-cars, and those buildings – you have to stand back and stretch your neck and you still can't see the top of them! And all those telephone wires, what a cat's cradle!'

'How long're you planning on staying, Mrs Sweeney?' asked Jack.

'Oh, not too long, don't you worry. Just long enough to look up some old acquaintances, and to dance, just once, if all my old dancing haunts haven't been torn down.'

Lucy said, 'There's a charity ball at the Waldorf tomorrow night, to raise money for the Henry Street Settlement. You can come along to that, if you'd care to. And you too, Jamie, I'd love it if you could come.'

'Don't you have an escort already?' asked Jamie. 'I've seen the society columns – "Miss Lightbulb," isn't it?'

'Oh, well, John was supposed to be taking me . . . John B. Harriot IV. But he won't mind if I tell him that you're escorting me instead. He's been dying to escort my friend Sylvia Park . . . not that he'll like her, once he gets to know her. She's so bossy with men, and John just hates to be bossed!'

Jamie smiled at her. 'You haven't changed, have you?' he told her.

She lowered her eyes. Her blue, blue eyes. 'I wish I could say that was true.'

That evening, Jamie and Mrs Sweeney were moved into the

Darling mansion; and they dined that evening on scrod and spit-roasted quail, sitting yards away from each other around a huge circular cherrywood table that they had imported from England, in what Jack loved to call 'the *cosy* dining room', as opposed to the 'grand dining room'.

The table was polished like a black pool. It reflected the electric chandelier and the whiteness of Lucy's face. She wore an off-the-shoulder evening gown of ice-pink silk, and a necklace of white diamonds, with diamond earrings to match. Jamie couldn't take his eyes off her.

'How are things in Oak City?' asked Jack, as Jeremy poured him another glass of champagne, the Dry Royal de Saint Marceaux, very popular in New York just then. 'I still miss it sometimes, you know; the old days around the stove.'

'Money always buys a man rose-tinted eyeglasses,' retorted Mrs Sweeney. She was dressed in black, as usual, with her hair scraped back and fastened with combs. 'Life's harder than ever. Samuel Blankenship died this summer; and Osage Pete's so blind now that he can scarcely find his way around.'

'Old Samuel Blankenship gone?' asked Jack, with distress. 'How come nobody wrote me?'

'What's the passing of some no-account railroad engineer, way out in the back-end of Kansas, to the sixteenth richest man in New York?' Mrs Sweeney taunted him. Lucy couldn't think why she was being so cutting.

'Samuel Blankenship wasn't no-account,' said Jack. 'He was my friend.'

'Oh, yes? How much of a friend? Soon as you got your claws on your money, you absconded, didn't you, Jack Darling, and never came back to visit him? And not a penny of all of your riches ever did anything for Oak City.'

'You listen here, I wrote off all my credit,' Jack retorted. 'There were folks in Oak City owed me hundreds. I wrote off fifteen hundred bucks' worth of clackers alone.'

'How much did you say them silver-plated banisters cost you?' said Mrs Sweeney. She lifted her solid gold fish-fork. 'And look at this here utensil. This here utensil would keep an Oak City family in pork and navy beans for an age of years.'

Lucy could see that her father was badly stung by Mrs Sweeney's gibes. She said, 'Poppa ... you did what you could. You can't support the whole world.'

But Jack asked Mrs Sweeney, 'Is that all folks've got for me now, back in Oak City? The black word? Do you say that I was tight? Do you think that I could have done anything at all to ease your burden? You listen to me, Mrs Sweeney, the only thing that could ever ease their burden is to bring back the cattle-drives, and you and me know that the cattle-drives are history, and never coming back.'

'They call you tight, yes,' said Mrs Sweeney. 'They say that you've forgotten them, and turned your back. Things are pretty bad these days, they've had the choleric fever, too.'

Jamie said, 'Mrs Sweeney ... let's change the subject, shall we? We're guests here, at Mr Darling's house, and we owe him our courtesy, at the very least.'

But Jack jabbed his finger at Mrs Sweeney and snapped, 'We'll see who's tight. You just wait, Molly Sweeney. We'll see who's tight.'

With that, he thrust back his chair, stood up, tugged the napkin out of his collar, and stalked out of the dining room.

There was a long, awkward silence. Then Mrs Sweeney turned sheepishly to Lucy and said, 'I'm sorry, Lucy. I guess I made a bad bust, talking like that to your pa. It's just that sitting here, eating with golden forks and drinking out of crystal glasses ... well, I can't help thinking of all the downright poorness back in Kansas – all the children dressed in flour-sacks, and the workworn wives, and your poppa thinking he's so all-fired much.'

Lucy said, softly, 'Poppa gave everything to Oak City,

Mrs Sweeney. His whole life; and my momma, too. Don't be too hard on him now. The money came by chance. He didn't ask for it, and to begin with, he didn't even want it. It may not last for ever, either. The oil-wells could run dry one day. So don't begrudge him this.'

'I'm sorry,' Mrs Sweeney repeated. 'But it's such a hard world; and here's the rich living like there's no poor folks at-all, like it's sunshine and money for everybody. And some of them rich folks not such good folks, neither.'

Lucy said, 'It's not all sunshine, Mrs Sweeney; even for the rich. Money never eased anybody's heartache.'

She glanced at Jamie. He didn't smile at her, but he continued to watch her with the wary intentness of a man who doesn't dare to think that he might be loved in return.

4

When Jamie saw Lucy rustling down the stairs in her dark crimson taffeta ballgown, he didn't say anything, but took one or two steps back, plainly impressed, and glanced at Mrs Sweeney, his eyes alive. Lucy's gown was deeply décolleté, in the latest fashion, and her white skin was decorated with a blood-black necklace of Czechoslovakian garnets.

'Well, there's the magical picture, isn't she?' said Mrs Sweeney, and she was crackling with pride, almost as if Lucy were her own daughter. 'And just to think that it was me what taught her to cut the pigeon wing.' – by which she meant elegant dancing. 'I looked just like that myself, once upon a time. Just like that! Thinner, maybe.'

Jamie held out his hand as Lucy crossed the hallway. 'You look simply fine,' he told her.

She curtseyed. 'You look very fine yourself, sir,' she replied. Jamie was wearing a high starched collar, and a new black tailcoat which Lucy had ordered for him from Woodbury's and which had arrived that morning accompanied by two tailors in case it required alteration.

Lucy thought Jamie looked distinctly dashing. In fact, now that he was dressed formally, the way that Henry Carson had always been dressed, she began to realize what a strong, attractive young man he really was. His tailcoat had given him unexpected style, and a look of masculine authority, in spite of his youthfulness, and his slow country drawl.

'We'd better be going,' said Lucy. 'Jeremy! Is the brougham ready? And where's poppa?'

'The brougham is waiting without, Miss Lucy,' Jeremy replied, from his position by the door. 'Your father will be down directly.'

'I hope he's still not sulking over what I said to him yesterday,' said Mrs Sweeney. 'I think a man should take his criticism, don't you think so? square on the chin. He needs a dance or two, that's what he needs. He needs some fun!'

But Jack — with the ludicrous promptness of a minor actor who has been waiting for his cue — appeared at that very instant at the top of the staircase. He took two or three steps, and then stopped. His face was as pink as anchovy sauce, and he was swaying very slightly from side to side, as if he were trying to keep his balance in a streetcar.

'I suppose you're waiting for me,' he announced. 'I suppose you're waiting for the tightwad of Oak City, Kansas, the man who turned his back on his needy friends.'

Lucy took two or three steps back up the staircase. 'Poppa, you've been drinking,' she said, resentfully.

Jack stared at her. 'Well?' he demanded. 'I'm in the best of spirits, the very best! Nothing like a few glasses of agurforty to make a man feel on top of the world! There you are, Molly Sweeney! Are you going to dance for me tonight? Are you going to show me what you're made of?'

'If he isn't fighting drunk!' whispered Mrs Sweeney; half in disgust and half in awe.

'Poppa,' said Lucy, gathering up her skirts and hurrying up the stairs to meet him halfway. 'Poppa, you can't go the ball like this. Everybody's going to be there! Mrs Vanderbilt! Even Mrs Astor. And Mr McKinley; and Mr Hanna, too. Poppa, *please*!'

Jack stopped and stared at her as if he didn't recognize her. 'I'm feeling *wonderful*,' he told her, confidentially, leaning forward so that she could smell the whisky on his breath. He'd been drinking Tightropes; but his own particular mix, which was more than half whisky and less than half champagne. 'Besides,' he whispered, 'Who are you to tell me where I should go, and when? Hm? You're not even my –'

Before he could say any more, Lucy snatched his sleeve, and braved the whisky fumes to whisper closely and directly into his face. 'Poppa, we're in society now! We've spent months and months, haven't we, making new friends, trying to learn how to do things properly, trying to give ourselves some standing. This is New York, poppa, not Kansas! If you go out drunk tonight, what will everybody *say*? We'll be cut by everybody, we'll never live it down!'

Jack wrinkled his mouth in disdain. 'Are these society folks such simlin-heads they never saw a fellow cheerful before?'

'Of course not, poppa, but this is a charity ball. And you're not cheerful, you're falling-down drunk. You don't go falling-down drunk to a charity ball!'

Jack stood up straight and stiff. He looked down at the hallway below, and pointed a finger at Mrs Sweeney. 'That woman accuses me of downright meanness. That woman accuses me of showing my back to my friends. Samuel Blankenship died because of me, that's what she said, and Oak City was ravaged by poorness, and what she said was, I never even cared.'

'Holy Godfrey's tonic, Jack Darling! I never said nothing of the sort!' Mrs Sweeney protested.

But Jack turned back to Lucy and now there were tears in his eyes. 'What have I done?' he sniffled. 'Look at this house! Look at me! Look at you! Your poor mother! What have I done?'

'Poppa, you'd better off in bed,' Lucy told him. 'Please – don't try to come tonight, you're far too upset. I'll find some dancing-partners for Mrs Sweeney.'

Jack stared at her. 'Mean, that's what she said! Mean, and didn't care!'

'Poppa –' said Lucy, reaching out for him.

He twisted himself away from her. 'Not you! Not you, too! I've had all the goddamned sympathy that any one man can stand! Even Casper felt sorry for me, and who can blame him? A faithless wife, no child of my own, a store that was nothing but grind and punishment! And now this! A fortune that I never deserved, heaped on top of me like – like saddlebags full o' rocks, heaped on top of a mule. It weighs me down, Lucy, it weighs me down! and I don't have the strength to get up again.'

Lucy made one more effort to take hold of his arm, but he wrenched it away, breaking one of her fingernails. 'Now don't you touch me,' he warned her, 'because you're no blood-relative of mine. You're anybody's child.'

Lucy felt stingingly hurt, as if she had smashed through a silverbacked mirror, and been sliced clean through to the bone. She turned to Jamie in distress. But Jamie clearly didn't understand what Jack was raving about, because he frowned, and mouthed, '*what*??' and shook his head.

It was Mrs Sweeney, mysteriously, who calmed Jack down. She came up the stairs neat-footed in her mourning-gown of stiffened black silk, and stood just two steps below him, composed, a little irritated, but contrite, too. 'Jack Darling,' she said, all Kansas-genteel. 'I spoke out of place. I'm sorry, that's what I've got to tell you, an awfully lot.'

'I never forgot them, none of them,' Jack insisted. He didn't even appear to have heard what Mrs Sweeney had said. 'Not Samuel, not Henry, not Osage Pete. I never forget the Lapps or the Foresters, nor yet the van Houtens.' He slowly tapped his right temple with his finger again and again, like a blind man determined to find a bellpush.

'They're all in here, all pictured in my mind's eye, every single one of them, forever and ever.'

Mrs Sweeney crooked her elbow as an invitation for him to link his arm through hers. 'Come on, Jack Darling,' she coaxed him. 'Some of that cold night air will fresh you up; that and some dancing. Look at me now, all dyked up in my brand-fired new dress! You can't let me step out without squiring me.'

'I never forgot none of them,' Jack repeated. 'Do you hear me? Do you hear what I say? And I was never untrue to Lucy's mother, not once, not ever.'

'Well, we hear what you say,' cooed Mrs Sweeney, 'but you just listen to this.' She beckoned him closer, and caught hold of his head, and lowered his ear close up to her mouth. She hesitated for a moment, but then she whispered something that only he could hear.

Whatever she said, the effect on Jack was instantaneous and extraordinary. He stood up straight, and stared first at Lucy, and then at Jamie, and all the alcoholic flush drained from his face.

'Poppa?' asked Lucy.

But Mrs Sweeney beckoned him yet again, and whispered something else; and Jack nodded.

'Poppa?' Lucy repeated.

'All in good time,' said Mrs Sweeney. 'Your poppa's just fine, now, aren't you, Jack? Ready for skipping?'

Mrs Sweeney guided Jack down to the hallway, where Jeremy was waiting to drape his evening-cloak around his shoulder. Jamie held out his hand for Lucy, and she could see that his face was congested with questions. *Anybody's child? What did that mean?* But Lucy was just as perplexed by what had happened as he was.

★

They drove to the Waldorf in the Darlings' high-varnished maroon brougham. The interior smelled suffocatingly of leather and perfume. As they passed one streetlamp after another, and the brougham's interior was intermittently lit by geometric patterns of gaslight, Lucy's face appeared and disappeared under the brim of her grey-beribboned evening hat. All the same Jamie kept staring at her from the opposite seat, his opera-hat perched in his lap.

Mrs Sweeney kept up a tireless excited commentary on everything she saw.

'Look at this, will you!' she exclaimed, as they turned south by the Grand Army Plaza. 'You should have seen it when I was here, when I was a girl! This was all garbage dumps, and quarries, and stockyards, with scarcely a house in sight, and it wasn't paved at all. Now look at all these buildings! It's a miracle!'

'All hotels here,' Jack told her, leaning so close to the brougham's window that his breath fogged the glass. 'The Savoy, the New Netherland, the Plaza. All hotels.'

But soon they were passing the huge mansions of the Vanderbilts; the house built by Cornelius Vanderbilt II on the entire blockfront between 58th and 57th Streets; the ravishing Gothic Revival house built by his brother William Kissam Vanderbilt on 52nd Street; and the two Renaissance-style houses built by their father William Henry Vanderbilt on 52nd and 51st Streets, one for himself and one for his daughters.

'The cost!' Mrs Sweeney exclaimed. 'What must these houses cost?'

In a glum voice, Jack told her, 'A. T. Stewart spent four million, so the yellow papers say; and the Vanderbilts spent fifteen million between them. The Vanderbilts could buy me and sell me twenty times in one day. And so could most of them, Astor and Gould and Carnegie. I'm small fry. You should tell them that, back in Oak City, those that give me the black word.'

Mrs Sweeney leaned across and touched Jack's hand. 'I've said I'm sorry, Jack Darling; and I've told you what you ought to know; so come along now. There's no call for making too much of it.'

Lucy said boldly to Jamie, 'You're staring.'

As they passed the next streetlamp, she could see that her challenge had made him blush. 'I'm sorry,' he said. 'I didn't mean to. But under that hat, I can scarcely see you.'

Lucy smiled. 'What were you thinking about?'

'I was thinking about you.'

'Oh, go on, tell the truth, you were thinking about business. You were thinking about how to run the Indians off the prairies, and tarts.'

'Torts,' he corrected her, laughing. 'But, no, I wasn't thinking about business. I was really truly thinking about you. You haven't changed, you know. Well, you *have,* your manners have changed, you're the blue hen's chicken these days. But you're still Lucy Darling, aren't you? Still the dreamer. I was thinking to myself, can you still see the clouds, for all of these tall buildings? Do they look like ships, and castles, and islands?'

'You're embarrassing me,' she told him; and he was, especially when Mrs Sweeney glanced across at her.

Jack coughed thickly, and said, 'There's rich, you see, and there's rich. There's some so rich they can't even count it, and they're the tightest, but who ever hears the black word about them?'

He paused, and then added, 'I can see it, you know. Still see it. The store, and the stove, and my Anna reaching up for the candy-jars.'

He frowned at Mrs Sweeney and asked her fiercely, 'Where did it *go*? Where did all of it *go*?'

Mrs Sweeney pursed her lips. 'Back in time, Jack Darling, where Sean lives now; and Samuel Blankenship, too; and all of those who went before.'

Without warning, Jack began to sob. He beat his fists on

his knees, and the tears coursed freely down his cheeks. Mrs Sweeney tried to shush him, but he wouldn't be shushed. Jamie watched him helplessly. What can you do for a man whose whole life has turned out to be nothing but bitterness and lost opportunities?

But Lucy put her arm around him and held him close. 'Poppa, they're jealous, that's all. Folks are always jealous when you have good luck. They don't mean you any harm, not really. If you went back to Oak City tomorrow, they'd welcome you just like always. Forgive them, poppa. That's all you have to do.'

'Wise words for such a young head,' said Mrs Sweeney. 'Forgive them, that's right; and forgive me, too, Jack Darling. And most of all, forgive yourself. Come along, tonight's for dancing!'

Jack wiped his eyes with his handkerchief, and blew his nose.

'Smile,' Lucy ordered him.

Jack gave her a grin as tight as a tourniquet.

'That'll do for now,' said Lucy, although when he stopped grinning, his eyes still flew from side to side, and his fingers pattered impatiently on the brim of his hat.

They pattered like hail on the roof of the store painted stray-dog yellow, on the very brink of the world.

Uneasily, Jamie said, 'Well, you know what it says in the Bible. Matthew, chapter nineteen. "It is easier for a camel to go through the eye of a needle, than for a rich man to enter the kingdom of God."'

They were waltzing in the Waldorf ballroom, under sparkling electric chandeliers; with more than three hundred other waltzers. The music and the laughter and the roar of chopped-up conversation made it almost impossible for Lucy to hear what Jamie was saying. The orchestra played *Love's Dreamland* and *Spring And Love*.

Lucy had already met Evelyn Scott and several of her friends; and been introduced to Mrs Astor and the John

Pierpont Morgans (she had met Jane before, and adored her). She had danced a polka with James Gore King, who had tramped blithely on her maroon velvet slippers. She felt aerated tonight, as if she *ought* to be enjoying herself, but Jack's drunkenness had unsettled her, and made her unpleasantly panicky. Much to Jamie's irritation, she kept twisting her head around to look for him. She hadn't seen him so drunk since her mother had died; nor behaving so oddly. What on earth had Mrs Sweeney whispered to him? She was terrified that he was going to do something stupid. He had always been a man of charity and deep humility, but lately Lucy had been able to see that he was charitable and humble only because he seemed to believe (quite falsely) that he had committed the most unforgivable wrongs, and deserved God's punishment. Lucy's greatest fear was that tonight he might feel that he deserved even greater punishment than ever, and humiliate himself beyond redemption.

If he humiliated himself, he would humiliate her, too; and that would jeopardize her tenuous new-found place in New York society. 'Sweet girl,' Mrs Astor had called her. But sweetness would not be enough to save her from the social consequences of having a drunk and publicly-embarrassing father.

'Can you see poppa anyplace?' she asked Jamie, worriedly.

Jamie looked over the heads of the waltzers. After all, he was six-foot-two 'above snakes', as Mrs Sweeney would have put it. 'Can't see him,' he said, after a lengthy inspection. 'Maybe he's gone for something to eat. Or something to drink, more like.'

Lucy said, 'I'd better look for him. He shouldn't have come tonight. I wish Mrs Sweeney hadn't persuaded him.'

'I can see Mrs Sweeney,' said Jamie. 'Just take a look at her! Talk about the Skipping Widder! Reckon she thinks she's still no more'n seventeen years old!'

Sure enough, Mrs Sweeney twinkled past them in the arms of Henry Sturgis Grew, the Boston millionaire, her eyes ecstatically closed, humming as she danced.

'Mrs Sweeney!' Lucy called her, but Mrs Sweeney was obviously dreaming of another time, and didn't hear her.

'Don't you go waking her up, now!' Mr Grew admonished Lucy, with a smile. 'I've never danced this good before! She tells me she walks the high-wire, too!'

'Once upon a time,' said Lucy, just as Mrs Sweeney mischievously opened her eyes.

Jamie and Lucy danced close to a prickly-moustached young man with spectacles, and a plainish girl with blonde ringlets and a big nose. The prickly-moustached young man called out, 'G'd evening, Miss Darling!' and out of courtesy, Jamie asked him, 'How're things?'

'That was Teddy Roosevelt, with Hester French,' Lucy explained, as they danced away. 'Teddy's something to do with the Navy. Very up-and-coming, although some people call him Moses, because he's always so righteous. Hester's one of those silly girls who dances with every young man who's up-and-coming, and then whines about them behind their backs, because none of them ever asks her to marry them.'

Jamie said, 'Not too much different from any society anywhere. What about you?'

'What about me?'

'Do you think you'll ever be married?'

'Nobody's asked me yet. Nobody that I *want* to marry, anyway.'

'What about your famous Englishman? Your Member of Parliament?'

Lucy gave him a scarcely imperceptible shrug of her bare white shoulders and looked away. She didn't know when she had stopped believing that Henry would ever write to her; but she had. All the same, she found it difficult to let his memory go. It was a little like taking a photograph out of her purse again and again, with the intention of throwing it away; but always hesitating, and putting it back.

'I'm still young,' she replied.

The orchestra finished the waltz; and everybody clapped and cried, 'Bravo!' so that whatever Jamie said next was swallowed by the noise.

'I'd love a glass of punch!' said Lucy, and Jamie steered her by the elbow to the side of the ballroom floor. Evelyn was there, in a pretty green gown tied with bows, in the company of a rigid young man who looked as if he didn't dare smile in case it compromised his perfect Grecian profile.

'Wait here, and I'll fetch us some punch,' said Jamie.

'What an *adorable* boy!' Evelyn exclaimed, after Jamie had shouldered his way through the crowd. 'But did I detect just a *soupçon de* Kansas accent?'

'He's just a friend from back home,' said Lucy.

'Well, they certainly grow them a generous size, "back home",' Evelyn observed, with an exaggerated relish that was obviously calculated to irritate her escort. Her escort, however, continued to stare into the middle–distance as if he were thinking about himself and his profile and nothing else.

'This is Ronald Prout,' Evelyn explained, raising her eyebrows to imply that Ronald wasn't up to much. 'Just another Gas House boy.' The Gas House was the most socially notable of all the Harvard 'final clubs' – even more prestigious than the Porcellian or the AD.

Ronald focused his bright grey eyes for a moment, and remarked drily, 'Kansas? Isn't that someplace out past 59th Street?'

Lucy was just about to ask Evelyn about next week's ball at the Holland House, when a strange commotion rippled through the crowd, the way that storms used to ripple through the Kansas grass. Heads began to turn towards the archway which led to the hotel lobby. A man's voice shouted, 'Don't touch her! Don't touch her!' and then another man's voice called, 'Stand away! Don't stand underneath!'

A young man with brilliantined hair came pushing his way across the ballroom. 'What's happening?' Lucy asked him.

'Great fun and games!' the young man replied. 'An old lady's balancing on the balustrade! Old enough to be my grandmama!'

Lucy clasped her hand over her mouth. *Oh God, Mrs Sweeney! It had to be!*

Evelyn frowned, 'Lucy? What's going on? Lucy!'

But without a word, Lucy elbowed her way through the excited throng of dancers, through the archway, and into the Waldorf's grandiose marbled lobby. As she did so, several of the women screamed, and the men let out a great low cry of alarm, like a mighty herd of beef on the hoof.

'Come down!' one of the men cried out. 'For the love of God, madam, come down!'

Henry Sturgis Grew was standing in front of the crowd, his arms outspread in perplexity. 'She said, "I'll show you!" That's what she said! "I'll show you!" And the next thing I knew, she was calling, and there she was, up on the rail!'

Lucy looked up, and felt a chilly prickling of fear all the way down her back. Mrs Sweeney was up on the marble balustrade of the hotel's mezzanine floor, her black widow's skirts raised up in one hand, balancing one black evening-slipper in front of the other. She was calmly smiling; but the look in her eyes was very far away. It was the look of a woman who has forgotten where she is, and whom the passing years have already robbed of almost everything.

There were crowds beneath her, in the lobby, and crowds all the way up the curving stairs, but those on the mezzanine kept well back, for fear of putting her off her balance. The lobby was thick with fear and cigar-smoke and expensive French perfume, and diamonds flashed everywhere, like fireflies.

'Has somebody sent for the engine company?' bellowed the Waldorf's portly manager. 'Ned! Bring blankets! If she falls, we might be able to catch her!'

Above the moans and the screams, Lucy could hear that Mrs Sweeney was singing to herself, high-pitched, off-key, a tremulous little song that must have dated back to her years with Forepaugh and Sells.

'Though in this sil-ly farce of love,
You've often tried to play . . .'

Lucy, tight-lipped, her heart pounding, pushed her way through to the foot of the stairs. When a large woman in a blue velvet gown turned to protest, her white breasts shivering like blancmanges, Lucy said, 'She's a friend, please, I know her. Please let me through!'

Halfway up the stairs, she called out, 'Mrs Sweeney! Mrs Sweeney!' but the crowd was too clamorous for Mrs Sweeney to hear; and even if she had, she probably wouldn't have taken any notice. She kept on balancing along the banister, thirty feet above the marble floor, one foot hesitantly in front of the other, and she was somewhere else altogether, in another time, walking the slack-wire in Omaha, perhaps, or Valley Falls, or Sutro, while upturned faces watched her in awe.

'Just rest assured that you'll not live . . .
To see your wed-ding day!'

She reached the end of the banister, hesitated, and swayed. The women screamed again, and the screaming at last seemed to penetrate Mrs Sweeney's fantasy, because she frowned down at the crowd below her through her glinting spectacles, and then she vaguely smiled.

'Mrs Sweeney!' called Lucy, thrusting her way up the stairs. 'Mrs Sweeney!'

It was then, right behind her, that she heard Jack bellowing, 'Molly! Molly Sweeney! You come down from there, you damp raddled old calico! What in hell do you think you're doing?'

Jack came plunging through the crowd, red-faced, bung-eyed, with the thrashing arm-movements of a man swimming to shore. 'Who are you shoving, sir?' one elderly man protested; but Jack lurched and staggered and stared at him so madly that the elderly man briskly turned away, pretending that he hadn't said anything at all.

'Molly Sweeney, you Goddamned biscuit-eater!' he raged. 'You come down from there right now!'

Although he had managed to remember the polite euphemism for 'bitch,' he was even drunker than before. He must have spent most of the evening in the bar, downing Tightropes. As he pushed Lucy, he glared at her, too, and snorted, and sniffed, and fumed, 'Your mother, by God,' whatever that meant. His face was smothered with sweat, and his pomaded hair was sticking up on end. Whisky fumes flowed after him like an invisible evening-cloak.

'Poppa, don't!' Lucy begged him. 'Poppa, if you distract her – if you surprise her – she'll fall!'

As it was, Mrs Sweeney was already standing sideways on the balustrade, her arms wide, right on the very brink of losing her balance. But she was still singing, in breathless little gasps, and still smiling.

'Just rest assured –'

'Molly Sweeney!' screamed Jack, as he reached the top of the stairs. Everybody around him stepped back.

'Is he a lunatic?' a plump elderly woman asked, inspecting Jack through lorgnettes.

'Drunk, more like,' her companion remarked.

'More like both, drunk, and a lunatic,' a tall ginger-haired girl put in.

Lucy turned around. 'He's my father,' she declared, bravely.

'Oh *dear*,' said the plump woman, and nudged her companion with her elbow. Mrs Sweeney swayed from side to

201

side, and at last managed to turn right around, so that she could balance her way back along the balustrade towards the stairs. She looked white-faced now, white as linen, and she was biting her lower lip in intense concentration.

'That you'll not live –'

Jack shuffled towards her. His shirt-tail was hanging out, and he had lost one of his collar studs.

'Molly, Molly, Molly,' he said, much more quietly now. 'If this is a punishment, Molly, I'm not going to take it. Is this the way you get your own back on me? Is this it?'

Mrs Sweeney didn't even glance at him, but came teetering towards him step by anxiously-adjusted step, her back straight, her arms outstretched, with a terrible elegance that somehow made her performance all the more frightening.

Right foot forward, poise on the toes, carefully place the weight on the arch. Pause, balance; then left foot forward, poise on the toes.

She wasn't doing it to punish Jack, Lucy knew that. She had heard Mrs Sweeney talk too often about 'my sparkling days, when everybody flocked to see me'. She was thinking of herself and nobody else. 'See Nile demencher,' that's what Doctor Cooper would have called it; the same way he called cholera morbus, the 'coloured marbles'. An old woman's sparkling days revived, as if all those years had never passed.

Mrs Sweeney stopped, and then hop-staggered one more step.

'To see –' she gasped, breathlessly. The crowd below her shrank farther back. Over by the elevators, on the opposite side of the lobby, two bellmen were struggling to drag blankets and pillows out of one of the elevator cars, anything to break Mrs Sweeney's fall, if she should fall.

'Molly,' said Jack, shuffling nearer and nearer, both hands outstretched, quivering. 'I was never such a bad man, Molly,

you know that. I've been wrong, Molly, I admit it. I had
my difficult times, that was for sure. And you're right to
punish me for it. But not this way, Molly. Come down,
Molly, I'll dance with you now.'

'— your —'

Mrs Sweeney smiled. She lowered her arms stiffly by her
sides. She looked at Jack for the first time, really *looked* at
him, really saw him, and the expression on her face was
exalted, like no human expression that Lucy had ever seen
before, only in paintings of saints and Jesus, with eyes that
followed you with pious regret wherever you went.

'— wedding —'

She toppled sideways. The crowd screamed; then instantly
stopped screaming. My God, she was still smiling as she fell!
Farewell, Forepaugh! Farewell, Sells! What a time to plum-
met, at the crescendo of her girlish dream. Farewell, all you
uplifted faces, all you laughing, glowing admirers!

But Jack covered the ten feet between them with two
extraordinary lopes, and lunged out across the balustrade, and
caught her around the waist, far too late, and the two of them
fell together, clinging tight. The crowd remained silent: so that
when they dropped into the outstretched blanket and then hit
the marble floor beneath, everybody heard the crack of Mrs
Sweeney's back as clear as a snapped-in-half walking-stick.

Now there were shrieks, now there was chaos. Arms
flung up. Women fainted on all sides, dropped like shot
cattle, and the crowd on the stairs swayed dangerously.
Lucy, dumb with panic, pushed her way back down to the
lobby, and in between the ramparts of heaving shoulders.

She found her way blocked by the broad unyielding back
of the Waldorf's manager. 'Get back!' he was bellowing.
'Give them air, will you, give them air!'

Lucy tried to wriggle her way past him, but he reached around behind his back and shoved her away.

'He's my father!' she screamed, pummelling his tight-shouldered frock-coat with her fists. 'He's my father!'

The manager stepped back, crushing the toes of a young girl in orange velvet, who was whimpering, 'Let me see! Let me see! I never saw anybody dead before!' He laid his arm around Lucy's shoulders, and said, 'I'm sorry, ma'am. You'd best think of saying goodbyes. It looks like he's broken his neck.'

Jack and Mrs Sweeney were lying side by side, Mrs Sweeney on her back, Jack face down. The fawn blanket had become tangled around them so that they looked as if they had restlessly slept together on the lobby floor. Mrs Sweeney's bleached green eyes were wide open, her spectacles lay broken on the floor beside her. She was staring sideways at Lucy with a quizzical smile on her face, as if she were asking, *What am I doing here, Lucy? I should be dancing.* There was no blood; no sign that she was dead except that she didn't blink, not once, and her black widow's dress had collapsed around her like a smashed umbrella.

Jack was quivering violently. His face was pressed against the floor, so that only his right eye was visible. The pupil darted desperately from side to side.

Lucy knelt beside him, and gently touched his hair. 'Poppa . . . oh, poppa, it's Lucy.' Tears poured down her cheeks, and sparkled as brightly as any diamond necklace. The women in their silk and velvet ballgowns stood around her and watched her in horrified fascination. 'Poppa, please speak to me. Please say something.'

He tried to look at her, but he couldn't seem to focus. 'Lucy . . .' he slurred, his eye wandering. 'What's happened to me, my darling? Am I dying, or am I dead?'

'No, poppa,' she told him. 'Everything's going to be fine. You've hurt your neck, that's all. They've sent for a doctor.'

'What about Molly?' he asked her. 'Is Molly hurt, too?'

Lucy glanced quickly at Mrs Sweeney's collapsed and angular body; at her fixed green eyes. A moment ago, Mrs Sweeney had looked as if she were sleeping, but still alive. Now death had claimed her completely, and she had stiffened like a waxwork.

Lucy wondered for a moment if she ought to tell Jack that Mrs Sweeney was still alive; that he hadn't broken his neck for nothing. But she couldn't lie to him, not now. She stroked his cold sweaty forehead two or three times, and then she shook her head.

'She's dead, poppa.'

His single eye stared without compassion at the floor. 'Dead? Well, she probably deserved it. You can't say that I didn't do my very best to save her, now can you?'

'She never blamed you, poppa.'

Jack said nothing for a very long time. Only his quivering reassured Lucy that he wasn't dead. At last, he hacked up a little mucus, marbled with blood; and then he said, 'I never knew she still felt so bad about me. I never knew.'

It was then, kneeling beside the man who had raised her, but who had never been her father, that Lucy understood for the first time that men and women know nothing of each other's ambitions, and nothing of each other's fears.

She looked up, and Jamie was standing close beside her. 'Lucy?' She lifted her hand, and he took it. 'The doctor's here,' he told her. He sounded as if he were speaking inside a belljar.

'Is he going to die?' asked Lucy.

The doctor sported white muttonchop whiskers and a gravy-stained cherry-red vest, and a slack brown bag, which he dragged behind him like a somnolent spaniel.

He cleared his throat, and looked around, as if he couldn't decide where Lucy's voice had come from.

'Die? Die? Good God, no. None of my patients ever die.'

He knelt beside Jack, and asked loudly, 'How're you feeling, old man?'

'Are you a doctor?' Jack retorted.

'Sure I'm a doctor.'

Jack coughed up more phlegm. 'I feel like I'm going, doctor.'

'Poppa!' Lucy pleaded.

'Can't help it,' Jack told her. 'It's dark and I'm cold and your momma's calling.'

The doctor opened up his bag and rummaged around. 'You die on me, friend, in front of all of these people, I'm going to kick your back end from here to eternity.'

'Can't help it,' Jack whispered. His quivering became more convulsive.

'He's not going to die,' the doctor said, confidently, gently squeezing Jack's neck. 'Can you feel that, friend? How does that feel?'

'Hurts,' Jack told him.

The doctor lifted Jack's tailcoat, tore open the peach silk backing of his fancy vest, and then tugged his shirt out of his pants, to expose his bare back. He looked around at the silent assembly of richly-dressed onlookers. 'Anybody lend me a brooch, or a hatpin?'

Without hesitation, Mrs Grew unfastened a diamond and emerald star that must have cost more than two hundred thousand dollars, and handed it over. The doctor opened it up and pricked Jack's shoulders with its pin, deeply enough to draw blood.

'How about that? You feel that?' the doctor demanded.

Jack said, 'What? Feel what?'

The doctor prodded the back of Jack's hands. 'How about that? You feel that?'

'I don't know what you're talking about. I don't feel nothing.'

The doctor stood up, sniffed, and handed Mrs Grew's brooch back. 'Obliged, ma'am,' he said, taking out a large soiled handkerchief and noisily blowing his nose.

'Well?' asked Lucy. 'Is he going to live?'

'Depends what you mean by "live", my dear. He aint a-going to die, if that's what you mean. God don't want him yet. But he aint never a-going to walk no more, nor move a solitary muscle below his chin.'

'You mean he's paralysed?' asked Lucy. Her head felt empty and echoing, as if she were going to faint.

'Is he rich?' the doctor replied. 'I suppose he must be, if he's here.'

Jamie had pushed his way forward, and now he took hold of Lucy's arm. 'He's rich all right,' Jamie told him. 'Jack Darling, the oil millionaire.'

'Well, that's going to help,' said the doctor, closing his bag.

Lucy said, with a surge of hope, 'Is there somebody you know who could give him his feeling back?'

'Oh, no, no, no!' the doctor told her. 'Nothing like that. Once your neck's broke, your neck's broke. Can't be undone. Just like bashing your brains out, can't scoop them back in again. But least, you see, he can pay for nursemaids, to feed him and wash him and generally take care of him. He's going to be just like a baby, for the rest of his natural life, but there's a bright side to it, seeing he's rich. Least he's going to be a *pampered* baby.'

Outside, a thin glittering drizzle had started to sift through the gaslit night. Crowds had gathered on the sidewalk outside the hotel, and Fifth Avenue was clogged with carriages as the guests called for their coachmen and went home early. Whistles blew, policemen shouted, people jostled and collided. Inside the hotel, on the floor, Jack's head was lifted a little by two bellmen, so that he could take a sip of brandy, as if he wasn't drunk enough already, and then lifted on to a stretcher, still face downward, and taken by ambulance to Bellevue Hospital. Mrs Sweeney was covered by a blanket and left on a table at the side of the lobby, her black dancing-slippers at ten to two. Eventually two painfully thin young policemen arrived, to carry her off to the morgue.

Lucy sat on a gilded bentwood chair, her face as transparently pale as a fairy queen, her shoulders draped in a borrowed ermine wrap. She had insisted on staying at the Waldorf until she had seen Jack carried away; but a little after ten o'clock she allowed Jamie and Evelyn to take her home.

On the way back towards Central Park, she sat in the most shadowy corner of the brougham, saying nothing. She felt exhausted, as if she scarcely had the strength left to walk up the steps to the house, and she felt guilty, too – guiltier than anybody would ever be able to understand. She felt as if every single event that had led to Mrs Sweeney's death and to Jack Darling's injury had been her doing – that it had been her vanity and her wilfulness and her immorality that had caused them both, at last, to topple from that balustrade.

If she hadn't bargained her lost virginity with Uncle Casper, she would never have become so rich. Jack would still be poor, and hard-worked, but at least he would be whole. Mrs Sweeney would never have relived her long-lost dreams of dancing in New York, but at least she would be still alive.

Lucy felt as if the glutinous stain of what had happened in the storeroom with Uncle Casper had crept wider and wider across her life like black oil spilled across unbleached linen.

Washing hadn't been enough to cleanse her. Nor had prayer. When she washed, when she prayed, there was always the unspoken question, *perhaps you enjoyed it, princess; perhaps you still think about it, what it was like, and wish you could have some more.* And then she would picture that grinning fiery face, with flames gushing out of its cheeks, and it would leave her trembling, and dry-mouthed, and disoriented.

Evelyn stayed with Lucy while Nora, flustered with shock and sympathy, undressed her and drew her a hot bath. Jamie stayed in the drawing room downstairs, drinking whisky, and pacing up and down in front of the reeking coal fire.

'Did they say how long your poppa might have to stay in the hospital?' Evelyn asked Lucy, through the partially-open bathroom door.

'A month at least, they weren't sure,' Lucy told her. 'The doctor said they have to find out which of his neck-bones are broken, and make quite certain that they heal properly. Otherwise he could catch the infectious fever.'

Frances the little cherry-cheeked kitchen-maid tiptoed in with a blue-and-white cup of hot chocolate, which she left on the table in the turret.

Eventually Lucy came out of the bathroom in a long nightdress of fine embroidered cambric, with Nora following her, trying to rub her hair dry as she walked.

'It's all right, Nora,' said Lucy. 'I'll wrap it in a towel, and sit by the fire.'

'You're sure, miss? I don't want to be the one responsible for you catching the grippe.'

Lucy held her close, and hugged her. 'You've been so kind to me, Nora.'

Nora blinked tears from her eyes. 'Such a poor man, your poppa. Always so confused. Do you know what he used to do, he used to call me to the morning room, and say, "Nora, you're wise, what should you do when you don't understand where your life has taken you to?"'

Evelyn looked up. 'What did you say to him, Nora?'

'What could I say? It was such a question! But I used to tell him what my grandfather always told me. "Today and tomorrow are just like gold and silver, one today is worth sixteen tomorrows; and don't forget that tomorrow is the day after you're dead."'

'Well, I'm sure *that* cheered him up no end' Evelyn replied.

Nora wound Lucy's straggly dark-blonde hair into a towel-turban. 'I'll come up by-and-by to brush it out for you, miss. And, miss – I'm so sorry, miss. Your poor dear poppa.'

She left the room, and Lucy sat in her plaited French basketwork chair by the hearth, and watched the flames licking and dancing for a while.

'How do you feel?' Evelyn asked her.

'I don't know quite. Numb.'

'You should have taken those powders the doctor offered you.'

Lucy shook her head. 'I don't want to sleep. Not yet.'

'Why do you think he did it?' Evelyn asked.

Lucy looked up. The fire sparkled in her eyes. 'You mean, did he do it on purpose?'

Evelyn hesitated, but then she said, 'I heard one of the policemen suggesting it. "Here's a classical suicide," that's what he said. And I saw your poppa for myself. He jumped right out, he couldn't have saved her, he couldn't have saved himself.'

Lucy was silent for a long time. A pretty little silver clock ticked above the hearth. She felt as if she ought to cry; and she knew that she would, but not just yet. At last, looking towards the fire, she said, 'He always thought that whatever went wrong, it was always his fault. My momma left him once, and he always blamed himself for that. She came back, but then she died, and he always blamed himself for that, too. He could never believe that he was any good.'

He blamed himself for Uncle Casper raping me, too, she thought, but she didn't tell Evelyn. If she told Evelyn, the whole of New York society would know it by dinner-time tomorrow; and they'd be talking about it in San Francisco by the week's end.

True or false, stove-talk or not, Mrs Sweeney's news that nobody thought well of him in Oak City had somehow been the last straw that had broken Jack's spirit completely. What more she had whispered to him on the stairs, Lucy couldn't guess. He hadn't achieved much in Oak City: a store, and just enough to live on, and a small circle of friends, but at least he had achieved it himself. At least it was something he could be proud of. When that last reassuring memory had turned into ashes, Jack Darling, for all of their money, had been left with nothing.

He had been a High Plains storekeeper. He knew all too well what happened to people who were left with nothing.

Lucy sipped her chocolate. It was rich and bitter and scalding hot. Evelyn said, 'I'd better go soon. Daddy and mommy always retire at ten. Daddy says it's the secret of a long life, retiring early. And about a million Mellons are coming for luncheon tomorrow. I think it's so impolite to have such hordes of people in your family, don't you?'

'I don't have anyone at all, except for poppa,' said Lucy.

'Well, it's high time you married,' Evelyn told her. 'You could start your own family then. But for goodness' sake don't propagate like the Mellons. I know they come from Pittsburgh, and that must excuse them some lapse in manners, but really! You should be nicer to John. You could do worse, and he's almost unbearably rich.'

Evelyn stood up, and came over to Lucy, and embraced her. 'I'll call by tomorrow, my dear, to see how you are. Don't despair, will you? There are simply dozens of people who love you dearly.'

Evelyn left. Lucy stood in her turret and watched the brougham turning around on Tenth Avenue to take her home. Nora knocked gently at the door, and said, 'Shall I brush your hair now, Miss Lucy? I should brush it out before it dries.'

Lucy nodded, and went through to her dressing room, and sat down in front of the mirror. She hadn't realized how anaemic she looked. The ghost of Lucy Darling.

Nora started to brush, counting under her breath.

'What's Jamie doing?' Lucy asked her.

'He'll be retiring now, Miss Lucy. Jeremy drew him a bath.'

'Would you tell him that I'd like to see him, before he retires?'

Lucy could see Nora's eyes flicker with uncertainty. 'Where, Miss Lucy?'

'Here, in my sitting room, of course. We'll be quite *safe*, for goodness' sake! I've known Jamie since I was a little girl!'

'You're not a little girl now, begging your pardon, Miss Lucy. And your poppa's not here.'

'Nora, please just tell him to come up and say goodnight.'

'Very good, then.'

'And ask cook for two more cups of chocolate.'

'Yes, Miss Lucy.'

Jamie knocked at the door, and Lucy answered it herself. Jamie had bathed, his hair was smartly combed back, and he smelled of eau-de-cologne. His long maroon dressing-robe was tightly tied, and underneath he wore a popular pattern of Sears Roebuck pyjamas, green-and-blue stripes.

'Hallo, Jamie,' she said, and immediately hugged him close.

He glanced around her rooms. 'I don't think your maid approved of my coming up here,' he told her.

'Oh, Nora! She's just being a fussbudget. Come on in, cook's sending up chocolate.'

They sat together by the hearth. The fire had died down now, almost to the bars, and Lucy reached for the bell for the scullery-maid. But Jamie said, 'You don't have to trouble about that. I don't think I've been living with you rich folks so long that I can't remember how to tip coal on to a hearth.'

He raked over the fire, and then shovelled on more coal. He hunkered in front of it, watching the thin flame-tongues licking, and then he said, 'I can't tell you how sorry I am. You know, about everything. Your father, Mrs Sweeney. It was just too bad.'

Lucy looked tired but unusually pretty in the firelight. Nora had brushed out her hair until it gleamed, and tied it with pale blue ribbons for the night.

'Jamie, can I ask you a question?' she said.

He frowned at her. 'Sure, whatever you like.'

'Well,' she hesitated. 'Do you think I'm at all – *evil*?'

'Evil? What makes you say that? Of course you're not evil.'

She wiped tears from her eyes with her fingers. 'I can't help feeling – well, I almost wish that poppa dies. Does that sound terrible to you? I don't know how he's going to stand it, being paralysed. Being spoon-fed, just like a child. I don't even know how I'm going to take care of him.'

'You can have nurses living-in, I guess. You can afford it, can't you?'

'Oh, I don't know. It's not just the nursing. It's living with him, when he's a cripple. How can I leave him? How can I think of getting married? I feel desperately sorry for him, but I feel so angry with him, too. He's spoiled everything.'

Frances tapped cautiously at the door, and then came in with two more steaming cups of chocolate, and a plate of wasps' nests and kisses. She curtseyed goodnight, and then hurried away, leaving the door slightly ajar. Lucy touched Jamie's hand, and said, 'You wouldn't close it, would you? I don't want Nora listening.'

Jamie got up from the hearth, crossed the room, and closed the door firmly. 'I don't think I could ever get used to servants. I'd miss my privacy too much.'

Lucy said nothing, but turned back to the fire. Jamie stood watching her for a while, the slender back of her neck, where fine blonde hairs gleamed.

'I guess you have a right to feel angry,' he said. 'You're still young. You have everything that any young girl could possibly want. And now this, poppa hurt so bad, and for no real reason at all.'

Lucy lowered her head. 'There was a real reason,' she said, softly.

'Anything you want to tell me about?'

213

'Come and sit down,' she asked him, and turned, and held out her hand. Jamie approached her slowly, trying to anticipate what she was going to say by the look in her eyes.

'He didn't have anything left,' said Lucy. 'When Mrs Sweeney told him that none of his friends in Oak City thought well of him any more . . .'

'He has *you*, doesn't he?' said Jamie. 'Why should he worry what his old cronies back in Oak City thought about him?'

Lucy whispered, 'No. He didn't have me. He didn't have anything.'

'He said something,' Jamie remarked. He was being careful now. 'Early this evening, on the stairs, before we left for the ball. He said something about your not really being his kin.'

Lucy nodded. Her blue eyes were blurred with tears, and now she couldn't stop them. 'The truth is, I'm not even his real daughter. My momma was my real momma – but –' she was so choked up with tiredness and shock that she could scarcely continue. Jamie knelt close to her, and held her close, and shushed her.

'You don't have to tell me any of this, not tonight,' he told her. 'The best thing for you to do is to finish your chocolate and get yourself some sleep.'

'Jamie – she died – and I never even *knew* – and she never told poppa who my father really was –'

'Come on, shush, he was always good to you, wasn't he?'

Lucy smeared her eyes against the sleeve of her robe. 'Oh God, Jamie, I feel so darned miserable.'

He held her and rocked her for nearly ten minutes, until the little pretty clock on the hearth chimed eleven o'clock. Then he passed over her cup of chocolate, and wiped her eyes for her, and kissed her forehead, and said, 'Come on, wash your teeth and then get yourself to bed.'

She turned to him, and nestled her face into his shoulder. She felt so sorely distressed; her throat and her chest hurt her from crying. But Jamie was so comforting. She gripped his arm through the sleeve of his robe, and his arm-muscle was broad and strong. She felt as if she wanted him to hold her like this, not just for tonight, but for day after day, and night after night, until the seasons flew flickering past her turreted sitting-room windows like dancing pictures in a nursery picture-show, and the fire flared and died, flared and died, year after year, until her grip failed at last, and she fell suddenly back to the carpet with silver hair and desiccated skin. If he held her like this for ever, she would never have to dress, never have to cry, never have to fall in love, never have to face the world of pain and surprises and irrational guilt.

Without raising her face, she said, 'Will you stay with me, at least till I fall asleep?'

Jamie kept on holding her tight, but she could feel the tension in him. 'You recall what happened in Denver,' he told her, and his voice sounded thick and vibrant beside her ear.

'I mean just holding me,' she said. 'I feel so all-alone.'

'Just holding you?' Cautious, but perhaps a little hopeful, too.

'Like now, till I can fall asleep.'

Jamie was silent for almost a whole minute. Then he said, 'Here? By the fire? Just until you fall asleep?'

'Umh-humh.' She was almost asleep already. Tiredness had risen up inside her like a moonless tide, and she found it almost impossible to keep her eyes open.

'Well . . .' said Jamie. 'I guess there's no harm.'

Lucy snuggled closer to him. 'I like you when you're all proud, and principled, and angry. You forgave me for Denver, didn't you?'

He stroked her hair. 'I'm not so sure that I ever did.'

'It wasn't *time*,' she murmured.

He kept on stroking her hair, over and over. 'Do you think that it could ever be time?'

She smiled. Even though her face was pressed close to his

robe, and he couldn't see her, he guessed that she was smiling, and he smiled too.

'You must keep on trying,' she said. 'You must keep on asking.'

'What happens if I don't?'

'You know what they say. He who doesn't ask, doesn't get.'

'What happens if I find somebody else? Somebody else who says yes, instead of no?'

She looked up at him. 'If you find somebody else, Jamie; then I shall cry. But I shall try not to be selfish. I shall try to be glad for you.'

She lowered her head again, and squeezed him tight. 'Anyway, I don't want to talk about it.'

A long silence passed between them. The clock chattered, the coals in the fire began to dislodge themselves. Somewhere far away, they heard the night-flattened clanging of a fire-bell.

Jamie said, 'Do you really not know who your father is?'

'Momma always refused to say,' Lucy told him. 'When she died, well, the secret died too; that's what Jack said; so nobody will ever know.'

'Does it bother you, not knowing?'

'I don't know. Sometimes it does and sometimes it doesn't. When I feel angry, or depressed, I think to myself, maybe that's my father's evil temper coming out in me. My momma always seemed to be so sweet. But sometimes I feel good and brave; like I think I'm beginning to feel good and brave right now; and then I think, maybe *that's* what my father was like, because I can't imagine my momma with any man who wasn't worthy of her.'

She paused, and she was about to say something else, but she stopped herself. She didn't want to tell Jamie about Uncle Casper. Only Jack knew about Uncle Casper, and what he had done to her; and even if Jack had ever suspected that Uncle Casper was her real father, then he certainly hadn't gone so far as to voice his suspicion out loud. It was more than Lucy could bear to think about.

Gradually, she fell asleep. She was conscious of Jamie embracing her, and of the fire fuming and crackling in the hearth, but she couldn't think about Jack any longer, her mind wouldn't let her. Jack and Mrs Sweeney remained frozen in her mind, tangled together as they toppled from the balustrade; but they fell no further. Perhaps, in her dreams, they would never hit the floor.

She didn't know how many minutes passed; but after a short while she felt Jamie easing himself away from her. He laid her gently on the rug. She felt the prickle of close-cropped wool against her cheek. Then Jamie stood up, hopping slightly, as if one of his ankles had gone dead.

'Don't go,' she heard herself whispering.

'Ssh, it's all right, I'm not going,' he reassured her. She heard him sitting with a complicated creak on the basketwork chair, and she opened her eyes for a quivering fraction and saw his faded green-and-blue pyjamas, and his slipper; and closed her eyes again, convinced.

She heard him yawn, and sigh; and the sound of his hands rubbing his chin. He must be exhausted, she thought to herself, and then she slept.

She didn't dream; but she thought she heard voices. Her mother was sitting in the next room, talking about ribbons. 'They haven't sent us ribbons, Jack.' She felt like calling out, but she knew that her mother was dead. If she called out, she might wake herself up, and then her mother would vanish. 'Momma?' she mouthed. 'Please don't go.'

The next thing she knew, Jamie was kneeling beside her, and carefully picking her up. She murmured something like, '*Don't . . . evening . . .*' but he lifted her right off the floor, holding her close against his chest. She kept her eyes shut, and she allowed her arm to swing limply, and she continued to breathe with the harsh and regular breathing of somebody who has fallen deeply and abruptly asleep.

But she was quite conscious as Jamie carried her through to the bedroom, and laid her on the bed, where the sheets had already been neatly folded back ready for her. When he laid her on the bed, and covered her up, and leaned over to kiss her goodnight, she half-opened her eyes, and reached out, and clung on to the lapel of his robe.

'Jamie?' she whispered.

'Goodnight, Lucy,' he breathed.

'You're not going?' she said, sleepily.

'I have to. I can't stay here.'

'I'm not asleep yet.'

He squeezed her hand. 'Lucy . . . it isn't right. I have to go.'

But through her treacly feeling of drowsiness, Lucy knew that she wanted him to stay with her. She clung tighter to his robe and refused to let go; and when he gently prised her fingers loose, she clung to his cuff with her other hand.

'Stay,' she demanded. She felt quite petulant about it now. He had to stay, he had to hold her, otherwise she would never be able to sleep. There would be two dreadful apparitions trailing their way through her dreams from now on: Uncle Casper, blazing like forty squibs; and her poppa, choke-throated, and stiff with paralysis.

She closed her eyes again, and dozed, but she didn't really sleep. She could feel Jamie sitting beside her on the bed, and staying there, even when she was too tired to keep her grip on his cuff. He waited beside her for what seemed like hours. But when he shifted, even a little, she took hold of his hand, with an even more possessive grip, and mumbled, 'Stay.'

He wasn't to go, she needed him there. Jack was waiting for her, somewhere down in her dreams; Jack and her Uncle Casper. She couldn't face them alone.

Jamie was still sitting beside her when the clock chimed a quarter after one. Then, gradually, she felt him fall sideways, until his head was resting on her hip. She closed her eyes, and the next thing she knew, the clock was striking two, and Jamie was still leaning on her, lightly snoring.

She shook him. 'Jamie? Jamie?'

'*Mmerrh?*' he replied.

'Jamie, get into bed. You're so tired.'

'*Mmhh.*'

The next time she opened her eyes, her bedroom was gradually filling with grainy grey light. She lay back on her pillow, staring at the ceiling. Then she turned her head, so that she could see the carriage-clock beside her bed. Five after seven. She lifted her head from the pillow, and there was Jamie, sprawled all over the other side of the bed, fast asleep, in his green-and-blue Sears Roebuck pyjamas.

She ruffled his hair. Then she kissed his ear. 'Jamie?'

It took him a long time to stir.

'Jamie?' she repeated. 'Jamie?'

He lifted his head and peered at her frowzily. 'Oh crims,' he told her. 'I must have fallen asleep.'

'It doesn't matter. Stop, don't go. It doesn't matter.'

He stared at her for a very long time. 'You're sure?'

She nodded, and smiled. 'Of course I'm sure. It's too late now, anyway. It's gone seven o'clock.'

Jamie sat up, and dry-washed his face with his hands. Neither of them said anything. But then Jamie turned and looked down at her, and said, 'I'm sorry.'

'What for?' she smiled.

'I fell asleep. Now what's your Nora going to think?'

'I don't know. I don't care. She's only my maid. I can dismiss her, you know, if I don't like her.'

'Guess I'm not so used to servants,' Jamie admitted. 'That Nora of yours, she can be pretty intimidating when she wants to be.'

Lucy reached up, and unfastened the top button of Jamie's pyjamas. 'I can sack her, whenever I feel like it.'

Jamie bent over and kissed her forehead. 'I guess you can.'

She ran her fingers into his hair, and she wouldn't let him go. 'I can do anything I like,' she told him. 'I can hire and fire, and who's to say different?'

'Jack?' Jamie suggested.

'Jack? It's not even Jack's money! It's mine! And Jack's not even my father!'

She hesitated, and then she added, 'Even if he was, he still couldn't tell me what to do; nor what not to do.'

She kissed him, forcefully, straight on the lips, but Jamie didn't close his eyes. She kissed him again.

'I love you,' she told him.

'No, you don't. I wish that you did.'

'I love you, simlin-head!'

She crossed her arms, and seized hold of her cambric nightdress, and wrestled it upwards, right over her hips and her breasts and her head, and then tugged it off, and threw it away. Then – naked – she clung close to Jamie, and kissed him, and kissed him again, while he tried to push her away, and to twist his mouth to one side.

At last, lifting himself up, panting, half-laughing, he had to look at her. Her tangled blonde hair, and her tiny pink-nippled breasts. Her narrow hips, and her long, slender legs.

She stared at him. She opened her thighs, on purpose. His eyes glanced sideways, he couldn't help it, then glanced again. She kept on staring at him, wanting him to want her, opening herself up, but irrationally fearful that just one look would reveal to him what Uncle Casper had done to her.

It was a test, a challenge, both dangerous and frightening. Her heart lolloped like a jackrabbit.

With a strangely grave face, Jamie unbuttoned the rest of his pyjama jacket. His chest was deep-tanned and ridged with muscles, from all those growing-up years of farmwork, with just the faintest whorl of dark chest-hair. He was breathing hard. He tugged loose the cord of his pyjama pants, and pulled them down; and up bobbed his penis, rearing out of its nest of hair, thick and knotted and sculptural and already glistening for her.

Lucy swallowed. Her cheeks felt hot, as if she were standing too close to a bonfire. She was so frightened by what she was doing that she closed her eyes. But then she felt Jamie's fingers stroking her cheek, and Jamie's lips kissing her face.

'I dreamed of this,' he murmured. 'You know that? I dreamed of this for years and years.'

She said nothing but, 'Sshhh, don't speak, . . .' and arched her head back on her pillow.

His hands cupped her breasts. They were small enough to fit perfectly into his palms; as if they had grown to just that size especially for him. Her tightened nipple brushed his lifeline. His lips brushed roughly against hers, and then brushed again.

'Jamie,' she said, although she wasn't sure that she had said it aloud.

He knelt between her parted thighs. He still looked so serious; almost reverential. Of course his father had brought him up to respect women and to fear God, and not to sin. With his paired thumbs, he parted the pale pink lips of her vagina, and stared in fascination as a single crystal drop of liquid ran slowly downwards, and disappeared like a lost diamond into the dark cleft of her bottom.

She felt the droplet slide. She looked into his eyes; and saw him smile; but failed to understand that, given the cause, he would have killed for her.

Lucy watched him, hypnotized by the expression on his face, as he raised himself up and pressed the swollen head of his penis between her lips; and then allowed the irresistible forces of gravity and desire to plunge him slowly inwards, until his dark curly hair tangled with her blonde silky hair.

His love-making was quite different from Uncle Casper's frantic coupling. Slow, rhythmic, with kisses and whispers of love. At first Lucy didn't think that it would excite her nearly as much. Perhaps she was a harlot after all, who could only enjoy love if she were forced into it, and degraded. But then the feeling of Jamie's penis pushing in and out of her began to give her a warming, vertiginous sensation that she had never experienced before. She clutched Jamie tight, and kissed and bit his muscular shoulders. And still his penis pushed, and pushed, and seemed to swell larger and larger inside her with every push.

She looked down, and as he half-withdrew, she clearly saw the thick reddened shaft of his penis, with her own petal-like lips moistly clinging to it as if they couldn't bear to let it go. She thought that she had never seen anything so strange or so beautiful. Two people, a man and a woman, actually joined together, one inside the other.

Jamie pushed harder and quicker, and he began to pant. His chest gleamed with sweat, and Lucy could feel the backs of his thighs tensing into knots of muscle. She gripped his buttocks and tugged him into her, deeper and deeper; and still his penis seemed to grow, until she couldn't imagine the size it must be. How could she possibly have room for it? It felt as if it were stretching her wide apart, filling up her whole body.

She felt as if she couldn't breathe. She couldn't even think where she was. She wanted to scream. She wanted to shudder. She wanted to bite him hard. He pushed and he pushed, and then suddenly he said 'Jesus God,' and pulled himself abruptly out of her, and she felt something warm and wet splatter across her stomach and her breasts, and touch her cheek.

Suddenly, everything seemed to have finished. She opened her eyes, and Jamie was kneeling between her thighs, gasping for breath. His penis was already sinking. She touched her cheek with her fingertips, and found that her face had been anointed with something like glutinous milk. There were more drops of it shivering on her stomach, and a drop sliding from her nipple.

Jamie was plainly embarrassed. He picked up one of Lucy's lacy handkerchiefs from beside the bed, and wiped her face, quickly, but with tenderness.

'I'm sorry,' he told her, hoarsely. 'I'm really sorry. I shouldn't have done that.'

She reached up and stroked his cheek. 'I loved it,' she whispered. 'I could do it again and again, for ever, as long as I did it with you.'

He tried to wipe her breast. 'I didn't want to risk you having a baby. That was why I –'

She looked down at herself, and curiously touched the droplets on her stomach. 'Is this what gives you babies? Truly? I somehow imagined you might be able to see them, swimming around. Very tiny, of course. I didn't expect them to be big.'

She frowned at the fluid, and sniffed it. 'What a strange smell it has. Does it really have babies in it? They can't feel anything, can they? It doesn't hurt them?'

Jamie began, 'Didn't your mother –' but then he realized what he was saying, and said, 'It has seeds in it, that's all. Human seeds. They have to be planted before they grow.'

Lucy reached for her nightgown. 'Was it so wrong of us, do you think?' she asked Jamie. 'It *was* wrong, wasn't it?' For some unaccountable reason, she suddenly felt as if she had sinned far more devastatingly than she had with Uncle Casper. She had seen Jamie naked; she had allowed him into her body; she had seen the seeds from which babies are made, and actually touched them. She felt as sinful as Mary Magdalene; but it had felt wonderful, too; and *important*; as important as living, as important as dying. How could anything so wonderful and so important be so sinful?

Jamie buttoned his pyjamas. Then he reached across the silk quilted bedcover and touched her hand. 'It wasn't wrong. God can always forgive human passion, that's what my father always said. Especially since we're going to be married.'

Lucy stared at him. 'Married?'

'We'll have to wait until your father's well enough, of course. We can't become engaged with his permission. I mean, he may not be your real father, but he's your legal guardian, isn't he, and you'll want him to give you away.'

'Jamie –' Lucy began. She loved him; she had adored making love to him; but she couldn't understand how one act of love had already become, in his eyes, a full and formal betrothal.

'We can wait, anyway, can't we, until I've finished my legal business with the Indians?' Jamie told her. 'Besides, we shouldn't make any announcement until Mrs Sweeney has been decently buried and decently mourned. Christmas would probably be the most appropriate time, what do you think?'

Lucy was trying to find the words to tell Jamie that she couldn't possibly think about marrying him; not yet, if ever; when Nora knocked at the sitting-room door.

'Miss Lucy? I've brought your tea.'

Jamie frantically tugged on his pyjama trousers, rolled off the bed, and looked around for somewhere to hide.

'Behind the drapes!' Lucy hissed at him, flapping her hand; and he stepped quickly into the window and wound himself into the heavy yellow velour curtains.

Nora came in directly, carrying a breakfast tray with tea and muffins, and the morning newspapers.

'Good morning, Miss Lucy,' she said, crisply. It was plain by the tight look on her face that she knew very well that Jamie was there. She never usually knocked before she came in; and she usually put down the breakfast-tray and chattered and fussed around opening the drapes and plumping up Lucy's pillows. This morning she set the tray down, arranged the newspapers beside it, and turned immediately to leave.

'There's no word from the hospital yet,' she said. 'But Doctor Crossley will be calling at twelve o'clock, to give us the latest intelligence.'

She hesitated. She was a chapel-goer, she disapproved of shenanigans with men, in fact she disapproved of men altogether, but she was too fond of Lucy to be difficult for very long. 'Perhaps you should look at the newspapers, Miss Lucy,' she said. 'I regret that they're rather on the excitable side.'

'Thank you, Nora,' said Lucy. 'I'll call you when I need you again.'

When Nora had closed the door behind her, Lucy, with shaking hands, picked up *The New York World*. The front-page headline read SOCIETY TRAGEDY AT THE WALDORF! Woman Killed – Oil Parvenu Critically Injured! They Plunge Thirty-Three Feet!

Trembling, she picked up *The Sun*. The headlines were even bolder. THE FATAL FALL! Oil Baron Paralysed, Woman Dies!

Both newspapers recounted every detail of the accident with breathless salacity. 'As they plummeted from the mezzanine, a dread hush fell across the assembled socialites. "Oh God, can no miracle save them!" a bejewelled woman was heard to scream.'

Worse than the sensational way in which the accident was described, however, was the bald statement at the end of the *World*'s article, which said, 'Coroner's Physician Donlin reported that Mr Jack Darling was in a state of acute intoxication, almost to the degree of alcoholic poisoning. In Dr Donlin's expert view, he would have been in no condition to effect a rescue of the late Mrs Sweeney, and his precipitate lunge towards her may even have contributed to her fatal fall.'

Jamie came out from behind the drapes. 'You haven't forgotten me?' he asked her.

She handed him the newspaper, and her eyes were filled with tears. 'They say that it was poppa's fault.'

Jamie studied the article for a moment, and then said, 'That's not true. We know that's not true. She was already falling when he jumped after her.'

'But he was drunk, wasn't he? Completely drunk. You can't deny that. And even if we say that it wasn't his fault, who's going to believe it?'

Jamie picked up his robe, and put it on. 'I'll write to the papers myself, and tell them what really happened.'

'Oh, Jamie,' said Lucy, miserably. She felt as if she would never be happy again.

Doctor Crossley arrived at the house just before lunch. He was very clean and dapper, and smelled of peppermints. He sat in the morning room with his case beside him, his hands clasped together just below his breast bone. Lucy sat opposite him, dressed in sober grey silk. Nora had braided her hair for her, and she wore a small black lace cap, fringed with dangling jet beads. In the foggy golden light that penetrated the room she looked far older than her eighteen years, but very collected.

Jamie stood behind her, in a tight off-the-peg suit from Hunt & Maxwell's in Manhattan, Kansas, nervously clearing his throat.

'I saw your father just an hour since,' said Doctor Crossley. 'His condition has not worsened, I am pleased to tell you; although it has not improved. His neck is broken, but this injury is not the direct cause of his paralysis. His tenth and eleventh vertebrae were displaced in the fall, resulting in irrevocable damage to his spinal column.'

'What does that mean?' asked Lucy.

'I am dreadfully sorry, my dear. It means that in common with the consultant surgeon at Bellevue, I have to conclude that your father will never regain any sensation below his chest. In time he will have limited use of his arms, and he will be able to breathe, to eat, and to digest without serious difficulty. However, all remaining bodily needs will have to be catered for by nurses; and he will never again be able to walk.'

Lucy clasped Jamie's hand. 'Oh God,' she said. 'He may as well be dead.'

Doctor Crossley shook his head. 'Not at all, my dear; although I quite understand your feeling. Many of the seriously handicapped lead comfortable, pleasant, and even useful existences. At least he will have the use of his hands. He will be able to get about quite nimbly in a wheeled chair.'

Lucy couldn't stop the tears from trickling down her cheeks. 'He's had such a terrible life, he's lost everything he ever wanted; and now this.'

'I will leave you a list of nursing agencies,' said Doctor Crossley. He paused, and then he said, very carefully, 'If I may, I will also recommend another physician.'

'Another physician?' asked Lucy. 'What for?'

Doctor Crossley tried to smile, but couldn't manage it. 'I regret that it will be difficult for me to continue as your doctor.'

'I don't understand.'

'When I took you and your father on to my list this summer . . . well, I may not have explained it very *clearly* at the time, but it could only be on what you might call a stop-gap basis. Now, I regret that the pressures of caring for so many patients has obliged me, well, to *prune* my list somewhat. I'm sure you can understand how sorry I am . . . but, truly, I have no choice.'

He took out a visiting-card, unscrewed his pen, and scribbled a name on to the back of it. 'Here – I'm quite sure that Dr Schumann will give you the greatest satisfaction.'

'But you were recommended by the Scotts,' Lucy protested. 'You were recommended most specifically.' In fact, what Evelyn had said was that 'Doctor Crossley is the *only* doctor in New York. Mrs Astor wouldn't be seen dead with anybody else. How many doctors do you know who spend the summer on E. C. Benedict's yacht?'

Doctor Crossley stood up. 'Of course, Miss Darling, and may I say that I have been honoured to make your acquaintance, and to be of service in some small way to you and your unfortunate father. But it is simply a question of practicality. I cannot effectively see to the needs of more than a hundred patients, especially when all of those patients demand the most personal and considerate attention.

'One of those patients is expecting me even now. My apologies, I really have to hurry.'

He handed Lucy the card with Doctor Schumann's name and address, and bowed his head. Lucy could see that he clipped the hairs in his nose. 'My heartfelt condolences on your tragic loss; my deepest regrets for your unfortunate father. My respects to yourself.'

Lucy tinkled the small silver bell on the table beside her, and Jeremy appeared to see Doctor Crossley to the door.

'May I visit my father?' Lucy asked him, as he sidestepped away.

'Oh – of course,' said Doctor Crossley. 'Any time you wish. At the moment, however, I must warn you – well, he is suffering considerable pain, and may not be in the most amenable of humours.'

'Thank you, doctor,' said Lucy.

'Thank *you*, Miss Darling,' Doctor Crossley grimaced, and left.

Jamie thrust his hands into his pockets. 'Didn't think much of him,' he remarked. 'Seemed to me like he couldn't get out of here quick enough.'

Lucy looked down at the card that Doctor Crossley had given here. Doctor Eli Schumann, 210 West 23rd Street. Not exactly a fashionable address. 'He said he was in a hurry,' she replied.

'There's being in a hurry and there's scurrying off like your tail's on fire,' Jamie replied, with a sniff.

'Oh, you're not familiar with *society*, that's all,' Lucy told him. 'Sometimes people seem like they're being brusque, but that's just etiquette. Evelyn's always telling me that it's ill-mannered to stay too long when you visit; or to behave too familiar. Why, a gentleman shouldn't even take his gloves off unless he's asked. A certain detachment, that's what Evelyn calls it.'

'Well, I don't think much to that, and I still didn't think much to *him*,' Jamie persisted. 'Leaving your gloves on, for pete's sake. Supposing there's a fire in the grate and you're sweating bullets?'

'Jamie,' smiled Lucy. Ever since last night, a new conspiratorial affection had grown up between them. But Lucy still wouldn't talk about betrothal, and whenever Jamie tried, she changed the subject, or thought of something she had to tell Nora, or called for the scullery-maid to bring more coals for the fire.

'You planning on visiting your poppa now?' asked Jamie.

Lucy nodded. 'He's suffered so much. Are you coming with me? We can take him some candy. He has such a sweet tooth for pecan penuche.'

She called for Jeremy to have the brougham brought around; and for Nora to bring her coat. Although Jack had contributed very little to the running of the household, apart from drinking whisky and dropping cigar-ash on the rugs and suggesting now and then that the cook should rustle him up some lamb shanks or pressed veal and horseradish, she felt very much this morning as if she were the mistress of the house. She would have revelled in it, if she hadn't felt so much unhappiness for Mrs Sweeney, and for Jack's accident. But as she waited in the hallway now, with Jamie standing silently beside her, she wondered whether she ought to have felt even more grief than she actually had; because she certainly didn't feel like crying. Perhaps she was shallow and wicked for having taken Jamie as her lover on the very night that Mrs Sweeney had died and Jack had been hopelessly crippled.

But this morning it was difficult for her to feel that Mrs Sweeney had died in any other way except the way that she had always wanted to die, spectacularly, and surrounded by gasping crowds. At least she hadn't died alone and sick, in

Kansas, and in a strange way Lucy could almost feel happy for her. As for Jack — Jack had been blaming himself and punishing himself for so long now that his paralysis seemed like a self-inflicted purgatory which he had deliberately — even hungrily — sought out.

She wondered how her mother would have felt today. Her mother had turned her back on Jack. Had that been easy for her? How much had her mother loved the man who had made her pregnant? Had it been easy to leave him behind?

That morning, as she waited for her carriage in one of the most opulent houses in New York, Lucy began to understand that she had no idea of the nature and measure of human love.

Quite simply, she had never had anybody to show her.

Being rich, Jack was lying in a room of his own at Bellevue, with a view of the East River. The room was whitewashed, and filled with blinding white October sunshine, so that it looked to Lucy as if Jack were already lying in an ante-room to Heaven. There was an overpowering smell of pine tar soap.

Jack's face was drawn tightly over his cheekbones. If she had passed him in the street, Lucy would have found it hard to recognize him. His eyes kept up that constant roaming from side to side that she had first seen when he was lying on the floor of the Waldorf lobby. His neck was supported by a high white celluloid collar, and his skull was wrapped in white bandages.

'Poppa,' she said softly. 'Poppa, it's Lucy.'

He pulled a taut, painful smile, but his eyes kept up their restless wandering.

'How are you feeling, poppa? Doctor Crossley said you were hurting.'

Jamie brought across a bentwood chair, and Lucy sat down beside Jack's bed. She lifted his hand from the knitted cotton bedcover, but it was limp and cold, like a piece of dead pork, and so she lowered it again. 'Poppa? I brought you some candies, some of the pecan penuche.'

Jack nodded. 'They say I can't feel nothing, that's what they say. Broke my back, broke my neck. What *I* said was, if I can't feel nothing, why in hell does it hurt so bad?'

Lucy said, 'Shush now, poppa. Doctor Crossley said you'll soon be better.'

Jack tried to cough, but he couldn't draw enough air into his lungs to clear out his throat. 'Feel like I'm choking, half of the time. I haven't eaten nothing yet, but it's going to be broth for the next few weeks, that's what they told me.'

He glanced at Jamie, and said, 'Is that you, Jamie?'

'Yes, sir,' Jamie told him, his hat in his hands.

'When're you leaving, Jamie?'

'I have to be in Washington by Monday, sir.'

'And then what?'

'Then it's back to Manhattan, Kansas, sir.'

Jack said nothing for a while, breathing harshly. Lucy said, 'We're going to find you a nurse, poppa. Somebody to take care of you every minute of the day.'

'They say I won't walk. Did Doctor Crossley tell you that? Not with my back broke. You don't remember old Dan Leuchars, do you? He was rolled on by a steer, had his back broke, saddest damned man I ever met.'

'Poppa, we're rich; you can have everything you need. Just because you can't walk, that won't mean you have to be unhappy. We can still go out; we can still go to the play; you can still go sailing with all of your friends.'

'Oh, sure enough,' said Jack bitterly. 'Jack the cripple, happy as a sandboy. Do you know what they used to call me at school? Jack-be-nimble, because I could run and jump so good. Now look at me. I should of died.'

His roaming eyes were blotted with bright tears. 'Guess you blame me for Molly Sweeney dying, too. Guess you think that's my fault. But I did what I could to save her. She was falling anyway, I didn't push her or nothing like that. I thought for that moment, I had to fly. *Had* to. Dear God, let me fly!'

Lucy took out her handkerchief and dabbed his eyes. He sniffled, and choked, and then he said, 'God thought different, I guess. "You're not going to fly, Jack Darling, no sir!" God decided in His infinite kindness that He wasn't going to grant me a miracle, not just then. But God alone knows that I did what I could to save her. And I just hope someday before I die that God has the heart to show me why He wasn't going to let me.'

'Poppa, why was it so terribly important?' Lucy begged him. 'I loved her, you know that. But she was old, and she didn't know what she was doing. I guess she thought she was back at the circus. Still young, you know? She was doing what she wanted.'

Jack pulled a face. 'Twinge,' he explained, trying to shift himself in his bed.

'Poppa, *why* did you jump?' asked Lucy.

But Jack began to cough; and wheeze painfully for breath; and to shake his head to show her that he couldn't answer; couldn't even find the air to answer.

'I'd better call the doctor,' said Jamie, and hurried from the room.

Lucy sat beside the bed, clutching Jack's hand, feeling not only powerless to help him, but powerless to understand him. Of all the people in the world she would have expected him to risk his life for, the Skipping Widder was the very last of them. There had never been love lost between them. Lucy remembered Jack calling her 'that boss-eyed old busy-body', and being so rude to her once in the store that her mother had spoken to him sharply about it, and they had argued in front of everybody.

The doctor bustled in, hog-moustached, with a yellow chequered vest, the kind that men wore to go to the track. He was closely followed by a big-faced frizzy-haired nursing sister in a floor-length apron.

'Now then, Mr Darling!' the doctor proclaimed, chafing his hands. 'You've been breathing again! What did I say about breathing?'

'Breathing!' the nurse admonished him.

Even though Lucy insisted that she wasn't hungry, Jamie took her for lunch at Delmonico's; firstly because he had always wanted to lunch at Delmonico's, and secondly because he thought that Lucy was looking pale and faint.

Delmonico's was comparatively quiet today. Outside the window of the main dining room, the trees of Madison Square were rusting sadly with approaching winter. She ate a few spoonfuls of asparagus soup and a small chicken salad, with a glass of sweet white wine. Jamie tried his best to restrain his appetite, but he made short work of the roast ribs of beef, although he wasn't sure if it was manners to pick them up in his fingers.

Jamie talked about going back to Kansas, and how he was planning to take on more work, and make a whole lot more money; and maybe think about politics, too, the state legislature had room for enthusiastic young lawyers. But even though he was talking about himself, it was plain that he was assuming that, by Christmas, he and Lucy would be betrothed, and that, by spring next year at the latest, they would be man and wife.

After all, wasn't it rare enough for a girl to allow a fellow to hold her hand, or to kiss her cheek, let alone encourage him to come into her bed?

In his euphoria, Jamie appeared to have forgotten the manifest difference in their destinies; that she was wealthy now beyond his imagination; that he could never hope to be the master in her house, in the way in which his own father had been master in his. He had forgotten what he had said to her on the beach in Los Angeles, that he could never follow her to New York. No duff, no Turkish delight.

But if Lucy had learned anything at all, it was that

manifest destinies are not to be tampered with; that the gods are not to be challenged. Jamie's cheerful assumption that they would soon be married filled her with a terrifying uncertainty, as if even to mention it would open a trapdoor beneath her feet, and set off another tragedy. She had never felt such panic in her life.

Jamie said, 'Are you all right, sweetheart? You still look pale.'

The restaurant seemed echoing and hot; and there was something about the chinking of forks on plates that Lucy found especially upsetting.

'I don't know,' she said. 'I think I'd like to leave in just a minute.'

Jamie wiped his mouth with his napkin, and smiled at her. 'You're tired, that's all. Yesterday was pretty much of a shock. I could use an early night myself.'

'Jamie –' said Lucy. First pale, she now began to blush. 'What occurred last night . . . between us. I'm sorry, Jamie, I truly am. But it cannot occur again.'

Jamie looked serious. 'Good Lord, Lucy, of course not!' He laid his hand across the table, but she made no move to take it. 'I never expected it to. It was a . . . what could you call it? A gesture. A statement, if you like, of something that we couldn't say in words. A statement of mutual affection. Gee, I wouldn't *expect* it to happen again. Not until we're – well, you know. Not until we're properly together, in the eyes of God, and of the law.'

Lucy didn't know what she could say to him; especially here, in a public restaurant. She toyed with the tiny spoon they had given her to eat her apricot sorbet, and said, 'It's so very soon, that's the trouble.'

She was about to say more; to explain that she hadn't yet seriously considered marriage to anyone at all, not even John T. Hollis who was embarrassingly handsome and scandalously witty and fifty times richer than she could ever be.

But Jamie said, 'I understand, Lucy. I understand!' even

though he couldn't have understood, couldn't *possibly* have understood, because Lucy couldn't even understand it herself. And just at that very moment, she caught sight of Evelyn Scott approaching them across the restaurant, in the company of her mother, and of two elderly but obviously very wealthy ladies, all of them plumed and feathered and with every square inch of sail on; the maitre d' ducking and dipping in front of them like a bow-wave.

'There's Evelyn,' said Lucy, and smiled at the ladies as they came nearer.

To her complete bewilderment, however, the entire party angled their noses very slightly upward and away from her, Evelyn included, and swept past her table, less than three inches away, with a contemptuous whisper of broadcloth and velvet and faille.

Lucy turned around in her chair. '*Evelyn!*' she called, but Evelyn didn't even flinch. The whole party were seen to a table at the back of the restaurant, and surrounded by waiters. They didn't even glance across at her. She might just as well have been invisible and inaudible.

'What's going on?' Jamie wanted to know. 'Isn't she speaking to you, or what?'

'She's my best friend!' Lucy declared. This was nightmarish.

'She's your best friend and she isn't speaking to you? Hasn't she told you why?'

'She hasn't said a word!'

Jamie made a face. 'Whyn't you go across and ask her?'

'I can't!'

'Why not?'

'I can't! It isn't *done!*'

Jamie was unimpressed. 'I don't think it's "done" to go marching past your best friend without so much as a "how-you-keeping?"'

Lucy pressed her hand across her mouth. 'Oh God, what if it's because of last night?'

'I don't get it.'

'What if they're cutting me because of last night?'

Jamie shook his head. 'I can't see how they can blame you for that. It wasn't you that fell off the mezzanine. And *you* sure weren't drunk.'

Lucy hesitated, her heart beating furiously. 'Go on,' Jamie coaxed her. 'Go on over and ask her. If she was ever a friend worth having, she'll tell you what's what. If she won't, then she's not worth knowing in any case. My father always taught me to face what I feared.'

Lucy lowered her head for a moment. Then she said, 'All right. I'll go.' She placed her napkin on the table, and immediately one of the waiters came across to pull back her chair for her. She stood up; and for the first time she was aware that several of the lunchers gave her a quick, shifty look out of the corners of their eyes, before concentrating too much attention on their plates.

They know, thought Lucy. *They all know. I've been cut, and not even my so-called best friend has had the decency to stand by me.*

She approached the corner table where Evelyn and Mrs Scott and their friends had just been handed their menus. Mrs Scott flickered a quick look at Evelyn, but none of them raised their heads.

'You'll excuse me,' said Lucy, her voice thinner than she wanted it to be. 'But you may be pleased to know that my poppa is recovering tolerably well today, although he is still in great pain, and although he has certainly lost the use of his legs.'

Mrs Scott sighed the sigh of the martyred, and at last looked up. Two stuffed swallows, transfixed in mid-dive by milliner's wire, quivered on the brim of her hat.

'Anyone who wishes to follow your father's misfortunes, Miss Darling, has only to read the yellow press.'

'And that's why none of you will speak to me?' asked Lucy.

'My dear Miss Darling, *all* societies, no matter how primitive, have certain standards of etiquette. It is for their own preservation; and the preservation of those values that are important to them.'

'You mean you're stuck-up,' Lucy retaliated.

Mrs Scott pinched her lips together. 'Our society, no matter what you may think of it, is unusually generous to those whom it welcomes into its embrace. We care not for background, Miss Darling, in this new nation of ours we cannot. But we do care for form; and for decent behaviour. Your father and his elderly lady friend showed neither last evening, and while the consequences of their lapse were tragic, they were also a scandal of the first degree.

'The charity ball was ruined; the charity committee was all but accused by the common newspapers of being a hotbed of drunks and circus-performers; and I can only quote Mrs Astor to you, who said that you may take the people out of the country, but you can't take the country out of the people.'

'Mrs Scott –' Lucy began; but Mrs Scott ostentatiously turned her head away, and presented Lucy with a conclusive view of the back of her hat. Two encircling wings, and a spray of dried flowers.

Lucy was right on the edge of tears. There was plenty that she wanted to say to Mrs Scott about form and decent behaviour, and about country people, too, but she couldn't trust herself not to cry. She looked quickly and hotly at Evelyn, and then went back to Jamie, who was standing waiting for her.

'I want to go now,' she said.

'You're not going to let those biggity old bitches drive you out?'

'I'm going to cry, Jamie, if I stay; and I don't want them to think that they can make me cry.'

'What in heck did they say to you? Are they really going to cut you? Can't you cut them back?'

Their waiter came up and asked if anything was wrong. 'Just bring me the check,' Jamie told him; and then to Lucy, 'I could go over there and give them an earful, if that'd do any good.'

'No,' she said. 'It would just make everything ten times worse.'

Jamie escorted her to the cloakroom. 'Well, who needs them, anyhow? If they think they're such big doings, just because they wear all that silk and satin, and they've built themselves an inside biffy.' He deliberately exaggerated his Kansas drawl.

He obviously thought it would make Lucy laugh. But she turned on him with all the fury she could muster up. '*I* need them!' she hissed at him. '*I* need them! They're the only friends I've got!'

Their white-stockinged footman Harry had already unfolded the carriage steps, and Lucy was about to climb aboard when Evelyn came rushing out of the restaurant, holding up her crimson skirts.

'Lucy! Lucy! Please, Lucy, wait!'

Lucy hastily wiped her eyes with her glove, but didn't turn around.

'Lucy,' Evelyn breathed, 'I'm so sorry! I'm really so desperately sorry!'

'And that's the way you show it, by sticking your nose up?' Jamie interrupted.

'Jamie, ssh,' said Lucy.

Evelyn said, 'It's all been so terrible! People have been calling all morning, poor mamma's beside herself! What on earth possessed your poppa to get himself so drunk? And that woman, that poor woman, balancing on the balcony-rail!'

'Just good old everyday country behaviour,' Lucy replied. 'Tell your poor mamma.'

'Oh, Lucy . . . please don't be angry with me. Everybody will

238

forget about it by Christmas. But they must blame somebody.'

'And what am I supposed to do between now and Christmas?' asked Lucy, turning to face Evelyn at last. 'Am I expected to sit alone in my mansion, talking to nobody, going nowhere? Am I still welcome at Mrs Vanderbilt's next week, or would everybody breathe a sigh of relief if I made my excuses?'

Evelyn reddened. 'Well, it really would be better all round if you –'

'Made my excuses,' Lucy finished for her. 'Thank you. I suppose, at least, that you're candid about it.'

'Lucy, mamma's right. There must be rules.'

'Oh, rules,' put in Jamie. 'Rules that ease your conscience when you turn your back on your best friend.'

'Please, Jamie,' said Lucy, touching his arm. 'Evelyn at least has said that she's sorry. Haven't you, Evelyn? Do you remember when Mrs Vanderbilt used to call us Primrose and West?'

Evelyn – who had been Primrose – was watery-eyed. 'I can't help it, Lucy. Mamma's quite furious that I'm talking to you now. And there are so many people who thought suspiciously of you and your poor poppa, right from the very beginning. Mrs Harris, of course. She's never forgiven you for the tennis-net.'

Evelyn paused, trembling, and then she said, 'They were quite prepared to accept you when you could give them harmless amusement. But now they feel that you're threatening them. Now they think that you're going to bring death and drunkenness and tightrope-walking to every party you attend. Lucy, forgive them – they're frightened of you.'

'And you, Evelyn?' asked Lucy. Her face suddenly looked very pretty in the opalescent October light. 'Are you frightened of me, too?'

Evelyn clasped her yellow-gloved hands together, and swallowed. 'Yes,' she whispered. 'I'm frightened of you, too.'

★

On Monday morning, Lucy came down to breakfast to find that only one place was set. 'Is Mr Cullen not having breakfast?' she asked Jeremy.

'Mr Cullen has taken his breakfast already, Miss Lucy,' Jeremy told her. 'He's packed now, and ready to leave.'

Lucy, in a soft billowing dress of blue-and-white striped silk, with a large bow at the back, crossed the polished hallway floor, and her reflection billowed beneath her. She opened the double doors to the morning room, and there was Jamie, sitting at the small French writing-desk, writing a letter.

'You weren't going to leave without saying goodbye?' she asked him.

He looked up, smiled, and shook his head. 'I was just writing down a few sentiments I want you to read once I'm gone. A few thoughts, that's all.'

She approached the desk and stood behind him, holding on to the back of the chair. He seemed to feel uneasy, sitting where he couldn't see her.

'Will you come back here, after you've finished in Washington?'

'I'll try, but I don't think it's likely. Once I get approval to clear those Indians off of that land ... well, then, the sooner they're off of it, the better the Kansas legislature is going to like it.'

He eased himself around in his chair. 'As soon as all *that's* cleared up, though, I can come back to visit. Just so long as all the restaurant checks don't mount up as high as Delmonico's.'

Lucy stood poised, not knowing what to say; not having the nerve for it; not having the experience for it. Her tongue touched her front teeth, and stayed there, as if she were trying to pronounce the one syllable which would begin her explanation that she loved him, she *loved* him, she knew that she loved him, but that they couldn't marry, couldn't even think of marriage. He would ruin her and worst of all she

240

would ruin him. She was making forty thousand dollars a week; he was making six thousand dollars a year. He couldn't even buy her three spoonfuls of soup and half a chicken salad without repeatedly expressing his disbelief at the size of the check. Seven dollars and fifty-eight cents! Plus tip!

But her tongue-tip remained where it was, pressed against her teeth; and although she knew that it was wrong of her not to speak; although she knew that it was actually *sinful* of her not to speak; she could not speak.

He loved her, and she had nobody else who loved her. She could tell him the truth, the flat truth, flat as a hoecake, that she had made love to him because she had been shocked and lonely and vulnerable, and because she had wanted to expunge the memory of her Uncle Casper. But she knew Jamie too well. If she told him that, he would walk out of here this morning and she would never see him again, never. And her whole world would shrink to just herself; a rich and lonely girl with no family and no friends, in a city that was frightened of her.

Jamie left just after eleven o'clock. The morning was sharp and metallic as a butcher's knife, and her breath smoked as she waved him goodbye from the doorway. The carriage circled around and rattled off on its way to Pennsylvania Station, and she stood for a long time watching it go, rubbing her arms through her thin silk sleeves to keep herself warm.

Eventually, Nora came up behind her, and said, 'The fire in the morning room's burning bright, Miss Lucy. Come along inside.'

Lucy nodded, and came in, and Nora closed the huge door behind her, blotting out the street. They walked together across the hallway.

'He's a fine boy,' Nora remarked; although it was scarcely a maid's place to make remarks of that kind. It was a mark of Lucy's isolation from New York society (which, of course, all of her servants knew about) that she could make it.

Lucy said, evenly, 'Yes, he is.'

'He told me –' Nora hesitated, and then she said, 'He told me you were going to be married. You and he. When he's back from the West, that is; and when Mrs Sweeney's been put to her rest; and when all this terrible Waldorf business is forgotten about.'

Lucy stared at her. 'Is that what he told you?'

'Yes, Miss Lucy, that's what he told me.'

'Well,' said Lucy. 'That's as may be.'

'It's not that I meant to be intrusive, Miss Lucy. He volunteered it, as it were.'

'Thank you, Nora, that's all.'

Nora put her head to one side and beamed at her. 'I have to say that I suspected his honour at first, Miss Lucy. But he's a fine boy. Any girl could do worse than him. And so pleasing to look at, too! My mother used to say that husbands should be like views from the kitchen window, always pleasing to the eye.'

'Nora,' said Lucy, and her words came out like chips of ice. 'That will be enough.'

Nora was undeterred. 'It's just advice, Miss Lucy. Sometimes the wisest of heads can do with advice.'

Lucy said nothing, although she was tempted. She and Jamie had spent the quietest and most reserved of weekends together. On Saturday they had taken the carriage over the Brooklyn Bridge, and ended up eventually on the cold beach at Coney Island, where they had walked along the shoreline with the sand whipping their ankles, saying nothing of love or promises, and not even talking of duffs or Turkish delight.

On Sunday they had not gone to church; but prayed at home with the servants, in the living-room, and sung *Rock of Ages*.

Late on Sunday afternoon, as it was growing dark, Jamie had knocked on the door of Lucy's turreted room and found her standing by the window, looking out over the lamplit carriages, and the shadowy trees of Central Park. He had stood a little way away from her, not speaking, and of course there had been no need. They had said everything they needed to say to keep their friendship intact. Anything more would have been dangerous for both of them.

Jamie had asked just one question: 'What will you do when I'm gone?'

Lucy had turned to him with eyes that were almost mauve. 'Wait. Think. Bide my time. What else can I do?'

'You could leave New York. There's always Washington. There's power in Washington, as well as society. There's Denver, too; or San Francisco; or Los Angeles. There's even Chicago.'

'Yes,' Lucy had replied, but her reply had meant nothing at all. She had turned back to watch the firefly lamps of the passing carriages. She had been sad, without tears. She had felt that her present existence was quite empty; as empty as a room. But she had also felt with extraordinary certainty that something new was waiting for her; and she was just as certain now, as she closed the morning-room door.

God may not have granted Jack the miraculous power of flight, as he hurled himself into off the Waldorf balustrade; but He still granted favours to the young, and the innocent, and the very beautiful.

Three weeks passed. October died; and November blew away its ashes. Mrs Sweeney was buried on a sharp sunny day with the soil so hard that the gravediggers had to be tipped extra. The priest said that she had danced, and because she had danced, she was blessed. Only Lucy and Nora and the rest of the servants attended the funeral. They wore black coats and black plumes, and carried black prayerbooks. The hearse stood in the background with its nodding, patient horses like a pen-and-ink drawing. Mrs Sweeney had no surviving relatives that anybody knew of. A bearded artist from the *New York World* sketched Lucy as she dropped a rose on Mrs Sweeney's casket, and the subsequent engraving appeared on the front page of the following day's paper, with the caption Shunned Millionairess Pays Last Respects To Tragic Childhood Dance Teacher.

After the funeral, Lucy visited Jack at Bellevue. His face had the look of sodden newspaper, grey, semi-transparent, slimily breakable. He was sleeping, mumbling, and occasionally weeping. The doctor with the hog-moustache and the racetrack vest was loath to make book on his chances. The nurse with the big face kept pushing gruel into his mouth, but all of it slid unswallowed on to his pillow.

'Jack?' Lucy whispered, but hopelessly; because his eyes kept roaming and he wasn't speaking any kind of sense any more. 'Jack, it's Lucy.'

That was all she said until it was time to leave. Then she clutched his dead-meat fingers and softly raged at him, 'Why did you do it? Why did you do it? Why? Why did you have to fly?'

The big-faced nurse was standing by the door watching her. Lucy pressed Jack's hand carefully back on to the bedcover, as if she had been caught trying to steal it. She stood up and tried to smile but discovered that she couldn't. The big-faced nurse remained in the doorway, and wouldn't stand aside as Lucy squeezed her way past. Lucy wondered what Jack might have been telling her.

'Goodbye,' she said, with a break in her voice.

The big-faced nurse watched her walk along the corridor, and was still staring at her as she reached the stairs.

When she came home from the funeral the young man was still waiting for her in the hall. He was rather wan, with a snubbish nose and polished brown hair thick with dandruff, and a lumpy frock-coat that seemed to be two-and-a-half sizes too large for him. He stood up as Lucy came in, and said, in a very swallowed English accent, 'Miss Darling?'

'Yes?' said Lucy.

'He's brought you a letter,' said Jeremy, as a grumbled aside.

'Miss Darling, I'm very gratified to make your acquaintance. My name's Clive Mallow, from the India Office.'

'The India Office?' asked Lucy.

'In London, Miss Darling. I'm a civil servant. I have a letter for you. I was charged to deliver it personally, by hand.'

He closed his mouth tightly, and stuck out his hand, and offered Lucy a large white letter. Lucy glanced at Jeremy, and then accepted it, and read the envelope. It was addressed in the firmest, most elegant handwriting, in purplish ink, to her; *Miss Lucy Darling, New York.*

She knew who had sent it at once. But she walked across the hallway, into the morning room, and opened it there, with the gold letter-opener that Jack had bought from Tiffany.

St Ermin's Mansions, SW,
October 1, 1894.

My own dear Lucy,

I apologize profusely for not having written to you sooner, but I have been travelling widely on affairs of study and affairs of Parliament, and this is the first opportunity that I have had to invite you and your father to visit me in England.

Of course I have no idea whatever if you have already made arrangements for the Festive Season, but if you would care to come over for Christmas and the New Year, I would be delighted to entertain you both at Brackenbridge, where we always have the most wonderful celebrations. We invariably eat until we explode, and spoil our guests with far too many presents.

My dear, while this letter may sound jovial, I have missed you with all my heart since I left, and have sat down several times to write to you, telling you of my travels, and of my feelings. But each time I have destroyed what I have written, because it has sounded far too maudlin.

Please write back just as quickly as may be, and tell me that you will be able to gladden my Christmas with your presence. I dispatch this letter with a kiss. No, not a singular kiss, a crowd of kisses, a bewildering sequence, an ardent succession, an ecstatic pell-mell!

Your
Henry

Lucy turned back towards Clive Mallow and her eyes were shining.

'Good news, I trust?' he asked her, although he must already have known what Henry's letter said.

'Yes,' she replied. 'Good news.'

5

Alfred George, 4th Baron Felldale, Henry's father, marched ahead of them through the fog, thrashing his knobby walking-stick, and shouting obscenities at his Dalmatians, a crowd of obscenities, a bewildering sequence. He was sixty-six, and the father not only of Henry, but of eleven other children besides, four boys and seven girls, and he daily took brandy and eggs for breakfast, but he kept up a cracking pace through the desiccated bracken, and was obliged several times to stop and wait for them, sniffing and saying, 'Come along, now, come along, now, plenty more to see.'

The 4th Baron wore a billycock hat, and a huge chequered cape. His eyes were bulbous, a little like Henry's, and his muttonchop whiskers were brambly and vividly white. His boots were wet and very muddy. Unlike Henry and Lucy, he didn't care a damn where he walked.

'You get a fine view of the lake from here,' he told Lucy,

loudly. 'At least you do when it's not quite so foggy. Here, Willy, you disobedient bugger!'

Henry walked close beside Lucy, his hands clasped behind his back. He wore a plain grey coat and a grey gamekeeper's cap. His cheeks were pale and his nose was pink from the cold; but he was still just as handsome as Lucy remembered him. She was wearing a beautifully-cut overcoat of raspberry-coloured tweeds, and a velvet bonnet with a silver brooch and pheasants' feathers.

'My father loves Brackenbridge,' Henry remarked, his breath fuming in the fog. 'He feels the very fibre of it with every step! Do you know that Dr Johnson came here once, with Boswell, in the time of the 1st Baron Felldale. Johnson didn't care for it much, or he claimed that he didn't. He said that it would have made a handsomish town hall, but not much else. I don't think my ancestor ever forgave him.'

They passed through a row of massive and ancient oaks, and now, through the sun-gilded fog, Lucy could dimly see the classical outlines of Brackenbridge itself. It was a huge, pale, Palladian house, with hundreds of faintly-glittering windows, and two curving staircases that swept down in front of it with all the grace of a ballet-dancer's arms.

In the chill of late November, the surface of the artificial lake in front of the house looked like a breathed-over mirror; but ducks still swam across it, leaving ripples behind them that caught the sun, and sparkled.

Leading down to the lake was a series of white marble steps: a classical cascade which Henry had been working on.

'This house means everything to me,' said Henry. 'It is romantic, historic, and noble. It runs through my life like a shining thread. Do you know something, when I was only eight, I was furious with my sisters for cluttering up the Adam fireplaces with their little ornaments, because it spoiled their classic lines.'

'I don't suppose your sisters cared much for that,' smiled Lucy.

Henry obviously didn't understand that she was joking. 'Those who strive to uphold the finer things in life are never popular.'

Lord Felldale had made his way down the hillside towards the house, and had almost reached the lake. His Dalmatians went bounding after him, like nursery rocking-horses. 'Come along, Jumper, you stupid sod! Billy! If you chase those ducks again, I'll damnwell gut you!'

'Your father's a hot potato,' Lucy remarked.

'The Carsons always have been,' Henry told her. 'It runs in the blood. Can't stand to be idle, that's the thing.'

Lucy lifted the hem of her coat to keep it clear of the long wet grass. As she started to walk down the hill, Henry said, 'I haven't had an awful lot of experience with women.'

Lucy stopped, and turned. He had remained for a moment in the foggy green shadow under the oaks, but then he emerged into the pearly-grey brightness and stood very close to her. 'I've travelled, yes; twice around the whole world; and I've made my name in politics; and when we see an end to this miserable Liberal government, which we most assuredly will, I know that I will be called upon to do great things. At least my friends expect me to, and so does the Press. But in front of you, I find myself tongue-tied. What can I say to you, except that you quite captivated me, right from the second I first saw you, and that nobody fairer of face or brighter of heart has ever walked the grounds of Brackenbridge, nor ever will?'

Far from being tongue-tied with her, Henry appeared to Lucy to be immensely talkative. He talked incessantly — about British policy in India, about the restoration work at Brackenbridge, about writers that he knew, about art, about the Persians, about Lord Rosebery and the Liberals, about food, about money, about servants, about living in London. He told her jokes and anecdotes; he described his arduous travels in Persia, and how (sick from exhaustion and self-neglect) he had subsequently gone to convalesce in Athos and Meteroa. 'I was hauled up hundreds of feet of rock face, like a trussed quail in a net, to look at the vinegar and sponge that were offered Christ upon the Cross.'

It was possible, however, that he found it difficult to talk to Lucy about matters of the heart. He had asked his father to take them out on this walk on purpose, so that he could speak to her privately, with all of the glories of Brackenbridge held up grandly and temptingly in front of her; for all that Brackenbridge was not yet his.

But now he had to talk about his feelings; about his real emotions; and there was no sharp anecdote to fit.

There was a very long pause. Lord Felldale, who was now skirting the lake, suddenly stopped, and shielded his eyes with his hand against the foggy glare, and stood watching them for two or three minutes before he shouted at his dogs, 'bastards! buggers!' and continued his walk back to the house.

'Do you love me?' asked Lucy.

Henry took off his cap. 'My dearest Lucy, I feel like such an amateur. I want you to be my wife.'

Lucy smiled, and said, *hmh!* just to tease him. Without even waiting for an answer, Henry looked away, and slapped his cap against his coat, and protested, 'It's no use at all. I simply can't find the right words. It was love at very first sight, Lucy! The instant I saw you walking across that tennis-net, you snatched my heart and you squeezed it in that little fist of yours, and you have never once let it loose. I want you to marry me. In May, my dearest, when the buds are out. Here – at Brackenbridge, in the family chapel.'

He unbuttoned his brown leather glove, and tugged it off, and offered Lucy his bare right hand. She lowered her eyes for a moment. He had amused and embarrassed her; but at the same time she felt extraordinarily meek and feminine. She had always been wilful. She had always teased the boys that she had known; especially the shy and the lovestruck boys; and even Jamie. But somehow she realized that Henry was not to be teased. For all of his apparent shyness with her, Henry was iron-willed and determined that he should have her.

'Of course,' Henry added, 'you don't have to decide anything directly. You can think about it for as long as you wish, although the sooner you make up your mind, the happier you will make me.' He didn't seem to have considered the possibility that she might refuse him.

He turned around and stared for a while at the ghostly views of Brackenbridge, and its woods, and its spectral lake. 'I can't offer you very much, my dearest. None of *this*, at the moment; although we can come here as often as you wish, and one day, God preserve my dear father, it all shall be mine. All I can lay at your feet at this particular moment is my Parliamentary stipend, which will hardly keep you in emeralds, and my book royalties, which were not much more than £34 last year. But – ' and here he lifted a single finger, and smiled at her triumphantly, ' – I can certainly offer you glory.'

Lucy had never been offered glory before. She wasn't even sure what it was. She had been offered money, and fun, and a great deal of undying passion, of one kind or another, but never glory.

She said, uncertainly, 'You'll have to give me time to think about it.'

Henry grasped her hand. 'You're cold! We'd better get back. But you won't keep me waiting, will you? As soon as I saw you disembark from the ship, I knew that I hadn't made a mistake. You're quite perfect, my dearest; in looks and in temperament. To have you as my wife would be the crowning achievement of my life.'

They walked down the hill together towards the lake – close, but not holding hands. Lord Felldale had already packed off his Dalmatians to the kitchens for a meaty bone, and he would be going upstairs to change now, and take his bath, before coming downstairs to the drawing room, for tea and scones, and a noisy half-hour snore in front of the fire.

'When do you have to go to London?' Lucy asked Henry.

'Tomorrow morning, I regret. It won't be for long. Two days at the very most. Next Saturday I wish to take you to see the dearest friend of mine, Margie Asquith. You and she will make such friends!'

They had crossed the wide shingled driveway, and reached the foot of the curving stone steps, when Lucy stopped, and said, 'Henry – I'm none too sure about this.'

'But my dearest Lucy, what is there not to be sure about? My God, look at this! This driveway hasn't been weeded in a month of Sundays.' He bent over and plucked up two or three tiny clumps of grass, and a straggling dandelion.

'Henry, all of my money came by chance. I wasn't highly born, I didn't work for whatever I got. I was rich by accident, and nothing else.'

'I know that,' said Henry, levelly, watching her, still holding the weeds in his hand. 'I know that, and it really doesn't matter two hoots.'

Lucy covered her eyes with her raspberry-gloved hand. 'I'm not too sure what I'm trying to say to you, Henry. I think I'm trying to tell you that I'm not very well learned, and so you soon might find me very uninteresting to talk to. I think I'm trying to tell you, too, that I wasn't naturally bred to manners, so no matter how much I learn, not to mix the fish-knives with the cake-forks, there could always come times when I let you down. I guess I'm trying to tell you that I'm frightened.'

'Lucy –' said Henry, warmly, and reached out to hold her hand.

'It's true!' she protested. 'You meet the Queen, and lords, and all kinds of aristocracy. You're going to be a lord yourself one day. You said yourself, you talked to the what's-his-name of Afghanistan, just like you'd played cricket together. I was born and raised a storekeeper's daughter in

No-Place-At-All, Kansas, and educated with chalk and black-board, and you and me just aint suited.'

Henry stared at her, stiff and expressionless. Then his face gradually cracked into a smile. 'Say that again,' he coaxed her.

She didn't understand. 'All of it?'

'No, no, just the last bit, *please*, when you said that you and me just aint suited.' His accent was so clipped that, to Lucy's ears, he sounded hilarious, like a gobbling turkey.

'You and me just aint suited,' she repeated, in fullblown High Plains whirligig Kansas.

'Again!' Henry begged her, with glee.

'Yewnme jessayn sootud.'

Very slowly, very precisely, Henry tried to imitate her accent. 'You-en-me, jist, aint, sewted. Ha! ha! Is that it!? You-en-me jist ent-sewted.'

'No!' Lucy giggled. 'Not sewted! *Sootud*! Yewnme jessayn sootud.'

Henry, without warning, took her into his arms, and held her much closer and tighter than was usually respectable. He stared at her very steadily, and said, 'You're wrong, Lucy Darling. Yewnme, we're sootud excellently!'

'An awfully lot, that's what we say in Kansas, when we're trying to be posh.'

'All right, then. We're sootud an awfully lot.'

Lucy looked into his eyes for a moment, and then gently pushed him away.

'There's nobody else?' he asked her.

She shook her head. 'There's nobody else.'

'Then please consider marrying me, Lucy; and please don't keep me waiting for too long. We've both been waiting far too long for each other already. Yes, my dearest, I know! It's been my fault, not yours! But I've written you so many poems, although I haven't dared to send them to you, and I thought about you every day, and everywhere I went, even in the castle of Baltit, when I was guest of the

Thum of Hunza, on my way to the high Pamirs, I thought of you, and spoke your name; and when I became the first known traveller to climb behind the glaciers of the Pamirs, and see the head waters of the Oxus, I whispered your name to the wind there, too.'

Self-satisfied, almost smug, he turned around, smiling, and clapped his hands together.

'Don't you *understand?*' he asked her. 'The name of Lucy Darling has been spoken in places where no man had ever been before, nor may ever go again; and if that isn't proof of the intensity of my affections for you, my dearest, then I cannot think what may be.'

Lucy stared back at him wide-eyed, and couldn't think what to say. Her feelings wobbled like a spinning-top. She was flattered – yes; exhilarated – yes; and she thought that Henry was everything that she could possibly want. Ever since she had received his invitation to come to England, she had known that she was going to say yes to him. But now she was terrified that he was far too much for her; that she would never be able to please him. Lucy had seen her own small share of the world. She had clung tight to fenceposts, deafened, while cyclones bath-watered their way across black Kansas skies. She had yachted with millionaires and lunched with visiting princes. She had danced along Fifth Avenue in the middle of the night, in a white silk ballgown. She had crossed the Atlantic on a German steamer (vomiting, most of the time, most dreadfully sick). But what was any of that, compared with what Henry had done?

Henry had been to Persia and China and India and places that most people had never heard of, like Chitral and Mastuj and Bozai Gumbaz.

Henry had hobnobbed with potentates. Henry had taken tea with Queen Victoria, and advised Her Majesty on the manners of the Persians. ('No manners, ma'am.')

Although Lucy had arrived at Brackenbridge only yesterday afternoon, Henry's abrasive energy and unstoppable outpourings of knowledge and wit had already made her feel that it might have been better for both of them if she hadn't come at all.

A summer flirtation on Rhode Island was one thing. But a serious proposal of marriage in the Derbyshire countryside, in winter, was quite another.

For goshsake, Henry knew French and Italian and classical Greek; he could quote foreign sonnets by the tailor's yard; he wrote articles and poems and worked furiously at his desk from first light until lunchtime; and his lamp was always burning until well after midnight, every night. As far as Lucy could make out he was expert at absolutely *everything,* from the plastering restoration in Brackenbridge's great gallery, to the political future of India, to what the cook was preparing for lunch.

This morning, Henry had been outraged when the kitchen-maid had come up with a suggested luncheon menu of lobster mayonnaise and cold rabbit pie. 'On a raw, chill day like this? You must be losing your senses!'

Lucy was excited and desperately flattered that he should have asked her to marry him. He was handsome, he was strong, he had offered her glory. Not only that, if she were to marry Henry Carson, the shameful shenanigans at the Waldorf would be expunged for ever. She would be able to step back into society; she would shine with even more social incandescence than before. Her only reservation was whether she could manage the task of being his wife. A girl who knew nothing about politics of any kind; a girl whose knowledge of society was limited to one summer season on Rhode Island, and a few months of dancing and theatre-going in New York?

What was more, she would have to live in England; and England seemed like such a damp and suffocating place, with stunningly offensive drains and air like a cold wet quilt. Nobody was welcoming or pleasant. The customs officers at Liverpool had rummaged through her trunks for hours, and reduced Nora's immaculate packing to a blizzard of tissue paper and crumpled dresses. The fat-legged maid who had taken Lucy up to her room at Brackenbridge had said, accusingly, 'Tha'll be axing for hot water, I don't suppose?' – an unmistakable warning that hot water was a nuisance, because hot water had to be fetched.

'Lucy – you will try to be quick, coming to your decision?' Henry insisted, with impatience.

'Have you asked poppa?'

'Indeed I've *tried*.'

'What did he say?'

Henry made a face. 'To be truthful, my sweet, I'm not altogether sure. He sang me a sort of song.'

Lucy tried to smile, but she found it difficult. Henry was not at all abashed by Jack – Jack with his fits and his roaming eyes, all bundled up in his invalid-chair like a huge and helpless infant. Henry was used to madness and senility. But Lucy found Jack an embarrassment, and a terrible burden, too – and in some ways worse than a burden, because he reminded her every time she looked at him of Uncle Casper's viciousness and her mother's unfaithfulness, and the enigma of her own birth. *Whose little girl are you, Lucy Darling?* Jack's eyes always asked her, helplessly; and how she hated those eyes.

Lucy said, 'Poppa's been worse, these past two days. He's probably tired.'

'Perhaps I ought to let Dr Roberts take a look at him,' Henry suggested. 'He's very modern, Dr Roberts, trained in Vienna. He did wonders for father's liverishness. Gave him Kissingen salts, and some kind of electrical treatment on his skin.'

Lucy asked, 'Is that all that poppa did? Sing for you?'

Henry nodded, obviously amused. 'It was something about dancing. "Swing them up, swing them down."'

'Swing them pretty girls round and round,' Lucy finished.

'You know it,' said Henry.

'Yes.'

Henry hesitated for a moment, and then cleared his throat. 'I love you, my darling; you have quite changed the way that I think. I used to believe that celibacy was the only sensible way of life; and that marriage was a puzzle. Now it seems as if it is celibacy that is a puzzle, and that marriage will provide me with the answer to everything.'

'Just give me a little time, Henry,' Lucy begged him.

'Thank you, my dearest, I will,' Henry replied; although he was plainly disappointed. 'But you won't keep me waiting for too long, will you?'

It was raining hard the next morning when the station fly was brought around to take Henry to Derby. Lucy stood in the high-pillared portico in her high-necked plum-coloured dress, and waved to him with her handkerchief. She felt like a character out of Jane Austen (she had found the author's early work, *Love and Friendship* in her bedroom). Henry lifted his hat to her and called, 'You will think very hard, won't you, my darling child? And you will try to say yes?'

The fly scrunched off across the wet shingle. Brackenbridge had taken on an exceptionally dismal cast today, with the rain driving through the oak trees and lashing at the laurel bushes around the house, and cascading noisily from the gutters. A stablehand walked across the driveway with a sodden coat over his head, leading behind him a large bay mare, her blanket black with rain.

Tessie, the disagreeable fat-legged maid, was waiting for Lucy when she came back into the hallway. 'Dr Roberts will be calling to see your father this morning, miss,' she said. 'Will you see him in the morning room, or in the library?'

Lucy was surprised. 'I don't know,' she said. 'Mr Carson didn't even mention to me that he was coming.'

Tessie sniffed. 'Well, *that* don't surprise me one bit. That's Mr Carson all over, that is. Arranges owt, but never tells nobody nowt.'

'Well, if he's arranged it — I guess, yes. We'll see the doctor in the morning room.'

'The morning room, miss. Very well, miss.'

Lucy would have done anything to have Nora with her now — even fussy, inquisitive Nora. But on their way from New York she had allowed Nora to disembark at Dun Laoghaire, in Ireland, so that she could visit her family in County Carlow. Nora hadn't seen her grandmother since she was three years old, when her father and mother had taken their nine children across to America. She would be coming to Brackenbridge to join Lucy just after Christmas, but at the moment Lucy felt as if she had no friends at all, nobody with whom she could talk about her feelings for Henry, no matter how obliquely. Jack had grown more and more morose and uncommunicative with every passing day, and Mary — the nurse whom Lucy had employed in New York to take care of him during their journey to Europe — had turned out to be so long-suffering and martyred that Lucy scarcely dared to speak to her.

If Lucy had asked Mary whether she should marry Henry or not, Mary would most likely have said, 'Don't ask *me* such a question. I was never asked to marry by anyone.'

Lucy went through to the morning room, where Mary was reading Jack a tract about the evils of travelling on a Sunday. Jack was lying back in his invalid-chair at an odd angle, his head half-propped on a stained needlepoint cushion, his eyes furiously roaming from side to side. Although he was sitting close to the fire, he was wrapped up head to toe in a large green blanket, and this blanket had been strapped around his waist with a leather belt. He was startlingly white, and he smelled of vinegar and urine, and something else, like cabbage that isn't quite fresh.

Mary looked up. She was Lithuanian by birth, gargoyle-like to look at and professionally despairing. She wore a nurse's cap of her own devising, which looked rather like a deep-sea fisherman's hat, in thick brown felt; and a coarse beige linen apron. Her eyebrows met thickly in the middle, and one of her cheeks was semi-circled with a bright crimson scar, where, during her public nursing days, a patient at Bellevue had attempted to kill her with a broken iodine bottle.

'Mary, did you know that Mr Carson had arranged for a doctor to visit Mr Darling?' asked Lucy.

Mary said, 'He did mention it, Miss Darling.' She had an odd, reflexive accent, that always sounded to Lucy like somebody talking backwards. 'Darling Miss, it mention did he.' There was an expression on her face that showed she was well-prepared to be sullen.

'I mean, you don't *mind* if a doctor comes to take a look at him?' asked Lucy.

'Not my position to mind, Miss Darling. This is Mr Carson's house, if Mr Carson wishes to send for the doctor, then who am I to say no?'

'He's supposed to be very up-to-date, this doctor.'

'I'm sure that he is, Miss Darling. But that won't make my duties any less burdensome, will it? And if I know doctors, and I *do* know doctors, he'll give me more to do than ever. "Now, then, nurse, make sure you cup the patient four times the day, and dose him up with Vichy salts eight times the day." It's always the nurse that suffers the extra work.'

Lucy sat down on the opposite side of the fireplace. 'I'm sure there won't be any extra work, Mary. If this doctor can make poppa just a little better, you might even have *less* to do.'

'Well that's the unlikeliest story I ever heard,' said Mary, gloomily.

'I'm just surprised that Mr Carson forgot to tell me he was coming, that's all,' Lucy replied.

'Has Mr Carson gone for long?' Mary wanted to know.

'No, no. Two days, that's what he told me. He had some important business, he couldn't get out of it. Something to do with Parliament.'

'I suppose he will travel back on Sunday,' Mary remarked. She shook her head and her huge brown hat flopped from side to side. 'What godlessness.'

Lucy looked across at Jack, but made no effort to speak to him, or to catch his attention. He lay tilted in his invalid-chair with his eyes darting around in his face like flies around a milk-pudding, and nobody could guess what he was thinking, if he was thinking anything at all.

Mary took out her noisy pocket-watch, ignoring the gilded clock above the fireplace. 'I will bathe him after the doctor has gone; and he can wait for his syrup of poppies, too.'

Without saying anything else, she lifted the pamphlet in her lap, and continued to read, 'Sunday travelling, encouraged by specially low prices, is a great evil. It encourages idleness, and the use of bad tobacco, bad drink, bad language, and bad company, while the profits go to the railway company.'

It was impossible to tell if Jack was listening or not. He appeared to Lucy to have hidden himself somewhere inside his own head — to have shut himself tightly in some dark cupboard without pain or memories or hopelessness.

'We'll be visiting London ourselves next week,' said Lucy, interrupting Mary's reading. 'Mr Carson has promised to take me to see the sights.'

'I hope that your father will be well enough to travel,' Mary replied, threateningly. 'In my opinion, it was ill-advised to bring him all the way to England; and in such rough weather.'

Lucy didn't answer. They had argued about this before. Lucy wouldn't have brought Jack to England at all, but propriety had demanded it and Henry had insisted. He didn't want to compromise Lucy's reputation or his own Parliamentary career by entertaining her at Brackenbridge for the whole of the Christmas season, unchaperoned, particularly since he intended to announce at the end of her stay that they would be married in the spring.

The London newspapers were far more discreet than Hearst's and Pulitzer's rags in New York, but there would have been smiles and raised eyebrows and a few 'aye-ayes' among Henry's Oxford set, and at the India Office, and even at Marlborough House, and Henry could not bear to be thought of as anything but spotlessly honourable, in particular when it came to women.

Besides, Henry believed that a change of scenery would do Jack some good; lift his morale; show him that life could still be interesting and profitable; and quicken his convalescence. With any luck, he could be out of plaster by Christmas.

For Lucy, the journey to England would have been heaps more fun if she could have brought Evelyn instead; or any of her erstwhile New York friends. But the six or seven telephone calls that she had made to the Scott mansion the week before she left New York had been stuffily rebuffed by the butler's 'not at home, Miss Darling, I regret,' and it had been the same story at the McPhersons and the Vanderbilts and the Frosts. None of her friends had come to wave her goodbye, even though her departure for England on the *Fürst Bismarck* had been announced in the social columns.

Mary closed her pamphlet. 'He is worse every day, your father. He used to speak just a little. Now he does not speak to me at all. I never know what he requires. I never know when he feels hungry; or when he feels thirsty; or when he wishes me to read; or when he wishes me to stop reading. I never know when he wishes to sleep. I never know when he wishes to wake up. It really is intolerable. I have always thought that patients have an obligation to their nurses to show a little consideration.'

She was still complaining when Tessie came into the morning room to say that Dr Roberts had arrived. Lucy asked her to show him in and Mary turned her head away.

Lucy didn't know what she had been expecting from Henry's 'up-to-date' doctor. An excitable young man with spectacles and wild hair, she supposed. But when Dr Roberts appeared in the doorway – extremely tall, extremely handsome in rather a satanic way, with black hair combed back from his forehead and slightly greying sidewhiskers, and lips that seemed to be curled up at the thought of all the mischief that doctors could get up to, if they chose, Lucy stood up quickly and said, 'Oh!' as if she had been caught in the act of doing something she shouldn't.

'My apologies,' said Dr Roberts, in one of the deepest voices that Lucy had ever heard. 'I had no intention of startling you. You must be Miss Darling. Dr William Roberts, at your service.'

He took Lucy's hand. There were dark circles under his eyes, as if he rarely slept. 'Mr Carson explained that your father had accidentally fallen, and broken his spine.'

'It happened in New York, two months ago now. He's still in plaster; but his doctors said it wouldn't hurt him to travel. They said it might cheer him up.'

'Which, quite manifestly, it has not,' remarked Dr Roberts, turning towards Jack and removing his gloves.

'He is worse than ever,' Mary volunteered. 'He never speaks, he never tries to feed himself. These days I am not very much better than his slave.'

'Who is this person?' asked Dr Roberts.

'My father's nurse Mary,' Lucy explained.

Dr Roberts approached Jack; leaned forward, and stared him closely in the face. 'Well, Mary,' he said, without looking at her, 'a nurse in a sense is always a patient's slave. She must give of herself without asking what is the cost. She must be gentle and attentive at all times, and think of nothing but her charge's welfare.'

Mary glanced indignantly at Lucy, her eyebrows dense, her mouth puckered.

'What is your father's name?' asked Dr Roberts.

Lucy came forward and stood beside him. 'It's Jack,' she said, quietly. 'He's not dying, is he?'

Dr Roberts ignored that question. Instead, he lifted Jack's eyelid with his thumb and watched his eyeball coursing from one side to the other. 'Jack?' he called him. 'Jack, can you hear me? I'm a doctor.' He asked Lucy, 'Can he normally speak? I mean, he's spoken since his accident?'

'He is play-acting, if you ask me,' Mary put in. 'Trying to win himself some sympathy.'

'I did not ask you,' Dr Roberts squashed her. He stood up straight again, frowning. 'What medication do you give him?'

'Something for the pain, that's all,' said Lucy.

'Laudanum,' Mary explained.

'How much laudanum, and how often?'

'As much and as often as he needs.'

'What is that unpleasant smell?' asked Dr Roberts.

'I was waiting until you saw him before I gave him his bath,' Mary explained.

'When was his last bath?' Dr Roberts wanted to know.

Mary was silent.

'When did you last bathe him?' Dr Roberts demanded.

'I could not say for sure. Not too many days ago. He complained the last time that it hurt him, so I left it for a while. It was his own wish.'

'I presume that he isn't continent?'

Mary shook her head.

'What does he eat? What does he drink?'

'Well,' said Mary, 'porridge mostly, and water. He cannot trouble himself to chew anything solid. He asks for a whisky now and again, but I do not like to give it to him, not while he's so sick.'

Dr Roberts unbuckled the belt that held Jack's blanket in place. He lifted one corner of the blanket a little, peered inside, sniffed, then dropped it again.

'Miss Darling?' he said, turning towards her.

Lucy had just lifted her hands to rearrange the dried flowers on the mantelshelf. She could see by Dr Roberts' face that something was badly amiss.

'I'm afraid it looks to me as if your father is in a very grave condition,' he said. 'You ought to leave the room. Perhaps you would be good enough to arrange for a carriage, so that your father can be taken to the hospital.'

'What's wrong with him?' asked Lucy. She felt a sudden cold sensation of panic. Ever since his accident, she had secretly prayed that Jack would die; she had believed with all of her heart that he would be better off dead. But now that Dr Roberts was looking at her with such dreadful gravity, she couldn't bear to hear what he was going to say. Jack might be better off dead, but if he were dead, then Lucy would have nobody.

Dr Roberts said, 'I have to examine your father thoroughly. You ought to leave the room. Please. This, er – this *nurse* can stay and help me.'

Lucy swallowed. Then she nodded. 'Very well. I'll ask for a carriage. Is the hospital very far?'

'Not quite twenty miles. But he has to go. He may very well need surgery.'

Lucy left the room without another word and closed the doors behind her. Tessie was crossing the hallway, and she stopped. 'Miss Darling? Are you all right?'

'Yes,' Lucy whispered. 'Could you ask the coachman to bring a carriage around?'

She took three steps forward across the hallway and her eyes switched off and her knees buckled underneath her. She heard Tessie crying out; she heard her own dress whooshing as she fell. She knew that she had cracked her head on the marble as she collapsed, but she was surprised to discover that it didn't hurt at all.

She opened her eyes and a dark man with glittering black eyes and a cleft chin was looming over her. She didn't feel afraid of him, but she was curious to know why he was here, in her bedroom. And why was he staring at her so intently? His chin was very dark, as if it had been rubbed with lampblack. She couldn't think why any man should want to rub his chin with lampblack.

She said, 'Lampblack. Why?'

The man abruptly turned away from her. A woman with a dying bird on her head was standing by the door. The room was so gloomy that Lucy could barely see. She heard a noise like somebody tossing gravel against the window, and then a roll of drums.

The dark man turned back to her. 'Miss Darling?'

She was recovering consciousness very quickly. She began to understand that the gravel against the window was rain; heavy rain; and that the drums were thunder. She recognized the woman with the dying bird on her head as Mary, Jack's nurse, and she recognized the dying bird as her nurse's hat, not a dying bird at all. But she still didn't understand who the man was, or what he was doing here.

'You swooned, Miss Darling,' the man told her. 'Just rest for a while. You'll be quite all right.'

Lucy looked around her. She realized now that she was lying in her bed in the yellow company suite at Brackenbridge. She reached up with one hand, and felt the embroidered initial F on the linen pillow-slip. F for Felldale. On the opposite side of the room stood a large mahogany bureau, and beside it hung a painting of Agnes, 2nd Baroness Felldale, who had died in childbirth the very same year that she had married. The baroness's face was pale, bulbous-eyed, and infinitely regretful.

'I swooned?' asked Lucy. 'I don't remember. My head hurts, though. My head hurts something awful. Did I hit my head?'

Mary stepped forward and the dark man stepped away. Mary looked even more displeased with life than ever. 'Are you recovered, Miss Darling?'

Lucy was exploring her forehead with her fingertips, and suddenly found a large and painful bump. 'Ow! There it is! It's enormous! How in the heck did I manage to do that?'

The dark man reappeared on the other side of the bed. 'You were lucky it wasn't any worse, Miss Darling. I'm afraid you'll have a magnificent black eye, though, for a week or two. You should eat more regularly. Eating doesn't have to be fattening. Small regular meals are quite sufficient; and they are an excellent insurance against such swoons.'

'You're Dr . . . *Roberts*,' said Lucy.

'Yes, my dear,' he smiled at her. 'That's right.'

'How's poppa? Have you had time to look at him yet?'

Dr Roberts nodded. 'You've been unconscious for almost an hour. I've examined your father as well as circumstances would allow. I wanted to talk to you, however, before dispatching him to the hospital.'

Lucy tried to focus on him. Her vision was still blurry, and she couldn't quite manage to make out if he were smiling or not.

Dr Roberts sat on the bed beside her, and took her hand. Now that he was closer, she could see that his expression was very serious indeed. It was so serious that she had an almost irrepressible urge to laugh; especially since he was so good-looking (in his satanic fashion) and he was holding her hand with such uninvited familiarity.

'I must be truthful with you,' he said. 'Your father has very little time left to live. Amputation may stave off his demise; possibly for several weeks. He may even last until Christmas, but not longer. You will at least be glad to know that his pain will not be great, and he will be given sufficient opiates to render his last hours bearable.'

'Tell me,' Lucy whispered.

Dr Roberts lowered his eyes. Like many dark men, he had very luxuriant eyelashes. Lucy stared at them in fascination.

'It would probably be better for all concerned if your father were removed to the hospital; and that you said your goodbyes to him quite soon.'

'What's wrong with him? The doctors in New York said that he would live.'

Dr Roberts said, 'There is no point in trying to spare your feelings, Miss Darling. He is suffering from what we call necrosis. In other words, his nerves and his blood-vessels were subjected to such injury that his legs below the knee are already dead. The rest of him is speedily following.'

He paused and licked his lips, and then he said, 'It may be some consolation to you that nothing could have been done for him, not by the doctors in New York; nor by anybody here; and that while his nursing was sometimes lax, it was not the direct cause of his condition. He was beyond hope, Miss Darling, the very moment he fell and broke his back.'

In spite of herself, in spite of everything, Lucy's eyes filled up with blistering-hot tears. She felt so wretched, as if she were to blame for what had happened, as if she had been Jack's cross, from the moment she was born. She bent her head forward on the quilt and sobbed until it hurt; while Mary stood by the door in her fisherman's hat looking as if she were about to go to sea and Dr Roberts uncomfortably patted her back and told her to *sshh, ssshh*, everything was going to turn out all right, Jack would scarcely suffer, he would die by quiet degrees, as he was dying already, and that the Lord would welcome him quietly home.

She entered Jack's bedroom silently, and stood for a long time watching him. It was a sombre room, with dark blue walls and carved oak panelling. Through the window she could make out the greenish-grey outlines of the oaks, bowing and dancing in the rain. Jack was lying back on his pillow, awake, his eyes still flickering, but somehow less fretfully than usual. Lucy approached his bed and smiled at him with the smile of the truly sad.

'Jack?' she called him.

'Hello, sweetheart,' he croaked at her. He hadn't spoken a word to her for over a week, but now he seemed quite rational.

'Jack, they're going to take you to the hospital.'

'They could save themselves some time, and take me straight to the cemetery.'

'Jack, you're not dying.'

'I'm dying, sweetheart. Dying, it's just like being in love. It's one of those things you know for sure. Nobody can fool you otherwise.'

He coughed, and then he said, 'That Dr Roberts told me, in any case. I asked him straight and he told me straight. Dry gangrene, that's what he said. Instead of dying all at once, I'm dying piece by piece. Let's just hope my head is the last to go. I'd hate my hands to be still alive when my head wasn't there to know it.'

Lucy drew up a small ribbon-backed bedroom chair and sat close to the bed. She didn't take his hand, she couldn't. His hands felt as if they had been dead and buried for weeks.

'I loved your momma, you know that,' Jack said, in a clogged-up voice. 'I loved her so much, if I just hadn't of hit her. This is my punishment, lying here today, half dead already.'

'Jack . . . she must have loved you too.'

Tears slid out of his eyes, and on to his pillow. 'If she ever did, I killed it, didn't I, then her, now me.'

They sat in silence for a very long time. The light died outside the window, but the rain continued to clatter, and the guttering chuckled at Jack's self-inflicted plight, and draughts blew soft mockery under the doors.

'Jack . . .' said Lucy, at last. 'Jack, why did you do it?'

Another long pause. Then, 'Why did I do what?'

'Why did you jump? Why did you try to save Mrs Sweeney?'

'Oh . . . that. Didn't I tell you? Well, maybe I didn't, at that. I had to jump. I had to save her. She was the only person who knew.'

'What do you mean? The only person who knew what?'

Jack coughed, and coughed, and then awkwardly wiped his mouth. 'She told me on the stairs . . . just before we went out. She said, you behave yourself, Jack Darling . . . and you dance with me tonight . . . and maybe, just maybe, I'll tell you something you'd truly like to know.'

He said nothing more for almost a minute, but lay back on his pillow wheezing. High-pitched, tubercular wheezes. Then he coughed again, and caught his breath, and coughed some more.

Lucy asked, in a voice as transparent as water, 'What was it you truly wanted to know? Nothing worth *dying* for, surely?'

Jack turned his face towards her, and for the first time since she had left Oak City railroad depot with Jamie, to go to California in search of her fortune, Lucy saw the Jack who had brought her up, lean and sad and kind, the Jack she had always believed was her father.

'Oh yes, it was worth dying for. More than worth dying for. Molly Sweeney told me she knew who your poppa was. Your true poppa. She knew for sure.'

'But how? How did she know?'

'She birthed you, that's how; she was the Oak City midwife; and your momma must've told her then. She and your momma were always close friends. She treated your momma like her own daughter; and your momma returned the compliment, and that's why she gave you all of those dancing-lessons for no charge at all.'

Lucy felt unreal, as if she were still half-concussed. 'Mrs Sweeney *knew*?'

Jack nodded, and coughed. 'She knew all right. Only person who did. Then and there, right on the stairs, that's what she told me. You behave yourself tonight, Jack Darling, you dance with me, and I'll tell you something you'd truly like to know.'

'But she didn't tell you?' asked Lucy. 'She didn't give you any idea?'

Jack was still fighting to catch his breath. 'She was — teasing me. Know what I mean? She was torturing me.

Paying me back. She never liked me . . . never liked me one bit. What she was doing was paying me back. Far as Molly Sweeney was concerned, your momma was just like a daughter . . . that's what she used to say. And when she died . . . when your momma died . . . Molly Sweeney laid the blame on me.'

He gasped, and coughed, and coughed again. 'That's what she came for . . . that's why she came to New York. She came to dance, and she came to settle that score. Well, she sure settled it. She sure settled it good. She told me she knew and then she died without telling me . . . and that's something I'm going to have carry with me on a handcart to Hell.'

'Jack,' said Lucy, her cheeks shining with tears. 'Jack, you're not going to Hell. Momma's waiting for you. You'll see, Jack, and all those people you took care of.'

Jack closed his eyes, anything to blot out his dancing vision.

'I wish,' he said. 'I only wish. At least, if Molly'd told me, you could have gone to your wedding-day knowing who your real poppa was.'

Lucy sat in silence beside the bed. The room was so dark now that she could hardly see. The tears dried on her face.

'Jack?' she said, after a long time.

'What is it, sweetheart?'

'Jack, do you want to go to hospital?'

Jack didn't answer.

Lucy said, 'If you don't want to go, we'll take care of you here. I can ask Henry to find us another nurse.'

Jack coughed. 'I'll go, sweetheart. I'd rather go. I don't want you to watch me dying. I know what it's like, watching somebody die – whether you love 'em or not.'

His breathing grew thicker. He shifted his hand on the quilt and Lucy thought for a moment that he was reaching out for her, but he wasn't. He was almost asleep.

'Jack?' Lucy whispered.

'The brooch, that's what she said,' Jack murmured, then coughed explosively.

Lucy felt the back of her neck prickle. 'The *brooch*? What brooch?'

But Jack had already fallen asleep, and his mumbling had degenerated into a thick, crackling snore.

Lucy sat in the darkness listening to him struggle for breath. *The brooch*, that's what Mrs Sweeney had told him. It must have been a clue; a teasing clue. Jack hadn't understood it. But Lucy did. It confirmed the dread that she had kept to herself, ever since Uncle Casper had taunted her about her mother. If the brooch were the clue to the identity of Lucy's father, then without a doubt it had been Uncle Casper. She was the daughter of a brother and a sister; the child of unholy intercourse.

She didn't shed any more tears. She had shed enough. But as she sat next to this dying man, with the rain rattling against the windows like the skeletal fingertips of death, softly seeking admission, she made up her mind that everything that had happened in Kansas would be forgotten now; that she would marry Henry, and become Mrs Lucy Carson.

Lucy Darling, whoever Lucy Darling had ever been, would die when Jack Darling died.

She was still sitting with her head bowed when the door creaked open slightly. She didn't turn around; the house was alive with creaks and groans and abrupt cracking noises. But after a very long pause she heard an incredulous voice say, 'Vanessa?'

She lifted her head. Silhouetted in the open doorway stood Lord Felldale, in a bulky woollen dressing-gown, perched heavily on his cane.

'Vanessa?' he repeated.

Lucy drew back her chair and stood up. She approached the doorway, so that the lamplight from the landing fell in a triangle across her face.

'It's Lucy, Lord Felldale.'

The old baron stepped back, and focused his clouded eyes. 'Lucy? Lucy? Well, I'll be buggered! I could have sworn for one moment that you were Vanessa. Back of your neck, identical! Good Lord! Gave me quite a shiver, I can tell you!'

Lucy glanced back into the room, listened for a moment, then closed the door. 'Poppa's sleeping,' she said.

Lord Felldale nodded towards the door. 'Is he poorly? Dr Roberts said he may not last the week.'

'He's very ill, yes, sir.'

'He can stay here, don't you know, if that's what you'd prefer. Don't mind visitors dying here, plenty have before.'

'He says he'd rather go to the hospital.'

Lord Felldale offered Lucy his arm, and together they walked around the galleried landing until they reached the wide white marble stairs. On all sides hung immense oil paintings of classical scenes, shipwrecks and thunderstorms and torrents of hugely-upholstered nudes. Lord Felldale remarked, 'A man, ideally, should die at home; his own home; with a small orchestra to play him out with his favourite airs; and perhaps a choir. I myself wish to close my eyes for the last time to the strains of the *Eton Boating Song*.'

They went slowly downstairs together. They had almost reached the hallway when Lucy said, 'Who's Vanessa?'

'Ah,' Lord Felldale smiled. 'Vanessa is my fifth daughter, a year younger than Henry. She's married now, married some banker bugger. What's his name, Y-Stancombe, some bally ridiculous name like that. Wealthy, but you should hear him laugh! Won't let him go near the horses, in case he laughs. But handsome enough. And wealthy, as I say. Very pretty girl, Vanessa, very pretty. Fair hair, like yours; could have sworn you were her, for just a moment.'

'I'm flattered,' said Lucy.

'Well, my dear, you deserve flattery,' Lord Felldale told her, as a footman opened the doors of the drawing room for them. 'You're quite pretty enough in your own right. No wonder Henry fell for you so hard. When he came back from America, he could talk of nothing else. And never seen him scribble so hard! Always scribbles when he's in love! Desperate drivel, of course, quite desperate; but the girls like it.'

From the way in which Henry had spoken to her, Lucy had supposed that he had known very few girls, and that his overwhelming interests in life had been politics, and exploration, and dinners with his friends from All Souls.

'Is he *often* in love?' she asked Lord Felldale. She couldn't help herself.

'Not often, always,' Lord Felldale replied. 'But I've never seen him so much taken as he is by you. Never. He talks too much, that's Henry's trouble; and he's what we call a Clever-Dick. But you shouldn't take too much notice of that. He's very sentimental, underneath. It's a Carson trait. Weakness, if you like; along with a certain amount of godlessness; and a belief in doing everything correctly; and a liking for the pork they serve on Sundays at the Bell Inn, in Derby.'

Lucy wasn't certain what she should make of this; but before she could reply, Lord Felldale inclined his head close to her ear, and said, 'I know that Henry has asked you to tie the knot, my dear girl; and if you find it in your heart to say yes to him, then all I can say is, I'd be very content.'

Lucy, unexpectedly, found herself blushing.

Dr Roberts was waiting for her in the drawing room, with a half-finished glass of tawny port on the mantelshelf beside him. He looked tired and serious. The drawing room was decorated in Adam green and gold, with green silk curtains, and figured green upholstery. In the summer it must have been exceptionally fresh and bright. On a wet November night with the curtains drawn tight and the log-fire sullenly filling the air with acrid oak-smoke, it felt damp and unwelcoming and claustrophobically enclosed, almost submarine.

'Another port, Roberts?' Lord Felldale asked him.

Dr Roberts shook his head. 'I have to be going. Do you wish me to take Mr Darling into hospital tonight?'

Lucy said, 'He'll go, Dr Roberts. He thinks it would be better if he did. But he'd prefer to go tomorrow, if that's all right. He's asleep now, anyway.'

'Very well,' Dr Roberts told her. 'Sleep is probably the best condition for him, the way things are. I'll call again tomorrow morning, if you could have a carriage ready for him, and blankets to wrap him in.'

He finished his port, then came up to Lucy and said, 'As for yourself, Miss Darling, how does your head feel?'

'Sore,' she declared.

'Remember what I told you about eating regularly,' he admonished her.

He collected his hat and his coat and his gloves, and went to the door. 'I gather you're still keeping well, Lord Felldale,' he added. 'You haven't complained of any twinges.'

'I wouldn't either, if it meant taking any more of your repulsive salts,' Lord Felldale retorted.

One of the footmen had been sent out in the rain with a message to be telegraphed to London, to summon Henry back to Brackenbridge.

Meanwhile, there was nothing that Lucy could do but take a bath, which Tessie filled for her without complaining, and prepare herself for bed.

In spite of what Dr Roberts had told her, she couldn't bring herself to eat more than a few mouthfuls of supper. It was cold spiced mutton and lentil soup, and she didn't fancy either. Henry was right to complain about the kitchens at Brackenbridge. She could have cooked better herself.

The kitchen-maid plainly didn't mind that Lucy had eaten so little. Any leftovers from the upstairs tables were immediately devoured downstairs. Henry had told her that he had once changed his mind about a chop which he had left on the side of his plate, and had called the footman (who had only just reached the dining-room door) to bring it back. The footman had about-faced, with the chop already gripped between his teeth.

273

Shortly after eleven o'clock, the great house began to close down. Fires were guarded or damped, dogs were kenneled, shutters were closed. Lucy went to Jack's room to see if he needed anything, but he was still asleep. She didn't go too close. He smelled sour. He smelled like a man dying. She stood beside his bed watching him, and thinking of Kansas, dust and sky, and thin-faced men and women with eyes like funeral beads, scratching a living out of nothing.

The windows rattled in the wind. Lucy said, quite loudly, 'Goodnight, Jack,' and went back to her bedroom.

In the middle of the night, the rain died away, but the gale blew even more fiercely. It screamed between the chimneys, and shook in frustrated fury at the shutters, and sent leaves and branches tumbling and galloping across the parklands, skeleton riders on skeleton horses.

Lucy heard the great Tompion clock at the end of the corridor chiming three. She lay in bed with her eyes open for a while; then she pushed back the covers and got up. The room was draughty, but now the rain had passed, and the south-west wind had risen, it was noticeably warmer. She stood by the window in her long white cambric nightgown, watching the clouds shrivel away to the east, and the trees toss themselves wildly from side to side.

It was then that she heard a creak; the same creak that Jack's door had made when Lord Felldale had opened it that afternoon. She listened; and then four or five minutes later she heard it again. She tiptoed to her bedroom door, quickly and quietly opened it, and looked out along the corridor.

She thought she saw a shadow, flickering for a second on the oak-panelled walls. A shadow that could have been a monk, or a fisherman. But there was nothing else; nothing but the wind and the rattling windows; and the stuttering bang of a kitchen-yard gate with a broken latch.

She drank a tepid glass of water, and went back to bed. She wondered if she ought to pray; but she didn't know what to pray for. She hoped she wasn't godless, like the Carsons. She needed God now; she needed Jesus; and the bland kind face of the Virgin. She hoped they were watching over her, even if she wasn't praying.

She hoped more than anything that they would save Jack from suffering; and give her strength; and help her to discover who she was.

Tessie woke her up shortly before seven o'clock, shaking her shoulder. She said, 'What? What is it?' then pushed Tessie away, and covered her shoulder with her hand as if Tessie had hurt her or dirtied her nightgown. It was unthinkable for a servant to touch her like that.

'Sorry, Miss Darling, but you'd best come.'

She sat up. Tessie was already crossing the bedroom with Lucy's robe billowing around her like wings. 'What's happened?' Lucy asked; although even as she asked it, she knew.

'Dr Roberts has been sent for,' Tessie told her.

Quickly (why was she hurrying?) Lucy walked along the corridor to Jack's room. The door was wide open, as if it were a prison cell from which a convict had escaped during the night (and, in a way, it was). Lord Felldale was standing just outside the door, looking weary and desiccated. His valet Michael was hovering at his elbow with a steaming glass of brandy and hot water, with an egg floating in it.

Lord Felldale opened his arms for Lucy and hugged her. He felt bony, and smelled of tobacco. 'I'm so sorry, my dear child,' he told her; and she couldn't reply, because her throat was tightly choked, but she managed not to cry. She didn't want to cry. She refused to cry for anything, ever again.

'When Dr Roberts said he might last until Christmas . . .' Lord Felldale began. 'Well, I didn't imagine for a moment that it would be so damn quick. Diagnosed and dead, all on the same damn day.'

Lucy looked into the room. Mary was standing by the

window, against the watered-milk light of morning, her face hidden in crumbly shadow under her nurse's hat. Lucy couldn't tell if she were sad or relieved or just indifferent. On the bed, Jack lay still, his head slightly tilted to one side, the pupils of his eyes still for the first time since he had fallen from the Waldorf's balcony. He seemed to be staring at a point somewhere on the left side of Lucy's robe, and Lucy instinctively looked down at her robe to see what he was staring at. He didn't look dead; but then he didn't look alive, either. His right hand lay open on the quilt; his left hand lay closed.

Mary said something that sounded like, 'Darling Miss, sorry am I.'

'Yes,' said Lucy. Then, 'Thank you.'

Her mouth was filling with saliva, and she felt suddenly flushed and hot.

'I'm sure that he didn't suffer at all,' Mary intoned.

Lucy glanced at Jack as if she were annoyed at him. But now she kept having to swallow more and more saliva, and she felt almost as if she were drowning. She took one last look at Jack, pushed quite abruptly past Lord Felldale, who was drinking his brandy-and-egg, and walked stiff-legged back to her room. She walked slowly at first, then quicker and quicker. She could feel her stomach tightening as she reached her door. Tessie had been hurrying along behind her, trying to keep up with her.

'Is there owt you'd care for, Miss Darling? Cup o' tea, mebbe?'

Lucy's mouth flooded with bile. Keeping her lips tightly pressed together, she shook her head.

'Mebbe some nice warm milk? The cows'll be milked by now.'

She couldn't answer, couldn't speak at all. She slammed her bedroom door behind her, crossed over to the washstand in three urgent strides, and vomited into the water-jug.

After a few moments, she lifted her head, her eyes

crowded with tears. Then her stomach curdled and groaned and she vomited again.

Tessie rapped anxiously at the door. 'Miss Darling? Miss Darling?'

Lucy didn't reply. She walked in unsteady criss-cross steps back to her bed, and sat down on it. She was shivering all over, and her nose was filled with sick. Tessie knocked again, and this time she opened the door. 'I don't want to intrude, Miss Darling, but are you feeling under t'weather?'

Without a word, Lucy rolled over on the bed, and entwined herself tightly in her sheets. How could she feel so hot and so cold, both at the same time? She couldn't stop shaking. She felt deaf and blind and suffocated, and her throat burned with stomach acids.

Tessie said, 'Dr Roberts is here. Best that I fetch him in, aye?'

Lucy was shivering too much to speak. She was conscious of Tessie waiting by the bed, then leaving the bedroom and closing the door behind her. She could see her own hand lying on the pillow in front of her, so close that she could hardly focus on it. She could see the pale green veins in her wrist. Jack's hand had looked like that. Not dead, but not alive. Perhaps she was dead, too.

After a long time, the bedroom door opened again and she heard voices outside, including the deep reverberating voice of Dr Roberts. He came around the bed, and drew up a chair. Lucy heard Tessie say, 'Shall I bring you your tea now, doctor?' but Dr Roberts saying, 'Not just yet, Tessie. You wait here. We have to think of proper appearances.'

'Yes, doctor.'

Dr Roberts reached across and held the palm of his hand very light and dry on Lucy's forehead. He left it there for a while, so low down over Lucy's eyes that she found it difficult to blink. Then he sat back, and waited for her to open her eyes naturally.

'How are you feeling?' he asked her. He was wearing a

tweed coat and a yellow silk cravat, as if he had dressed in a hurry.

'I don't know, just awful. Boiling hot and then freezing cold.'

Dr Roberts drew up the sheet over her shoulder. 'You've had a serious shock. I want you to stay in bed for the rest of the day; perhaps tomorrow, too, if you're still feeling upset.'

He waited for a moment, and then he said, 'There's nothing wrong with you, Miss Darling, don't worry. The death of someone close to them ... well, it affects different people in very different ways.'

'I saw my uncle die. He was burned to death, right in front of me. That upset me something awful but it didn't make me sick. Not like this.'

'Ah – but the deceased you saw this morning was your own father. That's quite a different kettle of fish. His very blood flows in your veins. You were related by destiny and by genetics; body and soul.'

Lucy almost felt like telling Dr Roberts that she was no more related to Jack Darling than she was to him; but somehow the protest seemed too futile to be worth finding the words for it. Dr Roberts stroked her hair, and her forehead, and said, 'Plenty of rest, plenty of fresh air. Keep the room well-ventilated, Tessie. Then some beef tea for luncheon, and something light for supper. Once the shock has diminished, you'll feel right as rain again. I promise.'

He was about to leave, when Lucy grasped his hand. 'He's dead, isn't he?' she asked. She did want to make absolutely sure. She didn't really believe in ghosts, or corpses that walked in the night, but she did want to make absolutely sure.

'Yes, Miss Darling, he's with God now.'

'He said he was going to go to Hell.'

Dr Roberts gave her a strained smile. 'I really don't think so. You've prayed for him, haven't you?'

'Yes,' agreed Lucy. 'I've prayed for him.'

Dr Roberts hesitated for a while, as if he were trying to make up his mind whether he should say any more to her or not. But then Lord Felldale's valet appeared in the doorway, and stage-whispered, 'Begging tha pardon, doctor. Lord Felldale's axing if tha wants t'send for t'pleece.'

'Please,' said Dr Roberts, irritably, waving him away.

'Sorry, doctor.'

Lucy lifted her head from the pillow. 'Did he say police?'

'It's nothing for you to concern yourself with, Miss Darling.'

'But why the police?'

Dr Roberts sleeked back his hair with the palm of his hand. 'I regret to say that your father did not pass away under entirely natural circumstances.'

'What do you mean?'

'As far as I can ascertain without a post mortem examination, your father died from a massive over-adminstration of some narcotic – most likely laudanum.'

'He was killed? Somebody *murdered* him?' Lucy tried to prop herself up on her elbow, but Dr Roberts immediately took hold of her arms and pressed her firmly back down on to the bed.

'Please, Miss Darling, we mustn't talk about murder! It's too early for me to say for certain. But I have my suspicions that Mr Darling's nurse Mary may have been – shall we say, less than attentive in her measurement of his nightly medication. That is all. I cannot say murder, nor must I. And nor must you.'

Lucy lay back on her bed with her hand across her forehead, watching Dr Roberts intently. Dr Roberts sat down at the small French bureau on the other side of the room, then reached inside his pocket for a pen. 'I'm going to prescribe something for you. Something to settle you, keep you calm. Laxative lithia . . . not a strong preparation. It should set your system to working again . . . improve your appetite.'

'I wish to see Mary,' said Lucy.

'I beg your pardon?' asked Dr Roberts.

'Mary, I wish to see Mary, my father's nurse.'

'Well, I'm not at all sure –'

She suddenly became irritated by his Englishness. 'I employ her, Dr Roberts, I pay her. She works for me. I wish to see her.'

Dr Roberts finished writing his prescription. He looked vexed, rather than grim. 'Very well, Miss Darling. If that is your wish. But I would like you to know that if you insist on doing anything but resting, and taking this medication, Lord Felldale cannot hold me responsible for your further wellbeing.'

He left the room with uptilted chin to call for Mary. If he had really been as satanic as he looked, he would have left behind him a sharp reek of sulphur smoke. Lucy lay back on her pillow. She still felt wretchedly nauseous: she wasn't sure if she was going to vomit yet again. But she managed to hold it back while she waited for Mary to appear.

When she came, Mary came so silently that Lucy didn't hear her. She opened her eyes and Mary was there, only inches away, white-faced, so grotesque in her appearance that she scarcely looked real. She could have been a changeling, or a troll. She had taken off her nurse's hat, and stood beside Lucy's bed with a shock of grey hair like a burst-apart telephone cable.

Lucy slowly inspected her, up and down. Her shapeless brown dress; her beige apron. Mary announced, 'The doctor said that you wanted to see me.'

'Yes, Mary.'

'If it concerns Jack, if it concerns the laudanum, then the answer is yes.'

Lucy said nothing, but waited, her hand on the pillow.

Mary said, 'He asked me.' It sounded to Lucy like 'Me asked he.'

'He asked you?'

'The doctor said that I was lax with Jack, but I cared for him, and both of us hated what happened to him. He was a burden and I made no pretence. He knew he was a burden. Why say otherwise?'

'He *asked* you?' Lucy repeated.

'Of course he did,' said Mary. Her tone was quite flat and repetitive, like somebody wiping a window with a leather cloth. 'He told me many times that he would be better off dead, and I agreed. He was dead already, I knew that and he knew that. His thighbones were dead, sequestrum they call it.'

'But he was alive,' Lucy protested. 'He was *alive*.'

'Oh yes.' Mary sounded unconcerned. 'But why was he alive? Jack himself, he would much rather have been dead. It was only you that wanted him alive because you have no family, and nobody in New York to speak to you now. And of course there was Mr Carson, who wanted him alive for the sake of appearances.'

'What are you saying to me?' Lucy whispered. 'What are you saying?'

Mary rocked up and down on her rubber-soled nursing shoes. 'Miss Darling, he was so fond of you. But I am saying that nobody wanted Jack alive for himself; not you; not anyone he knew; not even me; and that was why he was better off dead. Nobody had ever wanted him alive for his own self, that was what he told me. Nobody loves a storekeeper, that was what he said. The more you gave, the more they hated you, because they had to pay you back, and at the end you accepted their hatred because you deserved it, you should never have given them anything. A storekeeper with human sympathy is a fool, that is what he said; because who can reasonably ask a man to settle his credit for last week's beans. They have been eaten and become excrement. Cash for beans, yes. Cash for excrement, never.'

Lucy said blurrily, 'I don't understand any of this. You killed him! You gave him too much medicine!'

'Yes, I gave him too much laudanum. He asked me to. He begged me to. I am not ashamed of it. He was a miserable burden to me and I was a miserable burden to him. It was the very best way. That doctor, and all his talk of being a slave! If you are a slave to a patient, you take away his human dignity, in the same way that any slave strips his owner of his human dignity. You take away his reason for staying alive.'

Lucy couldn't follow what Mary was saying. It seemed like another language altogether. But she sounded so sure and so reasonable that Lucy found it impossible to be angry with her; or even to disagree with her. What was more, she could hear Jack speaking through Mary's mouth. A different accent, a different intonation. But it was Jack all right. By the time Mary had finished, and stood silent, Lucy could think only that she had done them all a service, and given Jack welcome relief from a life which had always been close to unbearable.

Dr Roberts reappeared. He stood darkly in the doorway, tugging at his fingers one by one.

'Miss Darling?' he inquired.

Lucy turned around. In a clear voice, she said, 'Doctor Roberts, I think we should wait for Mr Carson to return from London. It seems that my father took too much of his medicine on purpose; and that Mary tried to save him, but couldn't.'

'If this be true, how, pray, did he *reach* his medicine?' asked Dr Roberts. 'It was on the chest-of-drawers, on the opposite side of the room.'

'Dr Roberts,' said Lucy. She was aware that her accent sounded very American, in this temple of Englishness. 'We don't want to make too much of a damn fuss, do we?'

Dr Roberts looked at her with black glittering eyes. Then he smiled faintly, and nodded. Very well, *nolo contendere*. So long as everybody was content that Jack's passing had been all for the best; then he would be content, too. The very last thing that any of them wanted at Brackenbridge was an accusation against Mary of unlawful killing, with an inquest, and a court hearing, and newspaper reporters. Especially since the Liberal government was looking shakier every week, and it was accepted without question (in the better Press, anyway; and amongst his friends) that Henry would soon be called to some distinguished political office.

Boats were better not rocked.

Lord Felldale appeared. 'Lucy, m'dear!' he called her. 'Is everything all right? Roberts told me you'd been feeling queasy!'

'Everything's very well, thank you,' Lucy replied.

'Damned sorry about y'r pater,' Lord Felldale told her. 'Comes to us all, though, doesn't it? What?'

'Yes,' said Lucy. 'I guess that it does.'

Only a dozen weeks ago, nobody could have persuaded Jack Darling to believe that he would be buried in England, under a thunderous English sky, in the small medieval churchyard at Brackenbridge.

Rooks shrieked like fishwives from the nearby elms; and the church bell clanked; and the Rector of All Souls crisply declaimed, 'As he entered the world, unencumbered, so shall John Darling leave it; and face his Maker.'

There could have been no burial-place less like Kansas. The rector was unhealthily florid, everybody else's faces were as deathly-white as mushrooms. The cypress-trees rustled stiffly and proprietorially beside the grave. The tree of mourning, with somebody unfamiliar to mourn. But Lucy felt that Jack would be peaceful here; it was all God's earth; and when she turned away from the grave, to return to Henry, who was standing by the churchyard wall with his hat in his hand, she felt relieved, rather than sad.

Thunder rumbled in the distance; but for now, the churchyard was still radiant with coagulated orange light, and the cypresses were lit like flames. Henry asked, 'Are you well, my darling child? Do you want to go home directly?'

Lucy said, 'Yes, I think so.'

Henry offered his elbow. 'We're having drinks in the morning room, then luncheon afterwards. It's a pity there's so few.'

They had assembled only the smallest of funeral-parties: butlers and footmen and kitchen-maids, dressed in their Sunday-black; Dr Roberts; and Mary; but that was all. Lord Felldale had suffered an attack of gout in the early hours of the morning, and none of Henry's brothers and sisters had been able to come.

'Henry, you've been so kind,' Lucy told him.

Henry patted her hand. 'You're family now, Lucy, whatever you decide. Carsons always take care of Carsons. Look what it says on this gravestone *Let Courson Holde What Courson Helde*. My family have been here in Derbyshire for eight hundred years, since William the Conqueror.'

Lucy had never heard of William the Conqueror; but eight hundred years seemed like more than a coon's age, and she could understand that. Dressed in a black velvet hat, with a black silk veil; a black velvet dress and a black velvet coat; her breast patterned with glittering black beads, she walked beside Henry to the family clarence, be-ribboned with black.

They sat in silence as the clarence rattled and swayed up the hill towards Brackenbridge. The servants were taking the shorter path across the park. Raindrops sprinkled the carriage windows, and clung to the glass like tears, and Lucy could see the servants begin to hurry. A rainbow appeared behind the oaks, then faded.

'Ah, Blanche has arrived,' said Henry, as they reached the house. A small green victoria was standing by the steps, and a footman was carrying baggage into the shelter of the portico. Henry helped Lucy down, and gave her his arm as they walked into the house. Blanche was taking off her bonnet and cape, and giving them to Tessie, along with a teeming list of instructions about how to hang up her gowns, how to perk up the flowers on her hats, how to mix her hair-wash, how to clean her black boots. 'Treacle, sweet-oil, and an ounce of lampblack, and do it tonight, so that they have dried quite hard by the morning.'

'Blanche!' called Henry, taking off his hat. 'My dear Blanche, how perfect to see you!'

Blanche was also dressed in black; in respect for Jack. She was tall and fair and willowy and surprisingly unlike Henry, except that she shared that slight bump on the bridge of her nose.

'Blanche, I'd like you to meet Lucy Darling. Lucy – this is my beloved older sister, Blanche.'

'My poor girl!' Blanche declared. 'You must accept my heartfelt condolences!' She kissed the air on either side of Lucy's veiled face. 'Henry has never stopped talking about you!'

'I'm flattered, Miss Carson,' Lucy told her. She wondered if she ought to curtsey.

'You must call me Blanche, or Sha-sha, if you like. That's what Henry always called me when he was little. Tessie! Be careful with that hatbox!'

'It was very good of you to come,' said Lucy.

'My dear one, I was coming anyway, next week, to start the preparations for Christmas. One week early was no hardship. Besides, father could do with some looking-after. Less port, less snuff, and less rotten pheasant; more fresh vegetables and lentil soup. And less pretending to be twenty! Tessie! Tell the kitchen-maid to send for some ginger and Columba-root, as soon as she's back. Has Dr Roberts been?'

'He came this morning, before the funeral,' said Henry. 'He gave father a dose of Kissingen salts, and a telling-off.'

'Kissingen salts!' said Blanche, dismissively.

Outside, the rain began to lash hard across the park, and Lucy glimpsed the servants hurrying the last few yards to the back of the house, skirts lifted, hats held tightly on to their heads. Another carriage arrived: it was the Rector, Dr Williams, and Mrs Williams.

Henry said, 'When you're quite ready, Blanche, join us in the morning room.'

He caught Lucy's eye. Lucy looked back at him steadily but didn't smile. She felt too sad today to smile. But she knew that she had made up her mind. Or rather, fate had made up her mind for her.

'My dear Henry!' called Dr Williams, shaking out his frock-coat as if he expected rabbits to fall out of it. 'And my dear Miss Darling!'

She sat with Blanche in her sitting room overlooking the lake. The morning was dull and misty and silent, very late Novemberish. In two days it would be December. Blanche was busily embroidering a handkerchief. She had shown Lucy how to do French knots, but Lucy had given up after half an hour, and was sitting with her feet tucked up in the window-seat, watching the ducks make patterns on the water. It was the first Tuesday after the funeral. Henry was working in the library downstairs, but he had promised to take her into Derby that afternoon, for tea and a little shopping. Because of Jack's death, they had postponed their trip to London until the New Year.

Blanche kept glancing up at her. 'You ought to keep yourself occupied, you know. God gave us time in order that we might use it profitably.'

Lucy didn't know what was profitable about embroidering a handkerchief, especially since embroidered handkerchiefs could so easily be bought. But she was growing used to the Carson family's inexhaustible appetite for work; and especially their obsession with detail. Henry had been dissatisfied with the way in which one of the groundsmen had restacked a dry stone wall; and had spent two-and-a-half days dismantling it and rebuilding it himself.

From the minute that Blanche had appeared, the household had started running at double-quick time, everything polished, everything dusted, everything organized down to the last possible second. '*When* do we dust our hats?' she had demanded of Tessie. And to Lawrence, the coachman, she had given her own recipe for oil and Tripoli powder and instructed him to remove every last stain from the clarence's upholstery by four o'clock that day.

Blanche said, 'Henry is waiting on you, you know.'

Lucy leaned her head back against the shutter, but didn't say anything.

'He is absolutely captivated by you,' Blanche went on, satin-stitching as she spoke. 'He can scarcely sleep, waiting for your answer.'

Lucy said, 'I don't mean to upset him.'

'Will you marry him?' asked Blanche.

Lucy gave the slightest of shrugs.

'Do you care for him?' Blanche wanted to know.

'Yes,' said Lucy. 'I care for him very much.'

'Do you *love* him?'

'Yes,' said Lucy. 'I believe I do.'

'Then why not say yes to him? You would make him so happy!'

'I don't know,' Lucy frowned. 'I'm worried I won't be good enough for him. I mean *interesting* enough. I try to follow everything he's saying, and I try to take an interest in everything he does. But I wasn't schooled well, Sha-sha. What happens if I let him down, in front of Lord Salisbury, or even in front of the queen? What happens if he tires of my looks, and realizes that he's married a woman with no breeding and no education; nothing but money, and business-money at that?'

Blanche laid her embroidery in her lap. 'You have no idea, have you, how much Henry adores you? He wouldn't care if you were deaf-and-dumb, and knew nothing whatever. He is simply in love with you; and Henry has very seldom been in love. It is quite real, you know, quite genuine. He wouldn't have asked you to marry him if he wasn't completely sure.'

Lucy said, 'I want to say yes. I want to say yes with all my heart.'

'Then I'll tell you what,' Blanche enthused, 'I shall give you lessons in all of those subjects in which Henry has an abiding interest. I shall teach you history, and geography, and art. I shall acquaint you with politics, and protocol, and how to manage an English household. I shall give you some Horace, and some Ovid, and some Plato; but not Virgil, too liberal, *deus nobis haec otia fecit*, indeed! Moreover, I shall instruct you in French. I adore your American accent, you would sound wonderful speaking French!'

Lucy swung her legs down from the window-seat. 'Would you do that?'

Blanche set aside her embroidery and stood up and opened her arms. 'My dear Lucy, I have known you only a few days, but I feel already that I have known you since childhood! You have that sweet doubting nature that is a natural gift, and that is what Henry has fallen in love with! He adores your innocence, he is intoxicated with your uncertainty! But do not be uncertain about him. You will be the mistress of his heart for ever!'

Lucy hugged her. 'You'll really teach me to speak French?'

Blanche laughed. 'Of course I will! It's not at all difficult! Well – not as difficult as it might sound! Come here to the mirror . . . that's right, stand beside me. We can start straight away!'

They stood side by side in front of the large oval cheval-glass. Two slim, tall young ladies, dressed in black mourning silk, arm-in-arm.

'You must watch my lips as I speak, then imitate the same movements with your own lips,' Blanche told Lucy.

'Okay,' Lucy agreed.

'And you must *not* say "okay",' Blanche admonished her.

'Okay, then, I won't.'

'Very well,' Blanche began, 'say after me *faites énergique-*

ment votre tâche longue et lourde. Perform your long and onerous task energetically.'

Lucy hesitated, then stuttered, 'Fate zenner . . . fate zenner . . . *jeeka* mon –'

'Bravo!' Blanche applauded her. 'Now let's try it again! *Faites énergiquement votre tâche longue et lourde.*'

Slowly and hesitantly, Lucy copied Blanche's precise French pronunciation.

'There!' said Blanche. 'You have the accent! All we have to do now is to learn the grammar!'

Lucy laughed, and Blanche laughed, too, and they hugged each other. Seeing herself in the mirror, hugging Blanche so closely, Lucy was surprised how much they looked alike. They could have been sisters.

Henry was out in the garden that afternoon, supervising the finishing-off of his cascade. It would carry water three hundred and fifty feet down in descending steps all the way from the Brackenbridge brook to the lake beside the house. The cascade had been envisaged by Robert Adam when he was working on Brackenbridge, but the 2nd baron had run embarrassingly short of money (gambling, and a fertile and demanding mistress), and so the cascade had remained as nothing more than a sketch. That is, until Henry had written a short history of Brackenbridge, and discovered Adam's original drawings in the library.

Henry had determined to build the cascade, exactly to Adam's specifications, including the carrara marble steps, and the Venetian-style bridge across the top of it; and he had met almost the entire cost out of his own money.

Lucy walked diagonally up the hill on the south-west side of the house, her long black velvet coat sweeping the grass, her face veiled. She found Henry standing right at the top of the cascade, while three workmen struggled with the sluice mechanism. Henry was wearing a shapeless old shooting-cap and a huge muddy coat and mittens, and he was barking at the workmen relentlessly.

'Unjam it, you fool, if it's jammed! What's it jammed with? Twigs? What? Twigs?'

Lucy came up and stood a little way distant, watching him. He stretched out his arms like a penguin, and shook them. 'For goodness' sake, you blasted hammerheads! Easy with it, easy! This is machinery, not a mule!'

He wiped his mouth with the back of his hand, and stepped back, and almost stepped on Lucy's foot.

'Lucy!' His cheeks and his nose were bright red, like robins' breasts. 'I didn't realize you were here! My darling child! You must forgive my language!'

Lucy smiled and shook her head, but kept her lips pursed, as if she had a mouthful of water. She was desperately trying to remember the words that Blanche had taught her, as she left the house.

Henry took hold of her elbow, and led her towards the brink of the cascade's sluice. 'Here, look at this! You're just in time! As soon as these idiots open up the sluice-gate, the waters from the brook will be channelled all the way down these steps, and will pour straight into the lake.'

He lifted his fist triumphantly. 'Three-and-half years, it's taken, for me to finish this! But isn't it magnificent! Exactly as Adam first imagined it!'

One of the workmen lifted his head and said, 'Think we've cleared it now, Mr Henry sir! Twigs, sir, blown by that gale I shouldn't wonder.'

'Very well, then, open her up as soon as I give the word.'

Henry gleefully thrust his hands into the pockets of his coat. 'This will be quite magnificent! I did want father to be here, but he's suffering too much this afternoon, and I wasn't going to hold this up for *him!*'

Lucy touched his arm. He turned quickly and grinned at her, his breath smoking in the late-November sunlight.

'*Je . . . t'aime,*' she said, infinitely slowly.

Henry's grin gradually died away. 'What did you say?'

She could feel the tears prickling her eyes; but she had promised herself that she would never cry.

'Je . . . t'aime,' she repeated, trying to remember exactly how Blanche had pronounced it. 'Ma reponse . . . c'est oui.'

Henry stared at her for a very long time without saying anything. Untidy as he was, in his oversized coat, he looked even more handsome than ever – well-built, broad-faced, with that deep cleft in his chin, and those eyes that were sparkling with gusto and determination and irrepressible self-confidence. Looking at him then, Lucy thought how silly she had been to doubt that she could make him happy. He had known from the very beginning just how innocent she was; how little she understood of politics or classical literature or art. It was her apparent innocence that had attracted him so much – that, and the prospect of teaching her everything he knew – the priceless anticipation of instructing a beautiful and ingenuous young girl in the ways of the world, not to mention the ways of the Carsons, and the ways of Henry Carson in particular.

'You do, then, wish to marry me?' he asked her. Down below, in the stone-lined sluice, the workmen were patiently waiting for him; with the authentic patience of men who have been trained since birth to do their master's bidding. Lucy nodded, and whispered, 'Yes,' behind her veil, like a ghost whispering 'yes' behind a curtain of smoke.

Henry took hold of her black-gloved hands, and squeezed them with pleasure.

'Lucy,' he said. 'Lucy! You don't know what you have done to my life already! You have brought me light, and joy, and meaning. And, as my wife –'

He paused. Then, gently and cautiously, he raised her veil. He looked into her eyes as if he found it impossible to believe that she was true, and that she was going to be his. There was nothing sentimental in the way he looked at her. There was nothing romantic about it, either. It was a look of pleasure, of possession – and also, quite unexpectedly, of something that resembled alarm. Not fear, but the jangle of nerves.

Did she *frighten* him? she wondered.

'I always believed that you would say yes,' Henry told her. He sniffed from the cold. 'I always believed that you would. But until you did – well, I haven't been sleeping very well.'

'Sha-sha told me.'

'And that was why you decided to say yes?'

Lucy shook her head. 'No. I decided to say yes because I decided to marry you.' *And besides*, she thought, with Jack gone, I have no other family left. Just you, and Sha-sha, and your father.

'I am delighted beyond all telling,' Henry grinned. He turned to the workmen down in the sluice, and shouted out, 'Now! Open it up! The very moment!'

'Good enough, sir,' the workmen said, and turned the wheel. The wooden sluice-gate was gradually raised, and muddy water began to surge out across the white marble steps. It foamed over the first step, and then the next, and then the next, until it was rushing all the way down to the lake, a sparkling stairway of water.

Henry took in a huge triumphant breath. 'I shall remember this day for the rest of my life!' he declared. 'My dear God, Lucy, you have made me so happy!'

Far down below them, Blanche and several of the servants had come out of the house to see the cascade. After a few minutes, Lord Felldale appeared too, in an invalid-chair, pushed by their coachman, Lawrence. Blanche waved and Lucy waved back, and Lord Felldale raised his stick.

Then Henry cupped his hands around his mouth and bellowed out, 'She said yes, papa! She said yes!'

Early on Christmas morning, before it was light, snow fell across the Derbyshire dales as soft and as thick as if the angels had been plucking geese. Lucy woke up on Christmas morning and knew that something was different. Her room was filled with a strange blue fluorescence, and when she climbed out of bed and drew back the heavy velvet curtains, she gasped at what she saw.

The whole of Brackenbridge, white with whirling snow. Even the lake had vanished. She stood enchanted, with the palms of her hands pressed against the cold window-glass, and felt as if they had been transported while they slept into another world. A world of silence. A world of softness. A world of white.

She was still standing there when Tessie knocked, and came in with her tray of morning tea.

'Happy Christmas, Miss Darling!' said Tessie.

Lucy turned away from the window. 'And happy Christmas to you, too, Tessie!'

'Church at eight o'clock, Miss Darling,' Tessie told her, setting down the tray beside the bed. 'I'll be in to dress you directly.'

'Thank you, Tessie.'

'Oh, and Miss Darling –' said Tessie, almost coyly, as she turned to leave. 'Mr Carson axed me to point out his gift to you . . . there, on t' tray.'

Lucy glanced towards the tray and saw a small rectangular box, wrapped in red tissue, with a white silk ribbon around it. She turned back to Tessie and smiled, and Tessie giggled and rushed out, closing the door behind her.

'*Henry*,' Lucy said to herself, as she walked across to the tea-tray in her long white embroidered nightgown. She picked up the box, and turned it this way and that; and shook it. It seemed quite heavy, for its size, but it didn't rattle. '*Oh, Henry,*' she repeated.

She sat on the bed, untied the ribbon, and tore open the tissue paper with her thumb. Inside she found a cardboard box, decorated with patterned paper. Carefully, she lifted the lid, and inside the lid was more tissue paper, perfectly folded. Only Henry could have folded tissue paper like that.

When she spread open the tissue paper she found a necklace. It was an evening necklace, designed to decorate a deep *décolletage*. It was arranged as three sunbursts of gold, two lesser sunbursts, and one large central sunburst, each set with diamonds. The central diamond was enormous, nearly as large as Mrs Widgery's, one of those flawless but tea-coloured diamonds which some collectors spurn but others would kill for. Nine carats, nearer ten.

Her hands trembling, Lucy lifted up the necklace and carried it in front of her to the mirror in her dressing room.

'*Henry, what have you done?*' she whispered. She held the necklace up to her nightgown, but it didn't look right; so she unbuttoned her nightgown and slipped her shoulders out of it, so that she was sitting in front of the mirror bare-breasted. She fastened the necklace and arranged it over her bare skin and the effect was startling. She looked so classically beautiful. She lifted her hair at the back, and turned her face sideways. She could have been Cleopatra, or Helen of Troy. She could have been Marie Antoinette. Sha-sha had told her about Marie Antoinette.

She was still sitting in front of the mirror when she heard the door of her sitting room open. Immediately she tugged up her nightgown, and called, 'Tessie?'

There was a long silence. She hoped it wasn't that awful foot-dragging Matthew, who cleaned out the grates. She had caught him several times trying to spy through the keyhole into her bedroom, and Sha-sha said he was epileptic, and ought to be locked up somewhere safe.

'Tessie?' she called again. 'Is that you?'

'Actually, it isn't,' said Henry's voice.

'Henry?'

'I'm sorry, Lucy; I apologize. This is really not proper. But I wanted so much to wish you a happy Christmas; and to find out whether you cared for the necklace or not. I'm afraid my usual enthusiasm got the better of me.'

'Henry, I haven't dressed yet.'

'Well, yes, of course. I shall retreat. Have you tried on the necklace? Does it look well on you? The diamond was given to me as a parting gift by the Amir of Afghanistan, Abdur Rahman Khan, probably the cruellest man I shall ever meet. I never knew what I should do with it, until I met you.'

'You had this necklace specially made for me?'

'By Asprey's, yes. It arrived by special messenger two days ago. I was terrified that they wouldn't be able to finish it by Christmas.'

'But, Henry, it must be worth a fortune!'

'My dearest dear, compared to you, it is worth nothing at all.'

Lucy took a deep breath, watching herself in the mirror as she did so. She and Henry would be married in May: Lord Felldale was going to announce it today, after their Christmas dinner. They would be man and wife, sharing everything. And what could she not willingly show to Henry that she had not already been forced to show to Uncle Casper, her own father?

'Come in, Henry,' she said. 'Come and see your necklace, how well it looks.'

She turned on her seat; and as Henry came into the dressing-room, in his blue Chinese dressing-gown, she let her nightgown slip down.

Henry stood staring at her. She stared at him, challengingly, back.

'It's beautiful,' he said at last.

Lucy stood up, holding her nightgown around her waist,

so that it would slip down no further. She approached Henry and stood in front of him, quite close.

'Thank you,' she said, her voice catching. 'It's wonderful. I've never seen anything so wonderful.'

His eyes were searching her eyes. What was he looking for? What did he expect to find? Some kind of clue that Lucy wasn't everything he thought she was? She tilted her chin up just a little, and half-closed her eyes, and Henry kissed her. Not a long kiss, but a searching kiss, the kind of kiss that asked a question.

He lifted his left hand, hesitated for a moment, and then touched her bare breast. Her small pink nipple immediately crinkled. Lucy looked at him, looked at his eyes, but they were closed now, and he was breathing like a man asleep.

'Henry?' she said.

'*Couvrez ce sein que je ne saurais voir,*' he murmured. He was quoting, she didn't know what he was quoting, but she had learned enough French from Sha-sha to be able to understand it. '*Par de pareils objets les âmes sont blessées, et cela fait venir de coupables pensées.*'

His fingers encircled her nipple. She would have done anything then, if he had only touched it. *Touch it, kiss it.* But he wouldn't. He took one step away from her, and opened up his eyes.

'Molière,' he told her. "Cover those breasts, I must not see them. Souls are wounded by such sights, and they arouse wicked thoughts."'

'Is it wicked to look at your wife?' Lucy asked him.

Henry gave her the smallest shake of his head.

'But I'm not yet your wife,' Lucy suggested.

'No,' he told her. 'You're not yet my wife.'

'You're so proper, Henry.'

'And you're so innocent. What do you know of properness; or of improperness? And it's Christmas Day! And I shouldn't be here!'

'Henry –' she said. She didn't know what she was going to tell him. There was nothing to tell him. Her innocence had not been given freely, not with Uncle Casper, anyway. *Fumes! Fire! Laughter!* She was not to blame. Unlike Jack, she *knew* she was not to blame. So there was nothing to be gained from telling Henry what had happened. No forgiveness, no absolution. But, like all victims, she still felt guilty for what had happened. She still refused to believe that anything so drastic could have happened to her without her having been responsible for it.

She still dreamed of those ribbons cutting into her wrists. She still woke up, smelling the heated sourness of Uncle Casper's breath.

Henry said, 'I love you, Lucy. If you can be ready by ten minutes to eight . . . the carriages will be waiting outside to take us to church.'

Lucy came forward and kissed his cheek. She looked so young and slender and pretty in the strange reflected light from the snow; her blonde hair fastened in curl-papers, her nightgown around her waist, wearing the viciously-glittering diamond necklace of the cruellest of Amirs, her breasts tiny and upcurved and white, Arabian moons.

'You destroy me,' said Henry. 'You lay waste to me. But a happy Christmas, nevertheless.'

Brackenbridge became a noisy carnival on Christmas Day. A dozen of the Carsons' friends had arrived the previous day, as well as most of Henry's brothers and sisters, with all of their children. The corridors echoed with screaming and laughter and the scampering of little shoes. Henry was a genial uncle, but he was acutely conscious that, despite the fact that he was the eldest son, he had not yet married and produced any grandchildren of his own.

As they chattered in the carriage on the way back from church, his brother Charles recalled that Li Hung Chang, the Chinese diplomat, had expressed extraordinary surprise that a man of thirty-four should have no sons. The Emperor of Germany had six!

'Henry said, *very* stuffily, "I am not yet married, I regret." But Li Hung Chang had said, "So? What have you been doing all this time?"'

Charles shouted with laughter. 'You should have seen Henry's face! He couldn't answer him then; and if Li Hung Chang asked him the same question today, he *still* couldn't answer it!'

Henry did his best not to look annoyed. Lucy smiled behind her glove. She liked Charles. He was very robust, a much broader and more robust version of Henry, and he didn't seem to think very much of propriety or manners. He was astonished that Henry had summoned Blanche so promptly to act as Lucy's chaperone. 'But there we are, that's Henry for you, always watching his back! He wants to be Viceroy of India, when Elgin goes, and he daren't have anybody whispering about him. Everything proper, everything correct, and there had better *not* be any children to bob up and call him papa!'

'Charles, dear boy,' Henry scolded him. 'This is neither the day, nor the place.'

'Aha!' Charles retaliated. 'But haven't you chosen this day to tell us something special?'

'What do you mean?' retorted Henry.

'Oh, come along, Henry! Father can hardly contain himself! You know what father's like about lineage! "Let Carson Holde What Carson Helde." For ever, and ever, and you can't hold anything for ever, not without sons!'

'I don't know what you're trying to suggest,' Henry retaliated.

'Well, if you don't,' said Charles, clapping him on the back and winking at Lucy, 'you've been leading some young lady well up the garden path!'

Back at the house, they were greeted in the principal drawing room with hot punch and little mince pies, dredged in sugar. A tall aromatic pine stood in the window-bay, twinkling with dozens of tapers, and decorated with ribbons. The foot of the tree was heaped with gift-boxes, wrapped up in green and silver and gold, and an avalanche of nuts and sweets and gingerbread men had been spilled pell-mell across the floor, to give the impression that this profusion of presents had simply fallen from the sky.

Lord Felldale excitedly propelled his invalid-chair this way and that, toasting his guests and his family. 'Roberts says I shouldn't get myself aerated! Well, damn Roberts, that's what I say! This is Christmas! And this will be the very best Christmas ever!'

He rapped his cane against the side of his chair, and called to Blanche, 'Can't you let the children in yet, Sha-sha? I'm just bursting to see the little buggers' faces!'

Blanche waved and smiled, and said, 'Very well!'

She signalled the footmen to open the drawing-room doors; and all the children, fifteen or sixteen of them, came squealing and giggling into the room. They began to gather up the nuts and the sweets, the girls in their uplifted skirts, the boys in their knickerbockers, while their parents laughed and applauded and egged them on.

Then it was time for the gifts to be handed out; and Lucy had never seen so many clockwork monkeys and Dresden dolls and varnished toy yachts. One of Charles' boys, Edgar, came up to Henry with his face glowing, holding a cardboard box of painted lead soldiers, the 15th Bengal Cavalry.

'Uncle Henry, thank you!'

Henry scruffed Edgar's hair. 'Now you can play at putting down the sepoys,' he smiled. 'But if you play at the Mutiny, you must remember that in those days this regiment was known as Cureton's Multanis.'

'Yes, Uncle Henry.'

When he had gone, Lucy said, 'I would just adore to visit India. Poppa used to keep Indian spices in the back of the store. I used to take off the lids and smell them, when I was small, and imagine what India was like. Elephants, princesses, palaces! Poppa used to be cross with me, he said the spices would lose their smell if I kept on opening them.'

'You shall certainly see India,' Henry assured her. 'You shall see India and very much more. India is what I want out of life. I have never thought of myself as doing anything else, ultimately, than governing India. And if I govern India, then you'll be there beside me.'

'Just listen to him!' taunted William, Henry's youngest brother. 'The Viceroy of Pipe-dream!'

'You should do something about that moustache,' Henry replied. 'Shave it off, and put it out of its misery.'

'Have I met all of your family now?' Lucy asked.

'All save Vanessa,' said Henry.

'Will Vanessa not be here?'

'Vanessa . . . well, Vanessa doesn't come to family gatherings. She sees father two or three times a year, but usually when the rest of us are not here.'

'Have you quarrelled?'

Henry looked away. 'All families have their little differences, don't they? Would you like some more punch? We'll be opening the grown-ups' presents now.'

'That night that poppa died, your father actually mistook me for Vanessa.'

'Oh, yes? Well, he's growing a little old, you know. His sentiment waxes while his eyesight wanes. Look, here you are! This is the first of your gifts!'

'But I've already had this beautiful necklace!'

Henry took hold of her hand, and pressed it between both of his hands. 'I told you that we always over-indulge ourselves at Christmas; and you shall be the most over-indulged of all!'

Lucy was used to what wealth could buy. In New York, she had all the gowns and all the jewellery and all the ostentatious knick-knacks that eleven thousand dollars a day could stretch to. But she was not used to taste. When she opened her gift-boxes and discovered the most exquisite solid-silver dressing-table set, enamelled in France in rusts and golds; when she lifted out a Blue John vase; and a pair of perfect eighteenth-century miniatures; and a travelling-set of perfume bottles in crystal, fused with a tracery of gold; and French pearl earrings; she felt that she had graduated into a world in which wealth was regarded as something much more than champagne and carriages and dinners at Delmonico's. Wealth in this household had meaning and substance. It sustained tradition, it sustained artistic sensibilities. In a hundred years, her silk gowns would all be rags, but some unthought-of grand-daughter of hers would be wearing these earrings, and brushing her hair with this dressing-table set.

There were many more gifts. Brooches, rings, bracelets, a porcelain loving-cup, from the Derbyshire potteries. And Lucy had gifts of her own to give – a diary with a solid-silver binding, for Blanche; a silver monogrammed flask for Lord Felldale, both bought in Derby.

For Henry, however, she had a very special gift. It was wrapped in a large flat package, decorated with white paper flowers and green silk ribbons. He opened it up carefully, with a small reflective smile on his face which she would later recognize as a tell-tale sign of anxiety.

'I expected nothing,' he said, looking up at her; conscious that the rest of the family had now drawn around him to see what it was.

At last, he took off the paper, and held it up. An oleograph, in a gilded frame, of Lucy standing by Henry's beloved cascade, in her black velvet dress and her black velvet bonnet.

'I'm sorry,' Lucy told him. 'I didn't have the time to have my portrait painted. I asked in Derby; and Sha-sha offered to paint me in watercolour. But you don't mind an oleograph, do you?'

Henry shook his head without saying anything. By giving him this portrait, she had of course completely confirmed what everybody in the Carson family gleefully expected: that before Christmas Day was over, he would announce their forthcoming marriage.

At that moment, however, Lord Felldale wheeled himself over, demanding, 'What have you got there, Henry? Let me take a look at that!'

Henry tilted it around so that his father could see it. Lord Felldale frowned at it, and grunted.

'Do you like it, father?' Henry asked him.

'Like it, yes. It's pretty enough.'

'Father?' Henry queried, sensing the reservation in Lord Felldale's voice.

'It's pretty enough, that's all I said. But what do you want with a portrait of Vanessa?'

There was an embarrassed silence among the grown-ups. Only the unselfconscious laughter of the children kept the spirit of the room alive. Blanche knelt down beside her father, and stroked the back of his thick-veined hand, and said, 'Papa ... it's Lucy, not Vanessa. Mr Entwistle came from Matlock to take her picture just two weeks ago, by the cascade. You remember.'

Lord Felldale realized that he had said something out of place, but he still didn't understand what. He turned to Blanche in perplexity. 'Not sure that I —' he began. Then, 'Not sure that I —' He leaned forward in his invalid-chair and whispered hoarsely in Blanche's ear, 'Aint that Vanessa?'

'No papa, you're muddled-up. It's Lucy.'

'Ah, Lucy!' Lord Felldale declared. 'Lucy! Of course, Lucy! yes, yes, yes! *Lucy!*'

Henry stepped forward, and raised his hand. 'I had intended to save this announcement for later, when we were all well-filled with roasted goose and good red wine. But strong feelings are very difficult to conceal, especially amongst family and friends, and everybody here is more than aware of the affection I have for our American guest, Miss Lucy Darling.'

There was applause now, and a burst of relief, and Charles shouted out, 'Bravo!' The children cheered too; although not for Henry's sake. A division of dolls and Noah's-Ark animals had just broken through the ranks of Cureton's Multanis, and reversed the course of Indian history.

Henry said, 'I first came across Miss Lucy Darling in circumstances that, in American society, have now become legendary. She was slack-wire walking across the tennis-net, at the home of Mrs Gregory Harris, in Newport, Rhode Island. She impressed me so much with her beauty and grace that I decided, then and there, even before I had spoken one word to her, that I was in love with her, and that I would not be content until she consented to become my wife.'

Henry paused, and then he said, 'You all know me well. You know that I have always been one of the most determined bachelors of my age. But the minute I saw Miss Lucy Darling, the notion of bachelorhood suddenly appeared absurd. I could no longer think of a single reason why I should live without her.'

'Hear, hear,' William interrupted, but Blanche immediately shushed him.

'I have asked Lucy if she will be my bride,' Henry continued. 'To my unmitigated joy, she has said yes. Accordingly, we will be married in May, here at Brackenbridge, and the member for Southport will be wed not just to his country, not just to his party, but to the most beautiful lady in the western hemisphere.'

Charles cried out, 'Three cheers for Henry and Lucy! Hip-hip-hurra!' and William shouted, 'A toast! We must have a toast!' and Lord Felldale rapped his stick against the side of his invalid-chair and bellowed, 'Give the children some punch, poor buggers!'

At last, they drank to each other, Henry and Lucy, out of the loving-cup which Henry's sister Maude had given them. Everybody clapped and cheered, and the little girls skipped around them as if it were already May.

Henry took hold of Lucy's hand, and said, 'I love you, my darling, with my whole heart; and always will.'

'Henry,' she said, 'I love you too.' And she looked all around her at her new-found family. Charles and William and Blanche and Maude; even Lord Felldale, who had returned to his games with the children; and she felt secure again, and happy, and safe, and no longer alone in the world.

She began to feel sick about three o'clock, shortly after the family had finished their Christmas luncheon. The men had decided on a bracing walk through the snow, and a snowball fight, too, before it grew too dark, while the women retreated to the small drawing room to gossip. After only five or ten minutes, however, Lucy began to feel the lumps of roasted goose she had eaten sliding around in her stomach in their own grease, as if she hadn't even chewed them. She pressed the back of her hand to her forehead and it was chilled and perspiring, and she began to shiver.

'You must tell us what wedding-presents you want,' said Sha-Sha. 'You'll never guess what Arthur Balfour gave to Charles and Elisabeth: a silver-gilt tureen, in the shape of the galley of Sebastiano Venier at the Battle of Lepanto. Magnificent, but not at all suitable for leek-and-potato soup.'

Lucy tried to smile but found that she couldn't. 'You'll have to excuse me,' she said. 'I'm not feeling very well.'

'Too much excitement, for a Christmas Day,' Charles' wife Elisabeth suggested.

'You should lie down,' said Sha-sha.

She rang for Tessie and Tessie helped her upstairs to her bedroom.

'Stays too tight,' said Tessie, unbuttoning Lucy's dark red velvet dress, and then helping her out of her corset cover. 'You should do what Lady Brett always does, leaves off her stays at Christmas, and breathes in whenever a gentleman's looking.'

304

At that moment, Lucy felt herself turning shudderingly cold. She grasped Tessie's sleeve, and tried to say, *Help me*, but immediately she gagged and choked and splashed her lap with vomit. Goose, pease pudding, fricasséed kidneys, crimped cod, meringues; the very finest Christmas luncheon that Henry had been able to bully the kitchen into serving up.

There was nothing that Tessie could do, except to hold Lucy until she was finished; and then to help her weeping out of her dress, and bring hot wet towels to help her clean herself. Lucy felt as weak and as shaky as if she were dying, and her teeth were chattering so wildly that she was unable to speak.

'There,' Tessie soothed her. 'There, now. Let's sponge you, and put on your nightgown, and you can get into bed. Then I'll have young Kevin run for Dr Roberts.'

'What's wrong with me, Tessie?' Lucy shuddered. 'It isn't the typhoid, is it?' Henry had told her such grim stories about the bad drains that had killed his mother and several of his friends that she was always frightened to use the water-closets at Brackenbridge, and avoided every open drain-cover as if it were a trapdoor to Hell itself.

Tessie said soothingly, 'You're tired, that's all, Miss Darling. Over-excited. Dr Roberts'll doubtless give you something to calm you down. My goodness! Think of what happened today! No wonder you're feeling the way you do!'

Lucy managed to sip a little water. Then she lay back on her bed and tried to sleep, but sleep refused to come. Tessie sat in the chair beside her, saying nothing, waiting for Dr Roberts. The fire played criss-cross patterns on the ceiling.

It was almost dark outside. The windows were black. She heard laughter as the men returned from their walk. She touched Tessie's hand, and said, 'You'll tell Mr Henry, won't you? But don't alarm him, will you? Tell him I'm tired, that's all. Tell him I was over-excited.'

'All right, Miss Darling,' Tessie told her. 'Whatever tha likes.'

But it wasn't two minutes before Henry knocked at the door, and called, 'Lucy! Lucy! It's Henry! Sha-sha's just told me that you were sick!'

Tessie went to the door, and Lucy could hear their low, quick conversation. '– *over-excited, that's all – nothing to worry about – but called the doctor, anyway – well, you know, just in case –*'

Eventually, Henry said, 'All right, then, very well. She's your responsibility. But keep me informed.'

Tessie came back into the bedroom. 'Mr Henry's very upset, Miss Darling. But I told him it were nothing terrible. Just the collywobbles.'

'Thank you, Tessie.'

Tessie smiled in the firelight. 'Oh, miss, tha'll make a grand bride. I can't wait till May.'

'I hope I feel better than I do now.'

She didn't have long to wait, however. Dr Roberts appeared, chafing his hands, his face grey with cold.

'I'm sorry I brought you all the way out here on Christmas Day,' Lucy told him.

'No, no! Not at all! If we can't perform philanthropic works on Christmas Day, when can we do them? How are you feeling? Not too well, by the look of you. You look pale!'

Dr Roberts felt her pulse and checked her temperature. Then he asked, 'You haven't been lacing your stays too tightly?'

Lucy shook her head. 'I don't care for them too tight.'

'Have you noticed any swelling, however, of your bosom or your abdomen?'

Lucy was embarrassed; but Dr Roberts said gently, 'I'm sorry to be personal, Miss Darling; but I have to know.'

'Well – I'm putting on a little weight,' Lucy admitted. 'But Mr Carson is very insistent that I take my meals three times a day, even when I perhaps don't feel like it.'

306

'Have you seen anything this month?'

'Seen anything? Like what?' asked Lucy.

'Your period. Have you experienced any difficulties with that?'

Lucy swallowed. 'As a matter of fact, since coming to England . . .' she looked towards Tessie for support.

'Yes, Miss Darling?' asked Dr Roberts.

'Since coming to England, I haven't had a period at all.'

'Ah,' said Dr Roberts and rubbed his nose with the crook of his finger. 'No period at all? Not even a trace?'

Lucy shook her head.

'Ah,' Dr Roberts repeated.

'Do you have any idea what's wrong with me?' Lucy asked him. 'It isn't typhoid, is it? Henry and I are supposed to be marrying in May.'

'Yes, I heard about that, congratulations – and no, it's not typhoid. Would you mind if I were to feel your abdomen?'

Lucy stared at him blankly. 'All right. Go right ahead.'

Dr Roberts briskly rubbed his hands together. 'My fingers might feel rather cold . . . it's quite a journey from Matlock, on a night like this.'

He adjusted his expression to one of complete professional detachment, staring unfocused over Lucy's right shoulder while he carefully palpated her stomach. He took his time doing it, but he finished quite abruptly, and said, 'Thank you. You may cover yourself now.'

Lucy's stomach felt quite sore from all his prodding. 'Do you know what's wrong?' she asked him.

He nodded. 'I believe so. Would it be possible for your maid to step outside for just a moment, so that I can have a word with you alone? She may leave the door ajar, of course.'

'Tessie?' asked Lucy.

'Whatever you say, Miss Darling,' and went outside, into the corridor; where she stood sentry-duty over Lucy's honour.

Dr Roberts leaned forward, and in a peculiar throaty murmur said, 'You're pregnant. Do you understand? You're going to have a baby.'

Lucy stared at him. 'What?' she demanded. *Pregnant*? He must be making it up, like a character in a play. She couldn't possibly be pregnant. She had only made love once, with Jamie, and Jamie had made absolutely sure that his seed hadn't gone up inside her. She had read enough in *What A Young Woman Ought to Know* to understand that a woman couldn't become pregnant unless his seed 'entered the temple of her body'.

'I can't be pregnant,' she whispered.

'I will have to make some confirmatory tests,' Dr Roberts whispered back at her. 'But your symptoms are extremely unequivocal. You are pregnant, as much as two-and-a-half to three months. You can expect to have your baby sometime in mid-July.'

'I can't!' Lucy hissed back. 'I'm supposed to be marrying Henry in May!'

'Miss Darling,' Dr Roberts replied, 'it isn't a question of can't. "Can't" doesn't enter into it. You *are*.'

Lucy lay back on her pillow. Dr Roberts watched her with his dark-ringed eyes, not censorious, but not sympathetic, either. There was a shuffling noise outside the bedroom door, Tessie tying to position herself so that she could hear more clearly.

'Do you know who the father might be?' asked Dr Roberts.

Lucy glanced up at him. 'Yes,' she nodded, her mouth dry.

'It isn't –?' he asked, nodding towards the door, meaning Henry downstairs.

'No,' mouthed Lucy. 'It isn't Mr Carson.'

'Well,' said Dr Roberts after a while, 'you must consider what you are going to do. As you are probably aware, there are ways in which pregnancies may be terminated. But I should warn you that I will not personally be able to assist you in such a matter: it is something to which I am ethically opposed. Besides, there is danger enough in natural child-bearing, without tampering with God's intended procedure.'

He smiled at her. 'To die in the course of giving new life is a divine reward. To die while attempting to destroy new life is a divine retribution.'

Lucy whispered, 'When will it begin to show? I mean, really show?'

Dr Roberts shrugged. 'You have already noticed yourself your increase in weight, the swelling of your bosom and abdomen. Of course you may be able to conceal your condition for some time, with the aid of looser clothing. But it will be extremely difficult for you to keep it a secret until May; and impossible, of course, for you to keep it a secret on your wedding-night.'

Lucy lay back on her pillow. 'He won't marry me now, will he?' she said; more to herself than to Dr Roberts.

'That's impossible for me to say,' Dr Roberts replied. 'I *have* known men who have married women who are great with the child of another. There is a certain type of man who does; usually a man who is shy with women in his own right; but who is ready to take advantage of their special weakness at a time like this.'

'Henry's not that type of man,' said Lucy, emphatically. 'I'm glad he's not. I couldn't tolerate it if a man were to marry me out of pity.'

Dr Roberts reached down, picked up his bag, and snapped it shut. He stood up; and he looked peculiarly mournful, as if perhaps *he* were that certain type of man who would have married her. Sha-sha had already told her that he was single, and that he lived alone in a large grey-and-yellow stone house in Matlock, and that it was rumoured that he smoked opium, grieving for a long-lost love.

'Miss Darling . . . I can only say this . . . that if you have need of me, you have only to send for me. I will give you

309

all the attention that you deserve and require. Meanwhile I can recommend only that you exercise frequently, perhaps by walking; that you eat healthy foods; that you leave off your stays; and that you try to remain of carefree mind.'

'But I *must* have the baby?' Lucy asked him.

Dr Roberts nodded. 'Would you count it an honour to have a murderer for a friend? It's horrible to think about, isn't it? So how could you talk to yourself, if you yourself were the destroyer of a human life?'

Lucy said nothing. She didn't know what to say or what to think. Dr Roberts waited for a moment, and then called, 'Tessie! I think your mistress could be given some tea!'

Tessie reappeared, and looked from Lucy to Dr Roberts and back again for some clue to what they had been talking about. She had obviously heard whispers, and murmurs of distress, but very little else.

'Tea,' Dr Roberts repeated; and then 'I shall call again tomorrow, Miss Darling, if you should wish me to. Just to ensure that your fever has died down; and that you are feeling better.'

He left, saying nothing more. Tessie reached over and plumped up Lucy's pillows. 'Would you care for some tea, Miss Darling? And some Christmas cake, mebbe?'

Lucy tugged at her tangled hair. 'No, thank you, Tessie, nothing. I still feel sick.'

'Did Dr Roberts tell you what were wrong?'

'It's nothing,' Lucy told her. 'Woman's sickness, that's all.'

'It's t'change in climate, I reckon,' said Tessie. 'I spent a fortnight in Whitby once, and I didn't see anything for months afterwards.'

Lucy tried to smile.

'Then there's your da passing over'n'all,' Tessie added. 'Bound t'upset your workings, one way or t'other. I took glyc'rine suppotteries for it, got me going a treat.'

'I think I need to sleep for a little while,' said Lucy.

Tessie finished straightening out the bed. 'Whatever you like, miss. I'll tell Mr Henry not to disturb you.'

Tessie crept out of the room on tiptoe, and closed the door behind her as carefully as if Lucy were already asleep. But Lucy lay on the pillow with her eyes open, wide awake; and she would remain wide awake until morning.

Henry exlaimed, 'You look wonderful! Do you think you'll be well enough to come down to London tomorrow?'

Lucy had appeared for family breakfast the day after Boxing Day, looking pale but otherwise healthy. She was wearing a chequered wool walking dress which she had always disliked because of the way its pleated front concealed her waist, which she was proud of. But now she was grateful that she had brought it with her, because whatever she looked like in it, she didn't look pregnant, and that was all she cared about.

Blanche was being fussy with a pair of hairy-boned kippers. She glanced up at Lucy, and remarked, 'You look ready to storm up East Moor Peak.'

'I've reserved us a compartment on the ten-past-nine from Derby,' said Henry. 'We'll easily reach London in time for luncheon. Wilfred Blunt's meeting us at King's Cross. We've been invited to dinner with Lord Salisbury the following evening; and we'll be spending Saturday and Sunday with the Hawthornes. On Monday we'll go to Reigate. My friend Billiam's found us a house there, which we might rent. You'll have a marvellous time, my dearest child, I swear it!'

Lucy was trying to do her best with two triangles of toast and a little soft-scrambled egg. 'I'm sorry, Henry,' she said. 'I'm not sure that I'm well enough.'

Henry was crestfallen. 'But, darling . . . it's all arranged. I'm sure you won't find it strenuous. It will mean so much to me, to be able to show you off! Especially to Lord Salisbury! When it comes to preferment, it is a great advantage to be well married.'

Lucy signalled with the faintest lift of her fingers for the footman to take her plate away. She had forked her eggs over two or three times, but left them untouched. 'I'm sorry, Henry. I would love to go with you. You don't have any idea how much I'm longing to see London! But I still feel so weak. I would be a liability to you. You don't want Lord Salisbury to think that your wife is sickly. Surely, in politics, a sickly wife is worse than no wife at all.'

Henry finished his tea and set down his cup. 'I don't know what to say. I really don't. I care for you, Lucy, more than life itself. But it would be impossible for me to pretend not to be bitterly disappointed. First we had to postpone your coming to London because of your father's death; and now you're unwell. And I am simply exploding to introduce you to everybody I know!'

'Perhaps you are being saved from making a mistake,' said Lucy.

Blanche had been fighting with her kippers and keeping well out of this particular conversation; but now she looked up sharply. 'Mistake? What mistake?'

'I'm sorry,' said Lucy. 'I haven't been myself. I've been trying so hard not to let Henry down ... but I feel so unwell.'

Henry pushed back his chair and came to kneel down beside her. 'Lucy, my sweetest girl. I'm sorry! I'm allowing my own ambition and my own feelings to overtake me completely! You mustn't worry! I don't expect you to come to London if you don't feel strong enough! We can go in March, when the snows are all gone. Lord Salisbury won't have to see you in person to know how happy I am!'

Lucy laid her hand on his shoulder, then leaned forward in her chair and pressed her cheek against his. 'Oh, Henry. Sometimes I wish that you weren't so understanding.'

Blanche stared at Henry for a long, noticeable moment, and then returned to her kippers. Henry had seen her, and he said, with a false lightness in his voice, 'I'm not always known for being understanding. It's not a vice of mine, if that's what you mean.'

Lucy was aware that some kind of hostile communication had passed between Henry and Blanche, but she didn't have any idea what it was. But as an intensive, Henry snapped, in a surprisingly Northern accent, 'You're making a mess of that fish, Sha-sha. What did it do to deserve that?'

'If a kipper could but talk,' Blanche retorted.

Later that evening, after Lord Felldale had retired to bed, and Lucy was sitting in the green drawing room with Blanche, embroidering, Henry came in and drummed his fingers on the back of the sofa, and cleared his throat, as if he had something to say. Blanche had been brought up in a family of men, and knew what was required of her. She finished her knotting, and then put down her silks and her needles.

'Did you wish to speak to Lucy alone?' she asked him.

Henry was standing with his hands held tightly behind his back. 'General idea,' he told her.

'Very well,' said Blanche, rising from her chair. 'I shall see to tomorrow's luncheon. That is, unless *you* have already done so, Henry. I was thinking of pea-soup, made from the boiled-pork liquor; then boiled chicken perhaps, with celery sauce; and baked-apple dumplings for pudding.'

'Whatever you like,' said Henry, uninterested. 'I won't be here, whatever it is.'

He waited until Blanche had closed the door behind her. Then he approached the fire, where Lucy was sitting, and said, 'Well.'

Lucy didn't look up from her satin-stitch. 'You're angry with me,' she said.

Henry sat down in the chair beside her. He lifted his hand as if to touch her; then withdrew it, as if to touch her would be an act of commitment which he was not yet prepared to make. Not until he was sure that she loved him, anyway.

313

'I, er, I just wanted to ask you one question,' he said.

She paused in her stitching. Her needle gleamed orange in the firelight. 'I just wanted to ask you if your sickness was quite as serious as you purport; or whether it is a diplomatic sickness; so that you don't have to travel down to London with me.'

Lucy looked at him with more sadness than he could have understood.

He flapped one hand in frustration. He was very rarely lost for words. 'I *ask* – well, I hope you see why I feel I have to ask. Perhaps I'm making a fool of myself. But you seemed quite well before Christmas, before our betrothal was announced. Now you say hardly a single word to me, and spend all your time with Sha-sha, sewing. You said you despised sewing; but look. Needles and threads, cottons and silks.'

Lucy touched the flower-pattern that she had been embroidering. She had been thinking to herself, while she stitched it, imagine all the baby-clothes that I can embroider, all the little day slips and coats and nightgowns, all the bibs and bonnets. She had decided almost as soon as Dr Roberts had told her that she was expecting a baby that she would keep it. It wasn't that prenatal murder was a crime, and that she couldn't face the idea of killing her own baby. It wasn't that Jack had just died, and that one life seemed mysteriously to have replaced another.

It was partly the fact that the baby was Jamie's; and that Jamie represented another world for which she was still desperately homesick; and that Jamie was friendly and comforting and loved her dearly.

It was partly the fact that Henry loved her so intensely; and expected so much of her, *now*, at her very weakest, so far away from home, with Jack recently buried, and the Derbyshire countryside bleak and hilly and cold as a stone-bladed knife.

It was partly the fact that she was terrified of being

Henry's wife. And, most of all, it was the fact that she was terrified of *not* being his wife.

An extraordinary thought passed through her mind, as she looked at Henry in front of the fire. *You want to be my husband, yet I'm expecting another man's baby. You want to be my husband, and yet I've never even seen you naked. Another man's penis has been inside me, and made me pregnant, and yet I've never even seen your penis, let alone touched it.*

She flushed at what she was thinking. It aroused her, in a strange way, but it didn't embarrass her. If anything, it gave her a little strength, a little superiority.

Henry said, 'You agreed to marry me. You haven't changed your mind?'

'No, Henry.'

'Lucy – I need you, and I love you beyond all reason. You do know that, don't you?'

'Yes, Henry.'

Henry took a deep breath. 'Can you say that you love me, in return?'

Lucy stared at him boldly. 'Yes, I can say that I love you, in return.'

'And this sickness –'

'This sickness is a sickness. Maybe it's tiredness. Maybe it's the weather. Dr Roberts seems pretty sure that I'm going to survive.'

'You don't think that yewnme jessayn sootud?'

The fire hissed. Lucy's embroidery lay unfinished. It was almost nine o'clock, and 1895 lay not far away. Lucy felt that sense of fate that always characterizes the turn of the year, in that hushed week between Christmas and New Year. All you can hear is the billowing of dustcovers, shrouding old memories for ever; and new covers sliding silkily off. All you can hear are whispers and frustrated prayers and hollow regrets. How small things are, in the tiny hours of that week! Hopes for the future are as small and as bitter as caraway seeds, being thumb-pressed into infertile clay.

And still the clocks will strike to chime the New Year in; and still the bells will ring out across the dales, even when there is nobody to hear them.

There were days of terrible indecision. Sha-sha knew that something was crucially wrong but Sha-sha wouldn't say.

Sha-sha would turn her face away; but never speak an unkind word. Lord Felldale would come up to her (he was walking again now) and lay his hand on her shoulder, absent-mindedly and paternally. Sometimes he would stand like that for five or ten minutes at a time. 'Good girl,' he might say at last. 'Good girl.'

She had accompanied Henry to Derby station, and waved him off on the train. His disappointment and unhappiness had been so obvious that she could have cried. But how could she tell him what was wrong? She had stood on the platform in her black henrietta coat, amidst the noise and the steam and the piercing cold, and he had leaned from his compartment window and cupped his hands around his mouth and shouted, 'I love you! Never forget! I love you!'

And what could she say in return, except that she loved him too; but that another life had intervened which already she cherished much more? Not because it was Jamie's, but because it was hers, it belonged to her, and she knew who it was. Even if she never married, she could say to this dearest of babies, 'Your father is Jamie Cullen, of Oak City, Kansas; that is his name; and he is a lawyer; and you know who your mother is, because your mother is me.'

On the very last morning of the year, when she was doing a jigsaw on the sewing-table in front of her sitting-room window, Sha-sha came into the room and said, 'We've had a telegram from Henry.'

Lucy was trying to fit a brown piece into *Stanley in Africa*. She hesitated with the piece on her hand and said, 'What does he say?'

'He says he has to stay a few days more. He's going down

to Reigate on Thursday morning. He says he misses you very much.'

'I see,' said Lucy. She tried not to sound cold. She didn't mean to sound cold.

Sha-sha came up to Lucy and stood close beside her. 'Lucy, my dear . . . none of us wishes to see Henry hurt. If you feel no love for him . . . well, you really should say so. It is better that he knows the truth now, and suffers the pain of it, than suffers a loveless marriage.'

Lucy replaced the brown piece of *Stanley* into its box. She would never be able to find where it went, not now.

'The truth is, Sha-sha, that I do love him.'

'Sufficiently to be his bride?'

'Sha-sha, I love him.'

'Are you aware how much Henry fears that you don't? That you feel *obliged*, rather than impassioned?'

Lucy didn't know how to answer that question. She did know that Henry was unsure of her affections, yes. But she didn't know how far she herself was responsible for his uncertainty. She was beginning to learn that real love is a dangerous business, every man for himself, no prisoners. She had learned even more from her pregnancy. She had learned that love comes in many different and baffling guises. Love comes open-faced, love comes masked. But – just as Jack had said, '*It's one of those things you know for sure. Nobody can fool you otherwise.*'

She loved her baby. She loved Henry. She loved Jamie, after a fashion. But most of all she loved her baby.

This dark little mystery that was curled up inside of her!

Sha-sha said, 'What is it, Lucy?'

Lucy looked up at Sha-sha and couldn't stop herself from smiling. 'I can't tell you. But everything will work out fine, believe me.'

'You're crying,' said Sha-sha.

'No, I'm not. When poppa died, I made myself a promise, that I would never cry again; not once.'

317

'You're crying,' Sha-sha repeated, much more softly than before, and laid her hands on Lucy's shoulders.

But her mind was made up that first Monday morning of the New Year, which was blindingly bright. The sun shone brilliantly on the Derbyshire dales, and by eleven o'clock the frozen icicles along the guttering began to drip, and cook reported a flood in the scullery. Lord Felldale had taken his bloody buggers for a walk, whooping and whistling. Blanche was packing her trunks in preparation for leaving at the end of the week. There was a feeling of excitement in the air, although most of January was still to come, and February, too; and people died in those months in Derbyshire, just as they did in Kansas.

Lucy was standing by the window with her hands unconsciously clasped across her stomach. She was thinking of what she might say to Henry when he came back from London tomorrow. She had almost decided that – no matter how much it would hurt him – she ought really to tell him the truth. At least he would know that she really did love him, and that her sickness was genuine. The trouble was, he was so concerned about his honour and his reputation. He wanted so much to be Viceroy of India. A viceroy was stand-in for the queen herself. A viceroy was royalty, practically. How could a man who aspired to royalty marry a girl of no family, who was already pregnant by a two-bit Kansas lawyer?

How could a girl of no family expect him to give up everything for which he had been born and educated, just for her?

She was just about to turn away from the window when she saw a fly come struggling up the driveway through the snow. She paused, and raised the curtain a little, so that she could see better. The fly stopped a few yards away from the portico, because of the snow, and so Lucy was able to see who was stepping out. A long green coat, a snow-white face, a tilted black hat. It was Nora!

Lucy picked up her skirts and hurried along the landing. When she reached the head of the stairs, however, she stopped and allowed herself a very deep breath. The stairs were slippery, and she didn't want to fall. Not with Master Darling inside her. Or Miss Darling, whichever it was. She descended the staircase very sedately, holding on to the banister-rail; so that by the time she reached the hallway, Nora was already inside, kicking the snow from her shoes, and brushing herself down, and looking as vexed as always.

'Nora!' Lucy's voice echoed around the hallway.

Nora looked up, and then smacked her gloved hands together with delight. 'Why, Miss Darling, you've blossomed! I wouldn't have known you! And look at me, what a B-flat polony I am, after all those weeks of potatoes!'

They hugged tightly. Nora said, 'The driver told me your poppa was gone. Well, bless his soul to heaven, poor man. I shall miss him, him and his mournful ways. But is your Henry here? The driver told me all about that, too, how he proposed to you on Christmas Day! He said they was ringing the bells in the village, that's how pleased they were; and Lord Felldale sending around free wine for everyone.'

Lucy beckoned to one of the footmen. 'Could you leave those bags in the hallway, just for now?'

Nora frowned at her. 'What's the matter? Is my room not yet prepared?'

'It's not that,' said Lucy. 'It's just that we have to leave, as soon as we can. This morning, now, if I can arrange it.'

'This morning, Miss Lucy? But where are we going? I'm only this minute arrived!'

At that moment, Blanche appeared at the head of the stairs. 'Lucy?' she called. 'Is this your lady's-maid?'

Lucy turned around. 'Yes, Sha-sha. This is Nora, just arrived from Ireland.'

Blanche came halfway down the stairs. 'She can have the room next to Tessie's. It's most agreeable. It has a view of the lake.'

'Actually, Sha-sha –' said Lucy.

'Yes?'

'Actually, now that Nora's here, I've decided to go to London, to see Henry.'

'Well,' said Blanche, with a bowtie smile, 'that's what I've been hoping to hear. Nora – Matthew will take your bags upstairs for you. The downstairs-maid will fetch hot water, if you require it.'

'Actually,' said Lucy, 'we're going now.'

Blanche stared at her with eyes that couldn't quite seem to focus.

'Now? What do you mean? *Now?* You won't get to London until six or seven o'clock, even if you hurry! You have so much to pack!'

Lucy seized Nora's arm. 'Nora will help me, won't you, Nora? We'll pack together! We need only two trunks, at the very most!'

'Lucy,' said Sha-sha, with a little patronizing whinny through her nostrils, and a rustling downstairs of her skirts, 'this will never do! You cannot leave *now*. Not now-this-very-minute. I've arranged the menu for luncheon, everything; and the Pearsons will be here for tea. Diana Pearson is simply dying to tell you about her travels to Turkey.'

Lucy said, 'I'm sorry. I'm sorry, Sha-sha, I really am. But now that Nora's arrived . . . well, she's made me feel so much stronger. And she can act as my chaperone, of course. And I do miss Henry so dreadfully much.'

'Sure and you're talking like an Englishwoman,' Nora complained.

'Well, Englishwoman or not, I'm still going.' Lucy declared.

There was a moment's awkward silence between the three of them. Then Sha-sha clapped her hands and cried out, 'Why not? What a surprise Henry will have! He won't believe it, when you turn up on his doorstep! I'll help you to pack myself! Matthew, call for Lawrence! Tell him to bring the clarence around to the front, as soon as he can! And when I ring, bring him up for Miss Darling's trunks!'

Nora unbuttoned her brown broadcloth coat. 'If you please, Miss Lucy; if I mightn't have the smallest cup of tea before we start to pack?'

They folded and packed away Lucy's clothes as fast as they could; giggling and chattering as they did so. Tissue flew through the bedroom like soft and spectral seagulls. The sun shone; Nora's hands smoothed out silk. Dear fussy Nora! She had seen her uncles and her aunts and all of her cousins; and every one of them had treated her like royalty, and fed her on the best they could; the best fowls, and waxy potatoes, and the very best beer. And the general opinion in County Carlow was that she was beautiful, and fit for the Queen of America, and rich as Crazes.

They were ready by lunchtime. Blanche absolutely insisted that they stay for lunch. It was roasted hare with redcurrant jelly. Lucy could eat very little. She was far too tense and excited. But Blanche was thrilled by the idea of Lucy surprising Henry in London, and did enough talking and eating for the two of them.

'He'll be so serious! You know what moods he gets into! I really wish that I were invisible, and could be standing right beside you when he opens the door! You must telegraph, when you have the time, to tell me what happened!'

Blanche smiled at Lucy lovingly. 'At least I shall leave here knowing that Henry is happy at last.'

At half-past one, the clarence was loaded and they were ready to make their farewells. Lucy and Blanche embraced each other tightly, and Blanche's eyes were filled with tears.

'*Au revoir*, Sha-sha,' Lucy told her. 'Thank you for everything. You've taught me so much.'

'Goodbye, my dear,' said Blanche, kissing Lucy's cheek. 'I hope with all of my heart that you will be happy and contented.'

Lord Felldale was waiting by the clarence, with his dogs. He kissed Lucy, and patted her shoulder appreciatively, as if she were a glossy young mare. 'Good girl, good girl. Look after yourself. And look after that son of mine. Don't let him get above himself. Less of the Clever-Dickery, got it?'

Lawrence the coachman climbed up to his seat and took the ribbons, and Gerry, one of their more reliable footmen, climbed up beside him. Blanche and Lord Felldale waved to them as they drove away from Brackenbridge. A little way behind them, Tessie waved too, flapping her handkerchief frantically from side to side as if she were signalling to an express train that the bridge was washed away.

They circled around the lake, and through the trees, and at last the house disappeared behind a hawthorn hedge and a dry stone wall.

'Well, well, and that was hello-and-goodbye and no mistake,' Nora exclaimed.

'You're not too tired?' asked Lucy.

'Not at all. It was a wonderful rest, seeing all the relations. I've got plenty of stamina. And it'll do me good, to work off some of those potatoes.'

She opened up her purse, and took out a small packet of violet cachous, and offered one to Lucy. Lucy declined it, with a shake of her hand.

'They're marvellous for the breath, if you have to talk to somebody holy after you've been eating onions.'

She sucked for a while, and then she said, 'I'm looking forward to seeing London, that's one thing. I've always wanted to see London.'

Lucy continued to stare out of the window at the bleak Derbyshire skyline. 'We're not going to London,' she said, in a matter-of-fact tone.

'We're not? But you told Miss Shoo-shoo or whatever her name is –'

'It doesn't matter what I told Sha-sha. We're not going to London. We're going to Liverpool.'

'But didn't I just this very morning come off the boat from Liverpool?'

'Yes, you did, and now you're going back; and you and I are going to book ourselves a passage on the very first ship to New York.'

Nora was aghast. 'But what about your beloved? What about Mr Carson? You're not running out on him are you? You're still going to be married?'

'I can't marry him.' Lucy's throat felt tight with misery.

'What do you mean, can't? Don't you love him? You said that you loved him!'

'I do love him, very much. But I can't marry him. And the worst of it is, I can't even tell him why.'

Nora was silent for a very long time, as the clarence jiggled and jolted through the snowy landscape on its way towards Derby. 'Can you tell *me*?' she asked at last.

Lucy said, 'Give me a little time, Nora, and I will. At the moment, all I want to do is to escape.'

They reached Derby station. Lawrence and Gerry climbed down from their seats, banging their mittened hands together to warm them up. Their woollen scarves were thick with frozen breath.

'I'll take you to the London train, Miss Darling,' Lawrence told her. 'Gerry will find himself a porter, and buy your tickets for you.'

Nora frowned at Lucy, but Lucy pressed her fingertip to her lips. She didn't want anybody to know where she had gone; not until she could write to Henry herself. Besides, there might not be any sailings from Liverpool for two or three days, and the last thing she wanted was for Henry to come after her, and try to persuade her to come back. She would have time to send him a letter from Liverpool, before she sailed. She wouldn't vanish out of his life without an explanation. But she wasn't brave enough to tell him to his face.

Derby station was swept with gusts of wind as cold as

iron plates. Lawrence led them on to the London-bound platform, where the train was just about to arrive, and called for the porter to help them with their baggage. Gerry came hurrying up with the tickets just as the train came scraping and squealing and chuffing into the station; followed closely by three more porters, wheeling their trunks on barrows, brisk and professionally panicky, especially for a sixpenny tip. The slamming of doors and the echoing of whistles and the roar of steam was hellish; but dangerously exciting, too. Their trunks were loaded into the guard's-van; Lawrence saw them to their first-class seats. There were six seats in each compartment, Gerry had bought them all.

'Please, you don't have to wait until the train leaves,' Lucy told Lawrence. She pressed two half-crowns into his hand, and said, 'Thank you so much for taking care of us. You've been marvellous.'

'Any time, Miss Darling; any time at all. We're all looking forward to seeing you back at Brackenbridge.'

The instant that Lawrence had left the train, however, Lucy pushed down the window. She could see Lawrence walking through the barrier, sharing out his tip with Gerry. She waited until they had disappeared behind one of the iron pillars, and then she frantically beckoned to the short Kitchener-moustachioed guard, who had taken out his pocket-watch and his furled-up green flag, and was now waiting for the very second to be off.

'Conductor!' she called him. 'Conductor!'

The guard looked around, then caught sight of her. 'Talking to me, madam? I'm sorry, I'm the guard.'

'Well, guard, conductor, whatever you are! There's been a terrible mistake! I'm supposed to be going to Liverpool. My servants have put me on the wrong train!'

The guard stared at Lucy with a slight cast in his eyes. The 2:32 London express was due to leave Derby in fifty-five seconds; the platform barriers were closed; all the doors were closed; the engine-driver was leaning out of his cab waiting for the green flag; and a pale-faced young girl in a black-plumed hat was leaning out of a first-class compartment and telling him that she was on the wrong train.

At the same time, the Liverpool train was just arriving on the opposite platform, in an ill-orchestrated clamour of steam and protesting brakes.

The guard half-raised his whistle to his lips, watching Lucy all the time. Lucy immediately opened her purse, took out a sovereign, and held it up between finger and thumb. She turned it this way and that, so that it would catch the wintry sunlight.

'Guard, conductor – please! It's absolutely desperate!'

The bright whistle stayed where it was. 'Port-aaah!' screamed the guard. 'Porter! Quick as you like!'

Nora, being Irish, loved the hysteria of it all. The guard's-van was flung open, all of their trunks were found and unloaded, and madly carried over the footbridge; while passengers curious and irritable opened their windows and stuck out their heads to find out what was happening; and the Liverpool train was firmly held in its place like an impatient dog, *stay, sir*! by the stationmaster himself, with a stern expression and a red flag.

All of their baggage was re-loaded, the London express was whistled off; and Lucy and Nora were found a first-class compartment close to the front of the train. Another whistle, and they were off, too, with a jolt and a jerk, and a frenzied barking of steam.

They were gradually pulling out of the station, still going very slowly, when Lucy glimpsed a familiar figure on the platform, queueing just like all the other passengers to show his ticket. Immediately, she sat back in her seat, and pressed her hands over her face.

'Miss Lucy?' asked Nora, still panting from their frantic rush across the footbridge. 'What's the matter, Miss Lucy?'

'It's Henry!' Lucy exclaimed, quite aghast. 'He must have come home early! He must have come back from London on this very train!'

They were pulling clear of Derby now. Outside the window were rows of huddled houses, cluttered back yards, freezing washing-lines, and patches of snow. Smoke from the locomotive's chimney went rolling across the countryside like grubby cauliflowers. Lucy sat back in her seat feeling suddenly emptied of all of her energy, and tired, and despondent. Oh crims, poor Henry! She could picture so clearly his return to Brackenbridge, only to discover that she had just left for London. She could picture him telegraphing London; or hurrying back by this evening's train; and finding her gone.

She had saved her own feelings by running away; but what had she done to Henry's?

The train was late; and it rattled and rocked through Belper and Clay Cross and Chesterfield, shouting its way through tunnels and cuttings, blurting over bridges. Lucy watched the dales and the villages unravelling past the windows, grey and luminous. Nora kept an eye on her for as long as she could; then folded her arms and rested her chin on her collar and began to nod off.

Lucy stayed awake; grittily exhausted but unable to think of sleep; frightened by her own fear; frightened of what the future might bring; but determined to keep her baby safe, no matter what happened.

Liverpool, January 9, 1895
'On Board The American Line "St Louis".'

My dearest Henry,
I pray that I have not caused you too much suffering. I am leaving in an hour on the liner St Louis, bound for New York. I shall not return to England, nor trouble you ever again, as if I hadn't caused you sufficient trouble for one lifetime.

The truth is Henry that I feel I would disappoint you in so many ways. In disappointing you, I would disappoint myself. You deserve a wife who was born and bred to be the consort of an English nobleman. Whereas I am nothing of the kind. All the French I know was taught to me by Blanche, and I can still speak only a few words.

You will probably not be able to forgive me, after all your kindness and consideration too. However there are times when we must be honest with ourselves, and this is such a time.

You will never know how deep my affection was for you, nor how much I wanted to be your bride. I will dream of it for many years to come. Please do not think of me badly, or punish me by being unhappy.

With all my love,
Lucy.

It was the worst time of the year to cross the North Atlantic; for all that the *St Louis* had been launched less than a year ago, and that she had been blessed by President Grover Cleveland with American champagne. A savage January storm struck her shortly after she had left the shelter of the Irish coast, and she spent two days wallowing and lurching in thunderous troughs.

Lucy was chronically, painfully, seasick. She spent most of her time lying in her stateroom, praying that God should not punish her any more. The ship creaked all around her, and she was sure that it was going to burst, and let in the sea. Nora, on the other hand, seemed to thrive on the ship's friskiness, and ate more than ever – not only her own food, but the split-pea soup and milk-boiled haddock which the stewards brought for Lucy on a tray, and which Lucy couldn't touch.

After the third morning, however, the wind suddenly dropped, and the sea became surrealistically calm. The *St Louis* made speedy headway across an ocean as black and as glossy as India ink. The air was still bitingly cold; and even the bravest passenger could only remain on the promenade deck for five or ten minutes at a time. Ice floes spun past them, white on black, like frightened memories, and Lucy looked out for penguins, or stranded polar bears, but the floes were empty, as if the polar bears and penguins had deliberately hidden.

Several of the men passengers attempted to flirt with her. A bridge-building tycoon from St Louis, very handsome, like a lion, but far too old, with deeply lined cheeks and fetid breath. A German with Junkers ancestry, fresh breath, no lines, but very prickly-headed, with a broken nose. A Frenchman who pretended to be sad, an actor and an adventurer, who drank too much brandy and couldn't remember why he had decided to visit America at all, or so he said. Lucy tried to speak French to him, but he refused to understand, and kept bending his head forward and kissing her hand, as if he were a customs official, rubber-stamping a passport. '*Mam'selle, ce n'est pas le temps d'être prude à dix-huit ans.*'

But for most of the voyage, Lucy kept herself to herself, and spoke only to Nora; and not often to her. She had thought that she would confess to Nora that she was pregnant as soon as they set sail from Liverpool; but now that she had left Henry behind, she no longer felt such a pressing need for confession. As her pregnancy progressed, she lost interest in Henry. She lost interest in Nora. She lost interest in the whole wide world. All she cared about was what was growing inside her; stronger and more assertive every day. She wasn't ashamed. She thought sometimes that she ought to be. But she felt so happy and so much at peace with herself that she couldn't believe that it was wrong for her to bear this child.

The *St Louis* was delayed for another day because New York harbour was icebound. Lucy stayed in her stateroom most of the time, playing cards with Nora. They could see New York from the promenade deck, across the cracked white ice. The tall spires of the business district, the skyscraping palaces of Mammon. The Washington Building, the Produce Exchange, the Manhattan Life Building, the New York *Times*.

They were sun-gilded and self-enclosed, like the castles of haughty princes.

Nora tried her very best not to be inquisitive; but as evening fell, and the lights of Manhattan began to twinkle, she asked Lucy, 'Will you tell me what it was that made you run out on Mr Carson with such a rush?'

Lucy stared at her cards. 'I didn't really love him enough to marry him, I suppose.'

'But surely you could have told him that to his face, instead of rushing off? He didn't look like the kind of fellow who would have taken it so terribly badly, so long as you told him the truth.'

'Nora . . . I couldn't marry him. There wasn't anything more to it than that.'

Nora dealt her cards. 'I'm sorry that you can't confide in me, Miss Lucy. What else can I say?'

'Nora, I *will* confide in you. But give me time.'

'You're pregnant,' said Nora, boldly.

Lucy looked up, wide-eyed, white as the ice, startled by Nora's acumen; offended that her lady's-maid should have said such a thing; but relieved, too, because Nora had guessed it before she had found it necessary to confess.

'How did you know?' she demanded.

'Oh, come along now, Miss Lucy, I've guessed it for days. I'm a family girl. Isn't my own cousin Kathleen pregnant again, three months' gone, and isn't she behaving the same as you, sweet one minute, fickle the next? And all you can think about is baba, isn't that true?'

Lucy said nothing, but lowered her hand of cards with all the grace of a fan-dancer.

'I'm pregnant, yes.'

'But not with Mr Carson's child?'

'Mr Carson and I –'

Nora lifted both hands. 'Please, Miss Darling. You don't have to act like an Englishwoman when you're with me. You may sack me if you wish, for my impertinence. But it seems to me now that you have no family; and very few friends; and for all of your money you're just eighteen years old. It's a poor kind of human being that would let you fend for yourself just now, pregnant and confused.'

'Nora –' Lucy began, but didn't know what else to say.

'Have you told Mr Cullen yet?' Nora asked her.

Lucy shook her head.

'I'm suspecting that it's Mr Cullen's child? Him who hid behind the curtains, and all?'

'Yes,' said Lucy. She almost smiled. 'Him who hid behind the curtains.'

'Are you thinking of telling him?'

'I don't know,' Lucy admitted. 'I'm afraid.'

'Afraid?' What are you afraid of?'

'What do you think? I'm afraid that he'll want to marry me.'

Nora fanned out her cards. The king of clubs, the queen of hearts. 'You could do very much worse,' she said, with a moral neatness that would have finished a game of patience.

'I want to be married for love,' said Lucy.

Nora made a face. 'Hmph! There's many an old maid's said that, and no mistake.'

'Nora, I can't marry Jamie just because I'm having his baby. It's not the right reason! It wouldn't be fair! We'd end up like Jack and my mother; and the baby would end up like me!'

She paused, flustered, and then she said, 'I don't want any other child to end up like me; not ever.'

Nora stirred the cards around with her fingertip, without raising her eyes. She said nothing more; there was nothing more to say. Nobody could persuade a spoiled and hugely wealthy girl of eighteen years old to marry a man she didn't want to marry, could they? Especially when she wouldn't marry the man that she *did* want to marry.

Holy Mother, thought Nora; and they blame the Irish for being contrary.

It seemed colder in New York than Derbyshire. That hard New York cold; like somebody hitting you straight in the face with a roughcast brick, the second you step out into the street. New York seemed unfamiliar, too, not unfriendly but entirely self-interested, a city that had been carrying on with its business while she was away; a city that didn't care about her any more.

Lucy and Nora left their baggage at the American Lines office, and took a cab back home to Central Park West. It was a slow, traffic-jammed journey. The gutters were heaped with mountain-ranges of filthy cleared-away snow, and so at most places the streets would admit the passage of no more than a single line of carriages on each side. Lucy sat silently and shivered.

At last they reached Central Park West. Lucy had been so impressed with Brackenbridge that she had forgotten how titanic her own mansion was. It looked especially dark and bulky in the slate-grey light of a January afternoon. As Nora paid the cab-driver, Lucy stood on the icy sidewalk with the wind ruffling her furs, staring up at the turreted window of her bedroom.

They climbed the steps and Nora rang the bell. It took a long time for Jeremy to answer. When he did, he appeared diffident and strangely unsurprised. 'Miss Darling . . . come in.'

He took her fur coat. The house was echoing and dark and very cold.

'I received your wire concerning your father,' Jeremy told her. 'I was very sorry to hear of his death. Perhaps, under the circumstances, it was a blessing.'

'It's so *cold* here,' Lucy complained. 'In fact, it's *freezing*! Jeremy – haven't you been lighting the boilers?'

'We've been out of coke for a week now, Miss Darling.'

'Out of coke? Why didn't you order some more?'

Jeremy's hooded eyes slipped sideways. 'Obviously you haven't received my letter.'

'Letter? What letter?'

'Miss Darling . . . there is a fire in the morning room. Come warm yourself, and allow me to explain.'

Lucy followed Jeremy to the morning room. His shoes squeaked plaintively on the marble floor. She had a feeling that something terrible had happened. The house seemed so dead and dusty. And where were all the other servants? Nobody else had come to welcome her back.

A small fire of heaped-up slack was pouring out dense yellow smoke up the morning-room chimney. Outside the window, the stable roofs were thick with snow; which was odd, because the heat of the horses should have melted it by now.

Lucy sat down beside the fire. She kept her gloves on, because the room was so chilly. 'What's happened?' she demanded. Nora waited, standing, in the doorway.

Jeremy said to her, 'Nora, this is no concern of yours. You would be better occupied lighting a fire in your mistress's room, and unpacking her clothes.'

'Sure and why should *I* be lighting fires?' Nora wanted to know.

Jeremy turned back to her, his face a mask of well-trained superciliousness. 'Because there is nobody else to do it, my dear; that is why.'

Nora was about to protest further, but Lucy raised her hand and said, 'Nora, if you would. I must talk to Jeremy in private.'

'Very good, miss,' Nora told her, and gave her a formal curtsey; as if to indicate that the intimacy they had shared during their journey from England had now been summarily brought to an end.

Nora closed the door behind her. Jeremy waited until he

was sure that she was gone, and then he said, 'On the second of January, Miss Darling, your attorneys paid me a visit. Mr Greenbaum came in person. He said that he would be sending you a wire, and writing to you personally, but it seems as if the wire failed to reach you, and as if you and the letter crossed in mid-Atlantic.'

'What did he say?' Lucy asked. 'What on earth's the matter?'

'Mr Greenbaum could tell me very little, Miss Darling, since I am only your *major domo*. But was necessary for him to inform me that there had been legal action taken in California, and that the oil-wells which you believed to be yours had been successfully established in the California courts to belong to somebody else.'

'*What?*' said Lucy, shocked. 'What do you mean, they belong to somebody else?'

'Please, Miss Lucy ... I was told only what it was necessary for me to know. Mr Greenbaum said that all your bank accounts have been frozen, and that I should immediately cut down the household budget to the absolute minimum. I had to sell the horses and the brougham just to pay the rest of the staff their severance wages, Miss Darling; and I myself have not drawn wages for two weeks.'

'I don't understand,' said Lucy. She felt faint and shivery, as if she weren't here at all. This was a practical joke, surely? Any minute now, the boilers would fire up, and the coal would start to crackle brightly in the hearth. Any minute now, the electric lights would sparkle, and all her staff would appear to welcome her home.

But Jeremy continued to look at her through the strained winter light, the skin of his cheeks as criss-crossed with crumples as a handkerchief, and she knew with a terrible empty dread that he was telling her the truth.

'What am I going to do?' she whispered. (Who said that? Did I say that?) She really had no idea. In a few short weeks, she had fallen from being the incandescent darling of New

York high society, the Lightbulb Girl, pampered and flattered and followed by the gossip-reporters from ball to ball, asked to marry by English aristocracy, to nothing whatsoever, not worth a mention, a penniless parentless girl from Oak City, Kansas. All she had to show for her briefly-sparkling career was an illegitimate baby and a few steamer-trunks packed with silken gowns.

Jeremy intoned, 'I have sought other employment, Miss Darling. I hope you will forgive me. But I will remain here until you have sorted matters out with your attorneys.'

Lucy swallowed, and nodded, and said, 'Thank you,' although she didn't feel like thanking him. He should be taking care of her, especially now that she was pregnant; just like Mr Greenbaum should be taking care of her, and all of her servants, and Jamie, and Henry. Why had Henry been so full of himself? If Henry had been more sympathetic, she would have been able to tell him about the baby, and he wouldn't have minded, and then she wouldn't have had to run away.

And as for Jamie, it was *his* child; but what concern had *he* shown for her? He hadn't even written, when she was in England.

And as for Nora, all she could do was to sulk, because she hadn't been asked into the morning room; and because Lucy had treated her like a servant, which she was.

Jeremy said, 'Mr Greenbaum left me some money for you, Miss Darling, two hundred dollars; for incidental expenses such as food and carfare.'

'Thank you,' Lucy repeated, very quietly. She had a strange feeling that she had once said 'Thank you' in just that way before. Outside the window, it looked as if it were snowing again, but it was only a gust of chilly wind blowing around the corner of the house, and whirling flakes of snow from the stable roof.

Ira Greenbaum, she supposed, was as considerate as anybody

could have expected, for an attorney whose fees could probably not be met. He had a squat, compressed body, and his head rolled around in his collar like a large plum-pudding about to roll off a plate. His office was intensely dark and smelled of sour paper and sausage and damp flannel trousers.

As he spoke, he restlessly winnowed through sheets of paper and folded letters as if he were searching for something crucial which he never really expected to find.

'Shortly after you and the late Mr Darling had left for Europe, Miss Darling, we had a communication from Mr – what-was-his-name – your company attorney in Los Angeles –'

'Mr Thurloe Daby,' said Lucy. She was dressed in chocolate-brown velvet this morning, with darker brown piping, and a pheasant-feather hat. She felt tired. She knew she had mauvish circles under her eyes. But she felt much more composed than she had yesterday.

'*Daby*, that was his name . . . *Daby*. Odd name that, Daby. Sounds like Baby. But, anyhow, Mr *Daby* told us that a fellow called Beaumont had been arrested in mid-December by police in Charleston, South Carolina, after a fatal stabbing of a sea-captain on the dockfront. They charged him with murder in the first degree. Seems like Beaumont had been out to get his revenge on this sea-captain on account of some contraband deal between them that had turned sour.

'Anyhow, that isn't here and that isn't there. The point was that when the police searched Beaumont's house, looking for contraband as evidence, they found amongst plenty of other fascinating goods a gold ring and a boxful of papers belonging to a man called Nathaniel Touchstone, of Los Angeles, California.'

'What does that have to do with me?' asked Lucy. 'I don't know anybody called Touchstone. I *never* knew anybody called Touchstone.'

'Please, bear with me,' said Ira Greenbaum, still winnowing, still searching. 'It really isn't that complicated. When the South Carolina police wrote to the Los Angeles police, asking for information about Nathaniel Touchstone – asking for his whereabouts, you see, so that he could claim back his jewellery and his papers, they were told that Touchstone had once lived in Charleston, years ago, but that he had gone west to California to prospect for oil.

'He'd been pretty successful, too. Had a splendid house, plenty of land, owned an orange-grove, too. But, you know – in spite of all this – house, money – about three years ago, he committed suicide. Took poison.'

Ira Greenbaum's head wobbled from side to side, as if he were addressing a jury. '*Why* had he committed suicide? Well, because of remorse, apparently. He left a letter saying that about a year previous he had gotten very drunk one night with some old friends from South Carolina, and finished up the evening's entertainment by visiting a house of ill-repute in the Mexican district. He had woken up in the morning to find himself in bed with a young Mexican whore of not much more than ten years old, dead she was, stabbed to death, and himself covered in blood, and his own claspknife between the sheets.

'*God forgive me for what I did to that girl*, that's what he said in his letter, and he went to his grave convinced that he had murdered her. At the time, of course, what with the suicide letter, that looked to the Los Angeles police like the close of the matter. Great many people commit suicide in California, that's what they said, disappointment, broken dreams, whisky and suchlike. But now Nathaniel Touchstone's ring and papers had turned up mysteriously in Charleston, at the home of this fellow Beaumont.

'Well, the Charleston police talked to Beaumont; and in exchange for some leniency in the matter of the stabbed sea-captain, Beaumont told them what he knew about Nathaniel Touchstone.

'Years ago, Beaumont had been partners in the contraband

business with Touchstone, as well as a man called Weale and a man called Conroy.'

'Conroy?' asked Lucy. 'You mean *Casper* Conroy, my uncle?'

Ira Greenbaum nodded, and sharply sniffed. 'The same man, your uncle. Those three had made their living by smuggling everything and anything, apparently – guns, liquor, children. You name it. But after some kind of a disagreement, all three of them had broken up and gone their separate ways. Weale tended bar in Charleston for a while, your Uncle Casper went to Denver. At first, Touchstone seemed to have disappeared without trace. But it wasn't too long before Weale accidentally discovered from a California sea-captain that Touchstone had gone to Los Angeles and made himself a tidy profit in oil, legitimately, too . . . and that was when the mischief began.

'Weale rounded up Beaumont; and the two of them travelled by railroad to Los Angeles and re-acquainted themselves with Touchstone. Touchstone wasn't at all pleased to see Weale again, that's what Beaumont said. They had never been the best of friends, but Weale persuaded Touchstone to go out drinking. He knew from experience that Touchstone couldn't hold his liquor particularly well. By the time they took Touchstone to a house of ill-repute in the Mexican district, Touchstone was well-nigh unconscious.'

Ira Greenbaum paused, and looked sharply at Lucy, and asked, 'You're not feeling unwell, Miss Darling? You're looking a little pale.'

'I'm . . . fine,' Lucy told him. In actual fact, she felt as if the book-crowded office walls were shuffling closer and closer; and that she would soon be pressed to death between stacks of legal encyclopedias and choked on sheaves of musty paper.

'I could have my secretary bring you a glass of water? Or maybe some tea? She makes terrible tea, enough to revive anybody.'

337

Lucy shook her head. 'I haven't been quite myself, that's all.'

Ira Greenbaum rocked his head from side to side. 'It's this winter weather. *Paskudnak*, disgusting. I feel just the same.'

'You were telling me what happened to the man called Touchstone,' Lucy reminded him.

'Sure I was! And it was terrible, too. Weale and Beaumont found and killed a young Mexican girl. Killed her, just like that! Then they rolled her up in a blanket, and took her to the room where Touchstone was sleeping. According to Beaumont, Weale did the murdering . . . although of course there's nobody left alive to say that it wasn't Beaumont who did the dirty work himself. Then they left, so that Touchstone would wake up next to the dead girl, and think that *he* had committed the murder himself, when he was drunk.

'Which of course is what he *did* think, and went into a blind panic.

'He showed Weale the girl's body, and begged for help. He was a respectable oil magnate by now; the last thing he could afford was a scandal like this. Weale made a great pretence of shock and horror, but helped him to dispose of the girl's remains; and agreed to cover up the evidence. But in return, as insurance, Touchstone would have to make over to Weale a percentage of his Seal Beach oil holdings. Touchstone had two other equally profitable oil holdings further down the coast. What Weale was asking apparently didn't seem too much. Not to keep him from hanging, anyway.

'So that's how Weale got his hands on the title to the oil holding. By murder, you see; by blackmail. He even formed a company in the name of Ferris. Kind of a joke, you understand, Ferris Weale.

'But it wasn't long before Weale began to be discontented with his share of the oil, and he threatened Touchstone yet again, unless Touchstone gave him more. They had a terrific argument, apparently, but we don't know what the outcome of it was because Beaumont wasn't with them at the time. But the very next day Touchstone was found dead by arsenic poisoning. He had written a long suicide letter about "remorse" for murdering the Mexican girl, and another letter making over all of his oil to Weale.

'If Weale killed Touchstone, which he undoubtedly did, it was a pretty clever thing to do . . . the police were relieved that they had managed to solve two deaths at once. Two birds with one stone. They didn't take the trouble to look any further for murderers.

'The story doesn't end there, though. Weale told Beaumont that the oil-well wasn't producing more than a few barrels of poor-quality crude every day; and paid Beaumont off. Pretty well, fifty or sixty thousand dollars. Beaumont went back to Charleston and bought himself a grand house, and a carriage, and a wine-cellar, and a different lady every night. But it wasn't more than a year before he'd spent everything that Weale had given him. He returned to California and quickly discovered that Weale had been lying and that the oil-well was prospering, and had made Weale astronomically rich.

'Beaumont didn't have the wit to tackle Weale on his own. So he wrote to your Uncle Casper Conroy and asked him to come to California to help him. He had found a druggist who was prepared to swear that he had supplied Weale with arsenic, and that Weale had told him it was "for settling a score with Mr Touchstone". Beaumont intended to blackmail Weale, in just the same way that Weale had blackmailed Touchstone. But he needed money, to pay off the druggist; and a maid who would say that she had seen Weale writing Touchstone's so-called suicide letter, and was prepared to *say* that she had, in court, but only for a price.'

'How much?' asked Lucy, faintly.

'I'm sorry?'

'How much money did he need, to pay these people off, the druggist and the maid?'

'I'm not sure exactly. The figure of three hundred dollars was mentioned.'

Lucy thought of her mother's jewellery; of Uncle Casper's eyes, watching her.

Ira Greenbaum said, 'Your uncle went to California. He met up with Weale; and presumably threatened to tell the police about Touchstone, if Weale didn't give him a share in Ferris Oil. Your man *Daby* said there were furious arguments, but that Weale agreed, in the end, and signed over forty-nine per cent. Hm! Your uncle was a real forty-niner, and no mistake!

'But then there was a strange shooting incident, and Weale was killed, supposedly by Mexicans, but nobody knows why. Certainly not Beaumont; or if he does, he's not telling. The oil-field passed in its entirety to your uncle, and thus, when your uncle died, to you.'

'But my deeds are legal,' Lucy protested. 'They were legally drawn up. My friend Jamie Cullen did it for me. And nobody ever proved that my uncle killed Mr Ferris, or Mr Weale, or whatever his name was, did they?'

Ira Greenbaum shrugged. 'Your deeds are legal in the sense that *you* did nothing illegal. But Weale obtained his holdings in Touchstone's oil by fraud and murder and forgery; and so whether your uncle was implicated in the death of Mr Weale or not, the oil-holdings should rightfully have passed to Touchstone's closest next-of-kin, or failing that, back to the railroad company. Whoever those holdings belong to, Miss Darling, they surely don't belong to you.'

Lucy sat in silence for a very long time. Then she stood up. She didn't know what else to do.

'You mean that I have nothing at all?'

'I'm afraid that's the way of it. Strictly speaking, you may owe the legitimate leaseholders a great deal of money – everything you've spent. But I expect that I can negotiate you out of that one.'

'I can't even pay *you*.'

340

Ira Greenbaum's head tilted to the left; he smiled, a little archly. 'Let's just say that I prefer to tie up loose ends. What are you going to be doing for your dinner tonight?'

'I don't know. I hadn't thought.'

Ira Greenbaum lifted up papers, let them fall. 'Maybe I could take you to a restaurant I know. It's not exactly Delmonico's, but then it's not exactly Bode's, either.'

'Thank you, Mr Greenbaum, I'd rather not.'

'You have to eat, Miss Darling.'

'I can find ways to feed myself, thank you.'

Ira Greenbaum stopped shuffling his papers for a moment and watched her with passive regret. 'You have to vacate the house by the end of the month.'

Lucy swallowed, and nodded, but didn't say anything.

'I'm sorry things had to happen this way. My father always used to say that it's no disgrace to be poor, but it's no honour, either.'

'Your father sounds as if he was a wise man.'

'My father . . . I don't know. My father knew nothing about anything. And he was never rich, either. The *goldeneh medina*, that's what he used to call America, the Golden Land, but I could never tell if he was being serious or sarcastic.'

'Good day, Mr Greenbaum.'

'Good day, Miss Darling.'

In one of the fiercest February blizzards that the Middle West had ever seen, Lucy and Nora travelled westward through Indiana and Missouri to Kansas City, where they boarded the Kansas Pacific for the last leg of their journey through Topeka and Fort Riley and Salina, the snow blinding out the names of the towns at every stop, the snow turning the whole journey into a whirling, freezing dream.

The only warmth in the whole world seemed to be inside her, inside her own womb, where her baby nestled. As the train slowly clanked through the snow, she held her hands clasped over her stomach and closed her eyes and tried to feel what it was feeling; think what it was thinking. A tiny life, depending entirely on her.

Nora watched her with steady devotion. She had never been farther west than Elizabeth, New Jersey; but she and Lucy had developed a curious bond between them which seemed to have grown stronger and more intricate since Lucy had lost all of her wealth, and neither of them had questioned for a moment that Nora should accompany Lucy back home.

The blizzard was still screeching when they reached Oak City. They climbed down the ice-slippery steps to the ground. There was nobody to meet them: nobody knew they were coming. They carried their own bags across to the depot building. The snow was blown into snakes around their boots; their scarves whipped and curled and lashed their cheeks.

'Sure it's powerful chilly here!' Nora shouted over the blasting of steam from the locomotive. 'If this isn't the chilliest place on God's good earth!'

'It gets colder!' Lucy shouted back at her.

'That's a lie! It couldn't! I think that the tip of my nose just snapped off!'

They were lucky. They found old man Maeterlinck waiting outside the depot with his enclosed business-wagon, waiting for anyone who wanted a ride through the snow. He looked more like Santa Claus than ever, white-bearded, cherry-nosed, wrapped up in a thick green coat. He was too old for joinery these days, so he picked up pennies by giving rides, and doing oddjobs. He helped them with their bags, and then they climbed into the wagon, and brushed the snow from their coats, and unwound their scarves. Inside the business-wagon it smelled of pipe-tobacco and old man Maeterlinck's lunch, and it wasn't much warmer than it was outside, but at least they were protected from the wind.

'How's things?' old man Maeterlinck asked Lucy.

'Thought you would've had your own train by now, and twenty blackies to carry your bags.'

'I didn't want to appear too high'n'mighty,' lied Lucy.

'Well, something to be said for that,' old man Maeterlinck sniffed. 'Always said that poor folks never have no real enemies, but rich folks never have no real friends.'

He sniffed noisily, and then he said, 'Too bad about your pa, wodden it? And the Skipping Widder?'

'You heard about it?'

'It was all in the papers. How they fell off of that balcony and all. Don't know what the hell Molly Sweeney thought she was doing; but then she always was that way, wodden she? Always dancing and dreaming, dreaming and dancing.'

'There are worse things,' Nora retorted.

'Oh, sure, there are worse things,' old man Maeterlinck agreed. 'Like getting your great toe stuck fast in the faucet. Or biting into a cracky-wheat loaf and finding your wife's front tooth.'

Lucy didn't tell him that Jack was dead. She simply didn't want to.

They descended the gradient towards the Saline River. The snow was still flying, but not so fiercely now, and the wind appeared to have dropped. There wasn't much else for them to talk about, so they sat in silence. The wagon's springs creaked; old man Maeterlinck sniffed and cleared his throat; snowflakes pattered against the windows, soft as the finger-touches of forgotten women. Lucy could almost believe that they were the wind-blown spirits of all those wives who had died on the High Plains of Kansas, work-worn, bearing children, diseased, or just broken-hearted.

At last they reached the Cullen farm. Old man Maeterlinck whoaed his horses just outside the front door; and helped them down; and just as he did so, Jerrold Cullen appeared, in a thick sheepskin coat with the collar turned up, and the flaps of his muskrat hat pulled down over his ears.

'Lucy Darling!' he called out, in surprise. 'This is an honour!'

Lucy lifted her skirts as she stepped through the snow. She took hold of Jerrold Cullen's hand and squeezed it tight. 'Mr Cullen; it's so good to see you. This is Nora . . . she's my – well, she's my companion. And my friend, too.'

Old man Maeterlinck heaved down their bags and dropped them in the snow. 'You want to drag 'em into the house, m'friend?' Jerrold asked him.

'Not me,' coughed old man Maeterlinck. 'Getting a sight too old for lugging ladies' portmantooties.'

Jerrold shrugged. 'Don't worry about it. I'll have Martin carry them in.'

Old man Maeterlinck came shuffling up to them and took off his hat.

'How much do I owe you?' Lucy asked him.

'Three dollars even.'

Lucy lifted her purse and unfastened it, but made no attempt to open it. She knew that after their railroad fares and their meals she had only $1.78 left. She had been hoping to raise a little more money in Hays City tomorrow by pawning the remainder of her mother's jewellery; but right now she was almost flat-busted.

Her eyes caught Jerrold's eyes. At first he wasn't quite sure what she was silently asking him. But then she looked meaningfully sideways at old man Maeterlinck, and appealingly back to Jerrold, and Jerrold understood.

'Oh, sure, I'm sorry,' he said, and dug into the pocket of his sheepskin coat, and brought out two silver dollars, and handed them over. Old Man Maeterlinck bit them, sniffed, pushed them into his glove, and then shuffled away. Meanwhile Martin had appeared at the door.

'Dad?'

'Yes, Martin. How about carrying these bags inside for Lucy? Looks like she's staying for a little while. And this is Nora, Lucy's friend. Looks like Nora's staying for a little while, too.'

'Hi, Lucy,' grinned Martin. 'Thought you millionairesses had electro-plated carriages, and hundreds of servants.'

'Not me,' Lucy smiled.

'It's great to see you. Does Jamie know you're here? He's coming back from Manhattan Friday or Saturday. He'll go crazy to see you.'

'Well, I'm looking forward to seeing him, too.'

They went into the house. It was just as puritanical in its decor as ever, but all the fires were well stacked up, and it was wonderfully warm. Mrs Cullen came out of the kitchen with floury hands to kiss Lucy welcome. 'They tell us all about you, at the store. The new owner's a really good man. Nothing like your poor pappa, but a real good straight-forward man.'

Lucy was given a plain blue-decorated room overlooking the river valley; Nora was found a smaller room over the kitchen. Lucy's room was sparse. A single mahogany bed with a blue throwover; a blue rag rug; an oval cheval mirror, and a washstand. She unbuttoned her boots and then collapsed back exhausted on the bed. She couldn't believe that she was really back in Oak City, as poor as ever. But then she couldn't believe that she had really been away, either. The past months of silk dresses and champagne and handsome young men seemed no more substantial than something she might have read in a book. And she had been to England, too!

She had owned gold knives and forks, real gold. Now everything she owned was locked up in two large port-manteaux; and in her mind; and in her womb. But, strangely, it seemed like quite enough.

On the wall of her room hung an embroidered sampler. Its simple message read, *Naked came I out of my mother's womb, and naked shall I return thither: the Lord gave, and the Lord hath taken away; blessed be the name of the Lord.*

She closed her eyes. She slept for a while, and dreamed of trains, and flying snow, and half-remembered faces in a blur of winter whiteness, as if somebody had been trying to obscure them with fence-paint.

Jerrold said, with his fingers steepled, 'Lucy, you'd better tell me what's wrong.'

Lucy's eyes glistened in the firelight. It was after supper now. Nora was helping Mrs Cullen in the kitchen with the pots and pans. The boys had gone out to lock up the cattle and the horses. The house was still fragrant with the aroma of chicken pot-pie and freshly-baked bread. The clock ticked, the fire spat. The cat sat in front of the hearth with its paws tucked in, its eyes slitted, dreaming of Egypt.

Lucy's hands lay white on her dark maroon dress. The only jewellery she wore was her mother's cameo brooch.

'There's nothing wrong,' she replied. 'Really, there's nothing.'

'What made you come back here to Oak City? Don't tell me you're just visiting. If visiting was all you had in mind, you would've come in the summer.'

Lucy remained silent, staring at the fire.

'You know what it says in the Bible,' said Jerrold. '"The truth shall make you free."'

Lucy smiled, without looking at him.

'You've lost your money, haven't you?' Jerrold asked her, very gently.

'Yes,' whispered Lucy.

'Everything? You've really lost everything?'

'Everything. The oil-well wasn't even mine to begin with; never was; we had no right. A man was killed for it; and then the man who killed him was killed for it; and then the man who killed *him* was killed for it.'

She looked up; and her face was so sad that Jerrold could have taken her into his arms and comforted her like one of his own daughters.

'It was never mine. Not for one minute. I was lucky they didn't make me pay everything back. I was never the Lightbulb Girl, not truly: I was never anything at all.'

'How's Jack taking it?' asked Jerrold. 'Is he coming out to join you?'

346

'Jack's dead,' Lucy told him. 'He died in England. We buried him there.'

'I'm sorry,' said Jerrold. 'I really am truly sorry.'

'Spilled milk,' Lucy replied. 'Nothing but spilled milk, that's all.'

'He wasn't in pain?'

'No,' Lucy whispered. 'He wasn't in pain. Not in his body, anyway.'

'He was a tortured man, your father, if you'll forgive me.'

'Yes,' said Lucy; and in spite of the fact that she didn't want them to, her eyes filled up with tears. 'Yes, he was a tortured man.'

Jerrold reached across and laid his hand on top of hers. 'What are you going to do now? You're going to stay with us here for a while, I hope?'

'For a few days, if you'll let me. I have to go to Hays City to get some money. Then I'm going to start looking for some work. Maybe the new man at the store might have me.'

'Lucy, you can stay here, long as you like. There's plenty of work on a farm this size, and never enough people to take care of it. And your Nora seems a real friendly willing woman. You can both stay, however long you like.'

Lucy knelt down on the rug beside Jerrold, and took hold of his hands and pressed them between hers. 'Forgive me for coming here,' she pleaded. 'After they told me that everything was gone, I was stranded in New York with no money, no carriage, no servants, nothing – nothing except my railroad fare west, and Nora, and a memory of just what a loving family home this is. You can throw me out whenever you wish; and as soon as you wish. I know that. I don't want charity. But this house is home to me, Mr Cullen; the only home I have.'

Jerrold stroked her shining blonde hair. 'You can stay for ever if you want to. And you're certainly not leaving before Jamie gets home.' She could feel his voice rumbling like distant thunder. But it was reassuring thunder. The kind of thunder that makes you feel glad that you're at home.

Nora came in, and stood by the door, smiling; and it was then that Lucy knew that everything was going to turn out all right.

Jamie arrived home on Saturday afternoon, off the three o'clock train from Manhattan. Lucy hid behind the front door as soon as she saw the wagon arrive from the depot, and when Jamie came bursting in, stamping his snowy boots on the mat, she sprang out at him, and cried, 'Surprise!'

Jamie whooped like a cowhand, and lifted her up, and whirled her around.

'Careful!' she said. 'Careful!'

'Oh, I wouldn't drop you,' he grinned. 'You're precious to me like china.'

'When you were a kid, you broke half of momma's Carlsbad dinner service,' Martin reminded him.

'Hey now, you helped me,' Jamie retorted. 'I did the cups, but you did the saucers.'

He took off his cap and hung up his coat. 'What brings you all the way back to Oak City?' he asked Lucy. 'Thought you would have taken the grand tour of Europe, while you were there. Paris, Rome, Madrid.'

Mrs Cullen came up and kissed Jamie, and then put her arms around Lucy's shoulders. 'She's had some bad fortune, Jamie. You just be kind to her.'

They went through to the living room, where Nora brought them coffee (with just a nip of whisky for Jamie, to warm him up after his train-ride). Lucy told Jamie what had happened, and Jamie listened without saying a single word. It was only when she had quite finished that he knocked back his whisky, and wiped his mouth, and asked her, 'You're not going to marry Henry, then?'

'Of course not, I can't.'

Jamie rubbed the back of his neck. 'You can't? Just

348

because you lost your money? What difference should that make, if Henry really loves you? Rich or poor, shouldn't make no difference at all.'

'Oh Jamie, of *course* it makes a difference. Henry fell in love with an oil millionairess. He would never have fallen in love with a shopgirl.'

'Well, more fool him,' shrugged Jamie. 'Rich or poor, that doesn't make any difference to me. The only riches that are worth bothering about, as far as I'm concerned, are the riches of happiness.

'Amen,' said Jerrold, from the far corner of the room. 'The unsearchable riches of Christ.'

Lucy sat quiet for a moment, with her hands clasped in her lap. Then she said, 'There was another reason why I couldn't marry him.'

Jamie waited for her to tell him what it was, but she didn't.

'What other reason?' he asked, at last.

'Could I talk to you privately?'

'I don't think father's going to snitch on any of your secrets, are you, father?'

Jerrold grunted in amusement. He was reading *The True Measure of Christian Forbearance* – 'Wherefore, if meat make my brother to offend, I will eat no flesh while the world standeth, lest I make my brother to offend.'

'All the same,' said Lucy. 'I'd like you to be the first to hear it.'

Jerrold closed his book and tugged down his vest. 'Don't worry, I have work to do. I'll leave you two alone.'

When he had left the room, Jamie sat back in his chair with his cup of coffee, and Lucy thought that he was not only beginning to talk like a lawyer, he was beginning to *look* like one, too. He was just as handsome as ever, but he was too pale from sitting in offices and courtrooms; and paleness didn't suit him. 'What's this fearful secret, then?' he asked her, sucking his coffee-spoon. He would never have done that two years ago: that was an office habit.

'It wasn't the money,' said Lucy. 'It wasn't the money at all. I didn't find out about the money until I got back to New York.'

'Well, if it wasn't the money, what was it?' Still playing the lawyer.

'You don't have to *badger* me, Jamie. I'm not a witness in court.'

'I'm sorry. But you *can* tell me. Listen, I promise you! I won't snitch and I won't bite.'

'Maybe you won't. But you may get angry.'

Jamie laughed. 'Why should I get angry? I resigned myself a long time ago to the fact that you don't actually love me. You wrote and *told* me that you didn't love me.'

'Jamie, I do love you. You know I love you. I was confused.'

'*You* were confused? How do you think *I* felt?'

'I'm sorry, Jamie. I'm truly sorry. Henry was so −' Thinking of Henry, she couldn't stop the tears. Damn them! Tears, just when she didn't want them!

Jamie put down his cup of coffee and tugged a clean handkerchief out of his vest pocket. 'Henry was so *what*?' he asked her, quietly and kindly.

She wiped her eyes. 'I didn't mean to cry. I promised myself when Jack died − I promised myself that I never would.'

'That was a pretty stupid promise. How could you keep a promise like that?'

'I thought I'd try.'

She waited for a moment or two, and then she said, 'Henry was everything that I'd ever dreamed about. That was all. Well, that was more than enough. He was aristocratic and wonderfully educated and full of life and he would never take no for an answer.'

Jamie didn't say anything, but waited for her to tell him what her secret was. The secret why she couldn't marry the man she had always dreamed about.

When she actually said it, however, the words sounded like Chinese. He heard her speak; he thought that he had understood what she said; but his mind obviously refused to interpret the sounds that she had made into intelligible English.

'You're what?' he asked her.

Then, 'You're *what*?'

He offered, of course, more than once. But her mind was made up. She didn't want to think of marriage until the baby was born. She was still unsure of how she felt; and the last thing she wanted to do was to marry Jamie and turn his life into a never-ending purgatory of unreturned love. She had seen what a marriage like that had done to Jack Darling. It had eaten him like acid, inch by inch; and in the end it had killed him before his time.

Jerrold, to Lucy's relief, was neither angry nor disapproving. It would have been understandable for a Christian zealot to send Lucy out into the snow; and Jamie along with her. But when Jamie broke the news to him, with Lucy watching from the hallway outside, Jerrold said nothing at all. He seemed bemused, more than anything else, as if Lucy's pregnancy had presented him with a moral problem which he was unable to understand. If Jesus had been born in Oak City, what would Jerrold have done then? She saw Jerrold nodding; saw him frown; his hair shining in the blue-white light from the snowfalls outside the window.

When Jamie left, he said nothing; but sat in his rocking-chair with his hands clasped in front of him, not rocking, slightly hunched.

Later that day, Jerrold came into the parlour where Lucy was embroidering, and stood by the door watching her. Lucy looked up at him, and smiled, and then laid her embroidery down in her lap.

'You're not angry with me, are you?' she asked him.

'Angry? Why should I be? You know what the Lord said. Judge not, that ye be not judged.'

'This is your grandson,' said Lucy, laying her hand on her stomach.

Jerrold came into the room, and sat down, and looked at Lucy for a long time, his head couched in his hand.

'Do you know something, Lucy?' he asked her. 'I knew your mother very well. She used to come here often; for flowers, for cheese; or just to talk to Mrs Cullen, whenever she felt lonely. Your mother was what you might call an independent spirit; not like your father at all. She took whatever the world had to offer.'

Lucy didn't interrupt him, but watched him carefully. She could sense strongly that he was trying to tell her something; trying to give her clues to what she should do.

'The thing is,' said Jerrold, looking down at his hand as it rested on his knee; 'the thing is that your mother followed her own sense of what was right and what was wrong. Sometimes she shocked me, you know, the things she said; because she was pious and churchgoing and believed in the Lord, but she believed in happiness, too, everybody seeking their own fulfilment; she believed that the Lord expected every one of us to be happy and fulfilled.'

There was a long pause, and then Jerrold said, 'You've heard me talking strict to Jamie, specially when it comes to his law studies. But Jamie doesn't take too much notice of that, and nor should he. Jamie's going to be happy no matter what I say, Jamie's going to be fulfilled, because he's following the course that his heart dictates. The Lord has given him a path to tread and he's treading it. My advice to you, Lucy, honey, is that you should do the same. You've seen the elephant now, haven't you? You've seen New York, and London, and the way that rich folk live. There isn't much in Kansas that can match up to that kind of living.'

In a lacy-soft voice, Lucy asked him, 'Are you trying to say that I should leave?'

'Oh, no, not at all, sweetheart! you can stay for ever, if that's what you want!'

'Then what? I don't understand.'

Jerrold took a deep breath. 'I love Jamie, you know that; and I love you, too. And by all the Christian principles that I hold dear, I know that you should marry him. He's the natural father of your baby, after all. But if I'm going to be truthful, I think that you've been right to say that you won't. If you two married, then believe me, there wouldn't be nothing in it for either of you but pain.'

Jerrold had obviously said his piece, and had nothing more to say, because he sat back now, and watched Lucy anxiously, to see how she had taken it.

Lucy reached over and touched his hand. 'Thank you, Mr Cullen,' she told him. 'I can guess how hard it was for you to say that.'

'Sure thing,' said Jerrold, and stood up, and kissed her forehead, and went to round up his dairy herd for their evening milking.

But Lucy sat for a very long time alone by the fire, thinking about Jerrold's words, and almost feeling the world turning around her.

Spring came to the High Plains of Kansas; and then summer; and the grasses waved and whispered like the driest of oceans. Lucy spent her time helping Mrs Cullen in the kitchen, paring vegetables; or sewing. Her stomach was big, and very low, although she hadn't put on very much weight; and Mrs Cullen was sure that it was going to be a boy.

'What are you going to call him?' she asked Lucy one brilliant morning, as they sat together in the kitchen, cleaning wild fiddleheads for lunch.

Lucy could feel the baby pushing and stretching at her stomach. It kicked like an excited pony in the evening, when she sat down after supper, but during the day it stretched itself luxuriously and slowly, as if it were waking up from a long and befuddling dream.

I dreamed that I never existed, but now I do . . . She wondered if babies ever had dreams like that; or if they had memories of Heaven.

'I thought of Thomas,' she told Mrs Cullen.

'Well, Thomas is a good given name,' Mrs Cullen nodded. 'But what of a family name?'

'I don't know,' said Lucy.

Mrs Cullen stopped scraping the fuzz from the fiddleheads for a moment, and looked at Lucy with her intent grey Scandinavian eyes.

'Jamie worships you, you know that, don't you?' she said.

Lucy lowered her eyes.

'Jamie would die for you, Lucy, if you asked him to.'

'I never would. I would never do anything to hurt him, ever.'

'You're hurting him now, by carrying his child and refusing to marry him.'

'But what if I marry him and I just don't love him enough? What if I end up by being cruel to him, and vexatious, and hating him?'

Mrs Cullen took a deep breath. 'I don't think you would. I don't think that you have such spitefulness in you.'

'My momma wasn't spiteful; but she ruined my poppa. She *destroyed* him! I don't want Jamie to end up like Jack.'

'Perhaps Jamie's stronger than Jack,' Mrs Cullen suggested.

Lucy stared directly back at her. 'How can anybody be strong when the person they love doesn't love them in return?'

Mrs Cullen reached across the scrubbed deal table, and held Lucy's hand. 'What do you know about love and marriage, at eighteen years old? Some people marry for love; some people marry for money; most people marry for companionship. When you meet a man who loves you the way that Jamie loves you, you should think real seriously about what he is offering. Care, and friendship, and physical devotion. You must have found him physically attractive, that night you became pregnant.'

'I did and I do,' Lucy answered, boldly.

'So will you think of marrying him? Will you think of giving young Thomas his family name?'

Lucy scraped back her chair, and stood up, and walked across to the open door. A warm May wind was blowing softly through the oaks. On the grassy horizon, six or seven horses were galloping, as if they were runaways from a fairground carousel. Just in front of her, beside the brick pathway that led to the kitchen door, a bed of yellow-and-orange nasturtium flowers trembled. She thought: Jamie's so dear to me. Jamie's so good-looking. But I never wanted to have the family name Cullen; and I never wanted my children to have the family name Cullen, either. I know there's more, I've seen it! There are jewels and dances and fabulous people!

Please dear God don't let me end up here, married to Jamie. Please dear God. Otherwise my face will fade just like the faces of all those Kansas women fade; and my soul will tire of trying; and my spirit will end up pattering as a snowflake on some other poor girl's window, trying to warn her, trying to warn her, but melting too quickly to be seen.

She had a nightmare that hot July night of a moon that filled up the whole sky; and dragged everybody off the ground and into the air. Trees were wrenched up by their roots; shingles came flying off houses. Women screamed, cattle bellowed. Then the fences were ripped up and the soil itself was dragged into the sky in a blinding blizzard.

'*No!*' she shrieked, and woke up. She found that she was sweating, her nightgown was soaked and clung to her skin. Her stomach was drum-hard, and her muscles were gripping her as fiercely as Uncle Casper had gripped her.

'No,' she repeated, in a whisper, conscious that her first shriek had been silent, the swallowed shriek of a dreamer.

It was only when Mrs Cullen lifted the baby out of her that Lucy actually believed it. It was alive, an actual living baby. It steamed and it smelled and it coughed, and it clenched its tiny fists. In the fraction of a second, she had seen that she couldn't call it Thomas, because it was a little girl, and had counted its fingers and toes.

'A girl, God bless her, the little angel!' cried Mrs Cullen.

Mrs Cullen's face was ivory-white with exhaustion and varnished with perspiration, but she couldn't stop herself from clapping her hands together with joy, and saying, 'Thank you, Lord!' and 'Ettie, go tell your father, he's a grandpa! And it's a girl!'

The lamps around the bed were still alight; even though it was well past seven o'clock, and the sun had already dimmed their flames into flickering transparency. Jamie's fifteen-year-old sister Sarah was so affected by the baby's sudden appearance that she was giggling and sobbing at the same time, which made her sound as if she had hiccups. With serene deftness, Mrs Cullen tied and cut the baby's rainbow-coloured cord (she had cut several of her own) and handed the baby to Nora with no more ceremony than if it were a fresh-baked loaf, just taken out of the oven.

'Wash her, please, Nora. There's a towel on the chair. Now then, Lucy, one more push to get out the afterbirth.'

'Let me see her,' begged Lucy, in a croaky voice.

'Juh-juh-juh-juh! Just one minute. First of all, I want you to push.'

Mrs Cullen disposed of the afterbirth in a wrapped-up copy of the Kansas City newspaper. Then she sponged Lucy with cool water and her best lily-of-the-valley soap, and soothingly shushed her, and told her what a good girl she was, and helped her to change her nightgown. At last, Nora came forward holding her baby, washed and patted dry, and dressed in a daisy-cloth wrapper.

'She's not crying,' said Lucy. 'Isn't she supposed to cry?'

'Oh, she will, I promise you, she will,' said Mrs Cullen, 'Just as soon as she's hungry, or cold.'

Lucy held her daughter in her arms with caution and exhilaration and the feeling that her whole life had altered completely, that she wasn't even Lucy any more. Those tiny red crinkled hands, with miniature fingernails! That ugly crinkled red face, with plumlike eyes, and a mouth that pouted like a goldfish! and most of all that pungent and unforgettable aroma of somebody freshly-arrived from Heaven.

It was then that Jerrold came into the room, and stood in his shirtsleeves with his arms by his sides.

'My grand-daughter?' he asked Mrs Cullen; and Mrs Cullen nodded, with tears in her eyes.

Jerrold came forward and sat on the side of the bed. He delicately touched the baby's fingers, and brushed her cheek, and slowly shook his head.

'I'd forgotten,' he said, with a catch in his voice, 'I'd simply forgotten. You tiny one! Have you any idea what you're going to name her?'

'I'm going to call her Blanche,' Lucy told him. And then without warning she let out a sob as painful as a stab with a kitchen-knife; and clutched hold of Jerrold's shoulder; and cried so bitterly and uncontrollably that she started to gasp for breath, and Mrs Cullen had to lift the baby away from her.

'Oh God,' Lucy wept. 'Oh God, oh God, oh God.' But at last she managed to take in six or seven deep breaths, and steady herself, and wipe her eyes with the sleeve of her night-gown.

'There now, there now,' Mrs Cullen soothed her. 'It's just the birth. It's all the strength God gives you, letting itself out. Every woman cries, when she has her first baby.'

Lucy, with her lips clenched tight and her throat aching with emotion, looked across at tiny Blanche and nodded. 'Yes,' she tried to say, but she couldn't; because it wasn't true. She had wept when she had called her baby Blanche because it was the first time since she had left Brackenbridge that she had allowed herself to think about Henry, and how much she loved him; and how much Henry loved her.

Mrs Cullen said, 'Would you like her back now?' and Lucy nodded, and took her back.

'Sha-sha,' she whispered, in Blanche's petal-delicate ear.

Mrs Cullen smiled. 'We've sent Martin to the depot, to telegraph Jamie.'

Lucy said, 'Thank you,' without taking her eyes off Blanche.

Jerrold glanced at his wife, and twitched his head two or three times towards Lucy, to encourage her to speak. Mrs Cullen hesitated, and licked her lips, and then she said, 'You haven't yet thought any more about your baby having a father?'

'Sha-sha,' Lucy cooed at Blanche. 'You beautiful Sha-sha.'

'What I mean is,' said Mrs Cullen, 'you haven't thought any more about marrying Jamie?'

Lucy pretended not to hear, although she heard. She kissed Blanche's forehead, and hummed to her, and tried not to think about anything but babies and angels.

7

Old man Maeterlinck's business-wagon came rattling down the track between the oak trees a little after eleven o'clock on the ninth of August, a glaring Tuesday on the High Plains. Old man Maeterlinck came right up to the kitchen door and banged on the side of the hutch, and whistled between his teeth, and called out, 'Letter! Just arrived!'

Nora took the letter and tipped old man Maeterlinck two bits. 'It's for you, now, Lucy, from Washington.'

Lucy was sitting in the key-shaped arrangement of sunlight that fell through the kitchen door, stitching lace on to one of Blanche's bonnets, and at the same time easy-rocking Blanche's crib with her foot.

So far, Blanche had been the quietest of babies, except when she was bathed. Then she clenched herself up and screamed and shuddered without taking a breath until she was all wound up in her wrapper again, and rocked, and cooed to, and told what a darling little Darling she was.

It was obvious from the taut expression on Jamie's face that it hurt him to hear his daughter called 'Darling'. But Lucy still avoided talk about marriage. She was too happy as she was to talk about marriage. She loved Blanche, she loved the Cullen family; she loved Jamie, too. But she was terrified that if she married him that she would gradually tear him to pieces, and herself too.

And there was something else: if she married Jamie, she knew that she would be closing off forever any chance she might have of returning to that glamorous and privileged world of the wealthy.

She didn't allow herself to think about that very often. It seemed unbearably selfish. But when she was rocking Blanche's crib in the evening, after her feed, she would close her eyes and imagine herself sailing at Newport, or dancing at the Waldorf. It was bitterly hard to have been forced to give it all up.

After a week or two, Jamie no longer brought up the subject of getting wed. But he cuddled Blanche whenever he could, and played with her, and called her 'ma'am', or 'my little lady', and sang nursery-rhymes to her, and treated her just like his own daughter, which she was. Blanche, however, slept in Lucy's room at night; a room to which Jamie was not admitted; and when Blanche was breast-fed, she was breast-fed behind closed doors.

Lucy overheard Jerrold on several occasions trying to talk to Jamie about what he should do, but Jamie obstinately refused to discuss it. 'If she won't marry me, she won't marry me. There's nothing I can do about it.' Whenever he spent a few days at home, Jamie would go to his room early with a bottle of whisky and read law reports. Sometimes Lucy would hear him in the night, stumbling over his shoes or his bedside table, drunk with whisky and frustration.

Nora gave her the letter. She recognized the handwriting at once, and her heart tightened. *Now, though I toil to Samarkand, through rain and snow and stinging sand . . .*

'It's from Henry,' she said.

She opened it up carefully. Inside was a single sheet of paper embossed with the letter-heading of the British Embassy in Washington. Nora watched her while she read it, trying to discover what it said from her expression.

Washington, August 3, 1895

My dearest Lucy,

I have written you a score of letters, but posted none of them until now. I have to confess that your sudden departure from Brackenbridge filled me with the greatest grief, and in spite of your letter, I still find it inexplicable. I experienced a sense of loss unequalled in my life before, except when my dear mother died. This was superseded by a sharp resentment that you could not have confided in me.

Lucy, if you truly do not love me, then you have to do no more than tell me. I will accept whatever you say — not with joy, perhaps, but with good grace. Before I first saw you, I was a man for whom bachelorhood seemed to be the perfect state of affairs; after you left, I was a man for whom bachelorhood was the only future.

I was destined to have only one wife, or none at all; and that one wife is you.

If I am intruding on your new life, then please forgive me. I discovered your whereabouts from a colleague in the Embassy here in Washington, whom I had asked to monitor copies of the New York newspapers. Sure enough, he sent me two months ago the intelligence from the Wall Street Journal that your oil-holdings had been transferred to the Southern Pacific RR, and that you had returned to Oak City.

Lucy, if it was the loss of your wealth that caused you to run away from me, then have no fear whatsoever. I do not love you for your money; I love you for your darling self. You may not have heard in Kansas that Lord Rosebery's Liberal government was defeated in the House of Commons in June; and that there has since been a general election, which we have won triumphantly with a majority of 152.

Lord Salisbury has appointed me Under-Secretary of State at the Foreign Office, which was a slightly less exalted position than the Press and my friends had expected for me. But in order to assuage any possible embarrassment, he nominated me for membership of the Privy Council (a honour usually reserved for senior Ministers), and I have already been sworn in the presence of Her Majesty.

I am therefore financially capable of taking care of both of us; and I have rented excellent apartments at Carlton House Terrace.

My darling innocent Lucy, you broke my heart. If it is your decision that it must remain broken, then so be it. Only you have the wherewithal to repair it.

Give me at least the consideration of thinking carefully on this matter; and please reply, even if your answer is a final no. I am staying here in Washington until the last day of August, before returning to England. You may telegraph or write.

You are in my heart always,

Your loving, Henry.

Lucy re-read the letter, her eyes blurred and her hand trembling.

'What is it?' asked Nora, voraciously. 'What does he say?'

'He still wants me to marry him. He wants me to go back to England with him. He knows that I've lost all my money, but he says that it doesn't matter.'

'But what about Blanche? Does he know about Blanche?'

'I don't think so. All he knows is what appeared in the *Wall Street Journal*.'

'Do you still want to marry him?' asked Nora.

Lucy lowered the letter on to the table. 'I don't know. Yes, of course I do.'

'Would you take the baby with you?'

Lucy looked across at Blanche, sleeping in her crib, her eyes tightly closed, one little fist gradually uncurling.

'Henry thinks I'm innocent.'

'There's a difference between innocence and purity.'

'He thinks I'm pure, too.'

Nora laughed uncertainly, then stopped. 'You wouldn't leave Blanche, would you? You couldn't!'

'No,' said Lucy, 'I couldn't.'

She didn't sleep at all that night. She read Henry's letter again and again. Privy Councillor! Her Majesty the Queen! Carlton House Terrace! And more than anything else, those words of despairing endearment, '*I was destined to have only one wife, or none at all; and that one wife is you.*'

While she sat up in bed, reading the letter, she could hear Blanche's breathing from her crib. The harvest-dust had given her a little sniffle, so that each breath had a little catch in it. Lucy climbed out of bed and stood beside the crib, and thought that Blanche was the most perfect of all babies.

But then Lucy stood up, and saw her own face in the cheval mirror. A pretty young girl of eighteen years old, in a long cotton nightgown. A girl who had tasted wealth and society, and lost everything; but who had now been offered a second chance. Not just a second chance, either. A final chance. If she refused Henry now, then she might as well marry Jamie and stay in Kansas for the rest of her life, the wife of a country lawyer. Picnics in the garden, with blankets hung up on the clothesline to keep off the prairie wind; church socials and Kensingtons. Middle-age coming on before you know it. 'You want to trade that receipt for slipped custard pie?' She'd heard it.

'Sha-sha,' she sang to her baby. 'Oh, Sha-sha, my darling.'

Blanche stirred in her crib. Lucy picked her up, and held her close, breathing in her hot milkiness.

Take my heart sweet child of mine,
And promise to be true,
Then come what may I promise
I'll be overfond of you.

Blanche's head nestled against her neck, and her fingers clung tight to the ribbons of Lucy's nightgown. Even if she could have seen the tears that were streaming down Lucy's cheeks, she wouldn't have been able to understand them.

Mrs Cullen sat in the parlour window, with the sun shining through the bird-embroidered net curtains behind her, so that Lucy could hardly make out her face. However there was no mistaking the sadness in her voice.

'I don't know who you will be hurting the most,' she said. 'Your baby, or my son, or yourself.'

'I can't stay here in Kansas,' Lucy told her. 'Not when I have the chance to go. Mrs Cullen, I shall suffocate.'

Mrs Cullen turned her face in profile. Curved Swedish-looking forehead, tilted nose. 'Can you really leave Blanche?' she asked. 'Do you think you have the strength?'

'I can't take her, and I can't stay.'

'Does this man Henry mean so much to you? What can he give you that Jamie couldn't? If you were to stay here, and to marry Jamie, you would have a family, a complete family. You would always be cared for, you know that.'

'Yes,' said Lucy. 'I know that; and I'm grateful. I can never pay you back for what you've done for me.'

'You can pay me back by deciding not to go,' Mrs Cullen suggested.

Lucy bent her head forward and covered her eyes with her hand. Her mind refused to work any more. She had thought over Henry's letter again and again and again, until she was numb. But she had known from the moment she had opened it what she was going to do. No matter how agonizing it would be to leave Blanche behind. No matter how much she would be hurting Jamie and all the rest of the Cullen family; she had to go. She couldn't explain it in a way that Mrs Cullen could understand. Blanche was so desperately dear to her. Blanche was not only *hers*, Blanche was *her*.

But out beyond the embroidered net curtains, across the yard, far beyond the grassy horizons of the High Plains, the spires of New York rose like the castles of haughty princes, and beyond New York lay the whole Atlantic Ocean, and England, and Italy, and India. Cities teeming with thousands of people!

How could any of that be comprehensible to Mrs Cullen, who would probably meet no more than fifty more people in the whole of her life, and was apparently quite content?

Even if Lucy were to stay in Oak City, and bring up Blanche, what would she tell Blanche about the world beyond? And when Blanche was eighteen, and wanted to go off and live her own life, what would she say then? You can't go because I didn't?

Mrs Cullen said, very quietly, 'I'm more than happy to raise Blanche as my own daughter, you know that.'

Lucy nodded behind her hand. She wasn't crying. Just at the moment, she couldn't cry. But she didn't want to show her face, not yet. In the darkness behind her hand, no decisions had to be made, and the clock, for a few moments, stood still.

★

364

She wrote to Henry that same evening, and took the letter to the depot herself, on horseback. On her way back she reined in her horse at Overbay's Bend, where she and Jamie used to lie on their backs and watch the cloud-castles. The wind was warm; the sky was clear; the river was furrowed with ripples.

What a time in her life, she thought. Too old to dream; too young to bear any burdens.

When she arrived back at the Cullen farm, Mrs Cullen was already feeding Blanche in the kitchen. Lucy stood in the doorway watching her, and felt that she had already given her up. She could still change her mind, she knew that. She could leave and travel to Washington and *still* change her mind. But something was waiting for her, far away to the east; and whether it was love or destiny or something else altogether, she knew that she would have to go.

When Jamie arrived home the following Saturday, Lucy was sitting in the apple-orchard. Blanche was lying on a blanket in the long grass, looking up at the way the sunlight flickered through the leaves, and gurgling. Jamie walked through the lines of apple-trees and then rested his arm against one of the winesaps.

'Hallo, Lucy,' he said. His voice was expressionless and flat.

Lucy looked up from under her straw skimmer. She was wearing a green-and-white candy-striped blouse and a green skirt. The sunlight shone on her hair, and made it look to Jamie as if she had a golden halo.

'I brought you a telegram from the depot,' he told her, and held it up. 'Just arrived from Washington DC, that's what Mr Perkins told me.'

Lucy waited with her head held up and her back quite straight while Jamie walked across and gave her the wire. She didn't take her eyes away from his; not once.

Jamie watched her open it. 'Mother told me all about you and Henry,' he said.

The wire read, ECSTATIC STOP COME SOONEST STOP WIRE AHEAD STOP LOVE HENRY. Lucy folded it up, and tucked it back into its envelope. Then she took it out, unfolded it, and read it again.

Jamie said, 'I can't believe that you're going to leave Blanche. I just can't credit it.'

Lucy was silent for a little while, then she replied, 'I can't believe that I'm going to leave any of you.'

'Then why go?'

'Jamie, I have to.'

'I don't understand you at all.'

'Why? Because I'm acting on impulse? Haven't you ever done anything on impulse?'

'You're telling *me* about impulse?' Jamie demanded. 'Where do you think Blanche came from?'

Lucy smiled down at Blanche, who was kicking her legs in the air. 'She came from love, Jamie. And that's what she deserves. Nothing but love. Not arguing or bitterness or anybody feeling regretful because she was born.'

'Do you regret that she was born?'

Lucy shook her head. 'No. But I have my own life, too; and I haven't even started to live it yet.'

'I can give you a life. I love you, Lucy. I can give you everything that any wife could ever wish for.'

Lucy watched Blanche trying to snatch at the flickering patterns of sunlight. Maybe she was just the same, trying to grasp a bright illusion that wasn't really there. But she had to try.

Jamie said, 'I'll ask you just one more time, Lucy. Then I won't ask you ever again. Will you marry me, will you be my wife? Will you let me be Blanche's father?'

'You already are Blanche's father. Nobody will ever be able to take that away from you.'

But that was all she said. It was difficult enough to

explain to herself why she had to leave, without trying to explain it to Jamie. The apple branches nodded in the breeze, the grasses whispered, and bees hummed like snatches of half-remembered songs. Over to the west, thunder-bumpers began to rise, layer on layer, and by nightfall the sky would be crackling with electricity.

Jamie said, 'It's Blanche's feed-time. I'd better take her in.'

He picked Blanche up, and carried her away, and Lucy was left in the orchard by herself, among the Jonathans and the winesaps, with a crumpled blanket still warm from her baby daughter. Now she was innocent and pure and childless, but at a price which was impossible to guess.

She stepped down from the train that afternoon at the Baltimore & Potomac Railroad Depot; hesitantly, in her long coffee-coloured travelling-dress and her feathery hat, and Nora stepped down behind her.

Almost as soon as she did so, the steam vanished dram-atically, like a swirled-away curtain, and there stood Henry, bare-headed, in a grey frock-coat, carrying a stick.

They approached each other slowly, quite shyly, through the drifting fragments of steam. All around them, people hurried and shouted and called for porters, but Lucy scarcely noticed them. All she could see was Henry, not as tall as she had remembered, but very handsome, very relaxed-looking, smiling, with his hair swept back, and a beautifully-folded grey silk cravat, with a pearl pin.

They shook hands.

'Hallo, Lucy,' said Henry. 'I didn't truly believe until I saw you that you would come.'

Lucy was amazed how crisp and English his voice sounded, after only eight months in Kansas. 'I said I was coming,' she told him.

'I have a carriage outside the depot. There are rooms for you, at the Embassy. Lady Spiers will take care of you. She's absolutely charming. Is that your bag?'

367

They walked through the waiting-room, followed by Nora, and a porter carrying their two portmanteaux. 'Do you know something,' said Henry, 'President James Garfield was shot in this very waiting-room – July 2, 1881. And the interesting thing is that, while he lay in hospital, Alexander Graham Bell the inventor of the telephone hurriedly devised a metal-detector so that the doctors could locate the bullet in the president's body. Unfortunately, the metal-detector was confused by the steel springs in the hospital bed, and they couldn't find the bullet, and the president died.'

He suddenly stopped, and turned to Lucy, and grasped both of her arms. 'Why the devil am I rattling on about President Garfield, when I haven't kissed you since Christmas!'

He kissed her there and then, in the waiting-room where President Garfield had been shot, and he felt strong and urgent and passionate, like he always had before. There were whistles from waiting passengers, and laughter, and clapping; and Lucy blushed; but Henry stood and looked at her with his eyes steely-bright, and said, 'I love you more than life, Lucy. You are absolutely everything.'

He linked arms with her, tightly, and they left the depot. An Embassy barouche was waiting outside, with a spiffy top-hatted black man on the box.

'We're having a private supper tonight,' Henry told her, 'but tomorrow we're having a formal dinner with Mr McKinley and Mr Hanna, and we're going to talk about trade tariffs and protectionism; and then the following night we're going to the theatre to see *George and the Dragon*; and the night after that we're holding a party, with dancing, and service *à la Russe*.'

Lucy sat back in the deep-buttoned maroon leather seat and smiled at him, and then laughed. 'I'd forgotten how busy you always are!'

'Busy, nothing! Those are just the amusements! I have twenty-three meetings between now and next Thursday; as

368

well as three lunches, nine committees, and a formal visit to Gallaudet College.'

'And what am I supposed to be doing, while you do all that?' Lucy asked him.

'Shopping, I hope. One portmanteau can hardly be carrying all the gowns that you're going to need for half-a-dozen dinners, two operas, two visits to the theatre, and an Embassy party.'

'Henry —'

Henry raised his fingertip to his lips. 'Don't you dare speak to me about money. I know what ill-fortune befell you. I love you for what you are; and whatever I can give you, I shall.'

Nora obviously liked the sound of this, because she nodded her brown feathered hat enthusiastically.

They drove along Pennsylvania Avenue under a blotting-paper sky. Streetcars with tied-back curtains came clanging noisily alongside them; but the horses seemed not to mind. Lucy found Washington humid and suffocating after Kansas, where there was almost always a wind blowing. Washington was breathless and oppressive, and there was a smell of summer fever in the air.

'You're not alarmed by all these parties, I hope?' Henry asked her. He was referring to the letter she had written him, in reply to *his* first letter. She had explained her sudden flight from Brackenbridge by saying that she had felt 'terrified by all the responsibilities of being a politician's wife; and alarmed by your energy'.

'No,' said Lucy. 'I'm not alarmed.' She was quiet, though. She was thinking of Blanche; and the moment when old man Maeterlinck's business-wagon had rattled through the oak trees, and her view of Blanche had flickered, blurred, and at last been blotted out. Blanche, in Mrs Cullen's arms, waving at the sky, waving at the wind; but not realizing that she was waving goodbye to her own mother.

Lucy told herself strictly, almost petulantly, you've chosen this course. If it hurts you, you're going to have to endure it. But whenever she thought of Blanche, the pain was close to the brink of being unbearable, like a terrible scald.

'That's the White House,' Henry pointed out. 'That's where President Cleveland lives. He has the most memorable telephone number in Washington. It's 1.'

Lucy nodded, although she didn't look around. She didn't want either Henry or Nora to see that there were tears in her eyes.

It was peculiarly dark on the day they left Washington. Accompanied by Nora and by Henry's private secretary, Walter Pangborn, they travelled by rail to New York; where – on a far brighter morning – they boarded the Cunarder *Oregon* bound for Southampton. Lucy and Henry stood together by the rail of the first-class promenade deck as they sailed past the Statue of Liberty, and headed out for the open boats. A warm sea made Lucy's long white scarf wave like the wing of an albatross.

Lucy's single portmanteau had already been joined by three brass-studded steamer-trunks, carefully packed with new clothes. Most of her gowns had been bought ready-made, since there hadn't been enough time to have more than three evening-dresses fitted; but Henry promised her that when they arrived in London, she would be able to dress herself 'as befits the wife of a Privy Councillor'.

She had made such a determined effort to put Henry out of her mind that she had forgotten what amusing company he was; and how feminine and pretty he always made her feel. His energy could be tiring, and his insistence on supervising every little detail of daily life could be irritating. But he was always so boisterous, always so *interested,* and even when he was talking about foreign policy he never bored her.

He was particularly entertaining when he described the pomposity of Kaiser Wilhelm II, complete with an hilarious

German accent. Although the Kaiser was the nephew of the Prince of Wales, he insisted that his Uncle Bertie treat him like an emperor, not only in public but in private, and he had made that fact officially known through the German ambassador in London. The Queen had been outraged. Such *perfect madness*, she had complained to Lord Salisbury. It was really too *vulgar*. She added that '*if* he has such notions, he had better *never* come *here*'.

Lord Salisbury had bluntly told the Prince of Wales that he thought the Kaiser was 'not quite all there'.

'Shall I meet the Queen?' asked Lucy. 'And the Prince of Wales, too?'

Henry smiled widely, 'Of course you shall! I've already dined at Windsor twice this year; and there are always dozens of social occasions during the season when you can be presented. I'm sure Her Majesty will adore you. And His Royal Highness certainly will.'

The Atlantic crossing was so smooth that Lucy felt as if they were gliding across a dark blue ballroom floor. The journey seemed quite unreal. During the mornings they talked and played pontoon and made wedding-plans. Henry was drawing up a comprehensive list of guests and family, and arranging on a huge sheet of paper where they should sit in Brackenbridge's chapel, according to a seating-plan which he had drawn up entirely from memory. They had agreed that Lord Felldale should give Lucy away, in the absence of her own father, and that Blanche should be matron of honour. There were so many Carson grand-children that there would be no shortage of bridesmaids and pages.

During the afternoons, Henry retired to his cabin to work on Foreign Office papers, and to send scores of telegraphic messages to his parliamentary private secretary Ian Bruce and to other officials at the Foreign Office. Lucy was end-lessly amused by the way in which he addressed his colleagues as 'My Dear Beano' or 'My Dear Giglamps'. But most of

Henry's closest associates came from the same aristocratic class as himself, and all of them had been together at Eton and Oxford.

She noticed with an odd sense of unease that Henry gave Walter Pangborn very little to do. While Henry was still scribbling letters at eleven o'clock at night, Walter would be standing on deck smoking a small cigar and watching the stars.

'He always works so hard,' Lucy complained to Walter one evening, when Henry had left them in the *Oregon*'s lounge after dinner to finish off a long memorandum.

'Don't *trust* anybody, that's Henry's trouble,' Walter remarked, laconically. He was a slender, blasé young man with a hawklike nose and lidded eyes. 'Always says that by the time he's explained what he wants other people to do, he might just as easily have done it himself.'

He helped himself to a musty-looking chocolate. 'The Cussboss never keeps his valets for more than six weeks at a time. I think the valet who stayed the longest was a fellow called French, stayed for a year and a bit. When he gave his notice, Henry asked him to recommend a suitable replacement, and French said, "The only name that comes to mind, sir, is Jesus Christ." The Cussboss expects his servants to be perfect, you see, and they never are. He expects *himself* to be perfect.'

'You don't think that he'll always expect *me* to be perfect?'

Walter chewed and smiled. 'My dear Miss Darling, excuse my impertinence, but you *are* perfect. Henry's a fearfully lucky man.'

In her stateroom that night, when Nora undressed her, Lucy found that the front of her corset-cover was stained with milk. Nora said nothing, but Lucy looked at herself in the mirror and said, in a transparent voice, 'I shouldn't have left her, should I?'

Nora unfolded her nightgown for her. 'You did what you felt was right.'

'Right for me, yes,' said Lucy. 'But what about Blanche?'

Nora took hold of Lucy's hands. 'You must think no more about Blanche. Blanche is being well taken care of, and Blanche will flourish, just as you did, for all that you didn't know who your father was.'

'I miss her so much,' Lucy whispered.

Nora pretended not to hear. It was probably the best thing to do.

Lucy slept badly that night. It was almost dawn before the beating of the *Oregon*'s engines finally induced her to close her eyes. Even then she dreamed that she was walking down the slope beside the Saline River that led to the Cullen farm, and that Blanche was waiting for her in the orchard, under the dancing sunlight, under the winesap trees.

They were married in October, in the small York stone chapel at Brackenbridge, by the Rector of All Souls. The choir sang the *Salve regina* from the Eton choirbook; and then *Hail, Gladdening Light*.

Although it had been so chilly in the chapel that they could see their breath, it was unseasonably warm and sunny when they stepped outside, and on the bright green grass the leaves lay like huge curls of ship's rust. The bells echoed across the dales; and Lucy came down the chapel steps in a white silk dress, wearing a high crown of Belgian lace, and a three-layered lace-trimmed veil. Her fifteen-foot train was held up from the ground by a serious bevy of Carson grandchildren, pages and bridesmaids, the boys in blue velvet jackets and cream silk knickerbockers, the girls in cream silk gowns.

They posed for their wedding photographs on the steps outside the chapel; and in later years historians would trace their faces with their fingers, and say, here, this is Lord Salisbury, the Prime Minister, white-bearded and balding, his hat in his hand; and here is Lord Felldale, looking unnecessarily fierce; and here is Sir Thomas Sanderson,

Permanent Under-Secretary at the Foreign Office; and Francis Bertie, assistant Under-Secretary, son of the sixth Earl of Abingdon; and Eric Barrington, son of the sixth Viscount Barrington; and here are all the other Etonians, Ian Malcolm and Pom McDonnell and Eyre Crowe; as well as Henry Asquith (looking slightly detached) and Margot Asquith (looking secretly amused); Margot's sister Charty, now Lady Ribblesdale, with her husband Lord Ribblesdale; and Henry's chum George Wyndham, with his wife the Countess of Grosvenor, whom Henry had once 'fancied rotten', as his brother Charles put it.

As the photographer folded his tripods and packed away the last of his wet-plates, Henry took hold of Lucy's hand and said, 'Happy?'

Lucy nodded. 'If only my mother could have been here today.'

'I'm sure that she is, in spirit.'

Margot Asquith came up to them, in a coat of pale lavender trimmed with fur, and a hat crowded with pale lavender flowers. She kissed Lucy, and then she kissed Henry, and then she stood back a little way and smiled at them. 'You make such a picture, Lucy, there are many ladies here today who are quite *emerald* with envy.'

'I must thank you for that wonderful Dresden porcelain,' said Henry. 'We're going to take it down to Carlton House Terrace and use it right away.'

'Charty thought it too fanciful,' Margot told him.

'Margot,' said Henry, 'it's quite beautiful,' and there was a warmth in his voice which clearly suggested that, in his view, it was the giver of the gift which lent it most of its charm.

As Lucy met more of Henry's women friends, she began to notice a distinctive pattern in the way that he spoke to them. He always engaged them in a form of playful erotic teasing; the kind of teasing that takes place between adolescent boys and girls who are too shy to admit that they are attracted to one another. It was plain that Henry had never been short of admirers when he was younger, but Lucy was always left with the impression that none of his flirtations had developed into serious associations. They had been ball-room escapades; country house charades; winks and fumbles when nanny wasn't looking. He believed with an earnestness that Lucy found astonishing that only the comradely endearment of men for men could be truly noble. That was why he was fascinated by cricket, although he wasn't good at playing it.

There was no homosexuality in the love that Henry and his fellows felt for each other. In fact, it quickly became clear to Lucy that they were horrified by what Henry in his letters called 'b-gg-rs'. Until May of this year, one of Henry's closest and best-loved friends in the literary world had been Oscar Wilde; and in spite of Oscar's outrageous behaviour and his effusive notes of affection (he had once called Henry *'un jeune guerrier du drapeau romantique'*) Henry had been thoroughly shocked and surprised when he had been tried and found guilty of the love that dare not speak its name.

Although Henry made a special effort to include Lucy in his conversations, she always felt like an outsider when he began talking to his women friends; or for that matter to *any* of his friends. Almost all of them came from that closely-intertwined circle of English and Irish aristocracy; almost all of them had been educated at Eton, or Haileybury at the very worst; almost all of them had been to the same dinners, played the same pranks, travelled on the same Grand Tour. They would roar with laughter when they talked of the time that Henry had hit all of George Leveson Gower's tennis-balls at a snappish dog, although Lucy could never understand why. Or when they remembered the time that Henry had sent a footman in search of Charles at a crowded country-house ball, with no more helpful description than 'he looks like me, d'you see, and he'll be very hot'

375

– only to be presented ten minutes later with a complete (and very irritable) stranger.

But Lucy supposed that – in time – she would learn what all of the private jokes and all of the facetious undergraduate vocabulary meant. For the moment, she preferred to listen, to act demurely, and to keep her peace. This morning she had innocently asked Henry if Mr Laxer had arrived in time for the wedding, only to be met with peals of laughter because 'The Laxer' was Leveson Gower's university nickname, and not a particularly polite one, at that.

Yet, as the wedding party crossed the bright well-raked shingle to the Great Hall, Lucy was bursting with pride and happiness that she had married Henry, because it was obvious how much he was admired among his friends and colleagues; and how much of a catch the women considered him to be; and that the Carson family was already dearly fond of her. Lord Felldale called her 'my dove', and Blanche called her 'sweetness'. It was a small sharp sadness to her that she was unable to tell Blanche about the tribute she had paid her, by naming her baby Blanche.

The Great Hall was filled with sunshine; so dazzling that Lucy had to shade her eyes when she first walked in. A string quintet had been brought up from Oxford, and as she and Henry walked between the two long tables on which the wedding breakfast was spread out, the lutist played *Fair Oriana, seeming to wink at folly.*

Henry took hold of Lucy's hand, and held it high, in the manner of a medieval king entering a court with his queen, and smiled, and bowed, and everybody laughed and applauded.

'Bravo, Henry! Bravo, Lucy!'

'My darling Lucy,' Henry told her, 'I feel like Alexander, after he captured Tyre. Or Cortes, when he entered Tenochtitlán.'

'Oh, yes?' asked Lucy. 'And how was that?'

'Triumphant, my dearest! Triumphant!'

Henry had arranged the wedding-breakfast down to the last possible detail. He had chosen the menu, selected the china, supervised the floral displays, arranged the seating, and written out three hundred place-cards in the italic handwriting that Queen Victoria herself had praised for its clarity and grace. 'The wedding will be perfect from beginning to end', he had promised her; and in a strange unbelievable way it was. Yet because it *was* so perfect, and because Henry had insisted on supervising absolutely everything, she felt almost as if she were just another guest; or even as if she had dreamed it.

Henry had demanded that each of the two long tables should be embellished by a boar's head, garnished with aspic jelly. Then there should be mayonnaise of fowl; boiled chickens in Béchamel sauce; hams and ornamented tongues; raised game pie and galantine of veal; roasted pheasants; larded capons; lobster salads; prawns; meringues; custards and fruited jellies.

Cautiously — concerned that Henry's menu might be attractive on the eye but rather bland on the palate — Lucy had suggested panned oysters and scalloped turkey and some of Delmonico's devilled chicken — a chicken split open and seasoned in paprika and coated in breadcrumbs. But Henry had shaken his head without even looking up from his papers, and said, 'You see, my dearest, the tastes and the textures are all perfectly balanced; we don't want to upset the balance now.'

'I *can* cook, Henry,' Lucy had insisted.

'We have cooks to do the cooking,' Henry had replied. 'You are going to be my queen; and queens don't cook.'

'But I *like* cooking.'

Henry had laughed. 'Let me tell you something, my darling. Government House in Calcutta, purely by chance, was built by Lord Wellesley as a replica of Brackenbridge. The thing was, the Court of Directors of the East India Company didn't care much for Asiatic pomp and display.

So when they came to build a viceregal residency, they chose to imitate Brackenbridge, because of its purity, d'you see, and its elegance. And the copy in Calcutta, well, it's almost perfect, except that they have used lath and plaster for their pillars, instead of alabaster.'

His accent was part Derbyshire, part eighteenth-century. He said 'lăth and plăster, instead of alabăster'. His London friends were forever teasing and imitating him.

But he added, 'One day soon, God willing, I shall be Viceroy of India, and take my seat in Brackenbridge in Calcutta; as well as my seat in Brackenbridge here in England. And you shall not set one foot in the kitchens there; not one step; any more than you shall set one foot in the kitchens here. You are my queen. You are my empress. You are above everything but praise and adoration.'

He must have been rather pleased with that little speech, because he actually made notes in the margin of his writing-paper. His nib scratched, the ink gradually dried. In the huge family-room at Brackenbridge, with its sun-faded velvet curtains and its sun-faded oak panelling, Lucy had looked back at Henry for a moment, with the sun shining on the brilliant-blue iris of her left eye, and she had wondered then if she had misunderstood him, if he were quite another man from the man she had imagined him to be.

But the wedding was wonderful; and the wedding-breakfast was boisterous and happy. Lucy was kissed by more personable young men and more giggling young women than she had ever met in her life. Lord Salisbury, bearded and soft-spoken and avuncular, to her at least, gave her his 'dearest blessing'. Lord Felldale treated her so proprietorially and so kindly that she felt as if she had found a new father, as well as a husband. As they stood in the portico, wrapped in furs, to wave goodbye to the last of the carriages, Lord Felldale took hold of Lucy's hand and gripped it tight, and said, 'This is a great day for Brackenbridge, my dove. This is the beginning of a great new age! Brackenbridge shall have a new mistress, in years to come; and Henry shall have heirs; and although I shall not be here to see it, my God, it makes my heart glad!'

'I'm glad that you're glad,' Lucy told him, and kissed his cheek. 'I know that Henry adores Brackenbridge, and so do I.'

Henry came out, smoking a cigar, his black astrakhan coat hung over his shoulders, looking as pleased as Punch and smelling of brandy. 'What a wedding-day!' he declared. 'We should be married every day, my darling! Then all of our friends can come around!'

'Once is enough,' said Lucy, linking arms.

Henry kissed her. 'For you, my dearest darling, nothing will ever be enough.'

Lucy said, 'Your sister Vanessa didn't come, did she? I did so want to see Vanessa.'

Lord Felldale descended two or three steps, and whistled to his dogs. Henry smiled tightly, with his hands clasped behind his back, and shrugged, and said, 'Well . . . Vanessa has a mind of her own, you know. She always has. Do you want to come inside now? There are oysters for supper; oysters and champagne.'

'Just right for a wedding-night, eh?' Lord Felldale remarked.

'*Father*,' Henry admonished him, almost prissily.

Lucy turned to Henry with the luminous smile of a happy bride. Her blonde hair was brushed into curls, and pinned under her fur-trimmed hat. Her collar was raised up around her face, so that the fur sparkled in the lamplight like a dandelion-puff on the very brink of being blown. She looked like a winter-fairy; October's child. She felt transfigured; as if she had changed beyond any recognition; as if she had started life as somebody else. Lucy Carson. *Mrs* Lucy Carson. Elegant, well-connected, and envied. The correspondent from *The Times* had asked her a few respectful questions, and actually *bowed* to her when he was leaving. And even lords and ladies had stared at her, unabashed, as if she were an oleograph rather than a real person.

As she took Henry's arm, and walked back through crowds of applauding servants, butlers and valets and coachmen and kitchen-maids, she understood at last that she was home because she had been determined to make this her home; that her own beauty had created a heritage for her.

Henry said, '*Nunc scio quid sit amor*. Now I know what love is really like.'

But her wedding-night was frightening, like a night spent without friends in a fierce and foreign country, and by morning Lucy was left feeling perplexed and anxious. Henry loved her. There was no doubt about that. But it was *how* he loved her that confused her so much. Between Jamie's cautious tenderness and Uncle Casper's extreme violence, she had no experience of sex, so she was ready to accept that she was a victim of her own ignorance. Yet, in all the romances she had read, there had been nothing to prepare her for Henry's urgency, or for Henry's temperamental demands.

Lord Felldale had given them the Sun Room, so-called because it was painted in sunflower yellows, with curtains in saffron velvet. Originally, it had been decorated in cobalt blue, but because it faced north-eastwards, it had always felt cold and unwelcoming. Henry's mother had redesigned it in yellows to give it life and warmth; yet there was still something chill about it. Lucy had already sensed it when Nora came in to undress her, and prepare her for bed. A fire was crackling in the hearth, but the ceiling was so high that she could scarcely see it through the gloom; and a thin impertinent wind kept blowing under the door, *fyooooo, fyooooooooeeee, fyoooeeeeee!!*

Nora allowed the billowing silk nightgown to fall airily over Lucy's naked skin; a whisper, a promise. The hope of happiness.

'Well, you may not think too much of this,' said Nora, 'but my mother taught me how to sing it, years ago, and perhaps it might help. *"On the night of her wedding, a young maid will say, 'I have nothing, my Lord, but this tiny cup.' But give this same maiden a week and a day, and she will be begging, 'Please fill it right up!'"'*

Lucy said nothing but blushed; remembering Jamie's sperm scattered across her breasts. Pearls, seeds; and Blanche had already been conceived.

Nora brushed out her hair and at last she was ready for bed. Dry-mouthed, she looked at herself in the mirror. Nora smiled and kissed the top of her head.

'You love him, don't you?'

Lucy nodded.

'It's just nerves, then.'

Lucy said, 'He won't be able to tell, will he, that I've had a baby?'

'Is that what you're worried about?'

'He thinks I'm completely untouched. Perfect.'

'Then let him think it, if that's what he wants. He won't be able to tell. What most men know about the physical side of life wouldn't cover the back of a penny stamp, in big writing, too.'

Lucy swallowed. 'But when you're a virgin . . . isn't there supposed to be – well, *blood*? I read something about Italian women holding up the sheets, to prove that the bride was pure.'

Nora said, 'It isn't always so, believe me. A young girl can break her maidenhead just by horseriding or by carrying coals or scrubbing the kitchen step, and any man who looks to the linen for evidence is a fool. Besides, what does it matter, if you've given yourself to Mr Carson, in the eyes of God, that should be good enough for anybody, especially for him.'

She paused, however, and took a small glass-beaded hatpin out of the pin-cushion on the dressing-table. 'If you think it will make him feel better, you can prick your thumb with this, when he's sleeping, and mark the sheet. What you might call a little red lie.'

It was then that Henry knocked at the doors of the Sun Room, and immediately came in, smiling expectantly, and a little flushed. He was wearing a long woollen dressing-gown in bottle green. His hair was pomaded and combed sharply back from his forehead. Lucy caught the fresh floral smell of Floris toilet-water.

He looked at the huge curtained bed, with its ornate mahogany bedposts, its covers neatly triangulated on each side, ready for himself and his bride.

'Well, now,' he said, clearing his throat.

'Don't worry, sir, I'm all finished here,' Nora told him, rearranging the silver-backed brushes on the dressing-table, and quickly tidying up.

'You're a good woman, Nora,' Henry remarked, for no obvious reason. Perhaps he was trying to demonstrate to Lucy that he could handle servants appreciatively, after all.

'Thank you, sir. I wish the very best of happiness to you and Mrs Carson, in your married life.'

'Yes,' said Henry, without interest. Nora might just as well have wished that the weather would stay dry tomorrow. Without taking his eyes away from Lucy, he added, 'Would you cast a few more coals on the hearth, before you go?'

Nora briskly did as she was told, although Lucy could guess how she felt at being required to do the work of a housemaid.

'Goodnight, sir. Goodnight, madam,' she said at last, and closed the bedroom doors behind her.

Henry approached Lucy with an amused but cautious look on his face, as if he had just thought of a good joke, but didn't know whether he ought to share it or not.

'Well, my dearest; we are man and wife,' he announced. 'I could never have guessed that any woman could be so beautiful. I could never have believed that such happiness were possible.'

He took her in his arms, and he kissed her forehead, and her closed eyelids, and then her lips. 'I am not a man for praying, you know that. But every single night, I count it as a miracle that we should have met. If any of my friends had told me just eighteen months ago that I should marry a storekeeper's daughter from Kansas, I would have laughed in his face. And now look at me, with you in my arms!'

Lucy kept her eyes closed, enjoying the feeling of his arms around her, the warmth and the strength and the comfort of him. 'I always wanted to marry a prince,' she whispered, 'and look at me, I did. I wouldn't have laughed in anybody's face if they had told me that. I just plain wouldn't have believed them.'

'Think we're sootud?' he asked her, kissing her eyebrows, kissing her cheeks.

She nodded, and opened her eyes, and looked at him closely, every detail of his face, the mole on his cheek, the scar above his forehead.

'Let's lie down,' he suggested.

Henry helped Lucy out of her robe, and then untied his own dressing-gown, folding it over the arm of the chaise-longue. Lucy climbed into bed, and sat waiting for him. He went around in his ruffled nightshirt and his velvet slippers, turning down the lamps. 'I have always felt a special affection for this room,' he remarked, looking around. 'It reminds me so much of my dear mother. Always golden, always joyful.'

Lucy glanced at her bedside table. Underneath the lace cloth that covered it, her hatpin gleamed, ready to establish the loss of her virginity.

Henry climbed into the bed beside her, bouncing up and down as if he were testing the springs. 'Well, now,' he said. He leaned over and kissed her again, quite hard, so that she could feel his teeth pressing against her lips. Then he bounced up and down some more as he changed his position to make himself more comfortable – tugging his nightshirt where it

383

had become entangled between his thighs. His forehead knocked against Lucy's forehead, and he said, 'Sorry! Sorry, my darling!' and promptly rested his elbow on her hair.

Lucy suddenly felt panicky. All through their wedding-day, surrounded by guests and friends and affectionate relations, she had been ecstatically happy. But now that she was alone with Henry, she began to feel that she had somehow trapped herself; that she had married him not for love, but for all the things that he could give her – the home, and the family, and the place in society. He kissed her again, and again, and her panic began to rise. She felt that he was smothering her, that he was a relentless conglomeration of elbows and teeth and knees and tightly-twisted sheets, and that he was going to bruise her and suffocate her and crush her to death.

He squeezed her breasts through her nightdress, pinching and pulling her nipples. She tried to twist herself away from him, but he was much too strong and heavy for her, and he was her husband, so what possible reason could he have for believing that she didn't want him to make love to her, on their wedding-night of all nights?

He was clumsy more than violent, but he interpreted her struggling as shyness rather than panic, and so instead of giving her the opportunity to calm herself, and to catch her breath, he persisted in his kissing and squeezing and pummelling.

'Henry, please – !' she gasped. She was drowning in tangled sheets. She grasped at her pillow, but she succeeded only in pulling it down over her face, smothering her even more. 'Henry, mmmmmfff! Henry, please!'

He dragged up her nightdress, exposing her up to her waist. She felt the chill of the Sun Room's draught on her bare thighs. Henry kept pushing his face into hers, and leaning on top of her.

His breath roared in her ear. 'Oh, my darling Lucy . . . oh, my darling Lucy!'

His leg swung across hers. She felt the rubbery stiffness of his penis against her thigh. It was then that she managed to gasp out, 'No, Henry! Henry, please, no!'

He stopped thrashing. He lifted himself up on his elbow and stared down at her. His forehead was shining with perspiration, and he was panting.

'Henry,' she whispered, reaching up and touching his lips with her fingertips. 'Henry, you mustn't be so rough with me.'

She felt his penis curl. Very slowly, he lifted himself off her. All this time he didn't say a word, but continued to stare at her. He pulled down her nightgown, and straightened the sheets.

'I'm not —' he began, after a while.

'Henry, I'm your *wife*,' Lucy told him. She felt less frightened now, less panicky; but she still felt as if Henry were a stranger. As much of a stranger as Jack had turned out to be. As much of a stranger as Uncle Casper. She stroked his sidewhiskers. She wondered if she would ever be able to understand what went on inside men's minds. It seemed as if they were always in turmoil. An inexplicable churning of jokes, brutality, cleverness, violence, and senti-mentality.

Henry lay on his stomach with his fists clenched above his head and buried his face in the pillow.

'Henry,' Lucy coaxed him. 'If you can just be *gentle*.'

'I haven't had many women,' he told her, in a muffled voice. 'I'm not experienced. Only whores, like everybody else at Oxford, and they didn't mind what you did. I've never made love to anybody I really loved. Only once, and that experience crucified me, too.'

'Henry, my darling, I don't want to crucify you.'

'Perhaps I deserve it.'

Lucy reached across and stroked the hair at the back of his neck, but he still wouldn't lift his face from the pillow. 'Henry, I love you. I'm your wife.'

'But you don't want me to make love to you.'

'Of course I want you to make love to me.' (Did she? She didn't know. But now Henry had placed her in the extraordinary position of having to prove that she did, whether she did or not). She lay next to him for a long time, staring at the back of his neck, wondering what she should do. She was married to Henry; yet until he turned over and claimed her she remained unmarried. She was more married to Jamie than she was to Henry, if consummation were the test of marriage. She was more married to Uncle Casper, her own father.

'Henry, I didn't mean to make you angry,' Lucy begged him. She could feel the tears prickling her eyes.

'It's all right,' Henry replied. 'Whatever you said, I deserved it.'

She put her arm around his shoulders and kissed his hair. 'Henry, please. This is our wedding-night.'

'I know. And I have been cruel and unthinking. You should punish me.'

'Punish you? Henry, what are you talking about? You haven't done anything that I should punish you for. I'm your wife!'

He turned over at last. There was an expression in his eyes which Lucy found difficult to comprehend. She wondered if he were drunk. He could be drunk. The men had been downing magnums of Jacquesson champagne all day, and for most of the evening. But somehow Henry didn't *look* drunk. Not aggressive drunk, anyway. He looked cowed, like a dog that expects to be whipped for misbehaving; and yet eager, too, almost as if he *wanted* her to hurt him.

In a man who had first attracted her with his sophistication and social bravado, Lucy found this sudden change of demeanour to be highly disturbing, even frightening.

'My darling . . . perhaps you'd better get some sleep,' she told him.

'Are you that cruel?' he asked her.

'Henry, I don't understand what you're asking me to do!'

Henry took two or three deep breaths. His eyes remained piggy and glazed. 'I'm simply asking what any man would ask . . . if he had treated his bride so badly.'

'Henry, it isn't my place to punish you!'

'It is you who has been wronged,' Henry insisted. 'The meting-out of justice is your privilege. Accept it! You must!'

Lucy sat up in bed, propped up on one arm. The veins showed blue in her thin bent-back wrist. 'What do you want me to do?' she asked him. There had to be some way out of this alarming impasse; but Henry alone could tell her what it was.

He didn't take his eyes away from hers, but he dragged aside the sheet, and then lifted his nightshirt. His penis was half-erect, its head nodding to the beat of his heart. 'This is the real offender,' said Henry, his voice throaty. 'This is the one you must punish. Too eager by half. Too rapacious.'

Lucy said nothing, but waited for Henry to explain to her what she must do.

He reached up and unlaced the thin pink-silk ribbons of her nightgown. He handed them to Lucy as if they were reins. But still his eyes remained fixed on hers, scarcely blinking.

'He needs strict discipline,' said Henry. 'He needs to be taught to behave himself.'

'Henry . . .'

'Here,' said Henry. 'Wind the ribbons around him. That's right. Wind the ribbons around him, once, there, and twice.'

With shaking hands, Lucy wound the pink ribbons around Henry's penis, in the groove just below the dark-crimson glans. His breathing as she did so was harsh and erratic. In a series of pulses, his penis began to stiffen and rise. Henry said, 'You must never – ever – allow him to get away with it scot-free . . . he will only become worse . . . ill-behaved, undisciplined. Come on, now, punish him! Pull the ribbons tight!'

At first, Lucy couldn't understand what Henry wanted her to do. But then he seized hold of the ribbon himself, and tugged them hard, so that his glans swelled darker, and the ribbons cut deeply into his flesh.

'Tighter!' he demanded. 'He deserves to be hurt! If you let him get away with it, he'll be worse next time! Tighter!'

Terrified that she would injure him, Lucy nevertheless wound the ribbons around her fingers, and pulled them tight.

'Tighter!' Henry winced. 'Oh God, tighter! Make him suffer!'

Shaking with alarm, Lucy pulled tighter still. Henry's penis reared up like a runaway horse; its glans glistening and purple, its shaft hugely swollen. The ribbons were so tight now that they had almost disappeared into his flesh.

'*Now,*' said Henry, his voice constricted. He sounded like somebody else altogether, not Henry at all. He rolled on to his back, and grasped Lucy by the hips, and helped her to climb on top of him. Then without a word, he pushed his massively-distended penis – still tied around with pink night-gown ribbons – deeply and forcefully inside her – so deeply that she shuddered.

It took no more than two or three strokes, and Henry cried out, 'God, my God, Lucy!' and discharged himself inside her, making a sharp sucking sound between his teeth as he did so.

Lucy crouched on top of him for almost five minutes, feeling the hair of his chest against her cheek, listening to his heart beating. The fire spat; but the Sun Room still felt cold. The coldness leaked glutinously out between her thighs. Henry sidled after it. Cold wet nightgown ribbons stuck to her skin. She couldn't understand what had happened at all. She supposed that she was now Henry's fully-consummated wife; but had that been holy consummation or unholy punishment? It must have been agony for him, having his penis garotted so tightly, yet it seemed to have excited him hugely. He seemed to have *needed* it.

She thought: men are such a mystery, their lusts are so frightening. What kind of love can this be, where your husband wanted you to hurt him? Uncle Casper on the other hand had wanted to hurt *her*. Was pain a necessary part of making love? Would she always have to punish Henry, before they had intercourse?

Henry put his arm around her, and said, 'You're cold. You're feeling cold. Come under the covers.'

He sounded like himself again: the Henry whose voice had carried apple-crisp across Mrs Harris' lawns.

She climbed off and lay next to him. He made no attempt to hold her. The shadows from the fire danced across the ceiling. One day she would see an Indonesian shadow-play, and she would be reminded of her wedding-night. The shadows had curved noses and pointed ears, and jiggling insect arms like praying-mantises.

Henry said, 'Dearly beloved Lucy,' as if he were beginning a letter.

Lucy turned to look at him. He was lying on his back staring directly at the ceiling. The firelight outlined his sharp, aristocratic profile, and sparkled like a stray cinder in his eye. There were so many questions she wanted to ask him, yet she didn't know how to begin. She was a young bride, not even twenty years old. As far as Henry had been aware, she had never made love to a man before tonight. Yet he had immediately involved her in some private ritual of pain and humiliation without even explaining why.

'Henry,' she said, quite distinctly.

He didn't answer, but lay perfectly still, with his eyes open.

'Henry?' she repeated.

'Oh, I'm sorry, my dearest,' he replied, turning to smile at her. 'I was thinking of India.'

However, he didn't think about India all night. Shortly after midnight, when the fire was beginning to burn hot and low, he turned over in bed and lifted up her nightgown again.

She had been sleeping. Too much excitement, too much champagne. But she was woken up by the feeling of his hands caressing the curves of her bare bottom, and sliding down her bare thighs. 'Lucy, my dearest darling, are you awake?'

'Yes,' she murmured.

'Lucy, you must forgive me.'

'Forgive you? What for?'

Henry hesitated, then he thrashed away from her, turning his back. 'I'm always so selfish, Lucy, so intolerant. What must you think of me? You're the tenderest of children, the sweetest of brides. And what have I done but treat you with a worse depravity than any Persian?'

He paused, and took a deep breath, and Lucy could hear the catch in his throat. She thought: *He's crying. He's actually crying.* She lay in the dying firelight, horrified.

'Lucy,' he breathed. 'Speak to me. Tell me please that you'll try to find it in your heart to forgive me.'

'Of course I'll forgive you,' Lucy heard herself saying. 'There's nothing for me to forgive.'

'I won't ask you to punish me again, I promise.'

'Henry, ssh, don't talk about it.'

'I promise, I absolutely promise, that it will never happen again. Categorically, never.'

'Sssh,' she soothed him, and tangled her fingers into his hair. Perhaps after all he had been drunk earlier this evening, drunk and mad like Uncle Casper. She had recognized the flames that surrounded him, recognized the terrible brutal urgency.

He kissed her, his face wet with tears. He kissed her again and again. Then he heaved himself over her, with a great dragging of nightshirt, and opened up her thighs. He seemed to blot out the entire world like a total eclipse of the soul. She felt his fingers unstick her lips, she felt the blunt fleshy chisel of his member, pushing into her body.

In spite of his weight, in spite of the great drowned

dragging of nightshirt and nightgown and sheets, Lucy clung to him, and pressed her face against his shoulder, which smelled of fresh linen and sweat and flowery toilet-water, and thought at last that *this is love, this is loving. It was nothing but the drink before, nothing but shyness and inexperience. He's only been with whores, after all.*

He thrust deeper and harder, and her vagina stickily and audibly kissed him with every thrust. She closed her eyes and let her head fall slowly back on to the pillow.

'Oh Henry, my darling,' she whispered. 'I love you so much.'

It was then, however, that he began to soften. He tried to thrust quicker, his muscles tensed, Lucy heard him swear to himself under his breath. The only result was that he grew softer and softer, until he slithered out of her altogether. He gave a strange muffled roar, and pounded his fist against the mattress, and then rolled off her in a catastrophe of twisted sheets, and lay with his back to her, quivering with fury.

Lucy lay in silence for a while. Then she raised herself up again, and touched Henry's shoulder.

'Henry, please. It's not your fault. It's only the drink. You must be tired, too.'

But Henry continued to shake with humiliation and anger, and there was nothing that Lucy could do to console him. The clock in the hallway outside struck one; the fire died and the Sun Room darkened. Lucy remained wakeful for over an hour, hearing the clock strike again and again, and at last hearing Henry sleep.

They were to take a month's holiday in southern France, in the Var, in the house owned by Alfred Dunning, the painter, who had made friends with Henry at Oscar Wilde's house in Tite Street, in Chelsea. Dunning and Wilde had fallen out the year before, over a very gentle remark that Wilde had made about his epic painting *The Triumph of Divine Providence*. Now Wilde was in Reading gaol, disgraced, and

Dunning was painting the largest *Rape of the Sabines* ever commissioned.

Lucy had quite expected Henry to be bitter and morose after their wedding-night; but he was smiling and cheerful when he awoke and he kissed her as sweetly as if their whole night had been filled with fresh and fulfilling love-making. He had risen to go to the bathroom, and Lucy, when she had risen, too, to draw back the curtains and look out over the frosty grass, had heard him singing *Love's Sweet Delight* while he washed his hands and brushed his hair.

He had marched back into the bedroom, chafing his hands together. 'Well! I shall have to ring for the fire to be lit! They're too shy to disturb us, that's the trouble! But I could do with some breakfast, couldn't you? Finnan haddock, and poached eggs, and back bacon, and a good strong cup of China tea.'

Lucy had glanced towards the rumpled bed. She had suddenly remembered that she had forgotten to prick her thumb, and to mark the sheet with blood. She had glanced uncertainly at Henry, wondering if he would notice, but he had bounded back into bed, straightened the sheet, laced his fingers together, and sat waiting for his breakfast as if it were any other day of his life.

'Henry,' she had begun, sitting on the edge of the bed.

Henry had smiled at her. He had still looked so handsome; and so debonair! She could have been desperately in love with him, if he hadn't been so relentlessly difficult. It was almost as if he *worked* at being difficult.

He had taken hold of her hand, and kissed it. 'My bride,' he had told her, with pride.

Now they were sitting on a shaded veranda in the South of France, underneath a rust-coloured awning, drinking chilled rosé wine and watching the heat shimmer over the valley below them. Henry was very nattily dressed in a white coat and white ducks and a Panama hat, a real Panama hat which could be pulled through a wedding-ring (he had demonstrated, partly to show off the hat and partly to show off the wedding-ring.) Lucy wore an exquisite white linen dress, with a wide lace collar, and a white straw hat that looked as if it were about to take flight.

Alfred Dunning was spending his last day there. He was about to go to Algiers to spend some time with another artist from the Tite Street days. He was unexpectedly large and coarse-featured for an artist. At a guess, most people would have taken him for a coal-heaver, or a drayman. He talked very loudly, and was funny, most of the time, and very well-informed, and even his coarseness had a certain appealing immediacy about it. It was known that Alfred Dunning was never short of female companionship, and that every one of the fifty-three models who had posed for *The Triumph of Divine Providence* had been given plenty of opportunity to stretch her legs in between posing sessions.

'I still can't envy you, Henry,' Alfred said, fanning himself with his stained white hat. 'London winters, London fog, crowds of clerks all smelling like wet trousers.'

'My dear Dunners, it's the centre of the known world,' Henry had retaliated. 'I can stand at Charing Cross, and turn about on my heel, and know that in every conceivable direction, the great British Empire stretches out before me like a glittering paradise. Civilizing, educating, converting, enlightening. Bringing law where there was no law; bringing peace where there was only strife.'

'I know. And squeezing as much profit out of the poor befuddled darkies as possible.'

'Even enlightenment has its price.'

Alfred swigged back wine and, with his cheeks still bulging, poured himself some more. 'It's the light here. Marvellous for painting. But then you don't need light to be a politician, do you, Henry? Keep 'em in the dark, that's your motto.'

'I hope not,' Henry replied, a little priggishly.

'Still keen on India?' Alfred asked him.

Henry nodded, and narrowed his eyes, and gazed out across the claytiled rooftops. The heat distorted the olive-trees, so that they looked as if they were greenish-grey ghosts, waving to him silently and desperately from the opposite slope. He always narrowed his eyes like that when he wasn't particularly keen on answering the question.

'Well, I don't envy you India, either,' sniffed Alfred. 'Algiers is about as barbarous as I can stand. They have some entrancing ladies there; absolutely entrancing. Bellies like underfilled velvet cushions. Mind you, *you* have an entrancing lady here, so why should you worry?'

'Dunners, watch your language, there's a good man,' Henry retorted.

'Oh, he's not upsetting me one bit,' Lucy smiled. 'I can stand a little flattery as much as anybody.'

'That Kansas accent!' cried Alfred, sprawling back in his cast-iron chair as if he had been felled by a blow with a knobkerry. 'That derrr-awwwll! It runs right up my spine and circles twice around my head and comes tingling out of my tympani!'

Lucy laughed. Henry tried to join in, but was plainly too irritated. Their love life was still awkward; and after ten days of marriage the strain was beginning to show. Henry managed to be equable most of the time, but occasionally he was inclined to snap, or to drum his pen on his desk, or to stop suddenly in the middle of what he was doing and fix his eyes on the near-distance and look as if he had forgotten who he was.

They had made love two or three times, but on each occasion it had seemed to Lucy to be hurried and peremptory, as if Henry felt that he had something better to do. She couldn't understand it at all. When he talked of politics, when he talked of the British Empire, he was more eloquent and more passionate than any man she had ever known. He still amused her, still entertained her; and quite obviously loved her just as much as ever. It seemed quite out of character that when he made love to her, he was like a man running for a hopelessly-missed train. For Lucy, the fear that she had felt on her wedding-night had changed first to anxiety and then to frustration. She felt so much for him. She wanted to make him the very best of wives. But Henry kept stimulating her without giving her any satisfaction. It was worse than being served with a delicious plate of food, only to have it whipped away before she had eaten more than two or three mouthfuls.

She found herself drinking too much rosé and flirting with Alfred during the afternoon while Henry worked on his papers. Alfred certainly didn't mind, although he was cautious enough not to return Lucy's teasing when Henry was about. That afternoon, however, after Henry had finished his wine and vacated his chair on the balcony, Alfred crossed his legs and looked at Lucy from under the brim of his disreputable white hat, and she could tell that he had something on his mind.

'The *truite bleue* was marvellous,' she remarked.

'Your French pronunciation is improving,' Alfred replied, 'and so is your taste in food.'

'I've always liked trout. Once I had trout in the High Sierras, when I was travelling to California.'

'Ah, California! I must confess I've never been.'

'It's beautiful.'

'So I understand. But there are no artists there, are there? Only growers of beans. A land can have beans planted on it from one horizon to the other, but it never truly exists until somebody paints it.'

Lucy smiled at him in the glass-bright sunshine. He wore no socks, and he swung his suntanned ankle from side to side. 'Are you happy here?' she asked him.

'After a fashion. I enjoy it when my friends are here. The natives are a trifle crude.'

She turned away but he was still watching her. 'What about you?' he wanted to know.

'I'm newly-wed,' said Lucy. 'I must be happy.'

'There's no compulsion, you know. I've known scores of newly-wed couples who were really quite miserable'.

'I'm happy. I really am.'

Alfred poured her a little more wine. 'They take time, you know, marriages. They're rather like jigsaw-puzzles. They come in a brightly coloured box, with a pretty picture on the front, but most people are extremely disappointed when they open up the box and find that they have been given nothing but heaps of disassembled pieces, and that they have to put them all together themselves.'

He sipped, his ankle still swinging. 'Sometimes, of course, there are pieces missing. But you can't tell that for certain until you have sifted through them, tried to make some order out of them.'

They sat on the balcony in silence for a time, then Alfred said, 'Why don't I show you how my latest masterpiece is coming along? Bring your wine.'

He took her down the steep stone steps and across the angled garden to his studio; a high-raftered barn overgrown with vines. He unlocked the cracked oak door. Inside, the studio had walls of limewashed brick and a huge grimy north-facing window with dozens of broken panes. It was stacked with canvases, mostly Italianate landscapes and classical scenes, and broken pieces of stone statuary, female torsos mainly, although there was a row of six or seven Greek male torsos, all with their penises broken off. A pale bright light illuminated the whole studio with pearly evenness, and vine leaves fluttered against the window outside.

In the centre of the room stood a massive canvas, almost twice as high as Alfred himself, draped with cheesecloth. Alfred dramatically tugged the cloth away, and revealed a half-finished torrent of luminous nudity, and muscled horses' buttocks.

'The Sabines,' he announced. 'My *chef d'oeuvre.*'

'It's very dramatic,' said Lucy. 'And there's an awful lot of women with no clothes on.'

Alfred shrugged. 'It's a question of economics, I'm afraid. Nobody will buy a painting larger than three feet by two, not unless it's positively swarming with nudes.'

'They didn't really walk around nude in those days, did they?'

'My goodness, don't ask me. If they did, I don't suppose this would have been the first time they had been raped.'

Lucy laughed. She walked around the studio, fascinated by the pungent and oily smells of it, by the wriggling silver worms of half-squeezed paint-tubes, by the brushes and the bottles of turpentine. Long sticks of charcoal stood in a white glass jar like an incinerated flower-arrangement. She came to the row of male torsos. She sipped her wine, and said, 'They're all broken.'

'Yes,' said Alfred, watching her. 'Everybody thinks that they were damaged by centuries of erosion, but in fact they were broken off by vandals almost as soon as they were erected.' He added, daringly, 'If "erected" is the right word.'

Lucy turned. She set down her glass. Alfred approached her, and took off his hat. He stared directly into her eyes for a moment or two, then he tossed his hat all the way across the studio.

'You have the most exceptional beauty,' he said. 'Quite original; ceaselessly startling. You're like the sun shining through sunflower petals. You're like molten gold.'

Lucy opened her mouth slightly, her teeth resting on her glistening lower lip in the faintest of overbites.

Alfred said, 'I should love to paint you, you know.'

'Not as a Sabine woman, I hope?'

He took hold of her hands, clasped them both. 'Simply as yourself.'

Lucy looked away. Alfred gave her feelings that she couldn't comprehend. He seemed to be able to see through her, as if she were quite transparent, like water. Perhaps it was just his painter's eye. Perhaps she was revealing more of herself than she realized.

'Would you think it impertinent of me to give you some advice?' he asked her. 'I haven't known Henry for awfully long, but I do know something of what he's like.'

'Do you think I *need* advice?' Lucy challenged him.

'Perhaps. Only you can be the judge of that.'

He kept hold of her hands. His thumbs circled around and around on her knuckles. The sensation was soothing but peculiarly arousing at the same time.

He said, in soft, thick tone. 'Henry is the kind of chap who feels personally responsible for everything and everyone. He lives for toil! He eats blame for breakfast and sprinkles his supper with fault! Why do you think he wants so desperately to govern India? Only India is chaotic enough for him! Only India will burden him with enough administrative difficulties, enough tangled bureaucracy, enough political upheaval, enough poverty, enough pomp, enough pettiness, enough fanaticism! To be responsible for governing India is a martyr's dream!'

Alfred hesitated, and then he added, 'Henry believes for some reason which I fail fully to understand that he has to suffer. It is partly to do with the sense of historic mission with which a man of his birth and upbringing will always be encumbered. There may be something else, some other obligation which he feels he has to fulfil; or some stain on his soul which he feels he has to purge. Whatever it is, I sense that you have already become conscious of it, and that it is unsettling you.'

Again, Alfred paused, but he must have known that he was right, because Lucy didn't answer, and made no attempt to take her hands away.

Alfred said, 'You are Henry's wife. You have agreed to share his life. But you are not necessarily obliged to share his agonies. His agonies belong to him. You should remember that you are a woman in your own right, with your own desires, and your own free spirit.'

He smiled. 'You are also very young and very beautiful. You have a *duty* to enjoy yourself.'

He leaned forward. Lucy looked up. She realized at once that he wanted to kiss her. Their faces approached each other, sun and moon, until Lucy could feel his breath on her cheek.

'You don't have to think of anything at all,' said Alfred; and kissed her. The tip of his tongue ran along her lips, then penetrated them, and touched her teeth. She opened her mouth wider, and let him in.

They stood for long timeless moments in the pearly studio light, closely embracing, while behind them the Sabine women tumbled pink and plump across the canvas, like a basket of peaches being emptied, and the vines whispered and scratched at the window.

Alfred's hand gently closed over Lucy's breast, over her white linen dress. But then he kissed her one more time, and stood away.

'You're more than Henry deserves,' he told her. 'Don't let him turn you into a task; or a memorandum; or a column of accounts.'

Lucy said, 'Why did you kiss me?'

'Do you think it was wrong?'

'I'm Henry's wife.'

'You're Lucy. You're Lucy first, and Henry's wife after. You shouldn't forget that. Henry's wife is *what* you are; but Lucy is *who* you are.'

'We'd better get back,' said Lucy.

Alfred shrugged. 'As you wish. But you don't think that Henry will suspect us of misconduct, do you, if we linger too long in the studio?'

'I don't think I understand men,' said Lucy, brushing her dress straight and feeling quite cross about it.

'Nobody understands anybody. If they did – my God, if there were to be an instantaneous lightning-bolt of world-wide understanding, fellow for fellow – then the globe would be immediately be plunged into the fiercest and most destructive war in its history. It is only our failure to understand each other which keeps us from tearing each other's throats out.'

They left the studio and climbed back up the steps through the garden. Yellow roses nodded on either side of the path, making the afternoon air smell musky, and dropping their petals like thick curds of clotted cream. At the top of the steps, Lucy turned to Alfred, holding her hat against the katabatic breeze. 'Why didn't you want to make love to me?' she asked him, testing her own boldness, and his.

Alfred, with his disreputable hat pulled sideways over his forehead, laughed out loud. 'But I did, dear Lucy! I did!'

At that moment, Henry appeared on the balcony, in his shirtsleeves, looking pale and hot. 'Lucy! How are you?'

Lucy took hold of Alfred's hand. 'I'm very well, thank you, my darling. Alfred's been showing me his paintings.'

'Good man, Dunners,' said Henry. 'Nothing too risqué, I hope?'

Alfred gave Lucy's fingers the tiniest of squeezes. 'You know me, Henry. You know me.'

It was late November when they returned to England, and to the house that Henry had rented at Carlton House Terrace. Lucy had seen scarcely anything of London when they had stopped off for two days *en route* for France; but now she could see even less of it. The capital was plunged into raw and impenetrable fog; and all she could distinguish from her dressing-room window were the ghostly shadows of horses and carts, and spidery leafless trees, and guardsmen marching along The Mall.

Now that he was back in London, and back at work, Henry returned to the Foreign Office with a dedicated fury that almost made Lucy despair. He would rise every morning at six o'clock, shave and dress, and work by lamplight until breakfast. At half-past seven he would leave the house for the Foreign Office, which was only a minute's walk away, down the steps, across The Mall, and past Horse Guards' Parade.

Before he went, he would tiptoe into the bedroom, kiss her lightly on each cheek, and then on her lips, and tell her, 'Good girl, see you tonight.' That would be the last she would see of him until nine or ten o'clock, or sometimes later, when he would return white and stunned and semi-articulate with exhaustion. There were days when she felt that she wasn't married at all. Henry was nothing more than a stranger who came and went.

The sexual difficulties that they had suffered during the early days of their marriage soon ceased to trouble them. Henry was usually so tired when he returned home from the Foreign Office that the question of love-making became academic. Lucy took to shopping to satisfy her frustrations, and she and Nora could be seen almost every afternoon, in and out of the fashionable shops along Regent Street.

Carlton House Terrace was so close that most of her shopping had already been delivered by the time she got home. Hats and jewellery, and evening-purses and gloves. Sometimes she bought gifts for Henry: brandy-flasks or shooting-sticks or country hats, all of which he already owned in abundance. Once, to surprise him, she spent £55 on a French painting at a Bond Street gallery, but Henry insisted that the gallery took it back, because its subject-matter was too intimate (in the domestic rather than the sexual sense: it showed a kitchen) and because (in his opinion) it was hopelessly badly painted. The gallery's managing director wrote Henry a personal apology: Mrs Carson would be shown no more Bonnards.

However, there were moments of glitter and glory, and great delight. They were invited in early December to stay at Sandringham with the Prince and Princess of Wales, along with Lord Rosebery, Arthur Balfour, and Mr and Mrs Joseph Chamberlain. A week before Christmas they dined with Lord Salisbury, when he entertained the Russian Ambassador, M. de Staal; and every 'week-end' (as Saturday and Sunday were now being called), Henry contrived to invite somebody of amusement and interest to Carlton House Terrace. Leafing through her guest book at the end of her first winter with Henry, Lucy read the signature of the Duke and Duchess of Rutland; Thomas Hardy, the novelist; Henry Adams, the American historian; Henry and Margot Asquith; Alfred and D. D. Lyttelton, Evan Charteris, and many more.

They went to the theatre twice a month, at least; they attended official banquets with a great many colourfully-garbed men with shining black faces and ostrich plumes in their hair. They began to be mentioned almost every week in the society columns, and the *Evening Standard* called Lucy 'golden and ladylike', as if it were quite a surprise that an American girl could behave like a lady but, by the criteria of a nation that owned most of the profitable world, it was quite a compliment.

Then spring came, and Lucy began to know London better. She made more and more friends, mostly the wives of other Tory members of Parliament, but particularly the one-time Tennant sisters, Margot Asquith and Charty Ribblesdale. The Kansas accent which Evelyn Scott had vainly tried to Easternize was never lost altogether, but anybody in Oak City who heard it would have considered it well-nigh incomprehensible, clipped as a cow's ear. As if she were an actress in a play which she was making up as she was going along, Lucy found herself in high-ceilinged room with watered-silk walls, taking tea with elegant English ladies; riding side-saddle in a high silk hat along Rotten Row, between the budding elms; and although there were un-expectedly hurtful times, when she would glimpse a baby in a carriage in Kensington Gardens, and think of Blanche, *oh God, my poor Blanche*, she knew that she was living the life that she had always dreamed of. She had survived without parents, and found what she had always wanted. Blanche would do the same.

In May, to Lucy's undiluted terror, Henry and she were

commanded to dine and to sleep at Windsor Castle. Lucy thought that she would probably run away when she met the Queen. She had heard so many fierce stories about her. But when she was presented, she found the Queen to be tiny and articulate; softly-spoken, pale, almost girlish, and given to occasional giggles, and to making pointed remarks of her own.

After breakfast, as they stood in the sunshine waiting for their carriage, Her Majesty came up to Lucy in her rustling black dress and addressed her quite solemnly. 'You have a very agreeable husband, Mrs Carson. He is clever and well-informed. In an Empire such as ours, he has the ability to advance very far.'

'Thank you, ma'am,' said Lucy. She was amazed how white the Queen's hair shone; how white her lips were. Even her eyes looked bleached.

'I must say, too, Mrs Carson, that you are very handsome. I trust that you were not quiet yesterday evening because you found the conversation tedious.'

'No, ma'am,' Lucy replied. 'I found it real interesting.'

'Oh . . . it is never *interesting*,' the Queen replied. 'Diverting, perhaps. But never *interesting*.'

During the late summer, Henry (without consulting her) took Inverlochy Castle in Scotland, for the grouse-shooting. Lucy argued at first. She didn't want to leave London. But when Henry assured her that *everybody* left London in the summer, she eventually agreed. (In spite of tantrums, doors slammed, arguments up and down the stairs so that the servants could hear.) And, as it turned out, she adored Scotland. It was wildly different from Kansas, but she adored its mountains and its mauvish melancholy. She could open her bedroom window and the heather smelled like honey and the air smelled like slate.

Perhaps the only irritation was that Henry continued to work, even when they were on holiday. He was up at six o'clock as usual, sorting through papers that had been sent up in endless dispatch boxes by the Foreign Office, and by the time he and his friends left for the butts, he had already finished what (for most of his colleagues) amounted to a full day's hard work. After dinner, he returned to his desk, and worked until well after midnight.

Lucy had worked hard at Jack's store, dawn till dusk, but it was difficult for her to understand the ocean of paperwork with which Henry had to cope. Henry had told her with some pride that nearly ninety-two thousand telegrams and dispatches engulfed the Foreign Office every year, and every night Henry had to read the better part of them, so that he would be able to speak confidently and aggressively in the House of Commons. Every government minister suffered under the same burden of toil, and many of them were very much older and sicker than Henry. All for £1,500 a year, and the greater glory of Her Majesty's Britannic Empire.

Lucy was lying awake in her wide oak bed at Inverlochy Castle when Henry appeared at last. The clocks had long struck two, and she was so tired that she kept dropping off, and dreaming that she was still awake. She had been walking in the hills with Loulou Harcourt all afternoon, exercising Loulou's assorted dogs, and she had eaten too much grouse at dinner. But she had kept the lamp alight; and when Henry appeared, she sat up in bed and smiled at him.

'Finished at last?' she asked him.

He nodded. His face looked like a plaster-cast of himself. 'If you only knew what questions I have to answer.'

'Tell me,' she coaxed him, patting the green plaid blanket that covered their bed.

He shook his head. 'It's quite bad enough that I should have to worry myself with such matters, without you having to worry yourself, too. Can the Mayor of Portsmouth accept a foreign decoration? Can the Colombian Chargé d'Affaires be given a ticket of admission to the House of Commons? Does the Regius Professor of Physics at Cambridge University require a letter from the Russian Embassy in London before visiting Moscow? Should the Court of St James go into mourning for the Empress Dowager of Japan?'

Lucy pretended to think of some sensible answers, while Henry sat beside her, knowing that she couldn't. At last she lifted her head, and smiled, and unexpectedly kissed him. 'I don't have the first idea,' she said. 'But I know that I love you, my dearest.'

He loosened his necktie and eased out his collar-studs. 'It's more than I deserve. Your understanding is quite enough.'

'Ah, but I don't understand you. Nobody understands anybody. You know what they say. It's only our failure to understand each other that prevents us from tearing each other's throats out.'

She was tired. She had eaten and drunk too much. Henry was tired too. But he stiffened, right in the middle of unfastening his cufflinks, and demanded, 'What does that mean? What exactly does that *mean*?'

Lucy hopelessly shook her head. 'Henry, I'm really not sure. I just said it.'

He stood up, his eyes bulging, his face furious. 'Do you really mean to tell me that you believe in such sentiments? That our inability to understand each other is all that prevents us from falling on each other, like wild animals?'

'Henry, somebody said it, that's all, and I repeated it. It was only a joke.'

Quivering, Henry snapped at her, 'Do you have any idea how hard I have to work to achieve the most rudimentary of understandings between one country and another? Even between Englishman and Englishman? We live in Babel! We agree to talk to the Russian Ambassador, but everything he says is like Virgil's mysterious verses: you can only understand the first four words of every sentence. We agree to talk to the Society of Friends about slavery, provided they bring a shorthand-writer, so that we can check what they give to the Press, and we end up opening a file on who shall pay this shorthand-writer her one-guinea fee – a file inches thicker than our file on slavery! Every day is a thicket of misunderstandings, both accidental and intentional, through which I have to hack my path! And you try to tell me that misunderstanding is – I don't know, whatever you said that misunderstanding was.'

Lucy lowered her eyes, twisted her diamond-and-sapphire engagement-ring. 'Henry, I'm sorry. But we *don't* understand each other, do we?'

'Don't we?' he barked.

'Perhaps it's just that I don't understand you. I don't know, perhaps it's better that I don't. You seem to prefer to lead your own life, in your own way, without me.'

'How can you – ' Henry began, but then he clamped his hand over his mouth, as if he were the ugly step-sister in the Grimm's fairytale who coughed up frogs; and stood silent, staring at his collar-studs on the top of the black Jacobean table.

Lucy said, 'There's something wrong, Henry, isn't there?'

'Wrong? Of course not.'

'I don't mean wrong. There's something – something you've done – something you have to make amends for.'

Henry said nothing for a moment, then he let out a half-humorous, half-dismissive, *'hah!'*

'Isn't that true?' Lucy asked him.

Henry looked at her. He appeared to be wondering what to say next.

'Henry,' said Lucy, 'if it isn't true, if you're punishing yourself for nothing at all, then I swear to God that I'm going to leave you.'

Henry, with strangely jerky motions, undressed. He stood in the lamplight naked, deep-chested, a little too heavy around the waist, but very strong and athletic; a true gymnast, an exerciser in the nude.

He lifted the sheet and climbed into bed beside her. She waited for him, hardly daring to breathe. He said, in a voice like rubbed charcoal, 'I've been bad to you, Lucy, haven't I?'

'You've given me everything I could have wished for.'

'But love? What about love? Sometimes I feel that I have no capability to love.'

She held his wrist, and kissed the heel of his hand, again and again. 'You're tired, that's all. You work too hard.'

'I have to. God knows, we have an empire to run.'

'You also have a wife who cares for you, Henry, and doesn't wish to see you collapse from overwork.'

Henry was silent for a time. She felt his steady breathing on her hand. Then he said, 'I've thought for some time that you need to get out more, especially in London. My work keeps me tied to my desk, but that is no reason why you shouldn't go to dances and parties and enjoy yourself.'

'Henry, I'm quite content.'

'How can you be? I'm always so busy. I'm scarcely ever at home. But it's my nature, I would become quite mad if I were obliged to spend all my time at ease. There is so much work to be done!'

'What do you suggest?' asked Lucy. She wasn't sure what he was talking about.

'Well,' he said, 'it's this. I have a dear chum, Bruno Maltravers, we were at Oxford together. Malty, we always called him. His uncle's the Duke of Nantwich.'

'Didn't we meet the Duke of Nantwich at that reception for President Faure?'

'That's right. Bald, bearded, can't stick the man. Personally, I can never think for the life of me how he manages to have so much influence with the P.M. Malty always calls him the Mighty Coconut'.

'So what about "Malty"?'

'It's just that Malty doesn't do much for living; he's quite well off and he doesn't really need to. But he's the perfect escort. He's charming, he's amusing. You'll love him. I was thinking of inviting him to dinner, as soon as we get back to Carlton House Terrace, and putting a proposition to him, that he should escort you to dances, and to dinner-parties, whenever Parliamentary business makes it impossible for me to do so myself.'

Lucy said, 'Are you *sure?* I don't think I ever heard of such a thing.'

'My darling Lucy, it's quite common practice, especially among politicians. The administration of a global empire is a hugely time-consuming business, for all that we have junior clerks playing cricket in the corridors all afternoon. If you yourself have no particular objections, you and Malty would be doing me the very best of services. I could carry on with my work each evening without worrying that you were bored or fretful, or that you were privately blaming me because your life had turned out to be so drab.'

He kissed her, twice, on the forehead, more like a blessing than a gesture of husbandly affection, and then he said, 'These are great days for me, Lucy. I am approaching the destiny for which I was born. Unless I throw myself into my Parliamentary work night and day, I may easily lose the opportunity to become Viceroy. I was born to rule India; and I was born to rule her young. It is too much of a coincidence of destiny that the viceregal residence in Calcutta was built in imitation of Brackenbridge. Lucy – you talked of the cloud-castles that you used to see in Kansas. Brackenbridge in Derbyshire and Brackenbridge in India – *they* are my cloud-castles, and I must have them – I *must* have them – as you had to have yours.'

Lucy, taken by surprise, said nothing. She knew how Henry burned for India. But she had never realized how much he was prepared to sacrifice in order to make sure that it was his. Lord Elgin, the present Viceroy, was close to the end of his term. Almost everybody assumed that Henry would be offered the viceroyalty as his successor. Everybody, that was, except those who considered him harsh and incautious, like Lord George Hamilton, the Secretary of State for India; and those who were competitively interested in the viceroyalty for themselves, such as the Marquess of Lorne, heir to the Duke of Argyll and husband of Queen Victoria's fourth daughter, Louise, who didn't care for Henry one bit, and showed it, and never hesitated to tell the Queen what an arrogant self-serving bounder Henry was.

But Henry wanted India. And tonight Lucy had abruptly been brought to the realization that if he had to give up her love in order to win the viceroyalty, then by God, without hesitation, he would give up her love. He needed a wife; he would never be given India without a vicereine. But India came first. *He won't let me go, even if I say that I hate him to hell. He will endure my hating him, if he can have India.*

Henry appeared to have perfect confidence in Bruno Maltravers. But it wasn't his confidence in Bruno that made Lucy feel so estranged. It was his hunger for preferment; his terrible hunger for power and responsibility. Tonight, he had made her feel like a wife who had caught her husband at two o'clock in the morning in the pantry, stuffing himself with cream cake. His sexual character had mystified and worried her. But his greed for public duty was beyond her understanding.

When he slept that night, murmuring in his sleep as he always did, she lay awake staring at the darkness, trying to divine in it some reassurance, some shape, some form, some reason why she might be here, in this bed in Scotland, with her baby daughter half a world away, committed body and soul to an ambition that wasn't even hers.

Bruno Maltravers arrived at Carlton House Terrace just after noon on the first Thursday in December, as arranged, and sat waiting for Lucy in the front parlour, his legs elegantly crossed, his silk hat perched on his lap. Outside, the day was unexpectedly bright, although St James's Park was still blurred with fog, and the clattering of horses and the grinding of carriage-wheels sounded unnaturally flat.

Henry had left early on Monday morning for Berlin, to talk to Baron Marschall von Bieberstein, the German Foreign

Minister, about provocative German troop-landings in Portuguese East Africa. Antagonism between the German and the British governments was growing increasingly bitter; although Kaiser Wilhelm still wrote affectionately to his grandmother, Queen Victoria, and their ministers and their ambassadors were always received with the greatest courtesy.

Henry was attempting to use his long-standing friendships with German aristocracy to talk them into behaving with less truculence. He would be gone for two weeks at least, and he had warned Lucy with great solemnity that he might not even be back for Christmas.

'I am going to try to talk to the Kaiser personally,' he had confided in her. 'If I can do that, and convince him that the British government is interested not in conflict but in cooperation, then my future at the Foreign Office will be assured. Salisbury considers me an amateur, when it comes to European affairs. If I can mollify the Kaiser, as an amateur, then perhaps Salisbury will understand at last what I can do in Asia, where I am an expert. Think of it, Lucy! I will have India practically in my pocket.'

'Bruno promised to take me to see *Trilby*,' Lucy had told him. She was conscious that she was trying to make him feel jealous.

'I hope you enjoy it,' Henry had replied. 'I hate Tree.'

'Sometimes I think you hate anything that makes people laugh.'

Henry had stared at her and his face had looked oddly like a hawk — beakish nose and intensely-focused eyes. 'Nobody has ever accused me of being lacking in humour before,' he had retaliated.

'Perhaps you have never been lacking in humour before.'

'And what is that supposed to mean?'

'That you don't care for anything, anything at all, except India.'

Henry hadn't blinked. 'India is my destiny. Is it wrong of me to care so much for my destiny?'

Lucy had stood up, and clenched her fists, and almost screamed at him, 'Don't keep talking to me about your stupid destiny! Nobody has a destiny! You get – swept along, that's all! Just swept along!'

When Henry had left Carlton House Terrace that Monday morning, Lucy had begun to suspect from his turned-away face and his abrasive demeanour that nobody had ever said anything so hurtful to him in the whole of his life. He was a Carson, after all; and what was a Carson, but destiny incarnate? He had kissed her with all the limp lack of surprise of a steamed-open love-letter. Then he had cantered down the steps, heels clicking, climbed into his carriage, and gone to Germany.

But now (thank God) it was Thursday; and time for luncheon; and Bruno was here, morning-suited, dapper and shiny. Whether Henry had known it or not, the choice of Bruno as an escort for Lucy while he was away had been inspired. Bruno was tall, taller than Henry; handsome in a bashed-up upper-class way; exactingly fashionable; sardonic; but capable of huge acts of affectionate mischief.

Henry was a practical joker, but Lucy found most of his practical jokes to be cold and occasionally cruel. He thought it was funny if his friends fell off chairs and jarred their backs, or caught their fingers in mouse-traps. Bruno on the other hand preferred jokes against himself. 'There is nothing quite so funny as oneself. Once you understand that, you understand everything. God, the Universe, one's fellow man, you name it. It's an insight.'

Bruno's hair was chestnut-brown and crinkled. He was always straining his eyes as if he needed spectacles, and his short-sightedness had given him a slight stoop. His nose was broken, and his teeth were crooked, but he had a marvellously engaging smile. He was also the most attentive of escorts that Lucy could ever remember. He never failed to open carriage doors, to walk on the outside of the pavement, to send her gifts, to leave his card whenever he called. But there was nothing effete or weak about him. He took care of her because Henry had asked him to; and because he was a gentleman.

Lucy came down to greet him that Thursday morning dressed in a skirt of cobalt-blue velvet, with a Brussels lace blouse and a small fur bolero. She wore the six-strand pearl choker that Henry had brought her back from Madrid. Bruno stood up, and gave her an exaggerated bow. 'My dear Lucy, you look exquisite. Now I shall have to go home and change, to match up to your exquisiteness. Can you give me – what, an hour, perhaps? I shall have to spend at least ten minutes choosing a new tie.'

Lucy kissed him. 'You're as silly as ever.'

'Oh, you slaughter me,' Bruno protested. 'Actually, we'd better be going. We don't want to arrive later than the Prince of Wales, now do we? People would frown.'

Lucy said, 'Very well,' and she rang for Warren, the butler, to bring their coats. They climbed into Bruno's smart bottle-green brougham, and started to rattle along The Mall towards Buckingham Palace.

Bruno took hold of Lucy's hand. 'So, my dear, how have you been amusing yourself since Henry departed for the land of the midnight sausage? You know what they say about Germany, don't you? "Demand the best, but expect the wurst!"'

Lucy pressed her fingers to her forehead. 'Bruno . . .' she said. 'Do you really want to go to this luncheon? I wonder if I might persuade you to do something else.'

Bruno sat back in his seat, and frowned. They had passed the Palace now, and were progressing up Constitution Hill. 'Not so sure what you're driving at,' he told her, warily.

'Well, Bruno, I know we're supposed to go to this luncheon, and that the Prince of Wales will be there, and all about that . . . but I think I'd rather go the country.'

'The country?'

'I don't know, somewhere different, where nobody knows us.'

Bruno thought about this for a while – then, when they reached Hyde Park Corner – he rapped his cane on the brougham's roof, and his coachman Romney opened the hatch in the roof. 'Sir?' he demanded, out of the corner of his mouth.

'Epsom,' Bruno told him.

'Epsom, sir?'

'The racecourse, that'll do us.'

'No races today, sir.'

'Romney,' Bruno told him, with undisguised irritation, 'take us to Epsom.'

'Yes, sir,' said Romney.

In less than two hours they were standing on what seemed to Lucy to be the roof of the world. To the south, she could see thick hazy woods, and the single triangular spire of a church. To the west, she could see for miles and miles, all over Surrey, and farther; a pale countryside from which the sun was reluctantly dragging its watery-gold light, hedge by hedge, tree by tree, as it settled towards the horizon. The air was so raw that she could scarcely breathe in: not brittle-cold, like Kansas, but damp and sore-throaty.

A few yards away, by the deserted grandstand, Romney fed and watered the horses. He was in better spirits now, since Bruno had allowed him to visit the Derby Arms for bread-and-cheese and a pint of bitter beer. Lucy could hear him clicking to his horses and cajoling them and telling them how fine they were.

Bruno stood with his hands by his sides, his breath smoking, saying nothing, but looking right and left.

'It's marvellous here,' said Lucy. 'I feel like God, looking out over His new creation.'

'Well,' said Bruno, wryly, 'you could feel worse.'

'*Bruno*,' Lucy protested.

'I'm sorry,' Bruno told her. 'It's just that I really have no idea what all of this is in aid of.'

413

Lucy said, quietly, 'You do like women, don't you, Bruno?'

He swung his stooping shoulders around. 'I beg your pardon?'

'You do like women? You're not a buh-guh-ruh?'

Bruno opened his mouth and then closed it again.

'I'm sorry,' said Lucy. 'I'm truly sorry. That was quite unfair. What could you answer, if you were?'

'What could I answer, if I *weren't*?' Bruno retaliated.

Lucy turned to him. Behind her, the sun had fallen over Hampshire. In an hour-and-a-half, it would be dark. 'Bruno, why did Henry ask you to escort me?' she asked.

'He said he was very busy at the Foreign Office. Early mornings, late nights. He was afraid you might be bored.'

'Was that all?'

Bruno wouldn't answer. He stood leaning on his stick, looking out over the misty and mysterious undulations of the Downs, the shepherd of his own secret.

'That wasn't all, was it?' Lucy challenged him.

Bruno said, 'Perhaps I made a mistake.'

'What mistake?'

'Lucy . . . Henry is a very special chap. Henry is one of these chaps who only appears once a century or so and *he's* aware of it and everybody else around him is aware of it. You know what they say about him in *The Times*, and in *Punch*.'

Lucy stood very close to Bruno, her hands enclosed in her fur muffler, her face pale in the winter sunlight. 'Bruno, you're trying to tell me something.'

'Well,' he shrugged. 'I am, and I'm not.'

'What is it?'

'Don't you see?' Bruno demanded. 'It's all to do with Henry's what-d'you-call-it. His calling. His birthright. God said to Henry, you're going to govern India, and ever since God said that, Henry hasn't taken any notice of anybody else.'

Bruno looked around, sniffed, as if he could smell wood-smoke in the air, or blood. Lucy felt peculiarly afraid; but brave, at the same time. She wanted to know the worst. It almost excited her, to know the worst.

Bruno said, 'Henry, well ... he's unique. Just like the Duke of Wellington; or Disraeli. Ordinary people like you and me, we can love him or like him, we can give him all the semblance of friendship and family life ... But he's not like us, you know, Lucy. You and I, we're simply mortal. Henry will be remembered long, long after there is nobody in the world who can remember that you and I even existed.'

Lucy persisted, 'Why did Henry ask you to escort me?'

Bruno breathed steam. The day was falling fast, and it was already bone-cold. He could have said so many things. One explanation is as good as another. Why say anything complicated, or hurtful? Why say anything true? But Bruno had already gone too far, by agreeing to bring Lucy out to the country, when they should have been lunching in Park Lane. The moment he had said, 'Epsom', he had committed himself.

'Henry said –' Bruno began.

'Bruno, Henry said *what*?'

'Henry said, "The devil you know is preferable to the devil you don't."'

Lucy clutched his sleeve. She felt almost as if she were drowning, as if she couldn't breathe. 'Well, what did he mean by that? What does that mean, "the devil you know"?'

Bruno tried not to look at her; then looked at her. 'I'm obliged to tell you, aren't I?'

'Yes, goddamn it, you are!'

'What he meant was, Lucy ... what he obviously intended me to understand him as saying *was* – that he was too preoccupied with affairs of state at the Foreign Office – to give a young, vivacious wife everything that was required to make her happy.'

At that moment, Lucy grasped what Bruno was telling her; but the implications of it were so enormous that she remained silent, and waited for Bruno to say it out loud, word by word, as if it were a school recital.

Bruno said, 'You needed parties, that's what he said. Parties, and dances, and theatre, and entertainment.'

'That's what you've given me,' Lucy reassured him. 'That's exactly what you've given me!'

'I think he meant more,' Bruno told her, in a voice like wrung-out washing.

'More?'

Bruno was agonized. 'I have to tell you the truth, Lucy. I'm too fond of you now to lie to you. If you never want to see me again, then of course I'll understand.'

Lucy immediately tugged off her left-hand glove, and lifted her fingers to her eyes, to see if she was crying.

Bruno puckered his mouth, and said, 'I'm sorry. I'm sorry. Henry's my friend.'

They stood together on the Downs for almost ten minutes, in the biting wind. Romney came over, and took off his hat, and said, 'Horses gettin' cold, sir. Should we be gettin' back?'

Lucy looked at Bruno. She tried to keep her voice steady and level. 'There must be an inn, in Epsom.'

'Spread Eagle, sir,' Romney suggested. He didn't speak to Lucy, not even once. As far as he was concerned, Bruno might just as well have been standing on the Downs on his own. Romney was what most employers would have called 'the soul of discretion'.

'Spread Eagle?' asked Bruno. 'How far is that?'

In the darkest hours of the night, when the town of Epsom was completely silent, Lucy could hear the erratic thundering of Bruno's breath, and the sliding of the sheets. Then Bruno, naked, was on top of her, very lean, all bone and muscle. She reached down and clutched his stiffness; and almost at once guided it into herself.

He was very hard, like a long bone. He said nothing to her, while he pushed himself in and out; either because he had nothing to say, or because he was afraid to. She was conscious in a remarkable way that she was committing adultery, but she felt almost as if Henry had commissioned it, like a portrait, and whether he liked the portrait or not, he had to suffer the consequences.

Bruno shuddered. He was finished. He kissed her once, on the cheek; then he turned over on to his side and fell asleep. Almost an hour later, in the bathroom, Lucy stood in front of the mirror staring at her face. She didn't look like Lucy Carson at all. She was somebody else; although she didn't know who.

It was very cold, in the bathroom. The sun was very far away.

8

When Henry came home that thundery afternoon and stood in the hallway shaking his umbrella and called out, 'India, my darling! They've given me India!' her immediate thought was not of palaces or elephants or princes with diamonds in their foreheads.

As if they had flown open in her mind with a sudden and general clatter, she thought of those black tinplate boxes on the back shelves of the Darling General Store; and how she had breathed in their mysterious dust-dry pungencies; and wondered what kind of an extraordinary country it could be where people ate foods that tasted of shoe-leather and gunpowder and dried flowers and fire.

'The Queen has given her approval, and the P.M. will announce it next week,' said Henry, so excited that he couldn't stop stalking from one side of the parlour to the other, flapping his arms up and down.

'Fenugreek and cumin,' Lucy recited, holding out her arms for him. 'Chilli and turmeric and garam marsala.'

'What?' he laughed. 'Have you been learning Hindi already?'

She kissed him, and shook her head. His sidewhiskers were wet from summer rain. 'India!' she told him. 'I'm so proud of you, Henry! India!'

'Hamilton wasn't too pleased,' said Henry. 'He said I was too adventurous to be Viceroy. Too high-spirited! But there's nothing he can do about it now. He's written to Elgin already, giving him the news.'

'When do we leave?' asked Lucy.

'Well, not until December. We have so many domestic arrangements to make. I don't know whether Elgin will leave me an aide-de-camp; or a house steward. I don't even know if we're supposed to take our own carriages and plate and wine.'

Lucy said, 'You'll have to be a peer, won't you? Malty said you would, if they gave you the viceroyalty.'

'Ah, we've sorted that one out, too,' Henry told her, with a self-satisfied smile. 'They're going to make me an Irish peer, instead of an English peer, so that I can be free to seek re-election to the House of Commons when I get back. They haven't created an Irish peer for thirty years, and they may never create one again, but the Queen seems quite agreeable. I shall be Lord Carson of Brackenbridge.'

He gripped her arms tightly, and smiled at her wide-eyed with delight. 'And you shall be Lady Carson!'

Henry lunched at home, cold mutton and mustard pickles. Over the tapioca pudding, he asked Lucy, 'How *is* Malty these days? I swear that I haven't run into him for months!'

'Malty's well,' said Lucy, without looking up.

'Is he taking good care of you?'

'Excellent care, thank you. In fact we're going to Twickenham this afternoon, for a picnic tea on the river with Jeremy and Nellie Theobald.'

Henry nodded, meticulously spooning up the last of his pudding. 'I'm sorry you had to stay in Town so late. But as soon as they've announced my appointment, we can go up to Brackenbridge for a week or so. Shoot some grouse.'

'I really don't mind,' said Lucy, trying to sound offhand. 'I've enjoyed myself in Town. There's always something to do.'

'Would you like Malty to come up to Derbyshire with us?' asked Henry.

Lucy lifted her head and looked at him. The clouds must have been clearing outside, because a sudden gleam of watery sunshine illuminated the table, and sparkled on the glassware. Did he suspect that she and Malty had been going to bed together two or three times a week; in fact, almost every time they went out together? Lucy had taken every possible precaution not to be seen, unlike some other aristocratic ladies who flaunted their lovers as ostentatiously as they flaunted their new hats. Nora seemed to suspect her, but Nora had said nothing. Nora was concerned only that Lucy should be happy; and during this long busy summer of 1898, Lucy had been happier than Nora had ever remembered. She was twenty-one years old, the beautiful wife of a popular and successful politician. She was invited to all the balls and all the receptions and all the best banquets. The popular Press adored her, and had nicknamed her the Yankee Butterfly.

She and Henry were regularly invited to Windsor and to Buckingham Palace, and the Queen now called her by her first name.

She had all of that, and sufficient money to be able to dress herself in silks and velvets and furs. And even if it was a disappointment that Henry was so erratic and unsatisfying in bed, she had Malty. Equable, uncomplaining, ever-loyal Malty, who would take her wherever and whenever she wished, and make persistent love to her, on and on for as long as she could bear it.

He was always careful, however, and wore a French letter. The very last thing that she wanted was to be blessed with a wavy-haired baby with a slight stoop and a habit of humming *Another Little Patch of Red*.

She couldn't be sure that Henry didn't suspect her of adultery. Yet her love-making with Malty immeasurably improved their marriage. She became quieter, and more content, and because of her contentment, and the fact that she made no physical demands on him, Henry appeared to enjoy life much more, and to laugh more often.

The Carsons' obvious happiness was infectious, and they were popular hosts. They held scores of dinners and *soirées* at Carlton House Terrace; and early in 1897 Henry had taken a lease on a six-bedroomed Georgian house in Reigate, twenty miles to the south of London, called The Vines, where they held weekend parties, too.

The following week, when Henry's appointment as Viceroy was announced, there would be even more celebrations.

Henry wiped his mouth with his napkin, and then laid it on the table. 'I'll be back around eight o'clock this evening; no later. I have to write a letter to Elgin, and to my old Balliol chum, Walter Pinkerton. I'm going to need a first-class private secretary when I'm in Calcutta, and if anybody has any ideas who to go for, it'll be Pinks.'

He leaned over Lucy and kissed her.

'Henry, I'm very happy for you,' she told him, and kissed him back. Both were kisses of complete chastity, such as a brother might give to a sister, and *vice versa*.

There was a distant rumble outside, summer thunder. 'Better take your bumbersoll,' Lucy warned him.

But the same storm which came lashing down on Henry as he scurried across The Mall to the Foreign Office had already caused the abandonment of the Theobalds' picnic on the river at Twickenham. Lucy and Malty hadn't intended to go to the picnic at all. Malty had arranged to use the

Theobalds' house in Cheyne Walk while they were out, telling Jeremy and Nellie that he wanted to impress some friends on leave from India.

The Theobalds knew nothing of Malty's affair with Lucy. They were both good friends with Henry; and they certainly wouldn't have allowed their house to be used as a refuge for Lucy's adultery. Still, they were supposed to be picnicking in Twickenham until early evening, and what the Theobalds' eyes didn't see, Malty had declared, the Theobalds' hearts wouldn't grieve over.

It was a particularly convenient trysting-place because the Theobalds had taken all their servants, too, as a summer treat.

When Malty's brougham reached Cheyne Walk, however, the rain was clattering down furiously, drumming on the roof, and bouncing off the coachman's top-hat. Wiping the steam from the carriage window with his glove, Malty peered out and muttered, 'Oh, God!'

'What is it?' asked Lucy.

'Jeremy and Nellie. Look! They've been rained off.'

Sure enough, three coaches were drawn up outside the Theobalds' redbrick house, and servants were scurrying to and fro with umbrellas and hampers and folded tables.

'Well, that puts paid to that, I'm afraid,' said Malty. He rapped his stick on the roof of the brougham, and called out, 'Romney! Royal Academy! Let's go and look at some pictures!'

But Lucy snuggled up close to him and kissed his cheek, and said, 'Why do we have to go and look at pictures?'

'What else do you suggest? We have nowhere else. You're too well known for us to risk an hotel.'

'We could go home.'

'Home? You mean *your* home? Carlton House Terrace? You must be mad!'

'I'll give the servants the afternoon off.'

'And they won't suspect?'

'Not if you pretend to leave, and then come back later, through the kitchen.'

'Lucy, my darling, it's fearfully risky!'

She kissed him again, 'Perhaps it's about time we took some risks.'

An hour-and-a-half later, with the rain still pattering against the bedroom window, Lucy sat up completely naked in bed and wrote, '*My life in Kansas seems so far away that I find it difficult to remember it. Faces, names . . . they seem to have faded away, like a picture-book left on the windowsill. I remember the tornadoes, and I remember Uncle Casper, and Jack, and my mother. But they all seem like they never truly existed, something I read about, some story somebody told me . . . not real people at all.*'

She became conscious that the soft scratching of her pen had woken Malty up; and that he was watching her. The way the light shone faintly gold on the fine hairs of her forearms; the way her hair tangled across her cheek. He touched her shoulder, and then his fingers delicately circled her breasts, around and around and around.

'Do you know what I think?' Malty told her.

'No, what do you think?'

'I think that all men are monsters and all women are god-desses.'

'I'm not a goddess.'

'Yes, you are. Henry thinks you are. That's why Henry can never make love to you properly.'

'I don't want to talk about Henry.'

His fingers trailed down between her breasts, lingered around her navel. 'Do you think it's *de rigueur* for a vicereine of India to wear a ruby in her tummy-button?'

'I don't know. Do you think it would suit me? I don't think Lord Salisbury would approve. I'm surprised he gave Henry the viceroyalty in any case. He thinks he's too lively, too adventurous. He's quite sure that he's going to rock the boat.'

Malty said nothing for a while but ran his fingertips backwards and forwards in a light brushing motion on her bare thighs. She watched him. She wondered what he was going to say next. It looked as if he had something on his mind; something which he couldn't quite bring himself to express.

'Why didn't I meet you first?' she asked him.

'You mean, before Henry? With a view to what?'

'With a view to marriage, of course.'

'I wouldn't have married you. I'm not that kind of a fellow.'

'What do you mean?'

'Exactly that. I'm not that kind of a fellow. If we were married, well then, I'd have to work, wouldn't I, to keep you in dresses and hats and handmade shoes?'

'I thought you had a private fortune.'

Malty shook his head.

'You always gave me the *impression* you had a private fortune. You're always dressed so beautifully.'

'A man's clothes will never tell you anything.'

Lucy sat up. 'So, where *do* you get your income from?'

'From friends. From generous friends.'

'Not from Henry?'

'He gives me a little. He helps to defray the expense of taking you out.'

'But why should friends give you money, just like that, for nothing?'

'Because they're friends.'

Lucy supposed that she couldn't argue with the logic of that, but she lay back on her pillow feeling perplexed. She glanced at Malty, and he grinned at her, and touched the tip of her nose with his fingertip.

Lightning crackled, somewhere across the Thames. Then, almost at once, the house was shaken by a tremendous burst of thunder. It sounded as if it were directly overhead. The windows rattled in their sashes, and fine plaster sifted down from the ceiling. 'God's disapproval,' said Malty.

But Lucy clung to him tight and said, 'Please, make love to me. Please, while it's thundering!'

Malty kissed her, and then rolled over and busied himself with a French letter. Then he climbed on top of her, and made love to her with all of his usual slow and rhythmic grace. She closed her eyes. The lightning tore up the sky, like rotten linen; then the thunder collapsed. Malty pushed and pushed and pushed, murmuring sweet and filthy language to her while he did so.

She didn't know what it was that made her open her eyes. But as Malty's rhythm began to quicken, she turned her head on the pillow and glanced quickly towards the partly-open bedroom door. What she saw there made her go stiff with terror. She almost cried out, but all she could manage under Marty's ever-quickening onslaught was a high-pitched gasp. Malty thought nothing of it; she was always gasping when he made love to her.

It was Henry, standing tall and still and white-faced, in a light grey frock-coat with shoulders spotted darkly with rain. He was staring directly at her; unblinking. He had learned this morning that he was to be Viceroy of India, the glittering pinnacle of his career, the realization of his natural destiny. This afternoon, less than two hours later, he was witnessing his wife fornicating with another man. Worse than that, fornicating with one of his friends.

Malty shivered, and coughed, and then rolled off her, panting. Henry continued to stare at her through the half-open door, but Malty obviously hadn't seen him. Lightning sizzled over the Palace of Westminster; thunder bellowed. One second Henry was in darkness; the next he was bleached by dazzling blue-white light. Then he was plunged into darkness again, but the image of his face remained imprinted on Lucy's retina.

'What's the matter?' Malty asked her, as she reached for her robe.

She laid her hand on his shoulder. 'Ssh, nothing's wrong.'

However, she was quaking, and Malty detected the quivering in her voice, and lifted his head up. 'Where are you going? Lucy?'

'I'll be back in just a minute.'

She hurried out on to the landing. Henry had disappeared. She bit her lip anxiously, looking this way and that. She hurried along to his dressing room. It smelled strongly of leather brushes and Floris toilet-water, Henry's smell; but Henry wasn't there. She tried all the spare bedrooms. He wasn't in any of those, either.

'Lucy!' Malty called her. 'Lucy, what on earth are you doing?'

Lucy went back to the bedroom door and said, 'Shush, Malty, for goodness' sake!'

Malty said something in reply, but lightning filled the windows with unnatural brilliance, and his words were swallowed up by the subsequent thunder.

She ran barefoot downstairs. Henry wasn't in the parlour. Nor could she find him in the morning room. It was then that she heard a thrashing noise from the library. She crossed the hallway, and pressed her ear against the door. There it was again, *thrashh!* and then again, *thrashh!*

She laid her hand on the doorknob, but then she hesitated. Perhaps it would be wiser not to open it. Some things are better left unsaid, some things are better left unseen. Whatever Henry was doing, it sounded painful and it sounded dire. She allowed her hand to relinquish its grip on the doorknob, and slowly retreated.

Malty was waiting for her, dressed, at the top of the stairs. 'What the devil's wrong?' he wanted to know.

She mounted the stairs with the dislocated movements of a marionette. The thunder rumbled yet again, but distinctly further away, over towards St Paul's. Now it was raining, a gushing, bucketing summer storm. Gutters were flooded, omnibuses rolled through muddy lakes. Sightseers outside Buckingham Palace cowered doggedly under newspapers and stared at the grey-coated guardsmen as if they expected them to dissolve.

'Henry's here,' said Lucy. 'He saw us.'

'*What?*' asked Malty, wide-eyed.

'He saw us,' Lucy repeated, bleakly.

'God's witness!' said Malty. 'Where is he?'

'He's in the library. I'm not sure what he's doing.'

Malty took two or three steps downwards. 'I'd better –'

'No!' said Lucy, clutching at his sleeve. Then, much more softly, 'No. You'd better just leave.'

Malty slowly reached up and touched her cheek, letting his fingers slide into her tangly hair. 'Do you know something, Lucy,' he told her, 'I was more fond of you than any other girl I ever knew.'

'Aren't you fond of me any longer?'

He shook his head. 'I can't allow myself to be, can I? It's over, now that Henry's found out. I just hope that he doesn't punish you too severely; or himself, for that matter.'

Lucy stared at him and realized that this was probably the last time she would ever see him. Unless, of course, she was preparing to sacrifice Henry, and India, and everything for which she had abandoned Blanche. Malty had been escorting her for almost two years, and Lucy knew that it was his friendship she would miss, rather than his love-making. But he was right. It was over. She had too much to lose; and, in his way, so did he.

'I'll just get dressed,' he told her.

He put on his clothes as immaculately as usual, and tied his necktie perfectly. Then he leaned over and kissed Lucy's forehead. 'It was all wonderful fun,' he whispered. 'But listen, I can't find my *thing* . . . my *capote anglaise*.'

'Don't worry', said Lucy. 'I'll take care of it.'

Malty took one long look at her, and then he left. She heard him close the front door behind him. There were of course no servants to see him out.

She straightened the bed. She wasn't crying, but she

couldn't seem to make her arms do what they were told. She tugged the quilt, and as she did so, she saw Malty's French letter, which had dropped underneath the bed. She quickly picked it up, to dispose of it. She was on the point of flushing it down the water-closet, however, when she hesitated. Pearls, seeds, and a little baby like Blanche. Now that she was married, she could have a baby with no scandal at all. In fact, with nothing but joy.

She turned the slippery rubber inside out, and let its contents slide into her hand. 'Bruno Frederick James Maltravers,' she recited, in a whisper, as she cupped her hand between her thighs.

'Please be born. Please be a boy.'

She stood in the bathroom for two or three minutes. Then she washed, and brushed her hair. In the looking-glass she looked perfectly normal. A little flushed, perhaps, but otherwise composed. She finished dressing, and then she went downstairs.

She didn't know how she had expected Henry to react. With rage, perhaps. With icy fury. With disgust. With contempt. With bitterness and sorrow. Whatever it was, she certainly hadn't expected him to behave with such grace and equanimity, almost as if he were *pleased*, in a way, that she had hurt him. He was sitting at his desk in the library when she came down, wearing the half-glasses which he used these days for writing. The thunderstorm had passed away completely now, and although the library faced to the north, and was never sunny, it shimmered in reflected light from one of the windows opposite.

She remembered what Alfred Dunning had told her in the South of France: '*Henry believes for some reason which I fail to understand that he has to suffer.*'

In betraying him with Malty, perhaps she had somehow given him some perverse pleasure.

He looked up. His face had taken on the same swollen

appearance that she had seen on their wedding-night. Glazed, congested eyes; and piggy jowls.

'Has he gone?' Henry asked her.

Lucy nodded, still waiting for an outburst.

'Well . . .' said Henry, 'I suppose, when it comes down to it, I have only myself to blame.'

Lucy didn't say anything, but Henry smiled at her as if she had. 'Perhaps if I hadn't have been so preoccupied with work . . . perhaps if I'd paid you more attention.'

He kept opening and closing the lid of his brass inkpot. Open and shut, open and shut. 'Do you love him?' he asked.

Lucy shook her head. 'He doesn't love me, either.'

'So it's . . . carnal, that's all? Physical?'

'It's friendship.'

Henry's eyes wandered back to his desk. 'Friendship. Yes. I can understand that. I have been blessed throughout my life with true and loyal friends. I had hoped that, apart from being my wife, you were one of them.'

'Henry, I am. Or at least I would be, if you were to allow it.'

Henry thought about that, and then slowly nodded. 'I haven't given you much of a chance, have I? My poor Lucy.'

After a while, he got up from his desk and went to the window, and stood with his eyes slitted looking directly into the trembling reflected sunlight, as if he were daring it to blind him.

'How long?' he asked her, without turning around.

'Right from the very beginning, almost.'

'Was I really so careless?' He meant it in the sense that he hadn't cared for her.

'Henry – there's something inside of you I can't understand. I try to understand it but you always hide it. It's something to do with our marriage-bed; something to do with our love-making. But you will never explain it.'

Henry pinched his nose, and then wiped it.

'Henry,' Lucy continued, 'if you don't tell me what it is, then I can never help you.'

He looked around at last. His eyes were glistening, as if he were close to tears. 'Lucy,' he said. 'I ask only this. That you stay with me; that you be my Vicereine; and that all the matter of Malty be forgotten. I deserved it, and I was justly punished. Now perhaps we can forget recriminations and look forward. We have five years of greatness ahead of us! Let us open our hearts to it; and to our duty; and to each other.'

'Do you really mean that?' asked Lucy.

He gave a little wry grunt of amusement. 'My darling, I have very little choice. I have been chosen by fate; and so, in your way, have you. We *must* go to India. What else can we do? I could divorce you, I suppose, for adultery. But if all of those politicians whose wives had been adulterous were to be sued for divorce, the House of Commons would be a club for single men.'

He left the window and walked right up to her. 'As for what lies inside me . . . well, you're quite right. There *is* a feeling inside me to which I am not yet reconciled. A passion, as a matter of fact. But it is impossible for me to explain it to you. Not until I have conquered it myself.'

'Henry,' said Lucy, 'if you expect me to come to India with you, to be your Vicereine, then you must tell me what it is. Henry, you *owe* it to me. You're *obliged*.'

They heard the kitchen door slam. The servants were coming back. Henry said, 'If you imagine that you need forgiveness from me for what you did with Malty; then I forgive you. Nothing will ever shake my affection for you. We have a whole empire to administer, and that empire is far greater than either of our temperaments.'

Lucy said, 'Sha-sha taught me some French. *C'est une folie à nulle autre second, de vouloir se méler à corriger le monde.* It is a stupidity second to none, to busy yourself with setting the world to rights.'

Henry smiled faintly. 'I remember the time that I first quoted you Molière. At Brackenbridge, when I gave you that necklace.'

'Yes,' said Lucy.

Henry approached her. He laid his hands gently on her shoulder. My God, he was handsome; and the fatigue that was marked on his face from all of those hours at the Foreign Office – somehow that fatigue made him look even more appealing. Tired, vulnerable, the kind of man who needed a woman's care.

But she looked beyond him, towards his desk, and on his desk lay a flat black leather strap.

'What's that?' she asked. He knew at once what she was referring to.

'It's called a tawse,' he told her. His eyes challenged her to ask him any more.

'Is it yours?'

'Yes.'

'What's it for?'

'It's for anything you like'.

'What was it made for?'

Now he turned around, and focused on it, as if he had never seen it before. 'It comes from Scotland. They use them in their schools there, to maintain discipline, instead of the cane.'

'But what do you use it for?'

Henry picked it up, and slapped it into the palm of his hand, quite hard. 'I use it to remind myself that we are different from the animals only in that we are capable of punishing ourselves. Animals avoid pain at all costs. Only the human intellect understands that pain has a purpose.'

Lucy knew what she wanted to ask him, but didn't know how to phrase it. *Why are you punishing yourself? What for? And why must you always punish me, too?*

When she lay in their brass-pillared bed that night and

Henry slept, she began to see that they *had* to go to India; that only in India could their lives be fulfilled, for better or for worse. She also began to see that Fate had brought her India right from the moment that Uncle Casper had reappeared.

These days, she tried not to think about Uncle Casper. She still dreamed about him, still woke up dry-mouthed and quivering and panicky. And she could never bring herself to think about his being her father. It made her feel as if there were a madness in her from which she would never be able to escape.

Henry stirred, whispered, '*We are different from the animals only in that we are capable of punishing ourselves.*'

But why does Henry punish himself? And more to the point, why did he forgive me so easily?

In early October they abandoned their packing for two weeks and visited Lord Felldale at Brackenbridge. It was a wet and dismal autumn, all overcast skies and mud and slippery leaves, but their friends and colleagues had given them one farewell feast after another – the Old Etonians, Henry's contemporaries from Oxford, and his fellow civil servants at the Foreign Office (even the dour and disapproving George Hamilton).

Lord Felldale was looking drawn and unwell and peculiarly *shrunken*, but he was bursting with pride for Henry's appointment. When the news had first been announced, he had written to Henry. 'I begin to realize what a splendid position you have deservedly won. Congrats pour in from every quarter and the country generally is as proud of you as I, your father, am, and more I cannot say.'

In the afternoons, when Henry was busy with papers from the India Office, and with his endless inventories, Lucy went for long walks on her own. She felt different, calmer, she didn't know why. Perhaps it was because she now had something exciting to look forward to: a voyage to India, an

431

enticing new country, and the splendour of representing Her Majesty the Queen. She had been received with such affection by the Press and by Henry's friends, and even by those society ladies who might have been expected to wax exceedingly jealous that an American girl was soon to take up such an exalted position in the British Empire. She had received the kindest of letters from three other ladies of American birth who had established themselves in the English aristocracy, the Duchess of Marlborough, Lady Randolph Churchill, and Mrs Henry White.

On Sunday morning, at chapel, while the village choir sang a sweet and awkward hymn that had been specially written to speed them on their way to 'Eastern parts' (which of course rhymed with 'Loyal Hearts') Lucy felt so happy and so much at peace that she looked up to the foggy crimson light falling through the stained-glass window and wondered if God had seen fit to beatify her. On the way back to the house, she began to feel more and more light-headed. The darkness of the day grew darker, like an owl's eye closing. She collapsed on to the shingle and didn't even feel herself hitting the ground.

When she stirred, Dr Roberts was sitting beside her. The curtains were drawn, and the oil-lamp was lit. The bedroom door was open for decorum's sake, and Nora was standing outside in the hallway. Lucy wondered when Nora had started to look older. Perhaps she looked older, too. It was strange how the years passed, like walking through an empty house, room by room, and never being able to find your way back again.

Dr Roberts said, 'Hello, Mrs Carson.'

She smiled lazily. 'Am I ill?' she asked him.

'Do you *feel* ill?'

'I'm not sure. I ate some grouse yesterday. I knew that I shouldn't. Grouse never agrees with me, but I didn't want to hurt Lord Felldale's feelings.'

Dr Roberts took hold of her hand. 'I have good news for you, Mrs Carson. You're expecting your first child.'

Her smile faded, and she looked across at him with widened eyes. 'That's very diplomatic of you, Dr Roberts. But you and I both know that isn't true.'

'Nobody else has to know,' said Dr Roberts. 'By the way . . . purely out of medical interest, was the first child healthy?'

She nodded. 'A little girl. I named her Blanche.'

'You left her in America?'

'In Kansas, yes, with a family that I can trust.'

Dr Roberts could see that it hurt her to think about Blanche, and squeezed her hand. 'You mustn't blame yourself, you know, for leaving her. You're still young now. You were much younger then. At least you gave her the sacred opportunity of life.'

Lucy looked away, although she still held on to Dr Roberts' hand. 'Sometimes I wonder how sacred an opportunity that really is.'

Dr Roberts stood up. 'I think, in India, you will see that for yourself.'

On the first Saturday of December, on a morning stung with sudden snow-showers, Lucy invited a crowd down to The Vines, at Reigate, since Henry was packing the last of his library. Lord Elgin had warned him that 'in neither Calcutta nor in Simla is there a library worthy of the name.'

They had tried to underpack, but it had been difficult, since Elgin had advised them that the climate was not always warm, especially in the hills at Simla, at the beginning and the end of the season, where it could be 'bracing, if not actually cold'.

The hallway at The Vines was crowded with trunks and packing-cases, and the house itself was looking self-consciously half-dressed, like an old woman caught in the corset-cover. Still, it was a good time to have a weekend party, and Lucy had invited everybody for whom she genuinely cared, with the exception of Malty, who was spending the winter in Athens.

Margot Asquith and Charty Ribblesdale had come down; and so had the Brodricks, the Grenfells, Arthur Balfour, and (to Lucy's great delight) Charles, and William, and Blanche. She had invited Lord Felldale, but he was too ill to travel in the winter, and had sent instead a letter of farewell.

'My dears ... God speed, we know that the next five years will add lustre to a name that is already bright.'

The Vines was a plain but elegant Georgian house, white-painted, with green shutters, built in the lee of the chalky North Downs. It boasted only six bedrooms and two bathrooms, but both Lucy and Henry liked it because of its huge drawing room, where they could entertain twenty or thirty people at a time.

That morning, the drawing room was particularly noisy and crowded, and enough champagne had been passed around for the laughter to have reached a high pitch of hilarity. But Sha-sha drew Lucy aside, close to the windows that overlooked the garden, and said, 'You're looking pale, my sweet. This isn't too much for you? I know how Henry loves to pack. A place for everything, and an itemized list for every place. But it isn't really your *forté*, is it? Especially now that you're a mother-to-be'.

Lucy smiled. 'I'm just a little tired, that's all. I've only just gotten over my morning-sickness.'

'You have exacting days ahead of you, in India. You must take care of yourself, and your baby. And Henry will need all the support that you can give him. You must try to prevent him from overworking, you know. He has plenty of nervous energy but not much stamina.'

'I'll do my best,' said Lucy. 'It's not always easy.'

Sha-sha looked around the room at the Adam-green walls and the gold-framed paintings of horses and sheep. 'I've always adored this house, you know. If I had to choose a house to die in, this would be it.'

She was silent for a while, and then she said, 'Are things —
all right — between you and Henry?'

'All right? I'm not sure what you mean. He's delighted
about the baby. He's already decided to name him Horatio.'

'Horatio? *Horatio?* He must be losing his mind.'

'I thought of James, if it's a boy. Or maybe Jamie.'

'Too Scottish,' said Blanche. 'Still — at least you'll be
giving him a child. We were all beginning to think that you
never would. After all, my dear, you've been married for
three years. Most healthy women would have had four
children by now.'

'Perhaps I'm just the kind of woman who doesn't fall too
easily,' Lucy suggested.

On the other side of the drawing room, Henry was
laughing loudly and saying to Charlie, '. . . and there we
were at this tiny country halt, Cole Green, in the middle of
nowhere at all, and the local train had already left . . . so I
gave a telegram to the stationmaster, demanding that they
stop the express, and pick us up . . .'

At the same time, she caught a glimpse through the side
window of a maroon carriage arriving outside the house.
The maroon-uniformed coachman climbed down from the
box, opened the carriage door, and lowered the steps so that
a tall young lady in a moss-green coat and a green ostrich-
feathered hat could climb down. She was accompanied by a
slightly older woman in brown.

Blanche couldn't quite see who it was. 'More guests?' she
asked, craning her neck sideways.

Lucy said, 'Excuse me, Sha-sha, for just a minute.'

She pushed her way through the crowded drawing room.
Henry frowned and followed her progress across the room
as he finished off his story. '. . . and the stationmaster read it
out word for word . . . *Lord Carson of Brackenbridge, Viceroy
Designate of India, hereby requires you* . . . and in the end he
looked up and said, "Goodness me, sir, you'll get there
yerself before this wire does."'

Lucy reached the hallway just as the butler opened the front door. Immediately she was brought face-to-face with the woman in green. They stared at each other, not speaking, each seeking the resemblance that had brought them together.

'Vanessa,' said Lucy.

'Hallo, Lucy. I might call you Lucy?' She was blonde, tall, slight, and very beautiful, almost Germanic, with eyes of watered green.

'I didn't believe you would come,' said Lucy.

Vanessa stepped confidently into the hallway. 'To be truthful with you, neither did I.'

She stood quite still for a moment, listening to the chopped-up babble of conversation from the drawing room, then she smiled at Lucy benignly. 'What a pretty house,' she declared. Behind her, the woman in brown said, 'This is a pretty house. Very pretty. Bumpy ride from the station, though. All those ruts and troughs.'

Vanessa said, 'Oh, forgive me. This is Miss Hope Petworth, my sister-in-law. You don't mind? But she's been staying for a while.'

'How do you do?' asked Lucy.

The butler took their hats and their coats and their gloves. Miss Petworth said, 'You *do* look alike, you two, no question about it. Peas in a pod.'

Vanessa scrutinized Lucy with embarrassing intensity. 'Lucy is expecting a baby,' she declared. 'There's *that* much difference, at least. I don't know, Lucy, what do you think? Do you think we look that much alike?'

She took hold of Lucy's arm and guided her over to the wide hall mirror. 'There!' she said. 'Utterly different, when you compare us side by side.'

In fact (and Vanessa must have seen this, too), the resemblance was uncanny; and all the more uncanny because, feature for feature, they were quite unlike. Their hair was a different shade of blonde; Vanessa's darker, verging on the coppery.

Vanessa's eyes were green; whereas Lucy's were positively blue. Lucy was slightly shorter than Vanessa, with smaller breasts and narrower hips. And Vanessa's nose was incontrovertibly longer. But they still looked like sisters; and there was more than a physical resemblance. There was something about the way in which they spoke, and carried themselves. They were so alike that both of them could see at once that they could never be friends.

'I didn't want to upset any applecarts,' said Lucy.

'Of course not,' Vanessa replied. She spoke with the same distinctive accent as Henry, part North of England, part eighteenth-century. Very few people except Northern aristocrats spoke like that any more. 'Anyway, applecarts are specifically made for upsetting. Henry's still my brother, after all, and I have to feel proud of him, whether I like it or not'.

Lucy had written to Vanessa at her Lancashire address, although Sha-sha had told her that she would be visiting London. *My dear Vanessa . . . you are the only one of Henry's brothers and sisters I have not yet met . . . I understand that you and Henry have fallen out, although nobody has told me why. But may I appeal to you to come to Reigate for our farewell weekend party . . . because whatever has happened to divide you, we must all be proud of Henry's great achievement, in being appointed to India. He wishes to reconcile the differences of an entire people . . . surely, before he goes, his own family can reconcile their differences . . .'*

'Let's go in now,' said Lucy.

Vanessa primped her hair. 'I'm nervous,' she admitted.

'He's still your brother,' Lucy reminded her.

'Yes,' said Vanessa. 'Precisely.'

'I think I'd like to powder my nose,' Hope Petworth announced.

'The lavatory is on the left,' Lucy told her; and Hope Petworth disappeared.

Lucy said to Vanessa, 'You're not cross that I invited you?'

'I wouldn't have come, my dear, had I been truly cross,' Vanessa smiled at her. 'But, yes, I will admit to butterflies.'

'We'd better go in.'

Inviting Vanessa may have been reckless. Lucy couldn't tell. But nobody in the Carson family seemed to have been prepared to tell her just how reckless it was. The only way to find out for sure had been to invite her, and to worry about the consequences if and when they came. In any case, Lucy was much less vulnerable these days to the Carson family's displeasure. She was to be Vicereine, whatever they said; and Henry was to be Viceroy. Even Henry had to mind his Ps and Qs. He didn't dare to argue outspokenly with Lucy in front of their friends; and he certainly wouldn't risk a major scene. He and Lucy were always seen smiling, arm-in-arm; and he called her 'sweetheart' these days, as a matter of course.

They opened the drawing-room doors and joined the throng. As they did so, however, the group nearest to them abruptly fell silent; then the next group; then the next. In a matter of moments, the whole drawing room was deathly quiet; and all eyes were focused on Vanessa, standing in the doorway, and Henry, leaning against the fireplace, where he had been arrested right in the middle of the joke about the horse with two masters.

Henry slowly straightened himself. His eyes shone black and protuberant, lobster's eyes, and his cheeks were flushed. He tugged at his waistcoat, and adjusted his necktie. Then he stepped forward and said, slightly too loudly, 'Vanessa! What a surprise!'

Vanessa came forward in her rustling green dress and took hold of Henry's outstretched hand. 'Lucy invited me. She thought that you and I ought to make up, before you left to take up your illustrious post in India. After all, you're not simply my brother any more, are you? You're a national institution. You can't bear ill-will against a national institution. It would be just as absurd as hating the House of Lords.'

Henry couldn't stop staring at her. 'You've changed, Vanessa,' he told her, so quietly that most people in the drawing room were unable to hear. 'You've changed very much'.

'Have I?' said Vanessa. 'Marriage, Henry, that's what does it. Marriage, and time. Perhaps time more than marriage. Or perhaps you've grown so used to Lucy that you've forgotten what I look like.'

'You're still very –' Henry began. Lucy guessed that he was trying to say 'beautiful', or perhaps 'outspoken', but his mouth opened and closed and no words came out.

He stepped forward, two difficult steps as if he were trying to catch the timing of a waltz, and embraced her. She made no attempt to embrace him in return; but stood quite tall and still, smiling at everybody else over his shoulder.

'You must have a glass of champagne,' Henry insisted. 'Lucy . . . where's the champagne?'

Gradually, the conversation in the drawing room began to pick up again. Arthur Balfour told a story about Indian servants; and how they could only be persuaded to do what you wanted by suggestion, rather than direct demand. If your wife had left her hat in the carriage, for instance, it was more effective to instigate a roundabout conversation about how hats might suffer in the enclosed heat of a carriage, rather than give your servant a direct command to go and fetch the bloody thing.

Lucy stayed close to Henry, guarding him, almost, from Vanessa's obvious hostility. They talked about packing; about parties; about Afghanistan. A long, stilted and ultimately meaningless conversation which even somebody who didn't know either of them could have identified as the wariest of fencing-matches. Parry, riposte, parry.

After twenty minutes, Vanessa left Henry's circle in mid-conversation and started talking to Charty. Lucy noticed, however, that Henry didn't take his eyes off her, wherever she went; and that when she laughed – a high, trilling laugh

439

that everybody could hear – he actually winced, as if he had caught his finger in the door.

A little after two o'clock, when they had eaten *à la Russe*, pheasant hash and devilled whitebait and fruit-flavoured creams, Vanessa suddenly said, 'I should leave now, Lucy my dear. Henry! We have to go, I'm afraid. I want to get back to London in time to dress for the theatre.'

'Well, then, yes. It is a long trip back to Town.' Henry lifted his arms, and then let them fall. He looked terribly bowed and defeated, almost hunchbacked, and Lucy couldn't think why. 'I'm very gratified that you could come,' Henry told Vanessa. 'If you can possibly get out to Calcutta; or to Simla . . .'

Gratified? thought Lucy. Vanessa has treated him worse than a tramp who hasn't even asked her for sixpence. How can he be gratified?

She saw Vanessa and Hope Petworth to the door. Henry made a point of staying behind in the drawing room, laughing with unnatural loudness.

'Perhaps I made a mistake,' said Lucy, worriedly.

Vanessa smiled, and then kissed her, once on each cheek. 'Good luck,' she whispered.

'Good luck,' said Hope Petworth, and suddenly hugged her tight, as if they were cousins.

'Did I make a dreadful mistake?' Lucy repeated. She had invited Vanessa to The Vines in the hope that she might understand Henry more clearly; but now she was even more confused than ever. Why were Henry and Vanessa so antagonistic to each other? From the moment that Vanessa had walked into the drawing room, the air had been rattling with aggression.

Vanessa's carriage rolled away, leaving water-filled ruts in the mud. As she watched them disappear between the laurels, Lucy was conscious of Blanche standing close behind her. She turned, and climbed the steps, and then linked arms.

'Do you think I was wrong to invite her?'

'Adventurous, perhaps.'

'I don't see why.'

Sha-sha said, 'Henry is still our brother, you know, whatever happens. And Vanessa is still my sister.'

Lucy grasped Sha-sha's fingers. They were very cold. 'I know that,' she said. 'But I'm his wife.' She looked around. A thin wet snow was falling, but surprisingly it wasn't particularly cold. 'Can we talk in the garden?' she asked Sha-sha.

'All right. Let me get my coat. I could do with some good cold country air, to sober me up.'

They walked between the damp black rose arches, and the snow prickled on their furs. Somehow, in this silent bitterness, Lucy found it easier to talk.

She said, as bravely as she could manage, 'The truth is, our intimate life hasn't always been very easy. Henry is always working so late. Usually he doesn't come to bed until two or three o'clock in the morning, and then he's up again at half-past six.'

'So it's overwork, and nothing more?' asked Sha-sha.

Lucy shook her head. 'I think I could tolerate, if it were. But he seems to want to punish himself all the time. He doesn't seem to be able to make love to me unless he feels humiliated, or actually hurt.'

She hesitated. 'You don't mind my telling you this?'

'Of course not,' said Sha-sha. She thought for a moment, and then she stopped, keeping her huge fur coat wrapped tightly around her. 'Let me say something to you in utmost confidence. You are Henry's wife; you have a right to know. But nobody else must ever so much as *suspect* it.'

They carried on walking. It took Sha-sha a long time to find the right words to begin her story. Crows cawed harshly in the surrounding trees. The soles of their boots crunched on the gritty York stone pathway.

At last, Sha-sha said, 'One of the reasons that Henry fell for you so quickly and so absolutely was because of Vanessa.

You look very alike. Well, you must have noticed. But it's not just your looks. You have the same kind of personality as Vanessa, too. Sharp, amusing, independent. You could be Vanessa reborn.'

They reached the very end of the path, then stopped, and looked along the grey-green backs of the Downs, towards Box Hill.

Sha-sha said, 'You must have noticed by now that Vanessa never appears at family gatherings when there is the slightest possibility of Henry being there. I was quite amazed that she came today'.

'Sha-sha, he's the Viceroy Designate. It's almost like being the heir to the throne. I had to ask her. I had to give her the chance, if nothing else'.

'I know, Lucy. I know. But what happened between Henry and Vanessa . . .'

Lucy turned and faced Sha-sha, and clutched at her sleeve. 'Sha-sha, listen to me. I'm almost five months' pregnant, with Henry's baby. I'm going to India with him. I'm supposed to act as his Queen. If there's *anything* I ought to know . . .'

Blanche lifted her face; and in that wintry gum-coloured light she looked startlingly old, and tired, and the wrinkles under her eyes looked like badly-pressed silk.

She said, with self-protective weariness, as if she had become bored with telling it, 'They fell in love.'

'They did what?'

'They fell in love. Well, he more than her; but there was a time when she found him entrancing, and of course bad led to worse.'

'Tell me,' Lucy insisted.

'There's nothing to tell,' shrugged Sha-sha.

'I'm carrying his baby!' Lucy shouted at her. 'Who has more right to know than I?'

Sha-sha said nothing for a while, but tugged down her gloves and looked at Lucy pointedly.

'They fell in love,' Sha-sha said stiffly. 'Henry was just sixteen years old, and Vanessa was thirteen-and-a-half.'

'And they were in love?'

'How do you define love, my dear? Vanessa was infatuated, but Henry was obsessed. You can see how pretty she is, even today. When she was fourteen, she was magical. Henry was absolutely captivated. I know how hard he fought himself *not* to be in love with her. But there was nothing he could do. If you're obsessed, you're obsessed. He never left her alone. He was always writing her poems and drawing her pictures and buying her trinkets. He lived for every school holiday when he would see her again.'

Sha-sha's nostrils widened as she took a deep, steadying breath. 'You must remember that this is in the strictest of confidences, between you and me and nobody else. But you are going to a strange and difficult country, where every one of your personal resources will be tested to the utmost; and I believe that it will help you to improve your marriage and to understand your husband more sympathetically if you know the truth.'

'And what is the truth?'

Sha-sha took out her tiny lace handkerchief, and dabbed at her eyes, although she wasn't crying. 'Henry went into Vanessa's bed one night, and attempted to dishonour her.'

'You mean he —?'

'Forcibly, yes. And her screaming woke the entire household'.

'Oh, my God.' said Lucy. Her stomach tightened, and she held her hands across it. 'Oh, my God. What happened?'

'What do you think?' Sha-sha shrugged. 'The whole household came running. Henry was caught, Vanessa was hysterical. It was Bedlam. Henry — well, Henry was awash with shame and mortification. They would have sent him away, but he kept threatening to kill himself, and Vanessa pleaded that nobody should know that anything was wrong. In the end, the whole family decided that they would simply forget it – pretend that it had never happened. Far worse disasters had struck the Carson family since they came over to England with William the Conqueror. Poisonings, rapes, and incestuous acts. They decided, I think, that it was simply a part of English history'.

'But is that why Henry keeps punishing himself?' asked Lucy.

Sha-sha nodded. 'Mm!' she concurred. 'That's right! And poor Henry has never stopped punishing himself since. That was why we were all so pleased when he brought *you* home to Brackenbridge. We all believed that you would be the miraculous solution to all of his difficulties. After all, you look so much like Vanessa – we felt that at last he might be able to stop castigating himself.'

Lucy stood in the foggy garden feeling quite unreal. So that was Henry's terrible burden; that was why he demanded that she hurt him, and that she punish him. That was why he had forgiven her so easily for sleeping with Malty. In his eyes, that had been nothing, compared with the sin that *he* had committed.

'Well?' asked Sha-sha, after a while.

Lucy gave her a small smile. 'I'm pleased you told me. It explains a whole lot'.

'You won't tell him I told you? You won't even hint that you know? You would almost certainly destroy him, if you told him that you knew'.

'He needs to feel forgiven, that's all,' said Lucy.

'Well, yes, I suppose you're right. But Vanessa obviously hasn't forgiven him, and of course he doesn't care much for God. If only he were a Catholic, he might have got over it all years ago! Two dozen Hail Marys and twenty pounds in the poor-box, and his guilt would have been lifted for ever.'

Later, when the winter darkness had clamped itself over the Downs, Henry came into the bedroom where Lucy was brushing out her hair. He stood by the dressing-table for a while, twiddling his silver pen between his fingers, watching the way the lamplight gleamed on her curls. Her hair had all the glossiness of healthy pregnancy; her breasts beneath her nightgown were noticeably fuller.

'Why did you do that?' he asked her, his voice parched.

'You mean, why did I invite Vanessa?'

He was plainly trying to control his temper. 'I've told you countless times that Vanessa and I don't get on'.

She kept on brushing. 'I thought perhaps it was time that you did.'

'Lucy . . . certain events have taken place in this family about which you know nothing. I'd prefer it if they stayed that way. I can't stand your – meddling in affairs which don't concern you.'

Lucy was tempted to say that Sha-sha had told her every-thing about Vanessa; but she remembered her promise, and kept her peace. It was a pity, in a way, that she couldn't discuss it with him. She found his love for Vanessa quite understandable, especially in the light of the passion that Uncle Casper had exhibited for her; and for his own sister, her mother. Just because people were related, that didn't mean they couldn't find each other attractive. That didn't mean they were immune from falling in love.

Henry turned away, still fiddling with his pen. After a while he said, 'Well . . . I suppose no real harm has been done.'

Lucy laid down her hairbrush. 'Couldn't you find a way of making up with her? It seems such a pity that you can't be friends.'

Henry shook his head. 'No, she won't have it. You saw how damned frosty she was. I don't know why she came. Just to brag that she's seen me, I suppose, when she goes back to Lancashire.'

'Are you coming to bed?' Lucy asked him.

'Not yet. I still have to finish listing my reference books. I shan't be longer than two or three hours.'

'Henry –' Lucy began. He paused with his hand on the open door. 'Henry, don't you want to talk about Vanessa at all? Maybe I could help.'

Henry thought about that for a moment, and then replied, 'As far as Vanessa is concerned, my dearest, I believe I am probably beyond help.'

They sailed for Calcutta two weeks before Christmas on the British India Line's *Star of Bengal*. Henry went up on deck to watch England melt into the pewter-coloured afternoon light, but Lucy stayed in her stateroom, flipping through magazines and eating crystallized violets.

Out past the Isle of Wight, the steamer began that steady tilting and rolling that she knew would make her feel sick until she got to Calcutta. She closed the lid of the crystallized violets box, and wished she hadn't eaten quite so many.

Henry had instructed her to read up all she could about life and protocol in India – especially the guide to the daily round at Government House that had been painstakingly written for her in mauve ink by Lady Elgin. But she hadn't even opened the books that he had acquired for her, and Lady Elgin's close-written notes remained unread in their envelope. There would be plenty of time for that; and besides, she didn't yet want to think about India. At first she had been overjoyed at the prospect of visiting the continent that had been ground up like magic powder and shut up in Jack Darling's spice boxes. But Henry had been working so hard lately that they scarcely spoke; and it was like setting out for a strange land with a man she scarcely knew.

What was more, she felt as if Henry were taking her even farther away from baby Blanche, to a world so remote that she might never come back; and that upset her far more than she had imagined it would.

She had been appointed a travelling-companion, Mrs Nancy Bull, the wife of the Collector of Benares, who was returning to rejoin her husband after a Christmas at Home.

After fourteen years of living in India, Mrs Bull was bustling and bossy, a wide-hipped woman with a waddling gait and a face that was an explosion of peppery freckles. She knew everything and everybody, and brooked absolutely no impertinence or inefficiency from anybody, especially Indians.

'They will do as little as possible,' she warned Lucy, about Indian servants. 'And they will expect as much as possible in return. They are all scallywags.'

But she possessed an understanding of what it meant to leave one's home behind that was almost lyrical. 'The first time I came out, nobody had told me about the cord that is paid out behind one as the boat moves on, seeming to link one with the country and the life that one has left. As one travels farther, you know, it stretches; but it is always tugging at one's heart as if to prevent one from turning one's face forward, to go on, as a free person, to the East.'

Apart from Mrs Bull, and Nora, Lucy had also been appointed a lady's maid, Etta Brightwater, a brisk young widow from Sussex who had previously been employed by the Norfolks. Etta had worked as a maid in Lady Elgin's household when she first arrived in Calcutta, but she had returned home after only a year, widowed. Her husband had drunk unboiled water at an Indian feast, and died within two days of cholera. Etta was small and quick, sharp like a little mouse, and remarkably pretty in a countrified way. She had told Lucy that she couldn't wait to get back to India.

'I thought as how I missed Home so badly. But when I got back, there it was, same as usual, green and grey, same old faces, same old England. And no colour to it, just like it had been washed, and all the dyes had faded.'

Nora was suspicious of Etta at first. 'Even the Vicereine of Injure doesn't have the need for *two* lady's maids.' But when she began to understand how much work there was for them to do, constantly packing and unpacking clothes, cleaning gloves and mending stockings, she began to appreciate the wisdom of Etta's appointment, and to rub along well with her. It helped that Nora was marginally higher in the order of precedence, and could tell Etta which clothes to fetch from the 'Present Use' baggage, and which of Lady Carson's gowns to lay out, and which shoes to clean. Occasionally Lucy thought that Nora was far too demanding, all the sewing and sponging that she told Etta to do, but Etta didn't seem to mind, and Lucy guessed that once the novelty of exercising her bright new ha'porth of power had worn off, Nora would probably stop her ordering-about, and return to her usual tolerant and light-hearted Irishness.

Henry's moods changed wildly, almost by the half-hour. One minute he would be laughing and playing practical jokes – 'fizzy as champagne', as his valet described it. The next, he would be deeply morose, scarcely speaking to anybody. Then he would become furiously over-active, issuing dozens of instructions to his overworked staff, asking for letters, information, statistics, and estimates. Next he would become withdrawn and solemn and pompous. In those moments, Lucy knew that he was thinking about his glorious new position in the British Empire; not just as governor and superintendent of the greatest jewel in Victoria's crown, but as her embodiment.

He would speak almost mystically during moments like those; of noble duty; of dominions on which the sun never set; of the paramount power with which he would soon be invested.

But in those moments he would sound painfully lonely, too.

It wasn't just that, as Viceroy Designate, it was impossible for him to join in too boisterously with the social life of the ship. His private secretary Walter Pangborn was travelling with them, as smooth and as lazy as ever, as well as a relentlessly brisk wax-moustachioed ADC, Colonel Timothy Miller, eleven of his new staff, six officers of the Viceregal Bodyguard, and Sir Evan Maconochie of the

Indian Civil Service. But the remaining passengers were mainly Indian Army officers, engineers, civil servants, planters, and the wives and children of district officers and estate-managers.

The root of his loneliness was that, although Calcutta still lay thousands of miles distant, Henry was already becoming obsessed with the difficulties of governing a continent so vast and so tumultuous. In particular, it irked him that his mandate over India would not be complete. Historically, the Punjab government under its own British Lieutenant-Governor conducted its affairs more or less independently; and the British governors of Madras and Bombay – both important provincial presidencies – rarely felt it necessary to tell the Viceroy what they were up to.

They were talking about this difficulty as they sat at dinner in their stateroom, the night they passed through the Straits of Gibraltar. Henry suddenly raged, 'It's wrong! I can't understand how Elgin tolerated it! The Viceroy should govern India without any circumscription whatsoever!'

His loneliness was reflected in his day-to-day habits. He became obsessive about procedure and ceremony and correctness. He had always been an exact dresser, but these days he spent twice as long with his new valet, making sure that he always appeared immaculate. His valet was a Cockney called Vernon, a tall brown-eyed man with the looks of a handsome boxer, 'a little uncertain about his aspirates', as Henry liked to put it (he dropped his aitches), but always attentive and discreet. He was the first body-servant with whom Henry had been at all impressed. He was also the first body-servant who – within limits – could answer Henry back.

Lucy wasn't sure that she liked or trusted Vernon. She didn't like the deadness in his eyes. She always felt that he could see through her; that he could tell she hadn't been highly born. *Takes one to know one*, he was always saying, for no apparent reason whatsoever.

449

She talked to Henry about Vernon, in a roundabout way, but Henry ignored her. Henry thought of nothing but India, India, India. He could smell his power and his position, like the alluring smell of spices on the wind. He was so hungry for it that on his infrequent strolls on deck he would stand facing the East, cracking his knuckles.

He began speaking to everybody, even Lucy, with stilted formality. He would pay her compliments as if he were addressing an Indian maharanee. 'You have an exceptionally graceful air about you this evening,' or, 'your hair is combed in a very captivating manner.' At the same time, anybody who talked to her with what Henry considered to be a lack of deference to the Vicereine-to-be would be harshly and quickly brought to heel.

One critical reason for his stiffness towards her, Lucy guessed, was that he was tightly suppressing his sexual desires. He refused to risk making love to her, no matter how he might have wanted to. He wanted an heir, Horatio Henry Carson, and he would rather remain celibate for six months than risk provoking a miscarriage.

A few hours before the *Star of Bengal* was due to dock at Valletta for coaling, Sir Evan Maconochie took Lucy for a promenade on the deck. She wore a light French-grey coat and a plain hat tied with a scarf. Sir Evan wore a grey frock-coat.

'Lord Carson seems somewhat distracted,' Sir Evan remarked. 'I trust that everything is well?'

'I think he's preparing himself for India, that's all,' Lucy replied.

'Well, agreed, it won't be easy,' nodded Sir Evan. 'He knows India extremely well, of course. Better than some district officers. More *comprehensively*, anyway. But all the same, it is one thing to come to India as a district officer, and quite another to come to India as Viceroy.'

'It's difficult to understand what he's feeling,' said Lucy. 'He seems to be cutting himself off . . . shutting himself away from everybody.'

Sir Evan stood by the rail with his hands clasped behind his back and took a noisy breath of fresh air. 'He needs to *distance* himself, certainly. And so will you. To all intents and purposes, he will be king and you will be queen.'

'I thought kings and queens could do what they wanted.'

Sir Evan grunted with amusement. 'In fairy stories, perhaps. But not in India. In India, both British and natives will expect you to conduct yourselves as divine beings. Don't you understand? Both British and natives measure their standing by where *you* stand. The viceroyalty is the pinnacle of the entire society.'

Lucy leaned against the rail and let the cool Mediterranean breeze blow into her face. 'Mrs Bull was making a whole lot of fuss about – what did she call it? – the pecking-order.'

'Oh, yes,' said Sir Evan. 'I prefer to call it the order of precedence.'

'She said there was even a printed book about it, who's more important than whom.'

'Indeed, the Warrant of Precedence. The *burra memsahib's* Bible! No society hostess would ever dare to seat her guests without it. It's mostly a middle-class society, you see, a salaried society, in which the only way in which your social supremacy can be measured is by what you do, or by what your husband does.

'The élite are the members of the Indian Civil Service – governors, judges, district officers, members of the Viceroy's Council. Slightly below them are the members of the Indian Political Service, who take care of the Indian princes and the frontier people. Then comes the Indian Medical Service and the upper echelons of the Public Works Department. Then, Indian Army officers – depending on their regiment, of course – cavalry almost always preferred to infantry, although the Gurkhas are generally smiled upon. Members of the Education Department, however, tend to be sniffed at; and subordinate civil servants are right on the very frontiers of respectable society. Clergyman are practically pariahs;

and retail merchants are *never* invited anywhere, no matter how wealthy they may be.'

He paused, and took a small silver snuffbox out of his vest pocket, and helped himself to two sharp pinches of Rappee snuff.

'At the very base of the social ladder in British India are the Domiciled Europeans and those of mixed blood, the Eurasians, the *chee-chees*, so-called because of their sing-song accents. They are never invited to the best parties; or to join any of the clubs. Personally I think they are the saddest lot of all. They are always trying to ape their betters; and they are always talking with such nostalgia of a Home they have never seen, and never will.'

Lucy said, 'Do you know something, Sir Evan, I'm not at all sure I care for the sound of so much precedence. I mean, if there aren't any lords and there aren't any ladies, it just sounds like snobbery to me. Even in New York – '

Sir Evan gave her a tight smile, suppressing a sneeze. 'Calcutta is not New York, my dear Lady Carson. Precedence is the Indian way. The Indians themselves observe strict orders of caste. Amongst the Hindu, there are the pukka Brahmins, the heaven-born; the Kshatrias, the warrior-class; then the Vaisyas, the merchant and moneylending class, and so forth, down to the very lowest, the Untouchables. Lord Carson and your good self will be leading a very hectic life, socially. You will regularly be fêted with a lavishness which Her Majesty the Queen-Empress herself might envy. You will be regarded almost as demi-gods. But, after a fashion, yes, you will always be alone.'

Lucy slowly shook her head. 'I've never been alone in my life, Sir Evan. Believe me, I don't intend to be alone now.'

Sir Evan hesitated for just a moment, and then he cleared his throat, and sniffed, and added, 'This may sound impertinent, Lady Carson, but do believe me when I tell you that I intend it in the best possible of spirits. They say that it doesn't go down too well for women in India to be too –

well, this isn't meant to be denigrating – but women should make something of an effort not to appear too *clever*. There are some clever ladies, but generally they take considerable pains to keep it quiet.'

He paused, sniffed again, and looked at her warily. 'You do see what I'm driving at?'

The *Star of Bengal* stopped for twenty-four hours at Malta to take on coal. That evening, Henry and Lucy were given a dull dinner at Government House, under chandeliers so dim that they could scarcely see what they were eating (grilled sardines; followed by fatty leg of lamb, with carrots; and trifle for dessert). The dinner went on far longer than Henry had hoped, and he began to fret, especially when the Governor launched into an interminable story about a catastrophically incompetent butler who had once worked for him. 'Lifted the meat-cover, didn't he, with such a flourish, and there were my missing trousers, for all to see!'

That night, back in his stateroom, Henry stood quivering and speechless with tension for almost a minute. Then he clenched his fist and smashed it against his desk, so hard that he split the skin across his knuckles.

'Henry!' Lucy exclaimed.

'It's nothing,' Henry told her, winding a handkerchief around his hand. Then, much more quietly, 'It's nothing. I can't stand to waste time, that's all. Doesn't anybody realize how much I have to do?'

'Henry, you have to rest sometime.'

'When do you suggest?'

'Well, I suggest now. You're not going back to work tonight, are you?'

'Lucy, I have to. I have no choice.'

He turned to her. His face was grey with exhaustion. 'There's so much to do. So many dispatches to answer. An entire report on Kowait. Besides, I have to finish writing up our personal accounts. We have a salary of sixteen thousand

453

pounds per annum. How we're going to be able to afford to entertain all those nizams and maharajahs and rajas, I have no idea.'

'Henry, for goodness' sake, Walter is supposed to do your accounts.'

'It will take him twice as long, Lucy; and I will still have to satisfy myself that they're correct.'

'Henry, you're Viceroy now! You have a whole staff and hundreds of servants! When are you going to stop being your own servant?'

Henry tugged tightly at his necktie. 'Lucy, I'm a servant by destiny. Not only my own servant, but *your* servant, and my country's servant, and the servant of everybody in India, no matter what their colour, no matter what gods they worship.'

'Henry, your health is more important than India. Your health is more important than anything. Henry, I'm carrying your baby.'

She watched Henry's highly-polished shoes pacing from one side of the scarlet stateroom carpet to the other.

Then he stopped pacing, and walked across to his desk, and made a considerable performance of unrolling his large-scale map of India, all billowing paper and crackling folds, and weighing it down with a book and an inkwell.

'Come here,' he beckoned her. Then, 'Come here, Lucy, look.'

She came and she looked. 'Well?' she asked. 'It's pink and it's yellow.'

'That's right. It's pink and it's yellow. British pink, native yellow. In the west here, look – Baluchistan and Sind – separated from the rest of British India by a string of native states, running all the way from the Eastern Ghats to the mountains of Rajputana. In the south, we have the Central Provinces, and the two Presidencies of Bombay and Madras, divided from each other by the native states of Mysore and Hyderabad. In the east, we have the Bengal Presidency, and the province of Assam. And here, north-westward from Bengal, run the solid line of British provinces that make up the spine of British India: Bihar, the United Provinces, and the Punjab, all the way up to the North-West Frontier.

'There are ten British provinces, and five hundred and sixty-two native states. To all intents and purposes, they go their separate ways. We let the natives run their own affairs. Some of them are civilized; some of them are quite barbaric. There are two thousand three hundred recognized castes, sects, and creeds in India. We could not hope to administer them all closely, nor would we wish to. But they all have one thing in common: one thing! They all share a common allegiance to Her Majesty the Queen-Empress, in my person, the Viceroy.

'That is my responsibility. That is why I have to go on working, no matter how much of a burden it sometimes becomes. And that is why I am asking for your tolerance, and your strength, rather than your censure.'

He looked down at the map a moment longer; then lifted off the inkwell and rolled it up.

Lucy said softly, 'I'm sorry. I don't think I really understood just how hard it was going to be for you. I thought, well – I don't know. I thought you were going to be a figurehead, and that was all.'

'Well, you would, you're an American,' said Henry. 'But I am many other things besides. A king, an administrator, a judge, a general, a guiding light.'

'Thank goodness India has quite enough gods,' Lucy replied.

'You're not to mock,' Henry reprimanded her; although he knew that there was very little he could do to stop her.

'You'd better get to work,' Lucy suggested. 'I think I'll go to bed and read Lady Elgin's instructions. "At 9.35 pm their Excellencies will attend an out-of-door performance of *Merrie England* in aid of the Diocesan Women's Hostel."'

'You're going to be a queen, Lucy. You're not to mock.'

'Henry, I'm not mocking. I just don't want to be the queen in the nursery-rhyme, that's all, sitting in the parlour, eating bread and honey, while her king spends all his time in his counting-house, counting out his money.'

Henry walked back across the stateroom and took Lucy in his arms. Her stomach was protuberant enough now for him to have to stand a little way back.

'I will be your king, I promise you.'

She didn't hear Henry come to bed that night; and when she woke in the morning he was already gone. The sunlight was reflected from Valletta harbour, and played criss-cross patterns on the stateroom ceiling. She lay on her back for almost ten minutes, slowly waking herself up and thinking of India. When Henry had first told her that he had been appointed Viceroy, she had imagined a land of spices. But after what Henry and Sir Evan had told her, all she could imagine was a land as dark and stifling as a cupboard, a labyrinth of precedence and prejudice and never-ending toil.

A little after eight, she rang for Nora and Etta to dress her. She wore a skirt and jacket of maroon velvet, and a blouse of creamy-coloured lace, with lacy cuffs. She joined Mrs Bull for breakfast in the first-class dining room, with its parlour palms and its oil-painted landscapes of famous Indian landmarks, the Taj Mahal at Agra, the Palace of Winds at Jaipur, the Tower of Victory at Chitorgarh. She had lightly scrambled eggs. It was too windy and cool to eat out on deck; but it was just the weather for sightseeing.

'Do you think you could persuade that young officer with the Scottish accent and the black hair to take us on a tour?' she asked Mrs Bull.

Mrs Bull was mortified. 'Persuade him, Lady Carson? I'll *order* him!'

So by ten o'clock, they had made up a shore party with Mrs Bull and Nora and John McCrae, the *Star of Bengal*'s handsome young Aberdonian first officer, to act as guide, and two officers from the Viceroy's Bodyguard, Captain Roger Philips and Lieutenant Ashley Burnes-Waterton, in scarlet uniforms that were more gorgeous than anything worn by the Brigade of Guards. They took two victorias to the Strada Reale to shop for coral and silver and lace. Lucy managed to buy Henry a pair of coral cufflinks, and a silver hip-flask engraved with the cross of the Knights of St John, but it was only a few minutes before she was surrounded by noisy crowds of onlookers, some of whom guessed who she was, and cheered, 'Hooray for Lady Carson!' Captain Philips was looking strained and crimson in the face from all the jostling, so Lucy agreed to leave the Strada Reale and tour the rest of the town. Young Mr McRae reluctantly agreed to take them to see the embalmed bodies of members of the Carmelite Order, the famous 'pickled monks', but afterwards, in the brightness of the streets, Nora complained of feeling dizzy, and Lucy could feel her baby and her breakfast swimming together in one congealing emulsion, yellow and pink, like the Viceroy's map of India.

'You'll see worse than that in India, ma'am,' Mrs Bull promised her, waddling along beside her as they returned to their carriage, one hand keeping her wide-brimmed hat firmly clamped on top of her head. 'I hope we don't have that awful Solferino soup for lunch again.'

'Or pickled monk, what?' suggested John McCrae, grinning.

'That'll be quite enough of that,' Mrs Bull snapped back at him.

Slowly the *Star of Bengal* sailed the length of the Mediterranean, a blurred white ship on a misty blue sea. The weather was similar to an English September: sunny but cool. It was difficult to remember that they had left Southampton only a few days before on a scrapingly raw day, with threatened snow.

Port Said was the first truly oriental stop on the journey.

On a warm windy afternoon they were greeted at the dock by Sir Evelyn Bentley, the Consul-General, and Lady Bentley, and by the Khedive, Abbas Halmi, and by scores of ministers and officials and ADCs, and a fleet of black landaus that had been polished as bright as Army boots. For no comprehensible reason, a brilliantly-uniformed band played *Scotland the Brave* and then *It Came Upon A Midnight Clear*.

They were invited to a formal lunch at the Bur Said Hotel, in a huge cool dining room overlooking a blue-tiled courtyard, where a fountain splashed. Tall black-faced men in fezzes brought them *molokheya* soup, charcoal-grilled mutton, and *ful medames*, with marzipan *bakwala*. It was Lucy's first taste of Eastern food; but the white-haired Lady Bentley sat opposite her and gave her motherly guidance on what to eat, and how. 'The left hand, you see! Splendid!' and, 'for goodness' sake, don't try to eat that!'

The Khedive told a story about his father, Tewfit, and how he had won a wager when he was young by running all the way around the Pyramid of Cheops with an orange between his knees. Nobody knew whether to laugh or applaud or to receive the story in respectful silence, but the Khedive himself obviously thought it was hilarious, because he laughed so much that his servants had to bring him a glass of water.

Afterwards, the Khedive returned to Cairo and Henry withdrew to a private suite to talk to Sir Evelyn about Russian encroachment on the eastern Mediterranean and the Persian Gulf. Lady Bentley and an enthusiastic young ADC called Minchin took them on a sightseeing tour of Port Said, accompanied by Captain Philips and Lieutenant Burnes-Waterton, and two tall black officers of the Khedive's official bodyguard, who wore red fezzes and white uniforms with red epaulets, and carried ceremonial swords. Mrs Bull, of course, came too; and so did the bothersome lady wife of the Superintendent of Police at Coimbatore, in Madras, who was almost hysterically excited at being invited anywhere with the new Vicereine (whom she had been inspecting on deck from a distance, through opera-glasses).

'Duncan simply won't believe me!' she fussed. 'I'll be the talk of the *moorghi khana*.'

'What's a *moorghi khana*?' Lucy wanted to know.

'Strictly translated, a henhouse,' said Mrs Bull, grasping the handles of Lady Bentley's carriage as if she were preparing to wrestle it like an ox, and overturn it. 'A room for the ladies; most clubs have them these days.'

Port Said was noisy and chaotic and smelled like nothing that Lucy had ever smelled before: of dust, and charcoal-smoke, and heavy perfume, and sweet-potatoes, which were sold in the winter months like chestnuts and bagels in New York. As they left the Bur Said Hotel, their landau was surrounded by crowds of ragged boys, beggars, fortune-tellers, and men juggling with eggs and day-old chicks. They were pursued down the street as they were driven off, passing through light and shadow, past fruit-stalls and awnings and shops advertising Copperware and Best Quality Solar Topis.

'Just for fun, I'll take you to Simon Artz,' said Lady Bentley, fanning herself as they rattled through the streets. 'Everybody who comes out East has to go there at least once. They sell everything from topis to Turkish delight. And you'll see their striped shawls on the shoulders of practically every *memsahib* in India. But don't buy anything; especially their ghastly topis. I have a double terai for you, for the Cold Weather, and a Cawnpore Tent Club topi for the Hot. Much more practical. And some beautiful shawls I found in Cairo.'

They reached the marble-pillared entrance to Simon Artz's emporium, and young Minchin assisted Lucy and Lady Bentley down from the carriage. A party of Europeans were just leaving the store, fresh out from England on their first trip to India, all of them kitted out in huge and conspicuously brand-new topis. They were cleared aside by the Khedive's bodyguards, just like everybody else. One of the men declared, 'Here – I say!' and was about to remind the Khedive's bodyguard that white was white and black was black, but his girl companion caught his sleeve and pointed out that they were being pushed aside not just for anybody but for the new Vicereine of India.

'Sometimes I wonder how I bear it, you know,' Lady Bentley remarked, as they crossed the pavement. 'The heat, you know; and the general *hugger-mugger*. And I can't *tell* you how much I miss Eaton Square. But Evelyn adores it. He's in his element, all these *fellaheen* to bellow at.'

They had almost reached Simon Artz's doors when there was shouting and scrambling and shrieking from the English girls, and 'I say! Here! I say!' all over again from the English chaps. The crowds parted like the side of a water-filled *wadi* suddenly breaking down, and a staring-eyed long-haired beggar in a fluttering red cloak scrambled his way wildly through the crowds on the pavement and flung himself down at Lucy's feet, pressing his lips to her shoe.

He cried out, barely intelligibly, 'Oh queen, have mercy on me, for the love of Allah! Oh queen, have mercy on me!'

'Oh my God!' Lady Bentley declared. 'Oh my God, get him off!'

One of the Khedive's bodyguard stepped forward, and Lucy heard a sound which she had never heard before, but which she would never forget. Sharp steel, scraping against a scabbard. The bodyguard's sword flicked up, shining. Lucy glanced in horror at the bodyguard's face, and it was smooth and black and completely impassive, with tiny expressionless eyes. He looked as if he were doing nothing more interesting than cutting an offending bramble in the Khedive's garden. But his sword hacked into the beggar's face, right across the bridge of his nose; and like a conjuring trick the beggar's right eye fell out, and rolled across the pavement. Blood sprayed finely on to the bodyguard's leggings; and on to Lucy's shoes.

Lucy squeezed her eyes tight shut, praying that it hadn't happened, that she hadn't seen anything. 'Oh my God,' said Lady Bentley, in a voice like a French horn. 'Lady Carson, quick – back into the carriage! Mr Minchin, what on earth are you doing?'

Mr Minchin was windmilling his arms and staggering in bent-kneed indecision from one side of the pavement to the other. Captain Philips and Lieutenant Burnes-Waterton had run forward – Lieutenant Burnes-Waterton to stand in front of Lucy, brandishing his Webley revolver, although he hadn't cocked it – Captain Philips to guide her back to the landau. He seized her elbow and helped her up. 'Steady now, ma'am. All's well.'

On their way back to the docks, Lucy sat in the carriage trembling and cold. Lady Bentley gave her a shawl to cover her shoulders.

'What a shock, my dear. What a terrible thing to happen! But in the East, you know . . .'

'In the East, *what*?' Lucy demanded. 'That poor man wasn't doing anything at all!'

'My dear, he was touching you.'

'So? So what? He was touching me, so what? He was kissing my shoe, that's all. There's nothing threatening in kissing a person's shoe.' Lucy's Kansas accent came out serrated and twangy as a sawblade.

Lady Bentley patted her arm. 'My dear, he was a *lazar*, and you –'

'What am I?' Lucy wanted to know, her eyes wide, her face white in the Port Said sunshine.

'You are an empress. An *empress*, my dear. Haven't you understood that yet?'

At Port Said, cold weather wear was exchanged for tropical wear, which meant that Nora and Etta were furiously busy packing away all the dresses and skirts which had been marked as Lucy's cabin baggage, and unpacking all the

clothes which had been marked Wanted On Voyage –
embroidered linen blouses, white skirts, white cambric
dresses, white shoes. Double awnings were erected over the
decks, and Mrs Bull gave Lucy a stern warning to 'beware
the sun'.

'The sun is your enemy, Lady Carson, make no mistake
about that. You will never get used to it. Every time you
come out into the open in India, it will hit you like a
hammer. You should never venture anywhere between sun-
rise and sunset without your topi.'

Like a ship in a torpid dream, the *Star of Bengal* drifted its
way down the Suez Canal. The heat grew more intense
every day, and Lucy spent most of the time in her stateroom,
lying on her bed, fanning herself with a giant ostrich-plume
fan that Lady Bentley had given her, trying to read Jane
Austen but thinking of Blanche. '*I am the happiest creature in
the world, for I have received an offer of marriage from Mr
Watts.*' But where was Blanche now? Tucked up in her bed
in her upstairs room in the Cullen farmhouse, with the snow
all around, and the fires crackling? She could hardly believe
that Kansas in winter had ever existed. Perhaps it had all
been a dream. Every time she went out on to the promenade
deck to watch the dun-coloured desert gliding hypnotically
past her, she felt that Kansas had shrunk smaller and smaller,
like a toy snowstorm in a glass bottle, and that soon it
would dwindle away to nothing at all.

She wrote a letter to Blanche, and picked open the stitches
in the lining of her purse, and concealed it inside. Just in case
the ship sank; or she died of cholera, or circumstances made
it impossible for her to go back to Kansas, ever again. No
letter from a mother to a daughter was ever written with
such grief and pain, in spite of the fact that Lucy found it
difficult to express herself on paper.

'*My dearest darling Own One . . .*' the letter began. '*You
will never understand how hard it was to leave you. One day, if
we ever meet again, please don't turn your back to me, please*

don't blame me. I was young. I had my own life to lead. I gave birth to you, I gave you everything I possibly could. You always have a little crib-space in my heart, just like the crib that Mrs Cullen laid you in, when you were first born.'

Henry came into the stateroom, just as she was finishing her letter. He was dressed in immaculate white ducks, and a topi, and he was carrying a sheaf of papers which he had been working on. 'Writing?' he asked, in that same crisp carrying voice that she had heard on Mrs Harris' lawn.

She quickly picked up the letter so that he couldn't see it. He chuckled, and walked across to his desk, and filed his papers away. 'A *billet-doux* to your secret lover, perhaps? Who is it? Captain Philips? Or First Officer McRae?'

'I was trying to write a poem, as a matter of fact.'

'Aha!' He came across to her, rubbing his hands with his handkerchief. 'A love poem? For me? May I see it?'

She crumpled the letter up in her hand. 'It's not very good. Please. I'd rather you didn't.'

He tilted himself forward and kissed her forehead. 'Not to worry. Try and try again, that's my motto. *Fortuna transmutat incertos honores, nunc mihi, nunc alii benigna.'*

He kept on smiling at her. 'How's the child?' he asked her, at last.

For a hairsplit second, Lucy thought that he meant Blanche, that he had discovered everything. But then she realized that he was talking about the baby that was growing in her womb.

'Oh!' she smiled. 'Oh, the child is very well. I'm quite sure already that he's a he. And I'm already quite sure that he looks just like you.'

'You're not too bothered by the heat? It's going to get hotter, once we're past Aden.'

'Henry . . . whatever you can tolerate, I can tolerate too.'

He kissed her again. 'Do you know something, my darling? That first day I saw you, that very first instant, I knew that you'd make me a wonderful wife.'

Henry's ADC appeared, and asked him if he could spare some time to discuss the arrangements for their arrival in Bombay. Henry blew Lucy one more kiss, and then left. She waited for a minute or two, then she slowly uncrumpled her letter.

'*My Own One . . .*' she whispered.

They slid slowly through Ismailia, where bumboats came out to sell them an eclectic cargo of monkeys, onions, shoes and black bread. Some of the passengers amused themselves by throwing pennies at the small boys who ran alongside the ship, whooping and shrieking for money. Lucy had never seen monkeys before and was enchanted with them. One monkey in particular caught her eye: it was gingery and beady-eyed and mischievous, and reminded her of Malty. She would have bought it if Henry hadn't heard her calling out to the merchant, 'You! Hey, you! Let me see that monkey!' and stalked out on to the promenade deck.

'You're Vicereine-to-be, for God's sake! You don't buy flea-ridden monkeys from flea-ridden Arabs! You don't even *talk* to flea-ridden Arabs! As far as you're concerned, they don't exist!'

Lucy had felt hurt, and childish, and embarrassed. So embarrassed, in fact, that she didn't know how to say sorry; or even if she *should* say sorry. She rushed past him; and in through the doors that led to their stateroom, and threw herself on to her bed. *Jamie would have let me have it. Anybody would have let me have it. Anybody, except Henry.*

At last they reached Suez, a scruffy and bleached-out collection of rundown buildings, under a sky the colour of writing-ink. A few of the soldiers went ashore for donkey-rides and beer; the rest of the passengers stayed under the ship's awnings and began to realize what heat really meant.

The next day the *Star of Bengal* passed starkly through the Red Sea, dazzling white on intense blue. Already, Lucy had begun to notice signs that the passengers were arranging themselves into a strict social hierarchy. She and Henry, of course, were always treated with excruciating deference. But Lucy could see that, among the first-class passengers, certain little groups had begun to conglomerate. One group was made up of Henry's staff, and the officers of his Bodyguard, and the upper-crust members of the Indian Civil Service. Another group was made up of planters, who played cards as if their lives depended on it, and drank immense pink gins bobbing with pearl onions, and laughed much louder and much more desperately than the civil servants.

Among the women, it was glaringly obvious who were the *burra memsahibs*, the senior ladies. They sat at all the best tables; occupied all the best chairs; and were followed everywhere by shoals of lesser ladies. Lucy found herself looking eye-to-eye with *burra-mems* like Mrs William Smith-Carter, the wife of a cavalry colonel stationed at Meerut, and thought to herself: you ought to try living in Kansas. You ought to try eking out a living from the High Plains, those long dry summers when the wind blows everything away, those stone-hard winters when your cattle freeze solid. Then we'd see about you and your precedence.

Lucy had not yet encountered India.

Their last coaling station before they set sail across the Indian Ocean was Aden, which to Lucy looked like a dry and uncompromising collection of rocks with scarcely any vegetation to soften their the sun-blinded harshness. From Aden, they headed for the southern tip of India, and Ceylon, and every day the temperature increased. One morning, Lucy looked at the thermometer by the stateroom doors, and it was reading 115 degrees. She turned around to tell Henry, but he didn't even look up from his paperwork. 'That's nothing at all, sweetheart. In the plains, it goes up to one hundred and sixty, when it's really hot.'

But Henry didn't ignore Lucy completely. He remained formal, although he could occasionally act with surprising tenderness. One rare evening, he abandoned his letter-writing, and took her out on to the deck, to show her the Southern Cross glimmering in the night sky. Behind them, the ship's wake shone with silvery-greenish phosphorescence.

'It's all so strange,' said Lucy. 'I can hardly believe that I'm here at all.'

'That's the point,' Henry told her, obscurely.

They slept at night with all the stateroom portholes open, but the heat was still unbearable. Lucy envied all the passengers who had their bedding brought up on deck, the ladies on one side of the ship and the men on the other. In her own bedroom, she slept naked, the way she used to sleep on hot Kansas nights, her body shining with perspiration. Nora made some prudish noises about 'keeping the baby warm'. A pregnant woman with nothing on at all, holy St Anthony. But Lucy ignored her. Light as they were, her silk and cambric nightgowns all made her feel so sweaty and tangled-up.

During the day, whales and porpoises plunged alongside; and flying-fish sparkled in the water like showers of silvery needles. The women languished in the heat; the men competed (rather erratically) at clay-pigeon shooting. Lucy sat in a deckchair, with a tall glass of Rawlings' ginger-ale and ice, listening to the intermittent banging of shotguns, and thought, and dreamed. Inside, Henry sat at his desk in his shirtsleeves, writing and writing, and cursing quietly when his perspiring hand dimpled his paper, and caused it to repel his ink.

Scarcely anybody slept. The nights were too hot and starry; the excitement of India was in the air. Every morning the decks were hosed down with powerful jets of water. Every morning brought Lucy's empire closer.

They had sailed slowly all through the early-morning hours through the bright green Bengal countryside, manoeuvring

466

their way between the treacherous sandbanks of the Hooghly River, towards Calcutta. The sky was now the colour of beaten brass. The heat was overwhelming. On either side of the ship, Lucy saw date palms and coconut-groves and banana plantations; and, in the distance, rice growing as emerald-green as corn.

Lucy caught sight of three or four pariah dogs, tearing at something on the silty riverbank, something that was inter-mingled crimson and brown. It was only when the ship drifted nearer that she realized it was the dead body of an Indian.

'Oh, my God,' she exclaimed to Mrs Bull. 'That's a man, that's a dead man they're eating!'

But Mrs Bull didn't take her eyes away from a group of laughing passengers on the deck below, whom she considered had already drunk too much. Live and misbehaving Euro-peans were much more interesting than dead and half-devoured Indians. 'What did I tell you, your ladyship?' she said. 'That's India. In the midst of life, etcetera, etcetera. I went to a dinner party once, during the monsoon, and I smelled this most awful smell. I was sitting next to a colonel of the IMS, and he said, "For God's sake, don't touch the fish, it's stinking." Well, of course I was terribly embarrassed, and I asked him what should I do? He said, "You can't possibly touch it, it's death." And, do you know, he meant it.'

After breakfast, exhausted by the humidity and the an-ticipation of arriving, Lucy went to bed, and lay draped under mosquito nets listening to the low, steady thrumming of the ship's engines.

She slept uneasily, and as she slept she said the name, 'Jamie.'

Henry heard her murmuring; put down his pen and came into the bedroom.

'Jamie,' she repeated.

Henry leaned over her and watched her for a while. Then he asked, 'Who's Jamie? Lucy, who's Jamie?'

'Jamie,' she repeated. Then, 'Blanche. Poor Blanche.'

'Ah, a friend of Blanche, is that it?' Henry asked her.

He waited for an answer, but it was obvious that she was still asleep. He kissed her perspiring forehead, and then he left the bedroom and walked through to the parlour to pour himself a hugely-diluted whisky-and-soda.

His body-servant Vernon knocked at the door. 'Lord Carson? Half an hour, sir, thereabouts, so Colonel Miller says. I expect you'd care for your bath, yes, before you puts on your uniform?'

'Very good,' said Henry. 'And send Colonel Miller up to see me.'

'Hat the double,' Vernon responded.

Henry glanced towards Lucy's bedroom; then he turned away again, his forehead furrowed in thought. He could still picture Lucy slackwire-walking across Mrs Harris' tennis-net, that shining golden day in Newport. My God, how beautiful she had looked that day! How beautiful she still looked today! Vanessa reincarnate, only prettier, and younger, and shining even brighter, and carrying his child!

Perhaps it would have been better for both of them if he hadn't asked Lucy to marry him. The way things were, he had a dread that he might disfigure the very beauty that he cherished so much; because of his ambition; because of his guilt about Vanessa; because he burned for India so badly.

In his prouder moments, he saw his viceroyalty crackling up into the Indian sky like rockets and Bengal lights. He saw himself brightly illuminate the whole of India, its buildings and its people, its cultures and its castes; he saw them all lift their faces to his dazzling brilliance, all across the sub-continent, from the Rann of Kutch to the Bay of Bengal, from Cape Cormorin to the Himalayas.

Lord Carson of Brackenbridge, Viceroy and Governor-General, and God!

But there were times when he saw the rockets tumble, when their fire was spent; and he saw the Bengal lights winking out, and smoking to the ground. Perhaps he had married Lucy as a constant reminder that he was only mortal, and that there was darkness inside his ambition, as well as light.

He laid his left hand flat on his blotter, wrinkling the blotting-paper with his perspiration. Then he picked up his pen in the other hand, stiffly lifted it up, and stabbed himself between the knuckles of his third and fourth fingers. He clenched his teeth, and hissed with pain, but he didn't cry out. Pain was not enough. Pain was never enough. He would have to make far greater atonement than this.

Lucy, dozing in her bed, could smell Calcutta even before she was properly awake. A smell that was unique; a fragrance of tropical flowers and trees; a smell of garlic and spices and burning cow-dung; a smell of heat and jasmine and sandalwood and dust. And she could hear a band playing, too, a distant band.

She dreamed that she was sailing up the Hooghly River, but all the time she knew that she was dreaming, because the river was more like a lily-pond, and as warm as a bath, and Blanche, her baby Blanche, was calling her name. She slept more deeply for that single hour than she had slept since the *Star of Bengal* had left Port Said. When she awoke, the ship's engines had slowed almost to a standstill, and there was a peculiar quietness on board, a feeling of expectation and excitement; but a tingle of fear, too. For those who were returning, their Home Leave was irrevocably over. For those who were coming out for the first time, there were hundreds of anxieties. How would they cope with such a strange country? How would they fit into the social hierarchy? What would they do if they found themselves face-to-face with all those dangers they had been warned about – scorpions, and cobras, and rabid dogs, and beggars? What if they contracted cholera, or dysentery, or malaria, or plague?

Not the least anxious were the girls who had come out to

find themselves a husband, the so-called 'Fishing Fleet'. What they dreaded was that when the hot weather started, they would be 'Returned Empty'.

But for most of the newcomers, the worst nightmare was simply that they might make fools of themselves. Perhaps Henry's relentless letter-writing and scrupulous research had been a way of ensuring that he was never laughed at. Perhaps he was more concerned about making a fool of himself than Lucy had ever realized.

She reached across to the bedside table and rang for Etta to bring her robe and her mules. Etta seemed quite radiant as she helped Lucy to dress. As soon as she had tied Lucy's sash, she flung open the doors to the promenade deck, and declared, 'There you are, m'lady; Calcutta!' with as much pride as if she had constructed it herself, during the morning.

Lucy crossed the stateroom to the open doors, and looked out at the capital of British India. Under a flawless blue sky, she saw a white and colour-washed city of unbelievable grandeur, of magnificent pillars and domes and gateways, of classical mansions and palatial public buildings and hotels, of church spires and monuments and parks.

All of this imperial magnificence, sprawled around the hot, torpid bend of an alluvial river, thousands and thousands of miles away from Oak City, Kansas.

'It's wonderful!' she told Etta, and there were tears in her eyes. 'I had no idea!' But her tears were not shed out of awe, or romance, or even out of joy. They were shed for everything that she had left behind; and everything that she had decided to become. Now that she had arrived in Calcutta, those decisions were irreversible.

At that moment, a military band struck up with *Lillibullero*, and she heard cheering from the waterfront.

Like a tired but well-dressed old lady, the *Star of Bengal* was gradually manoeuvred into the Prinsep Ghat, the dock just south of Fort William. The fort itself was a remarkable star-shaped construction, based on a seventeenth-century principle of fortification. Behind it lay a vast area of dusty open ground, the *maidan*, created originally to give the fort an unrestricted field of fire, but now the most elegant part of Calcutta, with magnificent shining public buildings all around it – including, to the north, the house which Henry had been born to occupy, Government House, Brackenbridge in India.

The river was crowded with ill-assorted tugs and barges and punts, most of them decorated with flags and flowers. The cheering was deafening, and baskets of flowers were emptied into the river in thick blossomy cascades, until it looked as if the *Star of Bengal* were sailing not on water, but through somebody's ornamental garden.

The warehouses lining both sides of the Hooghly were all decorated with bunting, and every available inch of riverside space was crowded with thousands of dark-faced people in brightly-coloured Indian fabrics, violent yellows and fiery scarlets and livid greens. Lucy looked up, and saw that the *Star of Bengal* herself was fully dressed with flags, and that she was flying the Viceroy's standard.

Fireworks popped, whistles whistled, and the military band played *Hearts of Oak*.

'There you are, m'lady, that's all for you!' Etta told her. 'You and his lordship, of course!'

Nora came in and clapped her hands. 'Now then, Etta, her ladyship has to be dressed quick. Disembarkation in twenty minutes. I've already drawn your bath, ma'am. It's the white lace dress with the seed-pearls, your ladyship?'

'Yes, Nora.'

'And the tararah?'

'Yes, Nora.'

Lucy went through to the bathroom and Nora undressed her. If anything, Nora was more excited than she was. 'I never saw such a crowd. And all blackies! I never saw so many blackies! I went to the rail and they was whistling and shouting and calling me *memsahib,* and I'm sure I blushed to my roots and couldn't think *what* to do!'

'Do we have any Pears' soap left?' asked Lucy, as she turned to step into the tub. But just then, as she stood naked at the side of the bath, there was a cautious knock at the door. Lucy frowned at Nora. 'Who can it be?' she mouthed. The knock was repeated, louder this time.

'Lucy, it's Henry. May I see you?'

Nora clucked like a chicken in disapproval, but Lucy smiled, 'It's quite all right, Nora. We *are* married, after all.' Nora passed Lucy her white silk robe, and then reluctantly opened the door. Henry stepped in; and he was already dressed in his full formal uniform: gilt-embroidered jacket, white silk breeches, and buckled shoes. Around his shoulders was draped a full-length cloak in a sumptuous blue, with white be-ribboned epaulets, and tied with gold tasselled cords.

'Henry!' said Lucy. 'You look wonderful! Aren't you hot?'

'Nora, would you excuse us?' Henry asked her.

'Well, your lordship, it'll have to be just for a minute,' Nora protested. 'Her ladyship's supposed to be dressed by now!'

Henry came up to Lucy and clasped her shoulders. His eyes were bright with excitement.

'Have you seen it!' he exclaimed. 'Calcutta!'

Lucy smiled, and nodded. 'I've seen it. It looks – well, it's beautiful.'

'Oh, my dear, it's not just beautiful! It's the heart of all India! The heart, the brains! It's the centre of the world! Lucy, my darling, this is the moment! This is the moment when you and I step into the pages of British history!'

He kissed her forehead, then he kissed her lips. She clung to him tightly, and he enveloped her in his cloak. It was heavy, but it was silk-lined, and the silk felt cool. He kissed her again, his tongue trying to probe in between her lips, but she kept her mouth closed and resisted him.

Concealed within his cloak, she felt his hand loosening her waistband, and gently parting her robe. He caressed her neck and her shoulders, and then held her close, so that her bare breasts were pressed against the gilt embroidery of his jacket.

Nobody who saw them could have guessed that beneath his cloak, she was almost completely naked.

'You want me,' he whispered.

She said nothing, but pecked his cheek. 'Henry, I have to get dressed.'

He held her for a moment, trapped inside his cloak, then he let it fall away from her, and let her go. She fastened her bathrobe, not looking at him.

'There's something I want you to remember,' he told her, softly, so that Nora couldn't hear; but not so softly that Lucy couldn't detect the serious tone in his voice. 'India is very strange, and India is very hot, and we shall both be kept very busy here. But no matter what happens – no matter what arguments we have or what difficulties we get into, remember that I love you, now and for ever.'

She said nothing at first, but turned away, so that all he could see was her tangled hair and her quarter-profile. 'Love has to be proved, doesn't it?' she said at last.

She let the robe slip with a whisper to the floor. Then she stepped into the bath, and slowly sat down. All this time he watched her; her distended stomach, her swollen breasts; and didn't say a word.

'You do still love me, don't you?' Henry asked her.

She looked up, her eyes slightly hooded. 'What makes you ask that?'

He shrugged. 'Ha! It's damned silly, isn't it? I don't know. I suppose every expectant father asks the same question. Jealousy, I suppose. It sounds ridiculous; but you always seem to be paying more attention to the baby than you do to me.'

'But, Henry, *you* pay neither of us any attention at all,'

473

Lucy replied, although not bitterly. 'That's what I meant when I said that love has to be proved.'

He opened and closed his mouth in melodramatic astonishment. 'Do I have to prove to you that I love my own child?'

'Perhaps,' Lucy challenged him. She was speaking as a mother who had abandoned her own dearly-beloved baby. 'You have a child already, don't you? You have a son, called Ambition. It must be hard for you to find quite enough space in your heart for all of us. Me, and baby, and Ambition.'

'Lucy – ' Henry protested; but Lucy didn't even want to hear.

'Please, Henry, go. I have to get dressed.'

'Lucy – ' Henry repeated, but then he stopped himself, and shook his head.

'Lucy,' he said again, much more softly, but much more emphatically, as if he had just discovered her name.

He waited, but she wouldn't answer. 'All right,' he said, and wrapped himself up in his cloak, and swirled out of the bathroom without a word. Seconds later, she heard the double doors clashing.

'Now, what was *that* all about?' asked Nora, coming back in again.

Lucy shook her head. 'Oh, I don't know. Nothing. I always argue with him, even when I don't want to. I can't help it. He doesn't seem to be able to talk to me at all, unless we're arguing.'

'He'll do well here in India,' Etta remarked, from the bedroom, as she buttoned up one of Lucy's blouses, and carefully folded it. 'There's nothing your Bengali likes better than an argument. And he always thinks he's right, too!'

It was late afternoon on January 3, 1899, in the warm amber light of a sinking sun, that the state carriage carrying the incoming Viceroy and Vicereine of India rattled through the monumental lion-topped gates of Government House, Calcutta, and into the wide tree-planted compound that surrounded it. Their carriage was escorted by the Viceregal Bodyguard, almost ridiculously resplendent in scarlet tunics and gilded epaulets, their horses gleaming in the sunshine as if they were oiled. As the state carriage reached the foot of the ceremonial steps, a hoarse-voiced gunnery sergeant screamed *'Fire!'* and they were treated to a thirty-one gun salute, a deafening salvo that echoed and re-echoed all over the *maidan* and across the river to the crowded Indian district of Howrah.

Their arrival in Calcutta had been triumphant. Their progress through the streets had been greeted by a wall of noise, and they had been thronged by tens of thousands of cheering Indians, and blizzarded with flowers. Every building had been decorated with flags and banners and signs saying WELCUM LORD AND LADY CARSONS; or HELLO Y.E.s! and one – where the two halves hadn't quite managed to join up – had read A GAL A DAY.

'I think they flatter me,' Henry had said, squeezing Lucy's hand.

Lucy stepped down from the state carriage in her white lace gown, and her gold-and-pearl tiara. She looked tall, and pale, and very calm, and a murmur of curious approval rippled through the assembled company. Henry took her arm with obvious pride; and the two of them walked up the wide stone staircase towards the portico. Arrayed on the steps on either side of them was a rigid guard of honour, with sabres drawn. At the top, waiting for them with smiles of welcome, stood the outgoing Viceroy, Lord Elgin, in full uniform, and Lady Elgin, in yellow silk; as well as the governors of all the British presidencies; and the residents of some of the larger native states; and the political agents of some of the smaller native states; and more than fifty bejewelled and turbaned princes, including the Nizam of Hyderabad, the Maharajah of Benares, the Maharajah of Jodhpur; and the Maharajah of Mysore.

In that golden January sunshine, Lucy ascended the steps of Government House as if she were dreaming. Lord Elgin took her hand, and bowed his head, and said, 'Welcome to Calcutta, Lady Carson. I hope the guns didn't frighten you. The Viceroy gets more than anybody else. Practically deafened me, over the years. Even our pal the Maharajah of Gwalior only gets nineteen.'

Lady Elgin was dark-haired, grey-eyed, and very older-sisterly. She took Lucy's hand and said, 'No curtsey, please! I've been told of your condition. Congratulations! A new country, and a new baby!'

It took them nearly twenty minutes to be introduced to all of the residents and political agents and princes and deputy commissioners and members of the Viceroy's Council. Lucy was fascinated by the princes. The most plainly-dressed was the Nizam of Hyderabad, who wore a grey frock-coat and a fez-like hat with a feather in it, but Lady Elgin murmured to Lucy that he was by far the wealthiest of all of them, and that he used one of his two 180-carat diamonds as a paperweight. Some of the maharajahs were dressed spectacularly. The white-moustached Maharajah of Benares wore robes of Paisley-patterned silk, and a white silk turban decorated with green silk tassels and incredible emeralds, as green as glass and as big as birds' eggs, at least thirty of them. The Maharajah of the Punjab was dark and black-bramble-bearded, and wore a towering silk turban draped around with strings of pearls.

'I hail your Excellencies' advent,' he said, bowing low. 'Let us thank our Heavenly Father, whose grace has today enabled us to see your sublime Ladyship in all her great glory.'

'Well, thank you,' said Lucy. 'Thank you very much.'

As he conducted Henry and Lucy into the vast high-ceilinged Marble Hall, Lord Elgin noticed Lucy's amusement.

'Indians have a great love of florid language,' he remarked.

'You'll get used to it. Before you laugh at it, however, remember that comparatively few Europeans ever learn to speak Urdu or Marathi or Tamil or Telegu; and even those who do could never compose sentences as marvellous as that. Here! This is the Marble Hall! This is where we hold our state dinners.'

He let them admire the Marble Hall for a moment; then he ushered them through to the Council Chamber, where Henry's Warrant of Appointment was to be read. 'Just the other day, I was addressed by one petitioner as the father of all of his children. He had eleven. I'm just wondering when I ever had the time.'

Lucy looked around Government House with a mixed sense of familiarity and strangeness. This is my house now, this huge palace! Its similarity to Brackenbridge was striking. As Lucy walked along the corridors she felt almost as if she were home. But this house was very different in many ways; not the least of which was the fragrant Bengal breeze which blew softly through its pillared vistas. There was no central staircase: instead, there were four separate staircases to each of the four wings, and the walls were built not of softly-coloured Derbyshire stone, but of brick, rendered with Madras *chunam*, which had been polished and painted to resemble marble.

What had struck a keen note of sadness in Lucy's memory was that the outside walls of the entire residency had been washed in the same stray-dog yellow as Jack Darling's General Store.

'Don't worry,' said Henry, as if he had been reading her thoughts. 'We'll soon get rid of that yellow paint. There's only one colour for a viceregal palace, and that's white.'

They assembled solemnly in the Council Chamber. The falling sunlight glittered on jewels and silks and gold. Henry stood forward, and Lord Elgin unrolled his Warrant of Appointment, and cleared his throat. The chamber was noisy with coughing and shuffling.

'We do hereby give and grant unto you our Governor-General of India and to your Council as the Governor-General of India in Council, the superintendence, direction and control of the whole civil and military government with all our territories and revenues in India . . . and we do hereby order and require all our servants, officers and soldiers in the East Indies . . . to conform, submit and yield due obedience unto you and your Council.'

Lucy saw Henry gradually lift his head; and, as he did so, by divine stage-management, the sunlight pierced the chamber in a brilliant diagonal, and illuminated his face. His expression made Lucy tingle. It was stern, arrogant, triumphant. She had never seen a man to whom God had apparently given everything he could have wanted, and she felt charged with the most inexplicable emotions, excitement, fear – dread, almost – and an admiration for Henry which she would never be able to describe to him.

After the Warrant of Appointment had been read, the assembled officials and princes retired to the Tiffin Room for champagne and tea and a spectacular array of canapés and Indian snacks, from pheasant vol-au-vents to *karela masala,* fried bitter gourds, and bowls of lemon-flavoured rice.

Lucy noticed that all the Indians ate with their fingers, and most of them drank nothing but water. She tried eating a little rice with her fingers, until Lady Elgin shot her a friendly but cautionary look across the room which obviously meant 'not done, to imitate the natives'.

She was approached by the Maharajah of Baroda, Saraji Rao, a plump courteous man with an impeccable English lisp and a necklace of the largest natural pearls that Lucy had ever seen. 'I have seven children so far,' he told her. 'Have you and H.E. any comparable number of children so far?'

Lucy hesitated, and then shook her head. 'I'm afraid we have no children so far. Although we're expecting our first baby in June.'

'Well, please permit me to congratulate you in advancement,' the Maharajah told her. Then he said, 'You will find that a child brings H.E. and yourself great joy.'

'I hope so,' Lucy smiled.

'A man who has no children is like a house with no doors,' said the Maharajah.

'I'm sorry,' Lucy replied. 'I'm not too sure what you mean.'

'He is always *closed*, you understand. Thief-proof. He will never be opening himself up to anything novel. A man without children would be better taking himself to the cemetery and lying down in his mausoleum to wait for death.'

Lucy didn't know what to say to that; but she was rescued by Colonel Miller, who greeted the Maharajah effusively, and asked him if he would care for more *pethi halva*.

'You know my weakness!' laughed the Maharajah.

As darkness poured over the twenty-six acres of Government House as thickly as warmed-up treacle, Lady Elgin took Lucy on a tour of the southern wings of the house, to see the private apartments. The drawing rooms were cool and quiet, with pale walls and linen curtains across the windows to keep out mosquitoes. They were furnished in traditional English style, with comfortable shapeless sofas and huge armchairs, but most of the fabrics were Indian. Lady Elgin showed Lucy to her dressing room, where all her trunks had already been unpacked, and all her dresses and shoes and underwear exactingly folded and pressed and put away.

'You must be tired,' she said, at last. Outside the window it was almost completely black, except for a last smear of crimson on the western horizon. A distinctive and romantic fragrance filled the air, the distillation of tree-sap and flowers and spices in the rapidly-cooling air.

Lucy said, 'Yes, I'm a little tired. But what a day!'

'Dinner is at seven, for seven-thirty,' said Lady Elgin. 'You may of course retire early, once it's over, if you're feeling at all fatigued. You're the *burra-mem* now.'

'Are you sorry to be leaving?' Lucy asked her.

Lady Elgin looked around the dressing room. It was here that she must have dressed herself for countless dinners and receptions and balls and 'drawing rooms'.

'Yes, I'm sad,' she said. 'I'm looking forward to going Home, quite naturally. But once you've lived in India, you know, you can never forget it. It makes an indelible mark on you. You can meet people who haven't lived in India for twenty years, but you can always tell. They have a faraway look in their eyes. They may be sitting on a park-bench in Surrey, but some secret part of them is still stretched out on a long-sleever in Bengal.'

She ran her hand along the top of the bureau, and looked at her glove. Perhaps it was a habit that she had acquired over the years of her viceroyalty, checking for dust. 'I think perhaps my greatest regret is that I came to India as Vice-reine. I have been pampered, certainly, and entertained, and carried around like a queen. But there are so many aspects of a woman's life here in India that I have never experienced. Some nights, don't you know, I used to stand here by my window and think of all those women scattered across the length and breadth of the entire sub-continent. Lonely, frightened; struggling with Indian servants and snakes and dysentery and drunken husbands; trying to bring up children in remote stations in the *mofussil*. And I would think to myself . . . you never knew India at all.'

She turned, and touched Lucy's shoulder, as if she were conferring on her the isolation that she herself had been feeling for so long.

'I hope you leave India with fewer regrets than I. And do take care of your baby.'

480

Lucy woke up in the morning to find the sun shining bright through the gauze mosquito-nets, and the sheet wrinkled and deserted beside her. She rang for Nora.

'Nora, what's the time?'

'Ten before nine, your ladyship.'

'Where's Lord Carson?'

'He's taken his breakfast already, your ladyship. He's down in his office, with Lord Elgin, and Colonel Miller, and the rest of them.'

Lucy sat up. 'It's hot here, isn't it? Somehow I always imagined that Calcutta would be cool. It's the name, I suppose, "Calcutta". It just *sounds* cool. And this is the Cold Weather, isn't it?'

'I said the same thing to Etta, but Etta said this *is* cool. Compared with the Hot Weather, anyway. Would you care for a bit of breakfast, your ladyship?'

'No, just tea. And I'll dress first.'

'You should eat for two, your ladyship. Think of the babba. The babba needs to feed.'

'Nora, just tea!'

'Yes, your ladyship. Not even an egg?'

'Nora, please, I'm just not hungry!'

Nora drew back the mosquito-nets and Lucy climbed out of bed. She went across to the window and peered out over the compound of Government House. She could see the wide dusty-golden expanse of the *maidan*, and the zig-zag walls of Fort William, and across to the south, the Chowringhi Racecourse. A little farther to the east, the tall Doric spire of the Ochterlony memorial rose high into the morning sunshine, a hundred and fifty feet tall, with an odd Turkish cupola on top.

'I think I may like it here,' said Lucy.

'Well, it's all very peculiar, that's all I can say about it,' said Nora. 'If I want a cup of tea, I have to ask some fellow called the *khansamah*, and the *khansamah* tells the *khitmutgar*, and the *khitmutgar* tells the *biwarchi*, and the *biwarchi* makes the tea, and back it all comes, along the line, and if it isn't stone-cold by the time it gets to me. And there's about a hundred blackies milling around with nothing better to do than open doors and close them again. And not just that. Etta and me are nothing but what you might call supervisory, because there's four *ayahs* to care for your clothes and the Lord knows how many people to make the beds. It's an ant's-nest, so help me, not a servants'-hall. And I'm not at all sure about the smell. It's not corned-beef and potatoes for luncheon today, you can count on that. More like boiled-up mothballs.'

Nora went to ring for tea. 'They do a fair omelette, I'll admit that,' she coaxed Lucy. 'Will you not have an omelette?'

Lucy shook her head. She had eaten enough at yesterday's dinner: quail, and rice, and bright red chickens, and all kinds of fruits, and chopped almonds wrapped in gold and silver leaf. Mrs Bull had warned her against experimenting too enthusiastically with Indian foods. *'Calcutta tummy'*, she had warned, pursing her lips in the knowing way that only a collector's wife could purse her lips.

Lucy might not have been hungry; but as she sat in her private breakfast-room sipping milkless Darjeeling tea and talking to Nora, Henry suddenly appeared with a sheet of notepaper in his hand, and announced, 'Dinners!'

'Dinners?' asked Lucy. 'What do you mean, "dinners"?'

'Dinners, of course! Dinners! A formal dinner, every night of the week! And after the Inaugural Ball, dances every Saturday, without fail!'

'Did Lord Elgin hold dinners every night, and dances every Saturday?'

'No, my dearest, he didn't. But you and I will. Government House will become the social whirlpool of India. Dinners, and dances, and levées, too. Colonel Miller is drawing up a list of two thousand men who might profitably be invited to a "levée", so that they can meet their new Viceroy first-hand.'

'Henry, we've only just arrived.'

'All the more reason! I want to shake them up, Lucy! The Indian Civil Service in particular! I want to meet them, and inspire them! I want them to share my vision!'

Lucy smiled at him, and then laughed. 'All right, then! Dinners it is! So long as I can get used to the food!'

On Monday morning, as she sat drinking tea and eating rumble-tumble in the sun-blinded glow of her private dining room, the head *khitmutgar* appeared, Abdul Aziz, as if on wheels; and bowed his head, and informed her that Memsahib Morris had arrived.

'Who?' she asked, putting down her fork.

In spite of Nora's suspicions, Lucy had grown to like the *khitmutgar*, who was extremely tall and wore gorgeous maroon livery, with gilded braids. She had already nicknamed him 'Buffalo Bill'.

'Memsahib Morris, Your Excellency. Your so-shall secretary. His Excellency was especially requesting that you should see her as soon as humanly possible.'

'My social secretary? I didn't know I *had* a social secretary!'

'Memsahib Morris is your so-shall secretary, Your Excellency, madam.'

Lucy wiped her mouth on her napkin. 'You'd better show her in.'

There was a long pause, and then a bespectacled spinsterish woman of about fifty stalked through the doorway like a *kulang*, a crane, carrying a brown leather satchel. She wore a *terai* hat and an ecru linen suit, with a frilled white blouse.

Twenty years ago, she had probably been handsome, in her way. Today she was ordinary and very thin, with the fleshlessness of long-term malaria. She stretched out her hand.

'Elizabeth Morris, Your Excellency! Welcome to Calcutta!'

'I'm sorry,' said Lucy. 'Do I know why you're here?'

'First day at work!' Elizabeth Morris said, brightly. 'Must say His Excellency gets cracking, doesn't he! Golly!'

Lucy said, 'I'm really sorry, I don't know why you're here.'

Elizabeth Morris blinked behind her spectacles. 'I'm your social secretary, Lady Carson. Elizabeth Morris. Surely your hu – surely His Excellency mentioned my name.'

Lucy shook her head.

Elizabeth Morris said, 'Ah!' and clasped her hands together as if she were praying. For a moment, neither she nor Lucy said anything. Then Elizabeth Morris dragged out a chair, and sat next to Lucy at the breakfast-table, and said, 'The thing is, His Excellency interviewed me on Saturday afternoon, at two o'clock in the afternoon, on Lady Elgin's recommendation, d'you see, and said I was appointed, two hundred and fifty pounds per annum.'

'His Excellency hasn't mentioned anything to me,' Lucy retorted, although she was suddenly conscious that she might be betraying his trust.

'Well, he's a fearfully busy man,' smiled Elizabeth Morris. 'Perhaps he forgot! In any case, he was *very* scrupulous, when it came to interviewing me; and he asked all sorts of questions! Did I have my own teeth! Goodness me! What a question! Well, I do, as a matter of fact, touch wood and whistle. But my qualifications were obviously right! I've lived here for years, you see. My late brother was Sir Gordon Morris, you *must* have heard of Gordon, he was Chief Justice of the Supreme Court; and anyway I live in his house on the Chowringhi Road, which you can see from here, which is most convenient for both of us. You and me, if you know what I mean. But anyway, I've lived in Bombay, I've lived in Madras, I've lived almost everywhere in India that you could mention, well not Goa, of course, I'm not completely reckless, and not Udaipur, they're *very* strange there. They have a ritual of mass suicide called *johur*, and the Maharana wears full uniform and bare feet and stares.'

Elizabeth Morris picked up a rattan bag, and waved it as if it were a salmon she had just caught. 'I've bought a new leather-bound diary from the Army & Navy; and new pens; and a bottle of Stephen's blue-black. So, whenever you're ready, Your Excellency!'

Lucy stood up. 'Excuse me for just a moment, Mrs Morris,' she asked.

'*Miss* Morris, actually. Was engaged, once! But he was killed pig-sticking. Well, many years ago, now. Before Gordon passed over.'

Lucy left her breakfast room and walked swiftly through the long vista of *chunam* pillars, across the Marble Hall, to the Tiffin Room. Henry was sitting in a large gilded armchair, next to Walter Pangborn, and two other members of the Viceroy's Court whom Lucy didn't yet recognize, and the Nizam of Hyderabad, sitting elegant and perfectly-dressed in a grey silk frock-coat.

'Lucy!' said Henry, standing up as abruptly as if a spring had broken through the seat of his chair.

The Nizam and Walter and the other two gentlemen rose to their feet, and bowed, regardless of the fact that Lucy was wearing her white silk *negligée* and slippers, and that her hair was wound up in a white silk turban.

'Who is that woman?' Lucy demanded.

Henry made quick conciliatory faces to the Nizam, and then stalked across to Lucy and took hold of her arm. 'Have you no idea what face I will lose if I look like a man who can't control his wife?' he whispered at her, ferociously.

'Who cares about your face? Who's that woman? Elizabeth Morris, whatever her name is!'

'Elizabeth Morris is your new social secretary! I appointed her on Saturday! She knows the Warrant of Precedence off by heart, she knows everybody who's worth knowing in the whole of British India, she has tact, influence, and the ability to run your social life so smoothly and efficiently that you'll be able to organize the very best dinner-parties and the very best drawing-rooms that Government House has ever known!'

Lucy thought about that, and then, in a raging whisper, retorted, 'Good! Why the hell didn't you tell me before?'

Lucy and Elizabeth Morris became the kind of friends that are found only once in a lifetime. Elizabeth had been brought up with the Raj. She had seen Calcutta grow; she had seen great buildings rise and fall. She had seen terrible tragedies; friends dying of cholera; friends dying of drink or despair. At the age of eleven she had been taken by Lady Charlotte Canning to see the menagerie at the Viceroy's summer residence upriver at Barrackpore, and taken a pair of lynxes for a walk through Lady Canning's Italian garden.

The next year, 1861, Lady Canning had contracted malaria while returning from Darjeeling across the fever-ridden Terai, and died, aged 44. Elizabeth Morris had laid flowers on her tomb.

Every morning, Elizabeth took Lucy out in her carriage, to look round Calcutta. While Henry argued with his Council and his civil servants, Lucy went to Chowringhi to see the European stores, the Army & Navy, Hall and Anderson's, and Newman's. She saw Warren Hastings' house at Alipur, and the Esplanade, and Writers Buildings. But the saddest time was when she visited the South Park Cemetery, in Chowringhi, crowded with so many columns, urns, pyramids and obelisks that it looked as if they had been stored here, or washed ashore from a sunken funeral ship. Elizabeth said nothing as Lucy walked between the neatly-tended monuments, but watched her sharply. This was a lesson in the misery of Imperial India, as well as its glory. There were so many graves of girls who had married at 15 or 16, only to die of disease or in childbirth before their seventeenth birthday; and there were so many children.

After a long while, Elizabeth said, 'Two monsoons, no longer. That's how long most of them lasted. As Sir William Hunter wrote, "The price of British rule in India has always been paid with the lives of little children."'

The most regretful monument of all was the spiral column decorated with stone roses, dedicated to Rose Aylmer, who had died of dysentery at the age of 20.

Lucy read the elegy. *'Rose Aylmer, whom these wakeful eyes/May weep, but never see./ A night of memories and sighs/ I consecrate to thee.'*

Elizabeth said, 'That was written by Walter Savage Landor. He loved her, you know, and he never forgot her. My brother knew him. Rose died in 1800, and Walter lived until 1864. Sixty-four years of grief! He missed her every single day of his life.'

During the first weeks of their viceroyalty, Elizabeth guided Lucy through the treacherous brambles of Calcutta society. Together with Colonel Miller, she drew up the guest list for the first ball, and planned all the seating arrangements. The *memsahib* of a political officer would certainly not care to find herself sitting next to an assistant inspector-general of forests; and the wife of a lieutenant-colonel in Skinner's Horse would be mortified to be placed next to an officer of the 39th Garhwalis, for all that they were Gurkhas.

Their first ball was enchanting. Lucy had brought out from England a low-cut gown of white silk, with an overlay of white lace which had been especially made for her in Nottingham. The lace had the appearance of thousands of peacock feathers, and each feather was sewn with pearls.

Nora curled her hair for her and fastened it with two twists of pearls; and to crown her *coiffure* she wore her diamond tiara. When Henry led her into the ballroom that Saturday evening, all three hundred assembled guests broke out into spontaneous applause; and Colonel Miller led a call for three cheers.

'She has the appearance of a graceful swan,' wrote the correspondent for the London *Times*. 'If there is a woman more beautiful in the whole of India, then I have never seen her or heard of her.'

The ballroom at Government House was spectacular. It was supported on each side with shining white *chunam* pillars; and from its coffered ceiling a glittering array of cut-glass chandeliers hung down. Between the pillars were ranged sofas of blue satin damask, and sparkling mirrors that reflected the light even more brightly.

At the upper end of the ballroom, framed in an archway, a very rich Persian carpet was spread; and in the centre of that, a *musnud* of crimson and gold, which had originally formed part of the throne of Tippoo Sultan. On top of this stood a decorated chair and stool of state, for the Viceroy.

Henry and Lucy arrived in the ballroom at about nine o'clock, and the orchestra struck up, and dancing began.

'May I ask for this dance?' said Henry.

Lucy gave him a little curtsey. She was conscious that every man and woman in the whole ballroom was staring at her, swivelling their heads around so much as they danced that there were several awkward collisions in the middle of the floor.

Henry waltzed her sedately around the pillars.

'I haven't yet told you that you look very beautiful,' he said.

'Well,' she said, a little off-handedly, 'thank you.'

'Do you think you're going to like it here?' he asked her. 'How are you getting along with Miss Morris? She always reminds me of one of those umbrellas with a duck's head for a handle.'

'I'm getting along with her very well, thank you, and she does not look like an umbrella with a duck's head for a handle. If anybody looks like a duck's head with a handle, it's you. In fact you look like a duck. You certainly dance like a duck.'

Henry quickly glanced around, to make sure that nobody could overhear them. 'What on earth has got into you?' he demanded. 'We're supposed to be celebrating tonight, not arguing!'

'Oh, yes, and what are we supposed to be celebrating? Our first conversation in ten days? Henry, I didn't marry you to spend my life on my own. I haven't even *seen* you since Thursday morning!'

Henry was silent as they pivoted their way past a nodding, smiling group of senior civil servants. Then he said, 'I made it quite clear that my first few weeks would be very, very busy. I'm not starting up a mutton club, for goodness' sake, I'm ruling a continent!'

'Walter says you're doing it again.'

'Walter says I'm doing what again?'

'Walter says you're doing everything yourself. He says you're answering every single letter personally; he says that you've arranged to see the head of every civil service department at least once a week; he says you've arranged to make three speeches already; and to entertain almost a thousand people. He says you've been writing letters at breakfast, correcting proofs at luncheon, and working on your accounts halfway through the night.'

Henry said tautly, 'Shall we discuss this later?'

'How can we? You'll be talking to your Council about irrigation or something.'

'Lucy, I know I work very hard, but it's my nature. I can no more accept blame or credit for it than I could for having a well-turned calf, or a handsome nose.'

'There's nothing wrong with your nose.'

'For goodness's sake! I wasn't suggesting there was! I was

simply saying that I am industrious by temperament, and that I have more than enough to keep me fully employed.'

Lucy said, 'Your health's suffering. Look at you! You haven't been here two weeks and your hair's thinning and you skin's waxy and you cough all the time. And your temper's no better. I heard you shouting at Abdul the other day. Henry, you should have been ashamed of yourself. You sounded like a roaring lion.'

Henry was about to snap back something sharp; but Lady Ampthill beamed at him from across the ballroom, and he was obliged to beam back. 'It's very irregular,' he said, 'but let's go outside, and finish this conversation alone.'

He guided Lucy away from the dance-floor, between the pillars, and out on to the balcony. The night was fragrant, and echoed with music and laughter. The compound had been illuminated with lamps suspended from bamboos; and the wall of Fort William which faced towards Government House had been illuminated with dramatic starkness.

'Lucy,' said Henry, his face hidden in shadow, 'I have to ask you to bear with me, to give me time. I came here bursting with all manner of far-reaching ideas. I want to reform the tax system, so that people don't have to pay so much in times of dearth. I want to change the rules of famine relief. I want five thousand miles' more railways. I want better schools, and more doctors, and better safeguards against epidemic diseases.'

He paused, and took out his handkerchief, and wiped the perspiration from his forehead. 'I want all of those reforms, and I want them carried out urgently. This sub-continent will collapse if they're not! But the great slow-grinding bureaucracy that I have inherited! You cannot imagine how it frustrates me! If I suggest to my staff that something is done within six weeks, the attitude is one of pained surprise. If I suggest six days, one of pathetic protest. If six hours, one of stupefied resignation.

'I have the greatest and clearest vision for the transformation of the Indian sub-continent that any man has ever had. I could give India efficiency, profit, learning, and health. But what help do I have with which to implement these visions? The largest collection of chronic snobs, nest-featherers, hair-splitters, nose-pickers, blackguards and cretins ever assembled in one building, and a slow-grinding bureaucracy that dwarfs the Ziggurat of Ur.'

Lucy slowly shook her head. 'Henry – that is still no reason to do everything yourself.'

'For God's sake, Lucy, if I don't do it, who will?'

'You must *teach* them to do it! You must *expect* them to do it! I mean, Henry, this business about the chickens!'

Henry reddened. 'Who told you about the chickens?'

'Walter of course. He said you spent hours trying to balance the household budget.'

'And why not?' Henry protested. 'The cook was charging for literally hundreds of chickens which he never even bought! He returned five hundred and ninety-six as having been bought last month; but when we went to the trades-man, he said that he had sold us only two hundred and ninety. That's a saving of three hundred and six chickens in one month, for goodness' sake!'

'Henry!' Lucy crackled at him. 'You're running India, Henry, not a grocery store! What does it matter, three hundred chickens here, three hundred chickens there? There are three hundred little children lying dead in South Park Cemetery! How about making sure that there are never any more?'

Henry tightened his lips, nervously jerked his head, paced, preened. Then, much more quietly, he said, 'We have to get back to the ball. I'm glad we talked. I'll make a particular effort to talk to you every day. Perhaps then you'll gradually grow to understand that a moral principle is a moral princi-ple, and that it must be scrupulously applied to the petty things as well as the great. If fifty pounds is saved on chickens; if a hundred pounds is saved on wine; if a thousand

491

pounds is saved on misappropriated stores; then every year we will have that much more money to spend on saving children.'

Lucy took hold of Henry's hand. 'Henry, I know. Henry, I *know*. But why do all those petty things have to be done by *you*?'

He tugged his gloves, sniffed, looked away. He probably didn't know the answer to that.

'Perhaps you'd be good enough to save me the last dance,' he said, and went back inside, leaving Lucy alone on the balcony, under the starry Calcutta night, with the insects singing and the bamboo lamps flickering and dipping, and a faint cooling breeze blowing across the *maidan* from the Hooghly River.

But Henry kept his promise to talk to her every day for only three days; and even then he spared her only five or ten minutes, and paced, as if he wanted to be back at his desk. All he could talk about was the commissariat, or dinner arrangements, or what he should wear at next week's dance, or how much he distrusted Colonel Miller.

'I don't like all this moustache-tugging. Have you seen it? Tug, tug, tug; as if it isn't really his. I'm beginning to wonder if it's an insult. That's what the Sikhs do, you know, to challenge each other. They twirl their moustaches, and say, "Hmmm, hmmmm". That's exactly what Timothy Miller does to me.'

On the fourth day he sent Lucy a note with Muhammad Isak his head bearer, begging her forgiveness. '*Please look on me with mercy and sympathy, my dearest sweetheart, and don't be angry.*' Isak watched her with sad dark eyes as she read Henry's complicated excuse. He couldn't see her today. He had a critical meeting with his military secretary. He had just received news that the Russian War Minister intended to strengthen his country's defences in Central Asia and, what was more, to improve the Russian army's capability to attack India. To that end, he had ordered Russia's strategic railways to be advanced southward, toward the very borders of India.

That was on the first day of February. For the next two weeks, Lucy scarcely ever saw him, except at dinner, or their weekly dances, or whenever they were receiving princes or visiting dignitaries. Before February was out, he had instructed Muhammad to set him up a bed next to his office, so that he could stay up working late without disturbing her.

She lay in bed every night, listening to the endless chorus of the insects, and she had never felt lonelier. Sometimes she closed her eyes and pressed her pillow up against her ears, and tried to hear the wind blowing across the High Plains of Kansas, but she never could.

In the last week of February, however, while Lucy was out in the grounds of Government House, supervising the planting of a row of new *peepul* trees along the northern boundary, Henry unexpectedly appeared on their private verandah, and came walking towards her with great purpose along the diagonal paths of faultlessly-weeded Bayswater gravel.

It was an afternoon of glaring sun and black shadows, and sky that was crushingly blue. Lucy was dressed in a fine linen frock of saffron yellow, embroidered with knots of tiny white flowers. A *chaprassi* stood patiently behind her, holding up a huge white fringed parasol, to protect the *burra memsahib* from the slightest hint of the sun. He kept clearing his throat as if he were about to make a speech. Nearly thirty coolies were digging holes for each of the eleven trees, and raising them into position with ropes, while the head *mali* and the under-*mali* and six other *malis* argued and fussed and contradicted each other.

As Henry approached, the arguing and the shouting and the furious rustling of glossy green fig-leaves subsided, until

493

all that could be heard was the sawing of insects and the calling of *koels* and the crunching of Henry's shoes on the gravel.

'Henry!' called Lucy. Her voice sounded peculiarly stifled in the afternoon heat. 'This is a surprise!'

Henry gave her an irrepressible little smile of acknowledgement, and took off his wide-brimmed white hat and wiped around the headband with his handkerchief. 'I've just finished my meeting with Colonel Belloc,' he told her.

'Oh, you mean that architect fellow from the Royal Engineers?'

'That's right.' He replaced his hat and clasped his hands behind his back. He seemed to have made up his mind about something important. 'I must say that it was quite an experience. He's still here, as a matter of fact, I've asked him to stay for dinner. He's taking a bath at the moment.'

'You're smiling,' said Lucy.

'Yes, well, I suppose I am,' Henry admitted. 'Belloc's extremely *individual*. No doubt about it. Miller says that he and his brother once welcomed their Commander-in-Chief to their home in Simla by standing on their heads, on either side of the doorway, like matching pillars; and today, absolutely unabashed about it, he supped his tea out of his cakeplate.'

'But?' asked Lucy. She could sense an agitation in Henry's voice that she hadn't heard since they had left England. It excited her, too – and when the chief *mali* called out plaintively, 'Your Excellency, *ap mai ma-bap hai* (your are my mother and my father) but we are not being able to hold up this tree very much longer!' she scolded, '*Sssh!* Sukumar, do whatever you want!' and waved him away.

Henry said, 'Eccentric or not, Belloc has some remarkable ideas about the restoration of classical Indian buildings. Really – he's quite inspired me!'

'He must have done, to get you away from your desk,' said Lucy. She felt like adding, 'More than *I* can ever do,' but she held her tongue. Henry was in such an ebullient mood that she didn't want to spoil it. He took hold of her hand and swung it affectionately. Under her parasol, in her wide-brimmed primrose hat and her white chiffon veil, she looked delicately blonde and as pretty as a freshly-opened flower.

Henry said, 'I've given myself the afternoon off, as a matter of fact. Cancelled everything! I have some reports on the unadministered areas to look at later tonight, but they shouldn't take long.'

'I'm pleased.'

He looked around the grounds. 'So! These are the fig-trees you talked about!'

'They're beautiful, aren't they? They remind me of great green fans.'

'Make sure the gardeners water them properly. They should flood them twice a day, until they're well-established. They'll probably die, though. They don't like being disturbed.'

'Do you hear that, Sukumar?' said Lucy, defiantly. 'You must water these trees twice every day, plenty of *pani*! If they die, I will never forgive you!'

'Your Excellency *memsahib*, they will be attended as if they are my own children,' the head gardener promised her.

Henry led Lucy away from the fig-trees and across the gardens, with the *chaprassi* and his parasol shuffling after them. The heat made the gravel paths ripple as if Lucy were looking at them through a clear running stream. She almost expected to see trout flickering their way along them.

'You were right, you know,' Henry told her. 'I've been driving myself too hard. Not delegating; trying to be master and dog and tail, too.'

Lucy didn't know what to say. She had the strangest feeling that he was asking for her approval.

'It's Belloc, I suppose,' said Henry. 'He doesn't give tuppence for bureaucracy or protocol. But he cares just as passionately about India as I do, if not more. Since we rule

India, we have the obligation to protect its cultural heritage, that's what he says, even if the poor black heathens can't be bothered to do it themselves. Do you know that the British government spent less than seven thousand pounds last year, protecting India's historical buildings? Seven thousand pounds, for a whole sub-continent! That wouldn't buy a single plasterwork ceiling at Brackenbridge!'

'So what are you going to do about it?' asked Lucy. She couldn't pretend that she wasn't slightly put out that Henry's sudden new surge of ebullience had been inspired by an eccentric sapper – not by passion, nor by romance, nor even by guilt that he might be neglecting her.

Henry was looking tired, but he was no less charming and no less personable, and his appointment as Viceroy had invested him with an almost visible aura of political power which attracted men and women alike, and which attracted Lucy more than ever, even when she thought that she hated him. But her failure to reach to the very heart of him was making her feel a little less adequate and a little more defensive every day. Even when she saw him, she had stopped telling him how much she loved him, because it had begun to sound dangerously like pleading.

Sometimes his endless absences and his emotional stone-walling frustrated her so much that she felt like blurting out everything Sha-sha had told her about Vanessa, and to hell with the consequences. But if she did that, she was sure that he would shut her out completely; and then she wouldn't even have those few moments when he forgot his grinding official responsibilities and his haunting private guilt, and was amusing and gay and loving, as he was today.

She could have beaten her fists against the chest of this Viceroy, and demanded that he let the real Henry free. But how could one woman prevail against Eton and Oxford and Parliament, and eight hundred years of English family history – no matter how beautiful she was, no matter how furious she was, no matter what she was prepared to sacrifice?

Now that they were Viceroy and Vicereine, divorce or seperation were out of the question. Lucy had chosen glory, and so glory she would have to have. But she still loved him; she still needed him; and, more to the point, she still *wanted* him. She refused to believe, as Henry seemed to, that love and duty had to be mutually exclusive. Henry could love her back, if he allowed himself. What he needed was something to release his soul from its self-imposed captivity.

Perhaps, in the end, India would do it, by granting him the magnificent destiny that he had always craved. Perhaps their child would do it, when he was born, by granting him a heritage, and by presenting him with a responsibility that wasn't black, or bureaucratic, or a building.

Lucy knelt by her bed and prayed every night with her eyes tightly shut that Henry would be released; that he would suddenly blink and smile like a man shaken awake from a dream. But every night after she had whispered *amen* she would open her eyes and there in front of her would be her smoothly turned-down bedcover, and an empty marriage-bed, and nothing to look forward to but an hour's reading *Tess of the D'Urbervilles* under the thickly-draped mosquito-nets until she fell asleep, and Nora came slippered and curl-papered to turn out her lamp.

As they reached the house, Henry said, 'If nothing else, Colonel Belloc has at least encouraged me to get my hands dirty. Bricks and mortar, rather than paper! He's suggested that we make an excursion to see some of the buildings for ourselves, so that we can decide what needs to be done to preserve them, and how much we're going to have to spend. I used to do it at Brackenbridge, after all. And this is a far, far more momentous task than the preservation of one English country house.'

They climbed the steps at the back of the house and walked together along the arched verandah, their feet echoing on the marble-flagged floor. The fragrance of flowers and tropical vegetation had somehow become entrapped and distilled in the coolness of the arches, and was so strong that Lucy paused, and took a deep breath, and knew that she would never forget such a fragrance as long as she lived.

'I promised to show you the Taj Mahal,' said Henry, 'So we're going on a tour. We're travelling to Agra and to Delhi, setting off on Wednesday morning next week.'

'Well, that sounds wonderful,' said Lucy.

Henry heard the flatness in her voice. 'You don't seem to be exactly overjoyed.'

'I'm pleased, yes. But it sounds like more work to me. More responsibility.'

Henry grasped her hands and looked brightly into her eyes. 'Lucy, it's just what I need! Something to lure me away from all of my beastly paperwork! Something recreational!'

'Isn't your wife enough to lure you away from all of your beastly paperwork?'

'Of course, my darling. But I can't be selfish. You have your own life to lead, your own pursuits. Your drawing-rooms, your embroidery, your reading, your gardening. I can't expect you to give those up just to entertain me.'

'My God, Henry,' said Lucy.

Henry frowned. '"My God?" What's that supposed to mean?'

'It means, here we are, emperor and empress, but what's become of us?'

'Oh, Lucy,' Henry chided her. 'You're not going to start being temperamental again? Beloved, it's the heat, nothing more. It's your pregnancy, too. It's bound to make you feel disaffected at times. Major French did warn me about it, you know.'

'Oh, did he? Well, well, a medal for Major French! I don't suppose it occurred to Major French that I could be disaffected by trying to live with a husband who nevers stop playing Emperor of India, not even when it's time to go to bed?'

'Lucy, please, there are servants around.'

'There always are. Goddammit, Henry, a women can't even break wind in this house without a *punkah-wallah* rushing in to wave it away.'

Henry was tight-lipped, shocked. 'Lucy, for goodness' sake, you're forgetting yourself.'

'Oh really? Maybe I'm remembering myself. Maybe I'm remembering that I'm a storekeeper's daughter from Oak City, Kansas, who was wooed by a charming and considerate Englishman, and who was innocent enough to think that when she was married, she would be treated not just like a social asset but like a wife.'

'Actually, I think that's quite enough,' said Henry. He turned his back on her, and began to walk away.

'Henry!' Lucy called him, in tight-throated desperation.

Henry slowed, stopped, turned. He took off his hat. 'Lucy, it's no good railing against destiny.'

'I don't care a toot about destiny, Henry. I care about you and I care about me, and I care about my baby.'

Henry stiffly lifted his arm, still holding his hat, and gestured toward the heat-hammered grounds, and to the Palladian rooftops of Calcutta beyond, and to India. 'It's an empire, Lucy, and I'm responsible. I've been responsible for it from the very second I was born.'

'Henry, nobody is *born* responsible for anything. Do you think that I was born to be an empress? You could turn your back on India tomorrow, the same way you just turned your back on me. India wouldn't sink into the sea.'

'I'm not pretending that it would. But I have to do my duty.'

'Why is it so damned important that you do your duty to India and so damned unimportant that you do your duty to me?'

Henry lowered his arm. 'I will make every possible effort to forget that you said that.'

'I hope you don't, Your Excellency. I hope you *never* forget it.'

499

Henry hesitated, then came back along the verandah. Dark eyes were watching them from all around: eyes that glittered from the garden, from the open doors that led to their private drawing room, from behind the billowing net-curtains of their bedroom suites, from the steps where the Untouchables were sweeping, those whose wealth would be measured only in dogs and donkeys, and whose clothes were the garments of the dead.

'Lucy,' Henry coaxed her, 'the very last thing I wanted to do was to make you unhappy. If I have, then I beg your forgiveness with all my heart.'

Lucy looked away, and said nothing.

'This trip to Agra . . . I dearly hope that it will be affectionate, as well as useful. Perhaps you can give me another opportunity to show you how deeply I care for you.'

Lucy swallowed, and nodded. 'I'm sorry,' she said, and she was; although not for what she had said. She was simply sorry that it had been necessary to say it.

'What, then, friends again?' asked Henry.

'I suppose.'

He kissed her cheek. 'Sometimes you sound just like a Kansas storekeeper's daughter.'

She gave him a small tart smile. 'Sometimes you sound just like an Honourable I once knew.'

At that moment, Walter Pangborn came battling his way through one of the breeze-blown curtains, in a cotton suit that looked like a slept-in bed. 'You've had a telegram from London, Lord Carson. It concerns that last dispatch you sent to the Russian War Minister. Yes, *that* dispatch. I think perhaps it would be wise if you could attend to it right away.'

'What? Very well,' Henry replied, without any hesitation whatsoever. 'My darling . . . I'll be back as soon as I can. Timothy Miller is taking care of Colonel Belloc for the time being, but it would be nice if you could make yourself known to him before dinner.'

In obedience to their usual parting ritual, Lucy obediently lifted her cheek so that Henry could peck it, and she watched him without smiling as he strode away.

Sukamar the head-*mali* appeared below the verandah as promptly as if he had been hiding in the bushes. 'Your Excellency *memsahib*' – and to Walter, 'pardon me, *hazur*, – is Your Excellency *memsahib* wishing to inspect the tree-planting now? They are all prodigiously straight and up-right.'

'Thank you, Sukamar, but later,' Lucy told him. 'Don't forget to give them plenty of *peenika-pani*.'

'Of course, Your Excellency,' Sukamar told her. 'The inspection will be at your convenience.'

After Henry had walked off, Walter had remained behind, grasping the stone balustrade. He seemed uncomfortable, as if he wanted to tell her something.

'Fine trees,' he remarked.

'Well, I don't know,' Lucy told him. 'Henry's quite convinced they're going to die.'

'Henry's not very optimistic about anything much these days,' Walter replied. He took out a silver cigarette case and asked, 'D'you mind if I smoke?'

Lucy shook her head, and watched him light up. 'Why isn't Henry very optimistic?'

'I don't think I ought to gossip,' said Walter.

'Walter, I'm Henry's wife. I think I have a right to know, don't you?'

Walter winced, and blew out smoke. He hadn't taken very well to India. Since his arrival, he had suffered from constant diarrhoea and he was looking waxy and sweaty and noticeably gaunt, and twenty years older than thirty-one. He kept insisting that he was quite well, but when Elizabeth had first met him at one of their weekly dances, she had remarked to Lucy that he had the unmistakable appearance of a man who would be celebrating Christmas in South Park Cemetery.

'Everything's about a hundred times slower and a hundred times more difficult than Henry expected,' Walter explained. 'He likes action, don't y'know – immediate results! But the ICS wallahs are grumbling and procrastinating and causing all manner of complications because Henry is trying to cut down their paperwork and reorganize their offices. The governors are going their own sweet way as usual, regardless of what Henry tells them. The maharajahs and the swats and the walis are jolly polite, but utterly unhelpful. The residents are utterly unhelpful without even bothering to be polite. And the Foreign Office has been screaming at Henry to stand up to the Russians, and then giving him all kinds of stick when he does.'

Walter paused, and smoked, and then he added, 'Henry came here with such a vision of what he was going to do. India was going to be reformed overnight! But, d'you know, he's like a man in a swamp, the more he struggles, the more he protests, the deeper he sinks. He can manage an awful lot, you know. And he'll change India quite dramatically, I'm sure. But he won't be able to achieve what he came here believing that he could achieve, he'll end up desperately disappointed, and that's the tragedy of it.'

Lucy said nothing for quite a long time. Then she smiled quickly, and nodded her hat, and said, 'Thank you for telling me, Walter. I appreciate it.'

Walter said, 'I hope I haven't –'

'No, no. You were quite right to tell me. And I won't say a word to Henry.'

Walter coughed. 'The Cussboss finds it quite difficult – well, I've known him for years and years, and he finds it quite difficult to admit that he might have made a mistake. India is India, don't y'know, and it has enough graves of disappointed men to prove it.'

He winced again, and coughed.

'Are you all right?' Lucy asked him.

'Oh, it's nothing. Just another twinge.'

'You should take some leave,' Lucy suggested. 'Did Henry tell you that we'll be taking a trip to Agra next week?'

'Yes, he has.' Walter didn't sound very enthusiastic. 'An architectural excursion, no less.' He peered out at the garden, squinting his eyes to focus against the sunlight. His pomaded hair shone, his eyes looked unusually bulbous. 'I expect H.E. will want me to tag along.'

Lucy suddenly realized that Walter's shoulders were shaking. 'Walter, you're shivering! You're not feeling ill again, are you?'

'No, no. It's nothing. I'll survive. We Pangborns were always made of sterling stuff. Unsinkable, that's us!'

Lucy laid a hand on his shoulder. 'I don't know, Walter; maybe you should talk to Major French again. Miss Morris says that even a chill can be ten times more serious here than it would be in England.'

'England!' Walter declared, with cheerful bitterness. 'My God, what I wouldn't give to be sitting in the Marlborough Arms, in Oxfordshire!'

'Do you really want to go back?' Lucy asked him. She hesitated, and then she said, 'You could, you know. Henry would understand. What do they call it? Getting your Blighty-ticket?'

'No, no, of course not,' said Walter. 'We've scarcely arrived, and there's so much to do. Can't let a little tummy trouble get me down. Anyway, look at the time! I've got heaps of accounts to sort out.'

He briefly grasped Lucy's gloved hand, and gave her a flustered smile, and went back inside. Just then, the head *khit* came out and bowed his turbaned head. 'Her Excellency would be caring for some refreshment? *Meta-pani*, perhaps?'

Lucy wasn't particularly fond of the head *khitmutgar*, a portly pale-faced Hindu called Tir' Ram, who was endlessly obsequious, but who managed to convey with his measured squeaky-sandalled walk and his slow, immaculately-accented English that he considered himself somehow superior to everybody around him, European or Indian.

'Just bring me some *cha*,' snapped Lucy – cross with him for no particular reason, except that he was full of himself.

She passed through the floating curtains into the drawing room. Inside, it was shaded and cool and she took off her hat. She saw that the latest issue of *The Illustrated London News* had been laid on the brass-topped table, and she went across to pick it up. The previous issue had contained an article on New York society, complete with photographs, and she had read it again and again, carried back for almost half an hour to the city that Mrs Sweeney had dreamed about; and that had once been hers.

As she flicked through the first few pages, however, she heard a hissing sound like a snake, suh-suh-suh-suh! and she turned in alarm and caught sight of Walter at the end of the corridor that led from the private wing to the state reception rooms. He was crouched tensely against the wall, as if he were battling with a stomach cramp.

'Walter!' she called. Then, when he didn't answer, she hurried up to him, lifting her skirts as she ran, and called shrilly for the servants. '*Koi-hai! Jeldi! Jeldi!* and tell His Excellency!'

'Walter?'

Walter was rigid with agony. Lucy gently took hold of his elbow, and helped him to slide down the wall into a crouched sitting position on the floor. His face was shining with perspiration, his mouth drawn as thin and as tight as scrimshaw.

'Walter, what's wrong?'

'I'm all right, really, I promise you,' he gasped. 'Just the *khrab*, that's all. I'll get over it.'

'We'd better get you to bed,' said Lucy. 'I'll call for Major French, too.'

'I'm quite well, really,' Walter insisted. He relaxed gradually, and straightened out his legs, and took out his crumpled-up handkerchief to wipe his mouth. Muhammad Isak had arrived now, with two other bearers.

'His Excellency will be coming immediately straightway instanter,' Muhammad Isak announced.

'Can you help the *sahib* on to his feet?' Lucy asked him.

But Walter said, 'Wait, Lady Carson, please, just one moment.'

He tilted his head back against the wall, and closed his eyes, breathing evenly but very harshly, as if his lungs were clogged.

At length he opened his eyes, and said, 'There's something I have to ask you. One small favour you could do for me.'

'Of course,' said Lucy. 'Just tell me what it is.'

Walter leaned forward, and spoke to her in the hoarsest of whispers. 'If I do have to go back Home ... you know, because of my health – you will make sure, won't you, that Henry doesn't lose heart.'

'I can't imagine Henry losing heart.'

Walter shook his head. 'He doesn't want you to worry. The only person who knows how hard it is, is me. But if I have to go back Home ... well, then, he won't have anybody but you. Nobody else understands him. Nobody else wants to. And – what I said to you before –'

Lucy waited. 'What is it, Walter? What's wrong?'

'Well, it was something of an understatement. Henry's panicking, almost, if you want to know God's honest truth.'

'But what can I do?' asked Lucy.

Walter coughed, and winced. 'You can't do any more than I've been doing ever since we got here. Give him courage, keep his chin up.'

Lucy grasped Walter's hand. 'Walter, this isn't the time or the place. You're ill, and I want you in bed.'

'I'm all right. Just let me sit here for a moment.'

'Walter, you'll feel better for a rest and some stomach powders. And I'm sure they won't send you back Home. Not unless you really want to go.'

Lucy stood up. 'Muhammad, please help Mr Pangborn upstairs,' Lucy told him. 'And be particularly careful, he's precious to us.'

Muhammad Isak had a thin ascetic face of extraordinary calmness; and the thinnest of black moustaches. 'The *sahib* will be regarded as china,' he replied. 'We have sent a runner for the doctor-major, too, Your Excellency.'

'Good,' said Lucy.

Walter was assisted to his rooms by Muhammad Isak and three more over-solicitous bearers ('pleased to be putting your next foot on to the stair, heaven-born sir.') After he had gone, Lucy stood at the foot of the staircase for a short while, with her hand raised to her mouth, thinking.

Of course it was quite likely that Walter was slightly delirious. Fever came with terrible suddenness in Calcutta. Elizabeth had told her of women who had woken fresh and healthy in the morning, and yet by nightfall the same day had died raving and screaming that their husbands were murderers and that their servants had all turned into monkeys.

But Walter was certainly right about one thing. Since he had arrived in India, Henry had become increasingly diffident and difficult to please. Even if it hadn't yet affected his health, the Augean task of administering India had already begun to take its toll on his morale. It had brought to the surface all of his worst characteristics: his short temper, his chronic inability to delegate, and his fear of showing how much he loved anybody and anything, apart from himself and public duty.

Lucy could begin to see why he had embraced Colonel Belloc's ideas with such enthusiasm. To restore India's architectural heritage would present him with a task of monumental detail; something grand and historic and far beyond the ambitions of anyone who wasn't obsessively seeking ever greater burdens with which to punish himself.

But it was a task at which he could achieve some immediate and visible success.

She had just turned away from the staircase when Henry appeared, closely followed by Timothy Miller. '*Khit* told me that Walter had been taken ill.'

'Henry, he's in a dreadful state. They've taken him upstairs.'

Henry propped his hands on his hips. 'I really can't understand it. He told me this morning he was feeling so much better. He's even put his name down for the polo competition.'

'Henry, he said that to please you. He says everything to please you.'

'Lucy, for goodness' sake!'

'I'm sorry, Henry, but it's true. I'm surprised you didn't see it for yourself.'

Henry looked at Lucy for a long, difficult moment. Behind him, Timothy Miller cleared his throat and tugged at his moustache and tried to appear as if he wasn't there at all.

'You've called Major French?' asked Henry.

'Of course.'

'Then I'll see you at dinner.'

'I thought you said you were giving yourself the afternoon off.'

Henry didn't even look at her. 'I was. Unfortunately Her Majesty's Government had other ideas. Besides —' and here he waited until Colonel Miller had begun to walk back towards the state reception rooms '— there isn't very much joy to be had in giving yourself an afternoon off if there is nothing to do during this afternoon off but to listen to interminable criticisms about how insensitive one is, and what a boorish husband one is, and how one's destiny is not a desiny at all, but simply a job, like ragpicking, or delivering coal, or selling cat's-meat from a wheelbarrow.'

'Henry —' Lucy began; but she could see that he wasn't listening; and that he didn't intend to listen.

'I'll see you at dinner, then,' she agreed. But, before he could turn to go, she added softly, 'And in bed, afterwards, Your Excellency.'

Henry gave her a look which she couldn't interpret. Not

hostile, but very strange, like a man dreaming with his eyes open.

They crossed the arid plains of Bihar, running north-west-wards under a dark carmine sky. The viceregal train was decorated with flags and ribbons, and the lacquer of its carriages gleamed so brightly that it ran along the horizon like the dawn breaking. As the train passed, peasants rose from their dusty fields and watched it, not waving, not moving. Bihar was one of the poorest and most backward states in India, run by wealthy landowners as if it were a feudal country from the Middle Ages.

Lucy sat for hour after hour by the curtained window of their silk-upholstered railway carriage with her chin resting on his hand, staring at the thin figures standing in the grainy morning twilight, just as they stared back at her. Crystal table-lamps set up a soft persistent jingle, like a rich man jingling his money.

When the sun rose higher, she saw that the plains were almost colourless, dun and flat and stretching to eternity. Occasionally the landscape was lit by the scarlet flame of a *mohur* tree, and as evening settled she saw horizontal lines of smoke from village fires, and the last golden veils of dust stirred up by cows. The thick perfume of evening penetrated the carriage's ventilation; and she began to feel the strong romantic pull of the continent of which she could call herself empress.

The train was running on Working Time Bill No. 25, a gilt-edged requisition announcing in printed copperplate that Their Excellencies Lord & Lady Carson were travelling from Howrah Railway Station in Calcutta to Agra Cantonment on February 23, 1899. It consisted of ten carriages, including a lounge car, a dining car, and a sleeping car, pulled by a locomotive called the *Empress of India*. More than ninety servants and bearers attended to the needs of the viceregal party, which included Colonel Belloc, Timothy

Miller, Walter Pangborn, two secretaries from Government House, two captains from the Royal Engineers, Nora, and eleven officers of the Viceregal Bodyguard, as well as horses, tents, and wardrobes.

Lucy was delighted by Colonel Belloc. He was a small, smart, tightly-corseted man of sixty-one with florid cheeks and huge white muttonchop sidewhiskers. He wore white and canary-coloured coats, and embroidered vests with innumerable pockets, in which he carried a variety of six or seven pairs of spectacles – 'for mighty vistas' – 'for reading railway timetables and the personal columns of *The Times*' – 'for sizing up handsome ladies' – 'for the front stalls of the theatre'.

The first night she had met Colonel Belloc at Government House, he had talked incessantly about the great palaces and temples of India, and how so many of them were collapsing from neglect. 'You should see the palace of Udaipur, at sunset, white marble rising from the middle of a lake. Or Shatrunjaya, which is a temple-city of eight hundred shrines, in the mountains of Gujarat. Golden, with a thousand spires! Or the Temple of Konarak, south of Calcutta, which positively writhes, positively wriggles, with thousands of stone carvings of human carnality. Made me tremble, the first time I set eyes on it! Made my teeth shake! And all I had with me were my hymnbook-reading spectacles!'

On the long train-journey to Agra, Colonel Belloc divided his time between reading the works of the Bengali poet Chandidas, writing minuscule and copious notes in his black-covered notebook, and drinking *burra-pegs* of brandy. In the evening, however, when Henry had retired to his study at the further end of the lounge car to work on his papers, he relaxed in his armchair and talked to Lucy about Tantric Yoga and the Hindu view of life and love.

'Hindus believe, you see, that there is no such problematic thing as "life", with "you" confronting it. The problems of "life" are simply ridiculous games which you yourself have

509

set in your own path. But the Hindus believe that "life" and "you" are one and the same thing – *Tat tvam asi,* "You are It".'

Lucy sat very upright, very correctly, dressed in a lace-trimmed evening gown of ice-blue silk, her shoulders bare, a pearl-and-diamond star shining on the white skin of her bosom. Her blonde hair gleamed in the lamplight. 'What of love, then?' she asked.

Colonel Belloc sniffed sharply and took off his half-glasses. 'Love?' he asked her. He glanced towards the other side of the lounge car, where Walter, pale-faced and gaunt, but reasonably animated, was reading *The Field*; and Timothy Miller was reclining in his chair with his eyes closed, humming Gilbert and Sullivan songs and waving his hand like an orchestra conductor.

Colonel Belloc had obviously sensed that she was doing more than making polite conversation. She was young, she was pregnant. She was married to one of the most powerful men in the British Empire.

'The *Brihadarankaya* says, "When a man is in the embrace of his beloved spouse, he knows nothing as within and nothing as without." In other words, my dear Lady Carson, real love – what the Buddhists call *vajra,* or diamond-like love – is achieved by concentration of both partners not on themselves but on their love.'

He could see that Lucy didn't quite understand him, but he leaned forward and continued gently, 'Lust comes in black and clerical habits, or bustles, crinolines, impenetrable corsets, black stockings and gloves, layers of lacy pettitcoats, leather riding-boots, derby hats and breeches and whips. But love in the Hindu world is nothing, or rather "no thing". When a couple come together they transcend their earthly personalities and become the primordial pair, Shiva and Parvati. He is *purusha,* the witnessing self; she is *prakriti,* the natural world. Each is both.'

Lucy said, 'I *think* I know what you're saying.'

Colonel Belloc leaned back again, and smiled at her

paternally. He wasn't in the least intimidated by her vice-regality. 'This evening, Lady Carson, you think that you know. One day, when you experience it for yourself, you will *know* that you know.'

Very softly, Lucy said, 'I hope you're not trying to suggest that I'm not really in love?'

'Should I answer such a question?'

Lucy hesitated, then nodded. 'Yes, you should.'

Tir' Ram was approaching with a decanter of brandy on a silver tray, balancing his pale bulk against the swaying of the train. She waited while he poured Colonel Belloc-*sahib* another *burra-peg*.

When he was gone, Colonel Belloc said, 'It's hardly my place to judge. But I know from experience that it is always difficult to give of oneself, when one is not at all sure that anything is being given in return.'

'You're very astute,' Lucy told him.

'My nanny always said that I was.'

The viceregal train crossed the border between Bihar and the United Provinces in the small hours of the morning, under a March sky bristling with stars. Lucy slept alone in her bed, on embroidered linen sheets, in the thinnest of linen night-gowns. Henry eased open the door of her sleeping-compartment to say goodnight to her before he turned in, but she was already asleep. He stood beside her bed, looking down at her with a sad and distant expression on his face. Her toes were slightly curled as she dreamed some dream, and he could have touched them and caressed them, but he didn't want to wake her up. Her skin glowed through the linen of her night-gown.

He kissed her curls. More gently, he kissed her cheek. Then he closed the compartment door behind him, and returned to his desk.

Although the United Provinces were watered by the holy river Ganges, they were almost as desolate as Bihar. The Hot

Weather was only two or three weeks away now, and the sun beat down on the plains with all the relentnessness of a brass gong. All that Lucy could see out of the window was beige dust and glaring sunlight.

She spent most of her afternoons lying on her bed, fanning herself and reading a book of Indian poetry that Colonel Belloc had lent her, while the viceregal train clattered and swayed, and the miles sped past beneath her. She was used to endless horizons and interminable train-journeys, but India seemed to unravel forever.

The poems of Chandidas brought her unexpected comfort, and she read them again and again.

> *I have taken refuge at your feet, my beloved.*
> *When I do not see you, my mind has no rest.*
> *You are to me as a parent to a helpless child.*
> *You are the goddess herself, the garland about my neck, my very universe.*
> *All is darkness without you; you are the meaning of my prayers.*
> *I cannot forget your grace and your charm, and yet there is no lust in my heart.*

Late the next evening she was reciting this poem to herself when Henry knocked on her door, and stepped into her compartment. He was wearing shirtsleeves and khaki shorts, and his armpits were dark with sweat. Lucy put down her book and looked up at him.

'You can come in, if you like,' she told him.

'Thank you.' He came into the compartment, and closed the door. Then he sat down on the end of her bed.

'There's something I seem to have forgotten to say,' he told her, with some awkwardness.

'Oh, yes?'

He gave her a boyish, evasive smile. 'Actually, I was talking to Belloc. About India, about buildings, all that kind of thing. And Belloc reminded me that Indian culture is inspired not just by aesthetics but by love. One human for another; and humans for their gods.'

Lucy smiled back at him. 'Belloc sets great store by love, doesn't he?'

Henry picked with his fingernails at the stitching of Lucy's bedspread. 'There was a time when *I* did, too. There was a time when I wrote you poems.'

'So what is it that you've forgotten to say?' Lucy asked him.

Henry's voice was unusually gentle. 'Hundreds of things; on hundreds of occasions. How pretty you looked, on the day we were married. How regretful I feel, for having hurt you so many times.'

He hesitated, and took hold of her hand, twisting her wedding-band around and around. 'Belloc reminded me that I should look on this tour as something of a romantic journey, not only for me, because I feel such an affinity with the classical buildings of India, but for both of us. This is the first time that you and I have travelled anywhere in India as husband and wife, not on official duty. On this journey, my darling, you are more than my Vicereine, you are my bride; and what I have forgotten to tell you is that in spite of all of the burdens I have to bear —'

He stopped, his eyes bright with tears, his mouth tightly-clenched, as if all the pain and the passions that he was unable to tell her about were bursting at last to be released. 'I do love you, Lucy, that's what I've forgotten to say. I worship you. I know that I can be difficult to love. I know that I can be irascible; inattentive; and selfish. I find it hard to express my adoration for you in words, and even harder to express it with my body. But never forget that I am yours, completely, and that I have entrusted you with my heart, for your safekeeping, for ever.'

With that, he leaned forward and kissed her lips, lightly at first, the faintest of brushes. Then he kissed her more urgently, again and again and again.

A surge of warmth and excitement rose up inside Lucy; a feeling that Henry hadn't aroused in her since they had first been married. She clung to him tightly and kissed him fiercely back, tangling her fingers into his hair, tugging up his shirt and his cotton undervest, and feeling the sweaty muscularity of his back.

'Oh, Henry, if you only knew . . .' she whispered, kissing his eyes, kissing his cheeks, kissing and biting at his lips.

'Lucy . . . my darling . . .'

He kissed her again, and then he sat up straight. He was searching for a way to explain something to her. 'Of course we cannot make love.'

Lucy swallowed, and nodded. Major French had warned her that 'husbandly penetration would pose an unacceptable risk to the foetal wellbeing.'

Henry took a deep breath, and allowed his words to stumble recklessly on, in case he lost his nerve and couldn't say anything at all. 'There are ways, however, you see, in which a man can worship a woman . . . Belloc was showing me drawings from the Temple of Konarak, well, not only drawings from the Temple of Konarak but other drawings as well, rooftops, spires, architectural plans – but at Konarak there literally hundreds of sculptures of every conceivable act of love. Erotic, but not lewd, if you understand what I'm saying. Lustful, but not corrupt. The pure enjoyment of the flesh – of a man for a woman, and a woman for a man.'

Lucy said nothing. It was plain that Henry had been highly stimulated by the pictures that Colonel Belloc had shown him; and perhaps that had been Colonel Belloc's deliberate and particular intention. Perhaps Colonel Belloc in his knowing old-India-hand way was encouraging Henry and Lucy to rekindle the natural urges which the pomp and formality of the viceregality had vitiated.

'I adore you, Lucy,' Henry repeated, and lifted the poetry book from the bedcover, and set it aside. He kissed her, and then he lifted aside the bedspread, too.

Lucy said nothing as Henry took hold of the hem of her thin linen nightgown, and drew it up over her knees. He kissed her bare thighs – then, serious-faced, he pulled away the pillow which she had propped behind her back while she was reading, and drew her gently down the bed, until she was lying almost flat.

She felt breathless, and she could feel her stomach tighten. But she allowed Henry to lift her nightgown right up to her breasts. He knelt on the bed, staring down at her naked body with an expression that she had never seen on his face before; reverent, but hungry, too.

He parted her thighs with his hands; and then with his fingers she felt him open the lips of her vulva. Their kissing had moistened her, and her lips parted with the tiniest of sticky sounds, as if they were the wings of a freshly-emerged butterfly. He lowered his head, and with a quake of shock and pleasure, she felt his tongue-tip sliding right down the cleft of her vulva and into her body.

'*Henry –*' she protested, grasping his hair.

But he refused to lift his head; and his tongue ran up and down, exploring every fold and niche. Then he began to lick her faster and faster, his tongue-tip flying across her clitoris in a dazzling *pizzicato*, scarcely touching it, but stirring up a feeling inside her that was deep and dark and tumultuous.

She lifted her head, panting. She watched in excited fascination as the dark red of his tongue flickered between the blonde curls of her pubic hair. His eyes were tight shut, his lips glistened. His face looked like a beautiful mask. Calm, intent, concentrated.

Beneath the bed, beneath the bedroom car, the train-wheels beat out a ceaseless clattering rhythm on the rails, and India flew by.

Lucy lay back, panting even more quickly. Something was happening to her, she hardly knew what. The beating of the wheels and the swaying of the carriage and the flickering between her legs seemed to compress themselves within her head; as if the whole sub-continent of India were being poured like black molasses into a single tin.

'Henry,' she said. Or perhaps she didn't. The train-wheels echoed; the carriage swayed. 'Henry, you mustn't.' But the flickering of his tongue-tip grew faster than ever, and every muscle in her body was locked tight, tighter and tighter, until she felt that she could never move again.

Without warning her body was seized by a spasm that was so violent that she cried out loud, and jerked wildly up and down on the bed, as if she were being furiously shaken by an invisible demon; the Pretas, the Hindu demon of unquenchable thirst and insatiable hunger.

She lay on her side, shivering, weeping; her stomach-muscles rigid, clutching the pillow. She didn't know if she had experienced ecstasy or not. The feeling was beyond description, beyond putting a name to. Perhaps it really had been *vajra*, the diamond-like love.

Slowly she turned her head, and saw Henry standing over her. He stroked her forehead, and then he said, 'Are you all right, my darling? I haven't hurt you?'

'No,' she whispered. 'You haven't hurt me.'

He carried on stroking her forehead. His eyes were gentle but distant.

'Isn't there anything I can do for you?' she asked him, her throat dry.

He smiled at her. 'Not now. It was long overdue – the time for me to do something for you, without asking for anything in return.'

'You're not leaving, though?'

'Not if you don't want me to.'

'Then stay, please,' Lucy begged him. 'Sleep with me tonight. Tell me all about these Indian buildings you want to restore.'

'For a while, then,' said Henry.

The train continued through the indigo-dyed curtains of

the night, across the plain, with the warm dust sizzling between its wheels. At ten o'clock, Nora came into Lucy's sleeping-compartment to ask her if she wanted anything. She found Lucy fast asleep, and Henry sitting beside her, gently stroking her hair with one crooked finger.

Henry said, 'Ssh,' and smiled. Nora hesitated for a moment, and then closed the door behind her, and made her way back to her own sleeping quarters. On the way she met Colonel Belloc, who was standing in the corridor smoking a cigar and watching the night pouring past the windows.

'Colonel,' she nodded.

'Good evening, madam. Have you said goodnight to Lady Carson?'

'Yes, sir, I have.'

'She was well, I trust?' asked Colonel Belloc, with the faintest touch of amusement in his voice.

'Yes, sir, very well. Was there any particular reason why you asked?'

Colonel Belloc blew out smoke, and then admired the glowing tip of his Havana. 'No particular reason. But we must always be concerned for the wellbeing of others, don't you think?'

They descended from their carriage under a flawless turquoise sky, and Henry turned to Walter Pangborn and said, 'Please keep everybody back for just a while. I want to show this to Lady Carson on my own.'

'Of course,' said Walter. He was wearing a small pair of green glass spectacles, and Lucy thought that he was looking distinctly unwell. Colonel Belloc, who had accompanied them in the same carriage, was standing up, his face shaded by his huge Cawnpore Tent Club topi, looking this way and that, and clucking to himself, which he always did when he was considering some architectural problem, or a crossword puzzle, or the price of zinc (his family fortune had been founded on zinc.)

Henry took Lucy's hand, and led her across a wide and dusty forecourt, between rows of unkempt cypress trees, past dried-up water channels and heaps of rubbish and stones and weedy pathways. In front of them was a scruffy bazaar, with sagging awnings and piled-up baskets, and smoky cooking-fires. There was a strong smell of burning lamb-fat and fenugreek. Pi-dogs snuffled around the bazaar, morbidly searching for bones and chicken guts.

Beyond the bazaar, however, something magical rose into the sky. A snow-white palace that lifted itself from the darkness of the cypresses and sparkled like a dream.

'It's utterly pure, utterly perfect,' said Henry. 'I had the same feeling when I first saw you. That mixture of loveliness and sadness which is essential to the highest form of beauty.'

'I can't believe it's real,' said Lucy.

They made their way through the bazaar until they were standing beneath the walls of the Taj Mahal itself. Two officers of the Viceregal Bodyguard followed discreetly behind them; but to the fruit-sellers and pot-menders and curry-cookers in the bazaar, they might just as well have been any other European tourists taking their almost-obligatory *dekho* at the Taj. Henry had insisted that this visit to the Agra presidency should be informal and unofficial, as far as any of their visits ever could be.

Off to their left, the River Yamuna slid calm and turquoise-blue, a mirror to the sky.

Henry took hold of Lucy's white-gloved hand. 'If I could have one wish, it would be that you and I could be entombed in a mausoleum even half as exquisite as this.'

Colonel Belloc approached, in his huge mushroom topi, swishing a fly-whisk against the back of his breeches. 'Well, Lady Carson, what do you think? True love, as expressed in marble and semi-precious stones. Not that many of the stones have been left intact. The sad passion of Shah Jihan for his beautiful Mumtaz Mahal, and Moghul architecture at its very peak. What a combination!'

Henry said, 'The very first thing we're going to do is clear away this bazaar. Then we're going to tidy up the gardens and the forecourts, and dig out the water-channels. The Taj should be reflected not only in the river but in the gardens around it, so that it appears to float suspended in the air.'

'Excellent,' said Colonel Belloc. He turned to Lucy and gave her a curious look, half amused, half knowing. 'Great beauty should always be well attended-to. Those who are careless about great beauty should not be surprised if it falls forfeit.'

'Who said that?' Henry asked him.

'I did,' Colonel Belloc replied.

They returned to Calcutta on the second Friday in March. For Lucy, their journey had been dreamlike and magical; not only because of the strangeness and beauty of the Indian countryside and its palaces and forts and extraordinary temples, but because of Henry's affection and attentiveness. He had stayed almost over-attentively close to her side, and for the first time since they had been married, he had treated her like a virgin bride.

She would never forget the two days they had been taken on a steamboat-trip down the Ganges; past the crocodiles grilling their spines in the sun, and the Indian women gracefully balancing pots of water on their heads. They had floated silently between high wooded cliffs which rose sheer from the water, past ruined Hindu temples, clusters of huts, and beautiful stone *ghats*.

Under the stars that night, sitting on a sofa outside their heavily-furnished tent, Henry had told her, 'Lucy, I shall return to Government House not just refreshed, but inspired. Shah Jihan was inspired by his love for Mumtaz to build the Taj Mahal. I shall be inspired by my love for you to work the greatest changes in India that history has ever seen.'

His words had sounded as grand and glittering as a palace.

But only two days after their return to Government House, Henry began to show signs of the same irritability and the same obsessive working habits that he had travelled to Agra to forget. In the two weeks that they had been away, his paperwork had piled up, and there were countless telegraph messages from the Foreign Office to deal with, as well as urgent memoranda from Kuwait (for which Henry was also responsible) and the North-West Frontier.

He appeared at their weekly ball on Saturday evening, but only for half an hour. He danced with her only once, and said scarcely more than twenty words. There were dark smudged circles under his eyes. On Sunday evening he failed to come down for dinner altogether. He was still at his desk as dawn broke on Monday morning.

Lucy found him at ten o'clock, sitting at his desk with papers spread out in front of him, writing with his right hand and forking up a breakfast of kedgeree with his left.

'Henry?'

He glanced up, finished his sentence, then wiped his mouth with his napkin, 'Lucy? Is anything wrong?'

'Henry, you look dreadful. Have you had any sleep at all?'

'I snatched an hour on the cot. Please don't worry, I'm quite all right. It's just that we've had a few local difficulties up at Landi Kotal. Tribal stuff, nothing to worry about.'

Lucy came and stood beside his desk in her long white dress. He sat tensely, his pen poised, waiting to continue his work.

'Henry, I don't want us to forget everything that happened when we went to Agra.'

He put down his pen as if it were actually painful for him to do so, a sort of rheumatism of the soul. He took hold of her hand, and kissed it. 'We won't forget, I promise you.'

'Then please come to dinner this evening. And please don't stay up all night.'

'I promise.'

At that moment, Henry's valet Vernon appeared, looking as smooth and as insolent as ever. 'Your bath's drawn, Your Excellency.'

'Thank you,' said Henry. He kissed Lucy's hand a second time, although there was no more emotion in it than a post-office clerk franking a letter. 'And don't worry, my darling, I'll be there for dinner, no matter what.'

Lucy left the library, her gown whispering softly on the polished floor. Vernon watched her go, with eyes as bright as a monkey's.

Later that afternoon, while Lucy was resting on a long-sleever on the verandah, and Nora sat beside her embroidering a pillow-slip, Timothy Miller appeared.

'Colonel Miller!' said Lucy. 'What do you think of my *peepul* trees now?'

'Very fine indeed,' Timothy Miller agreed. 'In fact, it's beginning to look like a *pukkah* garden, since you've been here. Lady Elgin didn't get on tremendously well with the head *mali,* that was the trouble.'

'He has to be nagged,' Lucy smiled. 'I'm very good at nagging.'

'Actually, Lady Carson, I have a message for you,' said Timothy Miller. 'I lunched at Peliti's today with the commanding officer of my old regiment. Leonard Ryce-Bennett – you met him about a month ago, splendid chap. But anyway an American chap came up to me and said that he knew you very well from Kansas, and presented his compliments, and asked to be remembered.'

Lucy was astonished. She laid down her fan and said, 'You met somebody from Kansas in Peliti's?'

Timothy Miller opened his wallet and produced a calling-card. 'He said he was sorry for not leaving his card earlier; but he'd been travelling all around India; and he'd only just arrived in Calcutta.'

Lucy took the card with trembling fingers and read the

name on it. *James T. Cullen, Attorney-at-Law.* She looked up at Timothy Miller and she was unable to conceal the astonishment in her voice.

'He's here? He's really here?'

Timothy Miller nodded. 'Talked to him myself, Lady Carson. Bearded chap, tall, well-built. Strapping, you might call him.'

'That's him,' breathed Lucy. 'Did he tell you what he was doing here?'

'Something to do with the United States Diplomatic Service, so I believe. He's staying at Spence's.'

'Then you must send Muhammad Isak to go bring him here!' said Lucy, excitedly. 'Listen, I'll write a note, and you must send two bearers and a half-a-dozen coolies, so that they can carry his bags! He has to stay here at Government House, he must!'

Timothy Miller rang for one of the liveried bearers, who brought Lucy her portable writing-desk. She propped it on her knees, dipped her pen in the crystal inkwell, and wrote,

> *My dearest Jamie,*
> *While you are here in Calcutta it is positively unforgivable of you to stay in an hotel! You must come to Govt House at once, so that Henry and I can look after you! If you are not here within 1 hr I will come and get you myself!!*
> *Love, Lucy.*

She flapped the letter in the heat to dry it; then she sealed it and gave it to Timothy Miller. The aide-de-camp took it and bowed his head. But as he did so, he caught the concentrated look of misgiving on Nora's face. Behind Lucy's back, as she shut up her writing-desk, his lips formed the silent question, *'What . . .?'* but before Nora could give him any silent clues, Lucy said, 'Haven't you gone yet, Colonel Miller?'

'Ekdum, Your Excellency,' replied Timothy Miller; using

the Urdu word for 'immediately' to hint that she was treating him like a native servant.

When he had gone, Nora continued to frown at Lucy, with her embroidery in her lap. Lucy glanced at her, then turned away – then, when she realized that Nora wasn't sewing any longer, she looked back again.

'Well – what's wrong?' she wanted to know.

'You know what's wrong, your ladyship. You shouldn't have asked Jamie to come here.'

'Why on earth not?'

'You know why not. The Vicereine must always conduct herself in a manner becoming to Her Majesty herself.'

'But I've known Jamie all my life! I'm not going to ignore him, just because I'm the Vicereine. In fact – *because* I'm the Vicereine – I'm going to welcome him all the more warmly, so there!'

Nora shook her head. 'I just hope His Excellency will understand.'

'His damned Excellency is too busy working on his damned papers to worry about anything.'

'Didn't you say that you and his lordship had fallen in love with each other, all over again?'

'We did! In Agra, and in Oudh, and on the Ganges. But where is he now? Back at his desk, back with his papers and his worries and his government reports. Back with his residents and his commissioners and his deputy commissioners and his collectors and his clerks.'

'Lady Carson, it's his life's calling, you know that; and a wonderful calling it is, too.'

'Oh, yes!' said Lucy, bitterly. 'It's wonderful! Pomp and power, parties and balls! But men are all the same, Nora! They tie you up with silk ribbons, and they take your honour, and then they leave you to fend for yourself.'

Nora said nothing for a very long time. Outside in the gardens, it was baking hot, and the gardeners moved along the row of fig-trees, flooding the roots of each of them in turn.

'Well, I suppose it's not my place to criticize,' Nora decided. 'All I can say is that you should have a care. You may not think that Lord Carson is possessive about you; or that he loves you as dear as you believe he should. But I know a man who won't trust women when I see one; and I know a man who's jealous. I also know a man who's been badly hurt by a woman, once in his life, and won't let it happen again.'

'Nora, you're always looking on the black side,' Lucy chided her.

'Yes, your ladyship, perhaps I am. But at least that way I never get disappointed.'

The maroon-varnished carriage which Timothy Miller had sent to Spence's Hotel came rattling briskly through the gates of Government House less than fifty minutes later; and drew up beside the steps. The afternoon rippled with heat. The carriage door was opened by a liveried Indian servant, and the steps put down, and Jamie alighted, removing his double *terai* hat as he did so.

Lucy had asked Muhammad Isak to tell her immediately the carriage entered the grounds; and as Jamie took his first steps up towards the pillared portico, she came sweeping out in her long lawn dress and her wide white hat, and stood at the top of the staircase to greet him.

He came up slowly, his shadow zig-zagging behind him down the steps. He looked as if he had lost weight; but he was as tall and broad-shouldered as she always pictured him, and he was smiling in the same wry way.

'Your Excellency,' he said, bowing his head. His face was deeply suntanned, in contrast to most of the European men whom Lucy knew; who didn't want to look like *chi-chis*. He wore a plain grey suit and a soft-collared shirt, with a bolo necktie. His beard was streaked with fair hair, and made him look much older.

'Jamie! Of all the people I never expected to see in India!' shone Lucy.

'Well, then,' said Jamie, looking around at Government House. Scaffolding had been erected on the north-eastern side already, and the painters were busy with their white-wash. The lazy slap of their brushes punctuated the afternoon heat. 'So you found your cloud-castle at last?'

Lucy looked him up and down. She felt brimful with pleasure. 'You haven't changed! Well, you have, just a little! You're thinner!'

'I've been travelling, that's all,' Jamie told her. 'Hotel food, can't be helped.' He accepted her arm, and she led him into the house; through the cool echoing corridors. He nodded, and said, 'This is quite some place you've got here, isn't it? Befitting, I'd say.'

'You're teasing me,' Lucy protested.

'When did I ever tease you? It's befitting. You always dreamed of living someplace like this.'

His hat was taken, his cane disappeared. Abdul Aziz appeared, on silent slippers, and asked if he would care for tea. They were directed into the small white drawing room next to the main private lounge, where the curtains rose and sighed and fell back again; and a decorated brass dish stood on the low Benares table, heaped with *shakar parre* sugar puffs and the sesame-seed meringues called *tiltandula* and Darjeeling tea for two, in thin palmyra-decorated china that had been specially designed for Government House by Minton. Four servants stood attentively behind their chairs to pass their cups, and to help them to sweetmeats with silver tongs.

'So you're expecting another baby?' said Jamie. 'I didn't know.'

Lucy nodded; and couldn't think why she felt so shy about it. 'Henry's hoping for an heir to all the Carson estates. But how's Sha-sha? She must be so grown up by now.'

Jamie shrugged. 'She's fine. She's very pretty. She has blonde curls and ribbons, just like you. She can sing, she can dance. The last time I saw her was late last fall, just before they sent me out to Manila.'

'I miss her, you know,' said Lucy.

'Well, me too,' Jamie told her. 'But that was the way it had to happen, wasn't it? There's no sense in crying over spilled milk.'

'I wish I could see her, just once.'

Jamie picked up his tea, and sipped it. 'That wouldn't do anybody any good. She thinks that my father and mother are her real parents. It's real strange to see her sitting on my father's knee, and calling him papa, when all the time *I'm* the one she should be calling papa, not him.'

'Did the porters bring your bags?' asked Lucy. 'You can have the Aurangzeb bedroom, it's marvellous, it's all decorated in the Moghul style of the eighteenth century. You have a wonderful view of the garden I've been planting.'

'I'm sorry, I can't stay,' Jamie told her. 'I'm expected in Delhi by the end of the week. Then I have to travel north, to Kashmir.'

Lucy felt sharply disappointed; almost insulted. Since she had become Vicereine, she had been used to having her own way. For Jamie to decline her invitation was almost as unthinkable as turning down the Queen.

'You can stay for just two days, surely? I can have a special train requisitioned to take you to Delhi.'

Jamie shook his head. 'I'm sorry. I have to leave tomorrow. And the people I'm seeing wouldn't appreciate my arriving by specially-requisitioned train.'

'You can stay for tonight, can't you? Come for dinner!'

'Lucy, I'd love to, but no.'

'But why on earth not?'

'It just wouldn't be much of an idea, that's all. There are

times when what's past is best forgotten. Besides which, I don't want to be seen as too much of a pal of the Viceroy.'

'Who on earth's going to think that? And what does it matter, anyway?'

Jamie bit into one of the meringues. 'These are good,' he told her.

'My cook makes them specially for me. He calls them Lady Carson's Wishes. The recipe comes from a Hindu play that was written about two thousand years ago. Eggs, butter, brown sugar, limes, and a grain of sandalwood. But you're changing the subject.'

'I know,' Jamie agreed. He kept his eyes averted. 'But, you know – it's probably best for both of us if we don't discuss the reasons for my being here.'

Lucy widened her eyes in mock-disapproval. 'Can it be that terrible? You haven't taken up with pirates, have you, or opium-smugglers?'

'Lucy –'

But Lucy was irritated now. 'You used to tell me everything down at Overbay's Bend! All of your dreams, everything! So why can't you talk to me now?'

Jamie lowered his head for a while; then looked up at her and said, gently, 'Times have changed, Lucy; and so have we. You're not Lucy Darling any more. You're Her Excellency Lady Carson of Brackenbridge, the Vicereine of India.'

'I know that,' Lucy retorted. 'But what are you?'

Jamie pulled a wry face. 'Me? I'm not a lord or a viceroy or anything. I'm just a man who suddenly woke up.'

'What am I supposed to understand by that?'

Jamie sat back in his chintz-covered armchair. 'You remember all that legal work I was doing, on Red Indian affairs? I made quite a reputation for myself in Washington. My crowning achievement was when I dispossessed the Comanche around Spanish Peaks. No trouble, no fighting, they just folded their tepees and off they went. The government liked the way I could soft-talk the Indians into giving up their territories without provoking Little Big Horn the Second! "Can-Do Cullen", that's what they called me. It became my speciality, I guess: the legal rights of indigenous populations. In other words, how to gyp natives out of everything they've ever been entitled to. I was offered a job by Hector McAllen, doing legal work for the US Diplomatic Service. Good job, too, travelling the world, plenty of expenses. All I had to do was dispossess unsuspecting heathens wherever I found them, without breaking the letter of the law, or the solemn promises of Uncle Sam.'

A *khit* came forward, as silent as a shadow, to pour Lucy a second cup of tea. Lucy said, cautiously, 'Jamie, you sound so bitter.'

'No, I'm not bitter,' Jamie assured her. 'I've woken up, that's all. While I was working in an office, I didn't realize that the law had any particular connection with justice. But last year I went out to the reservations and saw some of those Comanche and Sioux families being moved off their homelands, in the middle of one of the coldest winters in living memory – old people, women, little children – and all because of legal work for which *I* had been personally responsible. Back at my office, in Manhattan, my boss had clapped me on the back, and given me a big cigar, "Have a cigar, Jamie, by thunderation you've earned it!" and a pay hike, too. He never saw those tiny babies in the snow. I thought of Sha-sha, then, and I thought of you; and I thought of me. We suffered, yes, when times were thin. But we never suffered like those Red Indians suffered. You wouldn't even know the meaning of the word suffering unless you saw what they had to endure. And we never suffered because of God-fearing human rapacity, and God-fearing human greed; and laws that twisted this way and that like the Saline River.'

'So what are you doing here in India?' asked Lucy.

'You could say that the wind just blew me this way. I was in Manila just a couple of months ago.'

'Manila, that's in the Philippines. You're fighting a war in the Philippines. Well, the United States is.'

'That's right,' said Jamie, 'and I was part of it. It was my duty to draw up papers that proved beyond a shadow of a legal doubt that the new Aguinaldo government was unconstitutional, and that the Spanish were still the legal administrators of the Philippines.'

Lucy was perplexed. 'But why would you do that? Surely the United States is at war with Spain.'

Jamie gave her a ground-glass smile. 'That's the whole point. The United States is at war with Spain, so if the Philippines still legally belong to Spain, we have the legal right to invade the Philippines and to shoot anything that moves. It's the old story, Lucy. I was supposed to be preparing legal pontifications in support of justice and human rights, but all I was doing was protecting the United States and its sugar industry.'

Lucy sat back in her chair. She had spent enough time with Henry and his political colleagues to understand that this was dangerous talk. It had been the golden conviction of every imperial administrator from Clive in India to Andrew Jackson in America that the inferior races 'have neither the intelligence, the industry, the moral habits, nor the desire of improvement which are essential to any favourable change in their condition' and that 'they must necessarily yield to the force of circumstances.'

To suggest that natives had rights of their own was close to blasphemy.

Jamie brushed meringue-crumbs from his lap, and then he said, 'One morning in Manila I was walking to the office and I came across a *negrito* woman lying in the gutter. Very black, very ugly, her dress pulled right up to her waist. She had a bullet-hole in her forehead and flies were crawling in and out of the bullet-hole like clerks crawling in and out of a law office.'

He didn't even look to see how Lucy was reacting to what he was saying. It was all too sharp in his mind; he had walked past this woman and she had actually been lying there, dead.

'What did you do?' whispered Lucy.

'What would you have done, if you had seen for yourself the effects on one poor woman of high-minded colonial rule? A bullet in the head, is that what it all amounts to? A gutter, and nobody even to pull your dress down and give you that last token of human respect? I'll tell you what I did: I kept on walking, right past the office door, and down to the docks. I caught the next steamer that was going, and I spent Christmas alone at the Gia-Long Hotel in Saigon, with *thit bhot to* for lunch, and nobody to sing carols with.'

He stood up; and walked across the drawing room to the beige-shaded window. Lucy was conscious that there was something in his posture which had changed. Maybe it was experience. Maybe it was age. Maybe it was harsh reality; and the burdens of fatherhood. Not just to a child; but to his own ideas. Men with no guilt never stoop their shoulders, not the way that Jamie was stooping.

'I travelled to Bangkok; and then to Rangoon, and up-country to Pyinmana and Mandalay; and then I read that Sir Humphrey Birdwood was giving a series of lectures on colonial law, here in Calcutta. It wasn't much of an excuse to come here; but it was good enough. And so I came.'

'You knew that I was here,' said Lucy, quiet as milk.

Jamie said nothing; but she could tell by the way he held his head that he had thought of her; and that he had been drawn to India as much by wanting to see her as he had by his conscience.

'Are you sure that I can't persuade you to stay?' she asked him, in an accent so English that she noticed it herself.

'No,' he replied, 'I don't know why it is, but life always seems to conspire to put us on different sides. You have your destiny; I have my conscience. Oil and water, I'm afraid, immiscible.'

Lucy said, 'Do you feel the same way about me now as you always did?' She hoped that the smooth-faced servants standing attentively behind their chairs wouldn't be able to follow what she meant.

Jamie tightened his mouth, didn't speak, but nodded.

'I feel the same way, too,' Lucy told him, trying not to sound breathless.

Jamie turned quite suddenly and stared at her. His expression was dark and hard: the expression of somebody who doesn't want to be played with. 'Are you serious?' he demanded. 'You're Empress of India, in everything but name. You have three hundred millions of people bowing down in front of you. You're pregnant with Henry's first child.'

Lucy took a deep breath. She felt giddy, and too hot; and even the ceaseless stirring of the gathered-muslin *punkahs* did nothing to make her feel any cooler. 'You and I grew up together. Nothing can change that. You and I know how Sha-sha came to be born, and nothing can change that, either.'

Jamie came over and held out his hand and smiled. 'Just like I said. No use crying over things that can't be helped.'

Lucy pressed her napkin against her mouth, and told herself strictly that she wasn't going to cry, no matter what.

Jamie watched her for a few moments, and then said, 'I think I'd best be going now. Is there someplace private, where we can say goodbye? Someplace – well, you have a whole herd of servants, don't you? It's kind of difficult to be yourself, with half of Bengal looking on.'

Lucy took Jamie's hand and climbed to her feet. 'Come to my sewing room.'

Immediately, the servants drew back Lucy's chair, and prepared to accompany her wherever she wanted to go, in case she should need something to sit on, or drop her handkerchief, or decide she was too cold, or too hot, or felt like a stroll in the garden. But Lucy raised her hand, and said, 'That will be everything,' and they bowed their turbaned heads, and said, 'Thank you, Your Excellency *memsahib*,' and let her leave the room, although their proprietorial anxiety was as thick and as cloying as vanilla *halva*. They didn't take their eyes away from Jamie until Lucy had swung the sewing-room door closed behind them.

In the buttermilk sunlight of a Calcutta afternoon, Lucy grasped Jamie's hands, and looked up into his face, and saw the whole of their childhood there, as country-simple as a book, but all of his years of work besides. She saw the hours of ambitious lawyering that Jamie had undertaken, to get himself to Washington. She saw the pain, and the disillusionment, and the care.

She loved him, she knew she did. She always had. But he wondered how much of her love was memories, and nostalgia; and whether it was easy to love him now because she wanted for nothing, and because no matter how preoccupied Henry might be, she was always well-cared-for.

Nora had once remarked, 'It's always the well-cared-for women who stray.'

Jamie held her in his arms, and she felt his unaccustomed beard against her cheek. But there was nothing unfamiliar about the way he embraced her, and when she kissed him, they kissed as deeply and as caringly as two people who had always been lovers; sharing their hearts, even if they had rarely shared their beds.

They kissed again. They didn't need to speak. If they had spoken, it could only have been to say goodbye, or to regret the circumstances that had kept them apart, and always would. Lucy closed her eyes. The hardness of her pregnant stomach pressed through her dress against the hardness of Jamie's penis. Their kissing had immediately aroused him; so that his grey trousers strained stiff. But their affection for each other was so strong that neither of them drew away. His excitement was a fact, just as Lucy's new baby was a fact, and they accepted both with silent – even mischievous – delight.

When their kisses had lingered; and died; and lingered again, they stood in the centre of the room still holding each other tightly.

'You'll be careful, won't you?' Lucy whispered, in a throaty voice.

'I'll be careful.'

'You won't die for any lost causes?'

Jamie squeezed her even more closely. 'Justice for people who have never been given justice before is never a lost cause.'

Lucy lifted her head. It was then that she saw in the mirror on the opposite side of the sewing room that the door behind her was slightly ajar, and that a pale-faced figure in a dark suit had been watching them steadily from the corridor outside. She turned, and gasped, and instantly the figure vanished, but she was quite sure that it had been Vernon, Henry's valet.

'What's wrong?' Jamie asked her. 'Lucy – what's wrong?'

She pushed his arms away. 'You'll have to go! Please, Jamie, you'll have to go!'

'I don't understand, what's wrong?'

'Somebody was watching us. One of the servants.'

'So what if they did? They wouldn't dare to say anything, surely?'

'It was a European.'

'All the same.'

'Jamie,' Lucy flustered, 'I'm Vicereine! And if you *knew* what Calcutta is for scandal!'

Jamie was about to protest, but when he saw the anxiety in her eyes he lifted both of his hands in resignation, and said, 'Very well. I have to go anyway.'

Lucy opened the sewing-room door wide and called for the servants.

'I'm sorry,' said Jamie. 'I just hope you don't have any trouble.'

'Will you write?' she asked him. 'At least let me know where you are.'

'I'll try,' he told her. 'I'm not sure that my friends are always going to be too happy about it.'

'You and I weren't put on this world to make our friends happy,' smiled Lucy, with tears in her eyes.

'Trouble is,' Jamie replied, 'we weren't even put on this world to make each other happy.'

Vernon's approach came much sooner than Lucy had expected. Jamie had been gone for only a half-hour, and she was sitting on the verandah with a glass of tonic water and fresh lime juice, when he passed through the floating gauze curtains like a shadow, and was suddenly there.

'Lady Carson?' he asked her, his hands clasped behind his back. 'I was wondering if I might have a word.'

Lucy had always considered Vernon to be coarse. His East End accent, she supposed. But when he approached her this afternoon she realized that she had quite dramatically misjudged him. His grey suit was perfectly tailored. His hair was cut with the precision that only a straight-razor and an utterly steady hand could achieve. Only his eyes reinforced the threat implicit in his voice. They were like the eyes of an intelligent but soulless primate; the eyes of a man who hit women. He moved with suppressed athleticism, which made him appear even more threatening. You knew that if he hit you, he would hurt you.

'How can I help you?' Lucy asked him; in a tone that tried to suggest that she wouldn't lift a finger to help him, even if she could.

Vernon pulled a face. 'I don't know, your ladyship. I think it's more like a case of *me* helping *you*.'

Lucy raised her eyes. 'And how exactly do you propose to do that?'

'Born and bred to be useful, your ladyship, that's me. Keep me mincers peeled, keep me lugs open. Knowing what's what, and who's doing what, and who wiv; that's John Vernon's particular stock-in-trade.'

'I thought you were a gentleman's gentleman, not a one-man newspaper.'

'Same thing, your ladyship. Part of the job. I mean, what use is a gentleman's gentleman if he can't serve his gentleman in every way there is; from polishing his toecaps to brushing his hats; and letting him know what's what, from time to time. I've always made it my business to tell my gentlemen everything what passes my way; from the favourite runners at the races to the latest intelligence about who was going bankrupt and who was misbehaving themselves wiv whom.'

Lucy said, with as much calmness as she could manage, 'What do you want?'

Vernon feigned surprise. 'What do I want? My dear Lady Carson, I never wanted nothing. Only to serve Lord Carson to the best of my ability and to find favour, if at all possible, wiv yourself.'

Lucy swung her legs off her long-sleever. 'Oh, come on, Vernon, what do you want? Five pounds? Ten pounds? A bottle of brandy?'

Vernon looked at her with those black soulless eyes; and then he slowly cracked an apeish smile. 'Fair dos, if you're going to play it so straight. Two hundred rupees a month, that would do it.'

'And how on earth do you think I can pay you two hundred rupees a month? I don't even know what a rupee looks like, if you want to know the honest truth.'

'It's quite all right, your ladyship. All you have to do is sign a chit. A little scrap of paper, promising to pay the bearer two hundred rupees. That'll be just as good as money.'

Lucy stared back at him and hated him so intensely that she could have stood up and slapped him and spat in his face. Perhaps if she hadn't have been pregnant she would have argued with Vernon, fought him. Perhaps if Henry hadn't been so unpredictable, she could have told him to do his worst. But she felt physically unbalanced and emotionally defensive. She wasn't at all confident that Henry would believe that whatever she felt for Jamie was nothing compared to her need to be wealthy, her need to be great, her need to hold the balance over other people's lives. She wasn't at all confident that she believed it herself.

It was the most tormenting of paradoxes. She had achieved greatness; she had achieved all the social influence that any woman could dream of. Yet here in front of her was another smiling man, nothing but a servant, making a victim of her.

She looked at Vernon and knew where she had seen such eyes before. They were the eyes of Uncle Casper; and of all the other Uncle Caspers; men who ran through the understructure of civilized society like rats through a derelict building.

She walked through to her drawing room, sat at her desk, took out a sheet of notepaper and unscrewed the cap of her Chinese-enamel pen. *Please pay bearer on receipt of this two hundred rupees,* and signed it.

Vernon accepted it with a nod, and blew on it steadily to dry the ink. 'I overheard Colonel Miller saying that your ladyship was a most extraordinary Vicereine. Must say that I have to concur wiv him, wholehearted-like.'

That night, however, she dreamed that she was back in Port Said; being jostled by crowds, under a thunderous sky. She was pushing her way through hundreds of hunched-up women, their faces completely covered with black veils. They knocked her with their shoulders and nudged their heads against her, quite violently, like undisciplined puppies. She was crossing the pavement towards Simon Artz's emporium when a dark figure flung himself at her. She tried to shout out, but her voice sounded strangled. A sword flashed, and the figure's face was cut completely in half.

There was no blood, only two halves of a head lying on the pavement like a sliced-open watermelon. Both halves were smiling at her. One half was Uncle Casper; the other was Vernon.

She sat up in a sweat, her sheets knotted, screaming for Nora.

The following morning, Henry came into the drawing room just before luncheon and stood fanning himself with a copy of *Punch*.

'Anything wrong?' Lucy asked him.

'Yes, as a matter of fact. *Punch* says that I believe myself to be divine, which is probably true; and we're losing Walter. He was very sick again last night, and Major French says he ought to be sent back Home.'

'Poor Walter!'

'Yes, and poor me, too. I shall miss him very sorely.'

Lucy said, 'You shall have to depend on me a little more.'

'You're expecting our baby. I can't make any more demands on you than I do already.'

'You can't make any fewer.'

Henry frowned. 'What do you mean by that?'

'I'm not quite sure. I think I'm beginning to understand something about men, that's all.'

'Oh, yes!' Henry laughed. 'And what great insight have you come up with that will dazzle the world and impress us all?'

'I'm not sure how to put it. But it's all to do with love and hatred.'

Henry sat down on the arm of Lucy's chintz sofa, took hold of her hand, and kissed it. 'Surely you haven't come to believe that I hate you?'

'No, I don't. But you hate the fact that you love me. It makes you feel weak. It makes you feel obliged. You always seem to think that you have to be punished for loving me. You keep trying my patience, and trying my love – as if you're deliberately provoking me into lashing back and saying something cruel to you, something unloving. Then you'll be able to forgive me, and feel like the great benevolent Sahib; and in secret you'll feel guilty because you made me beg your forgiveness, and you'll wallow in your guilt like you always do.'

Henry slowly lowered his head. A muscle worked in his cheek. Stiffly, he released Lucy's hand. 'You know, Lucy – I'm beginning to question whether you and I are suited.'

'There you are,' she challenged him. 'Doing it again!'

'Doing what again?' Henry demanded.

'Trying to make me feel guilty! Well, I won't!'

Henry tossed the copy of *Punch* across the room, so that its pages fluttered and burst out of its spine. 'Sometimes, my dearest, you're quite impossible. Will you dress for luncheon, please? We're entertaining the railway people today, as you probably know.'

'Henry!' Lucy called, as he marched off towards the door.

Then, 'Henry!' she repeated, her voice a little higher-pitched.

He turned, cross. She smiled at him with bright eyes. 'I love you, Henry, in spite of all.'

Walter came in to say goodbye. He was very thin; his face as yellow as the old newspapers you discover under twenty-year-old linoleum. He insisted, however, on walking unaided by his bearers, and in bowing to Lucy as a formal farewell.

'Goodbye, Walter,' she told him, taking his hand.

'You won't forget what I said? Won't let him lose heart?'

'No,' she whispered.

He nodded. 'Jolly good, then. I'd better be off. Nothing else I can do, is there?'

'Perhaps one thing,' said Lucy.

Walter raised an eyebrow.

'It's just that I was talking to a young ICS wife the other day . . . and it seems that she was seen by one of her servants doing something indiscreet.'

Walter leaned his hand against the table to support himself. 'Oh, yes? May I ask *how* indiscreet? It does happen, you know, especially in hills, before the men go up; and in the Hot Weather.'

Lucy tried to smile. 'Not *very* indiscreet ... a mistake, more than an indiscretion.'

'I see. So what are you asking?'

'Well, the fact of the matter is that her servant is demanding money not to tell her husband. Blackmail, I guess you'd call it, so that that *sahib* won't find out.'

Walter coughed, and narrowed his eyes. 'Is this an *Indian* servant?'

'I'm really not sure.'

'It doesn't sound like the kind of thing that an Indian servant would do. Not demand money from a European woman. They're too proud of their jobs; even the lower-caste servants. And they'd be too damned scared of the consequences if they were caught.'

Lucy said, 'I really have no idea. This young woman – she was, well – she was quite upset.'

Walter took out his handkerchief, and dabbed thoughtfully at his turkey-shrivelled neck. 'I don't know. The proper thing to do is to inform the police. But I suppose this young lady isn't keen.'

'She'd rather not.'

'I can't help you, then,' said Walter. 'I know what *I'd* do, if I were the young lady involved. But it's not a course of action I could cheerfully recommend, not to anybody.'

'What would you do?'

Walter gave a feeble grin, and cut his throat with his finger. 'There are plenty of obliging fellows in India, who would silence a chap like that for ever; and probably charge half what he's asking to keep silent now. That's India for you. Information is expensive, but life is extremely cheap.'

He hesitated, swayed on his feet, still grinning. 'But whatever you do, don't tell her I told you. Can't have young ladies assassinating their servants – now can we?'

★

On the last day of March, Lucy held a 'drawing room' for the wives of junior ICS officials. She always enjoyed the company of the younger women, even when they were stiff and shy (which they usually were). She could sympathize with their uncertainty: not only about the strangeness of India, but about the men who had brought them out here.

Most of them were fiercely snobbish, and all of them considered Indians to be racially and culturally inferior. But Lucy knew from her own experience how much of their prejudice was rooted in fear and ignorance. She also knew from meeting some of Elizabeth's friends that while the new arrivals seemed arrogant and reserved, they would eventually give almost everything to India. Their love, their loyalty; quite often their happiness, too; and their children's lives; and their own lives, too.

It wasn't easy for a young middle-class English girl to come out to India and run a household of six or seven servants, especially when she couldn't speak Urdu, and it had been firmly impressed on her that it 'wasn't done' for her to try.

It was an exceptionally hot day, even for the end of March, over ninety-five degrees, and all the shades were drawn, so that the Tiffin Room was bathed in a gloomy subaqueous light. The English ladies always shut out India, protecting themselves from its heat and its language and its customs. One of the young women was telling Lucy that she was worried about her garden. She always planted nasturtiums and phlox and chrysanthemums in the Cold Weather, and they grew wonderfully, but as soon as the Hot Weather started, they shrivelled to nothing. 'Every year, you see, you have to start all over again.'

Another young woman with a complexion like fresh milk sprinkled with cinnamon said that she found it difficult to get used to the idea of so many servants. If she dropped a spoon on the floor, she was not allowed by her servants to pick it up. If she went out in the garden, simply for a stroll, a *chaprassi* would patiently follow her around with a deck-chair, in case she should take it into her head to sit down. And when she had tried to plant some calendula seeds with a tiny little fork and trowel, an entire deputation of *chaprassis* and *babus* had called on her husband that evening and said that digging by the *memsahib* was not allowed. A dozen coolies would be summoned in the morning to do the digging.

Lucy had grown used to Nora and Etta's attentions for a long time now, but she still found it difficult to accept the constant and detailed care which she was given by their Indian servants. She was expected to do nothing for herself whatsoever. Not to wash herself, nor dress herself, nor brush her hair, nor lace up her shoes. Whenever she left Government House, even for a shopping trip to Chowringhi with Elizabeth, it was always in the company of twenty or thirty people, including four officers of the Viceroy's Body-guard.

She discovered, too, that the Indian caste system was even more rigorous than the European order of precedence. Only yesterday morning, she had gone out to find a dead bird lying on the ceremonial steps. She had asked a *mali* to remove it, but the *mali* refused, because it was forbidden for him to touch dead birds. She had asked the *mali* to call for the *masalchee*, but he also refused to touch it. Then she had called for a sweeper, who usually cleaned out the lavatories, but he had refused, too. In the end, they had been obliged to send for a low-caste *dome* boy from the bazaar, and he had removed it.

Lucy found it frustrating and unreal; as if she were being deliberately prevented by some elaborate conspiracy from making any contact with India herself. You may rule, *mem-sahib*, but you may not touch.

She was listening politely to a young wife telling her that she was trying to learn Urdu, because she had nobody to talk to during the day, except for her servants.

'I said to the cook, *kab* the sahib *yeh chiz dekhenge,* he will go *gonga.*'

As Lucy nodded and smiled, she saw Etta hurrying across the Tiffin Room, followed by Muhammad Isak and two other bearers. 'Excuse me,' she said to the young wife. She could tell at once that something was wrong. Etta was white and perspiring.

'Lady Carson, it's Nora.'

'What's wrong?'

'I'd rather not say within earshot, ma'am.'

'What's happened to her?' Lucy demanded.

'She's ill, ma'am.'

'Ill? She was all right this morning.'

Etta nodded and grimaced at the young wife who was trying to learn Urdu. 'It'd be better if I told you outside, ma'am; if you can spare just a minute.'

'Well, all right then,' said Lucy, a little irritably, and followed her into the Marble Hall.

As soon as they had passed the screens that separated the Tiffin Room from the Marble Hall, Etta flustered, 'She's terribly sick, your ladyship. They've called for the priest.'

'The priest? What for?'

'The last rites, your ladyship.'

'You mean she's going to *die?* How can she die? She dressed me this morning. She was perfectly well. She said she wanted to do some shopping.'

Tears began to stream down Etta's face. 'We went to the bazaar. We bought some silk and some beads and some musk. Then I met an old friend of mine from when I was here before, Katherine Anderson, who works for the Army & Navy, and all I wanted to do was to find out the latest *khubber.* And Nora wandered off on her own.'

'Yes?' Lucy demanded. 'Then what?'

'When I found her again – when I found her – she'd only bought herself some some *mottongost* from one of the stalls.'

'Some *what?*'

542

'Some *mottongost,* mutton on a stick; and she'd eaten it. I told her not to eat anything in the bazaar, but she said it smelled so good.'

Lucy didn't want to hear any more. She told Etta to take her straight to Nora's bedside.

'I'm sorry, your ladyship. Major French says no.'

'Then I want to see Major French.'

'Yes, your ladyship.'

Major French was already waiting for her in her private drawing room. He was grey-haired, very refined-looking, with long white hair that was combed back from his temples, and a large nose that was patterned with broken veins. For a man concerned with keeping people alive, his eyes were chilly grey and extraordinarily dead.

'Good afternoon, Your Excellency', he said, rising to his feet.

Lucy said, in a voice as empty as an embroidery frame, 'I'm told that my maid is going to die.'

Major French displayed a variety of shrugs.

'What's wrong with her?' Lucy insisted. 'She was perfectly well this morning, before she went shopping. Etta said that she'd eaten some meat or something.'

'I regret that she fell into a trap so often waiting in this country for the unsuspecting novice,' said Major French. 'You are obviously aware that we have been suffering something of a small epidemic in Calcutta recently, and it appears that your maid has become its latest victim.'

'Can I see her?' asked Lucy, swallowing back tears.

Major French shook his head. 'Not recommended, I regret, especially for the Vicereine.'

'She's my friend,' Lucy told him. 'Not just my maid, *my friend.*'

'You wouldn't count her as friend if she passed on *cholera morbus,*' said Major French.

'She has cholera?'

Major French nodded. 'The classic symptoms, I regret.

543

Painless but copious diarrhoea, with simultaneous vomiting. Blueish skin, hoarse voice – the notorious *vox cholerica* – terrible feelings of thirst. To be absolutely blunt, Lady Carson, I doubt if she will last the afternoon.'

Lucy found that she was shaking. 'I want to see her,' she said.

'I really can't sanction it,' said Major French, trying to smile. 'The *burra sahib* would have my guts.'

'I want to see her,' Lucy repeated.

'Lady Carson, I really must insist that you don't'

Lucy turned to him, full-face, and blazed, 'How would you like to posted back out to the *mofussil,* major? Somewhere really, really remote?'

Major French shrugged and nodded some more. 'Of course, if Your Excellency puts it that way . . .'

He led her upstairs, to the third floor where Lucy had never ventured before, to Nora's bedroom. Their footsteps echoed on the bare oak boards. Nora's room was white-washed plain, with a simple iron bed and a plywood locker. On top of the locker was a framed photograph of Nora's mother and father, hardbitten folk with wrinkled faces, frowning at the camera with deep distrust. On the wall above her bed hung a crucifix. The blinds were drawn, the room was stiflingly hot. Nora lay on her back, hollow-eyed, purple-skinned, and startlingly wrinkled, an indication of how much her body fluids had already drained away.

She was being attended by one of the *ayahs,* and a *punkah-wallah* was fanning her with a wide hand-held fan to keep her cool.

'You see she's very seriously ill,' said Major French. 'I must advise you not to approach too closely. You are wearing a cholera belt, I presume?'

Lucy whispered, 'Yes.' On Etta's advice, she always wore the white flannel belt that was supposed to give her protection against cholera; though nobody had yet been able to explain how it prevented one from catching a disease that was transmitted through the air like an invisible poison.

'All the same,' warned Major French. 'Not too near, please, for your own sake.'

Lucy rapped lightly at the door. 'Nora?' she called. 'Nora, it's Lucy! Can you hear me?'

Nora licked her lips with a tongue as dry as a lizard's, and coughed. 'Is the priest here yet?' she whispered. 'Is that the priest?'

'It's Lucy.'

'Who is it? Lucy? I've know so many Lucies. You're not Mrs O'Halloran's Lucy, by any chance? Or Lucy from the post office?'

'Nora, it's Lucy Carson.'

Nora was silent for a long time, still trying vainly to moisturize her lips, still trying to think. 'I known so many Lucies,' she repeated.

At that moment, there was a bustling sound along the corridor, the quick rip-rapping of men's shoes, and the jingling of medals and uniform. Lucy stepped closer to Nora's bed, and stood right at the very end of it, so that Nora could see her more distinctly. Nora frowned at her, and tried to focus, but she was very close to death now. Major French had given her tincture of Kino, and plenty of boiled water; but the cholera had taken hold of her so rapidly that there was very little else he could do.

'Nora,' Lucy called her. 'Nora, it's Lucy.'

'I knew a Lucy Darling once,' whispered Nora. 'She was such a pretty girl . . . whatever happened to Lucy Darling?'

'That's me,' said Lucy. 'I'm Lucy Darling!'

'*You're* Lucy Darling? You can't be Lucy Darling! Lucy Darling is dead!'

Lucy approached Nora and took hold of her hands. 'Oh, Nora. You're so cold!'

'No, no,' Nora contradicted her. 'I'm sleeping, that's all. I'm dreaming.' Then she looked up at her and smiled faintly, and said, 'You *are* Lucy Darling, aren't you? You really are!'

Lucy leaned forward and kissed her forehead. 'Yes, my dearest Nora. I really am.'

It was then that Major French grasped Lucy's arm, and respectfully but firmly pulled her away. She turned to protest, but then she saw Henry standing in the doorway, his face stony. Behind him stood Colonel Miller and two junior ADCs.

'I think you'd better return to your drawing room,' Henry told her, coldly. 'You have more than a hundred ladies in the Tiffin Room, all milling around with not the slightest idea whether they should stay or go.'

'Damned *moorghi-khana* down there,' added Colonel Miller, sarcastically.

With simplicity, Lucy said, 'Nora is dying.'

Henry glanced towards the bed. 'Don't you think I can see that for myself? *Cholera morbus*. And that is an even more convincing reason why you shouldn't be here.'

'Henry, Nora was more than a maid.'

'In two hours, my darling, or even less, she will be nothing at all but human clay.'

'Henry, she was my *friend!*'

Henry stepped into the bedroom himself, and took hold of Lucy's arm. She tried to struggle but he gripped her too tightly. She was watched with embarrassment by Colonel Miller and the junior officers as Henry pushed her past them, and out into the corridor. Once she was outside, however, she was able to wrench herself free.

'Who the hell do you think you are?' she snapped at him.

'Your husband, and the Governor-General of India,' Henry retorted.

'In which order?'

'For God's sake, Lucy, you're Vicereine!'

'Exactly,' Lucy told him. 'I'm Vicereine and my friend is dying in that room and I want to see her to say goodbye.'

'Do you have any idea how infectious she is? You've

kissed her! For God's sake, Lucy, you might have contracted it already!'

Lucy shook her head. 'Nora wouldn't do me any harm. Nora would never do me any harm!'

'That's absolute nonsense!' Henry bellowed at her. 'That's absolute bloody nonsense! That woman –' and here he jabbed his finger at Nora – 'that woman through her own stupidity has contracted one of the most fearful diseases known to mankind – and she has brought it back to our house – and *you* blithely tell me that she wouldn't do you any harm! That woman is as dangerous as a poisonous snake!'

There was a moment's pause; and right at that moment they all heard a whispering voice, calling to them from the bedroom. 'Do you remember now, the old songs we used to sing? Do you remember them at all?'

Lucy returned to the doorway; although Major French barred her access to the room with his arm. 'Which songs, Nora?' she asked.

'Oh, all of them ones. All of them ones we used to sing, walking to the horse-fair and all.'

'She's dying,' said Major French, emphatically.

'Which songs, Nora?' Lucy repeated.

'Well . . . you remember this one . . . *Tip, tip, my little horse?*'

Lucy's throat felt tangled up with grief. 'I remember it,' she said. Nora used to sing it when they were riding in their carriage down Fifth Avenue, on bright chilly days in New York.

'Will you sing it with me?' asked Nora.

Lucy wiped her eyes. 'Yes, I'll sing it with you.'

She stood in the doorway, allowed no nearer, while Nora's choleric whisper scratched out the words of her nursery-rhyme. Lucy sang high and pretty, although she was so sad for Nora that she could hardly manage to keep herself from crying.

'Tip, tip, my little horse;
Tip, tip, again, sir!
How many miles to Dublin town?
Fourscore and ten, sir!
Will I get there by candlelight?
Yes, and back again, sir!'

Nora's voice faltered, then failed. Slowly, Major French moved around the bed, and lifted up Nora's wrist. This time Lucy made no attempt to go any closer.

Major French raised his eyes. 'She's gone, I'm afraid.'

There was a difficult silence. Henry managed to say, 'Amen,' and Colonel Miller cleared his throat like a burst of rapid machine-gun fire.

But Lucy stood in the doorway with streaming eyes, and sang to Henry, as clear and high as she had before,

Tip, tip, my little horse
Tip, tip, again, sir!
How many miles to Dublin town?
Fourscore and ten, sir!
Will I get there by candlelight?

'*Yes —*' she began, but she was too miserable to finish. She turned her back on Henry and stormed off along the corridor, her primrose skirt flouncing as she walked.

Major French looked at Henry in embarrassment. 'I'm sorry I brought Lady Carson up here, Your Excellency. But she was so insistent.'

'Is there any danger that she may have caught the cholera?' Henry asked him.

Major French slowly shook his head. 'I doubt it. It usually seems to require very prolonged contact for the poisons to be passed through the air.'

'What about the kiss?' Henry demanded.

'I really couldn't say.'

Henry thought about that for a moment, tapping his order-papers against the palm of his hand. 'I suppose you can make funeral arrangements directly?'

'Yes, Your Excellency. A quick funeral would be my own recommendation, in view of the weather.'

'All right, then, do it. And you can tell that *punkah-wallah* that he can stop fanning her now. And – Major French?'

'Yes, Your Excellency?'

'I shall be talking to your commanding officer about a new posting for you. You are attached to Government House in order to protect lives; not to place them wantonly at risk.'

'If I might say so, Your Excellency –'

Henry walked right up to him and grasped the collar of his jacket and twisted it ferociously. His face was distorted like one of the caricatures of him that had appeared in *Punch*. 'If Her Excellency catches even so much as a cold, Major French, I will have you prosecuted to the fullest extent of the law. If she dies, then God help me I will kill you myself.'

The abruptness of Nora's death left Lucy utterly stunned. She returned to her drawing room white-faced, and told her bewildered guests that they would have to forgive her. Then she retreated immediately to her bedroom and lay face-down on her green silk quilt, staring at nothing, too distressed even to weep.

At six o'clock, Etta came in to ask whether she wanted tea; but she couldn't even answer. At a little after seven, Henry looked in on her, and sat on the bed beside her, and felt her forehead with his hand, but said nothing. At eight, when it was dark, Elizabeth Morris appeared, wearing a long grey dress, and a black tasselled shawl over her shoulders. She sat in the armchair close to Lucy's bed and watched her for quite a long time, with a saddened look on her face.

'Did Henry ask you to come?' said Lucy, at length.

Elizabeth said, 'Do you mind if I smoke?'

Lucy looked up at her. 'I didn't know you smoked.'

'Only in private,' she said, opening her large alligator handbag and taking out a tin of cigarettes. 'I'm afraid Gordon got me on to it. We used to play backgammon after dinner, almost every night. Backgammon and a cigarette; then a cup of cocoa and lights out.'

Lucy said, 'Did Henry tell you about Nora?'

'It wasn't Lord Carson, actually. It was Major French. He called in to see me, and suggested I might pay you a visit. Give you some sympathy, don't you know.'

Lucy sat up. She watched Elizabeth light her cigarette and blow out twin funnels of smoke from her nostrils. 'I never knew that anybody could die so quickly.'

'That's Corporal Forbes for you,' said Elizabeth. 'I beg your pardon, that's slang for *cholera morbus*. Some of my friends have taken days to die of it, but most go very speedily.'

'I think I could do with a lemonade,' said Lucy. 'I feel terribly thirsty of all a sudden.'

Elizabeth stood up and, still smoking, went across to the room to ring the bell for the servants. 'You should rest,' she told Lucy. 'I'll ask your lady's-maid to draw you a bath.'

Tir' Ram appeared, large and pale and supercilious, and asked what was wanted.

'*Meta-pani* for Her Excellency the Memsahib,' said Elizabeth. 'And *juldi!*'

While Lucy was waiting for her bath, Elizabeth told her about some of the friends she had lost from cholera and typhoid and dysentery. 'I think about them sometimes. I imagine their faces, almost like faces in a photograph album.'

Lucy thought about Blanche. She wished desperately that she had a photograph of her, just to know what she looked like now. She would be four this year. Lucy wondered if she looked anything at all like her.

Elizabeth said, 'I'm afraid that death is very close to us, in India. If you've lived here for a long time, like I have, you get quite philosophical about it. But it still hurts, of course; and all one can do is think that it's probably worth it, when you see what we've managed to do for the place. We've given them peace, and a common language, and a legal system that's second to none. We've built roads and railways and irrigated vast tracts of land.

'Even if the Indians hate us, there's something to be said for that, too. At least it will bind them together in a common cause, as one nation; and nobody could ever say that about India before.'

'I don't know where Nora fits into that,' said Lucy.

Elizabeth crushed out her cigarette. 'Everybody fits in somewhere. Even me.'

At two o'clock in the morning, Lucy awoke to find that she was sweating and shivering, and that her throat was raw. She reached out of her mosquito-nets for a glass of water, but she was shivering so much that she dropped the carafe on to the floor, and smashed it. Almost at once, Etta came in, with her hair in papers, in a huge balloon of a cotton night-gown.

'Lady Carson? Are you all right?'

'I d-dr-dropped my w-water j-ju –,' Lucy juddered. She could barely swallow, and she couldn't stop her teeth from chattering. Her stomach felt as hard as a drum.

Etta felt her forehead. 'You're burning hot!' she declared. 'Listen, cover yourself up, and I'll send for the doctor at once!'

Lucy said, 'It's not C-corporal F-forbes, is it?'

Etta didn't answer that. 'Let me send for the doctor,' she repeated. 'And I'll tell His Excellency, too.'

Lucy lay back on her sweat-wrinkled pillow, and clasped her hands over her stomach. *My baby. My poor baby. Please let me live, if only for my baby's sake.*

She had never really thought about dying before; although she had seen Uncle Casper die, and Mrs Sweeney die, and

Jack, too. Somehow their deaths had seemed like part of a play; part of a carefully worked-out drama. She could almost believe that they were still alive somewhere, like party guests hiding in another room to surprise their host.

It was only a few moments before Henry appeared, his hair ruffled, tying up the cord of his green silk robe.

'Lucy, my dearest, how are you?'

'Mind out, Your Excellency,' Etta warned him. 'There's glass on the floor.'

'Is Major French on his way?'

'I sent Muhammad Isak with a carriage.'

'Good girl,' said Henry. 'Could you bring us some water?'

Etta called for *pani,* and also for ice and a flannel cloth, so that she could bathe Lucy's forehead.

Lucy opened her eyes. Everything appeared to be warm and distorted and swimming. Henry's face was stretched out sideways as if it were made out of indiarubber, and Etta's voice was so low and blurred that Lucy couldn't distinguish what she was saying. Lucy tried to turn her head so that she could tell Etta to speak more clearly, but the bed seemed to pour away from under her, like a silent white waterfall, and she found herself floating in crimson darkness.

Someone was breathing harshly in her ear. She wasn't sure if it was herself, or Henry, or Vanessa. It could have been Vanessa. After all, they were practically twins. Perhaps the secret was that they were Siamese twins, joined by their destinies.

Henry had loved Vanessa. Perhaps he still did. Perhaps Lucy was nothing more than a substitute, someone to remind him of the woman he truly loved, until she forgave him, and came back to him.

Someone lifted her head and gave her a little cold water. She felt it dribble on to her nightgown. Her mouth wouldn't work properly, it wasn't her fault. Her throat was sore, too, so sore that she could hardly swallow. And even though her eyes were wide open, everything was dark.

She heard a deep voice saying, 'She's running a high fever. Let me look at her tongue.'

Then she heard Henry coaxing her. 'Lucy ... Lucy, my darling. Can you put out your tongue?'

She couldn't think what that *meant* − to 'put out your tongue'. Was it the same as putting out the cat? But in any case she felt a firm hand grasping her chin, and another hand grasping her upper jaw, and then the dry woody flatness of a tongue depressor.

'Is it cholera?' asked Henry, after a moment or two.

Lucy couldn't hear Major French's reply; but she did hear him say, 'She should be bathed in cool water and vinegar, then put to bed and kept warm. I'll make up a powder of scammony and jalap, grey powder and antimony, and this should be administered every four hours. I'll also give you a tonic of rose leaves and quinine and a little sulphuric acid. Give her ladyship one dessertspoonful before she sleeps, and then again in the morning.

'If her throat becomes intolerably sore, have a hot bran poultice made up, and apply it to her neck.'

There was a great deal of shuffling of feet in the room, and then Lucy was conscious of somebody leaning over to kiss her. It smelled like Henry. It must have been Henry. 'It's all right, sweetheart,' he told her. 'It isn't the cholera. You remember the children's hospital you visited last week in Ballyganj? You've caught the scarlatina. Can you hear me? You have the scarlatina. Major French says it isn't too serious.'

'What about the baby?' whispered Lucy. 'It won't hurt the baby, will it?'

'He doesn't think so. But just to make sure, we're going to send you up to Simla, in the hills. It's much cooler there, and you'll be able to rest.'

'I don't want to leave you, Henry,' she told him. She tried to cling on to him but she couldn't seem to find him.

'Sssh, my dearest. The best thing that you can do now is

to stay quiet. Then, when you're feeling better, I'll arrange transport to take you up to the hills.'

'As long as the baby's all right,' said Lucy.

There was a pause, and Lucy heard Major French murmuring something to Henry. Then Henry came back, and said, 'Don't worry, my dearest, really. You'll soon be as fit as a fiddle. And you'll adore Simla. It's almost like England.'

'Can Elizabeth come?' asked Lucy. 'I do want Elizabeth to come.'

'Of course Elizabeth can come. You'll have a wonderful time. I can finish off my work; and when the Hot Weather starts I can come up and join you.'

'Well, well,' said Elizabeth, somewhere in the background. 'It looks like early furlough this year.'

Lucy's scarlatina was more serious than Major French had first thought, and she was feverish almost all week, her skin reddened and prickly like a lobster's shell. By the following Tuesday, he had deemed her well enough to make the journey to Simla, although he warned her that if her condition began to worsen on the way, she should make a stop at Delhi. In any event, he would be sending a nurse along with her, Mrs Smallwood, whom he was privately glad to be rid of. Women were distinctly unwelcome in the Indian medical establishment, and Mrs Smallwood had only managed to make her way in Calcutta's hospitals by an attitude which the Civil Surgeon had described as 'untypical of her sex to the point of being terrifying'.

Messages were sent on ahead to Simla that the Viceregal Lodge should be made ready for the early arrival of the Vicereine. As usual, a tremendous entourage had to be assembled: not just Lucy herself and Etta and Elizabeth Morris and Mrs Smallwood and four *ayahs,* but a twelve-strong contingent of the Viceregal Bodyguard, and scores of bearers and *syces* to look after the horses, and more than seventy coolies, and Lucy's favourite cook, with all his scullions, and six large trunks containing Lucy's clothes, including all the new dresses which had just arrived from London and Paris, four chests to carry the clothes of the other European women, six casks of formal porcelain and ornaments, thirty cases of stores and provisions, two cases of books, two boxes of drawing-room sundries and coats for the servants, who were unused to the coldness of the hills, and four more boxes for saddlery, tennis poles, pardah bamboos, linen, and cheval-glasses. Last but most imposing was a German grand piano which would be carried up to Simla on a piano-cart.

There was no railway up to Simla yet, although a remarkable looping track was under construction in the lower reaches of the Hills, and was expected to be finished in four or five years' time. All of the Vicereine's baggage would have to be carried up to the hills by coolies and by camels, forty-one camels in all.

Lucy herself would be carried up the precipitous hill paths in a palanquin, an ornate ceremonial litter like a gilded sledge, with a folding tasselled hood which resembled the hood of a baby-carriage. Her four liveried porters had been given mercilessly strict instructions not to tilt her too much, or to carry her too close to the brink of the roads, or to drop her whenever they saw a poisonous snake, or to fall over any precipices.

By the time her party was ready to leave Calcutta late the following week, Lucy was still weak and shaky, but almost completely recovered, and on the whole she would have preferred to stay on the plains, at least until the Hot Weather started. But although she could have changed her mind about going to Simla if she had really wanted to, she felt that it would be wasteful and absurd to disassemble a company of over two hundred people who had worked so hard to pack so many things. Besides, she sensed that Henry wanted her to go, so that he could finish off his Cold Weather work uninterrupted, untroubled by any anxiety that he might be neglecting her.

He had still not quite forgiven her, either, for the way in which she had argued with him outside Nora's room, on the day that Nora had died; and once or twice, with ponderous sarcasm, he had called her 'Miss Darling' – presumably referring to the way in which she had spoken to Nora on her deathbed.

The morning she was due to leave, she walked with Elizabeth Morris through South Park Cemetery, to the Plot where Nora was buried. At the moment there was only a plain wooden marker. Lucy had asked Colonel Miller to commission a marble statue of an angel, her head bowed, her hands covering her face. She had seen a similar statue in a catalogue of monuments in Kansas, when she was a child, and it had always fascinated and saddened her.

'She's in brave company,' Elizabeth remarked.

Lucy looked around at the pyramids and pillars and domed mausoleums. It was another hot, humid day, with not a breath of wind. A bird chattered self-indulgently to itself in a nearby tree. Lucy said, 'I feel as if I've buried a part of myself here, too.'

'You have,' replied Elizabeth. 'So many of us have. Friends, little children. If you have sacrificed those for the sake of living in India, then nobody can ever say that you don't have the right to call it your own country, too.'

Lucy looked down at the marker on Nora's grave. 'I'll be seeing you,' she whispered, and then she turned and walked away, with Elizabeth following close behind.

Simla was both romantic and extraordinary, and Lucy fell in love with it as soon as they arrived. It was the most glamorous of all the hill stations, perched eight thousand feet on a series of ledges on one of the lower slopes of the Himalayas, a collection of English-style houses and boarding-houses and country retreats, all clustered around a main thoroughfare called The Mall.

It was like a dream about England, rather than England

itself; some said a nightmare. The Mall was lined with a remarkable collection of buildings that could only be described as Indo-Tyrolean; and these buildings housed cafés, shops that sold European goods, a theatre and a library. From The Mall, roads meandered off through stands of pine trees to English suburban houses, properly-constructed houses made of brick, with real glass in the windows, and fireplaces, and cosy names from Home like The Cedars, Ivy Glen, and Sunny Bank.

But it was all an illusion. Beyond Sunny Bank rose the pine-forested ramparts of the surrounding hills, and then the distant peaks of the snowcapped Himalayas; and monkeys clambered noisily on Sunny Bank's corrugated-iron roof.

Elizabeth Morris was personally sceptical of Simla. 'If I were told that the monkeys had built it all, I would say, "what wonderful monkeys, they must be shot in case they do it again."'

Lucy, however, was captivated by Simla's peace and its charm and its unselfconscious eccentricity. At the far end of The Mall stood a little Gothic church, just like a church in an English country village; but The Mall itself was busy with Indians pulling rickshaws and coolies carrying luggage. It was still early in the year, too early for the Hot Weather season to have started, and so the streets were comparatively quiet. The air was fragrant and cool, almost sharp, and as Lucy was carried towards Viceregal Lodge she closed her eyes and breathed in deeply. It was marvellous. She felt recovered already; and for the first time she was grateful to Henry for having sent her away.

The Viceregal Lodge was set on one of the most commanding sites in Simla; and, symbolically, one of the most commanding sites in all India. From one side of it, water ran westwards down to the Sutlej and on to the Arabian Sea. From the other side, the drainage flowed eastwards to Jumna, and into the Bay of Bengal. Beyond the trees of its silent and elegant gardens, the hills and the mountains were hazed in a silken blue that would have looked far too strange and silvery in any other country but India. The Lodge itself was approached by a winding sandy driveway, between a profusion of Alpine flowers and mature cypresses. Like every other building in Simla, it was highly idiosyncratic. It had all the appearance of an Elizabethan mansion, with a castle-like tower, and forbidding facings in blue and grey sandstone and limestone.

Elizabeth had complained to Lucy that she always found the Viceregal Lodge unbearably oppressive. 'It always reminds me of a Scottish hydro.'

They were carried to the *porte cochère*, and their palanquins set down. They were greeted by stiffly-saluting officers of the Viceregal Bodyguard, by an assembly of liveried servants, both European and Indian, and by Henry's assistant private secretary, John Frognal, who had set off on the seven-hundred mile journey to Simla as soon as he knew that Lucy would be convalescing in the Hills. Lucy liked him. He was young and amusing, with brushed-down hair and an unsuccessful foray at a walrus moustache, and although he was wonderfully diplomatic with all of the rajahs and maharajahs that Henry had to meet, he always found it difficult to take Government House protocol very seriously. When the ladies rose from Henry's formal dinners, and curtseyed to the Viceroy at the door, John Frognal would take bets on how many knees they would hear clicking.

'Your Excellency, you are heartily welcomed to Simla,' he told her, bowing. 'We all trust that you're feeling much recovered.'

'I think I'm better already, thank you,' smiled Lucy.

John Frognal helped her out of the palanquin and then introduced her to the Lodge's senior staff. They eyed her warily. Dressed as she was in mourning black, she looked very young and shy after Lady Elgin, and very pale too. The butler, Corcoran, a tall white-haired man with gelatinous eyes and caved-in cheeks, gave her a low bow, and said,

'Whatever Your Excellency requires can be provided, please be assured.'

'I presume that Your Excellency would prefer to rest for a few days before considering any social functions,' said John Frognal.

'Is there anybody here that I should meet?' asked Lucy. They had now walked into the Lodge's great galleried entrance hall. Although the hall boasted a huge teak staircase, which gave it enormous grandeur, it was teak-panelled right up to the ceiling, which made it feel dark and heavy and depressing. Large brass pots glowered in the corners.

'There are one or two interesting people around,' John Frognal told her. 'Not many, of course, yourself excluded. But I was thinking that you might care to hold a small drawing room, perhaps; or even a dinner-party, if you felt strong enough.'

'If I can endure being shaken up all the way up into these hills,' Lucy retorted, 'I truly think that I'm strong enough for anything. Half the time I thought they were going to drop me over the edge.'

'Well, it has happened,' John Frognal admitted. 'Lost a French ambassador once. But, look here, if Your Excellency is quite well enough to give a small function or two, I'll liaise with Mrs Morris,' he told her. 'There are two senior ladies from the Punjab secretariat; and Lady Leamington-Pryce from Delhi; and Mrs Talbot – Colonel Talbot's wife, Fane's Horse.'

'Aren't there any men?' asked Lucy. 'We're going to need some men to make up a dinner-party.'

'I'm expecting Sir Malcolm McInnes at the weekend; and Lord Pethick sometime next week, but I'm afraid that Lord Pethick is a little . . . well –'

'*Gonga*?' asked Lucy, irreverently; using the British Indian slang for batty.

John Frognal smirked in amusement. 'Yes, Your Excellency, *gonga* is just the word I was looking for.'

'Anybody else?'

'An American gentleman, Your Excellency. A special envoy from Washington, so I believe. I'm not quite sure of his rank, but he's visiting India on behalf of the United States Diplomatic Service.'

'Well, it would be pleasant to talk to an American.'

Accompanied by Corcoran, the butler, who walked ahead of them with creaking shoes and his hairy-nostrilled nose in the air, Lucy and her entourage were taken up to her suite of rooms. Corcoran flung open the double doors with a flourish, and revealed an enormous bedroom, with windows on two sides, and a view of the Sutlej valley, with the Suwalik range in the middle distance, and the ghostly outline of the Himalayas beyond.

Corcoran said, 'The Hindus believe, your ladyship, that the gods live in the hills; and who is to say that they don't?'

He walked around the massive Elizabethan-style four-poster bed, and opened the leaded casements. From down in the river valley came the sweet wooden notes of a cuckoo. 'First one this year,' smiled Etta, setting down her bag.

Corcoran added, 'All your trunks and boxes will be unpacked, Your Excellency, and your clothing made ready. Would you care to dine in your rooms this evening, after your long journey?'

'Yes, I think I would,' said Lucy. 'A very light supper; perhaps about seven o'clock. Do you have any quail?'

'Quail in abundance, Your Excellency.'

Corcoran left on his creaking shoes, and Etta took off Lucy's hat and coat and unlaced her shoes. 'Perhaps you'd like a bath, Lady Carson?' she suggested.

'In a while,' said Lucy. 'I think I'd like a rest first; just to take the place in. Look, there's the full moon up there, isn't it huge! Just over the mountains. I don't think I've ever seen anything so beautiful.'

'Oh, but ghostly, too, up here in the hills,' said Etta.

Lucy went out on to the balcony, and breathed in some

560

more of that crisp glorious air. The light in the garden was pale but very intense, like no light that she had ever seen before; and apart from the sound of the cuckoo she could hear another sound, much quieter, the sound of streams rushing deep in the valleys far beneath her.

Etta came and stood behind her. 'The Hindus are always superstitious about the hills.'

'I don't know why.'

'Oh, it's not just the Hindus, either. Everybody says there are ghosts in Simla. Some of the houses are haunted. People have seen women in white dresses walking around their verandahs, and it's turned out that a young *memsahib* died there, while she was waiting for her husband to come up from the plains. Always pacing the verandah, don't you see, waiting for him, and he never came. Or at least he came too late.'

Lucy shivered. 'I don't want to talk about death.'

'India *is* death, that's what I think, sometimes.'

'You told me you missed it.'

'Oh, I did. I wouldn't go back Home for all the tea in Darjeeling.'

'Are you really happy? It must be hard, not having a husband.'

Etta unfolded a white silk blouse, and shook the creases out of it. 'I miss the comfort of it. But I don't miss having a man around the place, especially in India. Men can get to grips with the country, can't they? See things, and meet people, and really get to live here. But how many Indians have *you* been introduced to, apart from rajahs? You might just as well be sitting in a bread-oven in England as coming out here. Just as hot, and you see just as much. And the same goes for most of the wives.'

Lucy said quietly, 'I wish Nora could have seen this place. She would have loved it.'

Etta nodded. 'I told her not to eat anything, you know.'

'Etta, I know. Nobody blames you.'

'I told her not to eat anything, nor to drink anything, neither. But she came up and said, "They smelled so delicious, I just had to have one." And do you know something, the fellow that was cooking them looked as if he had black shiny hair, but when he turned round suddenly you could see that his scalp was completely raw, and what he had on his head wasn't hair, but flies.'

Lucy swallowed. 'Etta – I really don't want to talk about it any more.'

'Sorry, your ladyship.'

'Can you find my blue silk robe for me? I want to undress, and have a rest. And get me some tea, would you? And find those powders that Major French gave me.'

'Yes, your ladyship.'

'And Etta?'

'Yes, your ladyship?'

'Nora's dead now, and buried, and she's at peace. Nothing we can say will bring her back.'

At that moment, from the far side of the pine-forested valley, they heard the highest of cries, almost like a woman calling out in grief. It echoed and re-echoed from one hill to another.

'Monkeys,' said Etta, and went to chivvy the *ayahs*.

Lucy ate a quiet dinner in her private dining room, waited on by Corcoran the butler and three maroon-liveried Indians, who stood to attention behind her chair and refilled her glass whenever it look as if the level of her wine had dropped a sixteenth of an inch, and whipped service plates away like conjuring tricks, and expertly removed the slightest crumb she might have dropped on the tablecloth with a complicated folding and unfolding of crisp primrose-coloured napkins.

She was served with *Potage St Germain,* followed by two perfectly-roasted quail, their skin crisp and seasoned with garam masala; and then a small portion of *gateau mille-feuille,* which was so light and creamy that it might have been brought direct from a *patisserie* in Paris.

Afterwards, she was joined in her drawing room by Elizabeth. They sat in large chintz-covered armchairs in front of a briskly-crackling fire, and Elizabeth told her stories about Simla in the old days, before it was decided to make it the viceregal seat of government during the Hot Weather. 'It was eccentric, even then, although it didn't matter so much in those days, because it was only a resort. We had marvellous gymkhanas at Annandale, which is a clearing in the forest among the hills. Not a meeting went past without some rider disappearing over the side of the precipice; sometimes horse and rider together. But there were some startlingly pretty girls here. I often wonder what became of them all. Married, I expect, or dead.'

Shortly after nine o'clock, with the moon shining across the hills, Lucy said, 'I think I'll go for a walk.'

Elizabeth frowned at her. 'A walk? On your own? You can't!'

'There's no danger, is there? You've said that plenty of young girls used to go around on their own.'

'But for goodness' sake, my dear. You're the Vicereine of India, you're seven months' pregnant, and you've only just recovered from scarlatina. What on earth would happen if you were taken ill? Or if some *dacoit* decided to kidnap you?'

'You could come with me.'

'And what use would *I* be? An old lady like me!'

'Oh, Elizabeth, I'm longing to go out without taking two hundred people with me. And it's such a beautiful evening!'

Elizabeth stood up and brushed down her dress. 'All right, then. But let's take our coats. And if we fall down a *khud* don't tell me that I didn't warn you.'

It wasn't as easy for Lucy to leave the Lodge as she had expected. She and Elizabeth took their shawls, and left her suite of rooms as quietly as they could. But in the corridor they were immediately confronted by one of the house-servants, in his green-and-gold livery, who bowed to them and asked their majesties what they required.

'Just going for a *howa-khana,*' said Elizabeth, imperiously.

'Then I am fetching you bodyguards and porters and torchbearers, your majesty.'

'Be off with you!' Elizabeth told him. '*Jow! Ekdum!*'

The boy couldn't understand why she was cross with him. With hurt eyes, he retreated along the corridor, and then disappeared around the corner.

'We'd better hurry,' said Elizabeth. 'He's probably gone straight to the *khansamah* and the *khansamah* will go straight to Corcoran, and then all merry hell will break loose.'

They crept together around the galleried landing, the teak flooring creaking with every step. Lucy began to get the giggles, and her stomach contracted so tightly that she had to stop and lean against one of the newel-posts and get her breath back.

'All right, my dear?' Elizabeth asked her, her eyes glistening with suppressed merriment.

'Lead on, Macduff!' Lucy told her.

They tiptoed down the grand staircase, across the entrance hall, and out by one of the side doors. Lucy had the presence of mind to take out the key and lock it after her, so that whatever happened they would be able to get back in.

Wrapping their shawls around their shoulders, they hurried as rapidly as they could through the gardens, keeping away from the winding path. There were two sentries at the front gates, but Elizabeth beckoned to Lucy, and led her through some dense rhododendrons and across the grass to a small side gate. 'I noticed this gate when we were being carried up here. The gardeners were using it, and if I know anything about *malis,* they never bother to lock up after them. Here, look, I was quite right, it's open!'

So it was that Lucy and Elizabeth found themselves strolling through Simla late on a moonlit evening, without bodyguards or ADCs or Indian servants.

Lucy said, 'I'd almost forgotten what it was like, to be alone.'

'You must have forgotten what it's like to dress yourself too,' Elizabeth remarked.

'No . . . I can still button up a button, if I have to. I still find it hard to remember just to stand there, and let my *ayahs* do it all for me. Sometimes I feel like I'm not a real person at all, just some large doll they're dressing.'

They had reached the junction of The Ridge and The Mall, where the Swiss-styled Post Office buildings stood. The streets were silent, only a few lights twinkled here and there. Somebody was playing a gramophone, some crackly tenor song that could only be English. The moonlight cast a pallid light on the Post Office buildings, so that they looked as if they had been fashioned out of cake.

Below The Ridge and The Mall, the hill tumbled steeply downwards in a labyrinth of bazaars and alleyways and shacks. It looked like a village that was forever frozen in a tumultuous landslide. From here came the strong smell of frying onions and cumin and *mehti,* and the sounds of arguing and plangent music.

'The native quarters,' said Elizabeth. 'We shouldn't really go farther. They're supposed to be a hotbed of spies and thieves. And they're quite a maze, too. Kipling said that if you knew your way around, from one verandah to another, the police could never find you in a thousand years.'

They stopped for a while, looking out over the hill, smelling the distinctive and unforgettable aromas of the Indian high country. But the moon was beginning to fall behind the mountains, and it would soon be dark. Elizabeth said, 'We'd better be getting back. They've probably sent half a regiment to look for us already.'

They turned to walk back toward the Viceregal Lodge. As they did so, however, a tall hatless man in a light grey suit appeared as if from nowhere, bare-headed, his hat in his hand, from the general direction of the native quarters, and began walking with apparent purpose straight towards them.

'European, thank God,' muttered Elizabeth. 'Probably just a poodle-faker, making his disreputable way home.' Poodle-fakers were men who took advantage of lonely married women while their husbands were still working down on the plains.

The man began to catch up with them, but neither of them could walk any faster. As they plodded up the hill towards Christ Church, he overtook them. He turned his head and glanced at them, unsmiling, and as he did so Lucy felt a thrill of terror so great that she gasped out loud, and flailed her hand out to catch Elizabeth's arm.

In the moonlight, the man's face was floury-white, and his eyes glinted like the eyes of the dead. Everything that Etta had told her about the ghosts of Simla rushed into her mind, and she felt the blood emptying out of her brain.

For a single occluded second – although she didn't fall – she fainted.

10

When she opened her eyes again, he was still there. Elizabeth was holding her steady and he was standing quite still, looking at her in pleasure and disbelief.

'Lucy,' he said, 'Lucy? Are you all right? I didn't mean to scare you.'

It was Jamie, although she could scarcely believe it. But he was quite real; and absolutely solid. The moonlight didn't shine through him; and he didn't float an inch above the ground.

'Jamie . . . what in the world are you doing here?'

'I guess I should be asking you the same question.'

Lucy let out two or three little coughs of surprise. 'I'm taking a *walk*, what does it look like! You gave me the shock of my life!'

'Well, ditto. But I did tell you that I was heading up to the hills.'

'Elizabeth Morris,' interjected Elizabeth, with ill-concealed impatience. Elizabeth wasn't fond of being ignored.

'I'm sorry; forgive me,' said Jamie, and shook Elizabeth's hand. 'James Cullen, I'm a friend of Lucy's from Kansas. That is, we kind of grew up together.'

'What a remarkable coincidence your being here,' said Elizabeth.

'Well, not exactly,' Jamie explained. 'I was in Delhi last week; and I read in the paper that the Vicereine was going up to Simla. I was on my way to Amritsar as a matter of fact; but I had some people to see hereabouts, so I made a particular point of being here. But I sure didn't expect to find the Vicereine taking walks. I mean – not like this – walks in the moonlight, without any kind of bodyguard.'

Elizabeth lifted her tightly-folded parasol. 'I can assure you, Mr Cullen, that I am bodyguard enough. Any *dacoit* who values his eyesight had better watch out.'

Jamie gave her an amused-alarmed grin, and fended off the aggressively-pointed ferrule. 'I can believe it, Mrs Morris.'

'*Miss* Morris,' Elizabeth corrected him. Then, to Lucy, 'Is he all right, my dear? What I mean to say is, is he *pukkah*?'

Lucy smiled, and nodded. 'He's perfectly *pukkah*. We used to go riding together, didn't we, Jamie, when we were children? We used to lie on our backs by the river, and tell each other what our dreams were.'

'Well, I *suppose* that makes him *pukkah*,' said Elizabeth.

Lucy suddenly and irrationally thought of Samuel Blankenship. She knew what *he* would have said. *You bet your rear-end that makes him pukkah!* Not that poor old Samuel would have known what *pukkah* meant.

Elizabeth took Lucy's arm. 'We'd better be getting back. They'll be kicking up all kinds of a fuss once they've found that we've gone.'

'Please . . . can I escort you?' asked Jamie. 'I thought that whenever the Vicereine went for a stroll, she took elephants, and bearers, and eight million coolies, and shot ibex and tigers.'

'Well, I do that, too,' said Lucy, a little haughtily. 'I haven't actually shot anything yet, but Colonel Miller's been giving me lessons with a gun. This is my first evening in Simla, that's all, and I wanted to see it on my own.'

Jamie looked up the empty street; and then back down again. 'It's real strange here, isn't it? It's not like India at all.'

'There are supposed to be ghosts,' said Elizabeth.

'Indian ghosts or British ghosts?' Jamie asked her.

'Both,' said Elizabeth.

'And which of those ghosts are in charge?'

Elizabeth gave him a quick, prickly glance. 'We British have given an awful lot to India, you know, including the lives of some of our bravest young men and women.'

'I'm sorry,' Jamie told her. 'I didn't mean to suggest that –'

'Quite all right,' said Elizabeth, briskly. 'I don't as a rule expect foreigners to understand what we've managed to achieve.'

Jamie shrugged, and said, 'Well . . .' but he didn't know what else to say to her, so he turned his attention to Lucy, 'You know something, your vicereineship, it's so good to see you. You're blossoming!'

'She isn't a bush,' Elizabeth complained.

'Listen,' said Jamie, 'I said I was sorry.'

Lucy laughed. 'Don't take any notice of Elizabeth; she's frightfully mother-hennish.'

'When is Henry coming up to the Hills?' asked Jamie, off-handedly.

'I'm not sure,' Lucy replied. 'He said he would come just as soon as he could, but he's terribly busy. Are you here for long? You haven't even told me what you're *doing*, not properly.'

Jamie shrugged. 'This and that, talking to people, not much.'

'Are you touring, Mr Cullen?' asked Elizabeth. 'Or are you on business of some kind?'

'Oh, touring, really. Looking around; meeting people.'

'You ought to go to Kashmir, if you get the opportunity,' suggested Elizabeth, in a tone which seemed to recommend that if he left this very minute it wouldn't be too soon. 'Kashmir is exceptionally pleasant during the Hot Weather. I remember punting across Dal Lake one August afternoon. It was quite wonderful . . . the white peaks of the Himalayas reflected in the water. And so utterly quiet, as if my boatman and I were the only people left alive in the whole world.'

'I don't think I'll have much time for boating,' said Jamie.

'Jamie's a lawyer,' Lucy explained.

'I see,' said Elizabeth. 'Is there anything in India which could possibly interest an American lawyer? India is run by British law.'

'I look around me, I see a whole lot that's relevant to American law,' Jamie replied.

Elizabeth seemed unimpressed. 'I was always led to understand that American law is very different from our own. My late brother was Sir Gordon Morris; perhaps you've heard of him. He used to say that American law was the law of vested interests. In trusts we trust.'

'Sounds like your brother was a cynic,' said Jamie.

'Perhaps. But he was a very gifted cynic.'

Jamie was silent for a while, as they slowly climbed the hill together; an incongruous party of three underneath a moon like a lamp. But then he said, 'The relevance of what's happening here in India today, compared with my recent experience in American diplomacy, is that in both cases, an indigenous population is being tricked, robbed, and buggered blind, and all in the name of the law.'

'Sir!' Elizabeth protested.

'Oh, you can "sir!" me all you like,' Jamie told her. 'But

ever since I arrived here in India, I've learned a whole lot. I've learned about oppression, I've learned about exploitation, I've learned about wholesale butchery in the name of some Queen who sits in a palace five thousand miles away and doesn't even think of her three hundred million native subjects from one weekend to the next.'

Elizabeth stiffened at this rabid affront to the British throne, and released Lucy's arm. 'Sir! You are not only foul-mouthed but unpatriotic. Our countries are bonded by a common language, a common ideal, and a common desire to do the right thing. The Raj is the jewel in the British crown. Long may it beam and glisten!'

'Well, hear, hear!' clapped Lucy.

But Jamie turned away and shook his head. 'You won't understand, will you? It's been staring you right in the face, Mrs Morris, from the moment you first arrived in India! The reason why India is the jewel in the crown is because the people here work for practically nothing. Without slave-labour – or the next thing to it – British India would collapse overnight.

He paused, and ran his hand through his hair. 'Let me tell you something, Lucy, I've been lucky, tonight, to meet you alone. Think how many people you normally take with you, wherever you go! What a magnificent spectacle it must be, when you and Lord Carson set out on your tours! Special train, two hundred servants! Who cares what it costs? But – well, as far as I can figure it out, one rupee spent on a specially-woven ceremonial carpet is one rupee taken out of the mouth of a starving child.'

'Oh, for God's sake, Jamie, stop it!' Lucy protested. 'I came out here to look at the moon, and the mountains, and to think what I might be wearing for Saturday's ball. I can't stand pomp, and I can't stand ceremony, and I don't want to talk about justice any more, either!'

Jamie gave her a look which she wasn't at all sure that she liked. 'Saturday's ball! Is that all you can think about?

Worrying your curls out of their curl-papers, stepping into your fine silk slippers. You're pretty beyond price; you're expecting a baby; and you're married to one of the most influential men who ever lived. Oh, yes – whatever you think about Henry, my darling, no matter how much you think you love him, no matter how much you think you hate him, he's clever and tenacious and he'll never give in to anybody. He represents the British Crown in India . . . he *is* the British Crown in India, and if there's one thing I know about him, he's totally dedicated to maintaining British rule, no matter what.'

'And what, may I ask, is so terrible about that?' Elizabeth demanded, quite white with indignation.

Jamie smiled. 'You don't see it, do you? You don't see what you've done, you British!'

'How dare you! I've seen exactly what we've done! We've taken a divided and primitive society – and we've pacified it, and educated it, and we've – we've bonded it together! We've given them law, and banks, and commerce, and a postal service second to none – and, and Scottish dancing – and goodness only knows what else!'

'Well, you're right, of course,' Jamie admitted. 'India these days – well, it's a spectacle. Buildings, railways, tea-plantations, docks, forts, cantonments. What a spectacle! But the spectacle can't exist without hunger, and filth, and disease, and beggary. It's a fact of history. The brighter the rooftops on the Golden City shine, the dirtier the sewers that run beneath.'

'You can talk!' Lucy protested.' 'What did you do to the Comanche? What did you do to the Sioux? Surely that was worse?'

'Yes, it was, in a way,' Jamie admitted. 'In Kansas and Colorado I took away their ancestral lands for ever. I desecrated their sacred burial-places. I robbed them of their self-sufficiency and I robbed them of their pride. In the end, to add injury to insult, I killed them, too. The American Raj is just as bad as the British Raj, and worse in some ways, because the sole aim of the American Raj was not to rule, not to administer, not even to exploit – but to destroy one people for the benefit and profit of another, under a banner called manifest destiny.'

'I'm glad to hear that you have *some* sense of shame,' put in Elizabeth, tartly.

'You're right,' said Jamie, 'I do. My father brought me up to believe in absolute fairness; and the sanctity of human life; and I betrayed both of those principles because I was flattered and because I was paid a lot of money to betray them.'

'In that case,' said Elizabeth, 'I really fail to see how *you* can be remotely qualified to criticize *us*.'

Jamie stopped. They had almost reached the crest of the hill, beside the dark Gothic silhouette of Christ Church. The trees whispered like conspirators.

'What I did in Kansas doesn't excuse what the British are doing here in India, what Lord Henry Carson is doing here.'

Lucy held her hand out. 'Jamie . . . let's forget about it for tonight. You sound as if you're all burning up!'

'And you don't know why?'

'Jamie, I don't even want to think about it, I'm too tired.'

'Yes,' he said; and suddenly he dropped his arms down to his sides, and looked away for a moment. 'Yes,' he acknowledged. 'I'm sorry. I've been tub-thumping and all you did to deserve it was to take a walk.'

'Perhaps we shall see you again, Mr Cullen,' said Elizabeth.

Jamie took her hand. 'Perhaps you shall.'

'At least you have manners,' Elizabeth smiled at him. In spite of herself, she had obviously begun to warm to him. 'It isn't often that one comes across a radical with manners.'

'Oh, I wouldn't call myself a radical,' said Jamie. 'Just because I don't believe in empires; and emperors.'

'And empresses?' asked Lucy. She was feeling very weary now, from talking and excitement and too much walking;

and she felt like provoking Jamie not so much because he irked her, but because she wanted him to go away; so that she could think about him when he was gone.

She thought to herself: Sometimes you can be so fond of somebody that you don't want them there. You want to relish them in memory and in anticipation and in dreams. Sometimes their actual presence is almost too much.

'Let me tell you something,' said Jamie. 'The British almost take it for granted, what they've achieved here in India. But they shouldn't. I mean what kind of a national character did it take to turn more than a thousand different ancient and holy civilizations into a single continent of obedient children – and then to swindle those children out of everything they have, year in, year out, for hundreds of years? You don't even have to invent some grand-sounding historical excuse, like manifest destiny! You just say, we know better, you ignorant little sooties, so behave yourselves! And the tragedy is that they do!'

Elizabeth asked, not altogether unkindly, 'Have you been drinking, Mr Cullen?'

'No,' said Jamie. 'I haven't been drinking; although I do. I've been visiting Indians, that's all. Indian villages, Indian towns, Indian families. Muslims and Hindus, makes no difference.'

He paused, and then he said, in a soft and almost regretful voice, 'I've been trying to understand what the people in this country have been suffering. That probably sounds ridiculous to you. Maybe it *is* ridiculous. Some of the people I've met, no education, no food, no sewage, no clean water – they don't even understand that they *are* suffering. They think that life is always like this – never known any different.'

He paused again. Lucy was very tired, but she was still listening.

Jamie said, 'You probably don't feel it, up there in Vice-regal House. But the ground is starting to shake. It's like an earthquake coming, you'll never be able to stop it, no matter what you do.'

Just then, they heard the clattering of horses from the direction of Viceregal Lodge. Down the hill, riding smartly and expertly and at very great speed, came Lieutenant Ashley Burnes-Waterton, followed by three more officers of the Viceroy's Bodyguard.

'Lady Carson!' called Lieutenant Burnes-Waterton, reining his horse to a spectacular sliding halt, its shoes striking bright orange sparks off the roadway.

'I'm quite well, thank you,' said Lucy, as clearly and as calmly as she could. 'I'm sorry that we alarmed you. I needed to walk by myself for a while. This gentleman was kindly offering his assistance.'

Lieutenant Burnes-Waterton nodded and saluted, and said, 'As you wish, ma'am. May we send for a rickshaw to take you back?'

'No, thank you,' said Lucy. She sounded like the young empress again. 'I walked here, and I shall walk back. Mr Cullen will escort me. You may follow at a distance if you care to.'

Lieutenant Burnes-Waterton dismounted, and led his horse along behind them, fully understanding that 'at a distance' meant out of earshot. The remaining officers walked their horses even farther behind, looking rigid and cross.

Lucy took Jamie's arm and the two of them walked up the hill very close together.

'When do you expect your baby?' asked Jamie.

'The middle of June, midsummer's day,' Lucy told him.

'What do you want? A girl or a boy?'

'Henry wants a boy. He's going to call him Horatio.'

'Jesus,' said Jamie; the old Jamie, from Oak City, Kansas, who once drank five shots of whisky in five minutes without taking a breath.

'How long are you going to stay here in India?' she asked him.

He made a face. 'I don't know. Until I've talked to everyone I feel I need to talk to, I guess.'

'You're not going to cause any trouble?'

'Trouble? What do you mean by trouble? Of course not. I'm just travelling around, asking awkward questions, and coming up with awkward answers. You know me.'

Lucy looked at him narrowly. 'I'm not so sure that I do.'

'I'm okay,' he reassured her.

'Are you happy?' she asked him.

'I'm still not married,' he told her.

'Courting?' she inquired.

'Unh-hunh.'

'You're not still pining for me? Now, that would be plain foolishness.'

He stopped, and Lucy stopped, and Elizabeth stopped, and Lieutenant Burnes-Waterton stopped, and all the other officers stopped. Jamie looked around him. 'By God,' he said, 'I sure know why you wanted to take a hike on your own.'

They carried on walking. They had almost reached the fence around the Viceregal Lodge. Lucy was beginning to feel chilly now, and tired.

'I don't know what it is,' said Jamie. 'I'm not ashamed to admit it, not now. The years have gone by and I've travelled all the way around the world and met dozens of women and lots of them were pretty. But I always felt that you and I were meant for each other, born for each other. I don't know why. It doesn't even trouble me any more. I just kind of take it as true. You know, like the world's round, and you and I were meant for each other.'

Lucy intertwined her fingers between his, and they were just as strong and reassuring as ever.

'I never took it for granted that the world was round,' she told him, in a voice too soft for Elizabeth to hear her.

'Maybe that's your trouble,' grinned Jamie. 'You're a dyed-in-the-wool flat-earther.'

She gave him a long, slow smile. 'You must come to dinner at the Lodge,' she said. 'I'll have Mr Frognal send you an invitation.'

'I'm staying at the Hotel Cecil,' he told her.

'That's pronounced Sessul; not Sea-sill,' she admonished him. 'And don't try to kiss me goodbye. Everybody in the viceregal court suffers from the same incurable disease, *gossipus rampantus*. We can't have the Viceroy thinking that his Vicereine is being pursued by a poodle-faker.'

Jamie slowly shook his head. 'Do you know how English you sound?'

'I love you,' mouthed Lucy, as he put on his hat and walked away.

She arranged a dinner for that very weekend, for the sole purpose of inviting Jamie; even though to balance her guest-list she had to invite the Reverend Hugo Watkins who was alleged by John Frognal to be a notorious bore on the subject of slavery, particularly about naked black women chained to trees, and particularly with his mouth full, so that he emphasized his evangelical fantasies by spraying out showers of crumbs all over the tablecloth. It had also been necessary to invite Doctor Kingston Lear, who lived in a huge rambling chalet on the brink of a hair-raising precipice on the south-eastern side of Simla. Doctor Lear had perversely called his chalet *Chota Bungla* – 'little bungalow' – because it was neither a bungalow nor little. It was rumoured among the service wives that if you were ever accidentally put up the spout while your hubby was still in Calcutta, Dr Lear was the man to go to. Fortunately the wives' behaviour (though flirtatious) was almost always so desperately honourable that even if Dr Lear had done that kind of work, he would have made very little profit out of it. Simla was not known for being a poodle-faking station.

It was a dull dinner party. Lucy hadn't realized how talented Henry was at talking, even with the silliest or most retiring of guests. Jamie said very little because he didn't want to appear too intimate with Her Excellency. The Reverend Watkins had plainly been warned by his wife not to talk about naked black women chained to trees, and so he spoke instead about trying to persuade the Simla Amateur Dramatic Society to put on *The Humility of Bishop Stewart on his Sickbed* at the Gaiety Theatre this season, instead of *The Geisha*.

Doctor Lear was yellow-skinned and hairy-wristed and almost equally morbid. He told two jokes as if they were physically painful to impart; one old chestnut about the brigadier who had dined a little too well at the Viceregal Lodge, and had tried to light his cigar with a geranium; the other a riddle asking, 'In which month do Indian civil servants drink the least?' The rest of the company had long turned to another topic of conversation before he perplexed them all by suddenly coming out with, 'February.'

After dinner, however, they retired to the panelled drawing room, where a large fire was roaring and *burra pegs* were poured, and everybody relaxed a little more. Lucy at last found herself able to talk to Jamie for a few minutes.

'I want to see you in private,' he said. 'I must talk to you.'

'Jamie, I can't.'

'Please. I can't stay in Simla too much longer.'

'Well, what do you suggest?'

'Come out to Mashobra. It's only six miles away. I don't know whether your ADC's told you, but there's a viceregal chalet there. It's real quiet and informal, not like this place. You won't have to take many servants. Maybe you could bring a picnic, something like that. I could meet you there about noon Monday.'

'I'm really not sure.'

'Lucy . . . I want to talk to you about Blanche.'

'Can't we do that here?'

Jamie looked around the gloomy drawing room at the chattering and laughing dinner-guests. The fire danced wildly in the hearth, and everybody's shadows swivelled around the carved-oak ceiling. There was a feeling of madness in the air; of a century that was coming to a close.

Lucy said, 'I mustn't come, Jamie. What if Henry found out? He's finding things difficult enough already, without thinking that –'

'Without thinking what?' Jamie demanded.

'Well – without thinking that I might be interested in another man.'

Jamie's eyes were very dark and steady. 'But you're not interested in another man.' Long pause. 'Are you?'

'Jamie, I'm married. And being Henry's wife – being Vicereine – that's more than just being married.'

'You mean your commitment to Henry is public as well as private?'

'I suppose so.'

'Even if you don't particularly love him?'

There was a very long-drawn-out silence between them, as slow and as viscose and as transparent as melted sugar.

Jamie said, softly and wildly, 'Lucy, I made a terrible mistake, letting you go. My God, I should have locked you in the root cellar and never let you out. I should have made you stay, at least until you understood how much I cared for you, and how much you cared for me, too.'

'Jamie,' Lucy warned him, 'this isn't the place.'

'Well, I'm not too sure that I care about that any more. I thought that I could forget about you, forget what you looked like, forget what you felt like. But I couldn't, and I can't, and I don't want to.'

'Oh, Jamie,' whispered Lucy, and touched his hand. It was the greatest intimacy that she could allow herself, here in the drawing room of Viceregal Lodge.

Jamie laid his hand on top of hers. He couldn't have failed to notice her diamond and sapphire and ruby rings; heirlooms from Brackenbridge and gifts from Henry's wealthier friends.

'Blanche is growing up to look just like you,' he told her. 'Same eyes, same curls, same skinny legs.'

Lucy swallowed with emotion. It was still painful to think about Blanche.

'Lucy . . . I want to be Blanche's father, bring her up to know who her real parents are. But I can't do that less'n she has her mother, too. I can't take all of that responsibility on my own. Wouldn't want to, wouldn't be fair on Blanche.'

'What are you asking of me?' Lucy demanded, in a soft, intense voice.

'Maybe it's impossible,' said Jamie.

'Yes,' Lucy told him. 'It's impossible.'

'Couldn't we talk some more?' Jamie asked her. 'Someplace private; someplace alone?'

'The last time we did that, we –' Lucy began, then thought better of it. She didn't want Jamie to know that she had been forced to pay Vernon to keep their last meeting a secret. She regretted now that she had given in to Vernon so easily. In fact she had regretted it the very next day. But how could she possibly stop paying him now? She didn't doubt for a moment that Vernon had the brass East End neck to tell Henry what had happened; and no matter how innocent the kisses that she had given Jamie might have been, Henry would assume that she *must* feel desperately guilty, or else she wouldn't have paid up.

Jamie said, 'I don't want to upset you, Lucy; I promise. But I do want to talk. You know, just the way we used to. Otherwise – I don't know – it all seems so goddamned *unfinished*. You left me with your child, Lucy, and you left me with a broken heart, too. At least give me the chance to understand why.'

Lucy said nothing. She knew why. But how could she really explain it to Jamie without breaking his heart even more; and her own heart, too?

And she was frightened of much more than that. She was frightened that if she came to know Jamie better – this new, bearded Jamie, with his strong political conscience and his worldlywise ways she might have to admit to herself that she loved him more than she could ever love Henry. She might have to face what she already knew to be true – that Jamie would love her just as demonstratively in return, which Henry never would.

'Come to Mashobra, please,' Jamie begged her. 'Just for an hour. Just to say goodbye.'

Lucy lowered her eyes and looked down at the silk embroidery on her evening gown.

Jamie said, 'I have a photograph of Blanche, back at the hotel. It's the only one I've got; but if you come to Mashobra, I'll give it to you.'

Lucy lifted her head. 'You have a *photograph*?'

'My father took it. He bought himself one of those folding cameras from Sears. He took some views, too. The house, the river. And a whole lot of mother.'

Lucy hesitated for a moment, but the thought of having a photograph of Blanche was too much of a temptation to resist. 'All right, then,' she said. 'I'll fix up a picnic. But I won't be able to stay for long.'

She was conscious that Elizabeth was observing her intently from the other side of the drawing room, and she smiled and nodded as if Jamie were telling her something tedious.

The *khit* came around with more cognac, but Jamie covered his glass with his hand. 'I have work to do, people to meet; thanks all the same.'

He started to tell Lucy about his work in the Phillippines, and Lucy watched him as he talked with the softly-focused look of deep affection. I could have married this man; we could have lived together in Kansas for the rest of our lives, where the sunflowers grow, and the wind blows fresh.

'You'll marry someday,' she said, interrupting him in the middle of a sentence.

'What?' he asked her, baffled.

'You'll find somebody some day. I'm sure of it.'

'Well . . .' he said, glancing around the room. 'Maybe I will.'

'Jamie, you mustn't love me for ever.'

He looked back at her. 'That's not one of those things you can decide for yourself. You can decide to change the way you are, like I can try to make up for what I did to the Cheyenne and the Arapaho by doing some good here in India. But you can't decide who you're going to be in love with.'

'Oh, you'll meet somebody, when you're least expecting it.'

'That happened to me a long time ago.'

'Jamie . . .' she cautioned him. You never knew who might be listening.

But he wasn't to be cautioned. He sat forward on the sofa and took hold of her hand. Under his breath, he said, 'Tell me.'

'Jamie, let go of my hand. Somebody will see.'

'Not before you tell me that you love me.'

Her eyes were bright and very blue. 'Of course I love you.'

'You mean it?'

She nodded. She said it to calm him; she said it so that he wouldn't feel too hurt.

'You mean it,' he repeated, releasing her hand and sitting back.

'Jamie,' she said, 'I loved you when we were young and I love you now and I will never stop loving you for the whole of my life. But I made my choice. I made it of my own free will. And my choice was to marry Henry.'

A picnic at Mashobra was surprisingly easy to arrange. All she had to say was, 'I want to have a picnic at Mashobra on Monday,' and at eleven o'clock on Monday morning Corcoran knocked politely at her door to assure her that her entourage was ready to depart. It was a soft, bright day, with the sun sparkling through the pines, and a light breeze stirring the Union Jack above the Lodge's crenellated tower.

As she and Elizabeth stepped out of the main door, she saw that Jamie had been right: she hadn't required more than a *khansamah*, two *khitmutgars*, three *musolchis*, Etta, with *two ayahs*, two *syces* to take care of the horses, four officers of the Viceroy's Bodyguard, eighteen coolies for pulling the rickshaws and carrying the charcoal stoves and the ice-pails and the tables and the linen-boxes and the supplies, and six or seven assorted boys who seemed to be coming along for the fun of it.

'I do so love a quiet outing in the countryside, don't you?' Elizabeth remarked.

'It would probably be more peaceful if we took a travelling circus with us, don't you think?'

Mashobra was one of the few retreats where the Viceroy and Vicereine could behave with genuine informality. Lucy and her party reached it by travelling through a long dark tunnel through the hills, and then along a narrow road which clung to the side of a sheer steamy precipice thousands of feet deep. Although it was only six miles away, it was a small haven of primitive peace among the trees, and even the viceregal chalet, for all the grandeur of its fretwork balcony, had no hot water, and only iron tubs to wash in.

Sunlight played shadow-theatre patterns on the road as they ascended; and monkeys laughed in the trees; and the rickshaw coolies puffed and groaned as they pulled Lucy and Elizabeth and Etta up steadily-steepening gradients.

'Don't worry,' said Elizabeth, dismissively. 'They only groan as a matter of habit, so that people will pay them more.'

At lunchtime, they reached Mashobra, and the entire noisy jingling entourage dismounted. The chalet had been opened already. Carpets had been rolled out, curtains had been hung, dust-covers had been dragged off chairs. Pots of geraniums had been brought up from the Lodge and arranged along the verandah, as if they had always been there. With all these scurrying scene-changers accompanying her wherever she went, Lucy wondered if it would ever be possible for her to see India as she really was. She was escorted up to the verandah by Lieutenant Venables, who saluted with quivering exactitude, and ask for permission to fall out.

Lucy and Elizabeth drank a glass of champagne on the balcony, while the *khansamah* got to work with his charcoal stove, and the rest of the servants busied themselves with setting up tables and arranging napkins and plates and silver-ware. In the middle of the forest, in a chalet with no hot water and a corrugated-iron roof, surrounded by the jabber-ing of monkeys and the calling of cuckoos, on a warm misty April day, they would be eating from Minton porcelain and patting their lips with Irish-linen napkins, as if they were lunching at an English country house.

The head *khitmutgar* came out from the kitchen and bowed. He presented both Lucy and Elizabeth with a type-written menu for their picnic. *Green Bean Toran, Biter Gourd with Union Stuffing, Hole Rose Chicken Vicereine, Stuff Okra, Black Lentle Chutni, Plantin Jaggery.*

'With your special allowance, Your Excellency, the *khan-samah* has dedicated to you this special new menu for the whole roast chicken, especially and deliberately devised on purpose for Your Excellency as an initial well come to Simla for the first time.'

'How is it prepared?' asked Elizabeth, quite sharply. Even as Vicereine, Lucy still couldn't quite get used to the demand-ing way in which Europeans spoke to their Indian servants; although Henry had told her time and time again that they would take advantage, otherwise, and run you ragged.

'*They're just like children,*' John Frognal had explained; and she had remembered then what Jamie had said, under the fast-disappearing moon.

The *khit* said, 'The chicken is taken leave of its skin, Your Excellency, and then it is suffocated for six hours long in onions and paprika and chilli and saffron and cumin and garam masala and coriander, but it is the great secret of this whole roast chicken that it is choked in its interior with the chest part of six quails tied together and covered with coriander leaves.'

'It sounds marvellous,' said Lucy, ignoring Elizabeth's wrinkled-up nose. 'Tell the *khansamah* that I am pleased by his compliment.'

'Very honoured, Your Excellency,' the *khit* acknowledged, and bowed again.

The picnic turned out to be wonderful; one of the most ravishing meals that Lucy had eaten since she had arrived in India. The 'Hole Rose Chicken Vicereine', was one of those truly great dishes that can only be created when the stars are in the right conjunction — when inspiration and traditional skill address themselves to a mixture of limited, odd, but superb ingredients, and come up shining in glory. Even Elizabeth had to admit that it was exceptional; and ate almost half of it.

Plantain jaggery turned out to be peeled plantains, boiled in raw sugar and chilled. Lucy adored it, but was too full to do very much more than taste it.

After luncheon, they were served coffee on the verandah, and Elizabeth began to doze on her long-sleever, her *terai* hat nodding lower with every deep breath. But Lucy was beginning to grow anxious. There was no sign of Jamie anywhere. Although she had enjoyed herself, and her servants had treated her like the empress she represented, it looked as if Jamie might have been prevented from getting here; in which case she would simply have to tell the servants to pack everything up and return to Simla.

The *khit* had just come out on to the verandah to ask them if they wanted more coffee when she saw a light flashing in the nearby trees; a mirror, catching the sun. It flashed three times, and then it stopped.

She waved the *khit* away, and said to Elizabeth, 'I'm just taking a walk around the bungalow. You don't mind, do you?'

Elizabeth was asleep, under the brim of her hat. She was snoring with the noise that her servants usually called 'memsahib singing hymns'. The coolies were eating their midday meal, leaning their backs against the gardening-shed. The officers of the Viceroy's bodyguard were stretched out on camp-chairs, eating *moorghi masala* and laughing. Lucy was able to rise from her long-sleever and leave the verandah without anybody seeing, and cross the chalet garden to the trees, where the mirror had been flashing.

She crossed the pathway like a ghost, or a memory.

Jamie was waiting for her in a small rocky hollow, almost completely overshadowed by ferns. Not far away, a small stream gargled over the rocks; and barbets twittered; and there was a pungent smell of woods and mountains.

This time she opened her arms to him and kissed him without hesitation. He held her as closely as he could, pressing her tautly pregnant stomach up against him, and kissed her hair, and her face, and her eyelids, and her cheeks, and her lips.

'You don't know how much I've missed you, Lucy. It's been worse than a pain that just wouldn't go away.'

She stepped back a little way and looked at him. He was dressed in a canary-yellow suit with patch pockets, and an open-necked shirt.

'Where *did* you get that suit?' she asked him.

He tightened his lips, and then laughed. 'Everybody asks me that. Goddamit. Abercrombie & Fitch, no less. They told me that this was what the experienced traveller always wore to tropical climes. I've never been laughed at so much in my life. My topi was so ridiculous that I threw it away. If I could afford the time, I'd have a *derzi* copy this suit in white, and then throw this away, too.'

'Oh, Jamie,' Lucy laughed.

Jamie said, 'There's a blanket here . . . why don't you sit down?'

Lucy perched herself on the double-folded *durry* that Jamie had arranged for her on a rock. 'Goddamit, you look pretty,' he told her.

'You didn't forget the photograph of Blanche?' Lucy asked him.

'No, no.' He reached into his jacket pocket, and took out an envelope. When he handed it to her, Lucy noticed that his hands were trembling.

'I wrote the date on the back,' he told her.

Lucy opened the envelope and took out the small sepia picture. It showed a small girl in a sunbonnet and an apron, frowning at the camera. Her arms were chubby; and around her left wrist was woven a chain of ox-eye daisies. Lucy recognized the background at once: it was the yard out at the back of Mrs Cullen's kitchen.

Lucy sat on the folded *durry* under the breeze-flickered leaves and her eyes blurred with tears.

'She's pretty, isn't she?' said Jamie. 'Every bit as pretty as you.'

'You're quite certain I can keep this?'

'Sure. See what I've said on the back.'

Lucy turned the picture over, and across the back was written *Blanche Cullen, Saline River, 1898. From her father Jamie to her mother Lucy, with love.*

Nothing could stop the tears that ran down Lucy's cheeks. Jamie offered her his handkerchief, but she shook her head and said miserably, 'No.'

'It was your choice,' said Jamie. 'You made it of your own free will.'

'I know,' Lucy replied, smearing the tears with her fingers. 'That doesn't make it any easier.'

Jamie stood still, watching her. Then he said, 'You're sure you won't come back to me?'

'Oh, Jamie, it's far too late for that.'

'You said that you loved me. You said that you always will.'

'I know. And it's true. But when you make a choice for yourself you have to stick to it, don't you? You have a duty to stick to it.'

'Is that one of Henry's platitudes?'

Lucy took another sad look at the photograph of Blanche, then tucked it back into its envelope. She stood up, and brushed the creases from her dress. 'I think I ought to go now, Jamie. I don't want to hurt you any more.'

'I shouldn't worry about hurting me, Lucy. You've already hurt me just about as much as one man can stand. Besides, there's somebody I want you to meet.'

Lucy quickly turned her head. 'Here? There's somebody else here?'

'It's somebody I trust, believe me.'

Lucy felt alarmed, and stepped back two or three paces. 'I though it was going to be you and me, alone.'

Jamie spread his arms wide. 'I'm sorry. It is. I mean, he hasn't been listening.'

'Well, that's very nice to know,' Lucy retaliated.

'Lucy, I'm sorry. Believe me, I asked you to meet me here today because I wanted to talk to you. I mean just about Blanche, and us. I thought by some ridiculous chance you might have changed your mind. I don't know, I guess I thought that you might have decided that Blanche needed both of us – that maybe you and Henry – I don't know. I guess I was grasping at straws.'

'Jamie, who's here?' She looked around the hollow, this way and that. 'And where is he? Or she?'

Jamie said, 'Please don't be angry, okay? It was after I left your dinner party the other night. I was talking to some of the people I met here in Simla, and I told them where I'd spent the evening. And they couldn't believe that I was actually friends with the Vicereine. They said it was such a great opportunity, and they were right.'

'*What's* a great opportunity?' Lucy wanted to know. 'Come on, Jamie, tell me!'

'These people – these friends of mine – they're trying to change things. Trying to persuade the people of India to help themselves – you know, rather than depending on the British for everything.'

'I don't understand,' Lucy replied. 'I'm not even sure that I want to. Listen, Jamie, I'll have to be getting back.'

'Lucy,' Jamie pleaded with her, taking hold of both of her hands. 'I wouldn't have asked you to come here if I didn't think you were sensitive enough at least to listen. All right, you've listened to me, and thank you for listening, but you've told me no. Now at least listen to Tilak. You can always say no to him, too.'

'Tilak, is that his name?'

Jamie said gently, 'You rule this country, Lucy. Don't you realize that? How can you rule a country without knowing how its people feel? What their needs are, what their hopes are? Every day millions of Indians say prayers that their gods will keep you and protect you and guide your hand. And yet you don't even know how much they're suffering; or what they want. You don't even know who they are.'

Lucy said, with deliberate sarcasm, 'You should have been a lawyer.'

'You'll listen?' asked Jamie. 'That's all I ask.'

Lucy nodded; and waited tall and still in the intricate light of the hollow while Jamie cupped his hands around his mouth and shouted, 'Tilak! It's all right! Tilak! Come here!'

Birds screeched and whooped in alarm, and startled monkeys crashed furiously through the trees. Jamie watched Lucy very closely as the clamour died down. The undergrowth rustled, twigs broke, and a short middle-aged Indian appeared, dressed in a rumpled buff-coloured business suit, and a dark red turban. He was plump and anxious-eyed and perspiring, with a small hooked nose and skin the colour

of cold tea; more like a Bombay shipping agent than anything else. He bowed his head to Lucy; but the look on his
face told her that he had very little respect for her, or at least
for the viceroyalty.

'This is Bal Gangadhar Tilak,' said Jamie. 'Tilak, this is
Her Excellency the Vicereine, Lady Carson of Brackenbridge.'

'*Salaam*, Your Excellency,' Tilak told her. 'Mr Cullen has
spoken to me much about you, extolling your virtues,
praising your beauty. I confess that he spoke no lies; and that
you are more beautiful than any European woman I have
ever been honoured to meet.'

'Why are you here?' asked Lucy, aware that she was using
the same sharp tones that Elizabeth had used when she was
asking about the Hole Rose Chicken. 'What do you want?'

Bal Gangadhar Tilak gave Lucy the tiniest of smiles, like a
heart-shaped hole in a pierced Indian screen. 'This is indeed an
unusual opportunity for me, to meet one of those who call
me a petty volcano. But Mr Cullen said that you would
listen with sympathy, and consider what I say, and if possible
pass on my message for the ears of His Excellency, so that he
would consider our feelings with greater care.'

Lucy was immediately aware that this was wrong; that
Jamie had coaxed her here not as Lucy, not as a lover, not
even as a friend, but as Vicereine of India. She said, 'Jamie –
I think I have to go. You shouldn't have asked me here,
really. Whatever I feel about you, whatever I feel about
Henry – Jamie, this isn't right.'

Jamie took hold of her hand, and gripped it tightly.
'Come on, Lucy, for once I want *you* to listen to *me*.'

'It isn't right,' Lucy reiterated.

Jamie ducked his head as if she had tried to slap him.

'Right?' he asked her. 'You tell me what's right! Is it right
that a whole civilization should be dominated by a handful
of people, your husband worst of all. Is it right that babies
should be starving before they're even born? Is it right that

five-year-old children should die of typhoid and cholera and dysentery? Let me ask you this – is it right that millions and millions of people should live their lives from birth to death without being given one single anna of the riches that their country has to offer them?'

'Jamie,' said Lucy, turning away, 'I can't do anything to help your guilt about the Cheyenne; and I'm not going to help you; and I'm not going to listen. Good day. And good day to *you*, Mr Gunga Din.'

She began to climb up the steep slippery sides of the hollow, holding her skirts up to help herself up, when Bal Gangadhar Tilak called, 'Mrs Viceroy! Wait!'

Lucy hesitated, and turned around. From out of the bushes, Tilak had beckoned a young girl, no more than four or five, only a little older than Blanche. She wore a blanket to cover her, but nothing else. Her hair was sticky with dirt and thick with nits, and her lips were crusted with yellow sores. All the same, her eyes were wide and dark and intelligent; and if she had been washed and dressed and treated by a doctor, she would have been captivatingly pretty.

'Your Excellency,' said Bal Gangadhar Tilak, 'this is the daughter of my cousin who lives close to Delhi. I visited him on my way to meet with Mr Cullen, and to talk to my people in Simla. I brought her with me because she is very sick, and will certainly die if she is left in the plains during the Hot Weather. Her name is Pratima, which means golden temple idol. She is almost starving; she has rickets and worms and many different diseases from which starving people suffer. Look at her, she is very dirty and sad.'

Bal Gangadhar Tilak laid his hand with great gentleness on Pratima's head. 'She is given to us from the gods, and if necessary the gods will take her back. But there is a way in which her suffering can be used to prevent the suffering of many other children, in many generations to come. Your friend Mr Cullen risked very much to bring me here to talk to you. I risked much; and so did you. I am a wanted brigand with a price on my head. I am supposed to be a dangerous man, a murderer! But – look at this little girl; and ask yourself what has she done to deserve such suffering. Ask yourself that. And then say to me that you cannot at least speak to His Excellency for just a few minutes about helping the plight of such innocents.'

Blanche, thought Lucy. She climbed slowly back down the hollow, and Jamie lifted his hand to help her. She leaned over Pratima and touched her cheek with her fingers, and Pratima shivered.

Bal Ganghadar Tilak made a resigned-looking face. 'She may survive, she may not. She has more chance than most, because I have brought her here. But if she has persuaded you to talk to the Viceroy about her plight; and about the plight of so many millions of our people ... well, she will have achieved something with her short life, won't she?'

'Pratima?' Lucy cajoled the little girl. 'Pratima?'

Then, softly, she sang to her:

'Tip, tip, my little horse,
Tip, tip, again sir!
How many miles to Dublin town?
Fourscore and ten, sir!
Will I get back by candlelight?
Yes, and back again, sir!'

Pratima smiled faintly, and then covered her eyes with her hand. Bal Gangadhar Tilak laughed. 'She is shy, you see! Even when you are starving, even when you are dying, you can be shy!'

Lucy thought of her picnic, of her Hole Rose Chicken, and her pain and her shame were almost too much for her to bear. She stood up straight, her lower lip trembling with grief and emotion, and said to Jamie, 'I'm sorry. I'm sorry I misjudged you.'

Jamie held her tightly in his arms. 'Sssh, hey. You don't have to be sorry. You haven't done anything at all.'

'But I love you!'

'I know. And I love you, too.'

She tugged a handkerchief out of her pocket and dabbed at her eyes. 'I'll do – I'll do what I can. I'll talk to Henry, in any case. How long are you going to be here?'

'Not more than two more days,' said Bal Gangadhar Tilak. 'We have very many people to see, up and down the whole country.'

'Oh, Jamie,' said Lucy, and hugged him close. 'What happened to those cloud-castles?'

'They're still there,' said Jamie. 'But, you know – I don't know. Maybe they were always just clouds, and nothing else.'

That night, in her study, by electric light, she sat at her small Regency desk and wrote Jamie a letter. Mauve ink, the same mauve that Lady Elgin had favoured, on vellum paper. On the wall beside her, engravings of Victoria and Albert regarded her with imperial seriousness. Outside, the monkeys still screamed.

'Viceregal Lodge, Simla
April 10 1899

   'My darling Jamie,
   There will be no opportunity for us to meet again before you leave. But never forget that I love you. Carry that thought with you wherever you go.
   As for Bal Gangadhar Tilak, tell him that I will talk to Henry; and that I will try to persuade him that Tilak is a man of honour who cares only for the welfare of the young and the old and the starving.
   Meanwhile, I love you, my darling Jamie. I love you, I love you. And in all the years to come.
   Your Cloud-Castle, Lucy.'

When she had blotted the letter, and dropped scarlet wax on to it, and impressed the wax with the viceregal seal, she called for a messenger to take it to the Hotel Cecil. 'And guard it with your life,' she told the small barefooted boy.

'Yes, *memsahib*,' the boy had assured her, and scampered off.

Elizabeth had walked into the room just as the boy was running away, and seen Lucy putting away her pen and her blotter, and frowned.

She heard no word from Jamie the following morning; nor the morning after that. She sent a bearer to the Hotel Cecil, inquiring about Mr Cullen; but the bearer came back with a three-toothed grin to say that Mr Cullen had left Simla at eleven o'clock, with two servants and four coolies. He had left no message; he had left no forwarding address. He had vanished, without a word, without a goodbye.

Lucy spent the rest of the afternoon in her drawing room, staring out over the mountains; but as night had fallen the mist had closed in; and the mountains had looked eerier and stranger than ever before. She heard a cry that wasn't monkeys and wasn't men; but something else altogether.

After Jamie's unaccountable disappearance, Lucy slept badly. She lay in bed night after night, thinking about him; hearing his voice. *I wanted Blanche to have a mother and a father.* And all the time the spring winds whispered and rustled through the Lodge, lifting curtains, turning over pages of magazines, stirring the dreams of the sleeping *ayahs*.

There was nothing that she could do. She couldn't send anybody to look for Jamie, or to find out where he might have gone. He had told her that his next stop was Amritsar, and then Kashmir, and she was tempted to send a telegraph to the resident at Amritsar, asking him to look out for Jamie on the pretext that he had left a valuable cigarette case behind, when he had visited Viceregal Lodge for dinner. But in the end she decided against it. She had already tied herself up into enough of a tangle over Jamie.

On Wednesday night she sat up reading until well after one o'clock in the morning. Etta had come in to see her just after eleven, to ask her if she wanted some warm milk or a powder to help her sleep. But Lucy had shaken her head. She was tired; but she wanted to think about Jamie. She needed to churn her feelings about him around and around in her head, like shirts in a washing-machine, until she was certain that she didn't love him more than she loved Henry. Or until she was certain that she did.

At one o'clock, she slipped out of her mosquito-nets, wrapped herself in her long white cambric robe, and stepped out on to the balcony. The night was the palest lilac; chilly but fragrant; and the sound of streams rushing down the dark and precipitous valleys was like the sound of blood rushing through her veins.

She felt as if she had been thinking for so long that her mind hurt. If only she could forget Sha-sha; if only Jamie hadn't kissed her in just that particular way. If only she hadn't slept with Malty. If only she hadn't ever set eyes on Henry.

She took the photograph of Blanche out of her pocket and angled it towards the moonlight so that she could see that serious little face, those chubby little arms. Jamie had said that she had skinny legs now; so she must have grown since this picture had been taken. If only I hadn't left you behind, my darling daughter.

She was still peering at the picture when she heard a soft knocking at the door of her bedroom. Quickly, guiltily, she turned around, trying to push the photograph back into the pocket of her robe. She missed her pocket, and dropped the photograph on to the tiled floor of the balcony; and just as she reached down to pick it up, the wind caught it, and tumbled it through the railings, and out into the night.

She was still anxiously trying to see where the photograph had fallen when Elizabeth appeared, in her nightcap, and the most severe and modest of missionary nightgowns.

'Why, Lucy! What on earth are you doing? You'll catch your death! That's if you don't tipple off the balcony!'

Lucy turned around, tearful. 'I dropped my – hairslide.'

'Your *hairslide*?' Elizabeth went to the edge of the balcony and looked over, into the shadows. 'Do you want me to send a *chokra* to go and look for it.'

'No, no, I don't want to wake anybody up.'

'Was it valuable?' asked Elizabeth.

'No, really, it was sentimental, more than anything else. Henry gave it to me.' She wiped her eyes. 'I'm too sensitive, right now. Anything makes me cry.'

Elizabeth put her arm around her, and guided her back into the bedroom. 'Well, we'll find it in the morning, when it's light. And I've just heard wonderful news from Mr Frognal. Henry's coming up to Simla tomorrow. He should be here by teatime.'

'Henry? That's marvellous.'

'Well, you may not think it, my dear, but it is. Once the Viceroy's arrived, the social whirl will *really* start! Which is not to say that you haven't started it already, my dear. But in your condition, of course, it has been rather difficult for you.'

Lucy sat down on her bed and looked towards the open balcony windows, as if she half-expected Sha-sha's photograph to come tumbling mysteriously back in again. But it was gone for good, she knew it was gone for good, and so was Jamie. Perhaps the wind and the night were trying to show her the right thing to do.

'Elizabeth,' she said, still staring at the balcony, 'have you ever been in love?'

Elizabeth had been tightening the ribbons around her wrists. She paused; uncertain at the tone in Lucy's voice.

'Yes,' she said, 'I've been in love.'

'What was his name?'

Elizabeth finished tightening her ribbon. 'Richard, that was his name. Captain Richard Watson, 13th Bengal Cavalry. He married a girl named Minnie Forrester, in the end. She had a thick black moustache, almost as magnificent as his. I heard later that he died in Egypt. Not heroically, either. Food poisoning.'

'I'm sorry.'

'Don't be. He was a beast, really.'

Elizabeth waited for a moment or two, and then she said, 'Why do you ask?'

'I'm not really sure,' Lucy admitted. 'I just wondered if you knew what it was like.'

Elizabeth let out a little laugh. 'You're the expert, surely! Married to the most dashing man in the British Empire!'

'I just wondered how you could ever be *sure*.'

Elizabeth came over to the bed and sat beside her. She smelled of lavender-water, and some kind of clove-scented rub. 'You're having a baby, you know. Your affections go quite topsy-turvy when you're having a baby.'

'I suppose so.'

'Are you worried about what you feel for Henry?'

Lucy said, 'I'm more worried about what I *don't* feel for Henry.'

'Well, don't think any more about it. These days, your brain is concentrating on loving your baby. It doesn't have much time for Henry; but it will.'

'Did your Richard make you shiver?' asked Lucy.

Elizabeth stared at her. She had begun to realize that perhaps Lucy wasn't talking about Henry at all; but about somebody else.

'At first,' she said. 'But when I saw him years and years later, with Minnie and four diminutive Minnie-ettes, I shivered! Not from excitement, my dear – but from profound relief.'

★

Lucy called Etta to dress her especially early that morning.

'Miss Morris told me that Lord Carson's coming this afternoon,' Etta smiled, as she brushed out Lucy's curls in front of the gilded dressing-room mirrors.

'Yes,' said Lucy. 'Now the fun's supposed to start.'

Etta obviously noticed the flatness in her voice, because she caught Lucy's eyes in the mirror; and paused in her hairbrushing. A small hand on a heavy silver-backed brush, a wedding gift from Lord Salisbury.

'You're looking a little tired, your ladyship, if you'll forgive me,' said Etta.

'Oh, it's nothing. Sleeping in a strange bed, that's all. And you know what they say about Simla. One of those unquiet places, crowded with ghosts.'

'I can't truthfully say that I've ever seen a ghost myself,' said Etta, carrying on brushing. 'Not sure that I want to, either.'

She brushed out the back of Lucy's hair, and caught a tangle.

'Oh, for goodness' sake!' Lucy snapped. 'Nora never –!'

She stopped herself, 'I'm sorry, Etta. That was wrong of me.'

'I miss Nora, too, you know, Lady Carson,' said Etta.

'Well, I suppose we all do. It's just that Nora worked for me when I was living in America. She was more of a friend that a lady's maid.' Lucy didn't add, of course, that only Nora had known about Blanche. If Nora had still been alive, she would at least have had somebody to talk to; somebody to tell how upset she was that she had lost Blanche's photograph.

Etta pinned up Lucy's hair. 'I hope that I can be your friend, too, Lady Carson; given time.'

Lucy turned, and took hold of Etta's hand. 'Of course you can. You are already.'

Somebody knocked at the door. Etta went to answer it, and it turned out to be Mrs Smallwood, Lucy's nurse. She was a neat, busy-mannered woman with black scraped-back hair and a white cotton apron and the efficient thinness of a truly dedicated nurse. It was said that she had lectured the Senior Surgeon at Madras so ferociously about the admission of women to the medical profession that he had broken down and wept (albeit after a half-bottle of Spencer & Co.'s cognac). She reminded Lucy of Mrs Noah in a children's Noah's Ark – hard, varnished, and bossy.

'You won't mind if I take your temperature, will you?' she insisted, setting her brown leather satchel on the nearest table and taking out her thermometer. She always spoke in the form of challenging questions, like a nanny. It must have been that maternal hectoring which had finally reduced the Senior Surgeon to tears.

'But I was going out for a walk,' Lucy protested.

'A walk? At this time of the morning? In your condition? After scarlatina? With all that dew on the ground? I'm sure you aren't serious, are you?'

'I feel like some exercise,' said Lucy. 'I feel so cooped up.'

'There is sensible exercise and there is silly exercise,' Mrs Smallwood replied, popping the thermometer into Lucy's mouth. 'I'm sure you know that, don't you?'

'Mmff,' Lucy replied.

'When the dew has evaporated, and the air is clear, you may take a short walk, if that's what you wish. But you do understand that His Excellency is coming this afternoon, and His Excellency wouldn't care to find you tired and out-of-sorts – now, would he?'

'Muffuff,' said Lucy.

Lucy breakfasted with Elizabeth Morris in the Plassey Room; a small quiet parlour with arches of saffron-coloured tiles, and long linen curtains which blew in the morning wind like the flags of some ancient order of Buddhist monks.

Elizabeth like *khagina* for breakfast, an Indian spiced omelette mixed with bessan, coriander, cardamoms and onions, and cut into thick diagonal slices. Lucy had her usual porridge, with a little cream. Mrs Smallwood had told her that any Indian spices would affect her unborn baby's digestion.

Elizabeth wore a rather arty dress of crimson-and-indigo printed muslin; and pearls. As she helped herself to the rolled-rice pancakes called *dosha*, she said, as if it had only just occurred to her, 'You meant, of course, have I ever loved more than one man at a time?'

'What?' asked Lucy, startled.

Elizabeth smiled, with her mouth full. 'When we were talking last night. You meant had I ever loved more than one man at a time. At least – forgive me – that's what I *thought* you meant.'

Lucy said nothing, but sipped her tea and waited to hear what Elizabeth was going to say next.

Elizabeth swallowed the last of her *khagina*, and fastidiously wiped her mouth. 'There's a famous Indian story, about a millionaire who was looking for a wife. He went to rich households and he went to poor households. He talked to girls who were beautiful and to girls who were plain. He asked them all the same question: *can you make a good meal out of two pounds of rice?*

'Of course they all laughed at him. That is – until he found a dazzlingly pretty girl who said, yes, she could. She took the rice, and carefully threshed it, keeping the grains and setting aside the husks. She sold the husks to jewellers, who use them to polish silver; and with the money she bought firewood and two pans.

'She lit the wood, and steamed the rice grains; and when the wood was all burned she sold the charcoal; and with the money she made from the charcoal she bought ghee and curds and oil and myrobalan and tamarind.

'She was able to serve the millionaire with rice broth, and kedgeree, and buttermilk, and soup. She served everything beautifully, with water scented with aloe wood; and of course he fell in love with her and married her.'

Lucy finished her tea. 'I'm not sure what you're trying to tell me.'

Elizabeth gave a little dismissive shrug. 'I think I'm trying to tell you to make the best of what you have. Your marriage to Henry may sometimes seem as unexciting as two pounds of rice. But if you work hard, and attend to what you have, it will one day bring you joy and happiness and great satisfaction.'

She paused for a while, and then she said, 'You were born in modest circumstances, my dear, in a place very far from here; and what happened to you happened by extraordinary chance and by dramatic good fortune. But now the responsibility for your future happiness is yours. You have more than most women ever dream of. I know that you feel uncertain. I know that you are sometimes simply bored. You doubt Henry's love. You doubt your own love for Henry.

'But like those two pounds of rice, a marriage needs care and work and constant attention; exchanging each reward for another reward; until you have not just two pounds of rice, but a banquet.'

Lucy looked back at Elizabeth for such a long time without speaking that Elizabeth eventually said, 'Lucy? You're feeling quite well?'

'Yes,' said Lucy. 'I'm fine.'

But then she said, 'What if I'd done that, a long time ago, with somebody else? I mean, what if I'd worked just as hard at loving *him*?'

Elizabeth smiled. 'What if I'd married Richard Watson? What if the world ended tomorrow?'

She reached out and touched the knuckles of Lucy's hand. 'In India, questions like that are called "flowers that grow in the sky". They have no point, Lucy. They are idle thoughts that will make you sad, and lead you nowhere at all.'

The two of them remained at the table while the servants cleared away the dishes, and the curtains rose and fell; and outside they heard shouting and laughter and the clattering of feet, as the Lodge was made ready for the arrival of His Excellency Lord Carson, Lucy's husband.

She managed to slip out into the gardens shortly after eleven o'clock, with a light shawl around her shoulders. She skirted around the Lodge until she was standing below her balcony window; and then she carefully searched through the flower-beds and the bushes, trying to work out where Blanche's photograph might have fallen.

She was picking through the Apline rockery when a *mali* appeared, wheeling a wheelbarrow.

'Hey, you!' called Lucy, as he made his way down the sloping lawns. *'Koi-hai!'*

The *mali* stopped, and set down his wheelbarrow. He was very young; and his face was pockmarked and pale. *'Mem-sahib?'*

'Have you been working here all morning?'

The *mali* clearly didn't understand. For the first time, Lucy felt infuriated that she hadn't learned any Urdu.

'Have – you – been – working – here –' she began, much louder, but then she realized that shouting made no differ-ence: all she was doing was frightening him.

'Have you seen a picture?' she asked him. 'A picture, of a little girl?'

He stared at her, nervous, desperate to oblige, but com-pletely uncomprehending.

'A picture,' she repeated, drawing tiny invisible squares in the air. 'A *photograph*. Picture of missy *baba*.'

'Missy *baba*?' frowned the *mali*, completely perplexed. He hadn't seen any little girls around Viceregal Lodge. There were no European children here at all; no *chota* sahibs or missy *babas*.

Lucy took a deep breath, and then she said, 'If – you – see – a – picture – of – a – missy – baba –' But it was hopeless. He didn't know what she meant.

She turned, and walked back across the shiny overwatered grass. Tin-pot birds called from the trees around her, alarmed by the comings and goings of the servants and the officers of the Viceroy's Bodyguard. Elizabeth was waiting by the stone steps that led up to the conservatory.

'Did you find it?' she called.

For a moment, Lucy was perplexed.

'Your hairslide,' Elizabeth reminded her.

'Oh,' said Lucy. 'No. It must have bounced, or gotten buried in the bushes.'

Elizabeth took hold of her arm. 'It'll turn up. You mark my words. I've sent boxes and parcels from one end of India to the other. Once I even sent some children, some young cousins of ours, with nothing but a picnic box, and a cardboard label saying *Bombay*. I've never lost anything yet.'

Together, they went back into the Lodge. Already the servants were sweeping and polishing and hurrying from one room to another with huge bowls of sweetpeas and daisies. Corcoran the butler creaked into view like a pirate ship under full sail, and asked, 'You *did* say the summer pudding, your ladyship?' Then John Frognal came jingling past, in full uniform, and saluted, and said, 'His Excellency should arrive at three o'clock, Lady Carson. I've just had the word.'

'Well, my dear,' said Elizabeth, talking hold of Lucy's hand, 'it seems as if your two pounds of rice are being delivered.'

Lucy couldn't help laughing. 'Henry would be *furious* if he heard you call him that!'

Henry strode into the gloomy panelled hallway of Viceregal Lodge with his hat in his hand, looking hot. Lucy was waiting for him inside, in one of the huge brocade armchairs by the foot of the staircase, fanning herself. She had chosen her blue linen tea-gown; the blue made her eyes look even more blue; and Etta had pinned up her hair for her in the soft, loose curls that she knew Henry adored.

Long pearl earrings swung from her ears.

Henry stopped quite still, and looked at her. 'Lucy,' he said; as soft and sharp as a nutmeg chipped against a metal grater.

Lucy stood up and faced him. He was dressed quite informally, in a linen suit and breeches, and a black silk necktie. He looked exhausted; as if his skin had collapsed around his face. But she detected a certain burned-down pleasure in the way he had walked in; as if he had completed his work in Calcutta to his immediate satisfaction, and was now quite prepared for some recreation and entertainment in the Hills.

He came forward and carefully kissed her. 'I've missed you,' he said; and he couldn't have said anything that pleased her more.

'I've missed you too. Things have been pretty dull up here.'

'You're well, though? You're feeling quite fit? Mrs Smallwood has been sending me daily reports.'

'Well done Mrs Smallwood! Yes, I'm feeling wonderful.'

Lucy took hold of Henry's sleeve. 'Master Carson's been kicking. Especially at night.'

Henry's eyes creased with pleasure. 'Has he now? The little blighter! And is everything well?'

'Everything's fine, Henry. Everything's wonderful.'

'Horatio Carson,' Henry enthused. 'And what a mark he shall make!'

'Henry,' said Lucy. She could see that his sense of his position was taking over; his sense of history and grandeur. Carson upon Carson, down the centuries! Let them hold what they held! She could scarcely speak to him when he behaved like that. It might be hours before he talked like a husband again; or like a lover.

He blinked at her.

'Henry,' she repeated. 'I'm feeling so good because I've been resting. I feel like myself again. I want you to do the same. Rest, and spend some time with me.'

Henry nodded, and smiled, and kissed her forehead. As he

did so, Lucy glanced towards the door. Caught in the afternoon sunlight stood Colonel Belloc, in a perfectly-pressed white suit; and behind him, dark and humourless and attentive, stood Vernon. Their eyes met, Lucy's and Vernon's; and although Lucy immediately looked away, she felt herself flush with guilt and embarrassment; and with the sheer hatefulness of what she had done.

Colonel Belloc came forward and took hold of her hand, and kissed her glove. 'Lady Carson, what a delight! I was planning on a visit back Home, as a matter of fact; but H.E. wanted to spend the Hot Weather talking about buildings, so here I am! Probably just as well. Time I opened up the old house and gave it an airing, don't you think? You and H.E. must come to dinner! It's just along the Ridge – Bellocgunge. Named after me and my brother, don't you see?'

Henry was already climbing the stairs, followed by Corcoran and Vernon and Muhammad Isak and twenty or thirty bearers and coolies carrying Henry's trunks.

Colonel Belloc waited until Henry had reached the half-landing, and then he murmured, 'As a matter of fact, I was much more interested in seeing you, than in talking about buildings. Please don't misinterpret my intentions, Lady Carson. I'm an honourable man. But I'm also a great believer in offering my services to all who seem to require them. Spiritual, political, artistic, sexual. I'm like a bazaar, don't you see, with insights for sale, instead of sweetmeats and incense.'

Lucy wasn't offended; but she wasn't sure that she was pleased, either. She gave Colonel Belloc a fleeting smile, and said, 'I'll see you at dinner, Colonel. And tomorrow we're going for a picnic. Perhaps we can talk then.'

'Be delighted to, your ladyship,' Colonel Belloc replied, and bowed, so that she could hear the laces of his corset creak.

That night, Henry and Lucy slept together; although Henry did no more than kiss her and hold her in his arms.

When Horatio started to kick, Lucy took hold of Henry's hand and pressed it against her stomach, so that he could feel it. He said nothing at first, but looked at her in wonder and amazement.

'Horatio,' he whispered.

'Perhaps,' she replied.

He slept very deeply for most of the night, with his back turned towards her. Towards dawn, however, he began to whisper and tremble, and say 'No, father,' over and over again.

She shushed him, and stroked his shoulder. Somehow, in Simla, away from his desk at Government House, he seemed very much more vulnerable, very much more human – very much more like the man who had once said to her, '*when you're in love, you're on fire.*'

Dawn began to lighten the sky beyond the balcony. Henry opened his eyes and stared at Lucy for a long time, as if he didn't know who she was.

She kissed him. He tasted like Henry. Cedarwood, salt, some particular masculine flavour.

'You're in Simla,' she told him, when he still failed to show any signs of recognition.

'My father's not here?' he asked her.

'No,' she mouthed. 'Your father's not here.'

He sat up. 'That's strange, you know. I dreamed that he was. I wanted to ask him about plaster of Paris.'

'Plaster of Paris?'

'Yes, to –'

But then Henry stopped. He had suddenly realized that he was talking dream-talk; and that in fact he was here, in bed with Lucy, in Simla.

'Do you know something?' he said, frowning around the bedroom. 'I could have *sworn* that –'

Lucy kissed him again. 'Simla is known for its ghosts. Perhaps you just met one.'

She went back into the gardens the following afternoon,

after she and Henry had given a 'delighted-to-meet-you' lunch to most of the members of the Simla Amateur Dramatic Company, all of whom were excessively noisy and pleased with themselves, and half of whom had drunk too much hock.

But now the rickshaws had all rolled away; carrying officers and wives and paramours, shouting out Shakespeare as they went, 'What's gone and what's past help!'; and Viceregal Lodge seemed extraordinarily quiet. Even the birds seemed disinclined to sing. All that Lucy could hear was the indolent flapping of the huge Union Jack on top of the crenellated turret, and the faint clamour of washing-up from the direction of the kitchens.

She found herself a stick, and began to probe through the bushes directly beneath her bedroom window. She found a small square of pasteboard, and her heart jumped; but it was only a visiting-card from somebody illegible. She picked up her skirts a little, and carried on jabbing and poking in the thickest places.

She was still searching when she heard a slight noise behind her. She lifted her head, and looked around, one hand on her large straw hat to prevent the breeze from lifting it off her head. Not far away stood Vernon, with his hands held so tightly behind his back that he looked as if he had no arms; as if his body were a black limbless sausage.

'Vernon!' said Lucy. 'You startled me!'

'Sorry about that, your ladyship,' Vernon replied. 'I'm not a startler by nature.'

'I suppose you want another chit,' said Lucy, stepping out of the shrubbery.

'Oh! Well – that, yes. All in good time.'

'I should never have agreed to it. It was quite absurd. Mr Cullen and I – well, Mr Cullen and I were childhood friends, that's all.'

Vernon nodded: 'Quite sure of it, your ladyship. Quite sure of it.'

Lucy looked at him keenly. 'Then you'll stop asking me for all this money?'

Vernon contorted his face in a complicated squinting grimace, giving Lucy what Cockneys called 'the north eye'. 'Can't say that,' he told her.

'Then what can you say? I used to work once, the same way you work. You're not Jack-out-of-doors and you're not the gentleman, either; so we can understand each other.'

Vernon sniffed, and stood uprighter. 'I like you, your ladyship. You're straight.'

Lucy waited, and Vernon remained upright. In the distance, they could hear hounds yapping, and the sound of somebody shouting, 'Heel! Heel, sir! Heel.'

'I wonder if you've been looking for something,' Vernon remarked.

'Looking for something? What do you mean?'

'Well, the way you was jumbling that bush with that stick of yours, I thought you might of lost something valuable.'

'My hairslide as a matter of fact,' Lucy replied, primly.

'Your *hairslide*?' grinned Vernon; as triumphant as a parent who knows all the time what his erring child has done wrong. He gave Lucy the same terrible feeling that Jack had given her when she was six years old, and had stolen three twists of cough-candy.

'Do you want your chit or don't you?' Lucy demanded. 'I could arrange for cash, two hundred rupees.'

'Well, now,' said Vernon, 'a kiss and a cuddle in the sewing room, that isn't worth more than two hundred rupees, that's agreed. But what about this? What do you think *this* is worth?'

He produced one arm from behind his back, and held in front of her nose the sepia photograph of Blanche. Dangled it, danced it, flicked it.

'*Where did you get that?*' Lucy snapped at him, snatching at it.

607

Vernon whipped it out of her reach. 'Lovely little girl, aint she? Pretty little thing. And such a sentimental message on the back.'

Lucy was shaking, and her eyes were filling with tears. 'You bastard,' she hissed. 'Where did you get that?'

'Easy,' Vernon told her. 'One of the *syces* found it on the path, and the *syce* gave it to the *dewan* and when we came in through the gates the *dewan* showed it to me, and asked me if I knew who it belonged to, and I took a look at the back and said serpently, course I did.'

He grinned even more widely. 'Providence, I'd call it. God's provision. Manna from heaven.'

'Give it to me,' Lucy insisted, her heart beating painfully against her ribcage.

'Give up the goose what lays the golden eggs? *Juwaub* to you, your ladyship.'

'Give it to me,' Lucy repeated. 'It's mine, and I want it.'

'I'm sure of it,' Vernon taunted her. 'But the question is, how bad do you want it? I mean to say, what would His Excellency say if he clapped his mincers on young Fanny Adams here? What would His Excellency think, if His Excellency found out that Her Excellency had been playing mummies and daddies with some Yankee nosper?'

'Give it to me,' Lucy begged him; and her voice was quite naked. 'It's all I have of her, that photograph.'

Vernon held it between two fingers, turning it this way and that.

'Thousand a month,' he told her.

'A thousand rupees? That's more than fifty pounds!'

'Seventy-five, to be precise.'

'I can't give you seventy-five pounds a month. I just can't!'

'Course you can. You're the Vicereine, you'll find a way. Colonel Miller spends twice that much on sherry. And bloody awful sherry it is, too.'

'I want my photograph.'

'Course you do. And I'll give it you back, if you're obliging. But I'll make myself a copy first, just to make sure. This is my jury, chummage and couter, this photograph is — knife, fork and spoon. I couldn't let you have it without making myself a copy, now could I?'

Lucy felt her stomach tightening in a contraction. 'I'm expecting a baby,' she whispered. 'How could you do such a thing?'

Vernon shrugged. 'It's the weak and the strong, aint it, your ladyship? Some live by noble birth, but most of us live on our wits.'

'I wasn't nobly born, you know that.'

'Ah,' Vernon smiled. 'But you're wealthy now; and you're weak. And if the Lord God don't find you out, then His Excellency will; and which is worster? Tell me that?'

'Give me my photograph.'

'Yes, your ladyship,' said Vernon. The sun shone on his brilliantined hair. 'Just as soon as I have your chit for a thousand rupees. Fair dos for all, that's what I say.'

The next evening, after dinner, Henry went to the library to work on his diaries; and Lucy was left by the fire with Colonel Belloc.

'You seem sad,' said Colonel Belloc, spinning his cognac around in his glass.

'Sad? Do I?' asked Lucy. Her hair shone in silk-fine strands in the firelight. She was wearing a green velvet evening gown, quite low-cut, that showed off the deep cleavage of her swollen breasts. She looked beautiful; she felt beautiful; with all the glow of pregnancy. But Colonel Belloc was right. She felt sad, too. Sad that she had abandoned Blanche; sad that she had lost her photograph. Sad that she was unable to seek the advice and comfort of her own husband.

For reasons she couldn't fully understand, she was beginning to feel closer to Henry than she had before. Perhaps she was simply growing more used to her life in India. Perhaps, by meeting and talking to Jamie, and seeing how much Blanche had grown up, she had accepted the reality that there could be no turning back.

There was something else, too. When she had watched Henry at work today – surrounded by governors and residents and maharajahs – constantly busy, constantly talking, constantly writing – she had felt proud of him, proud of what he was doing, and proud that she was a part of it.

Somehow that made her sadness all the more acute, because she had betrayed him, if only for a few moments – and if only in her heart.

Colonel Belloc said, 'You shouldn't be sad, you know. You'd be quite amazed how devoted Henry is to you. While we were travelling up here, you know, we had quite a talk. He's very concerned that he doesn't show you often enough how much he loves you.'

Lucy raised her eyes. 'He's very busy.'

'Of course. He has India to govern; and his own enthusiasms to pursue. But he thinks of you constantly, you know, and how to make you happy.'

'Henry hasn't made me feel sad,' Lucy replied. 'I just feel sad.'

Colonel Belloc swallowed more cognac. 'You're allowed to feel sad on occasions, my dear. Why not? Sadness is one of the nine moods of dramatic art. Whenever I see a woman looking pensive, I always remember the *ragini* of the rainy season.'

'The what?'

'Oh, I'm sorry, I'm being obscure as usual. During the medieval centuries, some Indian poets composed series of exquisite poems which they called Ragamalas, which means garlands of *ragas* – that's the male form – or *raginis* – that's the female form. Little mood pieces, as it were. And the *ragini* about the rainy season says that she is "pale and weak, her voice like the Kokil singing; some cadence of the song reminds her of her lord".'

Lucy started to smile.

'Mind you, it's spring, and the *ragini* for spring says, "My heart dreams of the firm-breasted Hindola with broad hips, who wears bright-coloured clothes; with the flower of the lotus she worships Lord Krishna who sits on a swing hung among the twisted roots of the banyan tree. She hears the notes of his flute, her heart full of love, her beautiful limbs adorned with jewels."'

Colonel Belloc's eyes were bright as he looked at her. 'That, my dear – that reminds me of you.' He coughed into his fist. 'Well, all except the broad hips, perhaps.'

They talked together until well after half past ten. After spending three or four weeks in Simla, Colonel Belloc was planning on a visit to Mount Abu in Rajputana, to examine the lavishly-carved Dilwara temple. He showed Lucy pages of drawings that he had made on his first visit there; sinuous stone figures intertwined with demons and gods and snakes and horses.

He told her about the God Vishnu. He recounted the adventures of Krishna, and how he had copulated so deliciously with the village women of Brindaban that they had pursued him through thorn-thickets, tearing off their clothes as they ran. He told her about the male followers of Chaitanya, who perceived the universe as feminine, and dressed up as giggling, flighty girls.

He was like a talking library on Indian art and music and religion; and through his eyes she began to see that she could reach Henry after all; that she had been immature and selfish and stubborn, and that the barriers between them would cease to exist the moment she said, 'they cease to exist'.

When at last Lucy excused herself to retire to bed, Colonel Belloc stood up and gave her the courtly bow, back straight, head bent. 'I hope I haven't bored you,' he said, taking her hand.

'Quite the contrary, Colonel. You've taught me more in one evening than my schoolteachers taught me in seven years.'

'Just remember,' said Colonel Belloc. 'There are no problems, only solutions. If something is standing in your way, all you have to say is, "*there is nothing standing in my way*."'

While Etta waited for her in the hallway, Lucy went to the library to say goodnight to Henry. She found him furiously writing, his head in his hand, with books and reports lying open all around him, as if a flock of dead albatrosses had landed on his desk. He put down his pen, and raised his head, his expression cautious, as if he expected her to be irritated that he was still working so late.

She stood behind him and laid her hands on his shoulders and kissed his hair. 'I'm going to bed now. Don't get too tired.'

He turned in his chair and looked at her carefully. 'How was your evening?' he asked her.

She kissed him again. 'I enjoyed it. Your friend Gordon Belloc is absolutely fascinating. Maybe a little too fond of talking about the things that men and women get up to; but fascinating.'

'He's the real stuff of the Raj,' said Henry. 'You know, half of these Indians you hear jabbering about *Swaraj* don't even know half as much about their own culture as Gordon does. Gordon's devoted his whole life to it – the buildings, the paintings, the literature. Do you know that he can even play a *sitar*? I'll get him to demonstrate it for you.'

'What's *Swaraj*?' asked Lucy. 'I head Colonel Miller talking about it at lunch yesterday, to Saraji Rao.'

'*Swaraj*, my darling, is a rude word in this house. It means independence, self-rule for Indians, by Indians.'

'You mean, without us? Completely on their own?'

Henry nodded.

'But they couldn't manage to rule themselves, could they?'

'Of course not. But a few fanatics seem to have got it into their heads that they could.'

'But how could they run the railroads, and the post; and plant tea; and everything like that?'

Henry picked up his pen, and twisted the nib. 'They may be capable of it one day, in a hundred years' time, when all the work that we're doing here today bears fruit. All of the education, and the restructuring of government, and the engineering, and the agricultural development. But they're certainly not ready for it yet. The trouble is, most Indians are so gullible that it takes only a few agitators to stir up trouble amongst thousands of them, millions of them; and then the innocent suffer as well as the guilty.

'In fact,' he said, leafing through the papers on his desk, 'we've been having unconfirmed reports from Army intelligence that one or two of the most notorious agitators have been seen around Chandigar and Simla; so it's probably best if you don't repeat your little expedition of the other night.'

'Oh,' said Lucy. 'Lieutenant Burnes-Waterton told you about that.'

Henry grasped her hand, and smiled, and then kissed her fingertips. 'It was his duty to report it. After all, your safety that night was his personal responsibility. Don't worry, no harm was done. But I had to give him and John Frognal quite a severe dressing-down.'

Lucy said, 'Oh, I hope not too severe. It was all my fault.'

'No, my darling, not too severe.'

She left the library and closed the door behind her. As she did so, however, a black-suited figure appeared out of the shadows. It was Vernon, with his hands clasped behind his back.

'Good evening, your ladyship. A word with you, before you go.'

Lucy opened her pocket, and took out a thousand rupees, in new folded notes. She had told John Frognal that she needed the money for new dresses and hats. How she was going to explain it to Henry, when he came to audit the accounts, she had yet to devise.

'Here, this is what you asked for,' she told Vernon.

He took the money, licked his thumb, and quickly counted it.

'Well, most grateful,' he said.

'What about my photograph?'

'Ah,' said Vernon. 'I've got a little problem with the photograph.'

'What do you mean? You said a thousand rupees and I've given you a thousand rupees.'

'Yes, I did, and you have. But what I was thinking was, am I selling myself short? I mean, if the photograph is worth a thousand rupees, as ready as that; then maybe it's worth two thousand.'

'I can't give you any more!' Lucy protested. 'I just can't!'

'In that case, p'raps I'd better let his lordship have a *dekho* at it.'

'Vernon, I beg you! Give me back my photograph!'

'One thousand more,' Vernon insisted. 'Then, on my life, you can have it.'

'Vernon, I can't!'

'In that case, Lady Carson, suit yourself, that's all I can say. Those are the terms. One thousand more, or else that photograph lands itself on Lord Carson's desk, no messing.'

Lucy was shaking with frustration and anger. 'I can't possibly get hold of one thousand more. Perhaps – I don't know, perhaps five hundred.'

'One thousand or nothing, your ladyship. Those are the terms, and terms is terms.'

'How long will you give me?'

Vernon sniffed. 'Ooh . . . I don't know. Forty-eight hours, how's that? Sooner if you get it sooner.'

At that moment, Etta appeared at the end of the corridor. 'Are you ready to retire now, Lady Carson?'

'Yes, Etta!' Lucy called back. Then, to Vernon, in a soft poisonous hiss. 'All right, then. But this had better be your last demand; because if it isn't I'm going to tell the Viceroy what you've been doing myself, and damn the consequences!'

'Sleep well, your ladyship,' Vernon grinned, and disappeared back into the shadows.

*

That night, she lay awake for hour after hour. All she could think of was Sha-sha's face, in that tiny photograph; and Vernon; and what Walter had said to her, before he went back Home.

'*There are plenty of obliging fellows in India, who would silence a fellow like that for ever.*'

And then she thought of what Colonel Belloc had said, that very evening. '*If something is standing in your way, all you have to say is,* "There is nothing in my way."'

Very quietly, she whispered, 'There is nothing in my way. *There is nothing in my way.*'

She was out in the grounds of Viceregal Lodge the following afternoon, taking the air, her *chaprassi* shuffling behind her with her parasol, when a very tall Indian bearer came walking across the sloping lawn towards her, unusually quickly, and with an unusual sense of purpose.

She glanced around her, a little worried. Elizabeth wasn't far away, sitting placidly in her garden-chair embroidering a tray-cover. Two of Lieutenant Burnes-Waterton's men were standing at the corner of the house, by the verandah steps. But all the same, Henry had impressed on her twice more this morning that nationalist extremists had been reported in the district, and that she should take particular care.

Elizabeth had told her some terrible stories of attacks by Indian servants on British officers and women on the North West Frontier. Garottings, stabbings, and axes between the shoulder-blades — even in the street. For a week or two afterwards, she had watched her servants' movements with deep suspicion, particularly Tir' Ram, who was a Pathan, but even her *ayahs*, too. 'You see,' said Elizabeth, 'the Indian mind works entirely differently from ours. They're like Alsatians. They can give you love and affection and devoted service for twenty years. Then they can suddenly turn and bite your leg off.'

'The Alsatians or the servants?' Lucy had asked her.

'The Alsatians, of course. Most of the servants are vegetarians.'

But now the tall Indian was only a few feet away. He came right up to her, and bowed, and said, 'Salaam, Your Excellency.'

'What is it?' Lucy demanded. 'What do you want?'

Without lifting his turbaned head, the bearer said, 'Just a few words, if you can spare the time.'

Lucy stared at him. 'Jamie?'

He lifted his head and gave her a tight-lipped smile. He had shaved off his beard, and rubbed dark make-up into his skin, but now that she looked at him closely, she wondered why she hadn't recognized him at once. Maybe she never really looked at her servants; not as people; not as anyone she might be interested to talk to.

Jamie said, 'Tell your servant to give me the parasol. Then send him away.'

Lucy instructed the *chaprassi* to hand over the parasol; and then she and Jamie started to walk slowly down the gardens, beside the flowering shrubs. Elizabeth looked up once from her embroidery, but obviously saw nothing unusual in the tall liveried bearer who was following Lucy with a measured pace.

'I got your letter, thank you,' said Jamie. 'I'm sorry I couldn't answer. I had to leave in a hurry.'

'Why are you wearing this ridiculous disguise?' Lucy asked him. 'You could have come for tea, if you'd wanted to talk to me.'

'Well, I'm afraid not. And that's all part of the reason I had to leave Simla so quick.'

'I don't understand.'

'I've got British agents looking for me. They think I'm some kind of subversive. You know, whipping up unrest and dissension, that kind of thing.'

'But that's ridiculous! I could tell Henry that you're not! Then you could take all that stuff off your face. You look so silly in a turban.'

'I'm afraid it's not quite as easy as that,' said Jamie, as they made their way along the lower part of the lawn. 'Because I've been meeting people like Bal Gangadhar Tilak . . . well, it's going to be difficult for me to prove that I haven't been involved in stirring up trouble.'

'I haven't had the chance to talk to him about Bal Gangadhar Tilak yet.'

'Well . . . it's probably better that you don't, not now. I thought maybe that the British were becoming a little more receptive to the idea of Indian independence. Prepared to listen to some new ideas, at the very least. But they've had people looking for me ever since I left Calcutta.'

'Jamie, let me talk to Henry. Let me explain!'

'You could tell him how you feel about Indian self-rule. You could tell him that maybe it's time for the British to start listening to the people they govern, instead of ordering them around like three hundred million dumb animals.'

'But you can't go around with a blacked-up face all the time! Let me tell him you're here. I'm sure he'll understand!'

'Lucy,' said Jamie, 'there's a particular reason why you mustn't tell him that I'm here, not yet. It's too dangerous. Will you please just trust me?'

'But —'

'Trust me, Lucy, please.'

'All right, then,' Lucy agreed. Did she trust him, though? Could she? 'But if it's so dangerous, why did you come?'

'Just to see you. Just to make sure you're all right.'

'I'm fine, I'm really well.'

'You look tired.'

'Well . . . even empresses have their problems.'

They stood by the flight of stone steps at the bottom of the lawn, and looked out over the distant peaks of the Himalayas. The day was so warm and hazy that, beyond the deodar trees, the snow caps appeared to be hanging in mid-air, like starched and crumpled white flags.

'I heard that the Viceroy had arrived,' Jamie coaxed her. '*He's* not the problem, is he?'

'No,' Lucy replied, so softly that it was more like a breath than a word.

Jamie turned to her, frowning.

'What's wrong?' he asked her. 'You really do have a problem, don't you.'

'It's nothing I can't sort out for myself.'

Jamie said, 'It's nothing to do with me, is it?'

Lucy shrugged. For some reason, she found she had a lump in her throat. Being pregnant had made her so emotional, made her so quick to cry, and she hated it.

'Lucy, tell me, is it something to do with me?' Jamie insisted.

'Well, in a way, yes.'

'Then tell me. Come on, tell me. How can I help you if I don't know what's wrong?'

Lucy took out her handkerchief and wiped her eyes. 'That day in Calcutta . . . when you came to visit.'

'What about it?'

'We went into my sewing room, remember? We kissed?'

'What of it?' Jamie wanted to know.

'Nothing. I mean it wasn't wrong or bad or anything. But somebody was watching. Vernon, Henry's body-servant. It wouldn't have mattered so much if it hadn't been him. The trouble is, he's white, he's British, and Henry trusts him, thinks he's the salt of the earth.'

'Did he tell Henry?' asked Jamie.

Lucy shook her head.

'Then what do you have to worry about?' said Jamie. 'Surely Henry isn't going to take a servant's word against yours . . . even if the servant *is* white. Even if he *is* the salt of the earth. He wouldn't be much of a husband if he did.'

Tears started to cluster in Lucy's eyes again. 'It's not just that. I paid Vernon some money. I gave him a chit in my own handwriting, two hundred rupees. I know it was stupid, but it's too late now. And what's Henry going to think if he finds out that I've been paying Vernon to keep quiet? He's going to think that something terrible's been going on.'

Jamie half-lifted his hand, as if he were tempted to put his arm around her. But he had to remember that he was supposed to be an Indian servant, and he couldn't even touch her sleeve. He watched and waited, serious-faced, while she recovered herself.

'Don't you think it would be better to tell Henry the truth?' he asked her, at length.

'I wish I had. But something else happened. Something worse. I lost Blanche's photograph, it fell in the garden. One of the servants gave it to Vernon, and he made me give him a thousand rupees. Now he wants another thousand, by tomorrow, or he's going to show it to Henry.'

'Let him show it to Henry, for God's sake! What does it matter? You're not ashamed of Blanche, are you?'

'Jamie, don't you understand? If Henry found out about Blanche, our marriage would be finished, absolutely torn to pieces. It hasn't been especially happy, these past two years, it's just beginning to get better. I'm just beginning to understand how to be the kind of wife that Henry needs. It's been hard, Jamie. You have no idea how hard. I couldn't bear it if it all came apart.'

'So, what are you going to do?' said Jamie. 'Are you going to go on paying this leech? You'll have to, if you don't want Henry to know about us.'

'Jamie, there isn't any "us".'

'Not at all?'

'There can't be.'

'Well, whatever, you're still going to have to go on paying the money, now you've started.'

Lucy was silent for a long and difficult moment. She had thought about this, ever since she had talked to Walter in Calcutta, but up until now it had only been play-acting in her head, a ridiculous fantasy that could never come true. *There are plenty of obliging fellows in India, who would silence a chap like that for ever.*

'I suppose this sounds really evil, and absurd,' she heard herself saying. 'But that man I met, Tilak . . . I mean, was he joking when he said he was a murderer?'

Jamie wiped the sweat from his forehead with the back of his hand, leaving a smear of berry-dye. 'What are you suggesting?'

'I don't know. I'm desperate. I can't think what else I can do.'

'You want to have Vernon *killed*?'

'I don't know. No, of course not.'

Jamie was very thoughtful. The day was growing hazier still, all around them, until they appeared to be standing in a fog of evaporated gold. Lucy could hear the barbets singing, the tinpot birds, down in the valley; and behind her the persistent and nearly-irritating tinkling of ice against glass, as Elizabeth swirled her glass of Rawlings ginger ale around and around and around.

'I'll think of something,' Lucy told Jamie. 'I didn't really mean –'

'No, no, listen,' said Jamie. 'I'm sure we can help you. Supposing we don't actually *kill* this Vernon fellow; but supposing instead we frighten him; warn him off. Tell him to give you back your photograph, and to stop blackmailing you, otherwise something very unpleasant is going to happen to him.'

'Could you really do that?' Lucy asked him. It seemed perfect. She had thought of killing Vernon over and over again; but the idea of frightening him half to death was so much better. So much more possible; so much more *exciting*.

Jamie said, 'All we'd have to do is smuggle one of Tilak's people into the Lodge . . . maybe dressed like a servant, like me. He could hide in Vernon's room; and when Vernon goes to bed, he could come out and hold a knife to Vernon's throat and tell him to behave himself.'

'Do you think it would work?'

Jamie grinned. 'What would *you* say, if somebody was holding a knife against your neck?'

Lucy laughed, a little hysterically. 'I think I'd say honest Injun!'

Jamie looked around. 'I doubt if I can find anybody to do it tonight. Let's say tomorrow.'

'There's a small side door by the verandah steps,' said Lucy. 'Tell the man to wait there about eight o'clock. I'll let him in, and show him the way to Vernon's room.'

'What about a password?' Jamie suggested.

'Kipling,' said Lucy.

'Kipling? For God's sake!'

'All right, then, *Swaraj*.'

'Very apt,' Jamie nodded. '*Swaraj* it is, eight o'clock tomorrow.'

'And your man won't do anything more than give Vernon a scare?'

Jamie said, 'Promise. He won't even be touched.'

Lucy tried to smile at him, but found that she couldn't. For the first time in all of the years that she had known him, she couldn't read in his eyes what he was thinking, what he was feeling. She had the disconcerting impression that she was looking into the eyes of a complete stranger; and it wasn't just the brown dye and the turban that made him seem so unfamiliar. She felt as if something had broken, somewhere inside of him. Hope, or ambition, or faith; or whatever it was that had made Jamie the boy she used to know.

Although she couldn't yet understand it, she felt intuitively that she was looking at a man who had loved and lost his only love; and in place of his love, embraced an ideal. An ideal that came knocking at poor men's doors.

'I'd better leave,' Jamie told her. 'I wish I could kiss you, but it wouldn't be very wise, would it? Especially if this Vernon fellow happened to see us. The Vicereine kissing the black help.'

'You'll tell your man, won't you, not to hurt him?'

'Not a whisker.'

Together, they walked back towards the Lodge. As soon as they reached the verandah, Jamie folded the parasol, propped it against the wall, and quickly made his way around to the side of the building, without turning back once. Lucy watched him go for a moment or two, then realized that it wasn't quite the thing for the mistress of the house to stare after one of the lowliest of her servants. She called for a *chaprassi*.

The next day was taken up with bitty little social events. In the morning, Lucy hosted a small bazaar in the conservatory in aid of Christian missionaries in Pondicherry. Very large women in very large hats stood behind rickety little card-tables draped with Union Jacks, stentoriously selling ma-cramé plant-holders and hand-painted fans and tins of Hunt-ley & Palmers Empire Assorted Biscuits.

Later, when the very large ladies had been bustled away in a procession of rickshaws, the Viceroy and Vicereine entertained to luncheon some of the more junior officers of the secretariat and their wives. The junior officers of the secretariat and their wives flushed a particular shade of boiled-ham-pink whenever they spoke or were spoken to, and afterwards Lucy remarked that for all their youthfulness she had seen more verve in a billiard-room full of stuffed bison.

'Thank you so much for your hospitality, Lady Carson,' one of the wives whispered. 'It was all so fearfully glam-orous.'

Lucy smiled, and looked around her; at the baronial chairs and the massive mohogany dining-table and the mahogany-panelled walls; and she suddenly realized that, yes, to a young middle-class girl freshly out from England, this must seem almost impossibly glamorous. She remembered the first gowns she had bought for herself, from Uncle Casper's oil money – expensive and dowdy and years out of fashion – and she flushed a little pink herself.

She rested all afternoon, or tried to. But she kept thinking about what she would have to do during dinner this evening – go to the side door and whisper the password *Swaraj*. That one word which was darkest tabu in Viceregal Lodge; and anywhere in India that Englishmen gathered.

Dinner at Viceregal Lodge when the Viceroy was staying there was always formal; although tonight's dinner was a little more jolly than most. Among others, they were entertaining the Blackguards Club, which was an association of Simla's wealthiest bachelors, and Lady Fitzsimmons, the wife of the Governor of Bombay, who was florid and excitable and possessed a notorious and distinctive shrieking laugh.

Lucy had taken a long time dressing, and felt more nervous than she could have imagined. She wore a simple grey silk evening gown, with a lace overdress to conceal her pregnant stomach, and a small pearl tiara, with matching pearl earrings. As she put the finishing touches to her hair, Etta remarked, 'You're looking a little pale, Lady Carson, if you don't mind my saying so.'

'Oh, tiredness, I suppose,' Lucy replied. 'I feel quite all right.'

As she went downstairs, she came across Vernon, on the first-floor landing. He paused, and bowed his head to her in the courtly bow, but said nothing. They both knew that Lucy's payment was supposed to be made tonight, or else Henry would be shown the photograph of Blanche. What only Lucy knew was that Vernon had another rendezvous arranged; a rendezvous with what she hoped would be fearsome retribution.

She was calmed a little by seeing him. He deserved it, after all; and Jamie had promised that he wouldn't be hurt. She couldn't wait to see his face tomorrow morning.

Henry approached her as she came downstairs, and offered his hand. 'You're looking very beautiful this evening, my dearest,' he told her. 'It looks as if Simla agrees with you. Come and meet Lady Fitzsimmons, but for goodness' sake don't say anything amusing. She might laugh.'

'Henry – ' Lucy began. She wanted to tell him that she was trying very hard to love him, that she was doing everything she could to come to terms with being his wife. But she couldn't find the words for it. When he said, 'Yes?' she simply shook her head, and said, 'Nothing. I'll tell you later,' and accompanied him into the huge panelled reception room, under the sparkling chandelier.

They sat down to eat at half-past seven, all forty of them, while the Viceroy's orchestra sat in their boiled shirts at the far end of the dining room and played light selections from the latest musicals. *We Shall Waltz Again In Springtime* and *Why Does Your Heart Tell Such Lies?*

Lucy scarcely touched her julienne soup; and ate only a tiny portion of her fillet of duck and peas. One of the Blackguards, a very handsome young cavalry officer called St John Teacher, asked her solicitously if she wasn't feeling well. It was almost ten to eight. It would take her only a minute to reach the side door, and open it, but Lucy was so tense that she took the opportunity to turn to Henry and say, 'You will excuse me, won't you, for just a moment? I need a little air.'

Henry rose, and immediately every man at the table rose with him. They stood silently to attention while Lucy was escorted to the door by two of the servants. Behind her, she heard them all sit down again, and resume their dinner.

'You wish to return to your room, Your Excellency *memsahib*?' asked Muhammad Aziz.

'No, please. I need a little fresh air, that's all.'

'I can escort you to the verandah, Your Excellency *memsahib*?'

'No, no. Please. I want to be alone, for just a few minutes.'

'Your Excellency *memsahib* is sure?'

'My Excellency *memsahib* is absolutely certain, thank you. Now, please, you have plenty of other duties to attend to.'

'Of course, Your Excellency *memsahib*.'

At last she was left alone in the hallway; apart from the two doorkeepers who stood waiting beside the entrance. She made her way quickly along the panelled corridor to the side of the house, holding up her grey silk gown so that it didn't rustle too noisily on the floor. The long-case clock in the hallway struck eight o'clock as she hurried down the short flight of stairs that led to the side door. She hesitated for a moment, took a deep breath, and then pulled back the brass bolts, using both hands, and turned the key.

She opened the door, and the cool night air flowed in. At first, she saw nothing, but she didn't dare to call out. She waited, feeling faint, her heart pounding against her ribs. Supposing he didn't come? Supposing the sentries had caught him? But then she heard quick, soft footsteps, and a small turbaned Indian appeared, dressed in the loose shirt and tight trousers of a rickshaw-coolie. He carried a wrapped-up bundle of cloth, which must have concealed his knife.

'*Swaraj*,' he whispered, in such a muffled voice that she didn't hear him at first.

'Oh, yes,' she said. 'Come in. Quick, I'll show you the way.'

She closed and locked the door while the Indian waited for her. She could smell garlic and onions and asafoetida on his breath, and his clothes were sour with sweat. He said nothing, but he had obviously understood what she said.

He followed close behind her as she led him to the servants' staircase. She was short of breath as she climbed, and she prayed over and over again with every step that none of the servants would appear, but they reached the second floor without being seen. Lucy led him along to the door of Vernon's room, and opened it for him.

'You know what to do?' she asked him.

His eyes glittered in the darkness. 'Yes, *memsahib*. I have been told what to do.'

'And you won't hurt him?'

'That is a promise, *memsahib*.'

Lucy waited for a moment, then closed the door behind him, and walked back along the corridor to the main staircase. As she slowly descended the stairs, her hands were trembling, and she was very close to fainting. On the first-floor landing, she stopped, and rested, listening to the sounds of laughter and conversation, and the orchestra playing *When We Meet Again, My Love*.

Then she went down to rejoin the dinner-party.

On her way up to bed that night, accompanied by Etta and two of her *ayahs*, Lucy paused on the first-floor landing outside Vernon's door. She was tempted for a moment to pretend that she had heard a noise, and to call for Lieutenant Burnes-Waterton, so that the rickshaw-coolie would be discovered and arrested.

On reflection, the idea of frightening Vernon into returning her photograph seemed much less appealing, even downright dangerous. Supposing the rickshaw-coolie were discovered, and caught? Supposing he admitted that the Vicereine herself had let him into the house?

Etta asked, 'Anything amiss, your ladyship?' but Lucy shook her head and said, 'No, nothing, thank you, Etta. I thought for a moment I might have forgotten something, that's all.'

She watched herself in the looking-glass as Etta prepared her hair for bed. She looked pale and preoccupied, an angel painted in thinly-diluted watercolours. Etta didn't seem to notice how pensive she was. She kept chattering on about a frilly blouse she had seen in Pearson's Modes, down by Scandal Point; and how pretty it would look with her new linen skirt. 'My very first mistress said to me, a lady's maid should always look smart, otherwise it reflects so poorly on her mistress.'

Etta brought Lucy a glass of hot milk to help her sleep, and 'to nourish young Horatio', but Lucy couldn't stomach it, and sat up in bed trying to read Jane Austen while the top of the milk crinkled, untouched, and formed a skin.

Shortly after eleven o'clock, Henry came in to bid her goodnight. 'Everybody's gone now, my darling. I'm spending a little time with Gordon Belloc; then I'm retiring to bed.'

She held his hand tightly. 'You won't be too late?'

'I promise,' he told her, and kissed his fingertip, and pressed it against her lips.

Lucy lay sleepless for another hour, listening to the servants preparing the Lodge for the night, closing doors and windows, extinguishing lights, carrying away empty glasses and dishes. Outside her open window the night sang with the steady chanting of insects; and the occasional whoop of a night-bird.

She wondered what Vernon would say to her, in the morning. Would he be angry? Would he be cowed? Would he give her photograph straight back? What if the rickshaw-coolie didn't frighten him at all? What if he called the guard?

She lay in bed listening and listening, until the clock in the hallway sonorously struck half-past midnight. She hadn't heard Henry come up; although she usually did, if she was awake. All those footsteps, and doors closing, and stage-whispered 'goodnights'. But Vernon would have returned to his room by now, to prepare Henry's clothes for the morning.

When the clock struck a quarter-to, Lucy couldn't stand the suspense any longer. She climbed out of bed, and went to the wardrobe and took out one of her dressing-gowns. Then she eased open her bedroom door, and looked out. The only illumination came from downstairs; otherwise the first-floor landing was in shadow.

She waited for almost a minute, listening. She could hear

servants talking quickly and softly downstairs, and the persistent *shushing* of a floorbrush. Then there was a long period of alarming silence.

It was high folly to think of going to Vernon's room. But she knew that she wouldn't be able to sleep until she had discovered what had happened, and she had a long and difficult day tomorrow, culminating in a visit to the Gaiety Theatre. Feeling more like an Oak City tomboy than an Indian empress, she gathered up her dressing-gown and tiptoed as quietly as she could across the galleried landing until she reached the mahogany-panelled door of Vernon's quarters; where she paused, and waited.

There was nobody around. No bearers, no cleaners. The lights were shining brightly downstairs, and so she assumed that Henry and Colonel Belloc were still talking in the library. Their plans for cleaning and restoring the Taj Mahal were already far advanced; and now they were working on the possibility of cleaning and repairing the Temple of Konarak.

Lucy knocked softly at Vernon's door. She waited, but there was no reply. She knocked again, and called, 'Vernon? This is Lady Carson.'

She waited almost a minute, but still Vernon didn't respond. Perhaps he was downstairs, attending to Henry. Perhaps he had fallen asleep. But if he had already been threatened with a knife at his throat by Jamie's rickshaw-coolie, it was highly unlikely that he had simply dozed off.

She knocked once more, as loudly as she dared. As she did so, the door swung open, by itself. Vernon must have left it unlatched. Inside, she could see that a lamp was still burning, on Vernon's desk, although the door wasn't open wide enough for her to be able to see any more.

'Vernon?' she whispered, Then, 'Vernon?'

Very cautiously, she eased back the door. Little by little, the room came into view. A smallish room, with slatted blinds, and a varnished desk, and a chintz easy-chair, and a single bed. On the wall, a frame photograph of an un-prepossessing girl with a large nose, holding a bouquet of lilies – his mother or his wife.

Lucy took only one step forward; but one step was all that was needed for Vernon to come into view. He was lying back on his bed, fully dressed, and he was staring at her. She thought at first that he was wearing a maroon scarf, and she couldn't think why. But then she realized with a frizzling chill that he was dead, and that his head had been almost completely severed from his body. The maroon scarf was congealing blood.

'Oh God,' she swallowed. 'Oh God.' Her stomach muscles tightened, and she had to hold on to the edge of the desk to keep her balance. Shocked as she was, however, she found it impossible to take her eyes away from Vernon's grotesque body. The rickshaw-coolie must have panicked, and cut his throat. Perhaps he had intended to cut his throat, right from the very outset. Perhaps he intended to cut *all* of their throats.

Because what had Jamie really been doing, wandering around the gardens of Viceregal Lodge, disguised as a bearer? Now she came to think about it again, Lucy found it difficult to believe that he had gone to all of that trouble just to find out how she was. He must have been reconnoitring; seeing how easy it was for an Indian assassin to slip into the house. Perhaps he had even been carrying a weapon himself.

Lucy took one step nearer the bed. She would have to call Henry now. If the rickshaw-coolie hadn't escaped already, he would have to be flushed out of hiding, and arrested. If he happened to reveal to Henry that his wife and Vicereine had allowed him into the Lodge, then Lucy would have to accept the consequences. Perhaps she could think of some explanation that wouldn't involve telling Henry that Vernon had been blackmailing her.

She was about to leave Vernon's room when she caught sight of a crumpled manila envelope on the bloodstained *durry* next to his hand. Swallowing back a throatful of vinegary-tasting bile, she reached over and picked it up. One corner of it was soaked dark red. On the front, in Vernon's particularly nasty backhand, was the name *His Excellency Lord Carson*.

Her hands shaking wildly, Lucy tore the envelope open. Inside was a note which said '*May it please Y.E., the inclosure speaks for itself.*' Pinned to the note was Lucy's photograph of Blanche.

She tucked the photograph into the pocket of her dressing-gown, and then she took three deep breaths, holding her stomach in an effort to relax her muscles. Thank God she had the photograph back. Now Henry would never have to find out about Blanche. All the same – no matter how vicious and unprincipled Vernon had been, no matter how relieved she was to recover the picture from him, Lucy couldn't bring herself to think that he had deserved to die for what he had done.

She turned to leave the room, and to call for Henry and Lieutenant Burnes-Waterton. As she did so, however, the door of Vernon's closet swung open just behind her, she glimpsed its dark diagonal movement out of the corner of her eye, and a muscular arm gripped her fiercely around the neck.

'Not to speak!' a voice hissed, close to her ear. She immediately recognized the strong smell of garlic and spices and sweat. Something hard and greasy was pressed against the side of her head, an inch behind her right ear. 'You are speaking only one word, unless I am speaking to you first, and I am shooting off your head!'

'Please,' Lucy begged him. 'Please, I'm pregnant.'

'I am telling you not to speak,' the rickshaw-coolie repeated. 'Where is the Viceroy?'

'I don't know. I really don't. I've been in bed.'

'This is not true! You know where he is!'

'How could I? I've been asleep!'

The rickshaw-coolie gripped her even tighter around the neck, half-choking her. 'I am waiting for him and he is not coming! Where is he?'

'Please - can't breathe - '

Now the rickshaw-coolie took the gun-muzzle away from her head, and dug it hard into her stomach.

'You are wishing that I kill your baby? Is that what you are wishing?' He dug at her stomach again and again.

Lucy coughed, her eyes filling with tears. 'Don't hurt my baby, please! He's probably - in the library - with - '

'Show me the way!' the rickshaw-coolie insisted. 'And no calling, no shouting!'

He pushed Lucy out of the door of Vernon's room on to the landing. Then he edged her towards the top of the stairs, prodding her stomach again and again.

'Please don't hurt my baby,' Lucy wept. She felt as if the whole world was collapsing on top of her. She could scarcely move one leg in front of the other. But the rickshaw-coolie kept on jabbing her, and breathing, 'You are not crying out! You are showing me where is the Viceroy!'

At the top of the stairs, Lucy begged, 'Wait, wait, be careful! I don't want to fall!'

The rickshaw-coolie hesitated. At that instant, one of the landing doors opened behind them. The rickshaw-coolie turned around; and Lucy turned, too; and there was Elizabeth, in her white broderie-anglaise robe, staring at them both in astonishment.

'Lucy?' she called. 'Lucy, what on earth - ?'

'Elizabeth, no!' Lucy screamed.

'Lucy, who is this man? What's going on?'

Elizabeth came towards them, around the corner of the galleried landing. Lucy tried to scream at her again, to warn her to keep away, but the coolie's arm pulled viciously tight at her throat, and all she could do was to let out a high choking noise.

She heard the rickshaw-coolie shout something in Urdu;

she didn't know what it was. Then a deep thunderous booming sound; and Elizabeth stopped in surprise. Another booming sound, and blood burst out of Elizabeth's iron-grey hair, and she threw up her arms like a puppet and fell backwards on to the carpet.

'No!' shrieked Lucy. She tried to struggle free, but the rickshaw-coolie snatched hold of her wrist, and twisted her arm behind her back. 'No!'

Downstairs, doors were flung open, and the hallway was flooded with light. The rickshaw-coolie cursed, and tried to pull Lucy down the stairs with him. There were shouts and banging noises and the sound of running boots. Lieutenant Burnes-Waterton appeared, in his mess trousers and shirt-sleeves, tugging his Webley revolver out of its brown-leather holster. Just behind him, Henry and Gordon Belloc were framed in the open doors of the library.

Lucy heard Henry shout, 'Lieutenant! For God's sake be careful! That's my wife!'

As he did so, the rickshaw-coolie lifted his revolver and fired twice into the hallway. Lieutenant Burnes-Waterton, with his gun still half out of its holster, performed a stagger-ing little dance, like a drunkard attempting a waltz. He fell on his side on to the floor, and lay shuddering and twitching. His blood ran across the polished floor.

'Which is the Viceroy?' the rickshaw-coolie screamed at Lucy. 'Which one is the Viceroy?'

'Please, you're hurting me!' Lucy gasped.

But Henry stepped across the hallway, and stood alone at the foot of the stairs, and announced clearly, 'I am the Viceroy. Release my wife at once.'

The rickshaw-coolie thrust Lucy aside. She staggered, and almost lost her balance, but managed to grasp the banister-rail. One silk slipper tumbled down the stairs by itself. Lucy watched in wide-eyed horror as the rickshaw-coolie took three steps further down the staircase, and lifted his revolver so that it was pointing directly at Henry's heart.

'I am being told to say that you and all of your people are oppressors and tyrants,' the rickshaw-coolie called out, his voice breathy with fear. 'This must be said by the newspapers when they tell of your death.'

Lucy thought she was screaming but she couldn't be sure. The rickshaw-coolie pulled back the hammer of his revolver and took two more steps down the stairs. Henry's face was extraordinary: rigid and bloodless, more like the face of a marble statue than a man. This was the way that a hero of the British Empire should die, facing his enemy, protecting his loved ones, his patriotism and his loyalty to the Crown untarnished.

Just then, though, with supreme casualness, as if he were out for a day's rough shooting in the *mofussil*, Gordon Belloc reappeared at the library door, holding up an enormous Savage 99 elephant-rifle. Calmly, but without any hesitation, he aimed it at the rickshaw-coolie and fired it.

The noise was devastating. Even the chandelier jangled. The hallway was filled with smoke. Lucy clapped her hands over her eyes as the rickshaw-coolie's body stood on the stairs for a moment, headless, and then flopped to the bottom of the stairs, to Henry's feet.

'*Facilis descensus averni,*' Colonel Belloc remarked. 'The way down to hell is easy.'

Henry, stiffly, climbed the stairs. He knelt down beside Lucy and held her in his arms. She was too shocked to weep. She shivered and shook like a small child with a high fever.

'Everything is all right now,' Henry soothed her. 'Everything is quite all right.'

Shortly after breakfast the following day, Etta came into Lucy's room and stood a little way away, as if she were afraid to come too close. 'They've arrested somebody,' she said.

Lucy shielded her eyes against the sunlight with her hand. 'They've arrested somebody? Who?'

'It was almost by accident, that's what they said, down in the native quarter. They wanted to talk to one of the rickshaw-coolie's cousins. They found a man sleeping in his house, somebody they didn't know. But it turned out it was somebody called Tilak, he's a well-known troublemaker. He's been around here for weeks, that's what they said! One of the gardeners said that he'd been planning to murder the Viceroy for months. It makes you shudder, doesn't it, just to think about it!'

Lucy stared at her. 'Where's Tilak now?'

Etta narrowed her eyes. 'Down at the police station, under guard, I'd say.'

'Has he talked to anybody?'

'Nobody's told me nothing, your ladyship.' said Etta. Then, 'Something wrong, your ladyship?'

'No, nothing. But I want you to find out what Tilak's been saying.'

'I'm surprised you care, your ladyship.'

'Of course I care! He killed Miss Morris! He killed Lieutenant Burnes-Waterton!'

'All right then, I'll do my best,' said Etta. 'Don't get fretful.'

Lucy said, 'Where's my hand-mirror? Bring me a flannel for my face.'

She looked at herself in her mirror while Etta poured out the water and wrung out the flannel. Very pale. Dark grey smudges under her eyes. She hadn't slept all night; except for a half-hour's fretful doze towards dawn.

'What do you think they'll do to him?' she asked Etta.

'What do I think they'll do to who?'

'Tilak, of course.'

'Oh, well,' said Etta. 'They'll hang him, won't they? No doubt about it.'

Lucy began to have a cold, sinking feeling of terrible dread. Now that Bal Gangadhar Tilak had been arrested, it was highly likely that he would soon tell the Simla police that he had talked on Monday to the Vicereine; and that the Vicereine had appeared to be sympathetic to what he believed in. In fact, Lucy's skin shrank at the thought that her meeting with Bal Gangadhar Tilak might have led directly to what had happened last night. What better way to demonstrate his impunity than to murder the Viceroy aided and abetted by herself?

Bal Gangadhar Tilak had been right. He was no 'petty volcano'. Bal Gangadhar Tilak could set India on fire, from end to end.

The confrontation between Henry and Bal Gangadhar Tilak's lawyer was informal but sober. Henry sat on a sofa beside the empty fireplace, while Tilak's lawyer sat brown and bespectacled nearby, ceaselessly rubbing his long brown fingers together, but obviously not intimidated by Henry's presence. It was plain that Henry found his lack of subservience to be irritating in the extreme. The day was bright and sharp. The light fell into the room like golden razor-blades. Henry was baffled and infuriated by Tilak's terrorism, and by his lawyer's intransigence.

'An act of political expression can scarcely be described as terrorism,' Tilak's lawyer suggested.

'None the less, he shot and killed a serving officer of the Viceroy's Bodyguard; and an innocent British lady; and a British manservant.'

'This is not denied.'

'What do you mean, "this is not denied"?'

'Exactly that, Your Excellency. The facts are unavoidable, and speak for themselves. The man who carried out the attack on Viceregal Lodge last night was one of the political fellowship of Bal Gangadhar Tilak; and was acting with Bal Gangadhar Tilak's approval, if not his specific knowledge. But I have to say that he was under the strictest orders not to harm the Vicereine.'

Lucy looked out of the windows. The peaks of the

Himalayas had vanished altogether behind a pearlized mist, like old Indian women concealing themselves behind their veils.

Henry was watching Lucy all the time, but he spoke to Tilak's lawyer. 'You realize what you're saying?'

'Yes, Your Excellency.'

'You realize what the penalty will be, if Tilak enters a plea of guilty.'

'Yes, Your Excellency.'

Henry took a deep, testy breath. 'Does he wish to be a martyr? I can certainly oblige him, if he wishes to be a martyr.'

'No, sir. He does not wish to be a martyr. He will plead guilty, you see, but with mitigating circumstances.'

Henry slowly took his eyes away from Lucy and focused on the lawyer. 'What mitigating circumstances? He sent an assassin to break into Viceregal Lodge to kill as many of us as he could, myself included.'

'Ah, but we have a letter, Your Excellency.'

The fire had reddened one side of Henry's face. 'Letter, what letter?'

'Here, Your Excellency,' said Tilak's lawyer, and shuffled in his case, and produced at last two sheets of paper. At once, with a sickening sense of shock, Lucy recognized the letter she had sent to Jamie at the Hotel Cecil, and a fair copy of it, written in large, angular italics.

'Here in my left hand the original copy which I do not wish to give to you in its actual bodily form at this moment, Your Excellency, for reasons that you will plainly understand. But this is a perfect copy in every respect.'

Henry read the letter with his hand faintly trembling. Then he handed it back to Tilak's lawyer in silence.

'It's a forgery,' he said.

'Your Excellency insults my intelligence. I am defending a man for his life. If I had only a forgery at my disposal, what chance would I stand in a court of law?'

'If it isn't a forgery, it was stolen. Stolen evidence is inadmissible.'

'Not stolen, great sir.'

'It's addressed to Mr Jamie Cullen, not to Bal Gangadhar Tilak. How else could Bal Gangadhar Tilak have acquired it, except by stealing it?'

'It was given to him freely,' said the lawyer, seriously. 'Mr Jamie Cullen wished to show Bal Gangadhar Tilak that the Vicereine was sincere in her intentions to intercede with you on matters of Indian independence.'

Lucy was so frightened that she could hardly swallow. Henry seemed to crouch lower and lower in his chair and she thought that he might crouch himself so small that he would concentrate himself into some black explosive demon, and turn on her with claws and horns and raging eyes.

But Henry was Viceroy; and he controlled himself. He sat without saying a word for nearly four minutes, and nobody dared to interrupt his deliberations, although Colonel Miller kept coughing and sniffing and shuffling his feet.

'Very well,' Henry said at last to Tilak's lawyer. His face was quite expressionless. 'No charges will be brought; Tilak will be released. I can only warn you that if anything like this ever happens again, mitigating letters or not, I will send up the Bengal Cavalry and I will order them to cut off your collective heads.'

The lawyer stood up, and bowed, and as he bowed, the firelight glinted from his spectacles. 'Your Excellency is very comprehending.'

He left. Henry sat silently for three or four minutes longer; then said to his own solicitor, and to Colonel Miller, and to Timothy Frognal, and to the small council of Indians who had accompanied them, 'The Vicereine and I wish to be alone for a while, thank you.'

Everybody shuffled quickly out of the room, and closed the doors behind them. Now there was just the two of them, husband and wife. Henry in his armchair, staring at the fire; Lucy on the sofa, staring at Henry.

'Henry?' asked Lucy.

Henry said nothing, but drummed his fingers on the arm of his chair.

'Henry, I'm sorry. I don't know what to say.'

He shrugged. 'There's nothing you can say. For some inexplicable reason you felt constrained to write Mr Cullen extolling the personal virtues of one of India's most unscrupulous nationalists. The letter is writ; the deed is done. All I can do is to make the best of it. That's part of a Viceroy's job, you know, making the best of things. Part of the burden.'

'But they killed Elizabeth, right in front of me! How could you let them go!'

Henry took a deep breath. 'I had to, Lucy. They knew from the very beginning that I would have to. I can't think why you wrote such a letter. I'm not even sure that I want to know. But if we were to try Tilak publicly, he would produce it in open court, and I would have no choice but to resign.'

'So for the sake of your job, you're letting that murderer go free?'

He turned to her and his eyes were chilling. 'Don't be so damned ridiculous. It's not for the sake of my job, it's for the sake of Her Majesty the Queen, and India, and the whole course of British history.'

'Henry, you're a man, not a god.'

He stood up, and walked stiffly across to the window. 'I have never once deluded myself that I am a god, Lucy. But when the Duke of Nantwich recommended my appointment to Lord Salisbury, he wrote, *"There are some men through whose spirits the magnetic forces of historical inevitability can be felt to flow, and Henry Carson is one of them."'*

Lucy sat watching him for a while. Something rang off-key. Something she couldn't quite understand. 'I didn't know the Duke of Nantwich had recommended you.'

638

Henry turned his head for a moment, and nodded. 'Yes, that's right. The Duke of Nantwich.'

'The Duke of Nantwich is Malty's uncle.'

'That's right, yes, so he is.'

Lucy frowned, 'Why did he recommend you? I thought he didn't like you. You didn't like him. You called him the Evil Coconut.'

'I really haven't the faintest idea why he recommended me,' said Henry. 'I'm glad he did, though. Salisbury's always taken his advice about India.'

Lucy stood up, her stomach very protuberant and low. 'Henry, you're lying to me.'

'Lying? I'm tired, that's all.'

'Henry, you're lying.'

He swivelled around. 'All right, lying about what? What reason could I possibly have to lie to you?'

'You're lying to me about Malty! You pushed us together on purpose!'

'You needed somebody to amuse you, that was all. I thought we'd forgotten all of this!'

'Amuse me!' Lucy protested. 'He was my lover! And you didn't care, did you? In fact, you *wanted* him to be my lover!'

'That's absurd!' Henry snapped.

'Is it? Is it really? Then why did the Duke of Nantwich the Evil Coconut who couldn't even stand to look at you – why did he recommend you to Lord Salisbury for Viceroy?'

Henry stood very still. He sniffed, and took out his handkerchief, and wiped his nose, and then patted the sweat from his forehead. 'You want the truth?' he told her.

'Yes, Henry, I want the truth.'

'Very well,' said Henry, 'since this seems to be the time when our mutual mistrust of each other has almost brought the British Empire down to her knees – the truth. And the truth is, yes, that I did encourage Malty to become friends with you. Not your lover, perhaps; but I suppose that had to be the inevitable consequence, with a woman as – physically active as you. A woman as young as you. As beautiful as you.'

He hesitated, but both of them knew that he had to finish what he was saying. Lives had been lost, reputations had been broken. He couldn't go back now.

'The day after you and Malty – well, the day after I found you together – I called on the Duke of Nantwich and explained what was happening between you. I said that there were several courses of action open to me. I could sue for divorce, citing Malty as co-respondent; but the scandal of that would have ruined the Nantwiches in society for several seasons, and would probably have killed Malty's mother. Or else I could say nothing and arrange for Malty to be reasonably employed in the India Office somewhere, playing cricket in the corridors for two hundred and fifty pounds a year; in return for which I would expect the strongest possible recommendation for my appointment as Viceroy.'

Lucy felt her stomach tighten, and she had to sit down.

'That's the truth, isn't it?' she whispered.

Henry couldn't even say the word 'Yes.' He simply nodded.

Lucy took five or six deep breaths, and gradually her contraction subsided. 'You sold me . . . you sold my body . . . you prostituted your own wife . . . so that you could be certain of becoming Viceroy?'

'That isn't the way that I would express it. You needed things that I just couldn't provide. You needed amusement, fun, parties. You needed somebody who could – well, you needed somebody who could give you comfort in bed. I confess that I haven't served you very well in that particular part of our married life.'

Lucy swallowed. Then she said, 'You should have told me about Vanessa right from the very beginning.'

'Vanessa?' Henry frowned.

'Henry, I know all about Vanessa. I could have helped you.'

Henry sat down. 'I'm sorry. I'm sorry you know. There's nothing that you could have done to help.'

'Perhaps if we start telling the truth to each other, that will help.'

'Lucy! You can't understand!'

'I can't understand that you're still in love with her? Of course I can!'

'And don't you think that being irredeemably in love with your own sister deserves punishment?'

Lucy thought for a while, and then she slowly nodded. 'Yes, Henry, perhaps it does. But I can give you both of those things now, truth *and* punishment, all in one.'

He lifted his head. He didn't understand her at all.

'You're going to tell me you love this Jamie Cullen. You're going to tell me that you've been having an affair with him, even though you're pregnant.'

'No,' said Lucy. 'I haven't seen Jamie Cullen for years and years. Well – not until he turned up in Calcutta last month.'

'You said in your letter that you loved him,' said Henry.

'I did. I do. I always will. I knew him in Kansas. I can't pretend that I didn't. But I could never love him the way I love you.'

Henry stood up. 'In that case, my dearest, how could you possibly have been persuaded to write what you did about Bal Gangadhar Tilak? You said in your letter that he is an honourable man, a great benefactor, and that you will try to persuade me what a saint he is.'

'I made a mistake,' said Lucy, sitting down.

Henry approached her, his face starkly shadowed by the electric light. 'Yes, my dearest, you made a mistake. You made an appalling mistake. You are Vicereine of India, the representative of the Queen-Empress, and yet you decided to meet in secret with the most vicious and squalid terrorist that India has ever known. And what did you do after that?

Did you repudiate him? Did you send troops to look for him? Oh, no! Nothing like that! You wrote a letter to your friend or your lover or whatever he is, and told him that you supported Bal Gangadhar Tilak, the terrorist, the nationalist, and that you would try to persuade me to treat him with respect!'

Lucy realized that Henry was in such an emotional rage that nothing could stop him. His fists were clenching and unclenching, spit flew from his lips, and the veins on his forehead bulged.

'With one letter,' he seethed, 'with one letter, you brought the viceroyalty to the brink of destruction; and gave me no option but to release one of the most determined of India's nationalists. The man who killed Elizabeth will never be punished. You saw to that.'

Lucy, without another word, rose from the sofa, and stood in front of him. Then she spread out her black mourning skirts, and knelt down on the floor. Then she lay spreadeagled in front of Henry, stretched out on the carpet and kissed and licked the toe of his black polished shoe.

'Lucy, get up! Lucy, you're expecting a baby, for God's sake!'

'Sahib,' she said. She was half-laughing, half-weeping. 'Oh mighty, mighty Sahib!'

'Lucy, get up!

'Not until I tell you the truth that will always be your punishment, oh mighty Sahib!'

Henry, fearful and enraged, seized Lucy's arms and lifted her bodily up off the floor. 'What in God's name is the matter with you? Are you demented! You're expecting a baby!'

She smiled at him, a saucy humorous anguished smile that she knew would provoke him beyond all measure. 'The truth and the punishment, Henry, is that this child that you're so concerned about may be yours; but on the other hand it may equally well be Malty's. In which case, you have paid the price for your precious viceroyalty in blood; and so have I.'

Then her shoulders began to shake, and she wept the bitterest tears that anybody could ever weep, for Elizabeth, and for Blanche, and for Henry, and for herself, too.

They caught Jamie as he was boarding the train at Delhi for Bombay. He was dressed like a clerk, in a grey suit and a *terai* hat, and he was carrying a briefcase. He was immediately escorted back to Simla. It had not been publicly announced, but it was generally known throughout the Indian Army and Police that the Viceroy was prepared to reward anybody who apprehended him; and generously.

Lucy saw him again from her bedroom balcony as he was brought under guard to the Viceregal Lodge, at six o'clock in the morning. The Sutlej valley was so misty that she couldn't even see the opposite hills. He was brought to the side entrance, with his head bowed. Lucy watched him, and prayed that he wouldn't raise his eyes.

Jamie was questioned for six hours by Henry and by various Indian Army officers. Lucy sat in her room, knowing that he was there, a pale pregnant widow wearing black. As it grew dark, Colonel Miller came up and knocked at her door and presented his compliments.

'Mr Cullen has asked to speak to you, Your Excellency, and His Excellency the Viceroy has assented.'

Lucy glanced at Etta, then gathered her skirts and stood up. 'Very well,' she said; and followed Colonel Miller along the corridor. His highly-polished shoes barked briskly on the teak flooring.

Jamie was waiting for her in a bare whitewashed room that had once been used for keeping guns. He looked tired and unwashed, but otherwise he seemed to be well.

'Well, well,' he said, as Lucy walked in. The sergeant standing behind him prodded him, sharply, to make him stand up.

'Hello, Jamie,' she said. She didn't sit down.

'Did His Excellency tell you what he was going to do to me?' asked Jamie.

Lucy shook her head.

'His Excellency is going to deport me; directly back to the United States of America, and His Excellency is going to lodge a formal complaint with the United States diplomatic service.'

Lucy said, very carefully, 'Don't you think you deserve it? You tricked me. You killed my best friend. You would have killed Henry, too.'

'Lucy,' said Jamie, 'that wasn't anything to do with me. That was just one of Tilak's hotheads.'

'You killed my best friend, Jamie.'

'I'm sorry about that. There isn't very much else I can say.'

'You're *sorry*?'

Jamie lowered his head, and said nothing.

Lucy watched him for a while, and then she whispered, 'I never knew that anybody could ever be so jealous. It's been burning inside of you, hasn't it, for years and years? It's burned you more thoroughly than Uncle Casper was ever burned. And you would have killed Henry, wouldn't you? You would have killed him. Nothing to do with *Swaraj*. Nothing to do with justice. It was jealousy, and nothing else.'

She paused, and then she took a small bloodstained photograph out of her pocket, and held it out to him. 'You'd better take this. You're responsible for both of them. The child, and the blood.'

Jamie swallowed, but still didn't speak.

Lucy looked away for a moment. Then she said, 'One thing more. That little girl. That little girl that Bal Gangadhar Tilak brought to see me. Was she really his cousin's child?'

'No,' Jamie whispered. 'I just thought – well, there wasn't

644

much hope of you changing your mind, was there? There wasn't much hope of you talking to Henry . . . not unless you could see some suffering that you understood.'

'You pulled my heartstrings, is that it?' asked Lucy.

'Something like that,' Jamie agreed.

'Where is she now? Do you know?'

'I don't know, somewhere in the native quarter; back where we borrowed her from.'

Lucy said, 'There's only one thing that I'm going to say to Bal Gangadhar Tilak, and that's to take care of that little girl. And there's only one thing that I'm going to say to you.'

'Oh, yes?' smiled Jamie.

'Oh, yes,' said Lucy. 'I've learned it from you and I've learned it from Henry. And that is, that I'm an empress. Not an empress of India; not an empress of anything at all, except the man I love, and myself.'

Jamie tilted his chair back, and leaned his head against the whitewashed wall. 'Empress,' he repeated, as if he would have to be satisfied with that.

On Sunday morning, June 24, 1899, to the sound of bells pealing from the Gothic tower of Christ Church, Simla, 'Horatio' Carson was born and named Nancy Victoria.

Nancy was blonde and curly, like her mother, but she seemed to bear no likeness at all to her father. To Lucy's secret relief, she didn't look at all like Blanche. She wouldn't have been able to bear it if she had given birth to yet another daughter just the same. Sha-sha would always have a very private individual place in her heart.

Although she didn't look like him, Henry was dearly fond of Nancy, and was always finding excuses to leave his desk and come through to the nursery and watch her; even if she was asleep. It didn't seem to upset him at all that she could have been Malty's daughter, instead of his. Quite the opposite; it seemed to give him a new calmness and balance in his life, as if at last he had been punished justly and sufficiently.

He never asked Lucy any more about Jamie, or why she had allowed him to introduce her to Bal Gangadhar Tilak. She sometimes suspected that he might have found out why, from the Simla Police, or from one of the Army's intelligence officers. Immediately after Henry had been obliged to let Tilak go, he had been noticeably distant with her; even testy at times.

But when Nancy was born, he seemed to make up his mind that whatever the failings of their marriage, whatever the burdens of his viceroyalty, he and Lucy had chosen their lives and they must live them honorably and affectionately, and with pride.

On Christmas Day, he gave Lucy a diamond-and-emerald ring. Inside it, he had inscribed the words, *I Will Love You Eternally, H.*

Lucy occasionally felt that she had been left with one unanswered question: whether it had been right for her to turn her back on Blanche and Jamie and choose the life of an empress, rather than the life of an Oak City wife and mother.

Jamie had killed with his jealousy whatever love she had once felt for him but she still thought about him; and about her younger days in Kansas, with the stormy sky hurtling above their heads as if it had a train to catch.

That is, until New Year's Day, 1900, the very first day of the new century, as she was being dressed by Etta in her dressing room at Government House for the traditional Viceroy's New Year's Day Parade.

Outside, she could hear the racketing echo of military drums across the *maidan*; and the clear-throated sound of bugles; mingled with the jingling of harnesses and the braying of elephants.

'Very well, I'm ready,' she told Etta, rising from her dressing-chair. 'I just want to say goodbye to Nancy.'

In her pleated and ruffled white dress, she crossed to the nursery, where Nancy was lying in her curtained crib, playing with her feet.

'How's my darling?' she asked her, leaning over her crib. 'How's my beautiful girl?'

The *amah* smiled fondly at Nancy, and said, 'Very sweet child, *memsahib*. Never weeping.'

'Well, she has nothing to weep about,' said Lucy. She reached into the crib to pick Nancy up. 'My darling, beautiful girl.'

Nancy tugged at Lucy's curls, and then at her earrings. Lucy kissed her, and was about to lay her back in her crib when her little fingers caught hold of Lucy's cameo brooch; the same cameo brooch which she had been left by her mother.

'Now careful, my sweetness!' Lucy cautioned her; but the brooch suddenly came apart, and the cameo dropped out of the silver backing, on to the baby's sheet. After it, a tiny oval photograph came fluttering, and landed beside it.

Frowning, Lucy picked the photograph up. It showed a serious-faced young man, with rather old-fashioned sidewhiskers. She turned it over, and on the back was written, *To My Only Love, On The Birth Of Our Daughter*.

It was only when she had studied the photograph for two or three minutes that it gradually dawned on her that she was looking at a photograph of her real father, Jamie's father, Jerrold Cullen.

That night, when the great New Year's Day Parade was over, she sat and wrote a short letter to Jamie. A letter without bitterness or cruelty; but a letter which told him who she had discovered herself to be; and a letter which she prayed would ease at last the pain of all of his wasted years.

She sat at her desk alone while the sun settled over Calcutta, thickening the shadows, turning the lazy reflective curves of the Hooghly River into polished bronze, and filling her room with a strange amber light, as if her dress were fading, as if her tiara were tarnishing, as if she were a photograph herself, a curio to be wondered about far in the future.

She turned, and saw Henry standing at the door.

'I have never seen you look so beautiful,' he said. Then he turned, and left the room, and closed the door very quietly behind him.

All Sphere Books are available at your bookshop or newsagent, or can be ordered from the following address: Sphere Books, Cash Sales Department, P.O. Box 11, Falmouth, Cornwall TR10 9EN

Please send cheque or postal order (no currency), and allow 60p for postage and packing for the first book plus 25p for the second book and 15p for each additional book ordered up to a maximum charge of £1.90 in U.K.

B.F.P.O. customers allow 60p for the first book, 25p for the second book plus 15p per copy for the next 7 books thereafter 9p per book.

Overseas customers, including Eire, please allow £1.25 for postage and packing for the first book, 75p for the second book and 28p for each subsequent title ordered.